英汉对照

巴黎速写

THE PARIS SKETCH BOOK

[英] 威廉・梅克皮斯・萨克雷 著
William Makepeace Thackeray
胡明华 译

凤凰出版传媒集团 | 江苏教育出版社
JIANGSU EDUCATION PUBLISHING HOUSE

图书在版编目(CIP)数据

巴黎速写/(英)萨克雷(Thackeray,W. M.)著;胡明华译.
南京:江苏教育出版社,2006.5
(凤凰苏教文库. 家庭书架)
ISBN 7-5343-7365-4

Ⅰ.巴...
Ⅱ.①萨...②W...③胡...
Ⅲ.小品文—作品集—英国—近代
Ⅳ.I561.64

中国版本图书馆 CIP 数据核字(2006)第 048089 号

出版者 江苏教育出版社
社 址 南京市马家街 31 号 邮政编码 210009
网 址 http://www.1088.com.cn
出版人 张胜勇

书 名 巴黎速写
著 者 [英]萨克雷(Thackeray,W. M.)
译 者 胡明华
责任编辑 胡群英
集团地址 凤凰出版传媒集团有限公司
(南京市中央路 165 号 邮政编码 210009)
集团网址 凤凰出版传媒网 http://www.ppm.cn

经 销 全国新华书店
印 刷 秦皇岛市昌黎文苑印刷有限公司
厂 址 河北科技师范学院(院内) 电话 0335—2039580
开 本 787×1092 毫米 1/16
印 张 40 插页 2
字 数 574 000
版 次 2006 年 12 月第 1 版
印 次 2006 年 12 月第 1 次印刷
定 价 42.80 元
发行热线 010—68003077
编辑热线 010—68002876

出版前言

在欧美诸国，普通家庭在客厅、壁炉旁或卧室等处，一般都置有一个书架，上面摆满了他们称谓的“家庭读物”。在中国，所谓的家庭常备读物似乎固有所指，通常为菜谱、医疗保健或旅游指南之类，但西方的家庭常备读物却主要是经典的文学艺术作品；这些书不是整整齐齐码在书架上，纯粹为了装饰或摆设，少有开卷，仅供观瞻，而是放在床头、茶几、阳台甚至卫生间，触手可及，可以随时翻阅。出门旅行前也可以顺便带上一册，在候机候车间隙捧而读之，既打发时间，又时时受益。这样的书，父母看过可以传给孩子，孩子看完再传给自己的孩子，子子孙孙，代代相传。文化的传承就这样在不知不觉间静悄悄地进行，伟大的文明就这样绵延于世。

令人遗憾的是，以文明悠久著称的中国，在经济飞速发展的今天，却缺少和自己的民族文化地位相对应的普通家庭常备读物。走进一个个越来越宽敞明亮的中国家庭，我们能看到琳琅满目、充满了艺术感的家具，能感受到灯光营造出的朦胧诗意的氛围，却很少能看到一个书架，一个承载人类文明积淀的书架；乘飞机或火车出行，多见旅人们百无聊赖无所事事地等候、聊天、打牌，亦多见时尚杂志或街头小报人手一份，却少见有人手捧一册文学艺术作品在喧嚣的环境中静静阅读。承续了五千年文明的中国人，在现时代表现出的对精神生活的漠视，让人生出一种巨大的遗憾和忧伤……

正是这样的感时伤怀，正是这样的遗憾和失落，正是这样一种久违了的文明意识，正是这样一种萦绕于心的担当，让我们起意策划出版这样一套充满着人文气息的“家庭书架”。

这是一套在西方文化发展和文明积淀过程中影响久远的读物，这是一套影响了欧美诸民族心灵世界和集体文明无意识的读物，这是一套可以让个体的精神世界变得无比丰富和无比强大的读物，这还是一套人人皆可阅读但充满着贵族气息的读物。

这套“家庭书架”，凝聚着人类文明中最美妙的智慧和最敏锐的灵感，一群最善于思考最长于想象的伟大作者，将神奇而微妙的精神活动进行到底，凝结成人类文明最璀璨的结晶体。

这些作品是思想的圣坛，回响着每个与之结缘的个体在文明深处徜徉徘徊时细微而悠远的脚步声；这些作品是人类语言的丰碑，文字垃圾在这里被无情地埋葬，快餐文化在这里灰飞烟灭。

这套大型汉英双语版图书大致可以分为文学艺术类、传记类、历史类、游记散文、社会文化类等。作者们虽然身份、职业不同——他们或为文学家，或为艺术家，或为政治家，但都以文辞优美著称，即使深奥难测的美学著作，如佩特的《柏拉图和柏拉图主义》，也因作者优美的散文笔法而让人亲近。其他如奥威尔的《政治与英语》、吉卜林的《谈谈我自己》、康拉德的《生活笔记》、罗斯金的《艺术十讲》、杰罗姆的《小说笔记》、兰姆的《兰姆书信精粹》、卢卡斯的《佛罗伦萨的漫游者》、萨克雷的《巴黎速写》、鲍斯韦尔的《伦敦日志（1762—1763）》等，皆出名家之手。这些游记或散文，不仅充满着精神感召的力量，而且因其文辞隽美，还可以作为美文来欣赏、诵读。执一册在手，当是畅快的精神旅行。

众所周知，译事沉疴业已成为当代中国知识领域难以治愈的顽疾，草率、随性、误译、漏译、跳译、畏难等等随处可见。虽然当前仍有少数译者在译事丛林中艰难爬梳并屡有优秀成果问世，但我们已经很难看到当年傅雷先生之于《约翰·克里斯朵夫》及王道乾先生之于《情人》的译事之工了。在今天的译著中，我们看不到修辞，看不到信达雅，看不到前人遗风，我们看到的是急功近利，看到的是用电脑翻译工具草译出来的种种无厘头。这是翻译者的悲哀，是出版人的悲哀，是读者的悲哀，是文化的悲哀。

在这种恶劣的翻译环境和悲哀的心境中，我们开始了充满挑战的组译议程。组织会聚了许多大师著作的“家庭书架”的翻译出版，于我们而言，与其说是建立出版功业，毋宁说是进入了布满陷阱的出版丛林。我们规避陷阱的种种努力，都是为了给读者朋友提供一个可资借鉴的阅读文本。

我们深知，大师著作的翻译是艰难的，用汉语来传达他们的思想总会留下或多或少的缺憾，甚至我们都怀疑这些思想是根本无法用另外一种语言传达的。这时候“迁就阅读”就必须成为我们出版人唯一的选择。尽管译者和我们都想“用优秀的作品来鼓舞人”，尽管译者和我们都努力地走在通往理想之塔的道路上，但在这些图书即将付梓之际，我们的内心仍然深感惶恐。我们深知，为读者奉献的译文仍然存在着有待克服的种种问题。

但是我们有勇气，有足够的勇气用这种英汉对照的方式将这些文本呈现给我们的读者。一则希望读者可以在英语与汉语的比照下更深地体察语言的精微和文本的精致；一则希望读者朋友在阅读过程中可以方便地提出自己的疑问，指出我们的不足，使这套丛书在今后不断的修订过程中日臻完备。

译事惟艰，出版惟艰。冀希读者朋友们一如既往地支持我们的翻译事业和出版事业。丛书如存有不当之处，希望读者朋友们宽容并谅解。

江苏教育出版社

2006 年 8 月

CONTENTS

目　录

巴黎速写

Dedicatory Letter

TO

M. ARETZ, TAILOR, ETC.

27, RUE RICHELIEU, PARIS.

SIR,—It becomes every man in his station to acknowledge and praise virtue wheresoever he may find it, and to point it out for the admiration and example of his fellow-men.

Some months since, when you presented to the writer of these pages a small account for coats and pantaloons manufactured by you, and when you were met by a statement from your creditor, that an immediate settlement of your bill would be extremely inconvenient to him; your reply was, "Mon Dieu, Sir, let not that annoy you; if you want money, as a gentleman often does in a strange country, I have a thousand-franc note at my house which is quite at your service."

History or experience, Sir, makes us acquainted with so few actions that can be compared to yours,—an offer like this from a stranger and a tailor seems to me so astonishing,—that you must pardon me for thus making your virtue public, and acquainting the English nation with your merit and your name. Let me add, Sir, that you live on the first floor; that your clothes and fit are excellent, and your charges moderate and just; and, as a humble tribute of my admiration, permit me to lay these volumes at your feet.

Your obliged, faithful servant,

M. A. Titmarsh.

献给裁缝师阿特兹先生的信

巴黎黎塞留街27号

先生：

在每个人的一生中，不管他在哪里发现了美好的德行，他都应该承认和赞扬这种品质，并把它指出来作为同胞们赞美和效仿的对象。

几个月以来，当您赠送给本书的作者一笔小数额的账单以换取您做的外套和裤子时，当您的债权人向您提出，这样仓促地处理您的账单会给他带来极大的不便时，您的答复是："上帝啊！先生，不要让这件事使你烦恼。就像一个绅士在一个陌生的国家经常出现的那样，如果你需要钱，在我房里有张一千法郎的支票正好符合你的需要。"

先生，历史或经验使我们认识到几乎没有什么别的行为能够与您的这种做法相提并论——像这样的来自一个陌生人和裁缝师的故事对我来说似乎是如此的惊讶，以至于您一定得原谅我就这样把您的德行公之于众，让英国国民知晓您的美德和名字。我还要再说几句，先生，您住在一楼；您做的衣服和样式都很出色，您的收费公道又合理；为了表示我对您的钦佩，请允许我把这本书作为一份微不足道的礼物呈现给您。

您感激不尽的、忠实的仆人，

迈克尔·安玑莱·蒂特马舍

Advertisement to the First Edition

ABOUT half of the sketches in these volumes have already appeared in print, in various periodical works. A part of the text of one tale, and the plots of two others, have been borrowed from French originals; the other stories, which are, in the main, true, have been written upon facts and characters that came within the Author's observation during a residence in Paris.

As the remaining papers relate to public events which occurred during the same period, or to Parisian Art and Literature, he has ventured to give his publication the title which it bears.

LONDON, July 1, 1840.

第一版声明

这册书里有大约一半的随笔已在各种不同的期刊上发表过。其中一个故事的部分情节、两个故事的全部情节都借鉴于法国原作。其余的故事，实际上绝大部分是作者以他本人在巴黎居住期间所观察到的人和事为基础而创作的。

剩下的内容主要涉及了同时期法国所发生的社会事件，或者和巴黎的艺术、文学有关，作者大胆地给它加了个书名就结集出版了。

伦敦，1840 年 7 月 1 日

THE PARIS SKETCH BOOK■

■ 巴黎速写

An Invasion of France

"CAESAR venit in Galliam summa diligentia."

About twelve o'clock, just as the bell of the packet is tolling a farewell to London Bridge, and warning off the blackguard-boys with the newspapers, who have been shoving *Times*, *Herald*, *Penny Paul-Pry*, *Penny Satirist*, *Flare-up*, and other abominations, into your face—just as the bell has tolled, and the Jews, strangers, people-taking-leave-of-their-families, and blackguard-boys aforesaid, are making a rush for the narrow plank which conducts from the paddle-box of the "Emerald" steamboat unto the quay—you perceive, staggering down Thames Street, those two hackney-coaches, for the arrival of which you have been praying, trembling, hoping, despairing, swearing—sw—, I beg your pardon, I believe the word is not used in polite company—and transpiring, for the last half-hour. Yes, at last, the two coaches draw near, and from thence an awful number of trunks, children, carpet-bags, nursery-maids, hat-boxes, band-boxes, bonnet-boxes, desks, cloaks, and an affectionate wife, are discharged on the quay.

"Elizabeth, take care of Miss Jane," screams that worthy woman, who has been for a fortnight employed in getting this tremendous body of troops and baggage into marching order. "Hicks! Hicks! for heaven's sake mind the babies!" "George—Edward, sir, if you go near that porter with the trunk, he will tumble down and kill you, you naughty boy! —My love, DO take the cloaks and umbrellas, and give a hand to Fanny and Lucy; and I wish you would speak to the hackney-coachmen, dear; they want fifteen shillings, and count the packages, love—twenty-seven packages,—and bring little Flo; where's little Flo? —Flo! Flo!"—(Flo comes sneaking in; she has been speaking a few parting words to a one-eyed terrier, that sneaks off similarly,

闯入法国

“恺撒极为谨慎地来到了高卢。”（原文为拉丁语）

大约十二点钟，班轮上向伦敦桥告别的钟声敲响了，并警告那些卖报纸的流氓男孩离开，他们一直在忙着把《泰晤士报》、《先驱报》、《保罗·普莱便士报》（保罗·普莱在英语中被用来比喻爱打听别人隐私的人，源自英国著名作品《保罗·普莱》中的人物）、《讽刺便士报》、《火焰报》等乱七八糟的令人生厌的东西兜售给你。钟声已敲响，犹太人、外国人、离家出行的人和上述的无赖男孩都匆忙挤向那块由“翡翠”汽船明轮的外壳搭就的通向码头的狭窄的厚木板。你看到那边有两辆出租马车正摇摇晃晃地沿着泰晤士街道驶过来，一直让你为之祈祷、担忧、希望、绝望、诅咒的一切，对不起，我认为诅咒这个词不是有礼貌的人使用的——在最后半个小时里终于出现了。终于，两辆四轮马车靠近了，一大堆数量惊人的皮箱、孩子、毛毡施行袋、女保姆、女帽盒子、装宽沿帽的盒子、装衣领的硬纸匣、书桌、斗篷和一个深情的妻子都从车里被卸到了码头上。

那位可敬的妇人叫道：“伊丽莎白，照顾珍小姐！”她两个星期以来都在忙着使这个庞大的队伍和行李能够有条不紊地前进。“乡下人！乡下人！上帝保佑，注意小孩！”“乔治——爱德华，先生，如果你带着这个皮箱去靠近那个搬运工，他将会翻倒下去并且会杀了你的，你这个淘气的孩子！——亲爱的，带上斗篷和伞，帮芳妮和露西一把。我希望你会跟出租马车的车夫讲讲价，亲爱的，他们想要十五个先令，还要数数那些包裹，

landward.)

As when the hawk menaces the hen-roost, in like manner, when such a danger as a voyage menaces a mother, she becomes suddenly endowed with a ferocious presence of mind, and bristling up and screaming in the front of her brood, and in the face of circumstances, succeeds, by her courage, in putting her enemy to flight; in like manner you will always, I think, find your wife (if that lady be good for two pence) shrill, eager, and ill-humoured, before, and during a great family move of this nature. Well, the swindling hackney-coachmen are paid, the mother leading on her regiment of little ones, and supported by her auxiliary nursemaids, are safe in the cabin; —you have counted twenty-six of the twenty-seven parcels, and have them on board, and that horrid man on the paddle-box, who, for twenty minutes past, has been roaring out, NOW, SIR! —says, NOW, SIR, no more.

I never yet knew how a steamer began to move, being always too busy among the trunks and children, for the first half-hour, to mark any of the movements of the vessel. When these private arrangements are made, you find yourself opposite Greenwich (farewell, sweet, sweet white-bait!), and quiet begins to enter your soul. Your wife smiles for the first time these ten days; you pass by plantations of ship-masts, and forests of steam-chimneys; the sailors are singing on board the ships, the bargees salute you with oaths, grins, and phrases facetious and familiar; the man on the paddle-box roars, "Ease her, stop her!" which mysterious words a shrill voice from below repeats, and pipes out, "Ease her, stop her!" in echo; the deck is crowded with groups of figures, and the sun shines over all.

The sun shines over all, and the steward comes up to say, "Lunch, ladies and gentlemen! Will any lady or gentleman please to take anything?" About a dozen do: boiled beef and pickles, and great red raw Cheshire cheese, tempt the epicure: little dumpy bottles of stout are produced, and fiz and bang about with a spirit one would never have looked for in individuals of their size and stature.

The decks have a strange, look; the people on them, that is. Wives, elderly stout husbands, nursemaids, and children predominate, of course, in English steamboats. Such may be considered as the distinctive marks of the

亲爱的——二十七个包裹——把小弗罗领过来，小弗罗在哪里？——弗罗！弗罗！”（弗罗偷偷摸摸地来了。她一直在跟那条只有一只眼的小猎犬说些告别的话。那只狗也偷偷摸摸地溜到了陆地上。）

当旅行的危险威胁到一位母亲时，她也会突然被赋予一种凶猛的意识和行为，就像一只鹰威胁到鸡窝里的母鸡那样，母鸡会毛发竖立，在她的窝前尖叫，面对接下来的情境，凭着她的勇气，成功地把她的敌人赶跑。我想你会经常发现你的妻子在举家搬迁时也以同样的方式（就为了两个便士）尖叫、激动、脾气暴躁。好了，已付钱给那些趁机敲诈的出租马车车夫，在随身保姆的帮助下，母亲领着一大群小孩也安全地到了船舱。你已经在二十七件包裹中数出了二十六个，并把它们放在了船板上，明轮的外壳上那个粗俗的伙计在过去的二十分钟里一直在号叫，现在，先生，——先生，现在别再说话了。

我从来都不知道一艘汽船是如何开动的，因为在头半个小时里，人们总是忙碌于众多的皮箱和孩子当中，根本就注意不到船的任何移动。当这些私人事情处理好之后，你发现自己的对面正是格林尼治（别了，亲爱的，亲爱的小银鱼！）[格林尼治在伦敦东南部三区。——译注]，你的心开始平静下来。而你的妻子在这十几天里第一次对你露出了笑容；你从船上的桅杆林、冒烟的烟囱林前经过；水手正在船的甲板上唱歌，船员讲着一套滑稽又熟悉的话语，微笑着庄严地向你敬礼；明轮的外壳上的人在吼叫：“让她放心，让她停住！”这句不可思议的话被船下面一个尖锐的声音重复着并蔓延出去，发出了回声：“让她放心，让她停住！”甲板上挤满了一群群的人，阳光在四周闪耀着。

阳光在四周闪耀，船上的服务员走过来宣布：“女士们，先生们，用午餐了！还有人想喝点什么吗？”大约一打的人会选择：煮沸的腌汁牛肉，很棒的未加工的红色柴郡[英国郡名。——译注]乳酪，就连美食家也会垂涎的小矮瓶的烈性黑啤酒也被供应，在这些食物的作用下，人们很快就得意忘形起来。

English gentleman at three or four and forty: two or three of such groups have pitched their camps on the deck. Then there are a number of young men, of whom three or four have allowed their moustaches to BEGIN to grow since last Friday; for they are going "on the Continent," and they look, therefore, as if their upper lips were smeared with snuff.

A danseuse from the opera is on her way to Paris. Followed by her bonne and her little dog, she paces the deck, stepping out, in the real dancer fashion, and ogling all around. How happy the two young Englishmen are, who can speak French, and make up to her: and how all criticize her points and paces! Yonder is a group of young ladies, who are going to Paris to learn how to be governesses: those two splendidly dressed ladies are milliners from the Rue Richelieu, who have just brought over, and disposed of, their cargo of Summer fashions. Here sits the Rev. Mr. Snodgrass with his pupils, whom he is conducting to his establishment, near Boulogne, where, in addition to a classical and mathematical education (washing included), the young gentlemen have the benefit of learning French among THE FRENCH THEMSELVES. Accordingly, the young gentlemen are locked up in a great ricketty house, two miles from Boulogne and never see a soul, except the French usher and the cook.

Some few French people are there already, preparing to be ill—(I never shall forget a dreadful sight I once had in the little dark, dirty, six-foot cabin of a Dover steamer. Four gaunt Frenchmen, but for their pantaloons, in the costume of Adam in Paradise, solemnly anointing themselves with some charm against sea-sickness!)—a few Frenchmen are there, but these, for the most part, and with a proper philosophy, go to the fore-cabin of the ship, and you see them on the fore-deck (is that the name for that part of the vessel which is in the region of the bowsprit?) lowering in huge cloaks and caps; snuffy, wretched, pale, and wet; and not jabbering now, as their wont is on shore. —I never could fancy the Mounseers formidable at sea.

There are, of course, many Jews on board. Who ever travelled by steamboat, coach, diligence, eil-wagen, vetturino, mule-back, or sledge, without meeting some of the wandering race?

By the time these remarks have been made the steward is on the deck

甲板上也有奇怪的，看，那就是它上面的人群。在英国汽船上有妻子、上了年纪的强壮丈夫、女保姆，当然最多的还是孩子。以下这样的表现可以被看做三四岁或四十岁的英国绅士的典型标志：其中有两三个男士已在甲板上扎起了帐篷。那边还有些年轻人，因为他们就要去大陆了，有三四个人已从上星期五就蓄起了胡子，看起来好像是上嘴唇被涂上了鼻烟。

一个来自歌剧院的芭蕾舞女演员也是去巴黎的。她后面跟着女佣和她的小狗，她在甲板上踱着步——这可是真正的舞蹈步伐——并四处抛媚眼。那两个会讲法语的英国青年是多么高兴啊！因为他们可借此接近她并讨好她，所有的人都是怎么评论她的姿势和步伐的！那边是一群年轻的女士，她们正准备去巴黎学习怎样成为家庭女教师。那两个盛装的女士是来自黎塞留街的女帽贩卖商，她们刚刚把带来的夏天流行的货品处理掉。这里坐着斯诺德格拉斯先生和他的学生，他正带着学生去他那靠近布洛涅［法国西北部城市，临加来海峡即多佛尔海峡。——译注］的住所，在那里，除了古典和数学教育（包括灵魂忏悔）之外，还有利于年轻的绅士们在法国本地人当中学习法语。因此，年轻的绅士们会被锁在一个东倒西歪的大房子里——离布洛涅有两英里远，除了法国招待员和厨子外连个鬼影也见不到。

那里有几个法国人，他们看起来好像是生病了。（我永远也忘不了我在一艘多佛尔汽船上那黑暗的、肮脏的六英尺宽的狭小船舱里所看到的那可怕的一幕。四个憔悴的法国人，要不是他们的裤子，穿着简直就与天堂里亚当的装束一模一样，正一本正经地往身上涂一些神秘的油来抵制晕船！）几个法国人在那边，但是他们中的大部分都带着一种适度的镇静去了船的前舱，你在前甲板（那是指船首斜桅内的区域吗？）上可以看到他们在极大的斗篷和无边帽下低着头。傲慢、可怜、苍白和喝醉的人都不再像惯常在岸上那样叽叽喳喳的了。我从未想到过在海上会有这么可怕的生理反应。

当然，在船上还有许多犹太人。凡是经常乘坐汽船、四轮大马车、公共马车、快递邮车、意大利的四轮马车、骡子或雪橇旅行的人，谁没遇到

again, and dinner is ready: and about two hours after dinner comes tea; and then there is brandy and water, which he eagerly presses as a preventive against what may happen; and about this time you pass the Foreland, the wind blowing pretty fresh; and the groups on deck disappear, and your wife, giving you an alarmed look, descends, with her little ones, to the ladies' cabin, and you see the steward and his boys issuing from their den under the paddle-box, with each a heap of round tin vases, like those which are called, I believe, in America, expectoratoons, only these are larger.

……

The wind blows, the water looks greener and more beautiful than ever—ridge by ridge of long white rock passes away. "That's Ramsgit," says the man at the helm; and, presently, "that there's Deal—it's dreadful fallen off since the war;" and "that's Dover, round that there pint, only you can't see it;" and, in the meantime, the sun has plumped his hot face into the water, and the moon has shown hers as soon as ever his back is turned, and Mrs. — (the wife in general) has brought up her children and self from the horrid cabin, in which she says it is impossible to breathe; and the poor little wretches are, by the officious stewardess and smart steward (expectoratoonifer), accommodated with a heap of blankets, pillows, and mattresses, in the midst of which they crawl, as best they may, and from the heaving heap of which are, during the rest of the voyage, heard occasional faint cries, and sounds of puking woe!

Dear, dear Maria! Is this the woman who, anon, braved the jeers and brutal wrath of swindling hackney-coachmen; who repelled the insolence of haggling porters, with a scorn that brought down their demands at least eighteen-pence? Is this the woman at whose voice servants tremble; at the sound of whose steps the nursery, aye, and mayhap the parlor, is in order? Look at her now, prostrate, prostrate—no strength has she to speak, scarce power to push to her youngest one—her suffering, struggling Rosa,—to push to her the—the instrumentoon!

In the midst of all these throes and agonies, at which all the passengers, who have their own woes (you yourself—for how can you help THEM? —you are on your back on a bench, and if you move all is up with you), are loo-

过这个四处漫游的民族呢？

在发表这些评论的时候，服务员已再一次出现在甲板上，晚餐准备好了。在晚餐大约两个小时后是茶点时间。服务员急切地把白兰地和水咽下去以防止晕船。大约这个时候你从海山甲那里经过，清新的海风吹着，甲板上的人群消失了，你的妻子警惕地看了你一眼，带着小孩下到女士舱房里去了，你看到服务员和他的同伴们从船舱下面的小屋里涌了出来，每人带着一堆圆圆的锡瓶，我认为那些东西就是在美国被叫做痰盒的东西，只不过这些要大点。

……

海风吹着，海水变得比以前更蓝了，也更美丽了——一脊一脊的长长白色岩石从身边越过。“那是拉姆斯基，”掌舵的男人说，一会儿又说，“那是迪尔——自战争以后它就衰落下去了，那是多佛尔港，小的圆圆那点，不过你看不见它。”在这个时候，太阳滚烫的脸突然跌落在水里，一旦太阳把身子转过去，就轮到月亮开始展示她自己了，太太（一般是叫妻子）自己带着孩子从那个可怕的船舱里出来，她说在那里简直无法呼吸，殷勤的女服务员和机敏的男服务员（用痰盂的）给那些贫穷的可怜小孩提供了毛毯、枕头和床垫，在这些成堆的用品之中他们都尽自己最大的可能蠕动着，在接下来的航行时间里，你可以从那些翻腾的成堆被褥中听到间断的虚弱哭喊声和痛苦的呕吐声！

圣母玛利亚！这就是刚才那个敢于对欺诈的出租马车车夫进行嘲笑和挖苦的女人吗？就是她抗议那些争论不休的搬运工人的傲慢无理，轻蔑地把他们的报酬降到最低价十八便士吗？就是这个女人的声音让仆人感到战栗吗？听她的脚步声是去儿童室或起居室了，她的脚步声还有次序吗？现在看看她，疲惫了，疲惫得没有力气去说话，还要省下力气去把她最小的孩子——她的正痛苦挣扎着的罗莎——推到一个器皿那儿去！

处于这种痛苦和折磨之中，所有的乘客都有他们自己的烦恼（你自己会怎样去帮助他们呢？——你正仰卧在一张长椅子上，如果你动一动，周

king on indifferent—one man there is who has been watching you with the utmost care, and bestowing on your helpless family the tenderness that a father denies them. He is a foreigner, and you have been conversing with him, in the course of the morning, in French, which, he says, you speak remarkably well, like a native in fact, and then in English (which, after all, you find is more convenient). What can express your gratitude to this gentleman for all his goodness towards your family and yourself? —you talk to him, he has served under the Emperor, and is, for all that, sensible, modest, and well-informed. He speaks, indeed, of his countrymen almost with contempt, and readily admits the superiority of a Briton, on the seas and elsewhere. One loves to meet with such genuine liberality in a foreigner, and respects the man who can sacrifice vanity to truth. This distinguished foreigner has travelled much; he asks whither you are going? —where you stop? —if you have a great quantity of luggage on board? —and laughs when he hears of the twenty-seven packages, and hopes you have some friend at the custom-house, who can spare you the monstrous trouble of unpacking that which has taken you weeks to put up. Nine, ten, eleven, the distinguished foreigner is ever at your side; you find him now, perhaps, (with characteristic ingratitude,) something of a bore, but, at least, he has been most tender to the children and their mamma. At last a Boulogne light comes in sight (you see it over the bows of the vessel, when, having bobbed violently upwards, it sinks swiftly down,) Boulogne harbour is in sight, and the foreigner says,—The distinguished foreigner says, says he—"Sare, eef you af no 'otel, I sall recommend you, milor, to ze 'Otel Betfort, in ze Quay, sare, close to the bathing machines and custom-ha-oose. Good bets and fine garten, sare; table d'hôte, sare, *à* cinq-heures; breakfast, sare, in French or English style;—I am the commissionaire, sare, and vill see to your loggish."

…Curse the fellow, for an impudent, swindling, sneaking French humbug! —Your tone instantly changes, and you tell him to go about his business: but at twelve o'clock at night, when the voyage is over, and the custom-house business done, knowing not whither to go, with a wife and fourteen exhausted children, scarce able to stand, and longing for bed, you find yourself, somehow, in the Hōtel Bedford (and you can't be better), and smiling cham-

围的一切好像也会跟着你立起来似的），他们正漠不关心地旁观——那边有一个男人一直很耐心地尽可能地照顾你，给你这个无助的家庭带来父亲般的关爱。他是一个外国人，而且在早晨的那段时间内你用法语和他交谈过，他说，你的法语讲得很好，简直就像本地人，后来他又用英语（终究让你觉得更方便了）和你谈话。鉴于他对你和你的家庭所施与的仁慈，怎样才能表达你对这位绅士的感激之情呢？——你就和他谈话，他曾经在皇帝手下服务过，也正因为这个原因，他明智、谦逊、易于接近。实际上他几乎是带着轻蔑说起他的国民，而且乐意承认不列颠人在海洋和其他方面所具有的优势。人们都喜欢在一个外国人身上遇到这种真正的慷慨，而且尊敬这个敢于牺牲虚荣心去尊重事实的人。这个杰出的外国人旅行过很多地方，他问你要去哪里？在哪里下船？在船上是否有很多行李？——当听到二十七个包裹时他笑了起来，希望你在海关能有些朋友，他们可以帮你分担卸货这一大麻烦，否则那将会花费你几周的时间。九点、十点、十一点，这个杰出的外国人一直在你的身边。你或许发现（由于忘恩负义的特点）他多少有点令人讨厌，但是，至少他对孩子和孩子的母亲是很体贴的。最后，有一盏布洛涅的灯光进入视线（你看见它在船首的上方，这个时候，船向上剧烈地振动起来，又很快地沉下去），布洛涅港已进入眼帘，这个外国人说——这个杰出的外国人说："先生，如果你还没定下旅馆，我愿向您推荐白特佛旅馆，在码头那里，离海滨浴场的更衣车和海关很近。绝对值得一住，在五点有客饭，法式或英式的早餐都有，先生——我是那儿的服务员，先生，欢迎您的光临。"

……诅咒这人家伙，原来他是一个厚颜无耻、冒失、鬼鬼祟祟的法国骗子！——你的语气立即变了，你告诉他还是到别处去兜揽生意为好。但现在是晚上十二点钟，航行已结束，海关营业也结束了，带着妻子和十四个疲惫的孩子又不知道去哪里，你们不可能站着，还是很需要一张床的，你发现你自己不知怎么就到白特佛旅馆了（因为没有更好的选择了）。聪敏的女服务员把你的孩子安置到舒适的床上，伶俐的侍者竭诚为你服务——

bermaids carry off your children to snug beds; while smart waiters produce for your honour—a cold fowl, say, and a salad, and a bottle of Bordeaux and Seltzer water.

......

The morning comes—I don't know a pleasanter feeling than that of waking with the sun shining on objects quite new, and (although you may have made the voyage a dozen times,) quite strange. Mrs. X. and you occupy a very light bed, which has a tall canopy of red "percale"; the windows are smartly draped with cheap gaudy calicoes and muslins; there are little mean strips of carpet about the tiled floor of the room, and yet all seems as gay and as comfortable as may be—the sun shines brighter than you have seen it for a year, the sky is a thousand times bluer, and what a cheery clatter of shrill quick French voices comes up from the courtyard under the windows! Bells are jangling; a family, mayhap, is going to Paris, en poste, and wondrous is the jabber of the courier, the postillion, the inn-waiters, and the lookers-on. The landlord calls out for "Quatre biftecks aux pommes pour le trente-trois,"—(O ! my countrymen, I love your tastes and your ways!)—the chambermaid is laughing and says, "Finissez donc, Monsieur Pierre!" (what can they be about?)—a fat Englishman has opened his window violently, and says, "Dee dong, garsong, vooly voo me donny lo sho, ou vooly voo pah?" He has been ringing for half an hour—the last energetic appeal succeeds, and shortly he is enabled to descend to the coffee-room, where, with three hot rolls, grilled ham, cold fowl, and four boiled eggs, he makes what he calls his first FRENCH breakfast.

It is a strange, mongrel, merry place, this town of Boulogne; the little French fishermen's children are beautiful, and the little French soldiers, four feet high, red-breeched, with huge pompons on their caps, and brown faces, and clear sharp eyes, look, for all their littleness, far more military and more intelligent than the heavy louts one has seen swaggering about the garrison towns in England. Yonder go a crowd of bare-legged fishermen; there is the town idiot, mocking a woman who is screaming "Fleuve du Tage," at an inn-window, to a harp, and there are the little gamins mocking HIM. Lo! those seven young ladies, with red hair and green veils, they are from neighbouring

一只冷鸡、一份沙拉、一瓶波尔多葡萄酒和矿泉水。

……

天亮了——我不知道还有什么能比伴随着照射在新鲜的、陌生的事物上的阳光一起醒来感觉更好的了（尽管你已经航行了十二次了）。太太和你睡在一张很精巧的床上，它有着用红色的高级密织棉布做成的高高华盖，窗户时髦地挂着廉价的绚丽印花棉布与薄纱，在房间的砖地四周还有小而简陋的条纹地毯，一切看起来都尽其可能的愉快和舒适——阳光比你一年以来所看到的任何一次都明亮，天空也更蔚蓝了，从窗下传来的院子里掺杂着尖锐急速的法语发音的叽叽呱呱的笑声是多么愉快啊！闹铃发出刺耳的声音，有一家人或许是正准备去巴黎。送快信的、车夫、旅馆侍者和旁观者在闲聊。房东大叫“三十三号的四份苹果牛排”。（哦，我的同胞，我喜欢你的口味和你的选择！）旅馆的女服务员笑着说：“这就好了，彼埃尔先生！”（他们会是什么样的呢？）——一个肥胖的英国人猛地打开他的窗户说：“小伙子，可以帮帮我吗，你在哪儿呢？”他已经打铃打了半个小时了——最后的呼吁终于成功，很快他被人扶着下楼到了咖啡间里，那里有三个热的面包卷、烤火腿、冷鸡和四个水煮蛋，他把这些称做他的第一份法式早餐。

布洛涅这个城镇是一个奇特的各种民族杂居的快乐的地方。矮个儿法国渔夫的孩子们都很漂亮，还有矮个儿的法国军人，四英尺高，围着红色的腰布，无边帽上有个巨大的毛球，褐色的脸庞，明亮锐利的眼睛，看，尽管他们矮小，却比在英国看到的在其驻扎军队的城市里虚张声势、笨重愚蠢的军人要精神和机敏多了。那边走过去一群光着大腿的渔夫；那边是个城里的白痴，正嘲弄那个尖叫着“塔日河”的女人，在一扇旅馆的窗户旁边，靠近一个竖琴的地方站着一些顽童，他们正嘲弄着那个白痴。瞧！那七位年轻的淑女，她们都有着红色的头发，戴着绿色的面纱，来自阿尔比恩［英格兰的雅称。——译注］，她们正准备去沐浴。这里来了三个英国人，很明显他们经常在这个地方出入，是我们国民中的花花公子的代表：

Albion, and going to bathe. Here come three Englishmen, habitués evidently of the place,—dandy specimens of our countrymen—one wears a marine dress, another has a shooting dress, a third has a blouse and a pair of guiltless spurs—all have as much hair on the face as nature or art can supply, and all wear their hats very much on one side. Believe me, there is on the face of this world no scamp like an English one, no blackguard like one of these half-gentlemen, so mean, so low, so vulgar,—so ludicrously ignorant and conceited, so desperately heartless and depraved.

But why, my dear sir, get into a passion? —Take things coolly. As the poet has observed, "Those only is gentlemen who behave as sich;" with such, then, consort, be they cobblers or dukes. Don't give us, cries the patriotic reader, any abuse of our fellow-countrymen (anybody else can do that), but rather continue in that good-humoured, facetious, descriptive style with which your letter has commenced. —Your remark, sir, is perfectly just, and does honour to your head and excellent heart.

There is little need to give a description of the good town of Boulogne; which, haute and basse, with the new light-house and the new harbour, and the gas lamps, and the manufactures, and the convents, and the number of English and French residents, and the pillar erected in honour of the grand Armée d'Angleterre, so called because it DIDN'T go to England, have all been excellently described by the facetious Coglan, the learned Dr. Millingen, and by innumerable guide-books besides. A fine thing it is to hear the stout old Frenchmen of Napoleon's time argue how that audacious Corsican WOULD have marched to London, after swallowing Nelson and all his gunboats, but for cette malheureuse guerre d'Espagne and cette glorieuse campagne d'Autriche, which the gold of Pitt caused to be raised at the Emperor's tail, in order to call him off from the helpless country in his front. Some Frenchmen go farther still, and vow that in Spain they were never beaten at all; indeed, if you read in the "*Biographie des Hommes du Jour*," article "*Soult*," you will fancy that, with the exception of the disaster at Vittoria, the campaigns in Spain and Portugal were a series of triumphs. Only, by looking at a map, it is observable that Vimeiro is a mortal long way from Toulouse, where, at the end of certain years of victories, we somehow find the

一个穿着航海服，另一个穿着射击服，第三个穿着宽松的上衣和一双没有踢马刺的靴子——全都在脸上蓄了自然或人工所能提供的尽可能多的毛发，全都把帽子歪戴在一侧。相信我，从这些脸上就能看出这个世界上还没有流氓会像英国人这样，没有无赖会像他们这些假绅士中的任何一个如此低劣、如此下贱、如此粗俗——如此无知和自负得可笑，如此极端的无情和堕落。

但是，我亲爱的先生，为什么要情绪激动呢？——冷静地看待事物。正如诗人已观察到的那样，“那只是个别绅士的行为”，有了这句话，一切就相称了，管他们是皮匠还是公爵。爱国的读者叫道，不要给我们的同胞（其余的人就可以）以任何形式的辱骂，最好以你刚开始的那种好脾气的、滑稽的描述方式继续下去。——先生，您的说法是完全正确的，向您的头脑和杰出的心灵表示敬意。

这里就没必要去描述布洛涅这个好城市了，那儿有高高低低的建筑、新的灯塔和海港、瓦斯灯、加工产品、修道院、一定数量的英国和法国居民，以及为纪念伟大的英格兰军队［原文为法语。——译注］而竖立的柱子，这样用法语来称呼是因为它去不了英格兰。这些都被滑稽的考格兰、博学的密令根博士和无数的旅行指南精彩地描述过了。在这儿，有趣的事情是听拿破仑时代勇敢的老法国人争辩：如果不是西班牙那场不幸的战争和奥地利的辉煌战役［在这场战争中，法军也蒙受了巨大损失。——译注］，还有在帝国后方积聚的皮特考伯格［Pitt（1759—1806），英国托利党人，曾任英国首相，英国、奥地利与俄国反对拿破仑联盟的创建者，耗费了几百万黄金建立起反法联盟，希望能够阻止法国向英国进攻。——译注］的黄金，这些黄金是为了建立联盟以防止这些国家总是在拿破仑的进攻下陷入无助的境地，那么，那个大胆的科西嘉人（即拿破仑）就会在吞掉纳尔逊［Nelson（1758—1805），英国将军。——译注］和他所有的炮舰后进军伦敦了。许多法国人仍向前挺进，声称他们在西班牙从来也没有被打败过；实际上，如果你读一下《当代人物传记》［原文中该书名为法语。——

honest Marshal. And what then? —he went to Toulouse for the purpose of beating the English there, to be sure;—a known fact, on which comment would be superfluous. However, we shall never get to Paris at this rate; let us break off further palaver, and away at once···

(During this pause, the ingenious reader is kindly requested to pay his bill at the Hotel at Boulogne, to mount the Diligence of Laffitte, Caillard and Company, and to travel for twenty-five hours, amidst much jingling of harness-bells and screaming of postillions.)

······

The French milliner, who occupies one of the corners, begins to remove the greasy pieces of paper which have enveloped her locks during the journey. She withdraws the "Madras" of dubious hue which has bound her head for the last five-and-twenty hours, and replaces it by the black velvet bonnet, which, bobbing against your nose, has hung from the Diligence roof since your departure from Boulogne. The old lady in the opposite corner, who has been sucking bonbons, and smells dreadfully of anisette, arranges her little parcels in that immense basket of abominations which all old women carry in their laps. She rubs her mouth and eyes with her dusty cambric handkerchief, she ties up her nightcap into a little bundle, and replaces it by a more becoming headpiece, covered with withered artificial flowers, and crumpled tags of ribbon; she looks wistfully at the company for an instant, and then places her handkerchief before her mouth:—her eyes roll strangely about for an instant, and you hear a faint clattering noise: the old lady has been getting ready her teeth, which had lain in her basket among the bonbons, pins, oranges, pomatum, bits of cake, lozenges, prayer-books, peppermint-water, copper-money, and false hair—stowed away there during the voyage. The Jewish gentleman, who has been so attentive to the milliner during the journey, and is a traveller and bagman by profession, gathers together his various goods. The sallow-faced English lad, who has been drunk ever since we left Boulogne yesterday, and is coming to Paris to pursue the study of medicine, swears that he rejoices to leave the cursed Diligence, is sick of the infernal journey, and d—d glad that the d—d voyage is so nearly over. "Enfin!" says your neighbour, yawning, and inserting an elbow in the mouth of his right and left hand companion,

译注］中的《苏尔特》［苏尔特（Soult，1769—1851），拿破仑部下的元帅。——译注］，你会想象得到，除了在维多利亚［西班牙城市。——译注］的灾难，法国人在西班牙和葡萄牙所取得的都是一系列的胜利。可是，从地图上可以看到维梅罗［葡萄牙地名。——译注］离图卢兹有一段极远的路程，正是在图卢兹这个地方，忠实的元帅终结了他的一系列胜利。然后发生了什么呢？——他去图卢兹是为了打败那儿的英国人，这是肯定的——一个众所周知的事实，评论是多余的。然而，我们绝不能就这样一路啰啰唆唆地到巴黎，让我们结束废话，立刻打住……

（在暂停期间，我们被委婉地要求去付布洛涅旅馆的账单，然后在很多马铃铛的叮当声和驾马者的尖叫声中爬上拉菲特、加亚尔［Lafitte和Caillard均为当时负责客车事务的官员。——译注］公司的公共马车，开始了二十五个小时的旅行。）

……

法国的女帽商占据着马车的一个角落，她开始拿掉在旅行中包裹着她头发的油腻的卷发纸。她摘掉了在最后的二十五小时内围着头部的颜色暧昧的“薄棉布”头巾，换上了黑色的天鹅绒软帽。自你离开布洛涅后，在马车的车顶上悬挂着的一件什么东西就一直对着你的鼻子上下跳动着。对面角落的一个老淑女一直在吮吸糖果和味道恶心的茴香酒，把她的小包裹安置在膝盖上那个巨大的篮子里，里面装着所有老女人带的让人讨厌的东西。她用一个布满灰尘的棉布手帕擦她的嘴和眼睛，把她的睡帽绑成一小捆，换了一块比较合适的头巾，上面布满了干枯的假花和弄皱了的缎带。她若有所思地看了一会儿同行的人，然后把手帕放在嘴前。她的眼睛奇怪地转动了一会儿，你听到了微弱的嘚嘚的噪音。老淑女把她的假牙装上了，假牙原来是放在篮子里糖果、大头针、柳橙、润发油、一块块的蛋糕、锭剂、祈祷书、薄荷水、铜钱和假发之间——都是旅行期间收藏在那里的。在旅程期间一直注意着女帽制造及贩卖商的那个犹太人绅士是个职业旅行推销员，他把他各种不同的货物都归在一起。那个脸色发黄的英国青年从

"nous voila."

NOUS VOILA! —We are at Paris! This must account for the removal of the milliner's curl papers, and the fixing of the old lady's teeth. —Since the last relai, the Diligence has been travelling with extraordinary speed. The postillion cracks his terrible whip, and screams shrilly. The conductor blows incessantly on his horn, the bells of the harness, the bumping and ringing of the wheels and chains, and the clatter of the great hoofs of the heavy snorting Norman stallions, have wondrously increased within this, the last ten minutes; and the Diligence, which has been proceeding hitherto at the rate of a league in an hour, now dashes gallantly forward, as if it would traverse at least six miles in the same space of time. Thus it is, when Sir Robert maketh a speech at Saint Stephen's—he useth his strength at the beginning, only, and the end. He gallopeth at the commencement; in the middle he lingers; at the close, again, he rouses the House, which has fallen asleep; he cracketh the whip of his satire; he shouts the shout of his patriotism; and, urging his eloquence to its roughest canter, awakens the sleepers, and inspires the weary, until men say, What a wondrous orator! What a capital coach! We will ride henceforth in it, and in no other!

But, behold us at Paris! The Diligence has reached a rude-looking gate, or grille, flanked by two lodges; the French Kings of old, made their entry by this gate; some of the hottest battles of the late revolution were fought before it. At present, it is blocked by carts and peasants, and a busy crowd of men, in green, examining the packages before they enter, probing the straw with long needles. It is the Barrier of St. Denis, and the green men are the Customs' men of the city of Paris. If you are a countryman, who would introduce a cow into the Metropolis, the city demands twenty-four francs for such a privilege: if you have a hundredweight of tallow candles, you must, previously, disburse three francs: if a drove of hogs, nine francs per whole hog: but upon these subjects Mr. Bulwer, Mrs. Trollope, and other writers, have already enlightened the public. In the present instance, after a momentary pause, one of the men in green mounts by the side of the conductor, and the ponderous vehicle pursues its journey.

The street which we enter, that of the Faubourg St. Denis, presents a

我们昨天离开布洛涅时就醉了，他正准备去巴黎进行医学研究，他发誓说真高兴要离开这个该死的公共马车了，这该死的旅程让人厌倦，很高兴旅行就要结束了。你旁边的那个人也伸展胳膊，把胳膊肘伸向左右邻人的嘴边，打着哈欠说："我们终于到了。"

我们到了！——我们到巴黎了！这一定要归功于女帽商的卷发纸和老淑女的假牙。因为在最后一程，公共马车的速度加快了。驾马的车夫把他那可怕的鞭子抽得劈啪作响，一路尖叫。带路的人不停歇地吹着喇叭，马具的铃铛声、车轮和链条的碰撞声、转动声，还有马蹄的嘚嘚声，混合着诺曼种马粗重的鼻息声，马车在最后十分钟里令人惊奇地加快了速度，本来一直以每小时一里格［大约三英里。——译注］速度前进的公共马车现在勇猛地向前冲刺，看来它至少能跑出每小时六英里的速度。这就像罗伯特先生在圣斯蒂芬时所做的一场演讲一样——他只在开始和结束时很用劲。开始时快速地讲，中间就拖延一会儿，结尾时再一次把已睡着的观众唤醒，他挥舞着讥刺的鞭子，大肆叫嚣他的爱国主议，用他的雄辩术来鞭策艰难慢跑的马匹，唤醒入睡的人，激发疲倦的人，直到人们不得不说：多么让人惊奇的演说者啊！多么一流的马车啊！自此以后我们不坐别的了，就坐这辆马车！

看看我们到巴黎的情景吧！公共马车在一扇看起来很粗糙的门（或是铁栅栏）前停下了，门的两侧是两间小屋，以前的法国国王都是从这个门出入，前不久大革命的一些激烈战役就是在这个门前进行的。现在，它被手推车、农民还有一群忙碌的人给堵住了，那群人穿着一身绿色的服装，用长长的铁钎刺探草捆检查进城人员的包裹和物品。这是圣丹尼斯［巴黎北部的一个区。——译注］的海关关卡，一身绿的人就是巴黎的海关关员。如果你是一个乡下人，想把一头奶牛带进城里去，对于这一特权，城市要求征收二十四法郎的关税；如果你有一英担的牛油烛，你一定要预先支付三法郎；如果是一群猪，每头猪九法郎。对于这些话题，布尔威先生［Bulwer（1808—1873），英国小说家，政治家。——译注］、特罗洛普

strange contrast to the dark uniformity of a London street, where everything, in the dingy and smoky atmosphere, looks as though it were painted in India-ink—black houses, black passengers, and black sky. Here, on the contrary, is a thousand times more life and colour. Before you, shining in the sun, is a long glistening line of GUTTER,—not a very pleasing object in a city, but in a picture invaluable. On each side are houses of all dimensions and hues; some but of one story; some as high as the tower of Babel. From these the haberdashers (and this is their favourite street) flaunt long strips of gaudy calicoes, which give a strange air of rude gayety to the street. Milk-women, with a little crowd of gossips round each, are, at this early hour of morning, selling the chief material of the Parisian café-au-lait. Gay wineshops, painted red, and smartly decorated with vines and gilded railings, are filled with workmen taking their morning's draught. That gloomy looking prison on your right is a prison for women; once it was a convent for Lazarists: a thousand unfortunate individuals of the softer sex now occupy that mansion: they bake, as we find in the guide-books, the bread of all the other prisons; they mend and wash the shirts and stockings of all the other prisoners; they make hooks and eyes and phosphorus boxes, and they attend chapel every Sunday:—if occupation can help them, sure they have enough of it. Was it not a great stroke of the Legislature to superintend the morals and linen at once, and thus keep these poor creatures continually mending? —but we have passed the prison long ago, and are at the Port St. Denis itself.

There is only time to take a hasty glance as we pass: it commemorates some of the wonderful feats of arms of Ludovicus Magnus, and abounds in ponderous allegories—nymphs, and river-gods, and pyramids crowned with fleurs-de-lis; Louis passing over the Rhine in triumph, and the Dutch Lion giving up the ghost, in the year of our Lord 1672. The Dutch Lion revived, and overcame the man some years afterwards; but of this fact, singularly enough, the inscriptions make no mention. Passing, then, round the gate, and not under it (after the general custom, in respect of triumphal arches), you cross the boulevard, which gives a glimpse of trees and sunshine, and gleaming white buildings; then, dashing down the Rue de Bourbon Villeneuve, a dirty street, which seems interminable, and the Rue St. Eustache,

[Anthong Trollope（1815—1882），英国小说家。——译注] 和其他的作家都已经告知过民众了。短暂的停留之后，一个一身绿的人爬到马车上来坐在管理人的一侧，这个沉重的车辆又开始继续它的旅程了。

我们进入了圣丹尼斯区的街道，这里的街道与黑咕隆咚的伦敦街道形成了鲜明的对比，整个伦敦街道都被包裹在弥漫的暗黑烟雾中，房子看起来好像是被涂上了墨汁，行人和天空都是黑色的。但在这里，一切都变得丰富多彩。在你面前，闪烁在阳光下的是一排长长的排水沟——尽管它在城市中并不是一个令人喜爱的事物，除非是在一幅珍贵的画作中。街道两边是各种尺寸和颜色的房子，有的只有一层，有的就像巴别塔（通天塔）那样高。街道上的男子服饰用品商店（这是男人们喜欢的街道）所展示出的印花棉布给这条街道带来了一抹清新的亮色调。每个挤奶女工的身边都围着一小群聊天的人，因为凌晨正是销售牛奶的最好时段，它也是巴黎牛奶咖啡的主要原料。装饰华丽的酒店被漆成了红色，还时髦地用葡萄藤和镀金的扶手做装饰，里面坐满了早晨饮酒的工人。右边那个看起来阴暗的监狱是所女子监狱，它原来曾是一所收容乞丐的女修道院。现在里面住着的是不幸的女犯，她们就如我们在旅游指南里所读到的那样在烘烤所有其他监狱的面包，缝补和洗涤其他所有囚犯的衬衫和长袜；她们做钮扣式的钩和孔、火柴盒，每个星期日去参加礼拜仪式。政府当局当然有足够的能力来帮助她们，但他们却让这些可怜的人继续不停地缝补下去，这难道不是对监督道德纪律的立法机关的当头一棒吗？但我们已过监狱很远了，现在到圣丹尼斯城门了。

当我们经过时，只有时间匆匆一瞥。圣丹尼斯城门是为了纪念伟大的路易十四而建的，城门上雕有女神和河神，顶部用百合花徽 [法国王室标志。——译注] 装饰。1672 年路易胜利渡过莱茵河，荷兰这头狮子就要死了。[1672—1678 年路易十四发动了对荷兰的战争。——译注] 但几年后，荷兰这头狮子复活了，并战胜了路易王。对于这个足够奇异的事实，铭文没有记载。绕着城门转过去（不从城门下面走是一种风俗习惯，同凯旋门

the conductor gives a last blast on his horn, and the great vehicle clatters into the courtyard, where its journey is destined to conclude.

If there was a noise before of screaming postillions and cracked horns, it was nothing to the Babel-like clatter which greets us now. We are in a great court, which Hajji Baba would call the father of Diligences—half a dozen other coaches arrive at the same minute; no light affairs, like your English vehicles, but ponderous machines, containing fifteen passengers inside, more in the cabriolet, and vast towers of luggage on the roof—others are loading: the yard is filled with passengers coming or departing;—bustling porters and screaming commissionaires. These latter seize you as you descend from your place,—twenty cards are thrust into your hand, and as many voices, jabbering with inconceivable swiftness, shriek into your ear, "Dis way, sare; are you for ze Otel of Rhin? Hotel de l'Amiraute! —Hotel Bristol, sare! —Monsieur, l'Hotel de Lille? Sacr-rrré nom de Dieu, laissez passer ce petit, Monsieur! Ow mosh loggish ave you, sare?"

And now, if you are a stranger in Paris, listen to the words of Titmarsh.—If you cannot speak a syllable of French, and love English comfort, clean rooms, breakfasts, and waiters; if you would have plentiful dinners, and are not particular (as how should you be?) concerning wine; if, in this foreign country, you WILL have your English companions, your porter, your friend, and your brandy-and-water—do not listen to any of these commissioner fellows, but with your best English accent, shout out boldly, MEURICE! and straightway a man will step forward to conduct you to the Rue de Rivoli.

Here you will find apartments at any price: a very neat room, for instance, for three francs daily; an English breakfast of eternal boiled eggs, or grilled ham; a nondescript dinner, profuse but cold; and a society which will rejoice your heart. Here are young gentlemen from the universities; young merchants on a lark; large families of nine daughters, with fat father and mother; officers of dragoons, and lawyers' clerks. The last time we dined at Meurice's we hobbed and nobbed with no less a person than Mr. Moses, the celebrated bailiff of Chancery Lane; Lord Brougham was on his right, and a clergyman's lady, with a train of white-haired girls, sat on his left, wonderfully taken with the diamond rings of the fascinating stranger!

一样），就到了林荫大道，在大道上能看到一排排的树木和耀眼的白色建筑物；接着又到了波旁维尔纳夫街，这是一条肮脏的街道，马车走起来似乎是没完没了；最后到了圣欧斯塔施街，带路的人吹了最后一次喇叭，这个伟大的交通工具嘚嘚地驶进了院子，旅程结束了。

进了院子之后，我们发现什么噪音也无法和迎接我们的喧哗声相比。我们现在是在一个很大的院子里，在这里朝圣的人们会把它称做马车的起源地。半打的公用马车都是在同一时刻到达的——它们都不是轻载的，这点不像英国的交通工具，非常沉重，里面承载了十五位乘客，比单马双轮的轻便车载的人多，车顶的行李都堆成了尖，一些人正在装货，院子里挤满了刚到的和正要离开的乘客，还有忙忙碌碌的搬运工和尖叫的旅馆看门人。你刚从座位上下来，那些看门人就抓住你，把二十张卡片强行塞进你的手中，还有许多声音叽叽喳喳地以难以想象的速度钻进你的耳朵："先生，你要去莱茵宾馆吗？""英国海军部旅馆！"……"布里斯多旅馆，先生！"……"先生，里尔旅馆？看在上帝的面上，让这个小孩过去，先生！你带的行李在哪儿呢？"

现在，如果你对巴黎陌生的话，就听蒂特马舍的话。如果你连一个法语音节也不会讲，喜欢英国式的舒适干净的房间、早餐和侍者；如果你想吃量多的晚餐，不是特别在意酒（你将会怎样呢）；如果在这个异域的国家，你想和你的英国同伴在一起，有你的门房、你的朋友和你自己的白兰地和水，那就不要听这些旅馆看门人中的任何一个，而是用你纯正的英国口音大胆地叫出来："莫里斯！"很快就会有一个人走上前来带你去利沃利街。

在这里你将会找到任何价位的公寓。例如每天三法郎的一个非常整洁的房间、一份水煮蛋或烤火腿的英式早餐、一份丰盛冷盘的晚餐，还有一个将会让你感到愉悦的团体。这里有来自大学的年轻绅士，闹着玩的年轻商人，有着九个女儿和胖胖的父亲、母亲的大家庭，龙骑兵的官员，律师事务所的职员。我们最后一次在莫里斯用餐时，在座的人有法庭的著名执行官摩西先生，布鲁厄姆大人［英国的法律改革者。——译注］坐在他的右边，还有一位牧师的夫人带着美丽的钻石戒指，领着一排白发的少女，

It is, as you will perceive, an admirable way to see Paris, especially if you spend your days reading the English papers at *Galignani's*, as many of our foreign tourists do.

But all this is promiscuous, and not to the purpose. If,—to continue on the subject of hotel choosing,—if you love quiet, heavy bills, and the best table d'hôte in the city, go, oh, stranger! to the Hotel des Princes; it is close to the Boulevard, and convenient for Frascati's. The Hotel Mirabeau possesses scarcely less attraction; but of this you will find, in Mr. Bulwer's *Autobiography of Pelham*, a faithful and complete account. Lawson's Hotel has likewise its merits, as also the Hotel de Lille, which may be described as a "second chop" Meurice.

If you are a poor student come to study the humanities, or the pleasant art of amputation, cross the water forthwith, and proceed to the Hotel Corneille, near the Odéon, or others of its species; there are many where you can live royally (until you economize by going into lodgings) on four francs a day; and where, if by any strange chance you are desirous for a while to get rid of your countrymen, you will find that they scarcely ever penetrate.

But above all, oh, my countrymen! shun boarding houses, especially if you have ladies in your train; or ponder well, and examine the characters of the keepers thereof, before you lead your innocent daughters, and their mamma, into places so dangerous. In the first place, you have bad dinners; and, secondly, bad company. If you play cards, you are very likely playing with a swindler; if you dance, you dance with a —— person with whom you had better have nothing to do.

NOTE (which ladies are requested not to read).—In one of these establishments, daily advertised as most eligible for English, a friend of the writer lived. A lady, who had passed for some time as the wife of one of the inmates, suddenly changed her husband and name, her original husband remaining in the house, and saluting her by her new title.

坐在他的左边！

你将会发现，还有一个轻松的方法了解巴黎，尤其是如果你像我们许多外国旅行者那样把一天的时间都花费在英文的《加里涅尼报》[这份报纸是入法国籍的英国人约翰·安东尼·加里涅尼（John Anthony Galignani）和威廉·加里涅尼（William Galignani）两兄弟合办的。——译注]上的时候。

但是所有这些话都是随便说说，不得要领的。让我们继续旅馆选择的话题——如果你喜欢安静昂贵的好旅馆，那就去王子旅馆，它靠近林荫大道。弗拉斯卡迪饭店也很方便。米哈博旅馆不太引人注意，但是你将会在布尔威先生《佩勒姆马勒衔的自传》中找到真实而完备的叙述。劳森旅馆同样也有它的优点，里尔旅馆也一样，可称得上是莫里斯第二。

如果你是一位来学习人文学科或艺术的穷学生，可以穿过塞纳河，向前走到高乃依旅馆，它离奥登很近，那里有许多同类的旅馆。你可以每天花四法郎光明正大地住宿（直到你身无分文不得不进寄宿处为止），而且你不用急于摆脱你的国籍，因为那里的人很少去在意这些。

同胞们，最重要的是要避开供膳的住宿处，尤其是如果你还带着一些女士，那么在把你纯洁的女儿、孩子的母亲带到危险地方之前要好好考虑一下，调查一下相关监护人的品性。第一，你的晚餐会很糟糕；第二，同伴也很糟糕。如果你玩牌，很可能是和一个骗子玩。如果你跳舞，最好是和一个没有任何关系的人跳。

注意（女士不宜读）：作者的一位朋友所住过的一家旅馆对英国人来说是个最好的广告。一位女士和她丈夫在一起住了一段时间，但是有一天她突然换了丈夫和名字。而她原来的丈夫仍住那里，用她的新名字跟她打招呼。

A Caution to Travellers

A million dangers and snares await the traveller, as soon as he issues out of that vast messagerie which we have just quitted: and as each man cannot do better than relate such events as have happened in the course of his own experience, and may keep the unwary from the path of danger, let us take this, the very earliest opportunity, of imparting to the public a little of the wisdom which we painfully have acquired.

And first, then, with regard to the city of Paris, it is to be remarked, that in that metropolis flourish a greater number of native and exotic swindlers than are to be found in any other European nursery. What young Englishman that visits it, but has not determined, in his heart, to have a little share of the gayeties that go on—just for once, just to see what they are like? How many, when the horrible gambling dens were open, did resist a sight of them? —nay, was not a young fellow rather flattered by a dinner invitation from the Salon, whither he went, fondly pretending that he should see "French society," in the persons of certain Dukes and Counts who used to frequent the place?

My friend Pogson is a young fellow, not much worse, although perhaps a little weaker and simpler than his neighbours; and coming to Paris with exactly the same notions that bring many others of the British youth to that capital, events befell him there, last winter, which are strictly true, and shall here be narrated, by way of warning to all.

Pogson, it must be premised, is a city man, who travels in drugs for a couple of the best London houses, blows the flute, has an album, drives his own gig, and is considered, both on the road and in the metropolis, a remarkably nice, intelligent, thriving young man. Pogson's only fault is too great an

对旅行者的一点忠告

当旅行者刚从我们离开的那个巨大的马车出来后，将会有一百万个危险和陷阱在等候着他。由于每个人都不可能在旅行期间把自己将遇到的事情考虑周全，或者在面临危险的时候未能保持警惕，就让我们利用这个非常及时的机会，透露给大家一些我们从痛苦的经验教训中所获得的智慧吧。

首先，就说巴黎市吧！需要注意，在这个繁荣的大都市里有着比其他欧洲城市数量更多的本国的和外国的骗子。去巴黎的年轻英国人，在他心里还没主意的时候，难道不愿意去获得一些快乐吗？即使是只有一次机会，他们也要去看看他们喜欢的东西什么样。当可怕的赌窟打开的时候，有多少人能抵制住不看它一眼呢？同样，当一个年轻人得到一次沙龙晚餐邀请的机会，而且他还天真地想去看看这种有许多公爵和伯爵经常光顾的“法国社会”时，难道他不会为此感到自豪吗？

我的朋友波格逊是一个年轻的小伙子，本性并不坏，虽然也许比他的朋友要软弱和单纯一些。他正是带着与其他英国年轻人一样的想法来到这个首都——巴黎的。去年冬天事情发生在了他身上，这里将要讲述这个真实的故事，顺便给大家提个醒。

故事的前提是波格逊是一个城里人，是伦敦最好的两家店铺的药材旅行商，他总是吹着笛子，带着一本文选，驾驶着他自己的轻便马车。需要注意的是，无论在路上还是在大都市里，他都被认为是一个值得注意的、有教养的、聪明而精力旺盛的年轻人。波格逊唯一的缺点是沉迷女色。正

attachment to the fair:—"the sex," as he says often "will be his ruin:" the fact is, that Pogson never travels without a "*Don Juan*" under his driving-cushion, and is a pretty-looking young fellow enough.

Sam Pogson had occasion to visit Paris, last October; and it was in that city that his love of the sex had liked to have cost him dear. He worked his way down to Dover; placing, right and left, at the towns on his route, rhubarbs, sodas, and other such delectable wares as his masters dealt in ("the sweetest sample of castor oil, smelt like a nosegay—went off like wildfire—hogshead and a half at Rochester, eight-and-twenty gallons at Canterbury," and so on), and crossed to Calais, and thence voyaged to Paris in the coupé of the Diligence. He paid for two places, too, although a single man, and the reason shall now be made known.

Dining at the table d'hôte at Quillacq's—it is the best inn on the continent of Europe—our little traveller had the happiness to be placed next to a lady, who was, he saw at a glance, one of the extreme pink of the nobility. A large lady, in black satin, with eyes and hair as black as sloes, with gold chains, scent-bottles, sable tippet, worked pocket-handkerchief, and four twinkling rings on each of her plump white fingers. Her cheeks were as pink as the finest Chinese rouge could make them. Pogson knew the article: he travelled in it. Her lips were as red as the ruby lip salve: she used the very best, that was clear.

She was a fine-looking woman, certainly (holding down her eyes, and talking perpetually of "mes trente-deux ans"); and Pogson, the wicked young dog! who professed not to care for young misses, saying they smelt so of bread-and-butter, declared, at once, that the lady was one of HIS beauties: in fact, when he spoke to us about her, he said, "She's a slap-up thing, I tell you; a reg'lar good one; ONE OF MY SORT!" And such was Pogson's credit in all commercial rooms, that one of HIS sort was considered to surpass all other sorts.

During dinner time, Mr. Pogson was profoundly polite and attentive to the lady at his side, and kindly communicated to her, as is the way with the best-bred English on their first arrival "on the Continent," all his impressions regarding the sights and persons he had seen. Such remarks having been made

如他经常说的那样，“女人将是他的祸因”。事实上，波格逊每次旅行都会把《唐璜》放在驾驶垫子下面，他也是一个足够英俊的年轻小伙子。

去年10月，山姆·波格逊有机会去拜访巴黎，就是在那个城市里他对女人的爱情让他大吃苦头。他自己来到英国东南部的港口多佛尔，一路上在两旁的城市里购置了他主人吩咐的大黄、苏打和其他货物（有“海狸油的芳香样品，它们闻起来就像是一丛花束——卖得挺火爆——在路彻斯特卖了一桶半，在坎特伯雷卖了二十八加仑”，诸如此类的），然后穿过英吉利海峡到了加来［法国港口。——译注］，接着又乘公共双座四轮马车到了巴黎。尽管只有他一个人，他却付了两个座位的费用，其中原因下文将会有所交代。

他在克拉克旅馆吃的客饭——这个旅馆是欧洲大陆最好的旅馆。这位年轻的旅客很高兴自己能被安排在一位女士旁边，他瞥了那位女士一眼，她可是贵族名流的典型。这位女士身材高大，穿着黑色的缎子衣服，眼睛和头发就像黑刺李一般黑，身上有金色的链子、香水瓶、黑貂披肩和精致的手帕，四根圆胖的白手指上戴着四个闪烁发光的戒指。她的脸颊是粉红的，像是用最上等的中国胭脂涂的。波格逊知道这种商品，他曾经购置过它。她的唇同样也是红色的，像是用了红宝石的唇膏，很明显，她用的都是最好的化妆品。

她当然是一个好看的女人了（眼睛低垂，不断地说着“我的三十二岁”）。波格逊这个可恶的年轻家伙声称自己不会喜欢年轻的女士，说她们闻起来就像面包和黄油，他认为这位女士才是个美人。当他跟我们说起她的时候，他说：“我告诉你，她是个尤物，非常的好，是我喜欢的那种类型！”这就是波格逊经商的信念，即他喜欢的东西就是最好的。

晚餐期间，波格逊先生对身边的这位女士极为礼貌和殷勤，友好地和她交流，如同第一次来到这个国家那些修养最好的英国人所做的那样，他谈论自己对所看到的风景和人的所有印象：绕着街垒和城镇漫步的半个小时所作的评论，沿着路走到海关期间所看到的一切，以及与看门人的亲密

during half an hour's ramble about the ramparts and town, and in the course of a walk down to the Custom-house, and a confidential communication with the commissionaire, must be, doubtless, very valuable to Frenchmen in their own country; and the lady listened to Pogson's opinions, not only with benevolent attention, but actually, she said, with pleasure and delight. Mr. Pogson said that there was no such thing as good meat in France, and that's why they cooked their victuals in this queer way; he had seen many soldiers parading about the place, and expressed a true Englishman's abhorrence of an armed force; not that he feared such fellows as these—little whipper-snappers—our men would eat them. Hereupon the lady admitted that our guards were angels, but that Monsieur must not be too hard upon the French; "her father was a General of the Emperor."

Pogson felt a tremendous respect for himself at the notion that he was dining with a General's daughter, and instantly ordered a bottle of champagne to keep up his consequence.

"Mrs. Bironn, ma'am," said he, for he had heard the waiter call her by some such name, "if you WILL accept a glass of champagne, ma'am, you'll do me, I'm sure, great honour: they say it's very good, and a precious sight cheaper than it is on our side of the way, too—not that I care for money. Mrs. Bironn, ma'am, your health, ma'am."

The lady smiled very graciously, and drank the wine.

"Har you any relation, ma'am, if I may make so bold; har you anyways connected with the family of our immortal bard?"

"Sir, I beg your pardon."

"Don't mention it, ma'am: but *Bironn* and *byron* are hevidently the same names, only you pronounce in the French way; and I thought you might be related to his Lordship: his horigin, ma'am, was of French extraction:" and here Pogson began to repeat,—

> "Hare thy heyes like thy mother's, my fair child,
> Hada! sole daughter of my ouse and art."

"Oh!" said the lady, laughing, "you speak of *LOR* Byron?"

交流，毫无疑问这些对于法国本地人来说都是很有意义的。这位女士不仅是带着善意的专注听波格逊的看法，她还说很高兴能听到这些。波格逊先生说没有什么能比法国肉更好吃的了，怪不得法国人要用独特的方法来烹调他们的食品；他还看到许多军人在这个地方列队行进，而且表达了一个真正的英国人对于军队的痛恨，并不是他怕这些人——妄自尊大的小人物，而是我们的军队会干掉他们的。关于这个话题，这位女士承认我们的护卫队是天使，但她请先生也不要太苛责法国人，因为“她父亲是皇帝手下的一名将军”。

波格逊对自己能和一位将军的女儿一起就餐而感到很荣幸，立即吩咐开一瓶香槟酒来继续他的谈话。

“比伦女士，”他说，因为他曾听到侍者这样称呼她，“如果你乐意接受一杯香槟酒的话，我会感到很荣幸的。他们说这种香槟非常好，比我们路边的便宜多了。——不，我不是在乎钱。比伦女士，祝你健康。”

那位女士非常亲切地微笑着，喝了酒。

“夫人，恕我冒昧，你和我们那位不朽的吟游诗人家族有什么联系吗?”

“先生，对不起，我不明白。”

“没关系，女士。但是比伦和拜伦明显是同一个名字，只不过比伦是法语的发音。我想你可能与他的贵族身份有关系，他的祖先有法国人的血统。”说到这里，波格逊开始背诵起来——

> 啊！你的眼睛就像你母亲一样，我美丽的孩子，
>
> 爱达［Hada（1815—1852），著名诗人拜伦唯一合法的女儿爱达·古斯塔·拉夫拉斯伯爵夫人。——译注］！我唯一挚爱的女儿。［引自拜伦的《恰尔德·哈洛尔德游记》。——译注］

“哦!”那位女士笑着说，“你是说拜伦勋爵吧?”

波格逊说：“《唐璜》、《哈洛尔德游记》和《该隐》的作者。”……“我

"Hauthor of '*Don Juan*,' '*Child Arold*,' and '*Cain, a mystery*,'" said Pogson:—"I do; and hearing the waiter calling you Madam la Bironn, took the liberty of hasking whether you were connected with his Lordship;—that's hall:" and my friend here grew dreadfully red, and began twiddling his long ringlets in his fingers, and examining very eagerly the contents of his plate.

"Oh, no: Madame la Baronne means Mistress Baroness; my husband was Baron, and I am Baroness."

"What! ave I the honour—I beg your pardon, ma'am—is your Ladyship a Baroness, and I not know it: pray excuse me for calling you ma'am."

The Baroness smiled most graciously—with such a look as Juno cast upon unfortunate Jupiter when she wished to gain her wicked ends upon him—the Baroness smiled; and, stealing her hand into a black velvet bag, drew from it an ivory card-case, and from the ivory card-case extracted a glazed card, printed in gold; on it was engraved a coronet, and under the coronet the words

BARONNE DE FLORVAL-DELVAL,
NÉE DE MELVAL-NORVAL.
Rue Taitbout.

The grand Pitt diamond—the Queen's own star of the garter—a sample of otto-of-roses at a guinea a drop, would not be handled more curiously, or more respectfully, than this porcelain card of the Baroness. Trembling he put it into his little Russia-leather pocket-book: and when he ventured to look up, and saw the eyes of the Baroness de Florval-Delval, Née de Melval-Norval, gazing upon him with friendly and serene glances, a thrill of pride tingled through Pogson's blood: he felt himself to be the very happiest fellow "on the Continent."

But Pogson did not, for some time, venture to resume that sprightly and elegant familiarity which generally forms the great charm of his conversation: he was too much frightened at the presence he was in, and contented himself by graceful and solemn bows, deep attention, and ejaculations of "Yes, my Lady," and "No, your Ladyship," for some minutes after the discovery had been made. Pogson piqued himself on his breeding: "I hate the aristocracy,"

确实是听到侍者称呼您比伦夫人，才冒昧地问您是否和他的贵族身份有什么联系。”波格逊意识到他猜错了，脸变得通红，用手指抚弄着他的长卷发，急切地看着他碟子里的东西。

“哦！不，比伦夫人意思是男爵夫人。我的丈夫是男爵，因此我就是男爵夫人。”

“什么！我很荣幸——对不起，夫人——您的身份是男爵夫人，我并不知道。请您原谅我叫您女士。”

男爵夫人很亲切地微笑——如此的神情就像朱诺想从朱庇特身上达到她邪恶的目的时对不幸的朱庇特所投去的表情。男爵夫人微笑着，私下里把她的手放进一个黑色的天鹅绒袋子里，从里面取出一张象牙制的卡盒，从象牙卡盒里抽出一张闪闪发光的卡片，金色的印刷体，上面刻了一个王冠，王冠下面有这几行字：

弗罗瓦勒·岱乐瓦勒男爵

麦勒瓦勒·诺瓦勒贵族出身

泰部街

珍贵的皮特钻石——女王自己的嘉德勋章［英国的最高勋位。——译注］，或者一滴玫瑰油的样品也不会比这个男爵夫人这张精美的卡片更受波格逊如此细心和恭敬的处理了。他颤抖着把它放入他的小俄式皮夹里，当他大着胆子抬头向上看时，看见了麦勒·瓦勒诺瓦勒贵族出身的弗罗瓦勒·岱乐瓦勒男爵夫人的眼睛正友好而宁静地注视着他，一种自豪的兴奋在波格逊的血液中流淌着，他觉得自己是法国大陆上最幸福的人。

但是波格逊有一段时间没有恢复他和夫人之间刚开始的优雅而亲密、充满魅力的谈话，他被眼前出现的一切吓坏了，在发现夫人身份之后的几分钟内，他用优美而严肃的鞠躬、真诚的关心和突然喊出的“是的，我的夫人”和“不，夫人（对家族有爵位的妇女的称呼——译注）”来安慰自

he said, "but that's no reason why I shouldn't behave like a gentleman."

A surly, silent little gentleman, who had been the third at the ordinary, and would take no part either in the conversation or in Pogson's champagne, now took up his hat, and, grunting, left the room, when the happy bagman had the delight of a tête-à-tête. The Baroness did not appear inclined to move: it was cold; a fire was comfortable, and she had ordered none in her apartment. Might Pogson give her one more glass of champagne, or would her Ladyship prefer "something hot." Her Ladyship gravely said, she never took ANYTHING hot. "Some champagne, then; a leetle drop?" She would! she would! Oh, gods! how Pogson's hand shook as he filled and offered her the glass!

What took place during the rest of the evening had better be described by Mr. Pogson himself, who has given us permission to publish his letter.

QUILLACQ'S HOTEL (pronounced KILLYAX), CALAIS.

"Dear Tit,

"I arrived at Cally, as they call it, this day, or, rather, yesterday; for it is past midnight, as I sit thinking of a wonderful adventure that has just befallen me. A woman in course; that's always the case with ME, you know: but, oh, Tit! if you COULD but see her! Of the first family in France, the Florval-Melvals, beautiful as an angel, and no more caring for money than I do for split peas.

"I'll tell you how it all occurred. Everybody in France, you know, dines at the ordinary—it's quite distangy to do so. There were only three of us today, however,—the Baroness, me, and a gent, who never spoke a word; and we didn't want him to, neither: do you mark that?

"You know my way with the women; champagne's the thing; make 'em drink, make 'em talk;—make 'em talk, make 'em do anything. So I orders a bottle, as if for myself; and, 'Ma'am,' says I, 'will you take a glass of Sham—just one?' Take it she did—for you know it's quite distangy here: everybody dines at the table de hote, and everybody accepts everybody's wine. Bob Irons, who travels in linen on our circuit, told me that he had made some slap-up acquaintances among the genteelest people at Paris, nothing but by offering them Sham.

己。波格逊夸耀他的出身：“我憎恨贵族，”他说，“但是我没有理由行为举止不该像个绅士。”

一个无礼、沉默的小绅士，一直是小酒店里的第三者，既不参与谈话也不喝波格逊的香槟酒，当这个快乐的旅行商高兴地想和他单独谈话时，他却拿起帽子，咕哝着离开房间了。那个男爵夫人还没有要走的意思。天很冷，有一堆火是很舒服的，她什么东西也没要。波格逊给她喝了几杯香槟酒，问男爵夫人是否会比较喜欢喝“热的东西”。男爵夫人庄重地说，她从不喝任何热的东西。“那么再拿些香槟酒来，再喝点?”她愿意！她愿意！噢，上帝！当波格逊把杯子盛满递给她的时候，他的手是多么颤抖啊！

在那天晚上剩余的时间里都发生了什么事最好还是让波格逊先生自己描述吧！他已经许可我们把他下面的这封信公开了。

克拉克旅馆，加来

亲爱的蒂特马舍：

我已在今天或者不如说是昨天到了加来，因为来时已过了午夜了。我正坐着回想那些发生在我身上的奇遇。当然是和一个女人有关，你知道，我经常碰到这种情形，但是，噢！蒂特马舍！如果你能看到她！法国的第一家族弗罗瓦勒·岱乐瓦勒，她像天使一样美丽，我宁愿去分豌豆也不在乎钱了。

我将告诉你它是如何发生的。你知道，在法国每个人都在小酒店里用正餐——很奇怪他们这样做。酒店里今天只有我们三个人——男爵夫人、我和一个一言不发的绅士。当然我们也不想他说话，你明白了吗?

你知道我和女人相处的方式是香槟酒。我请她们喝，让她们说话——让她们说话，让她们做任何事。因此我要了一瓶，装做是为自己要的，我说：“夫人，你愿意来一杯吗?——就一杯?”她真的喝了——你知道在这里这很普通。每个人都在供膳的旅馆里吃饭，每个

"Well, my Baroness takes one glass, two glasses, three glasses—the old fellow goes—we have a deal of chat (she took me for a military man, she said: is it not singular that so many people should?), and by ten o'clock we had grown so intimate, that I had from her her whole history, knew where she came from, and where she was going. Leave me alone with 'em: I can find out any woman's history in half an hour.

"And where do you think she IS going? to Paris to be sure: she has her seat in what they call the coopy (though you're not near so cooped in it as in our coaches. I've been to the office and seen one of 'em). She has her place in the coopy, and the coopy holds THREE; so what does Sam Pogson do? —he goes and takes the other two. Ain't I up to a thing or two? Oh, no, not the least; but I shall have her to myself the whole of the way.

"We shall be in the French metropolis the day after this reaches you: please look out for a handsome lodging for me, and never mind the expense. And I say, if you could, in her hearing, when you come down to the coach, call me Captain Pogson, I wish you would—it sounds well travelling, you know; and when she asked me if I was not an officer, I couldn't say no. Adieu, then, my dear fellow, till Monday, and vive le joy, as they say. The Baroness says I speak French charmingly, she talks English as well as you or I.

Your affectionate friend,

S. Pogson."

This letter reached us duly, in our garrets, and we engaged such an apartment for Mr. Pogson, as beseemed a gentleman of his rank in the world and the army. At the appointed hour, too, we repaired to the Diligence office, and there beheld the arrival of the machine which contained him and his lovely Baroness.

Those who have much frequented the society of gentlemen of his profession (and what more delightful?) must be aware, that, when all the rest of mankind look hideous, dirty, peevish, wretched, after a forty hours' coach-journey, a bagman appears as gay and spruce as when he started; having within himself a thousand little conveniences for the voyage, which common travellers neglect. Pogson had a little portable toilet, of which he had not

人都接受别人的敬酒。鲍伯·艾朗，那个经常在我们的路线上穿着亚麻布旅行的人，告诉我他在巴黎的最有教养的人群中已结识了许多上等人，除了给他们提供酒之外什么也没有做。

好！我的男爵夫人喝了一杯、两杯、三杯——那个老家伙走了——我们聊了好多（她把我当成了军人，她说：那么多人都愿意成为军人，难道不奇怪吗?），到十点钟我们已经很熟悉了，从她那儿我知道了她的整个来历，知道了她来自哪里，她要去哪里。只要让我单独和她们在一起，我能在半个小时之内知道任何一个女人的来历。

你想她是去哪里的呢？当然是去巴黎，她在他们称做“coopy”的交通工具中有位子（你在它里面不会像在我们的马车里那么拥挤，我曾去营业所见过其中的一辆）。她在“coopy”马车里有自己的座位，而它只能容纳三人。山姆·波格逊做什么了呢？他坐了另外两个位子。不是我大到需要两个座位，哦，当然不是，我要在路上让她全部都属于我。

我们将会在你接到这封信的第二天到达法国的首都。请为我找一个美观的旅馆，不必介意价钱。我说，在她听我们说话时，如果你可以的话，就在来到马车旁边时叫我波格逊上尉，我希望你能做到——你知道，这是次愉快的旅行。当她问我是不是一个军官时，我不能说不是。那么，再见，我亲爱的朋友，星期一见，如同他们说的一样，快乐万岁。男爵夫人说我说法语很迷人，她说英语说得像我们一样好。

你亲爱的朋友，

山姆·波格逊

这封信及时到了我们手中，我们给波格逊先生预定了房间，好与他在社会和军队上的地位相符。在约好的时间，我们也到了马车驿站，在那里注视着那辆载着他和他那位可爱的男爵夫人的马车的到来。

那些时常和波格逊那个职业的先生们（还有比他们更讨人喜欢的吗?）

failed to take advantage, and with his long, curling, flaxen hair, flowing under a seal-skin cap, with a gold tassel, with a blue and gold satin handkerchief, a crimson velvet waistcoat, a light green cut-away coat, a pair of barred brick-dust coloured pantaloons, and a neat Macintosh, presented, altogether, as elegant and distingue an appearance as any one could desire. He had put on a clean collar at breakfast, and a pair of white kids as he entered the barrier, and looked, as he rushed into my arms, more like a man stepping out of a band-box, than one descending from a vehicle that has just performed one of the laziest, dullest, flattest, stalest, dirtiest journeys in Europe.

To my surprise, there were TWO ladies in the coach with my friend, and not ONE, as I had expected. One of these, a stout female, carrying sundry baskets, bags, umbrellas, and woman's wraps, was evidently a maid-servant: the other, in black, was Pogson's fair one, evidently. I could see a gleam of curl-papers over a sallow face,—of a dusky night-cap flapping over the curl-papers,—but these were hidden by a lace veil and a huge velvet bonnet, of which the crowning birds-of-paradise were evidently in a moulting state. She was encased in many shawls and wrappers; she put, hesitatingly, a pretty little foot out of the carriage—Pogson was by her side in an instant, and, gallantly putting one of his white kids round her waist, aided this interesting creature to descend. I saw, by her walk, that she was five-and-forty, and that my little Pogson was a lost man.

After some brief parley between them—in which it was charming to hear how my friend Samuel WOULD speak, what he called French, to a lady who could not understand one syllable of his jargon—the mutual hackney-coaches drew up; Madame la Baronne waved to the Captain a graceful French curtsy. "Adyou!" said Samuel, and waved his lily hand. "Adyou-addimang."

A brisk little gentleman, who had made the journey in the same coach with Pogson, but had more modestly taken a seat in the Imperial, here passed us, and greeted me with a "How d'ye do?" He had shouldered his own little valise, and was trudging off, scattering a cloud of commissionaires, who would fain have spared him the trouble.

"Do you know that chap?" says Pogson; "surly fellow, ain't he?"

"The kindest man in existence," answered I; "all the world knows little

打交道的人一定知道，在四十小时的马车旅程后，一般人都会显得丑陋、肮脏、脾气暴躁、可怜兮兮，但是一个推销员却能像刚出门那样整洁愉快，因为他身上带着许多普通旅客所忽视的旅行用的小便利品。波格逊带着一个小小的梳洗包，他并没有忘记利用它。当他从马车上下来的时候，我们看到他戴着海豹皮的帽子，帽子下面是长长的、卷曲的、亚麻色的头发，帽子上面有金色的流苏，还有蓝色和金色相间的缎子手帕、深红色的天鹅绒背心、浅绿色的短外套、砖色的条纹裤子，还有一件整洁的雨衣，看起来是那样的优雅和高贵。他进海关关卡吃早餐时已换上干净的衣领和一双白色的小山羊皮手套，当他和我拥抱时，他看起来更像是一个从乐团里走出的男子，而不是从一辆在欧洲经历了慢吞吞、沉闷、单调、疲惫、肮脏旅程的马车里下来的。

令我惊讶的是，在马车里和我朋友在一起的有两位女士，而不是我预料中的一位。其中的一位是个强壮的女士，带着杂物篮子、袋子、伞和女人的外套，很明显是位女佣；另一个，一身黑色，很明显是波格逊的美人。我能看到她灰黄色的脸上有一道卷发纸的微光——暗黑色的睡帽在卷发纸上面摇晃着——但是这些都被一块饰带面纱和一顶极大的天鹅绒软帽隐藏起来了，帽顶的羽毛很明显是处在脱毛的状态中。她身上包裹着许多披肩和围巾。她犹豫着把一只美丽的小脚从马车里伸出来。波格逊立即来到她身边，很有骑士风度地用一只戴有小白山羊皮手套的手揽着她的腰，帮助这个美人从马车上下来。我从她走路的架势看出她有四十五岁了，但小波格逊已经被她迷惑住了。

他们之间还有一些简短谈话——其中很有意思的就是能听到我的朋友波格逊会怎样对一个听不懂他方言中哪怕一个音节的女士讲他自以为是的法语——他们彼此的出租马车靠近了。男爵夫人向上尉行了个法国式的屈膝礼。“再见（法语——译者）!”波格逊说，挥了挥他洁白的手。“再见，明天见（法语——译者）。”

一个活泼的矮个儿绅士是和波格逊乘坐同一辆马车旅行的，但他却很

Major British. ”

“He's a Major, is he? —why, that's the fellow that dined with us at Killyax's; it's lucky I did not call myself Captain before him, he mightn't have liked it, you know:” and then Sam fell into a reverie;—what was the subject of his thoughts soon appeared.

“Did you ever SEE such a foot and ankle?” said Sam, after sitting for some time, regardless of the novelty of the scene, his hands in his pockets, plunged in the deepest thought.

“ISN'T she a slap-up woman, eh, now?” pursued he; and began enumerating her attractions, as a horse-jockey would the points of a favourite animal.

“You seem to have gone a pretty length already,” said I, “by promising to visit her tomorrow. ”

“A good length? —I believe you. Leave ME alone for that. ”

“But I thought you were only to be two in the coupe, you wicked rogue. ”

“Two in the coopy? Oh! ah! yes, you know—why, that is, I didn't know she had her maid with her (what an ass I was to think of a noblewoman travelling without one!) and couldn't, in course, refuse, when she asked me to let the maid in. ”

“Of course not. ”

“Couldn't, you know, as a man of honour; but I made it up for all that,” said Pogson, winking slily, and putting his hand to his little bunch of a nose, in a very knowing way.

“You did, and how?”

“Why, you dog, I sat next to her; sat in the middle the whole way, and my back's half broke, I can tell you:” and thus, having depicted his happiness, we soon reached the inn where this back-broken young man was to lodge during his stay in Paris.

The next day at five we met; Mr. Pogson had seen his Baroness, and described her lodgings, in his own expressive way, as “slap-up. ” She had received him quite like an old friend; treated him to eau sucree, of which beverage he expressed himself a great admirer; and actually asked him to dine the next day. But there was a cloud over the ingenuous youth's brow, and I inquired still further.

谦逊，只乘坐一个座位，他从我们身边经过时，向我们致意——“你们好啊？”他用肩扛起他的小行李箱，迈着沉重的步伐，驱散开那些蜂拥而上的旅馆看门人，而他们也很乐意能省掉这个麻烦。

“你知道那个小伙子吗？”波格逊说，“难道他不是个无礼的家伙吗？”

我回答说：“他是现有的最仁慈的人，所有人都知道这个矮个儿英国少校。”

“他是一个少校，是吗？这个家伙和我们在克拉克旅馆一起用的餐，幸好我没有在他面前称自己是上尉，你知道，他也许不会喜欢的。”然后山姆陷入幻想之中——很明显能看出他在想什么。

“你曾见过这样的脚和脚踝吗？”山姆坐了一会儿后说，他也顾不得现场的新奇事物，把手插进口袋里，陷入沉思之中。

“难道她不是一个时髦的女人吗？”他继续说下去，开始列举她的迷人之处，就像一个赛马骑师评点他喜爱的一匹马。

“你看起来像是已经离开她很长一段时间了，”我说，“在答应明天拜访她之前。”

“好长的时间？——你说得对。让我单独待会儿。”

“但我以为马车里只有你和她两个，你这个捣蛋鬼。”

“马车里两个人？哦！啊！是的，你知道——为什么，也就是说，我不知道她带着女佣。（我是多么蠢啊，竟然认为一个贵族妇女会身边不带一个人旅行！）当她请求我让女佣上马车时我当然不能拒绝了。”

“当然不能。”

“你知道，作为一个男人，我不能拒绝。但是我得到补偿了。”波格逊说，狡猾地眨眨眼，以一种非常狡猾的姿势，把他的手放到他的小鼻头上。

“你怎么做的？”

“你这个小子！我可以告诉你，我是靠着她坐的，一路上坐在她和女佣的中间。我的背几乎就要累弯了。”就这样，波格逊描述着他的快乐，我们很快到了这个累弯背的年轻人在巴黎停留期间所要投宿的旅馆里。

"Why," said he, with a sigh, "I thought she was a widow; and, hang it! who should come in but her husband the Baron; a big fellow, sir, with a blue coat, a red ribbing, and SUCH a pair of moustachios!"

"Well," said I, "he didn't turn you out, I suppose?"

"Oh, no! on the contrary, as kind as possible; his Lordship said that he respected the English army; asked me what corps I was in,—said he had fought in Spain against us,—and made me welcome."

"What could you want more?"

Mr. Pogson at this only whistled; and if some very profound observer of human nature had been there to read into this little bagman's heart, it would, perhaps, have been manifest, that the appearance of a whiskered soldier of a husband had counteracted some plans that the young scoundrel was concocting.

I live up a hundred and thirty-seven steps in the remote quarter of the Luxembourg, and it is not to be expected that such a fashionable fellow as Sam Pogson, with his pockets full of money, and a new city to see, should be always wandering to my dull quarters; so that, although he did not make his appearance for some time, he must not be accused of any luke-warmness of friendship on that score.

He was out, too, when I called at his hotel; but once, I had the good fortune to see him, with his hat curiously on one side, looking as pleased as Punch, and being driven, in an open cab, in the Champs Elysees. "That's ANOTHER tip-top chap," said he, when we met, at length. "What do you think of an Earl's son, my boy? Honourable Tom Ringwood, son of the Earl of Cinqbars: what do you think of that, eh?"

I thought he was getting into very good society. Sam was a dashing fellow, and was always above his own line of life; he had met Mr. Ringwood at the Baron's, and they'd been to the play together; and the honourable gent, as Sam called him, had joked with him about being well to do IN A CERTAIN QUARTER; and he had had a game at billiards with the Baron, at the Estaminy, "a very distangy place, where you smoke," said Sam; "quite select, and frequented by the tip-top nobility;" and they were as thick as peas in a shell; and they were to dine that day at Ringwood's, and sup, the next night,

第二天五点钟我们见面了。波格逊先生已经看过他的男爵夫人了，向我描述了她的住所，用他自己的话说，是“时髦”的。她已经把他当做一个老朋友来接待了，用糖水款待他。他表示自己很喜欢这种饮料。她竟然邀请他第二天去吃饭。但是在这个天真的年轻人的眉宇间却有团愁云，我进一步询问下去。

他叹息着说：“唉！我以为她是一个寡妇，该死的！谁知道她的男爵丈夫进来了，那是一个高大的家伙，穿着一件蓝色的外套、一条红色的罗纹裤子，留着一把这样蓬松的大胡子！”

我说：“我猜，他没有赶走你？”

“哦，不！相反，极其亲切。这位爵爷说他尊敬英国的军队，问我是在什么军团，他说曾在西班牙和我们打过仗——还向我表示欢迎。”

“你还想要什么？”

波格逊先生这会儿只吹口哨，不说话了。如果是对人性有所了解的观察者在这里的话，他们会看透这个年轻推销员的心思。显然，那个络腮胡子的军人丈夫的出现阻碍了这个年轻流氓正在策划的一些计划。

我在遥远的卢森堡区爬了一百三十七个台阶才来到波格逊的住处，我不敢期望像山姆·波格逊这样口袋里装满金钱的时髦青年会经常到我住的地区来闲逛，因此，虽然他一段时间未曾露面，也不能指责他在友谊上的不冷不热。

当我到他旅馆里找他时，他恰巧也外出了。但是有一次，我幸运地碰到了他，他的帽子奇怪地歪戴在一侧，看起来像是木偶剧中的滑稽角色那样高兴，他坐在爱丽舍宫一辆敞篷的出租马车中。见到我，他说：“他是另一个上流社会的小伙子，你觉得一个伯爵的儿子怎样？尊敬的汤姆·瑞伍德，辛克巴伯爵的儿子。你对此是怎么想的，哦？”

我想他正在进入上流社会。山姆是个冲劲很足的小伙子，而且总是脱离自己的生活轨道。他在男爵家遇到瑞伍德先生，他们曾一起去过娱乐场所。那是一个值得尊敬的绅士，正如山姆称呼他的那样，他曾和波格逊开

with the Baroness.

"I think the chaps down the road will stare," said Sam, "when they hear how I've been coming it." And stare, no doubt, they would; for it is certain that very few commercial gentlemen have had Mr. Pogson's advantages.

The next morning we had made an arrangement to go out shopping together, and to purchase some articles of female gear, that Sam intended to bestow on his relations when he returned. Seven needle-books, for his sisters; a gilt buckle, for his mamma; a handsome French cashmere shawl and bonnet, for his aunt (the old lady keeps an inn in the Borough, and has plenty of money, and no heirs); and a toothpick case, for his father. Sam is a good fellow to all his relations, and as for his aunt, he adores her. Well, we were to go and make these purchases, and I arrived punctually at my time; but Sam was stretched on a sofa, very pale and dismal.

I saw how it had been. —"A little too much of Mr. Ringwood's claret, I suppose?"

He only gave a sickly stare.

"Where does the Honourable Tom live?" says I.

"HONOURABLE!" says Sam, with a hollow, horrid laugh; "I tell you, Dick, he's no more Honourable than you are."

"What, an impostor?"

"No, no; not that. He is a real Honourable, only—"

"Oh, ho! I smell a rat—a little jealous, eh?"

"Jealousy be hanged! I tell you he's a thief; and the Baron's a thief; and, hang me, if I think his wife is any better. Eight-and-thirty pounds he won of me before supper; and made me drunk, and sent me home:—is THAT honourable? How can I afford to lose forty pounds? It's took me two years to save it up:—if my old aunt gets wind of it, she'll cut me off with a shilling; hang me!"—and here Sam, in an agony, tore his fair hair.

While bewailing his lot in this lamentable strain, his bell was rung, which signal being answered by a surly "Come in," a tall, very fashionable gentleman, with a fur coat, and a fierce tuft to his chin, entered the room. "Pogson my buck, how goes it?" said he, familiarly, and gave a stare at me: I was making for my hat.

玩笑说要在一个特定的地方好好玩一番。山姆已经和男爵打了一场台球比赛，在埃斯塔米尼（Estaminy），“一个很特别、你可以吸烟的地方，”他说，“这个地方是特意挑选出来的，上流社会的贵族们经常光顾那里。”他们三人的关系已非常好了，经常聚在一起吃饭。那天他们是去瑞伍德家吃的饭。第二天晚上是和男爵夫人一起吃晚饭。

“我想一路上的小伙子都会注视我的，”山姆说，“尤其当他们听说我是从哪里回来的之后。”无疑，他们会注视的，因为很少有商人能有波格逊先生这样的机会。

第二天早晨我们已经计划好一起出去购物，买些女性服装之类的商品，山姆打算当他回国时送给他亲戚。给他的姐妹们买七本线装书；给他妈妈买一个镀金扣子；给他姨妈买一件漂亮的开司米披肩和软帽（这位老妇人在自治市镇中有一家旅馆，有许多钱，但是没继承人）；还要给他父亲买一个牙签盒子。对于他的亲戚来说，山姆是一个好小伙子，至于他姨妈，他很敬慕她。好吧！我们就要出去购买这些东西了，我按约定的时间准时到达，但是山姆却伸展着四肢躺在一张沙发上，脸色苍白，表情阴郁。

我知道这是怎么回事。“我猜，是瑞伍德先生的红葡萄酒喝得有点儿多了吧?”

他只是无力地看了我一眼。

“尊敬的汤姆住在哪里?”我说。

“尊敬的!”山姆用一种空洞可怕的笑声说，“我告诉你，蒂特，他并不比你值得尊敬。”

“什么，一个骗子?”

“不，不，不是那样。他是一个真正的贵族，只不过——”

“哦，嗬！我知道了——你有点儿嫉妒，哦?”

“该死的嫉妒！我告诉你，他是一个小偷，男爵也是个小偷。如果我认为他的妻子还好一点的话，那我真该死。晚饭前他赢了我三十八镑，把我灌醉了，送我回家——那是值得尊敬的吗？我如何才能负担得起这失去的

"Don't go," said Sam, rather eagerly; and I sat down again.

The Honourable Mr. Ringwood hummed and ha'd; and, at last, said he wished to speak to Mr. Pogson on business, in private, if possible.

"There's no secrets betwixt me and my friend," cried Sam.

Mr. Ringwood paused a little:—"An awkward business that of last night," at length exclaimed he.

"I believe it WAS an awkward business," said Sam, drily.

"I really am very sorry for your losses."

"Thank you: and so am I, I can tell you," said Sam.

"You must mind, my good fellow, and not drink; for, when you drink, you WILL play high: by Gad, you led US in, and not we you."

"I dare say," answered Sam, with something of peevishness; "losses is losses: there's no use talking about 'em when they're over and paid."

"And paid?" here wonderingly spoke Mr. Ringwood; "why, my dear fel—what the deuce—has Florval been with you?"

"D—Florval!" growled Sam, "I've never set eyes on his face since last night; and never wish to see him again."

"Come, come, enough of this talk; how do you intend to settle the bills which you gave him last night?"

"Bills ! what do you mean?"

"I mean, sir, these bills," said the Honourable Tom, producing two out of his pocket-book, and looking as stern as a lion. "'I promise to pay, on demand, to the Baron de Florval, the sum of four hundred pounds. October 20, 1838.' 'Ten days after date I promise to pay the Baron de et cetera et cetera, one hundred and ninety-eight pounds. Samuel Pogson.' You didn't say what regiment you were in."

"WHAT!" shouted poor Sam, as from a dream, starting up and looking preternaturally pale and hideous.

"D—it, sir, you don't affect ignorance: you don't pretend not to remember that you signed these bills, for money lost in my rooms: money LENT to you, by Madame de Melval, at your own request, and lost to her husband? You don't suppose, sir, that I shall be such an infernal idiot as to believe you, or such a coward as to put up with a mean subterfuge of this sort. Will you,

四十镑？它需要我两年才能节省下来——如果我姨妈听说了，她会取消我的继承权，该死!”这时的山姆处于极度的痛苦中，两手撕扯着他的金发。

当山姆在这种可悲的状态下悲叹自己的运气时，门铃响了，他粗鲁地回应了一声“进来”，一个高高的、穿着毛皮外套、下巴留着一簇硬胡须、非常时髦的绅士进了房间。“波格逊，我的花花公子，发生什么事了?”他用一种很随便的语气说，并看了我一眼，我正要去拿我的帽子。

“不要走。”山姆很急切地说，因此我又坐了下来。

尊敬的瑞伍德先生哼哼哈哈了一会儿，最后说，如果可以的话，他愿跟波格逊先生私下谈些事情。

“在我和我的朋友之间没有秘密。”山姆叫道。

瑞伍德先生停了停——最后大声说：“是关于昨晚的一件尴尬的事情。”

“我相信它的确是件尴尬的事情。”山姆冷淡地说。

“我真的为你的损失感到难过。”

“谢谢，我告诉你，我也一样。”山姆说。

“我的好朋友，你一定要注意，不要喝酒。因为，你一喝酒，你就会玩大的。天哪！是你让我们玩的，不是我们让你玩的。”

“我敢说，”山姆多少有点带着怒气回答，“损失就损失了，当事情已结束并付过钱之后，我们就没必要再谈论它们了。”

“付过钱了?”瑞伍德先生奇怪地说，“怎么，我亲爱的朋友——究竟怎么回事——弗罗瓦勒一直和你在一起吗?”

“弗罗瓦勒!”山姆咆哮起来，“从昨晚起我就没有见过他的面，而且再也不愿看见他。”

“好，好，到此为止。那你打算怎么处理昨晚你给他的账单?”

“账单，你什么意思?”

“先生，我的意思是，这些账单，”尊敬的汤姆说着就从他笔记本里抽出两张账单，他看起来很严肃，“‘我答应按要求支付给德·弗罗瓦勒男爵四百英镑。1838 年 10 月 20 日。’‘期满后十天我答应支付男爵利滚利共一

or will you not, pay the money, sir?"

"I will not," said Sam, stoutly; "it's a d——d swin—"

Here Mr. Ringwood sprung up, clenching his riding-whip, and looking so fierce that Sam and I bounded back to the other end of the room. "Utter that word again, and, by Heaven, I'll murder you!" shouted Mr. Ringwood, and looked as if he would, too: "once more, will you, or will you not, pay this money?"

"I can't," said Sam faintly.

"I'll call again, Captain Pogson," said Mr. Ringwood, "I'll call again in one hour; and, unless you come to some arrangement, you must meet my friend, the Baron de Melval, or I'll post you for a swindler and a coward." With this he went out: the door thundered to after him, and when the clink of his steps departing had subsided, I was enabled to look round at Pog. The poor little man had his elbows on the marble table, his head between his hands, and looked, as one has seen gentlemen look over a steam-vessel off Ramsgate, the wind blowing remarkably fresh: at last he fairly burst out crying.

"If Mrs. Pogson heard of this," said I, "what would become of the 'Three Tuns?'" (for I wished to give him a lesson:). "if your Ma, who took you every Sunday to meeting, should know that her boy was paying attention to married women;—if Drench, Glauber and Co. , your employers, were to know that their confidential agent was a gambler, and unfit to be trusted with their money, how long do you think your connexion would last with them, and who would afterwards employ you?"

To this poor Pog had not a word of answer; but sat on his sofa whimpering so bitterly, that the sternest of moralists would have relented towards him, and would have been touched by the little wretch's tears. Everything, too, must be pleaded in excuse for this unfortunate bagman: who, if he wished to pass for a captain, had only done so because he had an intense respect and longing for rank: if he had made love to the Baroness, had only done so because he was given to understand by Lord Byron's "Don Juan" that making love was a very correct, natty thing: and if he had gambled, had only been induced to do so by the bright eyes and example of the Baron and the Baron-

百九十八英镑。山姆·波格逊。’但你没有说你在哪个军团。”

“什么!”可怜的山姆喊道，他好像是从一场梦中惊起，看起来异常苍白和可怕。

“先生，你不要假装不知道，不要假装不记得你签过这些账单，你在我的房间里输的钱。是你自己请求德·弗罗瓦勒夫人借给你钱，又输给了她的丈夫，不是吗？你不要把我想象成一个会相信你的可恶的白痴或是一个能容忍你这种托词的懦夫。你愿不愿意付钱，先生?”

“我不愿意，”山姆坚定地说，“你这个——猪猡——”

瑞伍德先生跳了起来，紧紧抓着他的马鞭，看起来如此凶狠以至于把山姆和我吓得向后跳到了房间的另一端。“再说一遍那个词，老天在上，我会杀了你!”瑞伍德先生叫喊道，看起来他好像真会那么做，“再问一遍，你愿不愿意付钱?”

“我不能。”山姆无力地说。

“我会再来找你的，波格逊上尉，”瑞伍德先生说，“我会在一小时之内再来找你。除非你有别的安排，你一定要见我的朋友德·弗罗瓦勒男爵，否则我会向世人宣布你是个骗子和懦夫。”说着这些他就出去了，门在他身后砰地被关上，当他的脚步声渐渐远去了，我才顾得上回头看看波格逊。可怜的年轻人把胳膊肘支在大理石的桌子上，两手抱着头，看起来如同人们看到一位误了一辆离开拉姆斯盖特的轮船的先生一样无奈，风依然清新地吹着，最后他突然哭了起来。

我说：“如果波格逊太太听说这些，那会成什么样呢？（我希望能给他个教训）如果那个每星期日带你去聚会的妈妈，知道她的孩子喜欢已婚的女人；如果德伦克，格劳贝尔和公司，你的雇主们知道他们所信任的代理人是一个赌徒，他们的钱不保险，你以为你和他们的关系会持续多久，以后谁还会雇用你呢?”

可怜的波格逊一个字也没回答。他只是坐在沙发上痛苦地呜咽，即使是最严厉的道德家这时也会对他表示宽容，也会被这个可怜人的眼泪所打

ess. O ye Barons and Baronesses of England! if ye knew what a number of small commoners are daily occupied in studying your lives, and imitating your aristocratic ways, how careful would ye be of your morals, manners, and conversation!

My soul was filled, then, with a gentle yearning pity for Pogson, and revolved many plans for his rescue: none of these seeming to be practicable, at last we hit on the very wisest of all; and determined to apply for counsel to no less a person than Major British.

A blessing it is to be acquainted with my worthy friend, little Major British; and heaven, sure, it was that put the Major into my head, when I heard of this awkward scrape of poor Pog's. The Major is on half-pay, and occupies a modest apartment au quatrième, in the very hotel which Pogson had patronized at my suggestion; indeed, I had chosen it from Major British's own peculiar recommendation.

There is no better guide to follow than such a character as the honest Major, of whom there are many likenesses now scattered over the continent of Europe; men who love to live well, and are forced to live cheaply, and who find the English abroad a thousand times easier, merrier, and more hospitable than the same persons at home. I, for my part, never landed on Calais pier without feeling that a load of sorrows was left on the other side of the water; and have always fancied that black care stepped on board the steamer, along with the custom-house officers, at Gravesend, and accompanied one to yonder black lowering towers of London—so busy, so dismal, and so vast.

British would have cut any foreigner's throat who ventured to say so much, but entertained, no doubt, private sentiments of this nature; for he passed eight months of the year, regularly, abroad, with head-quarters at Paris (the garrets before alluded to), and only went to England for the month's shooting, on the grounds of his old Colonel, now an old Lord, of whose acquaintance the Major was passably inclined to boast.

He loved and respected, like a good staunch Tory as he is, every one of the English nobility; gave himself certain little airs of a man of fashion, that were by no means disagreeable; and was, indeed, kindly regarded by such English aristocracy as he met, in his little annual tours among the German

动。任何人也一定会找借口为这个不幸的推销员辩护。他假装成一位上尉是因为他对军衔有着强烈的尊敬和渴望；他向男爵夫人表白爱情是因为他愿做拜伦的“唐璜”，认为向女人表白爱情是一件很潇洒、有面子的事情；他去赌博也只是为男爵夫人的明亮双眼和男爵的做法所引诱。哦！你们这些英国的男爵和男爵夫人！如果你们知道有许多的小平民每日忙着研究你们的生活，模仿你们的贵族做派，你们将会多么在意你们的道德、举止和谈话啊！

一种自发的对于波格逊的怜悯之情占据了我的心灵，为了援救他，我考虑了许多计划，但没有一个看起来像是行得通的，最后我们终于想到了一个最明智的办法，决定找英国上校来商议此事。

幸亏我认识那个令人尊敬的朋友，矮个儿的英国上校。上帝啊！当我听说可怜的波格逊的尴尬窘境时，我脑子里猛然就想到了上校。上校是半薪退休的，他住在四层一间朴素的公寓里，也是波格逊根据我的提议而暂住的那家旅馆。实际上，我还是根据上校个人的推荐而把它选给波格逊的。

现在有许多类似的人物分散在欧洲大陆，但再也没有比正直的上校这样更好的向导值得人们去追随的了。喜欢舒适生活的人、不得不节俭生活的人，都发现在国外的英国人要比国内的英国人过得舒适、快乐而热情。至于我，在踏上加来码头时，总是感觉到有一个沉重的包袱被卸在了海的另一边。我总是回味起那种阴沉的心情，那种心情伴随我同葛文森［英国西南部，伦敦泰晤士河东岸的一个地方性的自治区。——译注］的海关关员一起在伦敦登上汽船，并且伴随我走向远处黑色阴沉的伦敦塔——它们显得那么拥挤、那么阴郁、那么巨大。

如果一个外国人敢说这样的话，英国人会切断他的咽喉，但这只是我个人的感想。上校今年与驻巴黎的司令部（前面提到的阁楼）一起在国外定期生活了八个月，只有每月的射击比赛才回到英国。他的老上校现在是一个老贵族，他相识的人都是值得人们去夸赞的。

作为一个坚定的保守派，他热爱并且尊敬每一位英国贵族，这使他自

courts, in Italy or in Paris, where he never missed an ambassador's night, and retailed to us, who didn't go, but were delighted to know all that had taken place, accurate accounts of the dishes, the dresses, and the scandal which had there fallen under his observation.

He is, moreover, one of the most useful persons in society that can possibly be; for besides being incorrigibly duelsome on his own account, he is, for others, the most acute and peaceable counsellor in the world, and has carried more friends through scrapes and prevented more deaths than any member of the Humane Society. British never bought a single step in the army, as is well known. In '14, he killed a celebrated French fire-eater, who had slain a young friend of his, and living, as he does, a great deal with young men of pleasure, and good old sober family people, he is loved by them both and has as welcome a place made for him at a roaring bachelor's supper at the "Café Anglais," as at a staid dowager's dinner-table in the Faubourg St. Honoré. Such pleasant old boys are very profitable acquaintances, let me tell you; and lucky is the young man who has one or two such friends in his list.

Hurrying on Pogson in his dress, I conducted him, panting, up to the Major's quatrième, where we were cheerfully bidden to come in. The little gentleman was in his travelling jacket, and occupied in painting, elegantly, one of those natty pairs of boots in which he daily promenaded the Boulevards. A couple of pairs of tough buff gloves had been undergoing some pipe-claying operation under his hands; no man stepped out so spick and span, with a hat so nicely brushed, with a stiff cravat tied so neatly under a fat little red face, with a blue frock-coat so scrupulously fitted to a punchy little person, as Major British, about whom we have written these two pages. He stared rather hardly at my companion, but gave me a kind shake of the hand, and we proceeded at once to business. "Major British," said I, "we want your advice in regard to an unpleasant affair which has just occurred to my friend Pogson."

"Pogson, take a chair."

"You must know, sir, that Mr. Pogson, coming from Calais the other day, encountered, in the diligence, a very handsome woman."

British winked at Pogson, who, wretched as he was, could not help feeling pleased.

己具备了一个上流社会的男人气质并受人欢迎。实际上他所遇到的英国贵族都很善意地对待他，在德国的宫廷，在意大利或巴黎的短途旅行中，他从没有错过任何一个大使的晚会。他还把消息告诉我们，我们从他那里能很高兴地得知晚会上都发生了些什么，以及关于饭菜、服装和一些丑闻的详细报道。

他还是在社会中尽可能让自己最有用的人之一，除了为自己的利益有些固执地倾向于决斗之外，对于其他人来说，他还是这个世界上最敏锐、最温和的顾问，他曾经帮助许多朋友度过窘境，比人道组织的成员所阻止的死亡事故都要多。众所周知，英国人从来不在军队中买一个官阶的。从所周知，英国人从来不在军队中买一个官阶的。在1814年他杀死了一个著名的法国吞火魔术师，因为这个人杀死了他的一位年轻朋友。他常常和快乐的年轻人打交道，并得到庄重年老的家庭成员的爱戴，“英国咖啡馆”里喧闹的单身汉晚餐、法布圣奥诺雷街贵妇人的饭桌上都有他固定的位子。我告诉你，这些举止文雅的老人彼此都是互惠互利的，能和他们中的一两位成为朋友那是年轻人的幸运。

我催促着波格逊赶紧穿上衣服，带着他气喘吁吁地爬到上校住的四层，到了那里我们很高兴能被请进去。这个矮小的绅士穿着他的旅行夹克，优雅地正忙着擦拭那些整洁长靴中的一只，他每天都要穿着这些长靴在林荫大道散步。两只双坚韧的黄皮革手套已被他用白黏土涂白了，还没有男人像他这样整洁地走出去过——他拿着一顶仔细刷过的帽子，在一张胖胖的小红脸下整洁地系着一个直挺的领结，穿着一件蓝色的礼服大衣，大衣对他来说是如此合身。关于这个英国上校，我们已经写了两页纸了。他开始时是有些严厉地注视着我的朋友，但他和我友好地握了手，我们很快就谈到正事上。“英国上校，”我说，“我们想就发生在我朋友波格逊身上的一件不愉快的事情征求您的意见。”

“波格逊，坐在椅子上。”

“先生，您一定知道，波格逊先生那天从加来过来，他在马车上遇到一

"Mr. Pogson was not more pleased with this lovely creature than was she with him; for, it appears, she gave him her card, invited him to her house, where he has been constantly, and has been received with much kindness."

"I see," says British.

"Her husband, the Baron—"

"NOW it's coming," said the Major, with a grin: "her husband is jealous, I suppose, and there is a talk of the Bois de Boulogne: my dear sir, you can't refuse—can't refuse."

"It's not that," said Pogson, wagging his head passionately.

"Her husband the Baron seemed quite as much taken with Pogson as his lady was, and has introduced him to some very distingues friends of his own set. Last night one of the Baron's friends gave a party in honour of my friend Pogson, who lost thirty-eight pounds at cards BEFORE he was made drunk, and heaven knows how much after."

"Not a shilling, by sacred heaven! —not a shilling!" yelled out Pogson. "After the supper I ad such an eadache, I couldn't do anything but fall asleep on the sofa."

"You 'ad such an eadache,' sir," said British, sternly, who piques himself on his grammar and pronunciation, and scorns a cockney.

"Such a H-eadache, sir," replied Pogson, with much meekness.

"The unfortunate man is brought home at two o'clock, as tipsy as possible, dragged up stairs, senseless, to bed, and, on waking, receives a visit from his entertainer of the night before—a Lord's son, Major, a tip-top fellow,—who brings a couple of bills that my friend Pogson is said to have signed."

"Well, my dear fellow, the thing's quite simple,—he must pay them."

"I can't pay them."

"He can't pay them," said we both in a breath: "Pogson is a commercial traveller, with thirty shillings a week, and how the deuce is he to pay five hundred pounds?"

"A bagman, sir! and what right has a bagman to gamble? Gentlemen gamble, sir; tradesmen, sir, have no business with the amusements of the gentry. What business had you with Barons and Lords' sons, sir? —serve

位漂亮的女人。”

英国上校对波格逊眨眨眼睛，而波格逊，尽管很可怜，也难免感到不悦。

“波格逊先生对这个可爱的人的兴趣并不比那个女人对他的兴趣多。因为，看起来是她先给了他名片，邀请他到她的住处，他就经常去那里，而且得到善意的接待。”

“我明白了。”英国上校说。

“她的丈夫男爵——”

“现在事情发生了，”上校笑了笑说，“她的丈夫嫉妒了，我猜想，在布洛涅树林还有场谈判。我亲爱的先生，你不能拒绝——不能拒绝。”

“不是那样的。”波格逊慌忙摇着他的头说。

“她的丈夫男爵好像与太太一样和波格逊说了好多，把波格逊介绍给他自己的一些有名的朋友。昨晚男爵的一位朋友举行了一个宴会招待我的朋友波格逊，在他被灌醉前玩牌输了三十八镑，天知道在这之后又输了多少。”

“不是一笔小数目，神圣的上帝啊！——不是一笔小数目！”波格逊大叫道。“吃过晚饭后我的头很痛，我什么也不能做，只好睡在沙发上。”

“你的‘头痛’，先生。”英国上校严厉地说，夸耀着他自己的语法和发音，很轻蔑波格逊这个伦敦佬的发音。

“头很痛，先生。”波格逊温顺地回答。

“这个不幸的人在两点钟被送回家来，醉得摇摇晃晃，被拖上楼去，没一点感觉，在床上一直躺到醒来。昨晚和他一起玩的那个人今天来拜访他——一个贵族的儿子，一个出色的小伙子——他带来两张单据，说是我朋友波格逊签字的账单。”

“好吧，我亲爱的朋友，事情很简单——他必须付钱给他们。”

“我不能付给他们。”

“他不能付给他们，”我们俩异口同声地说。“波格逊是一个旅行商，一

you right, sir."

"Sir," says Pogson, with some dignity, "merit, and not birth, is the criterion of a man; I despise an hereditary aristocracy, and admire only Nature's gentlemen. For my part, I think that a British merch—"

"Hold your tongue, sir," bounced out the Major, "and don't lecture me; don't come to me, sir, with your slang about Nature's gentlemen—Nature's Tomfools, sir! Did Nature open a cash account for you at a banker's, sir? Did Nature give you an education, sir? What do you mean by competing with people to whom Nature has given all these things? Stick to your bags, Mr. Pogson, and your bagmen, and leave Barons and their like to their own ways."

"Yes, but, Major," here cried that faithful friend, who has always stood by Pogson; "they won't leave him alone."

"The honourable gent says I must fight if I don't pay," whimpered Sam.

"What! fight YOU? Do you mean that the honourable gent, as you call him, will go out with a bagman?"

"He doesn't know I'm a—I'm a commercial man," blushingly said Sam: "he fancies I'm a military gent."

The Major's gravity was quite upset at this absurd notion; and he laughed outrageously. "Why, the fact is, sir," said I, "that my friend Pogson, knowing the value of the title of Captain, and being complimented by the Baroness on his warlike appearance, said, boldly, he was in the army. He only assumed the rank in order to dazzle her weak imagination, never fancying that there was a husband, and a circle of friends, with whom he was afterwards to make an acquaintance; and then, you know, it was too late to withdraw."

"A pretty pickle you have put yourself in, Mr. Pogson, by making love to other men's wives, and calling yourself names," said the Major, who was restored to good humour. "And pray, who is the honourable gent?"

"The Earl of Cinqbars' son," says Pogson, "the Honourable Tom Ringwood."

"I thought it was some such character: and the Baron is the Baron de Florval-Delval?"

"The very same."

周只有三十先令，天晓得他怎么能拿出五百英镑？”

“一个旅行商！一个旅行商有什么权利去赌博？先生，绅士和商人不应该去赌博。你一个商人和男爵、贵族的儿子有什么关系啊？你罪有应得。”

“先生，”波格逊有些愤怒地说，“品质而不是血统，才是判断一个人的标准。我蔑视世袭的贵族，敬慕真正的绅士。至于我，我认为英国商人——”

“闭嘴，先生，”上校跳起来，“不要教训我，不要走近我，带着你关于真正绅士的废话走开——真正的傻瓜！‘真正’会在银行给你开现金账户吗？‘真正’会给你教育吗？和人们竞争的时候，你以为‘真正’会给你带来好处吗？看紧你的口袋，波格逊先生，你这个旅行商，让男爵和他们自己的同伙都去一边吧！”

“是的，但是上校，”我叫喊道，作为忠实的朋友，我一直站在波格逊身边，“他们不会放过他的。”

“那个贵族先生说如果我不付钱，就必须要决斗。”山姆呜咽地说。

“什么！和你决斗？你的意思是那位贵族，你所指的他，将会和一个旅行商决斗？”

“他不知道我是——我是一个商人，”山姆红着脸说，“他以为我是个军人。”

上校的严肃神情被这一荒谬的插曲扰乱了，他冷酷地笑了起来。“事实是，先生，”我说，“我的朋友波格逊知道上尉这个称号的价值。因男爵夫人称赞他具有军人的外表，他就大胆地说他在军队。他假认军衔只不过是想迷惑那个男爵夫人浅薄的想象力，从没想过她还有一个丈夫和一群朋友，他后来还和他们认识了。然后，你知道了，抽身已迟。”

“你通过向别人的妻子示爱而自投罗网，波格逊先生，而且，你还用自己的真名，”上校的脾气又好转起来，“请问，那个贵族绅士是谁啊？”

“辛克巴伯爵的儿子，”波格逊说，“尊敬的汤姆·瑞伍德。”

“我想就是这类人物。男爵是弗罗瓦勒·岱乐瓦勒男爵？”

"And his wife a black-haired woman, with a pretty foot and ankle; calls herself Athenais; and is always talking about her trente-deux ans? Why, sir, that woman was an actress on the Boulevard, when we were here in '15. She's no more his wife than I am. Melval's name is Chicot. The woman is always travelling between London and Paris: I saw she was hooking you at Calais; she has hooked ten men, in the course of the last two years, in this very way. She lent you money, didn't she?" "Yes." "And she leans on your shoulder, and whispers, 'Play half for me,' and somebody wins it, and the poor thing is as sorry as you are, and her husband storms and rages, and insists on double stakes; and she leans over your shoulder again, and tells every card in your hand to your adversary; and that's the way it's done, Mr. Pogson."

"I've been AD, I see I ave," said Pogson, very humbly.

"Well, sir," said the Major, "in consideration, not of you, sir—for, give me leave to tell you, Mr. Pogson, that you are a pitiful little scoundrel—in consideration for my Lord Cinqbars, sir, with whom, I am proud to say, I am intimate," (the Major dearly loved a Lord, and was, by his own showing, acquainted with half the peerage,) "I will aid you in this affair. Your cursed vanity, sir, and want of principle, has set you, in the first place, intriguing with other men's wives; and if you had been shot for your pains, a bullet would have only served you right, sir. You must go about as an impostor, sir, in society; and you pay richly for your swindling, sir, by being swindled yourself: but, as I think your punishment has been already pretty severe, I shall do my best, out of regard for my friend, Lord Cinqbars, to prevent the matter going any further; and I recommend you to leave Paris without delay. Now let me wish you a good morning."—Where with British made a majestic bow, and began giving the last touch to his varnished boots.

We departed: poor Sam perfectly silent and chapfallen; and I meditating on the wisdom of the half-pay philosopher, and wondering what means he would employ to rescue Pogson from his fate.

What these means were I know not; but Mr. Ringwood did NOT make his appearance at six; and, at eight, a letter arrived for "Mr. Pogson, commercial traveller," &c. &c. It was blank inside, but contained his two bills. Mr. Ringwood left town, almost immediately, for Vienna; nor did the Major

“正是。”

“他妻子是个黑头发的女人，有双漂亮的脚和脚踝。她自称为雅典娜，总是谈论她的三十二岁？先生，当我们1815年在这里的时候，那个女人是林荫大道上的一个女演员。她那时未结婚，还不是他的妻子。岱乐瓦勒的真名是奇科。这个女人经常往返于伦敦和巴黎之间。在加来我看见她正引你上钩。在过去的两年中她用同样的方式已骗了十个男人。她借钱给你了，是不是?”“是的。”“而且她靠着你的肩膀，对你耳语，‘替我玩一半’，然后就有人赢了它，事情慢慢发展到了让你感到抱歉的地步。她的丈夫大发雷霆很愤怒的样子，坚持两倍的赌注。她又再一次靠在你肩膀上，把你手中的每张牌都告诉你的对手，这就是他们的伎俩，波格逊先生。”

“我被骗了，我知道我被骗了。”波格逊很谦卑地说。

“好吧！先生，”上校说，“让我告诉你，波格逊先生，不是考虑到你这个可怜的小流氓，而是考虑到辛克巴勋爵——先生，我很骄傲地说，我和他关系很好（上校深深地爱着每一个勋爵，并且，按他自己的说法，他和一半的贵族都相识），我会在这件事情上帮助你。你该死的虚荣心和本性一上来就使你和别的男人的老婆私通。作为惩罚你被人打一枪也是罪有应得。你一定在社会中做过骗子，现在你的上当受骗也让你付出了高昂的代价，你被自己骗了。但是，我认为对你的处罚已经够严厉了，所以，不只是考虑到我的朋友辛克巴勋爵，我将尽力避免事情进一步的发展。我建议你尽快离开巴黎。现在我祝你早安。”英国上校深深地鞠了一躬，开始继续擦拭他的靴子。

我们离开了。可怜的山姆非常沉默和沮丧。我在思索着这个“半薪哲学家”的智慧，对于他将用什么方法把波格逊解救出来感到好奇。

我不知道他采用了什么方法。但是瑞伍德先生在六点没有露面。在八点钟，我们收到一封给“旅行商波格逊先生”的信。信中除了两张账单外什么也没有。很快，瑞伍德先生离开了城镇到维也纳去了。上校也没有解释是什么原因导致他的离去，但是他喃喃自语了一些“知道一些他过去的

explain the circumstances which caused his departure; but he muttered something about "knew some of his old tricks," "threatened police, and made him disgorge directly."

Mr. Ringwood is, as yet, young at his trade; and I have often thought it was very green of him to give up the bills to the Major, who, certainly, would never have pressed the matter before the police, out of respect for his friend, Lord Cinqbars.

骗局”、“以报警相威胁，使他直接坦白了”之类的话。

瑞伍德先生在处事上还很稚嫩。我经常想，他对上校交出了账单这点说明他还是没有经验的，因为上校当然不会不顾他的朋友辛克巴的面子而把这件事情捅给警察的。

The Fêtes of July

In a Letter to The Editor of The"Bungay Beacon"

Paris, July 30th, 1839.

WE have arrived here just in time for the fêtes of July. —You have read, no doubt, of that glorious revolution which took place here nine years ago, and which is now commemorated annually, in a pretty facetious manner, by gun-firing, student-processions, pole-climbing-for-silver-spoons, gold-watches and legs-of-mutton, monarchical orations, and what not, and sanctioned, moreover, by Chamber-of-Deputies, with a grant of a couple of hundred thousand francs to defray the expenses of all the crackers, gun-firings, and legs-of-mutton aforesaid. There is a new fountain in the Place Louis Quinze, otherwise called the Place Louis Seize, or else the Place de la Révolution, or else the Place de la Concorde (who can say why?)—which, I am told, is to run bad wine during certain hours tomorrow, and there WOULD have been a review of the National Guards and the Line—only, since the Fieschi business, reviews are no joke, and so this latter part of the festivity has been discontinued.

Do you not laugh, O Pharos of Bungay, at the continuance of a humbug such as this? —at the humbugging anniversary of a humbug? The King of the Barricades is, next to the Emperor Nicholas, the most absolute Sovereign in Europe; yet there is not in the whole of this fair kingdom of France a single man who cares sixpence about him, or his dynasty, except, mayhap, a few hangers-on at the Château, who eat his dinners, and put their hands in his purse. The feeling of loyalty is as dead as old Charles the Tenth; the Cham-

七月的纪念日

——给《邦吉灯塔》编辑的一封信

巴黎，1839 年 7 月 30 日

我们在七月的节日开始时恰好来到巴黎。——毫无疑问，你一定获悉了九年前发生在这里的光荣革命，现在这里每年都要用一种相当滑稽的方式进行纪念。有炮火，学生游行，能得到银匙、金表和羊腿的爬杆比赛、关于君主政体的演讲等等，这些都要经过国民议会的批准，议会再拨款二十万法郎来支付所有的爆竹、炮火和前面提到的羊腿的费用。在路易十四广场有一个新的喷泉，路易十四广场另外还叫做路易十六广场或革命广场或协和广场（谁能说清楚是为什么?）我听说明天的某个特定时间在这里的喷泉将会喷出廉价的酒水，自从费埃希事件［Fieschi，1836 年暗杀菲力浦的未遂犯。——译注］之后，那里还将会有国民护卫队和正规军的检阅，检阅可不是开玩笑的，因此关于节日后半部分的报道就不得不省去了。

一个骗子竟然庆祝他的欺骗周年纪念日，难道你对此不感到好笑吗?“街垒国王”［即路易·菲力浦。1830—1844 年，七月王朝在巴黎人民革命中诞生，取得政权的不是人民而是资产阶级的上层分子。国王路易·菲力浦即位时五十七岁，他把自己打扮成“街垒国王”，身着便服，手持雨伞，在街上与百姓握手，他的宫廷向显贵们打开。——译注］是继尼古拉皇帝［1825—1855 年在位的俄国沙皇，曾镇压波兰起义和匈牙利革命。——译

bers have been laughed at, the country has been laughed at, all the successive ministries have been laughed at (and you know who is the wag that has amused himself with them all); and, behold, here come three days at the end of July, and cannons think it necessary to fire off, squibs and crackers to blaze and fiz, fountains to run wine, kings to make speeches, and subjects to crawl up greasy mâts-de-cocagne in token of gratitude and réjouissance publique! — My dear sir, in their aptitude to swallow, to utter, to enact humbugs, these French people, from Majesty downwards, beat all the other nations of this earth. In looking at these men, their manners, dresses, opinions, politics, actions, history, it is impossible to preserve a grave countenance; instead of having Carlyle to write a History of the French Revolution, I often think it should be handed over to Dickens or Theodore Hook; and oh! where is the Rabelais to be the faithful historian of the last phase of the Revolution—the last glorious nine years of which we are now commemorating the last glorious three days?

I had made a vow not to say a syllable on the subject, although I have seen, with my neighbours, all the gingerbread stalls down the Champs Elysées, and some of the "catafalques" erected to the memory of the heroes of July, where the students and others, not connected personally with the victims, and not having in the least profited by their deaths, come and weep; but the grief shown on the first day is quite as absurd and fictitious as the joy exhibited on the last. The subject is one which admits of much wholesome reflection and food for mirth; and, besides, is so richly treated by the French themselves, that it would be a sin and a shame to pass it over. Allow me to have the honour of translating, for your edification, an account of the first day's proceedings—it is mighty amusing, to my thinking.

Celebration of The Days of July

Today (Saturday), funeral ceremonies, in honour of the victims of July, were held in the various edifices consecrated to public worship.

These edifices, with the exception of some churches (especially that of the Petits-Pères), were uniformly hung with black on the outside; the hangings bore

注］之后欧洲最专制的君主，然而在法国除了宫廷中的一些吃饭拿钱的食客和奉承者之外，再没有一个人去关心他本人和他的王朝。对国王的忠诚已随着老查理十世［1824 年 9 月 16 日路易十八死去，查理十世即阿图瓦伯爵，是路易十六的弟弟，接替了王位。复辟王朝的反动政策遭到资产阶级和大多数人民的反对。国内外的政治、经济危机导致了 1830 年的七月革命，查理十世在 8 月 2 日放弃王位，最后逃往英国。——译注］的离去而消逝了。路易·菲力浦的议院、国家和所有一系列的内阁成员都遭到了民众的嘲笑（而你知道这个以他们所有的人来自娱的小丑是谁）。看，七月底的这三天［指 7 月 28、29、30 日。——译注］纪念活动开始了，大炮要开火，烟花爆竹要燃烧鸣响，喷泉要喷洒，国王要演讲，国民要去爬油腻的夺彩杆，所有这些都是为了愉悦公众，以示感激！亲爱的先生，这些法国人，自从君主政权趋向没落之后，在吃喝、演讲、扮演骗子的能力上超越了这个地球上其他所有的国家。看看这些人的举止、服装、观念、政治、活动和历史，它们都不可能维持其严肃的外表。我时常想，法国革命的历史应移交给狄更斯或西奥多·胡克［Theodore Hook，英国作家。——译注］来写而不是让卡莱尔［Thomas Carlyle（1795—1881），出生于苏格兰家庭，英国作家、历史学家和哲学家。——译注］去写。唉！大革命最后阶段的忠实历史学家拉伯雷在哪里呢？光荣的革命已过去九年了，最后阶段即我们现在纪念的革命的最后三天。

我已发誓对这个话题不再说只言片语了。在纪念活动期间，沿着爱丽舍宫的街道上摆满了姜饼摊，人们还竖立了一些"灵柩台"来纪念七月革命中的英雄，那里还有些学生和其他的人等等，他们和革命中的牺牲者既没有什么私人关系，也没有从牺牲者的死亡中得到丝毫益处，但他们都到这里来哭泣。他们在第一天所表现出的这种悲痛如同最后一天所表现出的快乐一样都是很荒谬和虚伪的。但人们还是需要这些能够给人带来欢笑的有益的思想反省和精神食粮，此外，它也得到法国人自身的郑重对待，如果把它给忽略了，在他们看来就是一件罪过和羞耻。在您的开导下，请允

only this inscription: 27, 28, 29 July, 1830—surrounded by a wreath of oak-leaves.

In the interior of the Catholic churches, it had only been thought proper to dress LITTLE CATAFALQUES, as for burials of the third and fourth class. Very few clergy attended; but a considerable number of the National Guard.

The Synagogue of the Israelites was entirely hung with black; and a great concourse of people attended. The service was performed with the greatest pomp.

In the Protestant temples there was likewise a very full attendance: APOLOGETICAL DISCOURSES on the Revolution of July were pronounced by the pastors.

The absence of M. de Quélen (Archbishop of Paris), and of many members of the superior clergy, was remarked at Nôtre Dame.

The civil authorities attended service in their several districts.

The poles, ornamented with tri-coloured flags, which formerly were placed on Nôtre Dame, were, it was remarked, suppressed. The flags on the Pont Neuf were, during the ceremony, only half-mast high, and covered with crape.

Et caetera, et caetera, et caetera.

The tombs of the Louvre were covered with black hangings, and adorned with tri-coloured flags. In front and in the middle was erected an expiatory monument of a pyramidical shape, and surmounted by a funeral vase.

These tombs were guarded by the MUNICIPAL GUARD, THE TROOPS OF THE LINE, THE SERJENS DE VILLE (town patrol), AND A BRIGADE OF AGENTS OF POLICE IN PLAIN CLOTHES, under the orders of peace-officer Vassal.

Between eleven and twelve o'clock, some young men, to the number of 400 or 500, assembled on the Place de la Bourse, one of them bearing a tri-coloured banner with an inscription, 'TO THE MANES OF JULY': ranging themselves in order, they marched five abreast to the Marchédes Innocens. On their arrival, the Municipal Guards of the Halle aux Draps, where the post had been doubled, issued out without arms, and the town-sergeants placed themselves before the market to prevent the entry of the procession. The young men passed in perfect order, and without saying a word—only lifting their hats as they defiled before the tombs. When they arrived at the Louvre, they found the gates

许我荣幸地翻译一篇在我看来比较有趣的关于第一天活动的报道。

七月纪念日庆祝会

今天（星期六）为了纪念七月革命中的牺牲者，为了表示民众对他们的敬意，许多礼堂都举行了葬礼仪式。

除了一些教堂（尤其是小教会的教堂）之外，这些礼堂都统一在外面挂上了黑布，黑布上只有这些题词：1830 年 7 月 27 日、28 日、29 日——它们四周围绕着橡树叶子编织的花圈。

在天主教教堂，主要是针对第三、第四等级公民的葬礼，他们只装饰小灵柩台。只有少许的圣职者参加，但是有很多国民护卫队的队员。

犹太人的犹太教堂全部挂上了黑布，有一大群人参加。宗教仪式的表演非常壮观。

在新教教堂内同样也挤满了等候的人群，牧师在宣讲，为七月革命辩护。

在巴黎圣母院，德纪兰先生（巴黎总教主）和许多上等圣职者的缺席被洛荷特圣母院议论纷纷。

城市的主管当局在他们各自的区域内等待仪式的开始。

从前放在巴黎圣母院上面的用三色旗装饰的杆子遭到洛荷特圣母院的议论，现在被藏了起来。奈夫桥上的杆子在典礼期间只有半墙高，而且被黑纱蒙着。

等等，等等，等等。

罗浮宫的墓碑上蒙上了黑布，上面用三色旗点缀着。在罗浮宫的前中央竖立着一个金字塔形的赎罪纪念碑，碑顶上有一个葬礼花瓶。

在大臣治安官的命令下，市政府的护卫队、正规军部队、城镇巡逻队以及便衣警察的特工队护卫着这些墓碑。

在十一点到十二点之间，有四五百名年轻人聚集在交易所广场上，

shut, and the Garden evacuated. The troops were under arms, and formed in battalion.

After the passage of the procession, the Garden was again open to the public.

And the evening and the morning were the first day.

There's nothing serious in mortality: is there, from the beginning of this account to the end thereof, aught but sheer, open, monstrous, undisguised humbug? I said, before, that you should have a history of these people by Dickens or Theodore Hook, but there is little need of professed wags;—do not the men write their own tale with an admirable Sancho-like gravity and naïveté, which one could not desire improved? How good is that touch of sly indignation about the LITTLE CATAFALQUES! how rich the contrast presented by the economy of the Catholics to the splendid disregard of expense exhibited by the devout Jews! and how touching the "APOLOGETICAL DISCOURSES on the Revolution," delivered by the Protestant pastors! Fancy the profound affliction of the Gardes Municipaux, the Sergens de Ville, the police agents in plain clothes, and the troops with fixed bayonets, sobbing round the "expiatory monuments of a pyramidical shape, surmounted by funeral vases," and compelled, by sad duty, to fire into the public who might wish to indulge in the same woe! O ,"manes of July!" (the phrase is pretty and grammatical) why did you with sharp bullets break those Louvre windows? Why did you bayonet red-coated Swiss behind that fair white façade, and, braving cannon, musket, sabre, perspective guillotine, burst yonder bronze gates, rush through that peaceful picture-gallery, and hurl royalty, loyalty, and a thousand years of Kings, head-over-heels out of yonder Tuileries' windows?

It is, you will allow, a little difficult to say:—there is, however, ONE benefit that the country has gained (as for liberty of press, or person, diminished taxation, a juster representation, who ever thinks of them?)—ONE benefit they have gained, or nearly—abolition de la peine-de-mort namely pour délit politique: no more wicked guillotining for revolutions. A Frenchman must have his revolution—it is his nature to knock down omnibuses in the street, and across them to fire at troops of the line—it is a sin to balk it. Did

其中一人披着一幅题字为“致七月革命的亡魂”的三色旗，他们依照次序排列好队伍，五人一排地来到英诺森呢绒市场。他们到这里的时候，呢绒市场的市政护卫队人员已增加了一倍，他们没带任何武装地出来了，城镇警卫官则排列在市场前以阻止游行队伍进入市场。年轻人对列整齐、一言不发地从市场前经过——他们只是在墓碑前列队经过时举起了他们的帽子向死者致意。当他们到达罗浮宫的时候，发现大门被关上了，杜伊勒里花园［杜伊勒里花园始建于1564年，最初的建造者是亨利二世国王的遗孀凯瑟琳·德美第奇。后来亨利四世和路易十四先后对它加以扩展。——译注］内的人员也被遣散了。军队以营为单位备好了武装。

在游行队伍通过之后，花园会再次向民众开放。

在第一天，从早到晚就是这样度过的。

从这篇报道的开始到结束，对于七月革命中的死亡人数一句也没提，难道它通篇不都是彻底、公开、怪异、荒谬、不加掩饰的欺骗吗？我前面说过，人们需要狄更斯或西奥多·胡克这样的人物来记录这段历史，并不需要专业的小丑。难道人们就不会用桑丘［塞万提斯《堂吉诃德》中一个朴实憨厚的人物形象。——译注］似的认真和憨厚的态度来写他们自己的故事吗？作者提到小灵柩台时的躲躲闪闪是多么好笑啊！天主教徒的节约与虔诚的犹太人不在乎花费的铺张所呈现出的对比是多么明显啊！新教牧师为革命的辩护论道是多么感人啊！想象一下市政府护卫队、城市警官、便衣警察和佩带刺刀的部队围着“碑顶被葬礼花瓶覆盖的金字塔形赎罪纪念碑”啜泣，但是出于命令，他们又不得不向那些自愿沉浸在悲痛之中的民众开枪！哦，“七月革命的亡魂”（这个句子很好且符合语法规则），你们用锐利的子弹打破那些罗浮宫的窗户是为了什么呢？你们用刺刀刺杀美丽的正面被涂为白色的建筑物（即凡尔赛宫。——译注）后身穿红色制服的卫兵，冒着大炮、步枪、马刀、上断头台的危险，冲破那边青铜色的大门，

not the King send off Revolutionary Prince Napoleon in a coach-and-four? Did not the jury, before the face of God and Justice, proclaim Revolutionary Colonel Vaudrey not guilty? —One may hope, soon, that if a man shows decent courage and energy in half a dozen émeutes, he will get promotion and a premium.

I do not (although, perhaps, partial to the subject,) want to talk more nonsense than the occasion warrants, and will pray you to cast your eyes over the following anecdote, that is now going the round of the papers, and respects the commutation of the punishment of that wretched, fool-hardy Barbés, who, on his trial, seemed to invite the penalty which has just been remitted to him. You recollect the braggart's speech:

> When the Indian falls into the power of the enemy, he knows the fate that awaits him, and submits his head to the knife:—I am the Indian!
>
> Well—
>
> M. Victor Hugo was at the Opera on the night when the sentence of the Court of Peers, condemning Barbés to death, was published. The great poet composed the following verses:—
>
> "Par votre ange envolée, ainsi qu'une colombe,
> Par le royal enfant, doux et fréle roseau,
> Grace encore une fois! Grace au nom de la tombe!
> Grace au nom du berçeau!"
>
> M. Victor Hugo wrote the lines out instantly on a sheet of paper, which he folded, and simply dispatched them to the King of the French by the penny-post.
>
> That truly is a noble voice, which can at all hours thus speak to the throne. Poetry, in old days, was called the language of the Gods—it is better named now—it is the language of the Kings.
>
> But the clemency of the King had anticipated the letter of the Poet. The pen of His Majesty had signed the commutation of Barbés, while that of the Poet was still writing.
>
> Louis Philipe replied to the author of "Ruy Blas" most graciously, that he had already subscribed to a wish so noble, and that the verses had only con-

穿过那个宁静的画廊，把王位、忠诚和千年的君主从那扇杜勒里花园的窗户里扔出来又是为了什么呢？

这不是一个容易回答的问题——人们已从这场革命中受益（获得出版自由或人身自由，降低税款，更为公正的议会代表，谁曾想过这些呢），国家还将要对轻度的政治罪犯免除死刑，废除断头台。一个法国人必须要从事他的革命行为——在街道上推倒公共马车，穿过它们向正规军部队开火是他的本性表现——去阻止它反而是罪恶的。法国国王不是欢送四轮大马车中的革命王子拿破仑吗？陪审团不是以上帝和正义的名义宣布革命的沃德利上校无罪吗？——人们由此可以预见，如果一个人能在众多骚乱事件中展现出适当的勇气和能力的话，他将会得到晋级和奖赏。

我不想除了必要的理由之外谈太多的废话（尽管，对国民也许有些不公平），我希望你能关注下面的一则逸事，它现在被各种报纸所转载，关于那个可怜的、愚蠢鲁莽的巴贝斯［Barbés（1809—1870），法国著名政治家，曾参加过1848年二月革命，被选为制宪会议议员，1839年他和白龙季两人领导反对路易·菲力浦的起义，起义很快遭到镇压，事后被捕，判为死刑。——译注］的减刑事件，在审判席上，他似乎是乐意接受死刑的判决，而国王刚刚赦免了他的死刑。这里有夸张的报道：

> 当这个印度人落入敌人手中时，他知道等待他的命运是什么，他把头放在刀的面前——我是印度人！
>
> 好——
>
> 在上议院宣判巴贝斯死刑的那天晚上，雨果正在歌剧院。他得知消息后，愤怒谴责了上议院的做法，并写了下面的诗句：
>
> 看在像鸽子一样飞去的你那天使的分上！
>
> 看在像芦苇一样幼弱的皇家赤子的分上！
>
> 再一次请开天恩；为坟墓增光，开恩吧！
>
> 为摇篮增光，开恩吧！

firmed his previous disposition to mercy.

Now in countries where fools most abound, did one ever read of more monstrous, palpable folly? In any country, save this, would a poet who chose to write four crack-brained verses, comparing an angel to a dove, and a little boy to a reed, and calling upon the chief magistrate, in the name of the angel, or dove (the Princess Mary), in her tomb, and the little infant in his cradle, to spare a criminal, have received a "gracious answer" to his nonsense? Would he have ever dispatched the nonsense? and would any journalist have been silly enough to talk of "the noble voice that could thus speak to the throne," and the noble throne that could return such a noble answer to the noble voice? You get nothing done here gravely and decently. Tawdry stage tricks are played, and braggadocio claptraps uttered, on every occasion, however sacred or solemn; in the face of death, as by Barbés with his hideous Indian metaphor; in the teeth of reason, as by M. Victor Hugo with his twopenny-post poetry; and of justice, as by the King's absurd reply to this absurd demand! Suppose the Count of Paris to be twenty times a reed, and the Princess Mary a host of angels, is that any reason why the law should not have its course? Justice is the God of our lower world, our great omnipresent guardian: as such it moves, or should move on majestic, awful, irresistible, having no passions—like a God; but, in the very midst of the path across which it is to pass, lo! M. Victor Hugo trips forward, smirking, and says, O, divine Justice! I will trouble you to listen to the following trifling effusion of mine:—

Par votre ange envolée, ainsi qu'une, &c.

Awful Justice stops, and, bowing gravely, listens to M. Hugo's verses, and, with true French politeness, says, "Mon cher Monsieur, these verses are charming, ravissans, délicieux, and, coming from such a célébrité littéraire as yourself, shall meet with every possible attention—in fact, had I required anything to confirm my own previous opinions, this charming poem would have done so. Bon jour, mon cher Monsieur Hugo, au revoir!"—and

维克多·雨果立即把这些诗句写在一张纸上，然后折叠了，用两便士的邮费把它送给了法国国王。

雨果的诗真是一种高贵的声音，它能在任何时候对国王讲话。诗歌在以前被称做上帝的语言——现在不妨被称为是国王的语言。

但是仁慈的国王已预料到诗人会写这封信。当诗人在写这首诗的时候，陛下已经签署了对巴贝斯的减刑令。

路易·菲力浦非常亲切地回答了《吕意·布拉斯》（雨果1838年的剧本）的作者，他已经同意了作者如此高尚的愿望，而作者的诗句只是再次确证了他先前的仁慈。

即使是在傻子盛行的国家，有没有人读过比这首诗还要怪异、露骨的诗作呢？除法国之外，在任何一个国家能找出一个诗人愿写这四行古怪的诗句吗？把天使比做鸽子，把小男孩比做芦苇，以天使或鸽子（玛丽公主[路易十六的王后，曾是奥地利公主。——译注]）的名义，以她的坟墓或摇篮中的婴孩的名义去呼吁执政者宽恕一个罪犯，他这番胡言乱语竟还收到了“仁慈的答复”？雨果会把这些胡言乱语派送出去吗？新闻记者会愚蠢得把它表述为“对国王讲话的高贵声音”，国王对这个高贵的声音作了极好的答复吗？这里根本就没什么正事。记者们耍着廉价而俗气的舞台诡计，在每种场合都夸夸其谈、华而不实地发表言论，对此他们还自认为是神圣而严肃的。面对死亡，就司法而言，像巴贝斯和他的骇人听闻的印度人身份，维克多·雨果和他的两便士邮出的诗，国王对这个荒谬要求的荒谬答复都不是什么理由！假设巴黎的伯爵是一枝芦苇的二十倍，玛丽公主是一群天使，难道法律就找不出它自身的理由吗？司法是我们尘世的上帝、我们伟大的无所不在的监护人，即使它要改变判决，也应该是严肃庄严，像上帝一样冷静地做出改变。但是，在它要做判决的过程中，瞧!! 维克多·雨果先生向前走了上去，傻笑着说，哦！神圣的司法啊！麻烦您听听下面我个人的一些微不足道的感情抒发：

they part:—Justice taking off his hat and bowing, and the author of "*Ruy Blas*" quite convinced that he has been treating with him d'égal en égal. I can hardly bring my mind to fancy that anything is serious in France—it seems to be all rant, tinsel, and stage-play. Sham liberty, sham monarchy, sham glory, sham justice,—ou diable donc la verité va-t-elle se nicher?

……

The last rocket of the fête of July has just mounted, exploded, made a portentous bang, and emitted a gorgeous show of blue lights, and then (like many reputations) disappeared totally: the hundredth gun on the Invalides terrace has uttered its last roar—and a great comfort it is for eyes and ears that the festival is over. We shall be able to go about our everyday business again, and not be hustled by the gendarmes or the crowd.

The sight which I have just come away from is as brilliant, happy, and beautiful as can be conceived; and if you want to see French people to the greatest advantage, you should go to a festival like this, where their manners, and innocent gayety, show a very pleasing contrast to the coarse and vulgar hilarity which the same class would exhibit in our own country—at Epsom Racecourse, for instance, or Greenwich Fair. The greatest noise that I heard was that of a company of jolly villagers from a place in the neighbourhood of Paris, who, as soon as the fireworks were over, formed themselves into a line, three or four abreast, and so marched singing home. As for the fireworks, squibs and crackers are very hard to describe, and very little was to be seen of them: to me, the prettiest sight was the vast, orderly, happy crowd, the number of children, and the extraordinary care and kindness of the parents towards these little creatures. It does one good to see honest, heavy épiciers, fathers of families, playing with them in the Tuileries, or, as tonight, bearing them stoutly on their shoulders, through many long hours, in order that the little ones too may have their share of the fun. John Bull, I fear, is more selfish: he does not take Mrs. Bull to the public-house; but leaves her, for the most part, to take care of the children at home.

The fête, then, is over; the pompous black pyramid at the Louvre is only a skeleton now; all the flags have been miraculously whisked away during the

看在像鸽子一样飞去的你那天使的分上！

威严的司法停住了，他听了雨果先生的诗，用真正的法国式的礼仪庄重地鞠躬，说："我亲爱的先生，这些诗是迷人的、令人陶醉的、美妙的，而且它还出自您这样一个著名作家之手，应引起各方面的注意——事实上，如果我需要什么东西来证实我先前的判决的话，这首迷人的诗倒是非常合适的。早安，我亲爱的雨果先生，再见！"他们离开了——司法脱下他的帽子鞠躬，这位《吕意·布拉斯》的作者果就确信他已受到平等的对待。在法国我想象不到还能有什么严肃的事情——一切看起来都是夸张、虚饰的，像舞台表演。虚假的自由，虚假的君主政体，虚假的荣耀，虚假的司法——真实的精灵藏到哪里去了？

……

七月纪念日最后的烟火才刚刚开始燃放、爆炸，它们发出了惊人的砰砰声，并放射出一道绚烂的蓝光，然后就全部消失了（就像许多荣誉一样）。纪念日最后的一声枪响也完了——一场视觉和听觉的盛宴就这样结束了。从明天开始，我们又将会忙于日常的事务。现在注意不要被宪兵和人群挤着。

我们刚刚离开的庆祝场景是那样的辉煌、快乐和美丽。如果你想见最多的法国人，就应该去参加这样的节日活动，在这里法国人的举止和单纯的快乐与我们国内相同阶层的人所展现的粗鲁和庸俗形成了好笑的对比——例如在埃普森赛马场或格林尼治展览会的英国人。巴黎附近一群愉快村民的叫喊声是我听到的最大的喧哗声，烟火一结束，他们就排成一个队列，三四个人一排，唱着歌走回家。至于烟火和爆竹就很难描述了，我只能看到它们中的很少一部分。对我而言，最美丽的场景就是庞大而有秩序、快乐的人群和孩子们，父母对这些小孩子都特别地照顾和仁慈。我看到那些曾在杜伊勒里花园陪小孩玩的父亲今晚都把孩子扛在肩膀上，为了让最小的孩子也能分享他们的乐趣，他们一扛就是几个小时。我觉得英国

night, and the fine chandeliers which glittered down the Champs Elysées for full half a mile, have been consigned to their dens and darkness. Will they ever be reproduced for other celebrations of the glorious 29th of July? —I think not; the Government which vowed that there should be no more persecutions of the press, was, on that very 29th, seizing a Legitimist paper, for some real or fancied offence against it: it had seized, and was seizing daily, numbers of persons merely suspected of being disaffected (and you may fancy how liberty is understood, when some of these prisoners, the other day, on coming to trial, were found guilty and sentenced to ONE day's imprisonment, after THIRTY-SIX DAYS' DETENTION ON SUSPICION). I think the Government which follows such a system, cannot be very anxious about any further revolutionary fêtes, and that the Chamber may reasonably refuse to vote more money for them. Why should men be so mighty proud of having, on a certain day, cut a certain number of their fellow-countrymen's throats? The guards and the line employed this time nine years did no more than those who cannonaded the starving Lyonnese, or bayoneted the luckless inhabitants of the Rue Transnounain;—they did but fulfil the soldier's honourable duty;—his superiors bid him kill and he killeth;—perhaps, had he gone to his work with a little more heart, the result would have been different, and then—would the conquering party have been justified in annually rejoicing over the conquered? Would we have thought Charles X justified in causing fireworks to be blazed, and concerts to be sung, and speeches to be spouted, in commemoration of his victory over his slaughtered countrymen? —I wish for my part they would allow the people to go about their business as on the other 362 days of the year, and leave the Champs Elysées free for the omnibuses to run, and the Tuileries in quiet, so that the nurse-maids might come as usual, and the newspapers be read for a halfpenny apiece.

Shall I trouble you with an account of the speculations of these latter, and the state of the parties which they represent? The complication is not a little curious, and may form, perhaps, a subject of graver disquisition. The July fêtes occupy, as you may imagine, a considerable part of their columns just now, and it is amusing to follow them one by one; to read Tweedledum's

男人还是很自私的，他不会带太太出门，而是让她留在家里照顾孩子。

节日就这样结束了。罗浮宫蒙着黑布的金字塔纪念碑现在成了一具残骸。所有的旗帜在晚上都奇迹般地消失了，沿着爱丽舍宫外足足有半英里长的闪闪发光的枝形吊灯现在也被存放到黑暗的仓库里去了。下一年的7月29日，这里还会举行庆祝活动吗？我想不会了。政府曾发誓不会再有迫害报刊的行为，但恰好是在29日，他们就因一些莫须有的对政府的敌对言论而查封了一份拥护王权的报纸。它已经开始逮捕，以后每天还要逮捕那些有嫌疑对政府抱不满情绪的人（你能想象到这里的自由是如何被贯彻执行的，当这些囚犯在经过36天的嫌疑拘留后，某一天他们会接受审判，然后法庭会宣判他们有罪并判一天的监禁）。我认为遵循这类体制的政府，对任何过度的革命纪念日都不可能感到忧虑，议院可以明智地拒绝给节日拨款。为什么人们会为他们在某个特定的日子里杀死了一定数量的同胞而感到骄傲呢？政府九年来所招募的护卫队和正规军除了炮轰饥饿的里昂人和用刺刀刺不幸的城镇居民外就没做过什么——他们只是履行了士兵的光荣义务——他的上级吩咐他去杀，他就去杀。如果他带着一点良心去执行命令的话，结果就会不同。难道胜利的政党每年都要为他们战胜了对方而欣喜、辩护吗？如果查理十世下令燃放烟火、举办音乐会和演讲活动来庆祝他残杀国民的胜利，我们会认为他的这种做法是正确的吗？就我个人而言，我希望政府能允许人们在这一年的其余362天里过自己的日子，开放爱丽舍大街让公共马车通行，让杜伊勒里花园保持安静，保姆也可以正常出入，每份报纸只卖半个便士。

文章后半部分对于政府的思索评议让您感到头痛了吧？这些议论其实并不难理解，或许它还能构成一个专题论文的主题。如今在法国的报刊专栏中，七月纪念日占有相当的分量，一张一张地去翻看它们是很有趣的。而读者读到的褒贬也都是半斤八两——读者在争议中知道了国王是怎样接受忠诚的万岁呼声的——在这个国家，人们说赞美的话时，舌头从来都不会在嘴里打颤，但是一旦国王离开，人们又在欢唱《马赛曲》并为它鼓掌。

praise, and Tweedledee's indignation—to read, in the Débats how the King was received with shouts and loyal vivats—in the National, how not a tongue was wagged in his praise, but, on the instant of his departure, how the people called for the "Marseillaise" and applauded THAT. —But best say no more about the fête. The Legitimists were always indignant at it. The high Philippist party sneers at and despises it; the Republicans hate it: it seems a joke against THEM. Why continue it? —If there be anything sacred in the name and idea of loyalty, why renew this fête? It only shows how a rightful monarch was hurled from his throne, and a dexterous usurper stole his precious diadem. If there be anything noble in the memory of a day, when citizens, unused to war, rose against practised veterans, and, armed with the strength of their cause, overthrew them, why speak of it now? or renew the bitter recollections of the bootless struggle and victory? O, Lafayette! O, hero of two worlds! O, accomplished Cromwell Grandison! you have to answer for more than any mortal man who has played a part in history: two republics and one monarchy does the world owe to you; and especially grateful should your country be to you. Did you not, in '90, make clear the path for honest Robespierre, and in '30, prepare the way for—

……

[The Editor of the "*Bungay Beacon* "would insert no more of this letter, which is, therefore, for ever lost to the public.]

但最好不要再说纪念日了。王权拥护者总是对此感到愤怒；上层的菲力浦政党则予以轻视和嘲讽；共和党人则为此而憎恨，仿佛纪念日是针对他们的一个玩笑。那为什么还要把它继续下去呢？在忠诚的名义和思想中如果还有点神圣的东西的话，为什么还要恢复这个纪念日呢？它只是展现了一个合法的帝王是怎样从他的王座上被赶了下来和一个机智的篡位者是怎样偷走了他的宝贵王冠。市民们自发地起义，推翻了波旁复辟王朝，有什么可称耀的呢？为什么要再现那些无用的争斗和胜利的痛苦记忆呢？哦！拉斐德将军［Marquis De LaFayette（1757—1834），法国将军，北美殖民地1775年到1783年独立战争的参加者，18世纪末法国资产阶级革命时期的大资产阶级的领袖之一；1792年8月10日后逃往国外，1830年七月革命的领袖之一，曾领导共和派，任国民军总司令，调解了革命敌对双方组织新政府。——译注］！哦，共和国、七月王朝两个朝代的英雄！哦，杰出的克伦威尔·格兰迪森！你必须为在历史中发挥作用的死亡的人负更多的责任，共和国［1789年7月14日，拉斐德带领起义人民攻下巴士底监狱，为法兰西第一共和国的建立立下了汗马功劳。拿破仑兵败下台后，拉斐德又出来重组议会政治，稳定了风雨飘摇的国家，成为安邦定国的大功臣。］和七月王朝［指路易·菲力浦的上台主要是得到拉斐德、塔列兰的支持和自由主义的资产阶级的成果。——译注］都把这个世界归功于你，你的国家尤其应该感谢你。可是，你没有给1790年忠实的罗伯斯比尔指明道路，也没有给1830年的国王指明道路。

……

［《邦吉灯塔》的编辑把剩余部分给删掉了，因此公众就再也看不到它了。］

On the French School of Painting: with Appropriate Anecdotes, Illustrations, and Philosophical Disquisitions

In A Letter To Mr. Macgilp , of London

The three collections of pictures at the Louvre, the Luxembourg, and the Ecole des Beaux Arts, contain a number of specimens of French art, since its commencement almost, and give the stranger a pretty fair opportunity to study and appreciate the school. The French list of painters contains some very good names—no very great ones, except Poussin (unless the admirers of Claude choose to rank him among great painters),—and I think the school was never in so flourishing a condition as it is at the present day. They say there are three thousand artists in this town alone: of these a handsome minority paint not merely tolerably, but well understand their business: draw the figure accurately; sketch with cleverness; and paint portraits, churches, or restaurateurs' shops, in a decent manner.

To account for a superiority over England which, I think, as regards art, is incontestable—it must be remembered that the painter's trade, in France, is a very good one; better appreciated, better understood, and, generally, far better paid than with us. There are a dozen excellent schools in which a lad may enter here, and, under the eye of a practised master, learn the apprenticeship of his art at an expense of about ten pounds a year. In England there is no school except the Academy, unless the student can afford to pay a very large sum, and place himself under the tuition of some particular artist. Here, a young man, for his ten pounds, has all sorts of accessory instruction,

论法国的绘画流派：兼有相应的逸事、插图以及论述

——给伦敦迈克吉普先生的一封信

罗浮宫、卢森堡美术馆和美术学院是巴黎的三大绘画作品收藏地，它们收藏了许多法国艺术的原作，它们从开始建立到目前为止，都给外国人提供了一个很好的机会去研究和欣赏美术作品。法国有许多出色的画家——虽然他们并不一定都是大师级的人物，除了普桑［Poussin（1594—1665），法国17世纪杰出的巴罗克大师。——译注］（除非克劳德［克劳德·洛兰（Claude Lorrain，1600—1682），与普桑同称为法国17世纪三大风景画家。——译注］的崇拜者愿把他列为伟大的画家之一）之外，我认为法国的绘画流派从来也没有像现在这样兴盛过。人们说只在巴黎这座城市就有三千名艺术家，在这些人中有相当一部分不仅画画得不错，而且很懂得他们的营生，会逼真地画插图，灵活地画素描，庄重地画肖像、教堂或饭店。

我认为，就艺术来讲，法国要比英国具有优势这点是无可争议的。而且，大家也一定知道，在法国画家这个行业是很不错的，它能得到人们较高的赏识和很好的理解，通常画家的报酬也比我们国内的高。这里有许多很好的美术学校可供青年选择，还有经验丰富的教师指导，每年大约花费10镑就能以学徒的身份来学习艺术。而在英国除了学院就没有这类学校，

models, &c. ; and has further, and for nothing, numberless incitements to study his profession which are not to be found in England;—the streets are filled with picture-shops, the people themselves are pictures walking about; the churches, theatres, eating-houses, concert-rooms are covered with pictures. Nature itself is inclined more kindly to him, for the sky is a thousand times more bright and beautiful, and the sun shines for the greater part of the year. Add to this, incitements more selfish, but quite as powerful: a French artist is paid very handsomely; for five hundred a year is much where all are poor; and has a rank in society rather above his merits than below them, being caressed by hosts and hostesses in places where titles are laughed at and a baron is thought of no more account than a banker's clerk.

The life of the young artist here is the easiest, merriest, dirtiest existence possible. He comes to Paris, probably at sixteen, from his province; his parents settle forty pounds a year on him, and pay his master; he establishes himself in the Pays Latin, or in the new quarter of Nôtre Dame de Lorette (which is quite peopled with painters); he arrives at his atelier at a tolerably early hour, and labours among a score of companions as merry and poor as himself. Each gentleman has his favourite tobacco-pipe; and the pictures are painted in the midst of a cloud of smoke, and a din of puns and choice French slang, and a roar of choruses, of which no one can form an idea that has not been present at such an assembly.

You see here every variety of coiffure that has ever been known. Some young men of genius have ringlets hanging over their shoulders—you may smell the tobacco with which they are scented across the street; some have straight locks, black, oily, and redundant; some have toupées in the famous Louis-Philippe fashion; some are cropped close; some have adopted the present mode—which he who would follow must, in order to do so, part his hair in the middle, grease it with grease, and gum it with gum, and iron it flat down over his ears; when arrived at the ears, you take the tongs and make a couple of ranges of curls close round the whole head,—such curls as you may see under a gilt three-cornered hat, and in her Britannic Majesty's coachman's state wig.

除非学生能付得起一大笔钱，他才可能得到专业艺术家的亲自教诲。在这里，一个年轻人只需10镑，就能得到各种各样附加的指导、模特儿等等，而且，学生在这里也能受到艺术的启发和激励，这在英国是没有的。法国的街道上布满了画店，人们自己就是走动的画像。教堂、剧院、小吃店和音乐厅里都挂满了画。另外，自然本身就很讨画家们的喜欢，因为这里的天空非常的明亮和美丽，在一年的绝大部分时间内太阳都是灿烂的。除了这些，还有一个强大的、更为自私的动力，那就是法国艺术家的收入很可观，在人们普遍收入不高的条件下，他们一年能挣五百镑就算是很多了。而且画家的身份只会提升他们的社会地位，却丝毫不会贬低他们的身价。在贵族受到嘲笑、男爵并不比银行店员富有的法国，他们是深受人们欢迎和爱戴的。

年轻艺术家在这里的生活可能是最舒适、最快乐的，也可能是最下流的。他或许是在十六岁从外省来到巴黎，他父母每年给他40镑的花销，还要支付老师的费用。他在拉丁区或在洛荷特圣母院新区安身（这里有许多画家）。他还能较早地来到他的绘画工作室，在许多像他一样快乐而贫穷的同伴之间劳动。每个人都抽着自己喜欢的烟斗，他们在这一团烟雾、一些粗话与齐声的吼叫相混合的喧闹中画画，在这种场合中，根本就察觉不到谁没来。

在这里你能看到人们所知道的各种各样的发型。一些有才气的年轻人留着披肩的长卷发——可是隔着街道你也能闻到他们身上的烟草味；一些人黑色的直发，油光光的很茂密；一些人留着著名的路易·菲力浦式样的小绺顶发；一些人是平头；一些人留着现在的时髦发式——把头发中分，抹上油，涂上胶，从中间往下一直到耳朵以上都烫平，耳朵以下的卷发则分成两绺，用夹子盘在头上——这样的卷发一般是出现在一顶金色的三角帽［三角帽代指军官。——译注］下，英国女王陛下的马夫在礼仪场合也戴这种假发。

这都是最近的流行样式。至于胡子，也有很多样式。我所有的艺术家

This is the last fashion. As for the beards, there is no end of them; all my friends the artists have beards who can raise them; and Nature, though she has rather stinted the bodies and limbs of the French nation, has been very liberal to them of hair, as you may see by the following specimen. Fancy these heads and beards under all sorts of caps—Chinese caps, Mandarin caps, Greek skull-caps, English jockey-caps, Russian or Kuzzilbash caps, Middle-age caps (such as are called, in heraldry, caps of maintenance), Spanish nets, and striped worsted nightcaps. Fancy all the jackets you have ever seen, and you have before you, as well as the pen can describe, the costumes of these indescribable Frenchmen.

In this company and costume the French student of art passes his days and acquires knowledge; how he passes his evenings, at what theatres, at what guinguettes, in company with what seducing little milliner, there is no need to say; but I knew one who pawned his coat to go to a carnival ball, and walked abroad very cheerfully in his blouse for six weeks, until he could redeem the absent garment.

These young men (together with the students of sciences) comport themselves towards the sober citizen pretty much as the German bursch towards the philister, or as the military man, during the empire, did to the pékin:—from the height of their poverty they look down upon him with the greatest imaginable scorn—a scorn, I think, by which the citizen seems dazzled, for his respect for the arts is intense. The case is very different in England, where a grocer's daughter would think she made a misalliance by marrying a painter, and where a literary man (in spite of all we can say against it) ranks below that class of gentry composed of the apothecary, the attorney, the wine-merchant, whose positions, in country towns at least, are so equivocal. As, for instance, my friend the Rev. James Asterisk, who has an undeniable pedigree, a paternal estate, and a living to boot, once dined in Warwickshire, in company with several squires and parsons of that enlightened county. Asterisk, as usual, made himself extraordinarily agreeable at dinner, and delighted all present with his learning and wit. "Who is that monstrous pleasant fellow?" said one of the squires. "Don't you know?" replied another. "It's

朋友都留着胡子。虽然自然赋予法国人的躯体和四肢并不是很强壮，但他们的毛发却很繁茂，你能看到许多的样式。而且，他们还戴着各种各样的帽子——中国式的帽子、清朝官员的帽子、希腊的室内便帽、英国的赛马骑师帽、俄国的无边帽、中世纪的帽子（这些带有纹章的帽子被称做官爵帽）、西班牙的网帽、条纹绒线的睡帽，可以想象一下他们帽子下的头发和胡子。还有他们的装束，都是你想不到、用笔也难以描述的。

在这样的人群和装束中，法国的艺术生就消磨着时日并学习专业。他是在剧院、城郊咖啡馆还是和迷人的小女工一起度过夜晚，就没必要说了。但我知道有一个人当掉了他的外套去参加一个狂欢聚会，六个星期以来他都是穿着罩衫高兴地到处走，直到能够赎回那件外套为止。

这些年轻人（同理科的学生一起）对待严肃市民的态度很像德国年轻的大学生对待庸俗市民的态度，或帝国时期的军人对待平民老百姓的态度——他们极端地蔑视贫穷、崇奉艺术，而市民们就被他们那种强烈崇奉艺术的精神给迷惑住了。在英国情况就很不一样了，在那里一个杂货店老板的女儿会认为嫁给一个画家是很不体面的，文人的地位要低于药剂师、代理人和酒商（尽管我们有理由予以反驳），他们在城镇中的地位是很暧昧的。举例来说，我的朋友里维·詹姆士·阿斯特瑞斯克，他有着优秀的家族血统和一笔可观的父辈财产，除此之外他还有一份生计。有一次他在沃里克郡和一些乡绅、牧师在一起吃饭，阿斯特瑞斯克像往常一样，在吃饭时表现得很愉快，凭着自己的学识和机智把在场的所有人都给逗乐了。“那个很愉快的小伙子是谁啊？”一个乡绅问。“你不知道吗？”另一个答道，“他是阿斯特瑞斯克，某某作家，某某杂志一个有名的投稿人。”“天哪！”乡绅十分惊讶地说，“一个文人！我还以为他是个绅士呢！”

另一个例子是法国的格佐特先生。当他做部长的时候，他拥有部长的公馆，能款待所有到场的贵族名流，宴会场面也很豪华。一位光彩照人、十分美丽的英国公爵夫人出席了其中的一场部长宴会。两星期后，她准备去拜访格佐特先生，但是凑巧，在这两星期内，格佐特先生不再是部长了，

Asterisk, the author of so-and-so, and a famous contributor to such and such a magazine." "Good Heavens!" said the squire, quite horrified! "a literary man! I thought he had been a gentleman!"

Another instance: M. Guizot, when he was Minister here, had the grand hotel of the Ministry, and gave entertainments to all the great de par le monde, as Brantôme says, and entertained them in a proper ministerial magnificence. The splendid and beautiful Duchess of Dash was at one of his ministerial parties; and went, a fortnight afterwards, as in duty bound, to pay her respects to M. Guizot. But it happened, in this fortnight, that M. Guizot was Minister no longer; but given up his portfolio, and his grand hotel, to retire into private life, and to occupy his humble apartments in a house which he possesses, and of which he lets the greater portion. A friend of mine was present at one of the ex-Minister's soirées, where the Duchess of Dash made her appearance. He says the Duchess, at her entrance, seemed quite astounded, and examined the premises with a most curious wonder. Two or three shabby little rooms, with ordinary furniture, and a Minister en retraite, who lives by letting lodgings! In our country was ever such a thing heard of? No, thank Heaven! and a Briton ought to be proud of the difference.

But to our muttons. This country is surely the paradise of painters and penny-a-liners; and when one reads of M. Horace Vernet at Rome, exceeding ambassadors at Rome by his magnificence, and leading such a life as Rubens or Titian did of old; when one sees M. Thiers's grand villa in the Rue St. George (a dozen years ago he was not even a penny-a-liner: no such luck); when one contemplates, in imagination, M. Gudin, the marine painter, too lame to walk through the picture-gallery of the Louvre, accommodated, therefore, with a wheel-chair, a privilege of princes only, and accompanied—nay, for what I know, actually trundled—down the gallery by majesty itself—who does not long to make one of the great nation, exchange his native tongue for the melodious jabber of France; or, at least, adopt it for his native country, like Marshal Saxe, Napoleon, and Anacharsis Clootz? Noble people! they made Tom Paine a deputy; and as for Tom Macaulay, they would make a DYNASTY of him.

他已经辞去部长职务，离开公馆，退休回家，住在自己的一套简朴公寓里，他还把这套公寓里的大部分房间都租了出去。我的一个朋友曾出席过这位前任部长的一次晚会，他在退休部长的家里遇到了公爵夫人。他说公爵夫人刚进来的时候，表情很惊讶，非常好奇地检查了房子，发现那里只有两三个破旧的小房间和普通的家具，一个退休的部长竟靠出租房屋来生活！在我们国家曾听说过这样的事情吗？没有。上帝保佑！不列颠人应该为这种差异而感到骄傲。

言归正传。法国的确是画家和穷文人的天堂。当人们获悉荷拉斯·维尔纳［Horace Vernet（1789—1863），19 世纪中叶法国浪漫主义画家。——译注］在罗马时，他的知名度都超过了法国驻罗马的大使，他过着以前的鲁本斯［Rubens（1577—1640），巴罗克艺术的代表人物。——译注］或提香［Titian（1490—1576），意大利文艺复兴盛期威尼斯派画家。——译注］式的生活。人们会在圣乔治街看到梯也尔［Thiers（1797—1877），法国政治家，历史学家。——译注］的壮观别墅（十二年以前他甚至都算不上是一个穷文人，没有这样的运气）。当人们考虑到居丹［Gudin（1802—1880），法国画家。——译注］这个擅长画海的画家因腿跛不能进入罗浮宫画廊时，就给他提供了一张轮椅，这可是只有王子才能享用的一项特权，除此之外还有人陪侍他——据我所知，他还是被陛下本人亲自推入画廊的。在萨克森元帅［Marshal Saxe（1696—1750），法军指挥官、陆军元帅。——译注］、拿破仑和阿那卡雪斯·克罗茨［Anacharsis Clootz（1755—1794），法国大革命时革命者，推崇理性，后和雅各宾左派一起被处死。——译注］这些名人的国度，谁不渴望成为这个伟大国家中的一员，把他的母语换成旋律美妙、急促不清的法国话呢？高贵的法国人啊！如果潘恩［Paine（1737—1809），18 世纪的启蒙思想家，资产阶级民主主义者。1737 年 1 月 29 日生于英国诺福克郡塞特福德镇，1809 年 6 月 8 日卒于纽约。——译注］、麦考莱是他们同胞的话，他们会让潘恩做下院议员、麦考莱［Macaulay（1800—1859），英国历史学家、作家。——译注］

Well, this being the case, no wonder there are so many painters in France; and here, at least, we are back to them. At the Ecole Royale des Beaux Arts, you see two or three hundred specimens of their performances; all the prize-men, since 1750, I think, being bound to leave their prize sketch or picture. Can anything good come out of the Royal Academy? It is a question which has been considerably mooted in England (in the neighbourhood of Suffolk Street especially). The hundreds of French samples are, I think, not very satisfactory. The subjects are almost all what are called classical: Orestes pursued by every variety of Furies; numbers of little wolf-sucking Romuluses; Hectors and Andromaches in a complication of parting embraces, and so forth; for it was the absurd maxim of our forefathers, that because these subjects had been the fashion twenty centuries ago, they must remain so in saecula saeculorum; because to these lofty heights giants had scaled, behold the race of pigmies must get upon stilts and jump at them likewise! and on the canvas, and in the theatre, the French frogs (excuse the pleasantry) were instructed to swell out and roar as much as possible like bulls.

What was the consequence, my dear friend? In trying to make themselves into bulls, the frogs make themselves into jackasses, as might be expected. For a hundred and ten years the classical humbug oppressed the nation; and you may see, in this gallery of the Beaux Arts, seventy years' specimens of the dullness which it engendered.

Now, as Nature made every man with a nose and eyes of his own, she gave him a character of his own too; and yet we, O foolish race! must try our very best to ape some one or two of our neighbours, whose ideas fit us no more than their breeches! It is the study of Nature, surely, that profits us, and not of these imitations of her. A man, as a man, from a dustman up to Aeschylus, is God's work, and good to read, as all works of Nature are: but the silly animal is never content; is ever trying to fit itself into another shape; wants to deny its own identity, and has not the courage to utter its own thoughts. Because Lord Byron was wicked, and quarrelled with the world; and found himself growing fat, and quarrelled with his victuals, and thus, naturally, grew ill-humoured, did not half Europe grow ill-humoured too? Did

做国王的。

通过以上的例子，人们就知道在法国有这么多画家是不足为奇的了。让我们回到原来的话题。在皇家美术学院，你能看到两三百件代表画家成就的作品。我想，从1750年以来，所有的得奖人必定会把他们的获奖素描或绘画留在这里。皇家学院里出来的任何作品都是好的吗？这在英国一直是被议论纷纷的一个问题（尤其在萨福克街道附近）。我认为，这几百件法国作品并不是很让人满意的。作品的主题几乎全部都取自古典主义题材。如俄瑞斯忒斯被各种各样的复仇女神所追赶；吮吸狼奶的小罗慕路斯；赫克托耳与昂朵马格分别时的拥抱场景等等。因为古典主义是我们祖先传下来的荒谬准则，因为这些主题在两千年前就是流行的，人们就要把它们无休止地延续下去；因为对这些崇高的英雄巨人，我们的祖先已按比例规定好尺寸。看呀！矮人也必须踩在和他们一样高的高跷上跳起来看！无论在油画上还是在戏院中，法国佬（对不起，开玩笑）都要像公牛一样尽最大的力气大声喊叫。

我亲爱的朋友，结果会怎样呢？可以预料得到，当他们努力把自己变成公牛时，他们却把自己变成了蠢驴。一百一十年来古典主义这个骗子一直束缚着这个民族。你可以在这个美术学院的画廊中看到由它所造成的七十年的单调沉闷的作品。

对于每个人，自然都赋予了他一个自己的鼻子和一双自己的眼睛，她还赋予了他自己的个性，然而我们愚蠢的人类却一定要尽我们所能地去模仿我们同类中的一个或两个，其实他们的思想和他们的马裤一样都不适合我们！事实上，探究自然而不是模仿自然才对我们真正有益。作为一个人，无论是清洁工还是埃斯库罗斯，他们都是上帝的作品，与自然的所有作品一样都是很好的鉴赏对象。但是愚蠢的人类却从不满足，总是在尝试着把他自己变成别的样子，想要否认他自己的特征，没有勇气表达他自己的想法。因为拜伦勋爵悲观傲世、对世界不满，难道一半的欧洲人也要随之模仿，对世界不满吗？难道每个诗人都觉得自己年轻的爱情枯萎，灵魂布满

not every poet feel his young affections withered, and despair and darkness cast upon his soul? Because certain mighty men of old could make heroical statues and plays, must we not be told that there is no other beauty but classical beauty? —must not every little whipster of a French poet chalk you out plays, "*Henriades*," and such-like, and vow that here was the real thing, the undeniable Kalon?

The undeniable fiddlestick! For a hundred years, my dear sir, the world was humbugged by the so-called classical artists, as they now are by what is called the Christian art (of which anon); and it is curious to look at the pictorial traditions as here handed down. The consequence of them is, that scarce one of the classical pictures exhibited is worth much more than two-and-sixpence. Borrowed from statuary, in the first place, the colour of the paintings seems, as much as possible, to participate in it; they are mostly of a misty, stony green, dismal hue, as if they had been painted in a world where no colour was. In every picture, there are, of course, white mantles, white urns, white columns, white statues—those obligés accomplishments of the sublime. There are the endless straight noses, long eyes, round chins, short upper lips, just as they are ruled down for you in the drawing-books, as if the latter were the revelations of beauty, issued by supreme authority, from which there was no appeal? Why is the classical reign to endure? Why is yonder simpering Venus de' Medicis to be our standard of beauty, or the Greek tragedies to bound our notions of the sublime? There was no reason why Agamemnon should set the fashions, and remains ἀναξ ἀνδρων to eternity; and there is a classical quotation, which you may have occasionally heard, beginning Vixere fortespost Agamemnona multi. , which, as it avers that there were a great number of stout fellows before Agamemnon, may not unreasonably induce us to conclude that similar heroes were to succeed him. Shakespeare made a better man when his imagination moulded the mighty figure of Macbeth. And if you will measure Satan by Prometheus, the blind old Puritan's work by that of the fiery Grecian poet, does not Milton's angel surpass Aeschylus's—sur-

了绝望和阴影吗？因为古代有几个杰出的人物创造了崇高的雕塑和戏剧，我们就被告知除了古典美之外没有其他的美了吗？难道一个法国诗人就不能以《欧里奥德》[伏尔泰的戏剧作品。——译注]之类的作品作为榜样，发誓说这才是真正的不可否认的杰出作品吗？

胡说八道！亲爱的先生，一百年以来这个世界都被所谓的古典艺术家们所欺骗着，现在又受到基督教艺术的欺骗。看看这里流传下来的绘画传统是多么的荒谬。它所带来的结果就是，展出的古典绘画作品没多少有价值的。首先，绘画的颜色很有可能就是从雕塑那里借鉴来的并运用于其中。它们绝大部分都是朦胧不清的石绿色，色调阴郁，仿佛是在一个没有颜色的世界里被画出来的。在每张画中，总会有白色的披风、白色的瓮、白色的柱子、白色的雕塑——这些都是崇高美所必不可少的因素。还有无数直而长的鼻子、细长的眼睛、圆圆的下巴、短短的上唇，它们就像是在画书中为你制定好的那样，仿佛后者就是至高的权威所发布的美的标准，而这些有艺术感染力吗？为什么古典主义要继续支配我们？为什么那边假笑的“麦迪奇的维纳斯”就是我们美的标准，为什么古希腊的悲剧要限制我们对于崇高的看法？就像以阿伽门农作为永恒的硬汉标准是毫无理由的一样，也得不到人们的信服。你或许听到过一段经典的引文，在贺拉斯[古罗马诗人。——译注]诗篇中有一句话，“Vixere fortes post Agamemnona multi (拉丁文)”，意思是“在阿伽门农之后生活过许多英雄”，即使它断言在阿伽门农之前有很多强壮的人，也不可能让我们轻易断言那些英雄会胜过阿伽门农。当莎士比亚用自己的创造力来塑造伟大的麦克白这个形象时，麦克白就成了一个很好的人物形象。如果你用普罗米修斯的眼光来衡量撒旦，用炯炯有神的希腊诗人的目光来衡量失明的老清教徒弥尔顿的作品[指弥尔顿的长诗《失乐园》。——译注]，难道弥尔顿的天使不是要胜过埃斯库罗斯的天使吗？它们不是具有基督教的因素吗？

在同类的美术学院中都可以看到大量模仿古代作品的缺乏生命力的复制品，梯也尔先生也在这股潮流的引导下促使画家去仿制同样大小的米开

pass him by "many a rood"?

In the same school of the Beaux Arts, where are to be found such a number of pale imitations of the antique, Monsieur Thiers (and he ought to be thanked for it) has caused to be placed a full-sized copy of "*The Last Judgement*" of Michael Angelo, and a number of casts from statues by the same splendid hand. There IS the sublime, if you please—a new sublime—an original sublime—quite as sublime as the Greek sublime. See yonder, in the midst of his angels, the Judge of the world descending in glory; and near him, beautiful and gentle, and yet indescribably august and pure, the Virgin by his side. There is the "*Moses*," the grandest figure that ever was carved in stone. It has about it something frightfully majestic, if one may so speak. In examining this, and the astonishing picture of "*The Last Judgement*," or even a single figure of it, the spectator's sense amounts almost to pain. I would not like to be left in a room alone with the "*Moses.*" How did the artist live amongst them, and create them? How did he suffer the painful labour of invention? One fancies that he would have been scorched up, like Semele, by sights too tremendous for his vision to bear. One cannot imagine him, with our small physical endowments and weaknesses, a man like ourselves.

As for the Ecole Royale des Beaux Arts, then, and all the good its students have done, as students, it is stark naught. When the men did anything, it was after they had left the academy, and began thinking for themselves. There is only one picture among the many hundreds that has, to my idea, much merit (a charming composition of Homer singing, signed Jourdy); and the only good that the Academy has done by its pupils was to send them to Rome, where they might learn better things. At home, the intolerable, stupid classicalities, taught by men who, belonging to the least erudite country in Europe, were themselves, from their profession, the least learned among their countrymen, only weighed the pupils down, and cramped their hands, their eyes, and their imaginations; drove them away from natural beauty, which, thank God, is fresh and attainable by us all, today, and yesterday,

朗琪罗的《最后的审判》，还有大师的许多雕像杰作。那就是崇高——你看——真正的崇高——希腊的崇高。看那边，天使围绕的世界审判者正在一团光轮中徐徐下降，他旁边是美丽温柔、庄严纯洁的圣母玛利亚。那里还有《摩西》，一直以来它都是最雄伟的石雕作品。也可以这样说，即它具有某种骇人的威严。仔细观察这幅作品和令人惊讶的《最后的审判》，甚至其中的任何一个人物形象都会让观众感到痛苦。如果把我安排在一个房间里单独和《摩西》在一起，我可受不了。那么在它们中间，创造它们的艺术家又是怎样挺过来的呢？他要怎样忍受着创作的劳累和痛苦啊？人们以为他会像塞墨勒［希腊神话中被宙斯雷电烧死的少女。——译注］一样被烧焦的，因为这些巨大的人物形象不是他的视力所能承受得了的。但人们也不要以为他是一个像我们这样具有平庸天资和缺陷的凡人。

就皇家美术学院来说，它的学生们在这里所创作的一切几乎都是毫无价值的。要等学生离开学院以后，他们才会真正做点事情，开始自己动脑思考。在我看来，成百的绘画作品中只有一幅画是很出色的（署名朱迪的一幅荷马吟唱的迷人作品）。学院对学生所做的唯一的好事就是把他们送到罗马，在那里他们可以学到更好的东西。在国内，这些人身处欧洲最孤陋寡闻的国家，由于本身职业的原因，在同胞之中也是最为孤陋寡闻的人。他们所传授的那种让人无法忍受的、愚蠢的古典主义，只能压制学生，束缚他们的手、眼睛和想象力；让他们感谢上帝，远离自然美。而自然美才是我们所有人在昨天、今天和明天所能感触到的新鲜东西，相反，古典主义只是让学生对人为的优雅亦步亦趋，缺乏正确判断和捕捉自然美的能力。

关于皇家美术馆的建筑还要再说一句。这座建筑很美丽，装饰得也很好，很实用。它有着灵巧精致的结构、美丽的喷泉、文艺复兴式的拱门和一些零散的雕塑，在一个美好的日子里，你几乎看不到还能有比这里更让人心旷神怡的地方。

从皇家美术馆里出来之后就到了风景如画的塞纳街，接着我们又步行到卢森堡公园，那里有保姆、学生、青年劳动妇女和留着辫子的老绅士，

and tomorrow; and sent them rambling after artificial grace, without the proper means of judging or attaining it.

A word for the building of these Palais des Beaux Arts. It is beautiful, and as well finished and convenient as beautiful. With its light and elegant fabric, its pretty fountain, its archway of the Rénaissance, and fragments of sculpture, you can hardly see, on a fine day, a place more riant and pleasing.

Passing from thence up the picturesque Rue de Seine, let us walk to the Luxembourg, where bonnes, students, grisettes, and old gentlemen with pigtails, love to wander in the melancholy, quaint old gardens; where the peers have a new and comfortable court of justice, to judge all the émeutes which are to take place; and where, as everybody knows, is the picture-gallery of modern French artists, whom government thinks worthy of patronage.

A very great proportion of these pictures, as we see by the catalogue, are by the students whose works we have just been to visit at the Beaux Arts, and who, having performed their pilgrimage to Rome, have taken rank among the professors of the art. I don't know a more pleasing exhibition; for there are not a dozen really bad pictures in the collection, some very good, and the rest showing great skill and smartness of execution.

In the same way, however, that it has been supposed that no man could be a great poet unless he wrote a very big poem, the tradition is kept up among the painters, and we have here a vast number of large canvases, with figures of the proper heroical length and nakedness. The anticlassicists did not arise in France until about 1827; and, in consequence, up to that period, we have here the old classical faith in full vigour. There is Brutus, having chopped his son's head off, with all the agony of a father, and then, calling for number two; there is Aeneas carrying off old Anchises; there are Paris and Venus, as naked as two Hottentots, and many more such choice subjects from Lemprière.

But the chief specimens of the sublime are in the way of murders, with which the catalogue swarms. Here are a few extracts from it:—

他们都喜欢在这个忧郁、古雅的老花园里闲逛。在这里，公民还拥有一个新的不错的法院来审理将来可能发生的所有骚乱。人们都知道，这里还有现代法国艺术家的画廊。对于现代艺术家，政府认为还是值得资助的。

从绘画展览的目录上我们可以看出，绝大部分绘画作品都是美术学院的学生画的，我们已在美术学院参观时看过他们的作品。他们已结束了在罗马的艺术朝圣，在艺术专业上也取得了一定的成就。这次展览很令人赏心悦目，没多少非常糟糕的作品，有一些作品确实非常出色，其余的也都展现出作者本人杰出而巧妙的艺术手法。

然而人们普遍认为，一个诗人只有写出一首伟大的诗篇，他才能被称为一个伟大的诗人。同样，在画家行业中也有这种看法。在这里我们看到了许多大幅的油画，油画上的人物形象都是按照适当的英雄高度和裸露度所画的。反古典主义一直到大约1827年才在法国出现，因此，直到那个时代为止，我们在这里看到的都是画家对古典主义的热忱信奉。这里有布鲁图［Brutus，罗马历史人物，为维护共和而处决了两个儿子。——译注］怀着一个父亲极度痛苦的心情砍下了他一个儿子的头，接着又叫下一个；有埃涅阿斯背着年老的安喀塞斯离开家园（特洛伊）；有帕里斯和维纳斯，他们赤裸得就像两个霍屯督人［西南非洲的一个种族。——译注］；还有许多从朗浦里埃［Lemprière，生年不可考，死在1824年，著名古典学者。著作有《希腊罗马古人名字典》。——译注］那里挑选的类似主题。

但是最主要的崇高题材还是谋杀。在作品目录中这个主题是出现最多的。这里抽出一小部分：

7. 博姆，荣誉勋位团的骑士。《垂死的法国皇太子妃》

18. 布隆戴尔，荣誉勋位团的骑士。《死亡的塞诺比亚》

36. 德贝，骑士。《卢克利希亚［罗马传说中的贞妇。——译注］之死》

38. 德热诺。《赫克托耳之死》

34. 柯罗，荣誉勋位团的骑士。《恺撒之死》

7. Beaume, Chevalier de la Légion d'Honneur. "*The Grand Dauphiness Dying.*"

18. Blondel, Chevalier de la, &c. "*Zenobia Found Dead.*"

36. Debay, Chevalier. "*The Death of Lucretia.*"

38. Dejuinne. "*The Death of Hector.*"

34. Court, Chevalier de la, &c. "*The Death of Caesar.*"

39, 40, 41. Delacroix, Chevalier. "*Dante and Virgil in the Infernal Lake,*" "*The Massacre of Scio,*" and "*Medea going to Murder her Children.*"

43. Delaroche, Chevalier. "*Joas taken from among the Dead.*"

44. "*The Death of Queen Elizabeth.*"

45. "*Edward V. and his Brother*" (preparing for death).

50. Drolling, Chevalier. "*Hecuba going to be Sacrificed.*"

51. Dubois. "Young Clovis found Dead."

56. Henry, Chevalier. "*The Massacre of St. Bartholomew.*"

75. Guérin, Chevalier. "*Cain, after the Death of Abel.*"

83. Jacquand. "*Death of Adelaide de Comminges.*"

88. "*The Death of Eudamidas.*"

93. "*The Death of Hymetto.*"

103. "*The Death of Philip of Austria.*"—And so on.

You see what woeful subjects they take, and how profusely they are decorated with knighthood. They are like the Black Brunswickers, these painters, and ought to be called Chevaliers de la Mort. I don't know why the merriest people in the world should please themselves with such grim representations and varieties of murder, or why murder itself should be considered so eminently sublime and poetical. It is good at the end of a tragedy; but, then, it is good because it is the end, and because, by the events foregone, the mind is prepared for it. But these men will have nothing but fifth acts; and seem to skip, as unworthy, all the circumstances leading to them. This, however, is part of the scheme—the bloated, unnatural, stilted, spouting, sham sublime,

39，40，41. 德拉克洛瓦［19 世纪法国浪漫主义画家。——译注］，骑士。《在地狱湖中的但丁和维吉尔》，《希阿岛的屠杀》和《屠杀孩子的美狄亚》

43. 德拉洛克，骑士。《逃离死亡的琼斯》

44. 《伊丽莎白女王之死》

45. 《爱德华五世和他的兄弟》（等待死亡）

50. 多令，骑士。《献祭黑寇芭［特洛伊的王后。——译注］》

51. 杜柏斯。《少年克罗维斯的死亡》

56. 亨利，骑士。《残杀圣·巴多罗买［十二使徒之一。——译注］》

75. 格林，骑士。《杀害亚伯的该隐》

83. 雅康丹。《阿德莱娜之死》

88. 《尤达米达斯之死》

93. 《海梅托之死》

103. 《奥地利的菲力浦之死》——等等。

你可以看出画家在作品中所描绘的都是多么悲痛的主题，而且他们是多么奢侈地用骑士身份来修饰自己。这些画家，他们喜欢黑布朗斯维克团（起初是一支由 700 名志愿者组成的轻骑兵/步兵团，组建于 1809 年，效力反法同盟。与之同名的油画也非常著名。——译注）应该被称为死亡骑士。我不明白，为什么这个世界上最快乐的人却要通过表现这类可憎的谋杀来愉悦自己，为什么谋杀就该被认为是杰出的崇高和理想化的题材。在一个悲剧的结尾出现谋杀和死亡是好的，好就好在是结尾，因为有了先前的情节铺垫，人们的思想已有所准备了。但是在这些绘画作品中除了第五幕（即结尾）之外什么也没有，看来它是被画家忽略过去了，他们认为不值得去表现那些导致结局发生的所有情境。这还只是目录中的一部分——夸张、做作、虚饰、呆板、虚假的崇高，我们的前辈就信奉这一套，对真实的生活则不予理睬，恭顺的学生和其他的反古典主义者应该利用他们自身的力量去尽力推翻古典主义。比如说，拉封先生真的在意尤达米达斯的死亡吗？

that our teachers have believed and tried to pass off as real, and which your humble servant and other antihumbuggists should heartily, according to the strength that is in them, endeavour to pull down. What, for instance, could Monsieur Lafond care about the death of Eudamidas? What was Hecuba to Chevalier Drolling, or Chevalier Drolling to Hecuba? I would lay a wager that neither of them ever conjugated τυπτω, and that their school learning carried them not as far as the letter, but only to the game of taw. How were they to be inspired by such subjects? From having seen Talma and Mademoiselle Georges flaunting in sham Greek costumes, and having read up the articles Eudamidas, Hecuba, in the "*Mythological Dictionary.*" What a classicism, inspired by rouge, gas-lamps, and a few lines in Lemprière, and copied, half from ancient statues, and half from a naked guardsman at one shilling and sixpence the hour!

Delacroix is a man of a very different genius, and his "*Medea*" is a genuine creation of a noble fancy. For most of the others, Mrs. Brownrigg, and her two female 'prentices, would have done as well as the desperate Colchian with her τεκνα φιλτατα. M. Delacroix has produced a number of rude, barbarous pictures; but there is the stamp of genius on all of them,—the great poetical INTENTION, which is worth all your execution. Delaroche is another man of high merit; with not such a great HEART, perhaps, as the other, but a fine and careful draughtsman, and an excellent arranger of his subject. "*The Death of Elizabeth*" is a raw young performance seemingly—not, at least, to my taste. The "*Enfans d'Edouard*" is renowned over Europe, and has appeared in a hundred different ways in print. It is properly pathetic and gloomy, and merits fully its high reputation. This painter rejoices in such subjects—in what Lord Portsmouth used to call "black jobs." He has killed Charles I. and Lady Jane Grey, and the Dukes of Guise, and I don't know whom besides. He is, at present, occupied with a vast work at the Beaux Arts, where the writer of this had the honour of seeing him,—a little, keen-looking man, some five feet in height. He wore, on this important occasion, a bandanna

黑寇芭是多令骑士的什么人或多令骑士是黑寇芭的什么人啊？我敢打赌他们两人从没有见过面。学院教育不但没有让他们领会作品的精神，反而让他们学会了石弹子游戏。他们是怎么被这类主题激发的呢？无非是看过塔尔马［拉封和塔尔马，法国当时的悲剧演员，后来曾受拿破仑赞赏。——译注］和乔治夫人穿着劣等的希腊服装招摇，熟读了《神学词典》中有关尤达米达斯、黑寇芭的文章。在红色的瓦斯灯和朗浦里埃神学词典的激励下，他们就以每小时一先令六便士的出价要么模仿古代的雕塑，要么模仿裸体的卫兵！

德拉克洛瓦［Delacroix（1798—1863），19世纪法国画家，代表作品有《但丁之舟》、《希阿岛的屠杀》、《自由领导人民前进》等。——译注］是个不同寻常的天才，他的《美狄亚》是一幅具有杰出想象力的天才作品。而其余的大多数画家只会把它处理成绝望的主题。德拉克洛瓦也创作过许多粗俗、野蛮的画，但它们全部都带有天才的印记——他充满诗意的伟大作品值得你全神贯注地欣赏。德拉克洛瓦还是一个享有崇高荣誉的人，如果没有一颗伟大的心灵，他也许就像其他人一样只是一个优秀杰出的制图员，一个出色的学科管理人。《伊丽莎白女王之死》表面上看来是出自一个没有经验的年轻人之手——但我却很中意它。《爱德华的孩子》在整个欧洲都很有名，它已被印出了一百多个版本。作者把悲哀和抑郁都处理得恰到好处，完全应得到很高的声誉。这个画家喜欢处理这样的题材——而朴次茅斯勋爵过去一直把这类题材称做“邪恶的工作”［因为里面有谋杀和死亡。——译注］。他已在作品中“杀死”了查理一世［1600—1649，英国斯图亚特王朝的国王，在断头台上被处死。——译注］、简·格雷女士［Lady Jane Grey（1537—1554），在位仅9天的英格兰女王，宫廷阴谋、男性权力贪欲的牺牲品，在断头台上被处死。这里指《简·格雷的处刑》这幅画。——译注］，还有居伊兹公爵，我不知道除此之外还有谁。目前他在美术学院忙于很多工作，本文作者很荣幸见到了他——一个矮小、热情的男人，五英尺高。在这个重要的场合上他头上围着一条印花大手帕，正在抽雪茄。

round his head, and was in the act of smoking a cigar.

Horace Vernet, whose beautiful daughter Delaroche married, is the king of French battle-painters—an amazingly rapid and dexterous draughtsman, who has Napoleon and all the campaigns by heart, and has painted the Grenadier Français under all sorts of attitudes. His pictures on such subjects are spirited, natural, and excellent; and he is so clever a man, that all he does is good to a certain degree. His "*Judith*" is somewhat violent, perhaps. His "*Rebecca*" most pleasing; and not the less so for a little pretty affectation of attitude and needless singularity of costume. "*Raphael and Michael Angelo*" is as clever a picture as can be—clever is just the word—the groups and drawing excellent, the colouring pleasantly bright and gaudy; and the French students study it incessantly; there are a dozen who copy it for one who copies Delacroix. His little scraps of wood-cuts, in the now publishing "*Life of Napoleon*," are perfect gems in their way, and the noble price paid for them not a penny more than he merits.

The picture, by Court, of "*The Death of Caesar*," is remarkable for effect and excellent workmanship: and the head of Brutus (who looks like Armand Carrel) is full of energy. There are some beautiful heads of women, and some very good colour in the picture. Jacquand's "*Death of Adelaide de Comminges*" is neither more nor less than beautiful. Adelaide had, it appears, a lover, who betook himself to a convent of Trappists. She followed him thither, disguised as a man, took the vows, and was not discovered by him till on her death-bed. The painter has told this story in a most pleasing and affecting manner: the picture is full of onction and melancholy grace. The objects, too, are capitally represented; and the tone and colour very good. Decaisne's "*Guardian Angel*" is not so good in colour, but is equally beautiful in expression and grace. A little child and a nurse are asleep: an angel watches the infant. You see women look very wistfully at this sweet picture; and what triumph would a painter have more?

We must not quit the Luxembourg without noticing the dashing sea-

荷拉斯·维尔纳是战争题材的绘画之王，他漂亮的女儿德拉罗克也结婚了。他是一个非常迅捷而敏锐的画家，用心记住了拿破仑所有的战役，画了各种姿势的法国士兵。他的这些战争题材的作品既自然生动又振奋人心。他很聪明，因此无论做什么都做得很好。他的《朱迪斯》或许是有些暴力的因素。而《丽蓓卡》就很好看了，没有一点做作的姿势和奇异的装束。《拉斐尔和米开朗琪罗》是一幅很巧妙的画——用巧妙来形容是非常合适的——构图和画法都很出色，颜色明亮绚丽，很悦目。法国学生都在不断地研究这幅画。如果有一个人模仿德拉克洛瓦的画那么就会有一打的人在模仿维尔纳的画。他有一部分木版画现在被印成《拿破仑的生活》出版了，这是一件无价之宝，再贵的价格也是物有所值。

柯罗［Court（1796—1875），法国风景画家。——译注］的《恺撒之死》在外观和工艺方面都很杰出。布鲁图斯（刺杀恺撒的罗马历史人物。——译注）的头部（看起来像阿曼德·卡雷尔）充满活力。画中有一些女人的头部画得很漂亮，色彩也不错。雅康丹［Jacquand，法国画家。——译注］的《阿德莱娜之死》还算漂亮。看来，阿德莱娜有个情人，他自己要去特拉斯比会修道院。阿德莱娜就扮成一个男人跟着他到了那里，立誓出家修行，但是一直到她临死时才被情人发现。画家用画笔非常动人地描述了这个故事。画中充满了热情和忧郁的魅力。物体也描绘得很好，光线的明暗和颜色都很好。迪塞森［Decaisne（1807—1882），法国画家。——译注］的《守护天使》在色彩运用上并不是很成功，但是画家的表现手法和风格都很雅致：一个小孩和一个保姆睡着了，一位天使看守着婴儿。女人们都若有所思地看着这幅温馨的画，还能有比这更让一位画家感到喜悦的吗？

居丹汹涌奔腾的海洋绘画、吉鲁［Giroux。——译注］的风景画还有艾力尼［Aligny（1798—1871），法国画家。——译注］的《普罗米修斯》都是值得一看的。《耶稣基督和孩子们》或许是法兰特连［Hippolyte Flandrin，19世纪法国画家。——译注］的一幅杰出的仿制品，尽管是模

pieces of Gudin, and one or two landscapes by Giroux (the plain of Grasivaudan), and "*The Prometheus*" of Aligny. This is an imitation, perhaps; as is a noble picture of "*Jesus Christ and the Children*," by Flandrin; but the artists are imitating better models, at any rate; and one begins to perceive that the odious classical dynasty is no more. Poussin's magnificent "*Polyphemus*" (I only know a print of that marvellous composition) has, perhaps, suggested the first-named picture; and the latter has been inspired by a good enthusiastic study of the Roman schools.

Of this revolution, Monsieur Ingres has been one of the chief instruments. He was, before Horace Vernet, president of the French Academy at Rome, and is famous as a chief of a school. When he broke up his atelier here, to set out for his presidency, many of his pupils attended him faithfully some way on his journey; and some, with scarcely a penny in their pouches, walked through France and across the Alps, in a pious pilgrimage to Rome, being determined not to forsake their old master. Such an action was worthy of them, and of the high rank which their profession holds in France, where the honours to be acquired by art are only inferior to those which are gained in war. One reads of such peregrinations in old days, when the scholars of some great Italian painter followed him from Venice to Rome, or from Florence to Ferrara. In regard of Ingres' individual merit as a painter, the writer of this is not a fair judge, having seen but three pictures by him; one being a plafond in the Louvre, which his disciples much admire.

Ingres stands between the Imperio-Davido-classical school of French art, and the namby-pamby mystical German school, which is for carrying us back to Cranach and Dürer, and which is making progress here.

For everything here finds imitation: the French have the genius of imitation and caricature. This absurd humbug, called the Christian or Catholic art, is sure to tickle our neighbours, and will be a favourite with them, when better known. My dear MacGilp, I do believe this to be a greater humbug than the humbug of David and Girodet, inasmuch as the latter was founded on Na-

仿，但艺术家至少是在模仿更好的样品了，人们开始意识到可憎的古典主义时代已一去不复返了。普桑的杰作《波吕斐摩斯》［希腊神话中的独眼巨人。——译注］（我只知道那幅杰作的一张版画）也许就预示了原创绘画的开端，而后者正是从对罗马绘画的狂热研究中被激发出来的。

在这场绘画革命中，安格尔先生［Ingres（1780—1867），法国画家。1806 年，安格尔赴意大利，1824 年回到巴黎。后来，1834—1841 年，他再度赴罗马，深刻地研究了文艺复兴时期意大利古典大师们的作品，尤其推崇拉斐尔。——译注］是其中的主力之一。他在荷拉斯·维尔纳之前是驻罗马的法兰西学院的院长。当他离开巴黎的画室去罗马赴院长职位时，他的许多学生也想方设法参与了他的这次罗马之行。有些人口袋里仅有一便士，也决定要追随他们的老师，他们徒步穿过法国，越过阿尔卑斯山脉，虔诚地去罗马朝圣。这样的行动对他们来说是很有意义的，与绘画职业在法国所占据的高等地位也是相称的。在法国，人们通过艺术所获得的荣誉仅次于在战争中所获得的荣誉。以前当一些伟大的意大利画家、学者跟随安格尔从威尼斯到罗马或从佛罗伦萨到费拉拉时，人们就曾听说过这样的旅行。作为一个画家，安格尔个人的功绩体现在哪里，本文的作者不能作出公正的判断，我只看过他的三幅画作，其中一幅就是他在罗浮宫的天花板彩画，那是深得他弟子赞美的一幅画。

安格尔的绘画风格处于法国艺术的专制古典主义流派和感伤神秘的德国流派之间，他的作品是要把我们带回到克拉纳赫［Cranach（1472—1553），是德国文艺复兴著名的女裸体人像画家。——译注］和丢勒［Albrecht Dürer（1471—1528），北部文艺复兴的代表人物。——译注］那个时代里去，也正是在这类作品中他取得了成就。

因为这里的每件作品都在寻求模仿，因此我们可以说，法国人具有模仿和讽刺的天赋。这种荒谬的被称做基督教或天主教的艺术也一定会把我们的邻人逗乐而得到他们的喜爱。我亲爱的迈克吉普，我确信这种艺术是比大卫［David（1748—1825），法国大革命时期的杰出画家，新古典主义

ture at least; whereas the former is made up of silly affectations, and improvements upon Nature. Here, for instance, is Chevalier Ziegler's picture of "*St. Luke painting the Virgin.*" St. Luke has a monk's dress on, embroidered, however, smartly round the sleeves. The Virgin sits in an immense yellow-ochre halo, with her son in her arms. She looks preternaturally solemn; as does St. Luke, who is eyeing his paint-brush with an intense ominous mystical look. They call this Catholic art. There is nothing, my dear friend, more easy in life. First take your colours, and rub them down clean,—bright carmine, bright yellow, bright sienna, bright ultramarine, bright green. Make the costumes of your figures as much as possible like the costumes of the early part of the fifteenth century. Paint them in with the above colours; and if on a gold ground, the more "Catholic" your art is. Dress your apostles like priests before the altar; and remember to have a good commodity of crosiers, censers, and other such gimcracks, as you may see in the Catholic chapels, in Sutton Street and elsewhere. Deal in Virgins, and dress them like a burgomaster's wife by Cranach or Van Eyck. Give them all long twisted tails to their gowns, and proper angular draperies. Place all their heads on one side, with the eyes shut, and the proper solemn simper. At the back of the head, draw, and gild with gold-leaf, a halo or glory, of the exact shape of a cart-wheel: and you have the thing done. It is Catholic art tout craché, as Louis Philippe says. We have it still in England, handed down to us for four centuries, in the pictures on the cards, as the redoubtable king and queen of clubs. Look at them: you will see that the costumes and attitudes are precisely similar to those which figure in the catholicities of the school of Overbeck and Cornelius.

Before you take your cane at the door, look for one instant at the statue-room. Yonder is Jouffley's "*Jeune Fille confiant son premier secret à Vénus.*" Charming, charming! It is from the exhibition of this year only; and I think the best sculpture in the gallery—pretty, fanciful, naïve; admirable in workmanship and imitation of Nature. I have seldom seen flesh better repre-

的代表人物。——译注］和吉洛底［AnneLouis GirodetTorison（1767—1824）。——译注］更大的骗子，因为后者至少还是建立在自然的基础上，而前者则是脱离自然、愚蠢的做作。以齐格勒骑士的《画圣母的圣徒路加》为例，圣徒路加穿着件僧侣服，然而在袖口周围时髦地绣了花边。圣母坐在一团巨大的金黄色光环之中，怀里抱着她的儿子。她看起来很严肃，圣徒路加也一样，他正以一种紧张不安的神秘表情看着他的画笔。他们就把这个叫做天主教艺术。我亲爱的朋友，生活中没有比这个更容易的了。首先选好你的颜料，把它们整齐地涂在调色板上——明亮的红色、明亮的黄色、明亮的黄褐色、明亮的深蓝色、明亮的绿色，然后给你画中的人物尽可能地穿上15世纪早期的服装。用上边所列举的那些颜色来画人物，如果底色为金色，那你的艺术就更"天主教"了。让你的使徒们的穿着就像神坛前的牧师那样，而且记住要有充分的日用品，如权杖、香炉和其他的这类小玩意，正如你在天主教的礼拜堂、萨顿街道和在别处所看到的那样。画圣母的时候，让她们的穿着就像克拉纳赫或凡·爱克［凡·爱克兄弟，荷兰画家，Hubert van Eyck（1395—1426）和Jan van Eyck（1395—1441）。——译注］所画的市长夫人那样，让她们全都留着垂到长袍上的长长的卷曲发辫，还有适当的角形衣饰。她们的头都偏向一侧，闭着眼睛，带着适度而严肃的假笑。在头的后面，画上镀金的光环或光轮，它们应是车轮的形状。这样你就完成基督教的艺术作品了。就像路易·菲力浦所说的那样，这就是从一个模子里刻出来的天主教艺术。在英国仍存有这种艺术，自它传到我们手里已有四个世纪了，它们就像纸牌上的国王和皇后被画在卡片上，千篇一律。看看它们，你会发现其服装和姿势与那些出现在奥佛贝克和柯内留斯（两人为拿撒勒画派的代表。拿撒勒画派以恢复纯粹的基督教精神为己任。——译注）

在你去门口拿你的手杖之前，再到雕塑室里去看一会儿。那边是朱弗雷（Jouffley）的《少女向维纳斯吐露她的第一个秘密》，太迷人了，太迷人了！它是唯一被选入今年展览会的作品，我认为它是画廊里最好的雕

sented in marble. Examine, also, Jaley's "*Pudeur*," Jacquot's "*Nymph*," and Rude's "*Boy with the Tortoise*." These are not very exalted subjects, or what are called exalted, and do not go beyond simple, smiling beauty and nature. But what then? Are we gods, Miltons, Michael Angelos, that can leave earth when we please; and soar to heights immeasurable? No, my dear MacGilp; but the fools of academicians would fain make us so. Are you not, and half the painters in London, panting for an opportunity to show your genius in a great "historical picture?" O, blind race! Have you wings? Not a feather: and yet you must be ever puffing, sweating up to the tops of rugged hills; and, arrived there, clapping and shaking your ragged elbows, and making as if you would fly! Come down, silly Daedalus; come down to the lowly places in which Nature ordered you to walk. The sweet flowers are springing there; the fat muttons are waiting there; the pleasant sun shines there; be content and humble, and take your share of the good cheer.

While we have been indulging in this discussion, the omnibus has gayly conducted us across the water; and le garde qui veille à la porte du Louvre ne défend pas our entry.

What a paradise this gallery is for French students, or foreigners who sojourn in the capital! It is hardly necessary to say that the brethren of the brush are not usually supplied by Fortune with any extraordinary wealth, or means of enjoying the luxuries with which Paris, more than any other city, abounds. But here they have a luxury which surpasses all others, and spend their days in a palace which all the money of all the Rothschilds could not buy. They sleep, perhaps, in a garret, and dine in a cellar; but no grandee in Europe has such a drawing-room. Kings' houses have, at best, but damask hangings, and gilt cornices. What are these to a wall covered with canvas by Paul Veronese, or a hundred yards of Rubens? Artists from England, who have a national gallery that resembles a moderate-sized gin-shop, who may not copy pictures, except under particular restrictions, and on rare and particular days, may revel here to their hearts' content. Here is a room half a mile long, with as many

塑——漂亮、朴实，又充满想象力，在工艺和逼真方面都是极妙的。我很少看到如此新鲜出色的大理石作品。仔细看看，还有雅雷（Jaley）的《害羞》、雅科（Jacquot）的《女神》、鲁德（Rude）的《男孩和乌龟》，这些作品表现的都不是很崇高的主题，它们展现的不外乎是些单纯、微笑的自然美。这有什么不可以呢？难道我们的上帝、弥尔顿和米开朗琪罗会像我们想象的那样离开地球，飞到不可测的高度吗？当然不会，但是学院的愚人们却不让我们有这样的想法。亲爱的迈克吉普，你和伦敦的许多画家不都渴望能有一个机会在一幅伟大的“历史性画作”中展示你们的才华吗？哦，盲目的人类啊！你有翅膀吗？你没有一根羽毛，否则你一定会膨胀起来，吃力地飞上高低不平的小山顶端。到那里之后，轻拍、摇动着你的肘部，让人看起来好像你真的会飞！下来吧！愚蠢的代达罗斯［希腊神话中尝试飞翔的工匠。——译注］，下来到这个上帝吩咐你行走的世俗之地。芳香的花朵正在开放，肥肥的羊肉正在那里等候，愉悦的太阳在那里闪光，让我们谦逊地满足现状，好好地享受现有的一切。

当我们沉迷于这场讨论中的时候，公共马车已轻快地带着我们穿过塞纳河，进入了罗浮宫。

对于法国的学生或旅居巴黎的外国人来说，罗浮宫的画廊是个怎样的天堂啊！在巴黎画家不仅有额外的财政供养着，而且他们在巴黎享受奢侈生活的方式也比其他的城市丰富，这都没必要说了。以罗浮宫为例，这里拥有价值连城的奢侈品，能够在这个宫殿中消磨时光是罗特希尔德家族［发迹于德国法兰克福的 Rothschilds 家族是当时的世界首富。——译注］花多少钱也买不来的。在法国，虽然有的艺术家可能是在阁楼上睡觉，在地下室用餐，但是在欧洲没有一个显贵能拥有这样的一间画室。国王的房间充其量也只有悬挂的缎子、镀金的壁带，而这些与一面布满了保罗·委罗内塞［Veronese（1528—1588）。——译注］或一百码的鲁本斯的油画的墙壁相比，又算得了什么呢？英国艺术家只拥有一个类似中等大小酒店般的国家画廊，除非是有特别的规定，他们不可以去模仿画作，偶尔，他们

windows as Aladdin's palace, open from sunrise till evening, and free to all manners and all varieties of study: the only puzzle to the student is to select the one he shall begin upon, and keep his eyes away from the rest.

Fontaine's grand staircase, with its arches, and painted ceilings and shining Doric columns, leads directly to the gallery; but it is thought too fine for working days, and is only opened for the public entrance on the Sabbath. A little back stair (leading from a court, in which stand numerous bas-reliefs, and a solemn sphinx, of polished granite,) is the common entry for students and others, who, during the week, enter the gallery.

Hither have lately been transported a number of the works of French artists, which formerly covered the walls of the Luxembourg (death only entitles the French painter to a place in the Louvre); and let us confine ourselves to the Frenchmen only, for the space of this letter.

I have seen, in a fine private collection at St. Germain, one or two admirable single figures of David, full of life, truth, and gayety. The colour is not good, but all the rest excellent; and one of these so much-lauded pictures is the portrait of a washerwoman. "*Pope Pius*," at the Louvre, is as bad in colour and as remarkable for its vigour and look of life. The man had a genius for painting portraits and common life, but must attempt the heroic;—failed signally; and what is worse, carried a whole nation blundering after him. Had you told a Frenchman so, twenty years ago, he would have thrown the démenti in your teeth; or, at least, laughed at you in scornful incredulity. They say of us that we don't know when we are beaten: they go a step further, and swear their defeats are victories. David was a part of the glory of the empire; and one might as well have said, there, that "*Romulus*" was a bad picture, as that Toulouse was a lost battle. Old-fashioned people, who believe in the Emperor, believe in the Théâtre Français, and believe that Ducis improved upon Shakespeare, have the above opinion. Still, it is curious to remark, in this place, how art and literature become party matters, and political sects have their favourite painters and authors.

也会来到这里陶冶性情。这里有一个半英里长的房间，房间像安拉丁的宫殿一样有许多窗户，它从日出到傍晚都是开放的，而且对各种方式和类型的学习研究都是免费开放。唯一让学生头疼的就是在琳琅满目的艺术品中，眼睛真的不知该从哪件看起。

带有拱门和喷泉的大阶梯，描画的天花板，闪闪发光的多利安柱子［希腊的一个部族柱子。——译注］都直接通向画廊，但是工作人员觉得工作日开放这里太奢侈了，因此它只在星期日对公众开放。有一个狭窄的后楼梯（通向院子，那里竖立着许多底层浮雕和一个磨光大理石的严肃的斯芬克司［狮身人面兽像］），这里在一周内是学生和其他人的日常入口。

最近这里运来了许多法国艺术家的作品，它们以前是挂在卢森堡美术馆的墙壁上的（死亡只不过是为法国画家能在罗浮宫占有一席之地提供了资格）。因信的篇幅所限，让我们在这里只谈论法国人的作品吧。

我曾在圣日耳曼区一件私人的收藏品中看到过一两幅极妙的大卫个人肖像画，它们都充满了生机、活力和愉悦的感情色彩。除颜色不好之外，其余的都很出色。在他的那些备受称赞的画作中还有一幅洗衣女的肖像画。罗浮宫里的这幅《罗马教皇派厄斯》的颜色也很糟糕，但它所展示的活力与生活面貌却很出色。大卫具有描绘肖像和日常生活的天赋，他却一定要尝试英雄题材——很明显，他的尝试失败了，但更糟的是，国内的画家都浮躁地跌跌撞撞跟在他后面效仿。二十年以前，如果你对一个法国人这样讲，他要么会让你亲口辟谣，要么至少会用轻蔑的怀疑态度来嘲笑你。他们说，我们的绘画已落后了却还不自知，他们则领先了一步，宣称他们的失败也是胜利。大卫是他们帝国荣耀的一部分，虽然人们也曾说过《罗慕路斯》是一幅糟糕的画，就像图卢兹之战是场失败的战役一样。那些老式落伍的人信奉皇帝和法国戏剧、认为丢西斯［Ducis（1783—1816），法国诗人，悲剧作家。——译注］比莎士比亚杰出，认为他们的失败也是胜利。还要注意，在这个国家，艺术、文学与政党都有所牵扯，每个政治派别都有他们各自喜欢的画家和作家。

Nevertheless, Jacques Louis David is dead, he died about a year after his bodily demise in 1825. The romanticism killed him. Walter Scott, from his Castle of Abbotsford, sent out a troop of gallant young Scotch adventurers, merry outlaws, valiant knights, and savage Highlanders, who, with trunk hosen and buff jerkins, fierce two-handed swords, and harness on their backs, did challenge, combat, and overcome the heroes and demigods of Greece and Rome. Nôtre Dame à la rescousse! Sir Brian de Bois Guilbert has borne Hector of Troy clear out of his saddle. Andromache may weep: but her spouse is beyond the reach of physic. See! Robin Hood twangs his bow, and the heathen gods fly, howling. Montjoie Saint Dénis! down goes Ajax under the mace of Dunois; and yonder are Leonidas and Romulus begging their lives of Rob Roy Macgregor. Classicism is dead. Sir John Froissart has taken Dr. Lemprière by the nose, and reigns sovereign.

Of the great pictures of David the defunct, we need not, then, say much. Romulus is a mighty fine young fellow, no doubt; and if he has come out to battle stark naked (except a very handsome helmet), it is because the costume became him, and shows off his figure to advantage. But was there ever anything so absurd as this passion for the nude, which was followed by all the painters of the Davidian epoch? And how are we to suppose yonder straddle to be the true characteristic of the heroic and the sublime? Romulus stretches his legs as far as ever nature will allow; the Horatii, in receiving their swords, think proper to stretch their legs too, and to thrust forward their arms, thus,—

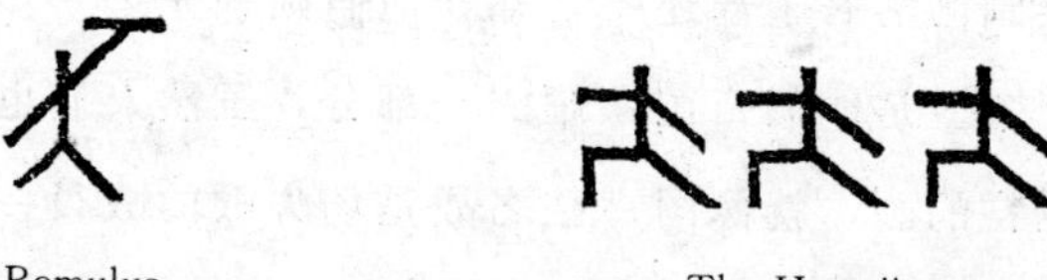

Romulus The Horatii

Romulus's is the exact action of a telegraph; and the Horatii are all in the position of the lunge. Is this the sublime? Mr. Angelo, of Bond Street, might admire the attitude; his namesake, Michael, I don't think would.

然而，雅克·路易·大卫死了，他实际上是在1825年身亡一年之后才在绘画界退位的。浪漫主义杀死了他。从阿伯兹福德（Abbotsford）城堡里出来的司各特［Walter Scott（1771—1832），英国19世纪著名历史小说家和诗人。——译注］，派出一支由年轻勇敢的苏格兰冒险者、快乐的亡命之徒、英勇的骑士和凶猛的苏格兰高地人所组成的军队，他们穿着紧身裤和短小的紧身皮上衣，背着马具，手持锋利的双刃剑来挑战、斗争，最终战胜了希腊与罗马的英雄和半神半人。圣母也赶来援助他们！布里恩·布瓦吉贝尔［《艾凡赫》中的骑士。——译注］把特洛伊的赫克托耳从马鞍上给推了下来，昂朵马格或许还在哭泣，但她丈夫已无法治愈了。看！罗宾汉砰的一声射出弓箭，异教徒的上帝咆哮着飞了起来。蒙特乔伊的圣徒丹尼斯！在杜诺亚的权杖下逃走的阿积士，那边是列奥尼达［Leonidas，古罗马时期斯巴达国王。——译注］和罗慕路斯向罗布·罗伊［罗宾汉（1671—1734），苏格兰绿林好汉的绰号，司各特所著同名小说中主角的原型。——译注］请求饶命。古典主义死了。约翰·傅华萨［Jean Froissart，14世纪的法国的编年史作者。——译注］先生已取代了朗浦里埃博士在法国所占据的统治地位。

关于已去世的大卫的杰作，我们就没必要说太多了。罗慕路斯是一个很不错的强壮青年是不用怀疑的了。如果他全身赤裸地（一顶漂亮的钢盔除外）出来战斗，那是因为这种装束是适合他的，能最大限度地展示他的身材。但是还有什么事情能比大卫时代之后所有的画家都热衷于画裸体更不可思议的呢？我们怎么能想到原来画家对英雄和崇高的真实特征其实是无动于衷的呢？罗慕路斯尽他所能地伸直腿，何拉提在接剑时当然也伸直了腿，他们也向前伸出自己的双臂，像这样——

罗慕路斯

何拉提

The little picture of "*Paris and Helen*," one of the master's earliest, I believe, is likewise one of his best: the details are exquisitely painted. Helen looks needlessly sheepish, and Paris has a most odious ogle; but the limbs of the male figure are beautifully designed, and have not the green tone which you see in the later pictures of the master. What is the meaning of this green? Was it the fashion, or the varnish? Girodet's pictures are green; Gros's emperors and grenadiers have universally the jaundice. Gerard's "*Psyche*" has a most decided green-sickness; and I am at a loss, I confess, to account for the enthusiasm which this performance inspired on its first appearance before the public.

In the same room with it is Girodet's ghastly "*Deluge*," and Géricault's dismal "*Medusa.*" Géricault died, they say, for want of fame. He was a man who possessed a considerable fortune of his own; but pined because no one in his day would purchase his pictures, and so acknowledge his talent. At present, a scrawl from his pencil brings an enormous price. All his works have a grand cachet: he never did anything mean. When he painted the "*Raft of the Medusa*," it is said he lived for a long time among the corpses which he painted, and that his studio was a second Morgue. If you have not seen the picture, you are familiar probably, with Reynolds's admirable engraving of it. A huge black sea; a raft beating upon it; a horrid company of men dead, half dead, writhing and frantic with hideous hunger or hideous hope; and, far away, black, against a stormy sunset, a sail. The story is powerfully told, and has a legitimate tragic interest, so to speak,—deeper, because more natural, than Girodet's green "*Deluge*," for instance: or his livid "*Orestes*," or red-hot "*Clytemnestra.*"

Seen from a distance the latter's "*Deluge*" has a certain awe-inspiring air with it. A slimy green man stands on a green rock, and clutches hold of a tree. On the green man's shoulders is his old father, in a green old age; to him hangs his wife, with a babe on her breast, and dangling at her hair, another child. In the water floats a corpse (a beautiful head) and a green sea and

[《何拉提之誓》。据说此画描绘的事件——三个何拉提家族的兄弟在家中的妇女和儿童面前，对着父亲高举在他们面前的利剑，宣誓效忠于罗马。——译注] 罗慕路斯摆出的是一种电报机似的准确姿势，何拉提则是一种向前冲的姿势。这就是崇高吗？庞德街道的安杰洛先生 [法国画家。——译注] 或许会赞同这种姿态，但他的同姓人迈克尔却不一定赞同——我这样认为。

我认为，大师大卫早期的小型绘画《帕里斯和海伦》是其最好的作品之一。画家对细节描绘得很精致。海伦看起来温顺得有些做作，帕里斯长着一双非常可憎的媚眼，但是这位男性的形体设计得很好，没有大师后期作品中所经常看到的那种绿色调。那种绿色意味着什么呢？是流行色，还是清漆？吉洛底的画都是绿色的；葛斯 [Gros，荷兰古典画家。——译注] 作品中的皇帝和掷弹兵一律得了黄疸病似的；杰拉德 [Gerard (1770—1837)，法国画家。——译注] 的《普赛克》很明显也患了黄萎病。这让我感到迷惑，我认为这是由于画中的人物首次公开露面所激发的狂热表现所致。

房间里还有吉洛底的可怕的《大洪水》和籍里柯 [Gericault (1781—1824)，代奥多·籍里柯是19世纪法国绘画浪漫派的先驱者，他开创了与古典派艺术分庭抗礼的局面。——译注] 阴郁的《美杜莎的木筏》。他们说藉里柯是因追求名誉而死的。他个人拥有一大笔财富，但是精神憔悴，因为在他活着时没人买他的画，也没人承认他的才华。现在，他的一幅潦草的铅笔画都能卖很高的价钱。他的所有作品都享有很高的声望。他的一生都是坦坦荡荡的。当他画这幅《美杜莎的木筏》时，据说他在自己要画的尸体中生活了很长一段时间，他的工作室成了一个陈尸所。如果你没见过这幅画，你或许也会对黎诺尔德 [Reynolds，法国雕刻家。——译注] 的雕刻版本比较熟悉。画上有一片巨大的黑色的海，海上颠簸着一只木筏，木筏上有一群可怕的死人和垂死的人，那些垂死的人由于可怕的饥饿和绝望而四肢扭曲、精神狂乱。远处黑色的地方是一艘迎着黄昏暴风雨航行的

atmosphere envelops all this dismal group. The old father is represented with a bag of money in his hand; and the tree, which the man clutches, is cracking, and just on the point of giving way. These two points were considered very fine by the critics: they are two such ghastly epigrams as continually disfigure French Tragedy. For this reason I have never been able to read Racine with pleasure,—the dialogue is so crammed with these lugubrious good things—melancholy antitheses—sparkling undertakers' wit; but this is heresy, and had better be spoken discreetly.

The gallery contains a vast number of Poussin's pictures; they put me in mind of the colour of objects in dreams,—a strange, hazy, lurid hue. How noble are some of his landscapes! What a depth of solemn shadow is in yonder wood, near which, by the side of a black water, halts Diogenes. The air is thunder-laden, and breathes heavily. You hear ominous whispers in the vast forest gloom.

Near it is a landscape, by Carel Dujardin, I believe, conceived in quite a different mood, but exquisitely poetical too. A horseman is riding up a hill, and giving money to a blowsy beggar-wench. O matutini rores auraeque salubres! in what a wonderful way has the artist managed to create you out of a few bladders of paint and pots of varnish. You can see the matutinal dews twinkling in the grass, and feel the fresh, salubrious airs ("the breath of Nature blowing free," as the corn-law man sings) blowing free over the heath; silvery vapours are rising up from the blue lowlands. You can tell the hour of the morning and the time of the year: you can do anything but describe it in words. As with regard to the Poussin above mentioned, one can never pass it without bearing away a certain pleasing, dreamy feeling of awe and musing; the other landscape inspires the spectator infallibly with the most delightful briskness and cheerfulness of spirit. Herein lies the vast privilege of the landscape-painter: he does not address you with one fixed particular subject or expression, but with a thousand never contemplated by himself, and which only arise out of occasion. You may always be looking at a natural landscape as at

船。画面充满力度且具有正统的悲剧情调，可以说，因为比较自然，它要比吉洛底的绿色的《大洪水》、青灰色的《俄瑞斯忒斯》或火红色的《克吕泰墨斯特拉》[希腊神话中阿伽门农的妻子。——译注] 更具有内涵。

从远处看，吉洛底的《大洪水》具有某种使人敬畏的因素。一个浑身是泥、脸色发青的男人站在一块青色的岩石上，他紧紧抓住一棵树。这个男人肩上背着他的老父亲，也是个脸色发青的老人。这个男人还携着他的妻子，他妻子胸前抱着个婴儿，肩上还背着个孩子。水上漂浮着一具尸体(头部很美丽)，绿色的海和绿色的空气包裹着这群阴郁的人。年老的父亲手里拿着一个钱袋，那个男人抓着的树就要断裂了。在批评家看来这两处都被画家处理得很好。这两处也扭曲了人们对法国正统悲剧的认识。因为这个原因，我从来也不能怀着愉悦的心情去读拉辛的作品——对话充满了阴郁的情调，忧郁的对偶句，活泼的下葬人的机智。但这是左道邪说，说时最好谨慎些。

画廊里还有许多普桑的画。画中物体梦幻般的颜色给我留下了深刻的印象，那是一种奇特、朦胧、艳丽的色彩。他的一些风景画是多么壮观啊！那边树林的肃静的阴影是多么深邃啊！在附近黑色的河水边，戴奥吉尼斯[希腊哲学家。——译注] 停住了脚步。天空中布满了雷电，空气很沉闷。你甚至可以听到从巨大阴郁的森林里传来的不祥的耳语。

在普桑的画旁边是卡瑞尔·杜亚尔丹 (Dujardin) 的一幅风景画，我认为它表达了一种与众不同的情绪，也很有诗意。一个骑马者正爬上一个小山，给一个邋遢的女乞丐钱。这位艺术家是采用了一种多么出色的方式来处理色彩啊！你可以看到早晨的露珠在草丛中闪闪发光，能感觉到新鲜益人的空气（“大自然自由地呼吸着”，如同收谷物的人唱的那样）在荒地上自由地飘荡，银色的水蒸气正从蓝色的平地上升起。你能明确分辨出这是在一年的哪个季节或是早晨的哪个时刻，但就是无法用言语来表述。它和上面所提到的普桑的作品一样，人们在看了之后一定会有种敬畏和沉思的愉悦、梦幻般的感觉。他的另一张风景画无疑也能给观众带来精神上的愉

a fine pictorial imitation of one; it seems eternally producing new thoughts in your bosom, as it does fresh beauties from its own. I cannot fancy more delightful, cheerful, silent companions for a man than half a dozen landscapes hung round his study. Portraits, on the contrary, and large pieces of figures, have a painful, fixed, staring look, which must jar upon the mind in many of its moods. Fancy living in a room with David's *sans-culotte Leonidas* staring perpetually in your face!

There is a little Watteau here, and a rare piece of fantastical brightness and gayety it is. What a delightful affectation about yonder ladies flirting their fans, and trailing about in their long brocades! What splendid dandies are those, ever-smirking, turning out their toes, with broad blue ribbons to tie up their crooks and their pigtails, and wonderful gorgeous crimson satin breeches! Yonder, in the midst of a golden atmosphere, rises a bevy of little round Cupids, bubbling up in clusters as out of a champagne-bottle, and melting away in air. There is, to be sure, a hidden analogy between liquors and pictures: the eye is deliciously tickled by these frisky Watteaus, and yields itself up to a light, smiling, gentlemanlike intoxication. Thus, were we inclined to pursue further this mighty subject, yonder landscape of Claude,—calm, fresh, delicate, yet full of flavor,—should be likened to a bottle of Château Margaux. And what is the Poussin before spoken of but Romanée Gelée? —heavy, sluggish,—the luscious odor almost sickens you; a sultry sort of drink; your limbs sink under it; you feel as if you had been drinking hot blood.

An ordinary man would be whirled away in a fever, or would hobble off this mortal stage in a premature gout-fit, if he too early or too often indulged in such tremendous drink. I think in my heart I am fonder of pretty third-rate pictures than of your great thundering first-rates. Confess how many times you have read Béranger, and how many Milton? If you go to the "*Star and Garter*," don't you grow sick of that vast, luscious landscape, and long for the sight of a couple of cows, or a donkey, and a few yards of common? Don-

悦。这两张画都显示出这位风景画家的杰出才华。他不是用一种固定特别的主题或表情来吸引你的注意，也不是靠他自己的沉思默想，而是靠灵感的触发来感染观众。你可能总是在看着一幅自然的风景画时，认为它是一件很好的仿制品，它似乎是要源源不断地在你内心中激起新的思绪，仿佛它自己也在不断更新着自己的美丽。我想象不出有什么能比书房里的许多风景画让人高兴、愉悦的同伴了。相反，肖像画和大幅的人物画往往都带有一种痛苦、僵硬的凝视表情，这种表情往往会让人产生不愉快的感觉。设想你住在一个房间，里面挂着一幅大卫的没穿短裤的《列奥尼达》，列奥尼达一直盯着你的脸，那种感觉会是怎样的呢？

这里还有一些让·安东尼·华托［JeanAntoine Watteau（1684—1721），是法国18世纪洛可可时期最重要的画家。——译注］的作品，我们看到的这幅是一张罕见的明亮而欢快的作品。画中的女士们在和她们的追求者调情，她们拖曳着锦缎裙裾四处走动的神情是多么做作啊！那些纨绔子弟是多么引人注意啊！他们一直假笑着，脚尖朝外，用宽宽的蓝色丝带束紧他们的卷发和辫子，穿着鲜艳华丽的深红色缎子马裤！那边，在一片金光之中，升起一群小小的、胖乎乎的丘比特，它们凑在一起突然出现就像是从香槟酒瓶子里飞出来的，分散在空气中。我确信，在酒和画之间有种隐喻关系。当眼睛被华托这些生动的画作激活后，人会不自觉地进入一种轻松、微笑、具有绅士风度的沉醉状态。就这样，如果我们还想去寻求更深一步的这类崇高的主题，那边还有克劳德的风景画［17世纪的风景画家克劳德·洛兰（ClaudeLorrain，1602—1682）曾经长期在意大利研究罗马附近的景色，他用一种理想化的山水给人们打开了新的眼界，使人们看到了自然的崇高之美。——译注］——宁静、新鲜、细致优雅、充满韵味——应该被比喻成玛古红酒［这种葡萄酒酒味细腻，有神秘感。——译注］。用罗曼尼果子冻酒来比喻前面提到的普桑［一种红葡萄酒。——译注］怎么样？——味道很重，甜腻——这种甘美的气味几乎能让你作呕，它是一种烈性的饮料，喝了它，你四肢瘫软，感觉好像是喝了热血一样。

keys, my dear MacGilp, since we have come to this subject, say not so; Richmond Hill for them. Milton they never grow tired of; and are as familiar with Raphael as Bottom with exquisite Titania. Let us thank Heaven, my dear sir, for according to us the power to taste and appreciate the pleasures of mediocrity. I have never heard that we were great geniuses. Earthy are we, and of the earth; glimpses of the sublime are but rare to us; leave we them to great geniuses, and to the donkeys; and if it nothing profit us aërias tentâsse domos along with them, let us thankfully remain below, being merry and humble.

I have now only to mention the charming "*Cruche Cassée*" of Greuze, which all the young ladies delight to copy; and of which the colour (a thought too blue, perhaps) is marvellously graceful and delicate. There are three more pictures by the artist, containing exquisite female heads and colour; but they have charms for French critics which are difficult to be discovered by English eyes; and the pictures seem weak to me. A very fine picture by Bon Bollongue, "*Saint Benedict resuscitating a Child*," deserves particular attention, and is superb in vigour and richness of colour. You must look, too, at the large, noble, melancholy landscapes of Philippe de Champagne; and the two magnificent Italian pictures of Léopold Robert: they are, perhaps, the very finest pictures that the French school has produced,—as deep as Poussin, of a better colour, and of a wonderful minuteness and veracity in the representation of objects.

Every one of Lesueur's church-pictures is worth examining and admiring; they are full of "unction" and pious mystical grace. "*Saint Scholastica*" is divine; and the "*Taking down from the Cross*" as noble a composition as ever was seen; I care not by whom the other may be. There is more beauty, and less affectation, about this picture than you will find in the performances of many Italian masters, with high-sounding names (out with it, and say RAPHAEL at once). I hate those simpering Madonnas. I declare that the "*Jardinière*" is a puking, smirking miss, with nothing heavenly about her. I vow that the "*Saint Elizabeth*" is a bad picture,—a bad composition, badly

如果一个普通人太早或太频繁地这样贪杯的话，他会像发烧似的头晕目眩，像得了痛风一样脚步蹒跚地步入死亡。我内心还是喜欢漂亮的三流作品的，而不是像你那样着迷于一流作品。坦白交代你读过几页贝朗瑞和弥尔顿的作品呢？如果你看过《功勋》这幅画，你难道不觉得那种壮观、华丽的景象让你作呕，你不希望看到一对奶牛或一只驴子和一些普通的庭院吗？亲爱的迈克吉普，我们还是不要再指责那些画家的愚蠢了，瑞奇蒙丘［地名。——译注］就是他们的全部。他们对弥尔顿从不厌倦，对拉斐尔像提香一样熟悉。我亲爱的先生，让我们感谢上帝赐予我们能力，让我们去体验和感受平凡生活的快乐。我从未听人说过我们是很伟大的天才。我们是地球上朴实的人类，所瞥见的崇高对于我们来说是太罕见的东西，把它们留给伟大的天才和蠢人吧！如果它们对于我们而言没有丝毫益处，那就让他们享用吧！但我们仍要快乐而谦逊地向他们表示感激。

我现在才有机会提到格瑞兹［Greuze（1725—1805），法国画家。——译注］的这幅迷人的《破碎的水罐》，年轻的女士都很喜欢描摹这幅作品。它的颜色（或许有些发灰）是很细致典雅的。这里还有画家另外的三幅画，画里都有着优美的女性头部和雅致的色彩。但是在法国评论家眼里的这些迷人之处，以英国人的眼光去看却很难发现得到。这些画在我看来太没有力度了。布隆格（Bon Bollongue）的那幅出色的画作《圣徒贝宁迪使一个孩子复活》应得到特别的注意，色彩很生动和丰富。你也一定要看菲利普·德·香槟（Philippe de Champagne）的大幅壮观、忧郁的风景画，还有雷奥波尔德·罗勃特（Leopold Robert）的两幅出色的意大利作品。他们或许是法兰西学院所创作的最好的画了——有着普桑作品的深刻内涵，描绘物体的色彩也很好，非常细致真实。

罗索［Lesueur（1494—1540），意大利佛罗伦萨画家。——译注］的每幅作品都值得细细观看和赞赏。它们充满了宗教的热忱和虔诚这种神秘的魅力。《圣徒思嘉》是神圣的。《下十字架图》是我见过的一幅非常杰出的作品，对他的其他作品我倒不是很喜欢。这幅画比较美，少些做作，在

drawn, badly coloured, in a bad imitation of Titian,—a piece of vile affectation. I say, that when Raphael painted this picture two years before his death, the spirit of painting had gone from out of him; he was no longer inspired; IT WAS TIME THAT HE SHOULD DIE!!

There,—the murder is out! My paper is filled to the brim, and there is no time to speak of Lesueur's "*Crucifixion*," which is odiously coloured, to be sure; but earnest, tender, simple, holy. But such things are most difficult to translate into words;—one lays down the pen, and thinks and thinks. The figures appear, and take their places one by one: ranging themselves according to order, in light or in gloom, the colours are reflected duly in the little camera obscura of the brain, and the whole picture lies there complete; but can you describe it? No, not if pens were fitch-brushes, and words were bladders of paint. With which, for the present, adieu.

Your faithful

M. A. T.

To Mr. ROBERT MACGILP,

NEWMAN STREET, LONDON.

这幅画上你可以发现许多大名鼎鼎的意大利大师的成就（这里就离题说说拉斐尔［Raffaello（1483—1520），意大利文艺复兴时期的画家。——译注］。我憎恨那些假笑的圣母玛利亚。我认为《美丽的女园丁》［La Belle Jardiniere，是拉斐尔1507年的一幅作品，他的主要代表作之一。——译注］是一位让人作呕、傻笑的女士，在她周围没有任何神圣的东西。我认为《圣徒伊丽莎白》是一幅拙劣的画——拙劣的构图、拙劣的画法、拙劣的颜色，是对提香的拙劣模仿——一幅可耻做作的画。我明白，当拉斐尔在他去世前两年画这幅画时，画魂已离他远去了，他不再有灵感，已走到生命的终端了。

在那里——谋杀结束了！我的信纸也写满了，没有时间再去谈论罗索的《上十字架图》，可以明确的是，这幅画的颜色令人作呕，但却是诚挚、温和、简朴、神圣的，这些都是很难用言语来表达的——一个人在放下笔后，想着想着，画里的人物形象就出现了，一个接一个地找好自己的位置，按照次序或明或暗地排列好，色彩也在脑海里及时浮现出来，但你能把它们描述出来吗？不能。只要我的笔不是乱写一通，关于绘画的谈论不是空话连篇就行了。就写到这儿，再见。

您忠实的
迈克尔·安玑莱·蒂特马舍
给迈克吉普·罗勃特先生的信
伦敦，纽曼街

The Painter's Bargain

SIMON GAMBOUGE was the son of Solomon Gambouge; and as all the world knows, both father and son were astonishingly clever fellows at their profession. Solomon painted landscapes, which nobody bought; and Simon took a higher line, and painted portraits to admiration, only nobody came to sit to him.

As he was not gaining five pounds a year by his profession, and had arrived at the age of twenty, at least, Simon determined to better himself by taking a wife,—a plan which a number of other wise men adopt, in similar years and circumstances. So Simon prevailed upon a butcher's daughter (to whom he owed considerably for cutlets) to quit the meat-shop and follow him. Griskinissa—such was the fair creature's name—"was as lovely a bit of mutton," her father said, "as ever a man would wish to stick a knife into." She had sat to the painter for all sorts of characters; and the curious who possess any of Gambouge's pictures will see her as Venus, Minerva, Madonna, and in numberless other characters: Portrait of a lady—Griskinissa; Sleeping Nymph—Griskinissa, without a rag of clothes, lying in a forest; Maternal Solicitude—Griskinissa again, with young Master Gambouge, who was by this time the offspring of their affections.

The lady brought the painter a handsome little fortune of a couple of hundred pounds; and as long as this sum lasted no woman could be more lovely or loving. But want began speedily to attack their little household; bakers' bills were unpaid; rent was due, and the reckless landlord gave no quarter; and, to crown the whole, her father, unnatural butcher! suddenly stopped the supplies of mutton-chops; and swore that his daughter, and the dauber; her husband, should have no more of his wares. At first they embraced tenderly, and, kissing and crying over their little infant, vowed to Heaven that they

画家的交易

西蒙是所罗门·甘姆布的儿子。众所周知，父亲和儿子在绘画行业中都是很聪明的人。所罗门画风景画，但是没人买；西蒙画的高级些，是肖像画，但也没人坐在他面前给他当模特。

由于他的这个职业每年挣不了五镑，而他至少已二十岁了，西蒙就决定娶个妻子来改善一下自己的处境——这也是许多明智的男人在相似的年龄和环境下所采用的一个计划。就这样，西蒙说服一个屠夫的女儿（因为肉排，他欠了她许多钱）离开肉店跟了他。那个女人叫格里斯基尼萨——她的父亲说她“像一块羊肉那样可爱，每个男人都想把刀子插进去吃一口”。她给西蒙做各种人物的模特。拥有甘姆布画作的人会发现，格里斯基尼萨以维纳斯、密涅瓦［雅典娜的别名。——译注］、圣母玛利亚和无数其他人物的形象出现在画像中。一位女士的肖像——是格里斯基尼萨、睡美人——也是一丝不挂地躺在一个森林里的格里斯基尼萨、焦虑的母亲——又是格里斯基尼萨。这时她和年轻的丈夫甘姆布有了爱情的结晶。

这位女士给画家带来了二百镑的可观嫁妆，如果这笔钱能持续维持下去，没有女人会比她更可爱、更值得爱了。但是这个小家庭很快就陷入了缺钱的窘境中。面包房的账单未付款；租金一直拖欠着，粗鲁的房东不再延期了；雪上加霜的是，她的父亲，没有人情的屠夫，突然停止了对他们供给羊排，还咒骂他的女儿和拙劣的画家（即她的丈夫）不应该再要他的东西。起初，他们在婴儿旁边温柔地拥抱、亲吻，发誓没有这些东西他们

would do without: but in the course of the evening Griskinissa grew peckish, and poor Simon pawned his best coat.

When this habit of pawning is discovered, it appears to the poor a kind of Eldorado. Gambouge and his wife were so delighted, that they, in the course of a month, made away with her gold chain, her great warming-pan, his best crimson plush inexpressibles, two wigs, a washhand basin and ewer, fire-irons, window-curtains, crockery, and arm-chairs. Griskinissa said, smiling, that she had found a second father in HER UNCLE,—a base pun, which showed that her mind was corrupted, and that she was no longer the tender, simple Griskinissa of other days.

I am sorry to say that she had taken to drinking; she swallowed the warming-pan in the course of three days, and fuddled herself one whole evening with the crimson plush breeches.

Drinking is the devil—the father, that is to say, of all vices. Griskinissa's face and her mind grew ugly together; her good humour changed to bilious, bitter discontent; her pretty, fond epithets, to foul abuse and swearing; her tender blue eyes grew watery and blear, and the peach-colour on her cheeks fled from its old habitation, and crowded up into her nose, where, with a number of pimples, it stuck fast. Add to this a dirty, draggle-tailed chintz; long, matted hair, wandering into her eyes, and over her lean shoulders, which were once so snowy, and you have the picture of drunkenness and Mrs. Simon Gambouge.

Poor Simon, who had been a gay, lively fellow enough in the days of his better fortune, was completely cast down by his present ill luck, and cowed by the ferocity of his wife. From morning till night the neighbours could hear this woman's tongue, and understand her doings; bellows went skimming across the room, chairs were flumped down on the floor, and poor Gambouge's oil and varnish pots went clattering through the windows, or down the stairs. The baby roared all day; and Simon sat pale and idle in a corner, taking a small sup at the brandy-bottle, when Mrs. Gambouge was out of the way.

One day, as he sat disconsolately at his easel, furbishing up a picture of his wife, in the character of Peace, which he had commenced a year before, he was more than ordinarily desperate, and cursed and swore in the most pa-

仍会生活下去，但是到了晚上，格里斯基尼萨饿了，可怜的西蒙只好当掉了他最好的外套买东西吃。

发现了典当这个方法，他们就像发现了爱尔多拉多［传说中的黄金国。——译注］一样。甘姆布和他妻子都很高兴，他们在一个月的时间内，当掉了格里斯基尼萨的金链子、她的长柄炭炉（睡前暖床用的）、甘姆布最好的深红色长毛绒裤子、两套假发，还有洗手盆、水罐、炉具、窗帘、陶器和扶手椅。格里斯基尼萨微笑着说，她已经在当铺里找到了第二个父亲——一个低级的比喻，这都透露出她的精神已堕落了，她不再是以前的那个温柔、单纯的格里斯基尼萨了。

很遗憾，她开始喝酒了。三天的时间里她喝光了当掉长柄炭炉的钱，一晚上就用当掉深红色长毛绒裤子的钱把自己灌醉了。

酗酒是邪恶的开端，也是所有恶习的开端。格里斯基尼萨的脸和她的内心都变得丑陋了。她的好脾气变成了暴躁和不满的抱怨；她文雅的语言变成了下流的辱骂和诅咒；她温柔的蓝眼睛变得暗淡和模糊，以前的红晕也从她的脸颊上退去，却爬上了她的鼻子，鼻子上很快又长出了些丘疹。此外，她还拖着一条又脏又湿的印花棉布裙子；长长的、粗糙无光的头发缠绕着遮住她的眼睛、披在她瘦削的肩上，有的都雪白了，这时你看到的是一幅醉酒的甘姆布太太的画像。

可怜的西蒙在他走运的日子里曾是个快乐、活泼的小伙子，现在则完全被不幸压倒了，并受到她凶悍的妻子的威胁。从早晨到晚上，邻居们都可以听到他妻子的牢骚，从而知道她正在做什么。房间里传出来的怒吼声、椅子摔在地板上的砰砰声，可怜的甘姆布的颜料和调色板被太太哗啦啦地扔出窗户或是扔下楼梯。婴儿整天都在啼哭。当甘姆布太太发脾气时，西蒙就面色苍白、无所事事地坐在角落里，一小口一小口地喝着白兰地酒。

一天，他在画架前寂寞地坐着，润饰一幅以他妻子做模特的画像，她妻子在画像中扮演的是平和的形象。这幅画他一年前就开始画了。这时的他已不是一般的绝望，而是以最悲哀的方式发出诅咒。“唉，天才的悲惨命

thetic manner. "O, miserable fate of genius!" cried he, "was I, a man of such commanding talents, born for this? to be bullied by a fiend of a wife; to have my masterpieces neglected by the world, or sold only for a few pieces? Cursed be the love which has misled me; cursed, be the art which is unworthy of me! Let me dig or steal, let me sell myself as a soldier, or sell myself to the Devil, I should not be more wretched than I am now!"

"Quite the contrary," cried a small, cheery voice.

"What!" exclaimed Gambouge, trembling and surprised. "Who's there? —where are you? —who are you?"

"You were just speaking of me," said the voice.

Gambouge held, in his left hand, his palette; in his right, a bladder of crimson lake, which he was about to squeeze out upon the mahogany. "Where are you?" cried he again.

"S-q-u-e-e-z-e!" exclaimed the little voice.

Gambouge picked out the nail from the bladder, and gave a squeeze; when, as sure as I am living, a little imp spurted out from the hole upon the palette, and began laughing in the most singular and oily manner.

When first born he was little bigger than a tadpole; then he grew to be as big as a mouse; then he arrived at the size of a cat; and then he jumped off the palette, and turning head over heels, asked the poor painter what he wanted with him.

The strange little animal twisted head over heels, and fixed himself at last upon the top of Gambouge's easel,—smearing out, with his heels, all the white and vermilion which had just been laid on to the allegoric portrait of Mrs. Gambouge.

"What!" exclaimed Simon, "is it the—"

"Exactly so; talk of me, you know, and I am always at hand: besides, I am not half so black as I am painted, as you will see when you know me a little better."

"Upon my word," said the painter, "it is a very singular surprise which you have given me. To tell truth, I did not even believe in your existence."

The little imp put on a theatrical air, and, with one of Mr. Macready's best looks, said,—

运!”他叫喊道，“我这样一个有着杰出才能的男人，却要忍受这些生活的不幸？就这样受妻子和朋友的欺侮，杰作被世人忽略，只能卖出几张画吗？诅咒这段误导我的爱情，诅咒这个不能给我带来温饱的艺术！让我去做苦工或偷盗，让我把自己卖了去做士兵吧！或把自己卖给魔鬼。没有比现在的我更不幸的人了!”

“恰恰相反。”一个很小的、愉快的声音叫道。

“什么!”甘姆布四肢发抖，很惊讶地叫道，“谁？——你在哪里？——你是谁?”

“你刚刚说到了我。”那个声音说。

甘姆布左手拿着他的调色板，右手上是管口冒着个气泡的深红色染料膏，他正要在红木的调色板上把染料挤出来。“你在哪里?”他又叫道。

“挤!”那个细小的声音叫道。

甘姆布把指甲从这个气泡上移开，然后挤了一下；这时，千真万确，一个小魔鬼突然在调色板上冒了出来，它以一种很特别很圆滑的神情开始笑了起来。

刚开始，他只比一个蝌蚪大一点，接着变成一只老鼠那么大，最后是一只猫那么大。他从调色板上跳下来，蹲在脚后跟上转着脑袋，问可怜的画家想从他那儿得到什么。

这个奇怪的小动物蹲在自己的脚后跟上转动着头部，最后坐在甘姆布的画架上——用它的后脚把肖像画上面的白砂和朱砂的颜料都涂抹开来。

“什么!”西蒙大叫，“你是——”

“你知道，确实是这样，当人们一谈到我的时候，我总是在附近的。另外，我并不像人们所画的那样坏，一半都没有。如果你了解我多一点，你就会知道的。”

“哎呀!”画家说，“你太让我吃惊了。说实话，我甚至不相信你的存在。”

小魔鬼摆出表演戏剧的架子，以麦克里迪［莎士比亚戏剧的导

"There are more things in heaven and earth, Gambogio,
Than are dreamed of in your philosophy."

Gambouge, being a Frenchman, did not understand the quotation, but felt somehow strangely and singularly interested in the conversation of his new friend.

Diabolus continued: "You are a man of merit, and want money; you will starve on your merit; you can only get money from me. Come, my friend, how much is it? I ask the easiest interest in the world: old Mordecai, the usurer, has made you pay twice as heavily before now: nothing but the signature of a bond, which is a mere ceremony, and the transfer of an article which, in itself, is a supposition—a valueless, windy, uncertain property of yours, called, by some poet of your own, I think, an animula, vagula, blandula—bah! there is no use beating about the bush—I mean A SOUL. Come, let me have it; you know you will sell it some other way, and not get such good pay for your bargain!"—and, having made this speech, the Devil pulled out from his fob a sheet as big as a double *Times*, only there was a different STAMP in the corner.

It is useless and tedious to describe law documents: lawyers only love to read them; and they have as good in Chitty as any that are to be found in the Devil's own; so nobly have the apprentices emulated the skill of the master. Suffice it to say, that poor Gambouge read over the paper, and signed it. He was to have all he wished for seven years, and at the end of that time was to become the property of the——; PROVIDED that, during the course of the seven years, every single wish which he might form should be gratified by the other of the contracting parties; otherwise the deed became null and non-avenue, and Gambouge should be left "to go to the——his own way."

"You will never see me again," said Diabolus, in shaking hands with poor Simon, on whose fingers he left such a mark as is to be seen at this day—"never, at least, unless you want me; for everything you ask will be performed in the most quiet and every-day manner: believe me, it is best and most gentlemanlike, and avoids anything like scandal. But if you set me about anything which is extraordinary, and out of the course of nature, as it were, come I must, you know; and of this you are the best judge." So saying, Di-

演。——译注］最好的表情说——

“甘姆布，在天地中有很多的事情，
比你在哲思中所梦到的还要多。”

甘姆布作为一个法国人，虽然不理解这句引语，但开始有些喜欢这位新朋友的独特谈话了。

魔鬼继续说道：“你是一个有才能的人，现在需要钱用。靠才能，你将来会挨饿的。你只能从我这儿得到钱。好吧！我的朋友，你需要多少？我只要这个世界上最低的利息。老莫迪凯这个放高利贷的，在这之前已经让你支付两倍的利钱了。而你只需在一张契约上签上名字，别的什么也不用做，这只不过是个仪式，转让给我一件东西，就这件东西来说，它本身是虚幻的，是你的一份没有价值、虚无、不明确的财产，我想它被你们人类中的诗人称做小小的柔弱的灵魂。——呸！旁敲侧击是没用的——我是指灵魂。来，让我拥有你的灵魂。你知道将来你也会以其他的方式把它卖了的，而且你不会得到比这个交易更好的报酬了！”发表了这番言论之后，魔鬼从他的口袋里抽出一张纸，有两张《泰晤士报》那么大，只不过在纸角上有个不一样的图章。

描述法律文件是沉闷而无益的，只有律师才喜欢读它们。他们写在单据上的东西和魔鬼在自己纸上所写的东西几乎都是一样的，学徒们豪爽地仿效师傅的技艺。只需说，甘姆布浏览了这张纸，签了字就够了。他在七年内将会实现他的所有愿望，在期满之后，灵魂就归魔鬼所有。条件是在这七年的时间内，魔鬼要满足甘姆布的每个愿望，否则，契约就是无效、行不通的，甘姆布就可以过自己的生活，不受契约束缚了。

“你将再也看不到我了。”魔鬼说。他和可怜的西蒙握握手，在他的手指上留下一个在这一天能看到的标志。“除非是你需要我的时候，因为你要求的每件事情将会以日常的方式静悄悄地进行。相信我，这是最好的绅士

abolus disappeared; but whether up the chimney, through the keyhole, or by any other aperture or contrivance, nobody knows. Simon Gambouge was left in a fever of delight, as, Heaven forgive me! I believe many a worthy man would be, if he were allowed an opportunity to make a similar bargain.

"Heigho!" said Simon. "I wonder whether this be a reality or a dream. I am sober, I know; for who will give me credit for the means to be drunk? and as for sleeping, I'm too hungry for that. I wish I could see a capon and a bottle of white wine."

"MONSIEUR SIMON!" cried a voice on the landing-place.

"C'est ici," quoth Gambouge, hastening to open the door. He did so; and lo! there was a restaurateur's boy at the door, supporting a tray, a tin-covered dish, and plates on the same; and, by its side, a tall amber-coloured flask of Sauterne.

"I am the new boy, sir," exclaimed this youth, on entering; "but I believe this is the right door, and you asked for these things."

Simon grinned, and said, "Certainly, I did ASK FOR these things." But such was the effect which his interview with the demon had had on his innocent mind, that he took them, although he knew that they were for old Simon, the Jew dandy, who was mad after an opera girl, and lived on the floor beneath.

"Go, my boy," he said; "it is good: call in a couple of hours, and remove the plates and glasses."

The little waiter trotted down stairs, and Simon sat greedily down to discuss the capon and the white wine. He bolted the legs, he devoured the wings, he cut every morsel of flesh from the breast;—seasoning his repast with pleasant draughts of wine, and caring nothing for the inevitable bill, which was to follow all.

"Ye gods!" said he, as he scraped away at the backbone, "what a dinner! what wine! —and how gayly served up too!" There were silver forks and spoons, and the remnants of the fowl were upon a silver dish. "Why, the money for this dish and these spoons," cried Simon, "would keep me and Mrs. G. for a month! I WISH"—and here Simon whistled, and turned round to see that nobody was peeping—"I wish the plate were mine."

Oh, the horrid progress of the Devil! "Here they are," thought Simon to

行为，能避免任何丑闻之类的事情。但是如果你要我做奇异的事情，超出自然控制的范围，你知道我必须要来的。对于这个，你是最好的法官。”说着这些，魔鬼就消失了。但他是爬上了烟囱，还是从钥匙孔里或其他的孔或装置里出去的，就没人知道了。剩下西蒙·甘姆布一个人处于极度的兴奋之中，上帝饶恕我！我相信许多高尚的人如果有这样的机会来做这笔交易的话，他们都会这样做的。

“嗨！”西蒙说，“我想知道这是真的还是做梦。我知道我是清醒的，因为谁会给我提供信用贷款让我喝酒呢？至于做梦，我又太饿了，根本睡不着。我希望我能看到一只阉鸡和一瓶白酒。”

“西蒙先生（法语）！”楼梯处有一个声音喊道。

“这里。”甘姆布回应着，赶紧开开门。瞧！门口站着一个饭店的男孩，手里托着个盘子，盘子上有锡纸盖着的菜肴和碟子，还有一个高高的琥珀色的细颈瓶，瓶子里是白葡萄酒。

“先生，我是新来的，”这个年轻人叫道，他走进房间，“但我相信就是这个门，你要了这些东西。”

西蒙笑笑说：“当然，我确实是要了这些东西。”但他意识到这都是他和魔鬼对话的结果。所以他接受了它们，尽管他知道这些东西是住在楼下的一个疯狂追求歌剧院女孩的犹太纨绔子弟——大西蒙的。

“走吧！小伙子。”他说，“很好。两小时后再来收碟子和杯子。”

年轻的侍者小跑着下了楼梯。西蒙急切地坐下来，开始津津有味地吃阉鸡，喝白葡萄酒。他狼吞虎咽地吃了鸡腿和翅膀，把鸡胸脯上的每片肉都给割下来吃——喝着美味的白葡萄酒来给这顿盛宴调节口味，不再理会随后不可避免要支付的账单。

当他舔着骨头的时候，他说：“上帝啊！多么好的晚餐！多么好的酒！——有人给端上饭菜是多么让人高兴啊！”有银制的叉子和匙子，剩余的鸡块也盛在一个银制的盘子上。西蒙叫道：“这些盘子和餐匙的钱可以够我和妻子花销一个月的了！我希望——”西蒙看看周围有没有人偷看，小

himself; "why should not I TAKE THEM?" And take them he did. "Detection," said he, "is not so bad as starvation; and I would as soon live at the galleys as live with Madame Gambouge."

So Gambouge shovelled dish and spoons into the flap of his surtout, and ran down stairs as if the Devil were behind him—as, indeed, he was.

He immediately made for the house of his old friend the pawnbroker—that establishment which is called in France the Mont de Piété. "I am obliged to come to you again, my old friend," said Simon, "with some family plate, of which I beseech you to take care."

The pawnbroker smiled as he examined the goods. "I can give you nothing upon them," said he.

"What!" cried Simon; "not even the worth of the silver?"

"No; I could buy them at that price at the 'Café Morisot,' Rue de la Verrerie, where, I suppose, you got them a little cheaper." And, so saying, he showed to the guilt-stricken Gambouge how the name of that coffee-house was inscribed upon every one of the articles which he had wished to pawn.

The effects of conscience are dreadful indeed. Oh! how fearful is retribution, how deep is despair, how bitter is remorse for crime—WHEN CRIME IS FOUND OUT! —otherwise, conscience takes matters much more easily. Gambouge cursed his fate, and swore henceforth to be virtuous.

"But, hark ye, my friend," continued the honest broker, "there is no reason why, because I cannot lend upon these things, I should not buy them: they will do to melt, if for no other purpose. Will you have half the money? —speak, or I peach."

Simon's resolves about virtue were dissipated instantaneously. "Give me half," he said, "and let me go. —What scoundrels are these pawnbrokers!" ejaculated he, as he passed out of the accursed shop, "seeking every wicked pretext to rob the poor man of his hard-won gain."

When he had marched forwards for a street or two, Gambouge counted the money which he had received, and found that he was in possession of no less than a hundred francs. It was night, as he reckoned out his equivocal gains, and he counted them at the light of a lamp. He looked up at the lamp, in doubt as to the course he should next pursue: upon it was inscribed the simple number, 152. "Agambling-house," thought Gambouge. "I WISH I

声说道，“我希望这个碟子是我的。”

唉，贪欲的得寸进尺是多么可怕啊！西蒙自己想：“它们就在这里，为什么我不收起来呢?”他真的动手了，还说，“让人发现也不会像挨饿那样糟糕，我会很快回到厨房假装我是和甘姆布太太在一起的。”

甘姆布把盘子和餐匙塞进外面的口袋，跑下楼梯，仿佛魔鬼在他后面，而事实确实是这样的。

他很快就来到他的老朋友当铺老板那里——“我的老伙计，我不得不又到你这里来，”西蒙说，“家里有些盘子，请求你照顾一下。”

当铺老板检查完物品后，笑着说：“这些东西，我一分钱也不能给你。”

“什么!”西蒙叫道，“银的还不值钱吗?”

“不是这样。因为我可以在玻璃制品街的莫里索咖啡馆以同样的价钱收买它们，我想，你是用更便宜的价钱得到它们的。”说着，他把每件物品上所刻着的咖啡馆的名字给犯了罪的西蒙看。

良心的惩罚确实是很可怕的。唉！报应是多么吓人，当罪行被发现的时候，会让人多么深刻地绝望，多么痛苦地悔罪啊！——否则，我的良心会很安宁的。甘姆布诅咒着他的命运，发誓以后一定要讲道德。

“但是，听着，我的朋友，”忠实的当铺老板继续说，“我不收买它们也没什么特别的原因，这些东西对我来说没有太大的用处。如果没有别的用途，它们只能被融化掉。给你一半的价钱，你觉得怎么样？——说吧，要不我就告发你。”

西蒙要讲道德的决心瞬间就被驱散了。他说：“给我一半的价钱。”当他从这个该诅咒的店里出来的时候，他突然喊了出来：“这些当铺老板都是怎样的坏蛋啊！他们抓住每个邪恶的借口来抢夺穷人得来不易的东西。”

当他向前走过一两条街道时，甘姆布数了数他所得到的钱，发现数目不少于一百法郎。因为是在晚上，看不清楚，他就到一盏路灯下数钱。他抬头看看路灯，拿不准下一步要做什么，路灯上面刻着简单的号码，152。甘姆布想：“是一个赌馆，我希望自己能拥有赌馆里桌子上一半的金钱，

had half the money that is now on the table, upstairs."

He mounted, as many a rogue has done before him, and found half a hundred persons busy at a table of rouge et noir. Gambouge's five napoleons looked insignificant by the side of the heaps which were around him; but the effects of the wine, of the theft, and of the detection by the pawnbroker, were upon him, and he threw down his capital stoutly upon the 0 0.

It is a dangerous spot that 0 0, or double zero; but to Simon it was more lucky than to the rest of the world. The ball went spinning round—in "its predestined circle rolled," as Shelley has it, after Goethe—and plumped down at last in the double zero. One hundred and thirty-five gold napoleons (louis they were then) were counted out to the delighted painter. "Oh, Diabolus!" cried he, "now it is that I begin to believe in thee! Don't talk about merit," he cried; "talk about fortune. Tell me not about heroes for the future—tell me of ZEROES." And down went twenty napoleons more upon the 0.

The Devil was certainly in the ball: round it twirled, and dropped into zero as naturally as duck pops its head into a pond. Our friend received five hundred pounds for his stake; and the croupiers and lookers-on began to stare at him.

There were twelve thousand pounds on the table. Suffice it to say, that Simon won half, and retired from the Palais Royal with a thick bundle of bank-notes crammed into his dirty three-cornered hat. He had been but half an hour in the place, and he had won the revenues of a prince for half a year!

Gambouge, as soon as he felt that he was a capitalist, and that he had a stake in the country, discovered that he was an altered man. He repented of his foul deed, and his base purloining of the restaurateur's plate. "O, honesty!" he cried, "how unworthy is an action like this of a man who has a property like mine!" So he went back to the pawnbroker with the gloomiest face imaginable. "My friend," said he, "I have sinned against all that I hold most sacred: I have forgotten my family and my religion. Here is thy money. In the name of Heaven, restore me the plate which I have wrongfully sold thee!"

But the pawnbroker grinned, and said, "Nay, Mr. Gambouge, I will sell that plate for a thousand francs to you, or I never will sell it at all."

"Well," cried Gambouge, "thou art an inexorable ruffian, Troisboules; but I will give thee all I am worth." And here he produced a billet of five hun-

上楼。”

他上了楼。许多游手好闲的人早已先他到了这里，他发现有五十多个人都挤在红色或黑色的桌子旁。甘姆布的五个金币与他周围成堆的金币相比就很不显眼了。但是由于当铺老板发现了他的偷窃行为，加上酒的作用，都对他构成了刺激。他坚定地把钱押在00号上。

00号是一个危险的号码，但对西蒙来说，它却比其他的号都要幸运。球开始转动了——在“注定的滚动圈数中”——它最后突然停在了双零上。一百三十五金币（也就是路易）被数了出来交给快乐的画家。“哦，魔鬼!”他叫道，“现在我开始相信你了！不要再谈什么道德。”他叫道，“谈金钱吧！不要和我谈论未来的英雄——告诉我中奖的号码是零。”他又在零上赌了二十金币。

魔鬼当然在球里，他使球滴溜溜地旋转，并如鱼得水地自然停在零上。我们的朋友在这笔赌注上又赢了五百镑。赌场里的管理人和旁观者都开始盯着他看。

在桌子上有一万两千镑。也就是说，西蒙赢了一半。从赌馆里出来后，他肮脏的三角帽里塞满了一沓厚厚的银行支票。他只在这个地方待了半小时，就赢得了一个王子半年所得的收入。

甘姆布一旦感觉到自己是一个富豪，并且和国家利害攸关的时候，他发现自己的思想也改变了。他为他罪恶的行为忏悔，他曾卑鄙地偷了饭店的碟子。“哦，诚实!”他喊道，“这种行为与我这个拥有大笔财产的人是多么不相称啊!”因此他又回到当铺老板那里，以一副可以想象得到的忧郁表情说：“我的朋友，我违背了我所坚守的神圣的信条，犯了罪过。我忘记了我的家庭和宗教。这是你的钱。看在上帝的面上，把我错卖给你的碟子还给我吧!”

但是当铺老板笑着说：“不，甘姆布先生。我决定以一千法郎的价钱把碟子卖给你，否则我不会卖的。”

“好吧，”甘姆布叫道，“你这个无情的恶棍。但我会把全部的钱给你

dred francs. "Look," said he, "this money is all I own; it is the payment of two years' lodging. To raise it, I have toiled for many months; and, failing, I have been a criminal. O, Heaven! I STOLE that plate that I might pay my debt, and keep my dear wife from wandering houseless. But I cannot bear this load of ignominy—I cannot suffer the thought of this crime. I will go to the person to whom I did wrong, I will starve, I will confess; but I will, I WILL do right!"

The broker was alarmed. "Give me thy note," he cried; "here is the plate."

"Give me an acquittal first," cried Simon, almost broken-hearted; "sign me a paper, and the money is yours." So Troisboules wrote according to Gambouge's dictation; "Received, for thirteen ounces of plate, twenty pounds."

"Monster of iniquity!" cried the painter, "fiend of wickedness! thou art caught in thine own snares. Hast thou not sold me five pounds' worth of plate for twenty? Have I it not in my pocket? Art thou not a convicted dealer in stolen goods? Yield, scoundrel, yield thy money, or I will bring thee to justice!"

The frightened pawnbroker bullied and battled for a while; but he gave up his money at last, and the dispute ended. Thus it will be seen that Diabolus had rather a hard bargain in the wily Gambouge. He had taken a victim prisoner, but he had assuredly caught a Tartar. Simon now returned home, and, to do him justice, paid the bill for his dinner, and restored the plate.

And now I may add (and the reader should ponder upon this, as a profound picture of human life), that Gambouge, since he had grown rich, grew likewise abundantly moral. He was a most exemplary father. He fed the poor, and was loved by them. He scorned a base action. And I have no doubt that Mr. Thurtell, or the late lamented Mr. Greenacre, in similar circumstances, would have acted like the worthy Simon Gambouge.

There was but one blot upon his character—he hated Mrs. Gam. worse than ever. As he grew more benevolent, she grew more virulent: when he went to plays, she went to Bible societies, and vice versâ: in fact, she led him such a life as Xantippe led Socrates, or as a dog leads a cat in the same kitchen. With all his fortune—for, as may be supposed, Simon prospered in all worldly things—he was the most miserable dog in the whole city of Paris. On-

的。”他填了张五百法郎的单子。他说：“看，这是我全部的钱，它是两年的房租。为了存这笔钱，我干了两个月的苦力。但就因为一念之差，我成了个罪犯。哦，上帝啊！我偷那个碟子是想还债，让我亲爱的妻子不再无家可归。但我忍受不了耻辱的负荷——我承受不了这种罪过的惩罚，我愿意挨饿，我愿意忏悔，但我会改正的！”

老板被吓住了。他叫道：“把你的支票给我吧，给你碟子。”

西蒙很伤心地大声说：“首先给我一张债务清偿单，在纸上给我签个字，钱就是你的了。”老板按照甘姆布口述的写了：“十三盎司的碟子，收款二十镑。”

画家叫道：“邪恶的家伙！恶棍！你掉进自己的陷阱里去了。你这不是把价值五镑的碟子以二十镑的价钱卖给我吗？可我的口袋里没有碟子啊？难道你不是一个有罪的偷东西的商人吗？交出来，坏蛋，交出你的钱，否则我会带你去见法官！”

受惊吓的店铺老板威胁抗议了一阵子，但最后他还是放弃了收钱，争论就此结束了。从这件事可以看出魔鬼和这个狡猾的甘姆布做交易还是挺困难的。魔鬼已经抓住了一个受害的囚犯，但也的确是逮住了一个难对付的人。现在西蒙回家了，为公平起见，他付了晚餐的钱，把碟子还回去了。

我再加几句（读者应该考虑考虑这种人性的复杂），甘姆布自他变得富有之后，他的德行也越来越多了。他是一个很模范的父亲；他给穷人供给，得到他们的爱戴；他轻蔑卑鄙的行为。我不怀疑瑟特尔先生或死者格林雷尔先生［英国19世纪20年代的罪犯。——译注］在同样的环境下，也会有尊敬的西蒙·甘姆布那样的行为表现的。

但是他的品质还存在一个污点——他比往常更憎恨甘姆布太太了。当他变得越来越慈善时，她却变得越来越恶毒。当他去剧院的时候，她去参加教会团体，反之亦然。事实上，她对待他的生活就像苏格拉底的妻子［一名悍妻，泼妇。——译注］对待苏格拉底一样，或是像厨房里的一只狗对一只猫那样。凭借着他所有的财富——可以想象得出，西蒙在世俗的世

ly in the point of drinking did he and Mrs. Simon agree; and for many years, and during a considerable number of hours in each day, he thus dissipated, partially, his domestic chagrin. O, philosophy! we may talk of thee: but, except at the bottom of the winecup, where thou liest like truth in a well, where shall we find thee?

He lived so long, and in his worldly matters prospered so much, there was so little sign of devilment in the accomplishment of his wishes, and the increase of his prosperity, that Simon, at the end of six years, began to doubt whether he had made any such bargain at all, as that which we have described at the commencement of this history. He had grown, as we said, very pious and moral. He went regularly to mass, and had a confessor into the bargain. He resolved, therefore, to consult that reverend gentleman, and to lay before him the whole matter.

"I am inclined to think, holy sir," said Gambouge, after he had concluded his history, and shown how, in some miraculous way, all his desires were accomplished, "that, after all, this demon was no other than the creation of my own brain, heated by the effects of that bottle of wine, the cause of my crime and my prosperity."

The confessor agreed with him, and they walked out of church comfortably together, and entered afterwards a café, where they sat down to refresh themselves after the fatigues of their devotion.

A respectable old gentleman, with a number of orders at his buttonhole, presently entered the room, and sauntered up to the marble table, before which reposed Simon and his clerical friend. "Excuse me, gentlemen," he said, as he took a place opposite them, and began reading the papers of the day.

"Bah!" said he, at last,—? "sont-ils grands ces journaux Anglais? Look, sir," he said, handing over an immense sheet of The *Times* to Mr. Gambouge, "was ever anything so monstrous?"

Gambouge smiled politely, and examined the proffered page. "It is enormous" he said; "but I do not read English."

"Nay," said the man with the orders, "look closer at it, Signor Gambouge; it is astonishing how easy the language is."

Wondering, Simon took the sheet of paper. He turned pale as he looked

界中还是很富有的——但他却是巴黎市最悲惨的人。只有在喝酒这点上，他与西蒙太太才能达成一致。有许多年，在每天的某段固定的时间内，他就会沉迷于酗酒之中，为他的家庭而懊悔。噢，哲学！我们也可以提到你，但是除了酒杯底外，你就像藏在井里的真理一样，我们在哪里才能找到你呢？

他过了这么长一段时间，世俗的物质已非常丰富，在实现他的愿望时几乎没有什么罪恶的迹象，随着他越来越富有，西蒙在六年就要结束之时开始怀疑他是否和魔鬼签过协议，就如我们在故事的开始所描述的那样。他已变得很虔诚，很有德行。他经常去做弥撒，此外还有个忏悔神甫。因此他决定把整件事情向那位牧师先生和盘托出，征询他的意见。

甘姆布讲完了自己的故事，故事显示出事情都是怎样通过一些奇异的方式使他实现了所有的欲望。他说："神甫，我想那毕竟只是我脑子里的想象，喝了酒之后，头脑发热，才导致了我的罪过和富有。"

神甫同意他的看法，他们轻松自如地一起走出教堂，然后走进一家咖啡馆，坐下来休息，以从礼拜的疲惫中恢复过来。

这时一位体面的老绅士走了进来，衣服的纽孔上戴有许多勋章，他闲逛着来到正在休息的西蒙和他的牧师朋友所坐的大理石桌子旁，他说："先生，打扰了。"然后就坐在他们的对面，开始读今天的报纸。

接着，他说，"呸！"——"这就是英国的大报啊？你看，先生，"他说着就把一张很大的《泰晤士报》递给甘姆布，"有这么荒谬的事情吗？"

甘姆布有礼貌地笑了笑，看了看递过来的报纸。他说："是很大啊！但是我不读英文报。"

"不，"这个人用命令的口气说，"仔细看看它，甘姆布，很奇怪，这种语言很简单的。"西蒙有些奇怪地接过报纸。刚看了一眼，他的脸色立即变白了，并开始诅咒冰块和侍者。"走吧！神甫，"他说，"这里的热度和阳光都让人无法忍受。"

陌生人和他们一起站了起来，"我亲爱的先生，很高兴又见到你。"他

at it, and began to curse the ices and the waiter. "Come, M. l'Abbé," he said; "the heat and glare of this place are intolerable."

The stranger rose with them. "Au plaisir de vous revoir, mon cher monsieur," said he; "I do not mind speaking before the Abbé here, who will be my very good friend one of these days; but I thought it necessary to refresh your memory, concerning our little business transaction six years since; and could not exactly talk of it AT CHURCH, as you may fancy."

Simon Gambouge had seen, in the double-sheeted *Times*, the paper signed by himself, which the little devil had pulled out of his fob.

There was no doubt on the subject; and Simon, who had but a year to live, grew more pious, and more careful than ever. He had consultations with all the doctors of the Sorbonne and all the lawyers of the Palais. But his magnificence grew as wearisome to him as his poverty had been before; and not one of the doctors whom he consulted could give him a pennyworth of consolation.

Then he grew outrageous in his demands upon the Devil, and put him to all sorts of absurd and ridiculous tasks; but they were all punctually performed, until Simon could invent no new ones, and the Devil sat all day with his hands in his pockets doing nothing.

One day, Simon's confessor came bounding into the room, with the greatest glee. "My friend," said he, "I have it! Eureka! —I have found it. Send the Pope a hundred thousand crowns, build a new Jesuit college at Rome, give a hundred gold candlesticks to St. Peter's; and tell his Holiness you will double all, if he will give you absolution!"

Gambouge caught at the notion, and hurried off a courier to Rome ventre *à* terre. His Holiness agreed to the request of the petition, and sent him an absolution, written out with his own fist, and all in due form.

"Now," said he, "foul fiend, I defy you! arise, Diabolus! your contract is not worth a jot: the Pope has absolved me, and I am safe on the road to salvation." In a fervour of gratitude he clasped the hand of his confessor, and embraced him: tears of joy ran down the cheeks of these good men.

They heard an inordinate roar of laughter, and there was Diabolus sitting opposite to them, holding his sides, and lashing his tail about, as if he would have gone mad with glee.

说，“我不介意在这位神甫面前说话，因为他将会是我近期内的一位很要好的朋友。但是我觉得有必要让你恢复记忆，关于我们六年来所做的一笔小交易。你知道，我们当然不能在教堂里谈这种事了。”

西蒙·甘姆布已经在有两张《泰晤士报》大的纸上看到了自己的签名，它正是小魔鬼从袋子里抽出来的那张纸。

关于这个问题已没有什么可怀疑的了。西蒙只有一年的时间了，他变得更加虔诚，比以前也更加小心。他向巴黎大学神学院的所有博士和宫廷的所有律师征求意见。但是他的伟大就像以前的贫穷那样让他感到疲倦。在他咨询的博士中没有一个人能给他一点有价值的安慰。

后来他对于魔鬼的要求开始变得蛮横起来，让他接受各种各样愚蠢荒谬的任务，但是它们都被准确无误地完成了，以至于西蒙想不出还有什么新的任务。魔鬼只好整天把手插在口袋里坐着无所事事。

一天，西蒙的忏悔神甫非常高兴地跳进房间。“我的朋友，”他说，“我找到了！我找到了——我找到办法了。送给罗马教皇十万克朗（欧洲某些国家货币，英国旧制五先令硬币），在罗马建一座耶稣会信徒学院，送给圣·彼得教皇一百个金烛台，告诉教皇陛下如果他能赦免你的罪过，你将会把所有的东西再加倍送给他。”

甘姆布听了这个计划后，急忙派一个信使快速去罗马。教皇陛下答应了他的请求，送给他一份按规定形式亲笔写的赦罪文。

甘姆布说：“现在，恶魔，我藐视你！出来吧，魔鬼！你的契约不值一文钱了。罗马教皇已赦免我，我的灵魂得到拯救了。”出于感激之情，他紧紧握住忏悔神甫的手，拥抱他，欢喜的眼泪顺着这个善良人的脸颊流了下来。

他们听到一声奇怪的哄笑，魔鬼就坐在他们的对面，垂着他的两翼，甩着他的尾巴，仿佛它就要快乐得发狂了。

他说：“胡说！你以为我会在意那个赦罪文吗？”他把教皇的信件扔到一个角落里。“神甫知道，”他点点头笑着说，“虽然罗马教皇的文件在这里

"Why," said he, "what nonsense is this! do you suppose I care about THAT?" and he tossed the Pope's missive into a corner. "M. l'Abbé knows," he said, bowing and grinning, "that though the Pope's paper may pass current HERE, it is not worth twopence in our country. What do I care about the Pope's absolution? You might just as well be absolved by your under butler."

"Egad," said the Abbé, "the rogue is right—I quite forgot the fact, which he points out clearly enough."

"No, no, Gambouge," continued Diabolus, with horrid familiarity. "go thy ways, old fellow, that COCK WON'T FIGHT." And he retired up the chimney, chuckling at his wit and his triumph. Gambouge heard his tail scuttling all the way up, as if he had been a sweeper by profession.

Simon was left in that condition of grief in which, according to the newspapers, cities and nations are found when a murder is committed, or a lord ill of the gout—a situation, we say, more easy to imagine than to describe.

To add to his woes, Mrs. Gambouge, who was now first made acquainted with his compact, and its probable consequences, raised such a storm about his ears, as made him wish almost that his seven years were expired. She screamed, she scolded, she swore, she wept, she went into such fits of hysterics, that poor Gambouge, who had completely knocked under to her, was worn out of his life. He was allowed no rest, night or day: he moped about his fine house, solitary and wretched, and cursed his stars that he ever had married the butcher's daughter.

It wanted six months of the time.

A sudden and desperate resolution seemed all at once to have taken possession of Simon Gambouge. He called his family and his friends together—he gave one of the greatest feasts that ever was known in the city of Paris—he gayly presided at one end of his table, while Mrs. Gam., splendidly arrayed, gave herself airs at the other extremity.

After dinner, using the customary formula, he called upon Diabolus to appear. The old ladies screamed, and hoped he would not appear naked; the young ones tittered, and longed to see the monster: everybody was pale with expectation and affright.

A very quiet, gentlemanly man, neatly dressed in black, made his ap-

行得通，在我们那里却两便士都不值。我为什么还要在乎教皇的赦罪文呢？得到教皇的赦免同下等的仆役的赦免都是一样的。”

“天哪！”神甫说，“这个恶魔说的是正确的——我忘了这个事实，他已很清楚地指出来了。”

魔鬼以一种让人厌恶的随便的口气继续说：“甘姆布，去你的吧！老朋友，那一手行不通的。”他为自己的机智和胜利感到得意，爬上烟囱离开了。甘姆布听到他的尾巴在烟囱里向上扫来扫去的声音，仿佛他是一个职业打扫烟囱的人。

西蒙又陷入了悲痛之中，就好像自己的罪行已通过报纸昭示于天下一样，这种处境是别人体会不到的，也是难以描述的。

让他更痛苦的是，甘姆布太太最先知道了他与魔鬼的契约和由此可能带来的结果，她就在西蒙的耳边鼓噪个没完，让西蒙恨不得现在他的七年期限就已到期。她尖叫、责骂、诅咒、哭泣、歇斯底里地发作，可怜的甘姆布完全被她给击垮了，对自己的生活感到厌倦。无论白天还是夜晚，他都得不到休息。他在自己的房子周围闷闷不乐，孤独而可怜，为娶了这个屠夫的女儿而诅咒自己的命运。

还有六个月的时间就到期了。

西蒙·甘姆布突然有了个孤注一掷的决定。他把家人和朋友都一起叫来——办了一场宴会，它可是巴黎市曾举办的最好的宴会之一——他坐在桌子的一端愉快地主持宴会，而甘姆布太太则盛装打扮地坐在桌子的另一端摆架子。

晚餐之后，按照计划的程式，他叫魔鬼现身。老女人都尖叫了起来，希望魔鬼不会光着身子出现；年轻人则嗤嗤地笑，希望看到这个怪物。每个人都由于恐惧和期待而面色发白。

一个温和、具有绅士风度的男人穿着一身整洁的黑衣出现了，他让在场的人都大吃一惊，并向所有人鞠躬。“我不会显示出我的真实面目，”他红着脸指着他的脚说，它们被浅口的皮鞋和鞋扣灵巧地隐藏了起来，“除非

pearance, to the surprise of all present, and bowed all round to the company. "I will not show my CREDENTIALS," he said, blushing, and pointing to his hoofs, which were cleverly hidden by his pumps and shoe-buckles, "unless the ladies absolutely wish it; but I am the person you want, Mr. Gambouge; pray tell me what is your will."

"You know," said that gentleman, in a stately and determined voice, "that you are bound to me, according to our agreement, for six months to come."

"I am," replied the new comer.

"You are to do all that I ask, whatsoever it may be, or you forfeit the bond which I gave you?"

"It is true."

"You declare this before the present company?"

"Upon my honour, as a gentleman," said Diabolus, bowing, and laying his hand upon his waistcoat.

A whisper of applause ran round the room: all were charmed with the bland manners of the fascinating stranger.

"My love," continued Gambouge, mildly addressing his lady, "will you be so polite as to step this way? You know I must go soon, and I am anxious, before this noble company, to make a provision for one who, in sickness as in health, in poverty as in riches, has been my truest and fondest companion."

Gambouge mopped his eyes with his handkerchief—all the company did likewise. Diabolus sobbed audibly, and Mrs. Gambouge sidled up to her husband's side, and took him tenderly by the hand. "Simon!" said she, "is it true? and do you really love your Griskinissa?"

Simon continued solemnly: "Come hither, Diabolus; you are bound to obey me in all things for the six months during which our contract has to run; take, then, Griskinissa Gambouge, live alone with her for half a year, never leave her from morning till night, obey all her caprices, follow all her whims, and listen to all the abuse which falls from her infernal tongue. Do this, and I ask no more of you; I will deliver myself up at the appointed time."

Not Lord G—, when flogged by Lord B—, in the House,—not Mr. Cartlitch, of Astley's Amphitheatre, in his most pathetic passages, could look more crestfallen, and howl more hideously, than Diabolus did now. "Take

女士很愿意看到它。但我就是你们想看到的人，甘姆布先生，请告诉我你的愿望是什么。”

“你知道，”甘姆布以庄严和坚定的语气说道，“根据我们的协议，在未来的六个月内你和我是密切相关的。”

“我听从您的吩咐。”新来的这位回应道。

“你要做我所要求的一切，不管它是什么，否则你会失去我签给你的这份契约，不是吗？”

“确实是。”

“你会在众人面前宣布这个条件吗？”

魔鬼把手放在他的背心上，鞠着躬说：“以我作为一个绅士的名誉担保。”

房间里都是人们赞赏的低语声。人们都被这个迷人的绅士所展示出来的和蔼风度给迷住了。

甘姆布继续说道，“我的妻子，”他温和地提到他的太太，“可以请你走过来吗？你知道，我很快就必须要走了，在这些善良的朋友面前，我很担忧，我要为那个与我同甘共苦、我最真挚和喜爱的伴侣做好提前的安排。”

甘姆布用手帕擦了擦他湿润的眼睛——在场的所有人也都这样做了。魔鬼也出声地啜泣，甘姆布太太羞怯地走到丈夫身边，用手温柔地拉住他，她说：“西蒙！这是真的吗？你真的爱你的格里斯基尼萨吗？”

西蒙严肃地继续说下去：“魔鬼，到这儿来。我们的契约规定在接下来的六个月内你一定要听从我的任何吩咐。那么你接受格里斯基尼萨·甘姆布吧！和她单独生活半年，从早晨到晚上都不要离开她，你要忍受她的反复无常，容忍她的任性，倾听从她恶毒的嘴里吐出的辱骂。就这样做吧！我对你不再要求别的了。在约定的时间我会把自己交给你的。”

议院里的G勋爵被B勋爵鞭打时，阿斯特雷戏院中卡特利奇先生在他最悲哀的情节中时，都不比这时的魔鬼更垂头丧气，更可怕地号哭。“甘姆布，再等一年吧！”他尖叫道，“要不两年——十年——一百年，把我放在

another year, Gambouge," screamed he; "two more—ten more—a century; roast me on Lawrence's gridiron, boil me in holy water, but don't ask that: don't, don't bid me live with Mrs. Gambouge!"

Simon smiled sternly. "I have said it," he cried; "do this, or our contract is at an end."

The Devil, at this, grinned so horribly that every drop of beer in the house turned sour: he gnashed his teeth so frightfully that every person in the company well nigh fainted with the colic. He slapped down the great parchment upon the floor, trampled upon it madly, and lashed it with his hoofs and his tail: at last, spreading out a mighty pair of wings as wide as from here to Regent Street, he slapped Gambouge with his tail over one eye, and vanished, abruptly, through the keyhole.

Gambouge screamed with pain and started up. "You drunken, lazy scoundrel!" cried a shrill and well-known voice, "you have been asleep these two hours:" and here he received another terrific box on the ear.

It was too true, he had fallen asleep at his work; and the beautiful vision had been dispelled by the thumps of the tipsy Griskinissa. Nothing remained to corroborate his story, except the bladder of lake, and this was spirted all over his waistcoat and breeches.

"I wish," said the poor fellow, rubbing his tingling cheeks, "that dreams were true;" and he went to work again at his portrait.

My last accounts of Gambouge are, that he has left the arts, and is footman in a small family. Mrs. Gam. takes in washing; and it is said that, her continual dealings with soap-suds and hot water have been the only things in life which have kept her from spontaneous combustion.

烤网上烤，放到热水里去煮都可以，但是不要让我做这件事。不，不要让我和甘姆布太太生活在一起!”西蒙严厉地笑了，“我已经说过了，”他叫道，“就这样做，要不我们的契约到此为止。”

这时，魔鬼可怕地笑了起来，以至于房间里的每瓶啤酒都在震动。他咬牙切齿的样子那么可怕，几乎每个人都被吓得昏倒了。他啪的一声在地板上放下一张很大的羊皮纸，发疯地在上面践踏着，用它的爪子和尾巴鞭打着羊皮纸。最后，展开它那巨大有力的翅膀，翅膀有从这里到摄政街那么宽，它用一条长有一只眼睛的尾巴抽打甘姆布，然后突然从钥匙孔里消失了。

甘姆布因为疼痛尖叫着突然站起来。“你这个醉鬼，懒汉!”一个尖锐、熟悉的声音喊道，“你已经睡了两个小时了。”这时他的耳朵上又挨了一拳。

他确实是在工作的时候睡着了。美丽的幻觉已经被微醉的格里斯基尼萨给驱散了。梦中的故事什么也没能留存下来，只有红色的染料溅满了他的背心和马裤。

可怜的小伙子擦着他兴奋的脸颊说：“我希望那个梦是真实的。”说完，他又去画他的肖像画了。

关于甘姆布最近的消息，他不干艺术这个行业了，现在在一个小家庭里做马夫。甘姆布太太开始洗衣物挣钱，也就是说，肥皂沫和热水成了她生活的全部，而这些也防止了她的自我毁灭。

Cartouche

I have been much interested with an account of the exploits of Monsieur Louis Dominic Cartouche, and as Newgate and the highways are so much the fashion with us in England, we may be allowed to look abroad for histories of a similar tendency. It is pleasant to find that virtue is cosmopolite, and may exist among wooden-shoed Papists as well as honest Church-of-England men.

Louis Dominic was born in a quarter of Paris called the Courtille, says the historian whose work lies before me;—born in the Courtille, and in the year 1693. Another biographer asserts that he was born two years later, and in the Marais;—of respectable parents, of course. Think of the talent that our two countries produced about this time: Marlborough, Villars, Mandrin, Turpin, Boileau, Dryden, Swift, Addison, Molière, Racine, Jack Sheppard, and Louis Cartouche,—all famous within the same twenty years, and fighting, writing, robbing *à* l'envi!

Well, Marlborough was no chicken when he began to show his genius; Swift was but a dull, idle, college lad; but if we read the histories of some other great men mentioned in the above list—I mean the thieves, especially—we shall find that they all commenced very early: they showed a passion for their art, as little Raphael did, or little Mozart; and the history of Cartouche's knaveries begins almost with his breeches.

Dominic's parents sent him to school at the college of Clermont (now Louis le Grand); and although it has never been discovered that the Jesuits, who directed that seminary, advanced him much in classical or theological knowledge, Cartouche, in revenge, showed, by repeated instances, his own natural bent and genius, which no difficulties were strong enough to overcome. His first great action on record, although not successful in the end, and tinctured with the innocence of youth, is yet highly creditable to him. He made a general swoop of a hundred and twenty nightcaps belonging to his companions, and disposed of them to his satisfaction; but as it was discovered

卡图什

我一直对一篇报道路易斯·多米尼克·卡图什英勇行为的文章很感兴趣，随着新的街道和公路在英国的普及，我们可以到国外来寻求这类故事。我们也很高兴地发现，无论是在穿木鞋的天主教徒还是虔诚的英国国教徒中，美德都是通行的。

摆在我面前的历史学家的著作记载，路易斯·多米尼克（即卡图什）是于1693年出生在巴黎的拉古尔第区［巴黎一个旧区的名称，其地酒店特多，每年狂欢节，更是热闹的中心，是假面具游车的出发站。——译注］。另一位传记作者则断言他是于1695年出生于马亥斯区，当然也是出身于一个体面的家庭。想想这个时期英国和法国所产生的天才人物：马尔波罗公爵［约翰·邱吉尔（John Churchill，duc de Marlborough，1650—1722），是英国名将，受封为马尔波罗公爵。——译注］、维拉尔斯、芒德汉、特平、布瓦洛［Boileau（1636—1711），法国文艺评论家。——译注］、德莱顿［德莱顿（1640—1716），17世纪英国诗人。——译注］、斯威夫特［斯威夫特（1667—1745），英国作家。——译注］、艾迪生［艾迪生（1672—1719），18世纪英国作家。——译注］、莫里哀［莫里哀（1622—1673），法国戏剧家。——译注］、拉辛［拉辛（1639—1699），法国古典主义戏剧家。——译注］杰克·谢帕德和路易斯·卡图什等等——他们在二十年的时间内都很有名并争先恐后地写作、战斗。

当马尔波罗开始显示出他的天赋的时候，他已不年轻了；斯威夫特年

that of all the youths in the college of Clermont, he only was the possessor of a cap to sleep in, suspicion (which, alas! was confirmed) immediately fell upon him: and by this little piece of youthful naïveté, a scheme, prettily conceived and smartly performed, was rendered naught.

Cartouche had a wonderful love for good eating, and put all the applewomen and cooks, who came to supply the students, under contribution. Not always, however, desirous of robbing these, he used to deal with them, occasionally, on honest principles of barter; that is, whenever he could get hold of his schoolfellows' knives, books, rulers, or playthings, which he used fairly to exchange for tarts and gingerbread.

It seemed as if the presiding genius of evil was determined to patronize this young man; for before he had been long at college, and soon after he had, with the greatest difficulty, escaped from the nightcap scrape, an opportunity occurred by which he was enabled to gratify both his propensities at once, and not only to steal, but to steal sweetmeats. It happened that the principal of the college received some pots of Narbonne honey, which came under the eyes of Cartouche, and in which that young gentleman, as soon as ever he saw them, determined to put his fingers. The president of the college put aside his honey-pots in an apartment within his own; to which, except by the one door which led into the room which his reverence usually occupied, there was no outlet. There was no chimney in the room; and the windows looked into the court, where there was a porter at night, and where crowds passed by day. What was Cartouche to do? —have the honey he must.

Over this chamber, which contained what his soul longed after, and over the president's rooms, there ran a set of unoccupied garrets, into which the dexterous Cartouche penetrated. These were divided from the rooms below, according to the fashion of those days, by a set of large beams, which reached across the whole building, and across which rude planks were laid, which formed the ceiling of the lower story and the floor of the upper. Some of these planks did young Cartouche remove; and having descended by means of a rope, tied a couple of others to the neck of the honey-pots, climbed back again, and drew up his prey in safety. He then cunningly fixed the planks again in their old places, and retired to gorge himself upon his booty. And, now, see the punishment of avarice! Everybody knows that the brethren of the order of Jesus are bound by a vow to have no more than a certain small sum of money in their possession. The principal of the college of Clermont had amassed a larger sum, in defiance of this rule: and where do you think the old

轻的时候也只是个迟钝、懒散的学院（现在的路易大帝中学）青年。但是如果我们知晓上面所提到的其他人物的事迹——尤其是小偷——我们就会发现他们成名都很早。就像拉斐尔和莫扎特在年幼时就表现出对艺术的痴迷一样，卡图什恶作剧的历史几乎是从他刚穿裤子时就开始了。

卡图什的父母把他送到克莱蒙学院（现在的路易大帝中学）接受教育，虽然管理那个神学院的耶稣会信徒没有使卡图什在古典或神学的知识上有所进步，卡图什却通过一系列的事实显示出他自身的天赋和爱好。对于他来说，没有什么强大的克服不了的困难。根据记载，他的第一件伟大的行动，尽管最后没有成功也带有年少的无知，却给他带来了很高的声誉。他抢走了周围朋友的一百二十个睡帽，自己还把它们随便地处理掉了。当整个克莱蒙学院的年轻人都丢失了帽子，唯独他带着帽子睡觉时，他很快就成了最明显的怀疑对象（哈哈，那是肯定的啦）。由于卡图什年龄还小，这次有着完美的构思并被灵活实施的计划被认为是年轻人淘气的表现。

卡图什很喜欢吃好东西。到学校里来供应食物的卖苹果的女人和厨子都被卡图什强迫着交出点东西。但是他并不想经常抢夺他们的东西，他偶尔还会和他们做公平的交易。当他把同学的刀子、书、尺子或玩具等东西弄到手之后，他就用它们来正当地换取果馅饼和姜饼。

看起来似乎是居于主导地位的邪恶天赋决定庇护这位年轻人。卡图什用了很长的时间，费了很大的劲终于从睡帽的窘境中摆脱出来。但是很快他又遇到了一个新的机会来满足他偷窃的癖好。这次不仅是偷，偷的还是糖果。事情是这样发生的。有一天学院的校长收到一些盛在罐子里的纳博讷的糖果，这件事让卡图什看见了，他就决定要把它偷出来。校长把糖罐存放在自己的房间，房间里只有一个门可以出入，没有其他的出口。房间里也没有烟囱，窗子是朝向院子的，晚上院子里会有杂务工，白天则会有人群经过。卡图什该怎么做才能得到糖果呢？

在这间房子的上面，有卡图什的灵魂所期盼的东西，校长的房间上面有套空闲的阁楼，灵巧的卡图什穿过房间，爬上了阁楼。校长的房间上面

gentleman had hidden it? In the honey-pots! As Cartouche dug his spoon into one of them, he brought out, besides a quantity of golden honey, a couple of golden louis, which, with ninety-eight more of their fellows, were comfortably hidden in the pots. Little Dominic, who, before, had cut rather a poor figure among his fellow-students, now appeared in as fine clothes as any of them could boast of; and when asked by his parents, on going home, how he came by them, said that a young nobleman of his schoolfellows had taken a violent fancy to him, and made him a present of a couple of his suits. Cartouche the elder, good man, went to thank the young nobleman; but none such could be found, and young Cartouche disdained to give any explanation of his manner of gaining the money.

Here, again, we have to regret and remark the inadvertence of youth. Cartouche lost a hundred louis—for what? For a pot of honey not worth a couple of shillings. Had he fished out the pieces, and replaced the pots and the honey, he might have been safe, and a respectable citizen all his life after. The principal would not have dared to confess the loss of his money, and did not, openly; but he vowed vengeance against the stealer of his sweetmeat, and a rigid search was made. Cartouche, as usual, was fixed upon; and in the tick of his bed, lo! there were found a couple of empty honey-pots! From this scrape there is no knowing how he would have escaped, had not the president himself been a little anxious to hush the matter up; and accordingly, young Cartouche was made to disgorge the residue of his ill-gotten gold pieces, old Cartouche made up the deficiency, and his son was allowed to remain unpunished—until the next time.

This, you may fancy, was not very long in coming; and though history has not made us acquainted with the exact crime which Louis Dominic next committed, it must have been a serious one; for Cartouche, who had borne philosophically all the whippings and punishments which were administered to him at college, did not dare to face that one which his indignant father had in pickle for him. As he was coming home from school, on the first day after his crime, when he received permission to go abroad, one of his brothers, who was on the look-out for him, met him at a short distance from home, and told him what was in preparation; which so frightened this young thief, that he declined returning home altogether, and set out upon the wide world to shift for himself as he could.

Undoubted as his genius was, he had not arrived at the full exercise of it, and his gains were by no means equal to his appetite. In whatever professions

有套空闲的阁楼，灵巧的卡图什穿过房间，爬上了阁楼。按照当时房间流行的样式，人们用一套穿过整个房间的木梁把屋子分为上下两部分，木梁上面还横着木板，它们构成了下层的房顶，上层的地板。年轻的卡图什移开几个木板，把一根绳子垂下去，吊着滑到房间，用几根绳子系住糖罐的颈口，然后爬了上去，把他的战利品放在安全的地方。现在，看看贪婪的惩罚吧！人人都知道誓约规定耶稣会的信徒们只能存有一定数目的钱，钱的数量很小。学院的校长却无视规定，自己私存了很多钱。你猜猜这个老先生把钱藏到哪里去了？就在糖罐里。当卡图什把匙子伸进去挖蜜饯时，他发现，除了一些金色蜜饯和两个金路易之外，还有九十八个金币被安全地藏在糖罐里。小卡图什以前在同学当中给人的印象是个穷孩子，现在却穿着足以让同学们夸耀的好衣服。当他回到家，父母就问起衣服是从哪儿来的，他说是他的一个贵族同学很喜欢他，送给他两套自己的衣服。老卡图什是一个好人，就去找这个贵族朋友谢谢他，但是却找不到这个人，年轻的卡图什也不屑于对他得到的钱做任何解释了。

在这里，我们再一次发觉到这个年轻人的粗心大意并为他感到遗憾。卡图什最后还是失去了那一百金路易——为什么？就因为那个不值两先令的糖罐。如果他把钱掏出来，再把糖罐和蜜饯放回原处的话，他就是安全的了，在以后的生活中也是个值得尊敬的市民。校长的钱丢了，也不敢公开坦白。但是他发誓要报复那个偷了他蜜饯的人，并开始了严格的搜查。卡图什像往常一样，又成了重点的怀疑对象。瞧！在他床上的褥子里发现了两个空糖罐！这次闯祸，如果校长没有急着去遮掩这件事情，真不知道他还会怎样逃脱。因此，校长让年轻的卡图什把剩余的钱都交出来，老卡图什又弥补了空缺，他的儿子才可以不受处罚，但是下次就不饶他了。

你能想象得到，这次闯祸离下次闯祸的时间间隔一定不会很长。尽管我们已无从得知路易斯·多米尼克下次闯祸的具体时间，但它一定是很严重的。对于卡图什来说，他能忍受学院里给予他的严惩，却不敢面对愤怒的父亲对他的斥责。在他闯祸后的第二天被允许出去走走，当他从学校里

he tried, —whether he joined the gipsies, which he did, —whether he picked pockets on the Pont Neuf, which occupation history attributes to him, —poor Cartouche was always hungry. Hungry and ragged, he wandered from one place and profession to another, and regretted the honey-pots at Clermont, and the comfortable soup and bouilli at home.

Cartouche had an uncle, a kind man, who was a merchant, and had dealings at Rouen. One day, walking on the quays of that city, this gentleman saw a very miserable, dirty, starving lad, who had just made a pounce upon some bones and turnip-peelings, that had been flung out on the quay, and was eating them as greedily as if they had been turkeys and truffles. The worthy man examined the lad a little closer. O, heavens! it was their runaway prodigal—it was little Louis Dominic! The merchant was touched by his case; and forgetting the nightcaps, the honey-pots, and the rags and dirt of little Louis, took him to his arms, and kissed and hugged him with the tenderest affection. Louis kissed and hugged too, and blubbered a great deal: he was very repentant, as a man often is when he is hungry; and he went home with his uncle, and his peace was made; and his mother got him new clothes, and filled his belly, and for a while Louis was as good a son as might be.

But why attempt to balk the progress of genius? Louis's was not to be kept down. He was sixteen years of age by this time—a smart, lively young fellow, and, what is more, desperately enamoured of a lovely washerwoman. To be successful in your love, as Louis knew, you must have something more than mere flames and sentiment; —a washer, or any other woman, cannot live upon sighs only; but must have new gowns and caps, and a necklace every now and then, and a few handkerchiefs and silk stockings, and a treat into the country or to the play. Now, how are all these to be had without money? Cartouche saw at once that it was impossible; and as his father would give him none, he was obliged to look for it elsewhere. He took to his old courses, and lifted a purse here, and a watch there; and found, moreover, an accommodating gentleman, who took the wares off his hands.

This gentleman introduced him into a very select and agreeable society, in which Cartouche's merit began speedily to be recognized, and in which he learnt how pleasant it is in life to have friends to assist one, and how much may be done by a proper division of labour. M. Cartouche, in fact, formed part of a regular company or gang of gentlemen, who were associated together for the purpose of making war on the public and the law.

Cartouche had a lovely young sister, who was to be married to a rich

出来回家时，在离家不远的地方遇到了家里的一个兄弟正要找他回家。他兄弟告诉他家里都准备好了，要惩罚他。这可把年轻的小偷给吓坏了，他拒绝回家，并开始在外面游荡起来。

虽然他是有天赋的，但是还没有经受过全面的锻炼，他的收获也并没有投其所好。在他尝试的各种各样的行业中——不管是加入吉卜赛群体，还是在奈夫桥上干老本行做扒手——可怜的卡图什总是挨饿。他饥肠辘辘、衣着褴褛，从一个地方游荡到另一个地方，从一个行业转换到另一个行业。他开始为自己在克莱蒙偷了糖罐而感到后悔并怀念起家里美味的肉汤来。

卡图什有位心地善良的叔父，是一个在鲁昂做买卖的商人。一天，当他在城市的码头上步行时，看到一个悲惨、肮脏、饥饿的男孩正扑向那些丢弃在码头上的骨头和萝卜皮，正贪婪地吃着它们，仿佛它们像火鸡一样美味。这个高尚的人走近看了看。上帝啊！正是那个逃跑的浪子——小路易斯·多米尼克！商人被他这种悲惨的情形感动了，忘掉了睡帽、糖罐的事情，把衣衫褴褛的小路易斯拉到身边，用最温柔的感情亲吻和拥抱他。路易斯也亲吻和拥抱他的叔父，向他哭诉了很长时间：他非常后悔离开家，当一个人饥饿的时候通常都会这样的。他和叔父一起回到了自己家里，他终于平安了。他母亲给他穿上新衣服，让他吃得饱饱的，在这段时间内路易斯还是个很乖的孩子。

但是为什么要试图阻止天才的进步呢？卡图什是任何力量也征服不了的。这时他十六岁了——一个聪明、活泼的年轻人，而且他倾心迷恋上一位可爱的洗衣女工。卡图什知道，要想在爱情上成功，仅有热情和感情是远远不够的——一个洗衣女工和其他的女人一样，不能整天唉声叹气地生活，还必须要有衣服和帽子，不时戴条项链，有些手帕和丝袜，被人邀请去赴宴或看戏。所有这些事情没钱能行吗？卡图什明白这是不可能的，因为父亲不给他一文钱，他只好去想别的办法。他又操起了自己的老本行，这里偷个钱包，那里偷块手表。此外，还遇到一个随和的绅士，把他手里偷到的物品又给拿去了。

young gentleman from the provinces. As is the fashion in France, the parents had arranged the match among themselves; and the young people had never met until just before the time appointed for the marriage, when the bridegroom came up to Paris with his title-deeds, and settlements, and money. Now there can hardly be found in history a finer instance of devotion than Cartouche now exhibited. He went to his captain, explained the matter to him, and actually, for the good of his country, as it were (the thieves might be called his country), sacrificed his sister's husband's property. Informations were taken, the house of the bridegroom was reconnoitred, and, one night, Cartouche, in company with some chosen friends, made his first visit to the house of his brother-in-law. All the people were gone to bed; and, doubtless, for fear of disturbing the porter, Cartouche and his companions spared him the trouble of opening the door, by ascending quietly at the window. They arrived at the room where the bridegroom kept his great chest, and set industriously to work, filing and picking the locks which defended the treasure.

The bridegroom slept in the next room; but however tenderly Cartouche and his workmen handled their tools, from fear of disturbing his slumbers, their benevolent design was disappointed, for awaken him they did; and quietly slipping out of bed, he came to a place where he had a complete view of all that was going on. He did not cry out, or frighten himself sillily; but, on the contrary, contented himself with watching the countenances of the robbers, so that he might recognize them on another occasion; and, though an avaricious man, he did not feel the slightest anxiety about his money-chest; for the fact is, he had removed all the cash and papers the day before.

As soon, however, as they had broken all the locks, and found the nothing which lay at the bottom of the chest, he shouted with such a loud voice, "Here, Thomas! —John! —officer! —keep the gate, fire at the rascals!" that they, incontinently taking fright, skipped nimbly out of window, and left the house free.

Cartouche, after this, did not care to meet his brother-in-law, but eschewed all those occasions on which the latter was to be present at his father's house. The evening before the marriage came; and then his father insisted upon his appearance among the other relatives of the bride's and bridegroom's families, who were all to assemble and make merry. Cartouche was obliged to yield; and brought with him one or two of his companions, who had been, by the way, present in the affair of the empty money-boxes; and though he never fancied that there was any danger in meeting his brother-in-law, for he had no

这个绅士介绍他加入了一个杰出的、让人愉快的团体，在这里卡图什的优点很快得到众人的认可，他也了解到在生活中有朋友相帮是件多么愉快的事。有了合理的劳动分工可以做多少事情啊！卡图什事实上已成了这个固定的绅士团伙的一员，这些人联合在一起是为了向民众和法律开战。

卡图什有一个可爱的妹妹就要嫁给外省一个富有的年轻绅士了。按照法国的风俗，是父母给他们安排了这桩婚事。这对年轻人要等到结婚时，也就是当这个新郎带着他的地契、房产单据和金钱来到巴黎时才能见面。恐怕在历史上也找不出像卡图什这样忠心耿耿的例子了。他考虑到同伙的利益，既然如此（小偷们可以被称做他的乡亲了），就把妹夫来巴黎的事情告诉了他的首领，要牺牲他妹夫的财产。他们很快布置好计划，侦察了新郎的住所。一个晚上，卡图什和几个挑选出来的弟兄第一次光顾了他妹夫的住所。这时人们都已入睡了。当然为了不惊动门房，免了让门房开门的麻烦，卡图什和同伴们静悄悄地爬上窗户跳了进去。他们到了新郎存放大箱子的房间，开始卖力地工作，用锉刀锉、用工具撬那些锁着财物的锁。

新郎睡在隔壁的房间。尽管卡图什和他的同伴们尽量不让工具发出声音，以免打扰他妹夫的睡眠。但是他们仁慈的计划落空了，那些声音吵醒了新郎。新郎偷偷地溜下床来，来到一个可以俯瞰全局的地方。他没有叫出声来，或傻乎乎地吓唬自己。相反，他要观看这些盗贼的面目，这样他就可以在别的场合认出他们来。尽管他是一个吝啬的人，他对自己的钱柜也没有丝毫的忧虑。因为事实上他昨天就把现金和单据转移了地方。

很快，当盗贼们把所有的锁都打开后，发现箱子都空空如也。这时新郎大声叫了起来："这儿，托马斯！——约翰！警官！——守住门，向盗贼开枪！"这些人立即被吓坏了，灵活地跳上窗子，没有阻碍地逃离了房间。

这件事情之后，卡图什就不愿意见到他的妹夫。当新郎来到他父亲家里时，他就避免一切可能与他碰面的机会。婚礼的前夜到来了。他父亲坚持卡图什在新娘的亲人与新郎的家人见面时一定要出席——到时人们都欢聚一堂来庆祝两家的联姻。卡图什被迫屈服了，还带了一两个同伙去出

idea that he had been seen in the night of the attack, with a natural modesty, which did him really credit, he kept out of the young bridegroom's sight as much as he could, and showed no desire to be presented to him. At supper, however, as he was sneaking modestly down to a side-table, his father shouted after him, "Ho, Dominic, come hither, and sit opposite to your brother-in-law:" which Dominic did, his friends following. The bridegroom pledged him very gracefully in a bumper; and was in the act of making him a pretty speech, on the honour of an alliance with such a family, and on the pleasures of brother-in-lawship in general, when, looking in his face—ye gods! he saw the very man who had been filing at his money-chest a few nights ago! By his side, too, sat a couple more of the gang. The poor fellow turned deadly pale and sick, and, setting his glass down, ran quickly out of the room, for he thought he was in company of a whole gang of robbers. And when he got home, he wrote a letter to the elder Cartouche, humbly declining any connexion with his family.

Cartouche the elder, of course, angrily asked the reason of such an abrupt dissolution of the engagement; and then, much to his horror, heard of his eldest son's doings. "You would not have me marry into such a family?" said the ex-bridegroom. And old Cartouche, an honest old citizen, confessed, with a heavy heart, that he would not. What was he to do with the lad? He did not like to ask for a lettre de cachet, and shut him up in the Bastille. He determined to give him a year's discipline at the monastery of St. Lazare.

But how to catch the young gentleman? Old Cartouche knew that, were he to tell his son of the scheme, the latter would never obey, and, therefore, he determined to be very cunning. He told Dominic that he was about to make a heavy bargain with the fathers, and should require a witness; so they stepped into a carriage together, and drove unsuspectingly to the Rue St. Denis. But, when they arrived near the convent, Cartouche saw several ominous figures gathering round the coach, and felt that his doom was sealed. However, he made as if he knew nothing of the conspiracy; and the carriage drew up, and his father, descended, and, bidding him wait for a minute in the coach, promised to return to him. Cartouche looked out; on the other side of the way half a dozen men were posted, evidently with the intention of arresting him.

Cartouche now performed a great and celebrated stroke of genius, which, if he had not been professionally employed in the morning, he never could have executed. He had in his pocket a piece of linen, which he had laid hold of

席——撬妹夫的钱箱子时他们也在场。尽管他从未想象过遇见妹夫会有什么危险，因为他不知道偷窃的那晚他们已被妹夫看到了，但还是有种本能的羞怯，他还是很在乎自己的名誉的。他尽量不让妹夫看到自己，也不想把自己介绍给他。吃晚餐了，当他偷偷地溜到桌子的一边时，他父亲在后面叫住他："嗬，多米尼克，到这儿来，坐你妹夫的对面。"多米尼克过来了，他的朋友也跟着。新郎大方地用一个满杯向他祝酒，正要向他讲些好话，一般都是些很荣幸和他们这个家庭联姻，很高兴彼此成了兄弟这类话，当他向多米尼克脸上一看——上帝啊！他看到那个几天前的晚上撬锁的人就在眼前！在他旁边，还有两个同伙的盗贼。可怜的年轻人的脸色立即变得苍白，他把杯子放下，很快就从房间里跑了出去，因为他以为自己是和整个盗贼团伙在一起。他回到家里，给老卡图什写了一封信，谦逊地拒绝了与他们家庭的联姻。

老卡图什当然要愤怒地追问他，这么迅速解除婚约的原因是什么。让他更惊骇的是，原来是大儿子的所作所为所致。解除了婚约的新郎说："你不能让我和这样的家庭联姻吧？"老卡图什这个诚实的老市民，带着沉重的心情承认，他当然不会。他将会怎样处理这个年轻人呢？他不愿向政府申请一张监禁令，把儿子关进巴士底狱。他决定让卡图什在圣拉扎尔修道院接受一年的管制。

但是怎样才能抓住这个年轻人呢？老卡图什知道，如果他告诉儿子这个计划，他一定不会答应的，因此，他决定狡猾地行事。他告诉多米尼克他打算要和神甫做一笔交易，需要有个见证人。就这样他们一起上了一辆马车，没有任何猜疑地来到圣丹尼斯街。但是当他们靠近修道院时，卡图什看到几个面相不善的人聚集在马车周围，就觉得自己的厄运注定了。然而，他装做对这个阴谋一无所知的样子。马车停住了，他父亲下了车，命令他在马车里等一会儿，他马上就回来。卡图什向外边看了看，在路的另一边站着半打人，很明显是要捉他的。

卡图什实施了一个天才才能想出的杰出计划，如果他早晨没有特别准

at the door of some shop, and from which he quickly tore three suitable stripes. One he tied round his head, after the fashion of a nightcap; a second round his waist, like an apron; and with the third he covered his hat, a round one, with a large brim. His coat and his periwig he left behind him in the carriage; and when he stepped out from it (which he did without asking the coachman to let down the steps), he bore exactly the appearance of a cook's boy carrying a dish; and with this he slipped through the exempts quite unsuspected, and bade adieu to the Lazarists and his honest father, who came out speedily to seek him, and was not a little annoyed to find only his coat and wig.

With that coat and wig, Cartouche left home, father, friends, conscience, remorse, society, behind him. He discovered (like a great number of other philosophers and poets, when they have committed rascally actions) that the world was all going wrong, and he quarrelled with it outright. One of the first stories told of the illustrious Cartouche, when he became professionally and openly a robber, redounds highly to his credit, and shows that he knew how to take advantage of the occasion, and how much he had improved in the course of a very few years' experience. His courage and ingenuity were vastly admired by his friends; so much so, that, one day, the captain of the band thought fit to compliment him, and vowed that when he (the captain) died, Cartouche should infallibly be called to the command-in-chief. This conversation, so flattering to Cartouche, was carried on between the two gentlemen, as they were walking, one night, on the quays by the side of the Seine. Cartouche, when the captain made the last remark, blushingly protested against it, and pleaded his extreme youth as a reason why his comrades could never put entire trust in him. "Psha, man!" said the captain, "thy youth is in thy favour; thou wilt live only the longer to lead thy troops to victory. As for strength, bravery, and cunning, wert thou as old as Methuselah, thou couldst not be better provided than thou art now, at eighteen." What was the reply of Monsieur Cartouche? He answered, not by words, but by actions. Drawing his knife from his girdle, he instantly dug it into the captain's left side, as near his heart as possible; and then, seizing that imprudent commander, precipitated him violently into the waters of the Seine, to keep company with the gudgeons and river-gods. When he returned to the band, and recounted how the captain had basely attempted to assassinate him, and how he, on the contrary, had, by exertion of superior skill, overcome the captain, not one of the society believed a word of his history; but they elected him cap-

备的话，他就完成不了这个计划了。他口袋里有一块亚麻布，这是他在一个商店的门口顺手抓到的，他很快就把亚麻布撕成大小相当的三条。一条围在自己的头上，像个流行的睡帽；第二条围在他的腰部，像一件围裙；第三条盖住他的帽子，一个圆圆的宽边帽。他的外套和假发都被扔在马车里。当他从马车里出来的时候（他没有让车夫放下梯子），十足就像个送饭的厨师的孩子。就这样他在众人的眼皮下没有受到任何怀疑地溜走了，告别了圣拉扎尔修道院的信徒和他诚实的父亲。他们很快就出来抓他了，但在马车里只懊恼地找到他的外套和假发。

同那件外套和假发一样，卡图什把家、父亲、朋友、良心、懊悔还有社会都抛在了一边。他发现（就像许多哲学家和诗人在做了卑鄙的事情之后）这个世界出了毛病，他直率地埋怨这个世界。关于著名的卡图什，首先要讲的故事就是当他成为职业的公开的强盗后，他的声誉得到很大的提高，并且显示出他知道怎样利用各种机会来为自己牟利。经过几年的磨炼，他取得了很大的进步。他的勇气和足智多谋得到朋友们广泛的赞扬。以至于有一天，团伙的首领觉得有必要称赞他一番，发誓当他死了之后，卡图什将是一位可靠的总指挥。这些话很讨好卡图什。一天晚上，两个人在塞纳河边的码头上散步，又继续谈到这个话题。当首领最后又说到这些时，卡图什红着脸抗议，以他太年轻为理由，说因为年轻，他的同伴们还不能够完全信任他。“哼，年轻人！”首领说，“年轻就是你的优势。你是唯一可以活到带领着你的队伍走向胜利的人。至于力量、勇敢和狡猾，如果你像玛士撒拉［《圣经·创世记》中人物，据传享年九百六十五岁。——译注］一样老就会做到了。你不会比现在十八岁得到更好的支持了。”卡图什先生是怎么回答的呢？他不是用言语来回答，而是用行动。他从腰带里抽出刀子，立即刺向首领靠近心脏左侧的地方，接着抓住这个掉以轻心的首领，把他猛地投向塞纳河里，让他与河神和鱼做伴去了。当他回到团伙后，向众人描述首领是怎样卑鄙地想暗杀他，他又是怎样反过来凭借着自己高超技能的发挥，干掉了首领，没有一个人相信他的话，但他们即刻就推举他

tain forthwith. I think his Excellency Don Rafael Maroto, the pacificator of Spain, is an amiable character, for whom history has not been written in vain.

Being arrived at this exalted position, there is no end of the feats which Cartouche performed; and his band reached to such a pitch of glory, that if there had been a hundred thousand, instead of a hundred of them, who knows but that a new and popular dynasty might not have been founded, and "Louis Dominic, premier Empereur des Français," might have performed innumerable glorious actions, and fixed himself in the hearts of his people, just as other monarchs have done, a hundred years after Cartouche's death.

A story similar to the above, and equally moral, is that of Cartouche, who, in company with two other gentlemen, robbed the coche, or packet-boat, from Melun, where they took a good quantity of booty,—making the passengers lie down on the decks, and rifling them at leisure. "This money will be but very little among three," whispered Cartouche to his neighbour, as the three conquerors were making merry over their gains; "if you were but to pull the trigger of your pistol in the neighbourhood of your comrade's ear, perhaps it might go off, and then there would be but two of us to share." Strangely enough, as Cartouche said, the pistol DID go off, and No. 3 perished. "Give him another ball," said Cartouche; and another was fired into him. But no sooner had Cartouche's comrade discharged both his pistols, than Cartouche himself, seized with a furious indignation, drew his: "Learn, monster," cried he, "not to be so greedy of gold, and perish, the victim of thy disloyalty and avarice!" So Cartouche slew the second robber; and there is no man in Europe who can say that the latter did not merit well his punishment.

I could fill volumes, and not mere sheets of paper, with tales of the triumphs of Cartouche and his band; how he robbed the Countess of O—, going to Dijon, in her coach, and how the Countess fell in love with him, and was faithful to him ever after; how, when the lieutenant of police offered a reward of a hundred pistoles to any man who would bring Cartouche before him, a noble Marquess, in a coach and six, drove up to the hotel of the police; and the noble Marquess, desiring to see Monsieur de la Reynie, on matters of the highest moment, alone, the latter introduced him into his private cabinet; and how, when there, the Marquess drew from his pocket a long, curiously shaped dagger: "Look at this, Monsieur de la Reynie," said he; "this dagger is poisoned!"

"Is it possible?" said M. de la Reynie.

"A prick of it would do for any man," said the Marquess.

做首领。我想堂·拉菲尔·马洛托阁下（西班牙将军，1780—1848——译注），西班牙的调解人，是一个亲切和蔼的人物，对于他而言历史没有白写。

由于坐上了这个尊贵的位子，卡图什立下的功绩就一件接一件。他的团伙也因此声名大振，如果是十万人，而不是他们现在的一百人，谁能知道一个新的人民政权会不会建立呢？“法国第一个皇帝路易斯·多米尼克”或许会做出许多光荣的事迹，从而活在人民的心中，就像多米尼克死后一百年另一个君主［拿破仑。——译注］所做的那样。

与上面所讲的相类似的一个故事，也是关乎道德的。这就是卡图什和另外两个男子一起去抢劫从默伦来的班轮或邮船，在那里他们得到了好多战利品——他们让乘客们都躺在甲板上，好去任意地抢劫。当他们三人庆功的时候，卡图什小声对他身边的同伙说：“只不过这些钱在三个人当中平分就太少了，你只要在你同伴的耳边拉上手枪的扳机，它或许就走火了，那么就是我们两个人平分了。”当卡图什说着的时候，很奇怪，手枪真的走火了，第三个人死去了。“再给他一枪。”卡图什说，那个人却把枪对准了他。但是这个家伙的开枪速度不如卡图什动作快，卡图什狂怒地靠近前去抓住他。“听着，恶棍，”他叫道，“不要太贪财，你要为你的不忠和贪婪送命！”因此卡图什把第二个强盗杀死了。在欧洲没人会说后者不该受到惩罚的。

关于卡图什和他的团伙胜利的故事，我可以写几卷而不是几张纸。他是如何在去第戎的马车上抢劫了伯爵夫人，而伯爵夫人又是如何爱上了他，自此以后忠心于他。警官中尉悬赏一百支手枪来捉拿卡图什，一位侯爵坐着六轮马车，说有紧急事要见拉雷尼先生，后者就单独地把他带进私人密室。这时，侯爵从口袋里抽出一把长长的、锋利的匕首。“看着这个，拉雷尼先生，”他说，“这把匕首有毒！”

“会有毒吗？”拉雷尼先生说。

“刺任何人一下就会送命。”侯爵说。

"You don't say so!" said M. de la Reynie.

"I do, though; and, what is more," says the Marquess, in a terrible voice, "if you do not instantly lay yourself flat on the ground, with your face towards it, and your hands crossed over your back, or if you make the slightest noise or cry, I will stick this poisoned dagger between your ribs, as sure as my name is Cartouche?"

At the sound of this dreadful name, M. de la Reynie sunk incontinently down on his stomach, and submitted to be carefully gagged and corded; after which Monsieur Cartouche laid his hands upon all the money which was kept in the lieutenant's cabinet. Alas! and alas! many a stout bailiff, and many an honest fellow of a spy, went, for that day, without his pay and his victuals.

There is a story that Cartouche once took the diligence to Lille, and found in it a certain Abbé Potter, who was full of indignation against this monster of a Cartouche, and said that when he went back to Paris, which he proposed to do in about a fortnight, he should give the lieutenant of police some information, which would infallibly lead to the scoundrel's capture. But poor Potter was disappointed in his designs; for, before he could fulfil them, he was made the victim of Cartouche's cruelty.

A letter came to the lieutenant of police, to state that Cartouche had travelled to Lille, in company with the Abbé de Potter, of that town; that, on the reverend gentleman's return towards Paris, Cartouche had waylaid him, murdered him, taken his papers, and would come to Paris himself, bearing the name and clothes of the unfortunate Abbé, by the Lille coach, on such a day. The Lille coach arrived, was surrounded by police agents; the monster Cartouche was there, sure enough, in the Abbé's guise. He was seized, bound, flung into prison, brought out to be examined, and, on examination, found to be no other than the Abbé Potter himself! It is pleasant to read thus of the relaxations of great men, and find them condescending to joke like the meanest of us.

Another diligence adventure is recounted of the famous Cartouche. It happened that he met, in the coach, a young and lovely lady, clad in widow's weeds, and bound to Paris, with a couple of servants. The poor thing was the widow of a rich old gentleman of Marseilles, and was going to the capital to arrange with her lawyers, and to settle her husband's will. The Count de Grinche (for so her fellow-passenger was called) was quite as candid as the pretty widow had been, and stated that he was a captain in the regiment of Nivernois; that he was going to Paris to buy a colonelcy, which his relatives,

“你不要说这些！”拉雷尼说。

“好吧！更重要的是，”侯爵恶狠狠地说，“如果你不立即平躺在地板上，脸朝下，两手交叉放在背后，或者发出一点声音、叫喊，我就会把这把有毒的匕首刺进你的肋骨，你不相信我的名字就是卡图什吗?”

听到这个可怕的名字，拉雷尼先生立即俯卧在地板上，小心翼翼地向卡图什屈服。他被塞住了口，用绳子绑了起来。干完这些，卡图什又把这个中尉密室里的钱都收入自己囊中。唉！许多勇敢的法警和忠实的密探那天就领不到自己的薪金和食物了。

有一个故事是讲卡图什有一次坐马车去里尔，发现马车里有位叫波特的神甫，神甫很痛恨那个叫做卡图什的恶人，说他回到巴黎后，计划在大约两个星期内，会给警察中尉提供一些信息，到时一定会逮住这个坏蛋。但是可怜的波特的计划破产了，因为在他还没有实施计划之前，他就成了卡图什手下的牺牲品。

警察中尉收到一封信，上面说卡图什已到了里尔，在那里和波特神甫在一起。其实在波特神甫回巴黎的路上，卡图什拦路抢劫了他，把他杀害了，自己带着神甫的文件，穿上神甫的衣服，用神甫的名字在某一天坐着里尔的马车去巴黎了。里尔的马车到了，警察很快包围了马车。装扮成神甫的恶人卡图什确实在里面。他被抓了起来，关进监狱，又带出来进行检查，经过检查发现他正是波特神甫本人！读这些名人的娱乐故事，发现他们堕落到像我们这些平庸的人一样开玩笑都是很让人愉快的。

另一个卡图什马车历险的故事是讲他在马车上遇到一位年轻可爱的太太，她穿着寡妇的丧服，带着两个仆人正要去巴黎。可怜的女士是马赛一个富有的老绅士的遗孀，准备去巴黎和她的律师商定如何处理她丈夫的遗嘱。格瑞克伯爵（和她一起的乘客都这样称呼他即卡图什）像这位漂亮的寡妇一样坦率，声称自己是某个军团的上尉，他正要去巴黎买一个上校军衔，他的亲戚布永公爵，蒙莫朗西亲王［法国的一个大族。——译注］拉特雷穆瓦耶家族的荣誉勋位获得者，在宫廷都很有势力，不会给他弄不到

the Duke de Bouillon, the Prince de Montmorency, the Commandeur de la Trémoille, with all their interest at court, could not fail to procure for him. To be short, in the course of the four days' journey, the Count Louis Dominic de Grinche played his cards so well, that the poor little widow half forgot her late husband; and her eyes glistened with tears as the Count kissed her hand at parting—at parting, he hoped, only for a few hours.

Day and night the insinuating Count followed her; and when, at the end of a fortnight, and in the midst of a tête-à-tête, he plunged, one morning, suddenly on his knees, and said, "Leonora, do you love me?" the poor thing heaved the gentlest, tenderest, sweetest sigh in the world; and sinking her blushing head on his shoulder, whispered, "Oh, Dominic, je t'aime! Ah!" said she, "how noble is it of my Dominic to take me with the little I have, and he so rich a nobleman!" The fact is, the old Baron's titles and estates had passed away to his nephews; his dowager was only left with three hundred thousand livres, in rentes sur l'état,—a handsome sum, but nothing to compare to the rent-roll of Count Dominic, Count de la Grinche, Seigneur de la Haute Pigre, Baron de la Bigorne; he had estates and wealth which might authorize him to aspire to the hand of a duchess, at least.

The unfortunate widow never for a moment suspected the cruel trick that was about to be played on her; and, at the request of her affianced husband, sold out her money, and realized it in gold, to be made over to him on the day when the contract was to be signed. The day arrived; and, according to the custom in France, the relations of both parties attended. The widow's relatives, though respectable, were not of the first nobility, being chiefly persons of the finance or the robe: there was the president of the court of Arras, and his lady; a farmer-general; a judge of a court of Paris; and other such grave and respectable people. As for Monsieur le Comte de la Grinche, he was not bound for names; and, having the whole peerage to choose from, brought a host of Montmorencies, Créquis, De la Tours, and Guises at his back. His homme d'affaires brought his papers in a sack, and displayed the plans of his estates, and the titles of his glorious ancestry. The widow's lawyers had her money in sacks; and between the gold on the one side, and the parchments on the other, lay the contract which was to make the widow's three hundred thousand francs the property of the Count de Grinche. The Count de la Grinche was just about to sign; when the Marshal de Villars, stepping up to him, said, "Captain, do you know who the president of the court of Arras, yonder, is? It is old Manasseh, the fence, of Brussels. I pawned a gold watch

这个军衔的。长话短说，在这四天的旅程中，路易斯·多米尼克·德·格瑞克伯爵办事的手段是如此高明，以至于这个可怜的小寡妇几乎都要把自己刚刚去世的丈夫给忘记了，当伯爵亲吻她的手暂时离开时，她的眼睛里闪着泪光，而伯爵只是离开几个小时而已。

无论是白天还是夜晚，伯爵总是跟随着她讨好她。两星期后的一个早晨，在两人单独谈话时，伯爵忽然双膝跪下说："莱奥娜，你爱我吗?"这个可怜的女人发出了世界上最温柔、最甜蜜的声音，红着脸把头靠在他的肩膀上，喃喃地说："噢，多米尼克，我爱你!"她说，"啊！我的多米尼克是多么伟大啊，他是如此富有的一个贵族，却愿意接受一无所有的我!"事实上，老男爵的爵位和财产都转让给了他的侄子，他给这个寡妇只留下三十万里弗尔［古时的法国货币单位及其银币。——译注］，还有政府的一笔可观的年金，但是这些与多米尼克伯爵的地租、格瑞克伯爵的身份相比就不算什么了。他的财富至少让他有资格去追求一位公爵夫人。

不幸的寡妇从未猜想过将会有人在她身上实施残酷的诡计。在这个与她定有婚约的丈夫格瑞克伯爵的请求下，她把她的钱都兑换成了黄金，在他们签婚约的那天就把这些金子转交给他。这天来到了。按照法国的风俗，男女双方的亲人都要参加。寡妇的亲戚虽然都是些令人尊敬的人物，却并不是高等的贵族，主要都是些财政人员或法官。有阿拉斯法院的院长和夫人、一个农场主、巴黎法院的一个法官，还有其他类似这样庄重、令人尊敬的人物。至于格瑞克伯爵，他还没有准备好名字，因此就从贵族名册中选了一些，带了一群叫蒙莫朗西、克里克、德拉图尔的同伙来支持他。他的办事员把他的文件放在硬纸袋里带来了，展示了他的财产计划和荣耀的祖先爵位。寡妇的律师把她的钱放在硬纸袋里。在黄金和羊皮纸之间放着一份契约，契约上把寡妇的三十万法郎变成了格瑞克伯爵的财产。格瑞克伯爵正要签字，这时叫马歇尔·德·维拉的那个家伙走过来说："上校，你知道那边谁是阿拉斯法院的院长吗？那是在布鲁塞尔买卖赃物的老玛拿西。我曾把一只金表当给了他，那是我在佛兰德斯的玛尔白鲁军队时从卡多根

to him, which I stole from Cadogan, when I was with Malbrook's army in Flanders."

Here the Duc de la Roche Guyon came forward, very much alarmed. "Run me through the body!" said his Grace, "but the comptroller-general's lady, there, is no other than that old hag of a Margoton who keeps the —" Here the Duc de la Roche Guyon's voice fell.

Cartouche smiled graciously, and walked up to the table. He took up one of the widow's fifteen thousand gold pieces;—it was as pretty a bit of copper as you could wish to see. "My dear," said he politely, "there is some mistake here, and this business had better stop."

"Count!" gasped the poor widow.

"Count be hanged!" answered the bridegroom, sternly, "my name is CARTOUCHE!"

偷的。”

这时叫德·拉罗克·盖恩公爵的那个家伙也很警觉地走上前来说：“让我走吧！”“那边审计部长的夫人正是那个放荡的老丑妇，她——”德·拉罗克·盖恩公爵的声音变小了。

卡图什亲切地微笑着走到桌子旁。他拿起寡妇十五万金币中的一块——就像一块美丽的铜。“亲爱的，”他彬彬有礼地说道，“这里面有些误解，这笔交易最好终止吧！”

“伯爵！”可怜的寡妇气吁吁地说。

“该死的伯爵！”新郎严肃地回答说，“我的名字是卡图什！”

On Some French Fashionable Novels

With a Plea for Romances in General

THERE is an old story of a Spanish court painter, who, being pressed for money, and having received a piece of damask, which he was to wear in a state procession, pawned the damask, and appeared, at the show, dressed out in some very fine sheets of paper, which he had painted so as exactly to resemble silk. Nay, his coat looked so much richer than the doublets of all the rest, that the Emperor Charles, in whose honour the procession was given, remarked the painter, and so his deceit was found out.

I have often thought that, in respect of sham and real histories, a similar fact may be noticed; the sham story appearing a great deal more agreeable, life-like, and natural than the true one: and all who, from laziness as well as principle, are inclined to follow the easy and comfortable study of novels, may console themselves with the notion that they are studying matters quite as important as history, and that their favourite duodecimos are as instructive as the biggest quartos in the world.

If then, ladies, the big-wigs begin to sneer at the course of our studies, calling our darling romances foolish, trivial, noxious to the mind, enervators of intellect, fathers of idleness, and what not, let us at once take a high ground, and say,—Go you to your own employments, and to such dull studies as you fancy; go and bob for triangles, from the Pons Asinorum; go enjoy your dull black draughts of metaphysics; go fumble over history books, and dissert upon Herodotus and Livy; OUR histories are, perhaps, as true as yours; our drink is the brisk sparkling champagne drink, from the presses of

论法国的几则流行小说

为小说辩护

有这么一个关于西班牙宫廷画家的老故事，这位画家收到参加国家列队行进要穿的一块缎子，因为急需钱用，他就把缎子当掉了。在出场的时候，他身上穿了件用上好的纸张做的衣服，他把纸画得就像真的真丝一样。而且，他的外套看着比其余人所穿的马甲要奢华得多。这次列队行进正是为了向查理国王表示敬意，国王注意到这位画家，他的骗局才被戳穿。

我时常想，就虚构的和真实的历史而言，虽然它们关注的是同样的事实，但虚构的故事要比真实的故事更讨人喜欢、更贴近生活、更自然。无论是懒散的还是有原则的人都愿意从事舒适的小说研究。他们或许是用这样的想法来安慰自己，即他们所研究的事情和历史一样重要，他们所喜爱的十二开本的小说和世界上最大的四开本的历史著作一样对人都很有教益。

然而，一些太太、名人开始嘲笑我们所研究的这个行业，认为我们所钟爱的小说是愚蠢的、琐屑的、使人道德败坏的、智力衰弱的表现，只会让人无所事事，等等。让我们理直气壮地对他们说——做你们自己的事，做你们那种沉闷的研究去吧！从“驴桥”定理［此命题曾被称为“愚人的桥”，因为这个命题的图形很像一座简单的支架桥，它深到了新手们难以越过的程度。——译注］开始去研究你的三角形吧！书写你那沉闷枯燥的玄学草稿吧！在历史书中摸索，论述希罗多德［古代希腊历史学家。——译注］和李维［Livy，罗马史学家。——译注］吧！其实我们所做的事情和

Colburn, Bentley and Co. ; our walks are over such sunshiny pleasure-grounds as Scott and Shakespeare have laid out for us; and if our dwellings are castles in the air, we find them excessively splendid and commodious;—be not you envious because you have no wings to fly thither. Let the big-wigs despise us; such contempt of their neighbours is the custom of all barbarous tribes;—witness, the learned Chinese: Tippoo Sultaun declared that there were not in all Europe ten thousand men: the Sclavonic hordes, it is said, so entitled themselves from a word in their jargon, which signifies "to speak;" the ruffians imagining that they had a monopoly of this agreeable faculty, and that all other nations were dumb.

Not so: others may be DEAF; but the novelist has a loud, eloquent, instructive language, though his enemies may despise or deny it ever so much. What is more, one could, perhaps, meet the stoutest historian on his own ground, and argue with him; showing that sham histories were much truer than real histories; which are, in fact, mere contemptible catalogues of names and places, that can have no moral effect upon the reader.

As thus:—

Julius Caesar beat Pompey, at Pharsalia.
The Duke of Marlborough beat Marshal Tallard at Blenheim.
The Constable of Bourbon beat Francis the First, at Pavia.

And what have we here? —so many names, simply. Suppose Pharsalia had been, at that mysterious period when names were given, called Pavia; and that Julius Caesar's family name had been John Churchill;—the fact would have stood in history, thus:—

"Pompey ran away from the Duke of Marlborough at Pavia."

And why not? —we should have been just as wise. Or it might be stated that—

你们一样真实；我们饮用的是科尔波恩、本特利等公司酿造的起泡香槟酒；我们在司各特和莎士比亚所展示给我们的阳光普照的大地上散步；即使我们所居住的是空中楼阁，它也是极为明亮宽敞的。——如果你们不羡慕，那是因为你们没有翅膀可以飞到这里来。让那些大人物轻视我们吧！像这样轻视他们邻人的表现是所有野蛮部落的习惯。他们根本就体会不到小说的独特魅力，例如博学的中国人、声称整个欧洲没有一万个男人的提普·苏丹（18世纪印度南部国家的统治者，多次抵抗英国殖民者），还有斯拉夫游牧民族：据说他们从方言中抽出一个词语来尊称自己，这个词语的意思是“说话”，他们设想自己具有这种令人满意的才能，而其他所有的民族都是聋哑的。

小说家有着洪亮、雄辩、启发性的语言，虽然有些人不听，虽然它的敌对方会非常轻视和否认这种语言。而且，它还可能会在自己熟悉的领域内遭到顽固的历史学家的异议。它在与历史学的争议中显示出其虚构的历史要比真正的历史更真实，历史实际上仅仅是些无足轻重的名字和地点的目录，对读者没有什么精神上的影响。

例如：

> 尤利乌斯·恺撒在法撒利亚打败了庞培。
>
> 马尔波罗公爵在布伦海姆打败了马歇尔·塔拉尔。
>
> 波旁王朝的总管在帕维亚［意大利的地名。——译注］打败了第一方济会。

我们从这里得到了什么？——只是许多名字而已。假如法撒利亚在那个神秘的时代被叫做帕维亚，尤利乌斯·恺撒家族的名字是约翰·邱吉尔，历史事实就会变成这样了：

> 庞培在帕维亚从约翰·邱吉尔那里逃走了。”

"The tenth legion charged the French infantry at Blenheim; and Caesar, writing home to his mamma, said, 'Madame, tout est perdu fors l'honneur.'"

What a contemptible science this is, then, about which quartos are written, and sixty-volumed Biographies Universelles, and Lardner's Cabinet Cyclopaedias, and the like! the facts are nothing in it, the names everything and a gentleman might as well improve his mind by learning Walker's "*Gazetteer*," or getting by heart a fifty-years-old edition of the "*Court Guide*."

Having thus disposed of the historians, let us come to the point in question—the novelists.

On the title-page of these volumes the reader has, doubtless, remarked, that among the pieces introduced, some are announced as "copies" and "compositions." Many of the histories have, accordingly, been neatly stolen from the collections of French authors (and mutilated, according to the old saying, so that their owners should not know them) and, for compositions, we intend to favour the public with some studies of French modern works, that have not as yet, we believe, attracted the notice of the English public.

Of such works there appear many hundreds yearly, as may be seen by the French catalogues; but the writer has not so much to do with works political, philosophical, historical, metaphysical, scientifical, theological, as with those for which he has been putting forward a plea—novels, namely; on which he has expended a great deal of time and study. And passing from novels in general to French novels, let us confess, with much humiliation, that we borrow from these stories a great deal more knowledge of French society than from our own personal observation we ever can hope to gain: for, let a gentleman who has dwelt two, four, or ten years in Paris (and has not gone thither for the purpose of making a book, when three weeks are sufficient)—let an English gentleman say, at the end of any given period, how much he knows of French society, how many French houses he has entered, and how many French friends he has made? —He has enjoyed, at the end of the year, say—

为什么不能是这样呢？——聪明的人们会明白的。它还可以被叙述为：

第十军团在布伦海姆袭击了法国步兵团。恺撒给家里的妈妈写信说：夫人，除了荣誉外，一切都完了。”

这是一个多么无足轻重的学科啊！仅围绕着这些事情历史学家就写了四开本六十卷的通用传记，还有拉德纳的袖珍百科词典等诸如此类的东西！其实，它里面的事实一点儿也没有意义。想要记住每个事物的名字还不如学习沃克的《地名辞典》，或者把五十年前旧版本的《士绅录》烂熟于心。

抛开历史学家，让我们回到问题的重心上来——小说家。

读者无疑已注意到，在这本书的扉页上所列的内容条目中，有一些是“仿作”，有一些是“作品”。有许多故事是从法国作者的作品中所借鉴来的（把它们删改得支离破碎，按老话说就是不让它们原来的作者识别出来）。至于作品，我们是想提供给读者一些关于法国现代作品的看法，我们认为，这些作品还没有得到英国民众的注意。

这类作品已出现几百年了，从法国的目录册中可以看到它们。但是作者的这本书和政治、哲学、历史、玄学、科学、神学作品没有太大的关系，由于他在小说方面花费了很多时间去研究，因此他在这里主要是为小说而辩。不管是一般的小说还是法国小说，我们都要谦逊地承认，我们更多地是从小说中来了解法国社会，而不是通过自己个人的观察去得到你想要的东西。让一个在巴黎已居住了两年、四年或十年的英国先生（如果他不是为了写书而去那里，三个星期就足够了）在限定的日期内说一说，他对法国社会都了解多少，他进入过多少法国人的家庭，他结交了多少法国朋友，他就会说：

在英国的大使馆里有那么多的晚会。

在他取信的房子里有那么多的茶会。

At the English Ambassador's, so many soirées.

At houses to which he has brought letters, so many tea-parties.

At Cafés, so many dinners.

At French private houses, say three dinners, and very lucky too.

He has, we say, seen an immense number of wax candles, cups of tea, glasses of orgeat, and French people, in best clothes, enjoying the same; but intimacy there is none; we see but the outsides of the people. Year by year we live in France, and grow gray, and see no more. We play écarté with Monsieur de Trêfle every night; but what know we of the heart of the man—of the inward ways, thoughts, and customs of Trêfle? If we have good legs, and love the amusement, we dance with Countess Flicflac, Tuesdays and Thursdays, ever since the Peace; and how far are we advanced in acquaintance with her since we first twirled her round a room? We know her velvet gown, and her diamonds (about three-fourths of them are sham, by the way); we know her smiles, and her simpers, and her rouge—but no more: she may turn into a kitchen wench at twelve on Thursday night, for aught we know; her voiture, a pumpkin; and her gens, so many rats: but the real, rougeless, intime Flicflac, we know not. This privilege is granted to no Englishman: we may understand the French language as well as Monsieur de Levizac, but never can penetrate into Flicflac's confidence: our ways are not her ways; our manners of thinking, not hers: when we say a good thing, in the course of the night, we are wondrous lucky and pleased; Flicflac will trill you off fifty in ten minutes, and wonder at the bêtise of the Briton, who has never a word to say. We are married, and have fourteen children, and would just as soon make love to the Pope of Rome as to any one but our own wife. If you do not make love to Flicflac, from the day after her marriage to the day she reaches sixty, she thinks you a fool. We won't play at écarté with Trêfle on Sunday nights; and are seen walking, about one o'clock (accompanied by fourteen red-haired children, with fourteen gleaming prayer-books), away from the church. "Grand Dieu!" cries Trêfle, "is that man mad? He won't play at cards on a Sunday;

在咖啡馆里有那么多的晚餐。

在法国人的私人家庭里，有三次正餐，很不错。

我们说，他看到了许多蜡烛、茶杯、装有甜饮料的玻璃杯和穿着漂亮衣服享受这一切的法国人。但是我们并不了解他们，我们看到的只是人们的外表。一年又一年，我们住在法国，即使变老了，也没有看到更多的东西。我们每晚都和泰福勒先生打牌，但我们对于这个人的内心——他内心的状况、想法和他的生活习惯了解多少呢？如果我们腿脚灵便、喜欢娱乐，在周二和周三就和弗利克弗来克伯爵夫人跳舞。从我们和她在房间里第一次旋转开始到现在，我们对她熟悉了多少呢？我们知道她的天鹅绒睡衣、她的钻石（顺便说一句，其中四分之三是假的），我们知道她的微笑、她的假笑、她的胭脂——但是再也没有别的了。她在星期四晚上的十二点钟可能会变成一个厨房的女佣也未可知；她的轻便马车或许只是一个南瓜；她的氏族里其实有许多可耻的人。对于真实、不涂胭脂、内在的弗利克弗来克，我们却并不了解。英国人没有被上帝赋予这种特权。我们或许会像勒维扎克先生一样了解法语，但却从来也不能看透弗利克弗来克的内心。我们的行为与她不同，我们思考的方式也和她不同。当我们在晚上说起一件有意思的事情时，我们会异常得健谈和愉快，弗利克弗来克则会对我们这些不善言谈的不列颠人的这种不合时宜的言行感到惊讶。我们结婚了，有了十四个孩子，除妻子之外，我们会向罗马教皇及其他的人表示我们的喜爱。而在法国，如果从弗利克弗来克婚后那天起直到她六十岁，你没有向她表示爱意的话，她会以为你是个傻子。我们周日晚上就不和泰福勒打牌了，而泰福勒先生常看到我们一点钟从教堂里出来（在一起的还有十四个红头发的孩子带着十四本祈祷书）。泰福勒叫道："上帝啊！那个人疯了吗？他星期日不打牌，却去教堂，他有十四个孩子！"

同样，法国人对英国人的了解呢？让我们回到讨论的话题上来，由于我们英国人的观念、道德和气质与法国人有很大的不同，所以我们很难和

he goes to church on a Sunday: he has fourteen children!"

Was ever Frenchman known to do likewise? Pass we on to our argument, which is, that with our English notions and moral and physical constitution, it is quite impossible that we should become intimate with our brisk neighbours; and when such authors as Lady Morgan and Mrs. Trollope, having frequented a certain number of tea-parties in the French capital, begin to prattle about French manners and men,—with all respect for the talents of those ladies, we do believe their information not to be worth a sixpence; they speak to us not of men but of tea-parties. Tea-parties are the same all the world over; with the exception that, with the French, there are more lights and prettier dresses; and with us, a mighty deal more tea in the pot.

There is, however, a cheap and delightful way of travelling, that a man may perform in his easy-chair, without expense of passports or postboys. On the wings of a novel, from the next circulating library, he sends his imagination a-gadding, and gains acquaintance with people and manners whom he could not hope otherwise to know. Twopence a volume bears us whithersoever we will;—back to Ivanhoe and Coeur de Lion, or to Waverley and the Young Pretender, along with Walter Scott; up to the heights of fashion with the charming enchanters of the silver-fork school; or, better still, to the snug inn-parlor, or the jovial tap-room, with Mr. Pickwick and his faithful Sancho Weller. I am sure that a man who, a hundred years hence should sit down to write the history of our time, would do wrong to put that great contemporary history of "Pickwick" aside as a frivolous work. It contains true character under false names; and, like "*Roderick Random*," an inferior work, and "*Tom Jones*" (one that is immeasurably superior), gives us a better idea of the state and ways of the people than one could gather from any more pompous or authentic histories.

We have, therefore, introduced into these volumes one or two short reviews of French fiction writers, of particular classes, whose Paris sketches may give the reader some notion of manners in that capital. If not original, at least the drawings are accurate; for, as a Frenchman might have lived a thou-

自己的邻人形成亲密的关系。像摩根女士和特罗普夫人这样的作者，她们经常光顾巴黎的许多茶会，对法国人和法国的生活方式夸夸其谈——虽然我们对这些女士的才能表示敬意，但我们认为她们所提供的信息没有什么价值。她们讲给我们听的不是人而是茶会。全世界的茶会都是一样的，只不过法国人的衣服要更华丽、漂亮些，我们的茶锅里会有更多的茶而已。

然而，这里有个廉价、快乐的旅行方法。一个人可以不用在护照和驿车上有所开销，只要坐在他的安乐椅上就能完成。从隔壁开放的图书馆里借来一本小说，乘着小说的翅膀，展开想象力去认识和了解他在现实生活中不可能知道的其他人以及他们的生活方式。两便士的一册书就会把我们带到想要去的任何一个地方。——与瓦尔特·司各特一起回到艾凡赫和国王狮心理查、威弗莱［《威弗莱》，1814 年出版，司各特的小说。——译注］和詹姆士二世孙子的时代；和银叉派（从 1825 年至 1850 年在英国出现的描写上层阶级婚姻和时髦生活的最流行的小说——译注）使用魔法的巫士们升到上流社会的顶峰；或者，更好的是在隐匿的旅馆休息室或愉快的酒吧间和匹克威克先生，以及他忠实的仆人山姆·维勒［《匹克威克外传》中的人物。——译注］在一起。我确信一百年之后也会有人坐下来写我们这个时代的故事，会错误地把那部伟大的叙述匹克威克同时期历史的书当做无意义的书扔在一边。在这些作品中，虚构的人物所反映的都是真实的人物性格。劣等的小说《蓝登传》［18 世纪英国斯摩莱特的作品。——译注］和不可多得的上乘之作《汤姆·琼斯》［18 世纪英国小说家菲尔丁的代表作。——译注］都很好地展示了英国人的生活状况和社会风俗，那是我们从浮夸或真正的历史著作中所得不到的。

因此，在这本书中我们就介绍一两篇关于法国小说家和特定人物阶层的短评，对于巴黎的生活风俗，这本书或许能给读者提供一些见解。如果不是原汁原味，至少它的描述是精确的。作为一个法国人，即使是在英国生活了一千年，也写不出《匹克威克》这样的作品，因此一个英国人也不要指望能够对法国人的内心想法和状况做出很好的描绘。

sand years in England, and never could have written "*Pickwick*," an Englishman cannot hope to give a good description of the inward thoughts and ways of his neighbours.

To a person inclined to study these, in that light and amusing fashion in which the novelist treats them, let us recommend the works of a new writer, Monsieur de Bernard, who has painted actual manners, without those monstrous and terrible exaggerations in which late French writers have indulged; and who, if he occasionally wounds the English sense of propriety (as what French man or woman alive will not?) does so more by slighting than by outraging it, as, with their laboured descriptions of all sorts of imaginable wickedness, some of his brethren of the press have done. M. de Bernard's characters are men and women of genteel society—rascals enough, but living in no state of convulsive crimes; and we follow him in his lively, malicious account of their manners, without risk of lighting upon any such horrors as Balzac or Dumas has provided for us.

Let us give an instance:—it is from the amusing novel called "*Les Ailes d'Icare*," and contains what is to us quite a new picture of a French fashionable rogue. The fashions will change in a few years, and the rogue, of course, with them. Let us catch this delightful fellow ere he flies. It is impossible to sketch the character in a more sparkling, gentlemanlike way than M. de Bernard's; but such light things are very difficult of translation, and the sparkle sadly evaporates during the process of DECANTING.

A French Fashionable Letter

"MY DEAR VICTOR—it is six in the morning: I have just come from the English Ambassador's ball, and as my plans, for the day do not admit of my sleeping, I write you a line; for, at this moment, saturated as I am with the enchantments of a fairy night, all other pleasures would be too wearisome to keep me awake, except that of conversing with you. Indeed, were I not to write to you now, when should I find the possibility of doing so? Time flies here with such a frightful rapidity, my pleasures and my affairs whirl onwards together in such a torrentuous galopade, that I am compelled to seize occasion by the fore-

我们要给那些喜欢研究轻松滑稽小说的人推荐一位新作家的作品，这位作家就是德·贝尔纳（De Bernard）先生，他在作品中描绘了现实社会的生活风俗，没有那种当今法国作家们所热衷的荒谬、可怕的夸张手法。虽然他有时伤害了英国人的体面（现实生活中的法国男人和女人不也会这样做吗），但更多的是出于一种怠慢的态度，而不是羞辱，就如许多作家会对各种想象中的恶行做矫揉造作的描写一样。德·贝尔纳先生笔下的人物都是些上流社会的男男女女——他们也足够卑鄙的了，却没有什么让人震惊的犯罪行为。对于这些人物的生活方式，他是用活泼、讽刺的笔调来进行描述的，而不像巴尔扎克或大仲马的作品那样会给读者带来惊骇的感觉。

让我们举个例子，那就是《伊卡洛斯的翅膀》[Icare，希腊神话中的建筑师代达罗斯的儿子，父亲给他用蜡与羽毛制成双翼，借以逃遁；但伊卡洛斯因飞近太阳，蜡遇热融化，翼羽纷纷脱落，便堕海而死。——译注]这本有趣的小说。对于法国时髦的无赖，它给我们提供了一张很新颖的画像。流行几年一变，当然无赖也要随之发生变化。就让我们抓住这个愉快的飞行同伴吧！在人物速写上不会有人比德·贝尔纳先生写得更活泼、更文雅的了。但是这种轻松的风格也很难翻译，因为语言的魅力往往在翻译的过程中很遗憾地被折损掉了。

一封时髦的法国信件

我亲爱的维克多——现在是早晨六点。我刚从英国大使馆的舞会上回来。按照我的计划，今天没有睡觉的时间了，我就给你写封短信。因为这会儿我心里还在迷恋着那个优雅的夜晚，除了跟你谈话之外，其他的欢乐都让我感到厌烦。事实上，如果我现在不给你写信，那什么时候才能找到时间来做这件事呢？在这里光阴似箭，我的快乐和事情也飞速地向前旋转着，我不得不抓住时机，因为每一刻都有要紧的事情要做。不要指责我的疏忽。如果我的通信不是那么的有规律，我很乐意把这个过失归咎于我所生活于其中的社会风气，是它随着自己

lock; for each moment has its imperious employ. Do not then accuse me of negligence: if my correspondence has not always that regularity which I would fain give it, attribute the fault solely to the whirlwind in which I live, and which carries me hither and thither at its will.

"However, you are not the only person with whom I am behindhand: I assure you, on the contrary, that you are one of a very numerous and fashionable company, to whom, towards the discharge of my debts, I propose to consecrate four hours today. I give you the preference to all the world, even to the lovely Duchess of San Severino, a delicious Italian, whom, for my special happiness, I met last summer at the Waters of Aix. I have also a most important negotiation to conclude with one of our Princes of Finance: but n'importe, I commence with thee: friendship before love or money—friendship before everything. My dispatches concluded, I am engaged to ride with the Marquis de Grigneure, the Comte de Castijars, and Lord Cobham, in order that we may recover, for a breakfast at the Rocher de Cancale that Grigneure has lost, the appetite which we all of us so cruelly abused last night at the Ambassador's gala. On my honour, my dear fellow, everybody was of a caprice prestigieux and a comfortable mirobolant. Fancy, for a banquet-hall, a royal orangery hung with white damask; the boxes of the shrubs transformed into so many sideboards; lights gleaming through the foliage; and, for guests, the loveliest women and most brilliant cavaliers of Paris. Orleans and Nemours were there, dancing and eating like simple mortals. In a word, Albion did the thing very handsomely, and I accord it my esteem.

"Here I pause, to call for my valet-de-chambre, and call for tea; for my head is heavy, and I've no time for a headache. In serving me, this rascal of a Frédéric has broken a cup, true Japan, upon my honour—the rogue does nothing else. Yesterday, for instance, did he not hump me prodigiously, by letting fall a goblet, after Cellini, of which the carving alone cost me three hundred francs? I must positively put the wretch out of doors, to ensure the safety of my furniture; and in consequence of this, Eneas, an audacious young negro, in whom wisdom hath not waited for years—Eneas, mygroom, I say, will probably be elevated to the post of valet-de-chambre. But where was I? I think I was speaking to you of an oyster breakfast, to which, on our return from the Park

的意愿把我带往各处的。

然而，你并不是我唯一推迟回信的人。我向你保证，相反，你是我为数众多的时髦朋友中的一个，关于清偿我债务的问题，我今天要和你谈四个小时。对所有的人，我都会给你个优先选择的机会，甚至包括可爱的桑·塞维里诺公爵夫人，她是一个美妙的意大利女人，是我去年夏天在爱克斯湖畔幸运碰到的。今天我还和一位财政部长有项重要的谈判。但是这并不重要，我要先给你写信。友谊先于爱情和金钱——友谊先于一切。写完信之后，我还和德·格涅尔侯爵、德·卡斯蒂雅尔伯爵、哥伯汉姆勋爵约好了去骑马，以使我们的身体能恢复过来，因为格涅尔没吃早餐，昨晚在英国大使的盛会上我们也没吃好。我亲爱的朋友，以我的名誉担保，每个人都有反复无常令人难以置信的一面和令人舒适的一面。为了昨晚的那场宴会，一个皇家柑橘园内挂上了白色的缎子；果汁甜酒的盒子变成了许多餐具柜；灯光从叶子的缝隙中洒落下来；客人们都是巴黎最可爱的女人和最卓越的骑士。奥尔良公爵和内穆尔公爵也在那里，他们就像凡人那样跳舞和吃东西。总而言之，阿尔比恩把宴会办得非常好，我向他们表示我的尊重。

写到这里我要停住了，好叫我的男仆端杯茶来，因为我的头很沉，但是我根本就没时间头痛。这个叫费列德里克的小坏蛋在服侍我期间已打破了一个茶杯，以我的名誉保证，那可是一件真正的日本货——这个小坏蛋什么事情也不做。例如，昨天他不是在打碎了切利尼[Cellini（1500—1571），意大利16世纪后半期雕塑家、美术评论家，样式主义雕塑的代表人物。——译注]的那件花了我三百法郎买来的雕刻品之后，又打碎了一个酒杯吗？我一定要把这个小坏蛋扔出门外，以确保我家具的安全。因此，我的马夫埃内亚斯，一个大胆的年轻黑人，凭他的智能用不了几年或许就会提升为贴身男仆。但是我说到哪儿了？我想我正和你说到吃早餐。从公园回来后，我们邀请了一群讨人喜欢的小混混吃了些牡蛎。然后我们去了赌赛场地，哥伯汉姆勋爵

(du Bois), a company of pleasant rakes are invited. After quitting Borel's, we propose to adjourn to the Barrière du Combat, where Lord Cobham proposes to try some bulldogs, which he has brought over from England—one of these, O'Connell (Lord Cobham is a Tory,) has a face in which I place much confidence; I have a bet of ten louis with Castijars on the strength of it. After the fight, we shall make our accustomed appearance at the 'Café de Paris,' (the only place, by the way, where a man who respects himself may be seen,)— and then away with frocks and spurs, and on with our dress-coats for the rest of the evening. In the first place, I shall go doze for a couple of hours at the Opera, where my presence is indispensable; for Coralie, a charming creature, passes this evening from the rank of the RATS to that of the TIGERS, in a pas-de-trois, and our box patronizes her. After the Opera, I must show my face at two or three salons in the Faubourg St. Honouré; and having thus performed my duties to the world of fashion, I return to the exercise of my rights as a member of the Carnival. At two o'clock all the world meets at the ThéâtreVentadour: lions and tigers—the whole of our menagerie will be present. Evoé! off we go! roaring and bounding Bacchanal and Saturnal; 'tis agreed that we shall be everything that is low. To conclude, we sup with Castijars, the most 'furiously dishevelled' orgy that ever was known."

The rest of the letter is on matters of finance, equally curious and instructive. But pause we for the present, to consider the fashionable part: and caricature as it is, we have an accurate picture of the actual French dandy. Bets, breakfasts, riding, dinners at the "Café de Paris," and delirious Carnival balls: the animal goes through all such frantic pleasures at the season that precedes Lent. He has a wondrous respect for English "gentlemen-sportsmen;" he imitates their clubs—their love of horse-flesh: he calls his palefrenier a groom, wears blue birds's-eye neck-cloths, sports his pink out hunting, rides steeple-chases, and has his Jockey Club. The "tigers and lions" alluded to in the report have been borrowed from our own country, and a great compliment is it to Monsieur de Bernard, the writer of the above amusing sketch, that he has such a knowledge of English names and things, as to give a Tory

在那里建议我们试试他从英国带来的斗牛犬，以它们的争斗结果来打赌，其中一只叫欧康奈尔，它看起来还较有把握能赢，我就以十个金路易和德·卡斯蒂雅尔伯爵打赌它有力量获胜。这场战斗结束后，我们按照惯例又出现在巴黎咖啡馆（顺便说一句，这是唯一能看到男人自重的地方）——扔下罩袍和马刺，穿上外套去消磨晚上剩余的时间。首先，我要在歌剧院瞌睡上两个小时，在那里我的出现是不可缺少的。为了卡罗琳这个迷人的姑娘不受下流人物和上流人物的干扰，我们的包厢就是为了保护她而设的。离开歌剧院，我必须还要出席在圣奥雷诺区法布街的两三个沙龙。我这样对上流社会履行完自己的义务之后，就作为狂欢节的成员又回到正常训练中去。在两点钟，所有的人都在旺达多瓦剧院集合。好！让我们去吧！嚎叫、蹦跳着纵情狂乐，我们就是那么低俗。结束后，我们和卡斯蒂雅尔吃了些东西，这是我所知道的最喧闹混乱的狂欢。

信的其余部分是关于财政方面的事情，既荒谬又有所教益。但我们在这里暂停一下，考虑考虑以上这一部分内容。虽然作者用的是漫画式的表现手法，但真实生活中的法国花花公子还是给我们留下了一个明确的印象。打赌、早餐、骑马、巴黎咖啡馆的晚餐、发狂的狂欢节盛会。在四旬斋前的季节，这些人都要尽情地欢乐。作者对英国的“运动绅士”非常了解，他模仿他们的俱乐部——他们对马的喜爱。他用英国马夫的名字来称呼他的法国马夫，他戴着蓝色鸟眼花纹的领饰，穿着红色上衣出去打猎，骑着越野赛马，有他的赛马总会。德·贝尔纳先生报告中所提及的“老虎和狮子”借鉴自我们英国。对德·贝尔纳先生我们要好好地称赞一番，因为他对英国的姓名和事物是如此的熟悉，比如给保守党贵族一个体面的名称哥伯汉姆，把他的狗叫做欧康奈尔。保罗·德·柯克［Paul de Kock（1793—1871），法国作家。——译注］在他最近的一本小说中把一个英国贵族叫做布兰格罗格贵族，看到这些貌似真实的名称很让人高兴。

Lord the decent title of Lord Cobham, and to call his dog O'Connell. Paul de Kock calls an English nobleman, in one of his last novels, Lord Boulingrog, and appears vastly delighted at the verisimilitude of the title.

For the "rugissements et bondissements, bacchanale et saturnale, galop infernal, ronde du sabbat tout le tremblement," these words give a most clear, untranslatable idea of the Carnival ball. A sight more hideous can hardly strike a man's eye. I was present at one where the four thousand guests whirled screaming, reeling, roaring, out of the ball-room in the Rue St. Honoré, and tore down to the column in the Place Vendôme, round which they went shrieking their own music, twenty miles an hour, and so tore madly back again. Let a man go alone to such a place of amusement, and the sight for him is perfectly terrible: the horrid frantic gayety of the place puts him in mind more of the merriment of demons than of men: bang, bang, drums, trumpets, chairs, pistol-shots, pour out of the orchestra, which seems as mad as the dancers; whiz, a whirlwind of paint and patches, all the costumes under the sun, all the ranks in the empire, all the he and she scoundrels of the capital, writhed and twisted together, rush by you; if a man falls, woe be to him: two thousand screaming menads go trampling over his carcass: they have neither power nor will to stop.

A set of Malays drunk with bhang and running amuck, a company of howling dervishes, may possibly, at our own day, go through similar frantic vagaries; but I doubt if any civilized European people but the French would permit and enjoy such scenes. Yet our neighbours see little shame in them; and it is very true that men of all classes, high and low, here congregate and give themselves up to the disgusting worship of the genius of the place. — From the dandy of the Boulevard and the "Café Anglais," let us turn to the dandy of "Flicoteau's" and the Pays Latin—the Paris student, whose exploits among the grisettes are so celebrated, and whose fierce republicanism keeps gendarmes for ever on the alert. The following is M. de Bernard's description of him:—

至于“咆哮和蹦跳，狂欢作乐和纵情欢乐，该死的快步舞，安息日的轮舞曲诸如此类的”，这些描述狂欢节盛会的词汇给我们留下了清晰而不可言传的印象。人们几乎看不到比那样的场景更可怕的了。我曾亲眼看到，四千宾客尖叫着、嚎叫着离开了圣奥诺雷街的舞厅来到旺多姆广场上，他们绕着广场上的柱子开始尖叫着唱起自己的音乐，然后又以一小时二十英里的速度发疯般地往回狂奔。如果一个男人独自去这样的娱乐场地，这种情景对他来说是太可怕了。这种可怕的狂欢给他的印象更像是恶魔的作乐而不是人类所为。砰砰的撞击声、咚咚的鼓声、嘀嘀的喇叭声、椅子摔倒的声音、手枪射击的声音还有管弦乐队发出的声音都像跳舞的人一样疯狂了；子弹等在空中掠过的声音、刮起涂料和碎片的一阵旋风、太阳照射下的所有服装、帝国所有阶层的人物、巴黎的所有恶棍都在一起缠绕扭曲、互相推挤。如果一个人摔倒，那他就惨了，因为两千个尖叫暴怒的女人就会从他的躯体上践踏着走过去，她们既停不下来也不想停下来。

或许东方的马来人［东南亚的一个民族。——译注］也会吸着印度大麻疯狂奔跑，伊斯兰教徒也会这样嚎叫而疯狂。但我怀疑在欧洲除了法国人之外还会有哪些文明国度会允许和欣赏这样的场面存在。可是我们的邻人对此没有一点羞愧感。各个阶层的人，不管是高的还是低的，都在这儿集合，沉浸于狂欢之中。——让我们从林荫道和咖啡馆的花花公子转到拉丁区的纨绔子弟——巴黎的学生，在青年劳动妇女中他的英勇行为是很有名的，他是个狂热的共和主义者，这点让宪兵们对他始终保持着警惕。接下来就是德·贝尔纳先生对他的描述：

> 当我们是法学院学生的时候，我认识了丹姆布吉阿克。我们在先贤祠那个地方住同一家旅馆。女士们偶尔会遇到那些信奉圣母的小男孩，他们从头到脚都穿着白色的衣饰。我的朋友丹姆布吉阿克却接受了一次与众不同的献祭仪式。他父亲是大革命中一位伟大的爱国者，认定他的儿子也应该是共和主义的坚定拥护者，因此，让教母和代理

"I became acquainted with Dambergeac when we were students at the Ecole de Droit; we lived in the same hotel on the Place du Panthéon. No doubt, madam, you have occasionally met little children dedicated to the Virgin, and, to this end, clothed in white raiment from head to foot: my friend, Dambergeac, had received a different consecration. His father, a great patriot of the Revolution, had determined that his son should bear into the world a sign of indelible republicanism; so, to the great displeasure of his godmother and the parish curate, Dambergeac was christened by the pagan name of Harmodius. It was a kind of moral tricolour-cockade, which the child was to bear through the vicissitudes of all the revolutions to come. Under such influences, my friend's character began to develop itself, and, fired by the example of his father, and by the warm atmosphere of his native place, Marseilles, he grew up to have an independent spirit, and a grand liberality of politics, which were at their height when first I made his acquaintance.

"He was then a young man of eighteen, with a tall, slim figure, a broad chest, and a flaming black eye, out of all which personal charms he knew how to draw the most advantage; and though his costume was such as Staub might probably have criticised, he had, nevertheless, a style peculiar to himself—to himself and the students, among whom he was the leader of the fashion. A tight black coat, buttoned up to the chin, across the chest, set off that part of his person; a low-crowned hat, with a voluminous rim, cast solemn shadows over a countenance bronzed by a southern sun: he wore, at one time, enormous flowing black locks, which he sacrificed pitilessly, however, and adopted a Brutus, as being more revolutionary: finally, he carried an enormous club, that was his code and digest: in like manner, De Retz used to carry a stiletto in his pocket by way of a breviary.

"Although of different ways of thinking in politics, certain sympathies of character and conduct united Dambergeac and myself, and we speedily became close friends. I don't think, in the whole course of his three years' residence, Dambergeac ever went through a single course of lectures. For the examinations, he trusted to luck, and to his own facility, which was prodigious: as for honours, he never aimed at them, but was content to do exactly as little as was necessary for him to gain his degree. In like manner he sedulously avoided those

牧师不高兴的就是，丹姆布吉阿克洗礼时用哈马笛斯［Harmodius，是公元前6世纪的雅典人，曾杀死暴君伊巴尔克。——译注］这个异教徒的名字来命名。三色帽章［法国大革命时期革命军所戴的帽章。——译注］对于孩子来说是一种很好的道德激励，让他承受了所有即将到来的革命。就这样，我朋友的个性发展了起来，在他父亲榜样的激发下，在家乡马赛这种温和的气氛下，他成长为一个具有独立气概、政治上主张公正的人物。当我刚认识他的时候，这些特点正被他发挥到极致。

他很快就成长为一个十八岁的年轻男子。细高个，宽阔的胸膛，一双黑色的热情的眼睛，除此之外，他还知道如何去最大限度地施展自己的魅力。虽然他的骑士服装可能会招来异议，但他却有自己独特的风格——在学生当中，他是个领先的时髦人物。一件紧身的黑色外套，扣子沿着胸膛一直系到下巴那里，衬托出体形；一顶低帽顶的帽子，宽大的帽檐给他那被南方太阳照射过的青铜色的脸上投下了严肃的阴影。有一段时间，他把黑色的头发梳成蓬松平滑的发型，但很可惜的是，不久他又换成了布鲁图的发型，因为这种发型显得更革命。后来，他还随身携带着一根很大的棍棒，那是他的代号和象征，就像德·雷茨［法兰西元帅。——译注］过去也经常在他口袋里带一把匕首作为标志一样。

虽然在政治上我们的想法不同，但是某些性格和行为上的共同点还是把丹姆布吉阿克和我连到了一起，我们很快就成了亲密的朋友。我认为，在整个三年住校期间，丹姆布吉阿克没有通过任何一门课程的考试。对于考试，他相信运气，像他这样灵巧的人能有这种想法是很奇怪的。他追求的目标不是荣誉，只要付出最少的努力能获得学位，他就很满足了。他小心地避开讨厌的图书馆，在那里每天都聚集着我们学校的读书人。他是整个拉丁区服装店的常客，因此在穿着服饰方面，他完全是个时髦人物。据说他的英勇豪侠行为也不仅局限于塞纳

horrible circulating libraries, where daily are seen to congregate the 'reading men' of our schools. But, in revenge, there was not a milliner's shop, or a lingère's, in all our quartier Latin, which he did not industriously frequent, and of which he was not the oracle. Nay, it was said that his victories were not confined to the left bank of the Seine; reports did occasionally come to us of fabulous adventures by him accomplished in the far regions of the Rue de la Paix and the Boulevard Poissonnière. Such recitals were, for us less favoured mortals, like tales of Bacchus conquering in the East; they excited our ambition, but not our jealousy; for the superiority of Harmodius was acknowledged by us all, and we never thought of a rivalry with him. No man ever cantered a hack through the Champs Elysées with such elegant assurance; no man ever made such a massacre of dolls at the shooting-gallery; or won you a rubber at billiards with more easy grace; or thundered out a couplet of Béranger with such a roaring melodious bass. He was the monarch of the Prado in winter: in summer of the Chaumière and Mont Parnasse. Not a frequenter of those fashionable places of entertainment showed a more amiable laisser-aller in the dance—that peculiar dance at which gendarmes think proper to blush, and which squeamish society has banished from her salons. In a word, Harmodius was the prince of mauvais sujets, a youth with all the accomplishments of Göttingen and Jena, and all the eminent graces of his own country.

"Besides dissipation and gallantry, our friend had one other vast and absorbing occupation—politics, namely; in which he was as turbulent and enthusiastic as in pleasure. La Patrie was his idol, his heaven, his nightmare; by day he spouted, by night he dreamed, of his country. I have spoken to you of his coiffure à la Sylla; need I mention his pipe, his meerschaum pipe, of which General Foy's head was the bowl; his handkerchief with the Charte printed thereon; and his celebrated tricolour braces, which kept the rallying sign of his country ever close to his heart? Besides these outward and visible signs of sedition, he had inward and secret plans of revolution: he belonged to clubs, frequented associations, read the Constitutionnel (Liberals, in those days, swore by the Constitutionnel), harangued peers and deputies who had deserved well of their country; and if death happened to fall on such, and the Constitutionnel declared their merit, Harmodius was the very first to attend their obsequies, or

河的北岸，有时我们听到的消息是说他在很远的德拉派街和保梭尼亚大道地区的惊人冒险行为。对我们这些不太喜欢凡人的人来说，这样的叙述就像酒神巴克斯征服东方的故事，它激发了我们的雄心抱负，但没有招致我们的嫉妒。因为我们对哈马笛斯的优点都很了解，我们从来没有要和他敌对的想法。没人能像他那样带着如此优雅的自信骑着马慢跑经过爱丽舍宫；没有人在室内靶场能像他那样轻松自如地残杀木偶，能非常轻松地在弹子游戏中赢了你关键的一局；能用一种悦耳的男低音大声喊出贝朗热的诗句。他在冬天是帕拉多（地名——译注）之王，夏天是索米耶尔和蒙帕拿斯（地名——译注）之王。他经常出入时髦人物所光顾的场所，穿着奇装异服参加舞会——他那种打扮会让宪兵们都感到羞愧，而过于拘谨的上流社会也把他排除在沙龙之外。总而言之，哈马笛斯是个低俗臣民的代表，是一个有着自己独特的杰出魅力的年轻人。

除了胡闹和勇敢之外，我的朋友还有一个很大的爱好——那就是政治，他很热情地投入于其中。祖国是他的偶像、他的天堂、他的梦魇。他白天滔滔不绝讲的是国家，晚上做梦梦到的也是国家。我已经给你们说过他那具有政治隐喻性的发型。我还要提到他的烟斗，他的海泡石制的烟斗，烟斗上有富瓦将军［Foy，拿破仑部下的将军，在滑铁卢战役受伤，继在王朝复辟期间当议员。——译注］的头像。他的手帕上面印着国家宪章。他那有名的三色帽章会不会也在嘲笑他日思夜想的国家从没亲近过他呢？除了这些外在的可以看得到的煽动叛乱的迹象外，他内心还有革命的秘密计划。他参加俱乐部，经常光顾社团组织，读宪法（在那些日子里，自由主义者非常相信宪法）和那些有功于国家的高谈阔论的议院议员的文章。如果这些人死了，宪法宣布了他们的功绩，哈马笛斯会是第一个参加他们葬礼或用自己的肩膀扛他们棺材的人。

这些就是他的兴趣和爱好。他对自己所厌恶的事物也是极端反感

to set his shoulder to their coffins.

"Such were his tastes and passions: his antipathies were not less lively. He detested three things: a Jesuit, a gendarme, and a claqueur at a theatre. At this period, missionaries were rife about Paris, and endeavoured to reillume the zeal of the faithful by public preachings in the churches. 'Infâmes jésuites!' would Harmodius exclaim, who, in the excess of his toleration, tolerated nothing; and, at the head of a band of philosophers like himself, would attend with scrupulous exactitude the meetings of the reverend gentlemen. But, instead of a contrite heart, Harmodius only brought the abomination of desolation into their sanctuary. A perpetual fire of fulminating balls would bang from under the feet of the faithful; odors of impure asafoetida would mingle with the fumes of the incense; and wicked drinking choruses would rise up along with the holy canticles, in hideous dissonance, reminding one of the old orgies under the reign of the Abbot of Unreason.

"His hatred of the gendarmes was equally ferocious: and as for the claqueurs, woe be to them when Harmodius was in the pit! They knew him, and trembled before him, like the earth before Alexander; and his famous war-cry, 'La Carte au chapeau!' was so much dreaded, that the 'entrepreneurs de succes dramatiques' demanded twice as much to do the Odéon Theatre (which we students and Harmodius frequented), as to applaud at any other place of amusement: and, indeed, their double pay was hardly gained; Harmodius taking care that they should earn the most of it under the benches."

This passage, with which we have taken some liberties, will give the reader a more lively idea of the reckless, jovial, turbulent Paris student, than any with which a foreigner could furnish him: the grisette is his heroine; and dear old Béranger, the cynic-epicurean, has celebrated him and her in the most delightful verses in the world. Of these we may have occasion to say a word or two anon. Meanwhile let us follow Monsieur de Bernard in his amusing descriptions of his countrymen somewhat farther; and, having seen how Dambergeac was a ferocious republican, being a bachelor, let us see how age, sense, and a little government pay—that great agent of conversions in France—nay, in England—has reduced him to be a pompous, quiet, loyal

的。他厌恶三种人：耶稣会信徒、宪兵和戏院的捧场人。在那个时期，巴黎周围布满了传教士，他们通过教堂公开布道，努力去点燃信徒们的热情。哈马笛斯称他们为“卑鄙的耶稣会会士”！在超过自己的容忍限度，容忍不下去的时候，他就带领一伙像自己这样的学生去参加牧师们审慎的聚会。但哈马笛斯不是带着一颗忏悔的心，而是把厌恶和冷漠带进他们的教堂。在他们的参与下，信徒们的脚下会有持续爆炸的弹子起火，烟火的气味掺杂了香炉的气味，醉醺醺的合唱队员们站起来唱的是跑调的圣歌，让人看了还以为是以前祭祀酒神的秘密宗教仪式。

他对宪兵的憎恨也很强烈。至于戏院的捧场人，当哈马笛斯在剧院出现时，他们就惨了！他们在他面前会吓得发抖，就像地球在亚历山大面前会发抖一样。他那句有名的口号“太棒了”是如此可怕，以至于受公众欢迎的戏剧上演的时候，承办人也会在欧德翁剧院（那里是学生和哈马笛斯经常去的剧院）要求两倍的捧场人在场，让他们在演出的任何一处都要鼓掌。实际上，他们几乎挣不到双倍的价钱，有了哈马笛斯的光顾，他们的报酬应该大都是在座位下面挣得的。

在我们随便选入的这个片段中，巴黎学生的鲁莽、活泼和狂暴都会给读者留下一个非常生动的印象，它比任何一个外国人所能描述的都要好。这部小说中的女主角是青年劳动妇女。亲爱的老贝朗瑞这个玩世不恭的享乐主义者，已经用世界上最可爱的诗句赞美过这些人物了。对于这些，或许我们以后还有机会再说一两句。现在让我们跟随德·贝尔纳先生去看看对他同胞进一步有趣的描述。我们已经知道作为单身汉的丹姆布吉阿克是一个怎样极端的共和主义者，让我们看看年龄、观念和一些政府的报酬——在法国这都是谈话的主要内容，在英国也是——是怎样把他变成了一个傲慢、温和、中庸观念的忠实支持者。前半部分所描绘的是他的学生肖像，现在要呈现的是一个副区长的极妙、生动的肖像。

supporter of the juste milieu: his former portrait was that of the student, the present will stand for an admirable lively likeness of—

The Sous-Préfet

"Saying that I would wait for Dambergeac in his own study, I was introduced into that apartment, and saw around me the usual furniture of a man in his station. There was, in the middle of the room, a large bureau, surrounded by orthodox arm-chairs; and there were many shelves with boxes duly ticketed; there were a number of maps, and among them a great one of the department over which Dambergeac ruled; and facing the windows, on a wooden pedestal, stood a plaster-cast of the 'Roi des Français.' Recollecting my friend's former republicanism, I smiled at this piece of furniture; but before I had time to carry my observations any farther, a heavy rolling sound of carriage-wheels, that caused the windows to rattle and seemed to shake the whole edifice of the sub-prefecture, called my attention to the court without. Its iron gates were flung open, and in rolled, with a great deal of din, a chariot escorted by a brace of gendarmes, sword in hand. A tall gentleman, with a cocked-hat and feathers, wearing a blue and silver uniform coat, descended from the vehicle; and having, with much grave condescension, saluted his escort, mounted the stair. A moment afterwards the door of the study was opened, and I embraced my friend.

"After the first warmth and salutations, we began to examine each other with an equal curiosity, for eight years had elapsed since we had last met.

"'You are grown very thin and pale,' said Harmodius, after a moment.

"'In revenge I find you fat and rosy: if I am a walking satire on celibacy,—you, at least, are a living panegyric on marriage.'

"In fact a great change, and such an one as many people would call a change for the better, had taken place in my friend: he had grown fat, and announced a decided disposition to become what French people call a bel homme: that is, a very fat one. His complexion, bronzed before, was now clear white and red: there were no more political allusions in his hair, which was, on the contrary, neatly frizzed, and brushed over the forehead, shell-shape. This head-dress, joined to a thin pair of whiskers, cut crescent-wise from the ear to

副区长

丹姆布吉阿克让我在他的书房里等他，因此我就被用人带到了那里。在他的书房里我看到周围都是他这种身份的人所用的平常家具。在房子的中央是一个大的写字柜，写字柜周围是一些老式的安乐椅；房间里有许多架子，上面堆满了盒子；还有几张地图，其中有一张很大的地图就是丹姆布吉阿克管理的那个区。对着窗户的是一个竖立在木头垫座上的法国国王的石膏模型。想起我朋友先前所信奉的共和主义，我不由得对着它笑了起来。在我还没顾得上看其他的摆设时，一串沉重的马车车轮滚动的声音把我的注意力吸引到了院子里，车轮滚动的声音把窗户震得格格作响，看起来似乎是要把这幢副区长的房子给摇晃起来。院子里的铁门打开了，驶进一辆喧闹的四轮马车，马车旁边有两个佩剑的宪兵护卫着。一个高个儿的绅士从马车上下来，头上戴着插有羽毛的三角帽，穿着蓝色和银白色相间的制服外套。他用非常庄严的恩赐的态度向他的护卫敬了礼，然后就上了台阶。过了一会儿，书房的门被打开了，我抱住了我的朋友。

刚见面的寒暄和问候之后，我们开始好奇地打量起对方，从我们最后一次见面到现在已有八年了。

“你变瘦了，脸色也苍白了。”哈马笛斯过了一会儿说。

“相反，我发现你胖了，脸色也红润了。如果说我的形象是对独身生活的一种讽刺，那么你的形象就是对婚姻生活的颂扬了。”

他的变化确实很大。许多人或许会把发生在我朋友身上的这种变化称为一种好的变化。他长胖了，显示出果断的气质，变成了法国人所认为的好人，也就是说成了一个胖人。他以前青铜色的肤色现在变成了干净的白里透红的颜色。他的头发也没有什么政治上的隐喻了，它们整齐地卷曲着从额头上掠过，是贝壳形状的样子。这种发型再配上一把稀疏的从耳朵到下巴的月牙状的连鬓胡须，使我的朋友具备了

the nose, gave my friend a regular bourgeois physiognomy, wax-doll-like: he looked a great deal too well; and, added to this, the solemnity of his prefectoral costume, gave his whole appearance a pompous well-fed look that by no means pleased.

"'I surprise you,' said I, 'in the midst of your splendor: do you know that this costume and yonder attendants have a look excessively awful and splendid? You entered your palace just now with the air of a pasha.'

"'You see me in uniform in honour of Monseigneur the Bishop, who has just made his diocesan visit, and whom I have just conducted to the limit of the arrondissement.'

"'What!' said I, 'you have gendarmes for guards, and dance attendance on bishops? There are no more janissaries and Jesuits, I suppose?' The sub-prefect smiled.

"'I assure you that my gendarmes are very worthy fellows; and that among the gentlemen who compose our clergy there are some of the very best rank and talent: besides, my wife is niece to one of the vicars-general.'

"'What have you done with that great Tasso beard that poor Armandine used to love so?'

"'My wife does not like a beard; and you know that what is permitted to a student is not very becoming to a magistrate.'

"I began to laugh. 'Harmodius and a magistrate! —how shall I ever couple the two words together? But tell me, in your correspondences, your audiences, your sittings with village mayors and petty councils, how do you manage to remain awake?'

"'In the commencement,' said Harmodius, gravely, 'it WAS very difficult; and, in order to keep my eyes open, I used to stick pins into my legs: now, however, I am used to it; and I'm sure I don't take more than fifty pinches of snuff at a sitting.'

"'Ah! apropos of snuff: you are near Spain here, and were always a famous smoker. Give me a cigar,—it will take away the musty odor of these piles of papers.'

"'Impossible, my dear; I don't smoke; my wife cannot bear a cigar.'

"His wife! thought I; always his wife: and I remember Juliette, who really

一般中产阶级的相貌，像个蜡人一样。他看起来太好了。除了这些，还有他庄严的官员制服，使他外表上看起来红光满面，令人愉悦。

“你的光彩让我感到吃惊，”我说，“你知道吗？这身装束和那边的随从们都有种过分的庄重和华丽，你就像帕夏［土耳其等国的高级官员。——译注］走进自己的官殿一样。”

“我穿的这件制服是为了向主教阁下表示敬意的，他来参观他的主教管区，我刚刚带他去参观了所管辖的区域。”

“什么！”我说，“你有宪兵做守卫，还奉承主教？我想，不会有什么爪牙和耶稣会信徒了呢？”副区长笑了。

“我向你保证我的宪兵是值得尊敬的。在那些组成了牧师队伍的神职人员中，有许多人是很有身份和才能的。此外，我的妻子就是一位代理主教的侄女。”

“你是怎么处理你那部很大的塔索式的胡子的，可怜的阿尔芒迪娜以前很喜欢的？”

“我妻子不喜欢胡子。你知道适合一个学生的并不适合一位长官。”

我笑了起来。“哈马笛斯和长官！——我怎样才能把这两个词联系在一起呢？但是在你的信中，你说自己作为听众经常和乡镇镇长、下级地方议会的议员坐在一起开会，告诉我，你是怎样设法保持清醒的？”

“刚开始，”哈马笛斯庄重地说，“是非常困难的。为了让我的眼睛睁着，我常用针刺我的腿。然而，现在我已习惯了。我可以保证在坐着的时候不会吸鼻烟超过五十次。”

“啊！谈到鼻烟。这里靠近西班牙，你以前可是个很有名的烟鬼啊！给我来支香烟——好把房间里这些纸堆的霉味给驱除掉。”

“我亲爱的朋友，不行。我不吸烟，我妻子受不了烟味。”

他妻子！总是他妻子。我想起了朱丽叶，她真的是闻着烟斗的味道就恶心的，但哈马笛斯喜欢吸烟。最后，朱丽叶这个可怜的姑娘也

grew sick at the smell of a pipe, and Harmodius would smoke, until, at last, the poor thing grew to smoke herself, like a trooper. To compensate, however, as much as possible for the loss of my cigar, Dambergeac drew from his pocket an enormous gold snuff-box, on which figured the self-same head that I had before remarked in plaster, but this time surrounded with a ring of pretty princes and princesses, all nicely painted in miniature. As for the statue of Louis Philippe, that, in the cabinet of an official, is a thing of course; but the snuff-box seemed to indicate a degree of sentimental and personal devotion, such as the old Royalists were only supposed to be guilty of.

"'What! you are turned decided juste milieu?' said I.

"'I am a sous-préfet,' answered Harmodius.

"I had nothing to say, but held my tongue, wondering, not at the change which had taken place in the habits, manners, and opinions of my friend, but at my own folly, which led me to fancy that I should find the student of '26 in the functionary of '34. At this moment a domestic appeared.

"'Madame is waiting for Monsieur,' said he: 'the last bell has gone, and mass beginning.'

"'Mass!' said I, bounding up from my chair. 'You at mass like a decent serious Christian, without crackers in your pocket, and bored keys to whistle through?'—The sous-préfet rose, his countenance was calm, and an indulgent smile played upon his lips, as he said, 'My arrondissement is very devout; and not to interfere with the belief of the population is the maxim of every wise politician: I have precise orders from Government on the point, too, and go to eleven o'clock mass every Sunday.'"

There is a great deal of curious matter for speculation in the accounts here so wittily given by M. de Bernard: but, perhaps, it is still more curious to think of what he has NOT written, and to judge of his characters, not so much by the words in which he describes them, as by the unconscious testimony that the words all together convey. In the first place, our author describes a swindler imitating the manners of a dandy; and many swindlers and dandies be there, doubtless, in London as well as in Paris. But there is about the present swindler, and about Monsieur Dambergeac the student, and Mon-

开始像一个骑兵一样吸烟了。作为对我不能吸烟的补偿，哈马笛斯从他口袋里取出一个大的金制鼻烟盒，上面描绘着我前面提到的那个石膏的头像，在它周围还环绕着一圈漂亮的王子和公主，都是些很好的袖珍画。路易斯·菲力浦的雕像出现在官员的房间中是件自然的事情。但是这个鼻烟盒似乎就显示出他个人对国王的情感和信仰的程度，这在以前的保皇者看来可是件罪过。

“什么！你现在改信中庸了?”我说。

“我是副区长。”哈马笛斯回答道。

我没有什么可说的了，只好保持缄默，我不是为发生在我朋友身上的生活习惯、方式和观念的变化感到惊讶，而是对我自己的愚笨感到吃惊，正是这种愚笨引导我试图在一个 1834 年的官员身上去寻找那个 1826 年的学生的印象。这时，一个用人进来了。

“夫人正在等先生，”他说，“最后的铃声已响过，弥撒开始了。”

“弥撒!”我说着就从椅子上跳了起来。“你就像一个体面严肃的基督徒那样去做弥撒，你的口袋里没有爆竹，不吹令人厌烦的调子了吗?”——副区长站了起来，他的表情很平静，嘴上浮现出一丝宽容的微笑，他说：“我辖区的人们是很虔诚的。不去干涉人们的信仰是每个明智政客的准则。当局政府对我也有严格的命令，每周日十一点去做弥撒。”

在德·贝尔纳先生这篇诙谐的文章中，有许多措辞巧妙的地方值得我们去思索。但是，他没有写出来的东西更能激发我们的好奇心。我们更多地不是通过他描述的词语来判断他笔下的人物形象，而是通过把这些词语组合在一起的无意识的陈述。在我们节选的第一部分中，作家描述了一个仿效花花公子举止的骗子。无疑，在伦敦和巴黎都有很多骗子和花花公子。但是，就现在的骗子、学生时代的丹姆布吉阿克、副区长丹姆布吉阿克和他的朋友来说，他们平静的外表下所包含的是内在的堕落，让我们希望并

sieur Dambergeac the sous-préfet, and his friend, a rich store of calm internal debauch, which does not, let us hope and pray, exist in England. Hearken to M. de Gustan, and his smirking whispers, about the Duchess of San Severino, who pour son bonheur particulier, &c. &c. Listen to Monsieur Dambergeac's friend's remonstrances concerning pauvre Juliette who grew sick at the smell of a pipe; to his naïve admiration at the fact that the sous-préfet goes to church: and we may set down, as axioms, that religion is so uncommon among the Parisians, as to awaken the surprise of all candid observers; that gallantry is so common as to create no remark, and to be considered as a matter of course. With us, at least, the converse of the proposition prevails: it is the man professing irreligion who would be remarked and reprehended in England; and, if the second-named vice exists, at any rate, it adopts the decency of secrecy and is not made patent and notorious to all the world. A French gentleman thinks no more of proclaiming that he has a mistress than that he has a tailor; and one lives the time of Boccaccio over again, in the thousand and one French novels which depict the state of society in that country.

For instance, here are before us a few specimens (do not, madam, be alarmed, you can skip the sentence if you like,) to be found in as many admirable witty tales, by the before-lauded Monsieur de Bernard. He is more remarkable than any other French author, to our notion, for writing like a gentleman: there is ease, grace and ton, in his style, which, if we judge aright, cannot be discovered in Balzac, or Soulié, or Dumas. We have then—"*Gerfaut*" a novel: a lovely creature is married to a brave, haughty, Alsacian nobleman, who allows her to spend her winters at Paris, he remaining on his terres, cultivating, carousing, and hunting the boar. The lovely-creature meets the fascinating Gerfaut at Paris; instantly the latter makes love to her; a duel takes place: baron killed; wife throws herself out of window; Gerfaut plunges into dissipation; and so the tale ends.

Next: "*La Femme de Quarante Ans*," a capital tale, full of exquisite fun and sparkling satire: La femme de quarante ans has a husband and THREE

且祈祷，这种情况在英国不要存在。听听写信人德·吉斯坦先生，他为了个人的幸福等等，就私下里谈论桑·塞维里诺公爵夫人的事；听丹姆布吉阿克的朋友为那个闻到烟斗味就恶心的可怜的朱丽叶抗议，还有他对于副区长去教堂的事实所表现出来的天真的钦佩。对于读者的惊奇，我们可以这样解释，即巴黎人普遍是不信仰宗教的；在巴黎，风流艳事是如此普通，它被认为是理所当然的事情，人们不会对此大惊小怪。我们所流行的却恰恰相反。在英国一个人声称他没有宗教信仰会招致人们的议论和指责；如果有风流艳事的话，人们无论如何也要顾及面子，把它作为一个秘密不向众人公开以防弄得声名狼藉。在许多描述法国社会的小说中，人们仿佛又回到了薄伽丘的时代，对于法国人来说，拥有一个情妇和拥有一个裁缝师一样普通，不值得向外人炫耀。

举例来说，在我们面前就发现一些作品（警告女士们，可以跳过这些句子）写的都是极妙的诙谐的故事，作者就是前面赞美过的德·贝尔纳先生。他比其他的任何法国作家都更为卓越，按我们的观念来说那是因为他的作品就像一位绅士一样：风格闲适、优雅而且时髦，如果我们正确判断一下的话，就会发现在巴尔扎克或大仲马的作品中是找不到这种风格的。接着我们来看——《戈福特》这本小说。小说的内容是讲一个可爱的美人嫁给了一个勇敢、傲慢的阿尔萨斯贵族，丈夫允许她去巴黎度过冬天，他则留在家里继续交际、狂饮、猎杀公猪。这个可爱的美人在巴黎遇到了迷人的戈福特。很快，后者向她表示了爱意。接着，一场决斗发生了。贵族死了，妻子跳窗自杀了，戈福特沉迷于酗酒之中。故事就这样结束了。

《四十岁的女人》也是一个很好的故事，充满了优雅的乐趣和生动的讽刺。这个四十岁的女人有一个丈夫和三个情人。在一个布满星星的夜晚他们全都发现了彼此的关系。四十岁的女人性情非常浪漫，她给了三个爱慕者每人一颗星星。她对其中的一个和另外一个说："阿尔方索，当那边的白色星球在天堂里升起的时候，要想到我啊!""伊沙多尔，当明亮的行星在天空中闪耀的时候，记住你的凯若琳啊!"等等。

lovers; all of whom find out their mutual connexion one starry night; for the lady of forty is of a romantic poetical turn, and has given her three admirers A STAR APIECE; saying to one and the other, "Alphonse, when yon pale orb rises in heaven, think of me;" "Isidore, when that bright planet sparkles in the sky, remember your Caroline," &c.

"*Un Acte de Vertu*," from which we have taken Dambergeac's history, contains him, the husband—a wife—and a brace of lovers; and a great deal of fun takes place in the manner in which one lover supplants the other. —Pretty morals truly!

If we examine an author who rejoices in the aristocratic name of Le Comte Horace de Viel-Castel, we find, though with infinitely less wit, exactly the same intrigues going on. A noble Count lives in the Faubourg St. Honoré, and has a noble Duchess for a mistress: he introduces her Grace to the Countess his wife. The Countess his wife, in order to ramener her lord to his conjugal duties, is counselled, by a friend, TO PRETEND TO TAKE A LOVER: one is found, who, poor fellow! takes the affair in earnest: climax—duel, death, despair, and what not. In the "*Faubourg St. Germain*," another novel by the same writer, which professes to describe the very pink of that society which Napoleon dreaded more than Russia, Prussia, and Austria, there is an old husband, of course; a sentimental young German nobleman, that falls in love with his wife; and the moral of the piece lies in the showing up of the conduct of the lady, who is reprehended—not for deceiving her husband (poor devil!)—but for being a flirt, AND TAKING A SECOND LOVER, to the utter despair, confusion, and annihilation of the first.

Why, ye gods, do Frenchmen marry at all? Had Père Enfantin (who, it is said, has shaved his ambrosial beard, and is now a clerk in a banking-house) been allowed to carry out his chaste, just, dignified social scheme, what a deal of marital discomfort might have been avoided:—would it not be advisable that a great reformer and lawgiver of our own, Mr. Robert Owen, should be presented at the Tuileries, and there propound his scheme for the regeneration of France?

还有《美德的一幕》，我们正是从这篇小说里抽取了丹姆布吉阿克的故事。小说还包括一个丈夫一个妻子和两个情人的故事，当一个情人排挤另一个情人的时候就发生了许多有趣的事情。——确实很有道德寓意！

如果我们仔细看一位名叫贺瑞斯·德·维叶尔·卡斯代尔伯爵［Horace de VielCastel（1802—1864），法国诗人、作家。——译注］的作品，我们会发现，虽然他的作品里也有同样的阴谋私通，但缺少了诙谐的风格。一个贵族伯爵住在圣奥诺雷的法布街，他有一位高贵的公爵夫人做情妇。他把这位夫人介绍给自己的妻子伯爵夫人。伯爵夫人为了给他们的婚姻关系带来贵族的荣耀，在一位朋友的劝说下，就假装带了一个情人。而她所找的这个情人，可怜的小伙子！他竟把事情当真了。因此就有了故事的高潮——决斗、死亡、绝望等诸如此类的情节，不是吗？在他的另一部作品《圣日耳曼的法布街》中，他声称要描述法国社会——拿破仑视之为比俄国、普鲁士、奥地利更为可怕——的贵族名流。作品中当然会有一个年老的丈夫，还有一个多愁善感的德国贵族青年爱上了他的妻子。作品的道德寓意就体现在这位太太的行为上，她受到了人们的指责——倒不是因为欺骗了她的丈夫（可怜的家伙！）——而是她卖弄风骚有了第二个情人，并出于彻底的绝望和慌乱把第一个情人给消灭了。

上帝啊！法国人为什么还结婚呢？如果安凡丹［Père Enfantin，人称安凡丹老爹（1796—1864），法国空想社会主义者，圣西门的门徒。——译注］的高雅、公正、合理的社会体制能得以实施的话，多少婚姻上的不便就能被避免了。——我们国家伟大的改革者、立法者罗伯特·欧文先生应该出现在杜伊勒里花园为法国的复兴提出他的方案，这个建议不是很可取的吗？

在英国或许是用不着欧文了，因为我们国家还没有充分发展到能给一个哲学家以公平的待遇。在伦敦，目前为止还没有神圣的婚姻机构，一个老单身汉因为有钱就可以娶一个迷人的年轻少女，一个七十岁的寡妇因为银行账单上的可观数目就可以收买一个二十岁的快乐年轻小伙子。如果权

He might, perhaps, be spared, for our country is not yet sufficiently advanced to give such a philosopher fair play. In London, as yet, there are no blessed Bureaux de Mariage, where an old bachelor may have a charming young maiden—for his money; or a widow of seventy may buy a gay young fellow of twenty, for a certain number of bank-billets. If mariages de convenance take place here (as they will wherever avarice, and poverty, and desire, and yearning after riches are to be found), at least, thank God, such unions are not arranged upon a regular organized SYSTEM: there is a fiction of attachment with us, and there is a consolation in the deceit ("the homage," according to the old môt of Rochefoucauld) "which vice pays to virtue"; for the very falsehood shows that the virtue exists somewhere. We once heard a furious old French colonel inveighing against the chastity of English demoiselles: "Figurez-vous, sir," said he (he had been a prisoner in England), "that these women come down to dinner in low dresses, and walk out alone with the men!"—and, pray Heaven, so may they walk, fancy-free in all sorts of maiden meditations, and suffer no more molestation than that young lady of whom Moore sings, and who (there must have been a famous lord-lieutenant in those days) walked through all Ireland, with rich and rare gems, beauty, and a gold ring on her stick, without meeting or thinking of harm.

Now, whether Monsieur de Viel-Castel has given a true picture of the Faubourg St. Germain, it is impossible for most foreigners to say; but some of his descriptions will not fail to astonish the English reader; and all are filled with that remarkable naïf contempt of the institution called marriage, which we have seen in M. de Bernard. The romantic young nobleman of Westphalia arrives at Paris, and is admitted into what a celebrated female author calls la crême de la crême de la haute volée of Parisian society. He is a youth of about twenty years of age. "No passion had as yet come to move his heart, and give life to his faculties; he was awaiting and fearing the moment of love; calling for it, and yet trembling at its approach; feeling in the depths of his soul, that that moment would create a mighty change in his being, and decide, perhaps, by its influence, the whole of his future life."

宜婚姻出现在这儿（充斥着贪婪、贫穷、欲望和渴望财富的地方都会有这种婚姻），无论如何，感谢上帝，这种结合并不是一个正式的有组织的制度安排的，在这种结合中有我们虚构的爱情和在欺骗中寻求的安慰（“敬意”，根据拉罗什富科［拉罗什富科（1613—1680），法国作家，生于巴黎。——译注］的警句），“恶对德行是有利的”，因为正是谎言才显示出德行的存在。我们曾听到过一位狂怒的老法国上校痛骂英国女士的贞洁：“你想象一下，先生，”他（他在英国曾是一个囚犯）说，“那些女人穿着低胸的礼服来吃晚餐，独自和男人在外面散步！”——上帝啊！他们（在那些日子其中一定会有一个出色的中尉老爷）一起散步的时候，她竟没有一点儿一般女性的顾虑，仿佛她们生活在莫尔的乌托邦时代，可以穿金戴银地走遍爱尔兰而不用担心任何人的骚扰和伤害。

现在，不管德·维叶尔·卡斯代尔先生是否给我们描绘了一幅有关圣日耳曼法布街的真实图像，这都是大多数外国人所讲不出来的。但是有些描写还是会让英国读者感到吃惊。它们都充满了对于称做婚姻的这个制度的真正蔑视，我们在德·贝尔纳的作品里也看到了这点。威斯特伐利亚［德国的一个地名。——译注］的一位浪漫的年轻贵族到了巴黎，加入了一个团体，这个团体被一位著名的法国女作家称为巴黎上流社会精华的精华。他是一个大约二十岁的青年。“沉湎于自己的才能之中，从未遭遇过激情。他在等待着爱情的到来，也惧怕爱情的到来。既需要它，又为爱情的到来而激动。在灵魂深处他感觉到爱情到来的那一刻将会给他的生活带来很大的变化，或许还能影响并决定他以后的整个人生。”

这也并不奇怪，难道有这些想法的一个年轻贵族不应该至少要选择一位小姐或一个寡妇吗？但不幸的是，这个家伙一定要选择一位已婚女人。他的命运会是什么样的呢？我们的作家用一种法国流行的对话形式向我们讲述了以后的故事。

Is it not remarkable, that a young nobleman, with these ideas, should not pitch upon a demoiselle, or a widow, at least? but no, the rogue must have a married woman, bad luck to him; and what his fate is to be, is thus recounted by our author, in the shape of

A French Fashionable Conversation

"A lady, with a great deal of esprit, to whom forty years' experience of the great world had given a prodigious perspicacity of judgement, the Duchess of Chalux, arbitress of the opinion to be held on all new comers to the Faubourg Saint Germain, and of their destiny and reception in it;—one of those women, in a word, who make or ruin a man,—said, in speaking of Gerard de Stolberg, whom she received at her own house, and met everywhere, 'This young German will never gain for himself the title of an exquisite, or a man of bonnes fortunes, among us. In spite of his calm and politeness, I think I can see in his character some rude and insurmountable difficulties, which time will only increase, and which will prevent him for ever from bending to the exigencies of either profession; but, unless I very much deceive myself, he will, one day, be the hero of a veritable romance.'

"'He, madame?' answered a young man, of fair complexion and fair hair, one of the most devoted slaves of the fashion:—'He, Madame la Duchesse? why, the man is, at best, but an original, fished out of the Rhine: a dull, heavy creature, as much capable of understanding a woman's heart as I am of speaking bas-Breton.'

"'Well, Monsieur de Belport, you will speak bas-Breton. Monsieur de Stolberg has not your admirable ease of manner, nor your facility of telling pretty nothings, nor your—in a word, that particular something which makes you the most recherché man of the Faubourg Saint Germain; and even I avow to you that, were I still young, and a coquette, AND THAT I TOOK IT INTO MY HEAD TO HAVE A LOVER, I would prefer you.'

"All this was said by the Duchess, with a certain air of raillery and such a mixture of earnest and malice, that Monsieur de Belport, piqued not a little, could not help saying, as he bowed profoundly before the Duchess's chair, 'And might I, madam, be permitted to ask the reason of this preference?'

一段法国流行的对话

夏绿公爵夫人是一位精力充沛的女士，凭借着在上流社会所积聚的四十年的经验，其判断力已变得异常敏锐。对于到圣日耳曼区法布街的新人的命运和接纳程度，她都是个很出色的判断人——总而言之，她是那种能成就或毁灭一个男人的女人——在谈到杰拉德·德·施特尔贝格时，她曾在自己家里接见过他，并且在各处也能遇见他，她说："这个年轻的德国人在我们中间永远也无法为他自己获得高雅或幸运儿的称号。除了他的沉着和礼貌之外，我可以看出在他的个性中还有些粗鲁和难以克服的缺陷，它们只会随着时间的推移变得更加严重，并且将会妨碍他屈从于任何一种职业。不是我自己欺骗自己，有一天他将会成为一段真正的浪漫故事的主人公。"

"他，女士？"一个年轻的男人回应道，他有着女人的肤色，留着女人的发式，是时髦风气最忠实的奴隶之一。——"他，公爵夫人？为什么呢，这个男人充其量只是莱茵河里出来的一个脾气古怪的人，一个迟钝、笨重的家伙，如果说他能了解一颗女人的心，那我就是一个雄辩的下等布列塔尼人了。"

"嗯，贝尔波特先生，你会是一个雄辩的下等布列塔尼人的。施特尔贝格先生没有你那种闲雅的风度，没有你讲述琐事的灵敏，也没有——总而言之，就是那些让你成为圣日耳曼区法布街的最出色的男人。我甚至可以向你发誓，如果我仍然年轻，是个卖弄风情的女人，想要找一个情人的话，我会选择你的。"

这些话都是公爵夫人用一种戏弄的口气，同时还夹杂着一些诚挚和恶意说出来的，那位贝尔波特先生很好奇，他在公爵夫人的椅子前深深地鞠了一躬，禁不住说："夫人，我可以知道蒙您偏爱的原因吗？"

"哦，我的上帝啊！当然可以。"公爵夫人依然用同样的语调说，"因为像你这样的情人从来也不会把对一个人的依恋发展到激情的程度。你知道吗，在我的一生中，这种激情已吓坏了我。人们不能从一

"'O mon Dieu, oui,' said the Duchess, always in the same tone; 'because a lover like you would never think of carrying his attachment to the height of passion; and these passions, do you know, have frightened me all my life. One cannot retreat at will from the grasp of a passionate lover; one leaves behind one some fragment of one's moral SELF, or the best part of one's physical life. A passion, if it does not kill you, adds cruelly to your years; in a word, it is the very lowest possible taste. And now you understand why I should prefer you, M. de Belport—you who are reputed to be the leader of the fashion.'

"'Perfectly,' murmured the gentleman, piqued more and more.

"'Gerard de Stolberg WILL be passionate. I don't know what woman will please him, or will be pleased by him' (here the Duchess of Chalux spoke more gravely); 'but his love will be no play, I repeat it to you once more. All this astonishes you, because you, great leaders of the ton that you are, never can fancy that a hero of romance should be found among your number. Gerard de Stolberg—but, look, here he comes!'

"M. de Belport rose, and quitted the Duchess, without believing in her prophecy; but he could not avoid smiling as he passed near the HERO OF ROMANCE.

"It was because M. de Stolberg had never, in all his life, been a hero of romance, or even an apprentice-hero of romance.

"Gerard de Stolberg was not, as yet, initiated into the thousand secrets in the chronicle of the great world: he knew but superficially the society in which he lived; and, therefore, he devoted his evening to the gathering of all the information which he could acquire from the indiscreet conversations of the people about him. His whole man became ear and memory; so much was Stolberg convinced of the necessity of becoming a diligent student in this new school, where was taught the art of knowing and advancing in the great world. In the recess of a window he learned more on this one night than months of investigation would have taught him. The talk of a ball is more indiscreet than the confidential chatter of a company of idle women. No man present at a ball, whether listener or speaker, thinks he has a right to affect any indulgence for his companions, and the most learned in malice will always pass for the most witty.

"'How!' said the Viscount de Mondragé: 'the Duchess of Rivesalte arrives

个充满激情的情人的控制中随意地退出。而他也只能置个人道德于不顾，遗漏了实际生活中最美好的那一部分。如果激情没有把你毁灭掉，也会给你的人生带来残酷的折磨。总而言之，它可能是最粗俗的审美趣味。现在你知道我为什么偏爱你了，贝尔波特先生——你被认为是流行潮流的领导者。”

“完全正确。”绅士嘀咕道，他越来越好奇了。

“杰拉德·德·施特尔贝格将会是一个充满激情的情人。我不知道什么样的女人会中意他，或讨他的喜欢（这里夏绿公爵夫人更庄重地说），我再给你重复一遍，他的爱情将不会是场游戏。这些都让你感到吃惊，因为你作为一个时髦的首领人物，从来没想象过在你们这群人中会发现一个浪漫传奇的主人公。杰拉德·德·施特尔贝格——看，他过来了！”

贝尔波特先生站了起来，离开公爵夫人，他并不相信她的预言。但是从浪漫传奇的主人公身边走过时还是免不了向他笑了笑。

那是因为德·施特尔贝格先生在他的一生中从来也没有能成为浪漫传奇的主人公，甚至连主人公的学徒都没有做过。

到目前为止，杰拉德·德·施特尔贝格对于上流社会的许多历史行情还不曾入门。他只知道他所生活的这个社会的表面现象。因此，他把整个晚上都用来倾听周围人们的轻率的谈话，并从中收集信息。他整个人都只剩下耳朵和记忆存在了。施特尔贝格确信在这所新的学校里很有必要做一个勤勉的学生，这里所传授给他的是了解上流社会并取得进步的技巧。他在窗户的凹处站着，这个晚上学到的东西比几个月的调查所教给他的东西都要多。舞会上的谈话比一群无所事事的女人私底下的闲聊还要轻率。舞会上的每个人，不管是听的还是讲的，都认为他不应该假装表现出对于他同伴的好感，相反，最不友好的态度却往往被认为是最聪明的感情表达方式。

“怎么！”德·蒙达日子爵说：“列维萨尔特公爵夫人今晚一个人来

alone tonight, without her inevitable Dormilly!'—And the Viscount, as he spoke, pointed towards a tall and slender young woman, who, gliding rather than walking, met the ladies by whom she passed, with a graceful and modest salute, and replied to the looks of the men BY BRILLIANT VEILED GLANCES FULL OF COQUETRY AND ATTACK.

"'Parbleu!' said an elegant personage standing near the Viscount de Mondragé, 'don't you see Dormilly ranged behind the Duchess, in quality of train-bearer, and hiding, under his long locks and his great screen of moustaches, the blushing consciousness of his good luck? —They call him THE FOURTH CHAPTER of the Duchess's memoirs. The little Marquise d'Alberas is ready to die out of spite; but the best of the joke is, that she has only taken poor de Vendre for a lover in order to vent her spleen on him. Look at him against the chimney yonder; if the Marchioness do not break at once with him by quitting him for somebody else, the poor fellow will turn an idiot.'

"'Is he jealous?' asked a young man, looking as if he did not know what jealousy was and as if he had no time to be jealous.

"'Jealous! the very incarnation of jealousy; the second edition, revised, corrected, and considerably enlarged; as jealous as poor Gressigny, who is dying of it.'

"'What! Gressigny too? why, 'tis growing quite into fashion: egad! I must try and be jealous,' said Monsieur de Beauval. 'But see! here comes the delicious Duchess of Bellefiore,'" &c. &c. &c.

Enough, enough: this kind of fashionable Parisian conversation, which is, says our author, "a prodigious labour of improvising," a "chef-d'oeuvre," a "strange and singular thing, in which monotony is unknown," seems to be, if correctly reported, a "strange and singular thing" indeed; but somewhat monotonous at least to an English reader, and "prodigious" only, if we may take leave to say so, for the wonderful rascality which all the conversationists betray. Miss Neverout and the Colonel, in Swift's famous dialogue, are a thousand times more entertaining and moral; and, besides, we can laugh AT those worthies as well as with them; whereas the "prodigious" French wits are to us quite incomprehensible. Fancy a Duchess as old as Lady —— her-

的，没有她离不开的多米利了！”——子爵说话时指着一个高挑的年轻女士。她与其说是走，不如说是在滑动，她从一些女士身边经过时，优雅端庄地向她们致意，并用暧昧的充满媚态和挑逗的目光回应着男士打量的目光。

“当然！”站在蒙达日子爵旁边一位优雅的先生说，“你没看到多米利以一个搬运工的身份在公爵夫人身后来回走动吗？在长长的头发和一排浓密胡子的掩饰下，他还为自己的好运感到羞愧呢？——他们把他称做公爵夫人自传的“第四篇章”。小艾伯塔侯爵出于怨恨准备去死。但是最好笑的是，为了向他大发脾气，她只接受了可怜的德·望德作为情人。看他在那边正靠着烟囱。如果侯爵夫人不及时和他断绝关系，离开他去找别人，这个可怜的家伙就要变成白痴了。”

“他是嫉妒吗？”一个年轻的男士问，看起来好像他不知道什么是嫉妒，仿佛他也没机会嫉妒。

“嫉妒！很明显的嫉妒，而且还得到了夸大。他嫉妒得就像可怜的格瑞西尼一样，他会因嫉妒而死的。”

“什么！格瑞西尼也嫉妒？噢，它成了流行的了。天哪！我一定要尝试尝试嫉妒的滋味。”这位德·波瓦勒先生说。“但是，看啊！美妙的贝莉费奥雷公爵夫人来了。”……

这种时髦的巴黎式对话已够多的了。我们的作者把它们叫做“即席创作的一部奇妙作品”、一部“杰作”、一种“奇异的主题，在其中没有千篇一律的单调”，如果正确报道的话，它确实是一种“奇异的主题”。但对英国读者来说它至少还是有些单调的，我们只能说它很“奇妙”，因为让人惊奇的卑劣行为在所有的对话中都得到了暴露。在我们看来，斯威夫特小说中的人物对话要更为有趣并合乎道德。此外，我们也和他们一样可以嘲笑那些杰出的大人物。然而，这种“奇妙的”法国式的机智对于我们来说太难以理解了。设想一个老公爵夫人——自己会告诉我们“如果她想找一个

self, and who should begin to tell us "of what she would do if ever she had a mind to take a lover;" and another Duchess, with a fourth lover, tripping modestly among the ladies, and returning the gaze of the men by veiled glances, full of coquetry and attack! —Parbleu, if Monsieur de Viel-Castel should find himself among a society of French Duchesses, and they should tear his eyes out, and send the fashionable Orpheus floating by the Seine, his slaughter might almost be considered as justifiable COUNTICIDE.

情人的话，她会怎样做呢”；而另外一位公爵夫人带着第四个情人在女人群中端庄地迈着轻快的脚步，用暧昧的充满充满媚态和挑逗的目光回应男士的注视。——当然，如果德·维叶尔·卡斯代尔先生在一群法国公爵夫人当中出现了，她们会把他的眼睛给拔出来的，把这个时髦的欧夫斯［希腊神话中的歌手，善弹竖琴，传说他奏的音乐可感动鸟兽木石。——译注］扔到塞纳河里，让他顺水漂走，残杀他的刽子手或许还会被认为是有理的判官。

A Gambler's Death

ANYBODY who was at C— school some twelve years since, must recollect Jack Attwood: he was the most dashing lad in the place, with more money in his pocket than belonged to the whole fifth form in which we were companions.

When he was about fifteen, Jack suddenly retreated from C—, and presently we heard that he had a commission in a cavalry regiment, and was to have a great fortune from his father, when that old gentleman should die. Jack himself came to confirm these stories a few months after, and paid a visit to his old school chums. He had laid aside his little school-jacket and inky corduroys, and now appeared in such a splendid military suit as won the respect of all of us. His hair was dripping with oil, his hands were covered with rings, he had a dusky down over his upper lip which looked not unlike a moustache, and a multiplicity of frogs and braiding on his surtout which would have sufficed to lace a field-marshal. When old Swishtail, the usher, passed in his seedy black coat and gaiters, Jack gave him such a look of contempt as set us all a-laughing: in fact it was his turn to laugh now; for he used to roar very stoutly some months before, when Swishtail was in the custom of belabouring him with his great cane.

Jack's talk was all about the regiment and the fine fellows in it: how he had ridden a steeple-chase with Captain Boldero, and licked him at the last hedge; and how he had very nearly fought a duel with Sir George Grig, about dancing with Lady Mary Slamken at a ball. "I soon made the baronet know what it was to deal with a man of the n—th," said Jack. "Dammee, sir, when I lugged out my barkers, and talked of fighting across the mess-room table, Grig turned as pale as a sheet, or as—"

"Or as you used to do, Attwood, when Swishtail hauled you up," piped

一个赌徒的死亡

只要是十二年前在C学校的人都一定还会记得杰克·阿特伍德。他是那个地方最精神抖擞的青年，他口袋里有很多钱，比当时我们所在的整个五年级的人所拥有的钱都要多。

在他大约十五岁的时候，杰克突然从C学校退学了。很快我们就听说他在一个骑兵团里有委任权，等他父亲那个老绅士死了之后，他还会有一笔可观的财富可以继承。几个月之后，杰克来拜访学校的老朋友，自己证实了这些传言的真实性。他把小的校服夹克和漆黑的灯芯裤都搁置起来不穿了，现在穿的是一身很好看的军队制服，让我们都肃然起敬。他的头发上抹了油，手上戴满了戒指，在他的上唇上面有一抹暗黑色，那是胡子，而且在他的衣服上面还有许多挂剑环和镶边，足够一个陆军元帅用的了。当门房老斯威士泰尔穿着破烂的黑外套和绑腿套经过时，杰克轻蔑地看了他一眼，逗得我们所有人都笑了。现在轮到他笑了。因为在几个月前，当斯威士泰尔习惯性地用他的大手杖痛打他的时候，他经常用力地吼叫。

杰克的谈话全部都是关于那个骑兵团和团里的好人的：他是怎样和保德罗上尉一起越野赛马，在过最后一个障碍的时候超过了上尉；他又是怎样差点和乔治·格瑞格先生展开决斗，就是为了和玛丽在舞会上跳舞的事情。“很快我就让这个准男爵知道他是在和一个第N军团的人作对，”杰克说，“当我把手枪拔出来，说要和他站在餐室桌子的两端决斗时，格瑞格的脸色变得像纸一样白……”

out little Hicks, the foundation-boy.

It was beneath Jack's dignity to thrash anybody, now, but a grown-up baronet; so he let off little Hicks, and passed over the general titter which was raised at his expense. However, he entertained us with his histories about lords and ladies, and so-and-so "of ours," until we thought him one of the greatest men in his Majesty's service, and until the school-bell rung; when, with a heavy heart, we got our books together, and marched in to be whacked by old Swishtail. I promise you he revenged himself on us for Jack's contempt of him. I got that day at least twenty cuts to my share, which ought to have belonged to Cornet Attwood, of the n—th dragoons.

When we came to think more coolly over our quondam schoolfellow's swaggering talk and manner, we were not quite so impressed by his merits as at his first appearance among us. We recollected how he used, in former times, to tell us great stories, which were so monstrously improbable that the smallest boy in the school would scout them; how often we caught him tripping in facts, and how unblushingly he admitted his little errors in the score of veracity. He and I, though never great friends, had been close companions: I was Jack's form-fellow (we fought with amazing emulation for the LAST place in the class); but still I was rather hurt at the coolness of my old comrade, who had forgotten all our former intimacy, in his steeple-chases with Captain Boldero and his duel with Sir George Grig.

Nothing more was heard of Attwood for some years; a tailor one day came down to C——, who had made clothes for Jack in his school-days, and furnished him with regimentals: he produced a long bill for one hundred and twenty pounds and upwards, and asked where news might be had of his customer. Jack was in India, with his regiment, shooting tigers and jackals, no doubt. Occasionally, from that distant country, some magnificent rumor would reach us of his proceedings. Once I heard that he had been called to a court-martial for unbecoming conduct; another time, that he kept twenty horses, and won the gold plate at the Calcutta races. Presently, however, as the recollections of the fifth form wore away, Jack's image disappeared likewise, and I ceased to ask or to think about my college chum.

A year since, as I was smoking my cigar in the "Estaminet du Grand Balcon," an excellent smoking-shop, where the tobacco is unexceptionable, and

“阿特伍德，你还是就像斯威士泰尔责问你的时候，或你过去经常做的那样。”小希克尖声地说，这是个基础班的男孩。

无论攻击任何人都有失杰克的身份，尤其是个成年的准男爵。因此他饶恕了小希克，也不在乎别人以他为笑柄而发出的窃笑。但是他所讲的关于贵族绅士和贵妇人的故事逗乐了我们，还有“我们中”的某某人怎么怎么，一直讲到我们认为他是为陛下服务的伟大人物之一为止，讲到学校的铃声敲响为止。这时，我们怀着沉重的心情把书放在一起，在老斯威士泰尔棍棒的抽打下向教室走去。我敢保证，是因为杰克对老斯威士泰尔的轻蔑，他才这样报复我们。那天我至少挨了二十下，而这些本来应该属于第N军团龙骑兵阿特伍德的。

当我们冷静地回想起这位以前同窗的虚张声势的言谈和行为的时候，他所说的事迹并没有像他刚出现时的外表那样给我们留下多么深刻的印象。我们回忆起以前他是如何给我们讲些超乎寻常的故事的，它们是如此的怪异以至于学校里最小的男孩也会嘲笑这些故事。我们经常听出他在事实方面的一些漏洞，而他在承认犯错误的同时又是怎样的厚颜无耻。他和我虽然不是很要好的朋友，却一直保持亲密的关系。我是杰克的年级同学。但我还是因老同学的冷漠而受到了伤害，他在与保德罗上尉骑马、与乔治·格瑞格先生决斗的生活中已忘却了我们以前的亲密关系。

有好几年都没有听到任何有关阿特伍德的消息。有一天一个裁缝来到C学校，他曾在杰克上学的时候给杰克做过衣服，给他提供军装制服。他向我们出示了一张长长的账单，账单上有一百二十镑以上的欠款。他问我们到哪里去才能打听到这位顾客的消息。杰克很可能是和他的军团在印度射杀老虎和豺狼。有时也从那个国家传来一些关于他的活动的惊人谣言。有一次，我听说他因为某些不得体的行为，被传讯到了军事法院；还有一次听说他有二十四马，在加尔各答的赛马会上赢得了金牌。然而，现在随着对五年级记忆的慢慢消逝，杰克的形象也同样地消失了，我不再打听也不再去想我的这位同学了。

the Hollands of singular merit, a dark-looking, thick-set man, in a greasy well-cut coat, with a shabby hat, cocked on one side of his dirty face, took the place opposite to me, at the little marble table, and called for brandy. I did not much admire the impudence or the appearance of my friend, nor the fixed stare with which he chose to examine me. At last, he thrust a great greasy hand across the table, and said, "Titmarsh, do you forget your old friend Attwood?"

I confess my recognition of him was not so joyful as on the day ten years earlier, when he had come, bedizened with lace and gold rings, to see us at C—school: a man in the tenth part of a century learns a deal of worldly wisdom, and his hand, which goes naturally forward to seize the gloved finger of a millionaire, or a milor, draws instinctively back from a dirty fist, encompassed by a ragged wristband and a tattered cuff. But Attwood was in nowise so backward; and the iron squeeze with which he shook my passive paw, proved that he was either very affectionate or very poor. You, my dear sir, who are reading this history, know very well the great art of shaking hands: recollect how you shook Lord Dash's hand the other day, and how you shook OFF poor Blank, when he came to borrow five pounds of you.

However, the genial influence of the Hollands speedily dissipated anything like coolness between us and, in the course of an hour's conversation, we became almost as intimate as when we were suffering together under the ferule of old Swishtail. Jack told me that he had quitted the army in disgust; and that his father, who was to leave him a fortune; had died ten thousand pounds in debt: he did not touch upon his own circumstances; but I could read them in his elbows, which were peeping through his old frock. He talked a great deal, however, of runs of luck, good and bad; and related to me an infallible plan for breaking all the play-banks in Europe—a great number of old tricks;—and a vast quantity of gin-punch was consumed on the occasion; so long, in fact, did our conversation continue, that, I confess it with shame, the sentiment, or something stronger, quite got the better of me, and I have, to this day, no sort of notion how our palaver concluded. —Only, on the next-morning, I did not possess a certain five-pound note which on the previous evening was in my sketch-book (by far the prettiest drawing by the way in the collection) but there, instead, was a strip of paper, thus inscribed:—

一年前，我正在一个阳台上的小咖啡馆里抽着雪茄，这是一个很不错的吸烟的小店，烟草无可挑剔，独特的荷兰产杜松子酒也值得一尝。这时一个肤色偏黑、体格结实的男人坐在了我的对面——这个小大理石桌子的另一端，他穿着一件油腻的式样还不错的外套，一顶破旧的帽子歪戴在他脏兮兮的脸颊一侧，他叫了白兰地。我很不喜欢这位朋友的外表和冒失，也不喜欢他盯着我看。忽然，他从桌子上伸过来一只油腻的大手，说："蒂特马舍，你难道忘记你的老朋友阿特伍德了吗？"

我承认这次识别出他来并不像十年前那天识别出他来让人高兴。那时，他到C学校来看我们的时候是一身俗丽的装扮，戴着饰带和金戒指。一个人在十年之中会学到许多世俗的知识，他会把手自然地伸出去握住一位百万富翁或一位贵族老爷的带着手套的手，而在破烂的袖口所包裹着的一只脏兮兮的手面前则会本能地把手抽回去。但是阿特伍德的手一点也不退却，从他紧紧握住我被动伸出的手的动作可以看出，他要么是充满深情，要么是很穷。我亲爱的先生，正在读这篇故事的亲爱的先生是很了解关于握手的学问的。回忆一下那天你是怎样握贵族丹施的手的，而当可怜的布莱克来向你借五英镑的时候，你又是怎样甩开了他的手。

然而，在杜松子酒的作用下，我们之间的冷漠很快就被驱除掉了。在一个小时的交谈中，我们又变得像以前在老斯威士泰尔的戒尺管教下那样亲密。杰克告诉我他出于厌恶已离开了军队。他那位准备给他留下一笔财富的父亲去世了，死前欠了一万英镑的债务。他没有提到他个人的情况，但是从他那破旧的大衣中所露出的胳膊肘，我明白了他现在的处境。他说了很多，然而都是关于运气的好坏。他给我讲了一个确实可靠的计划，他要去破坏欧洲所有营业的银行——还有很多以前的诡计。当时我们喝了很多杜松子酒。事实上，我们谈了那么长的时间，以至于我羞愧地承认，当时是情绪或者某种更强烈的东西完全制服了我，直到今天，我还想不起来我们是怎样结束谈话的。——只不过到了第二天早上，我发现昨晚夹在速写本（里面收集了最好的素描）里的一张五英镑的钞票不见了，取而代之

I. O. U.

Five Pounds. JOHN ATTWOOD,

Late of the n—th dragoons.

I suppose Attwood borrowed the money, from this remarkable and ceremonious acknowledgement on his part: had I been sober I would just as soon have lent him the nose on my face; for, in my then circumstances, the note was of much more consequence to me.

As I lay, cursing my ill fortune, and thinking how on earth I should manage to subsist for the next two months, Attwood burst into my little garret—his face strangely flushed—singing and shouting as if it had been the night before. "Titmarsh," cried he, "you are my preserver! —my best friend! Look here, and here, and here!" And at every word Mr. Attwood produced a handful of gold, or a glittering heap of five-franc pieces, or a bundle of greasy, dusky bank-notes, more beautiful than either silver or gold:—he had won thirteen thousand francs after leaving me at midnight in my garret. He separated my poor little all, of six pieces, from this shining and imposing collection; and the passion of envy entered my soul: I felt far more anxious now than before, although starvation was then staring me in the face; I hated Attwood for CHEATING me out of all this wealth. Poor fellow! it had been better for him had he never seen a shilling of it.

However, a grand breakfast at the Café Anglais dissipated my chagrin; and I will do my friend the justice to say, that he nobly shared some portion of his good fortune with me. As far as the creature comforts were concerned I feasted as well as he, and never was particular as to settling my share of the reckoning.

Jack now changed his lodgings; had cards, with Captain Attwood engraved on them, and drove about a prancing cab-horse, as tall as the Giraffe at the Jardin des Plantes; he had as many frogs on his coat as in the old days, and frequented all the flash restaurateurs and boarding-houses of the capital. Madame de Saint Laurent, and Madáme la Baronne de Vaudry, and Madame la Comtesse de Don Jonville, ladies of the highest rank, who keep a société choisie and condescend to give dinners at five-francs a head, vied with each other in their attentions to Jack. His was the wing of the fowl, and the largest portion of the Charlotte-Russe; his was the place at the écarté table, where

的是一张纸条，上面写着：

借　据

五镑。

约翰·阿特伍德

第N军团龙骑兵

从阿特伍德这番明显客套的认可字据上，我知道是他借了钱。如果昨晚我是清醒的，一定不会借给他。因为，这张钞票对当时的我来说是至关重要的。

当我躺下来诅咒着我的坏运气，想到底该怎样设法度过接下来的两个月时，阿特伍德忽然闯进了我的小阁楼——奇怪的是，他的脸色发红——唱着叫着就像昨晚一样兴奋。"蒂特马舍，"他喊道，"你是我的保护神！——我最好的朋友！看这里，这里，还有这里！"每说一句，阿特伍德就从口袋里拿出一把金子或一堆闪闪发光的五法郎的钱币或一堆油腻、黑糊糊的银行支票，但它们比银子和金子都要美丽——原来他在半夜从阁楼上离开我之后，就去赌场赢了一万三千法郎。他从那堆闪闪发光的钱币中把我可怜的一小部分即六个钱币分了出来。我嫉妒了起来，现在比刚才更焦急了，尽管饥饿是迫在眉睫，但我憎恨阿特伍德背着我赢了这么多钱财。可怜的家伙！如果他没有赢到一个先令或许还会好些。

然而，在英国咖啡馆的一份丰盛的早餐消除了我的懊恼。我愿为我的朋友说句公道话，他豁达地让我分享他财富的一部分。只要我和他在一起吃饭，从来都不用我付账单上的钱。

杰克现在换了住所。他有了名片，上面印着阿特伍德上尉，驾着一辆神气活现的出租马车四处跑，马车有植物园里的长颈鹿那么高。在他的外套上又和往日一样有了许多挂剑环。他经常光顾巴黎的豪华饭店和旅馆。德·圣·劳伦特女士、德·旺德瑞男爵夫人和德·琼维勒伯爵夫人，这些上流社会的女士、这些属于精英社会的人为了争着目睹杰克的风采经常屈尊设宴——以每人五法郎的标准——款待他。他成了一个幸运儿。在牌桌

the Countess would ease him nightly of a few pieces, declaring that he was the most charming cavalier, la fleur d'Albion. Jack's society, it may be seen, was not very select; nor, in truth, were his inclinations: he was a careless, dare-devil, Macheath kind of fellow, who might be seen daily with a wife on each arm.

It may be supposed that, with the life he led, his five hundred pounds of winnings would not last him long; nor did they; but, for some time, his luck never deserted him; and his cash, instead of growing lower, seemed always to maintain a certain level: he played every night.

Of course, such a humble fellow as I, could not hope for a continued acquaintance and intimacy with Attwood. He grew overbearing and cool, I thought; at any rate I did not admire my situation as his follower and dependant, and left his grand dinner for a certain ordinary, where I could partake of five capital dishes for ninepence. Occasionally, however, Attwood favoured me with a visit, or gave me a drive behind his great cab-horse. He had formed a whole host of friends besides. There was Fips, the barrister; Heaven knows what he was doing at Paris; and Gortz, the West Indian, who was there on the same business, and Flapper, a medical student,—all these three I met one night at Flapper's rooms, where Jack was invited, and a great "spread" was laid in honour of him.

Jack arrived rather late—he looked pale and agitated; and, though he ate no supper, he drank raw brandy in such a manner as made Flapper's eyes wink: the poor fellow had but three bottles, and Jack bade fair to swallow them all. However, the West Indian generously remedied the evil, and producing a napoleon, we speedily got the change for it in the shape of four bottles of champagne.

Our supper was uproariously harmonious; Fips sung the good "*Old English Gentleman*;" Jack the "*British Grenadiers*;" and your humble servant, when called upon, sang that beautiful ditty, "*When the Bloom is on the Rye*," in a manner that drew tears from every eye, except Flapper's, who was asleep, and Jack's, who was singing the "*Bay of Biscay O*," at the same time. Gortz and Fips were all the time lunging at each other with a pair of single-sticks, the barrister having a very strong notion that he was Richard the Third.

上，伯爵夫人会每夜为他分担几场，宣称他是最有魅力的骑士、英格兰的精华。可以看得出，杰克的交际朋友并不是很杰出的人物，实际上也不是他所喜欢的。他是个粗心、胆大妄为、马克席斯［一统整个伦敦街区的乞丐，拦路强盗，整日被各式各样的女人簇拥着。——译注］似的人物，每天都可以看到他双臂上各挎着一个女人。

可以想象得到，按照他的这种生活方式，他赢得的五百镑也持续不了很长时间。事实也是如此。但是有段时间，他的运气很好。他的钱不但没有减少，反而经常能够保持一定的数目。他每晚都赌博。

当然，像我这样一个卑下的人不可能指望和阿特伍德永远熟识和亲密的。我想，他变得傲慢和冷漠了。无论如何，我不喜欢自己在他旁边处于一种侍从和家眷的处境，宁愿离开他丰盛的餐桌去普通的饭店吃饭，在那里花九便士能吃到五个主菜。然而，阿特伍德有时也来拜访我，或在他壮丽的出租马车后面载我一程。他身边也有了一群朋友。他们是菲浦斯，一个律师，天知道他在巴黎做什么；高兹，一个西印第安人，也同样是个混混；还有弗拉普，一个学医学的学生。一天晚上在弗拉普的房间里我遇到了他们三个，他们邀请了杰克，已备下"丰盛的酒席"来欢迎他。

杰克来迟了——他看起来脸色苍白，有些焦虑。尽管他没吃晚餐，却喝了很多纯白兰地酒，喝得弗拉普直眨眼。这个可怜的家伙只有三瓶酒，杰克很有可能把它们全都喝了。然而，西印第安人高兹慷慨地做了补救，他拿出一块金币，我们很快用它换来了四瓶香槟酒。

我们的晚餐非常融洽，也非常吵闹。菲浦斯唱那首好听的《老英国绅士》，杰克唱《英国的掷弹兵》，把谦卑的仆人也叫过来，他唱了那首美丽的小曲《麦田里的花朵何时开放》，每个人都被感动得流出了眼泪，弗拉普除外，因为他睡着了。杰克还唱了《哦，比斯坎的海湾》。高兹和菲浦斯一直在用棍子互相戳对方，律师有种很强烈的想法即他就是理查三世。最后，菲浦斯在西印第安人高兹的头上打了一拳，这个挨打的人发怒了。他抓起一个香槟酒瓶子，幸亏它是空的，从房间的另一端扔向菲浦斯。如果这个著名的

At last Fips hit the West Indian such a blow across his sconce, that the other grew furious; he seized a champagne-bottle, which was, providentially, empty, and hurled it across the room at Fips: had that celebrated barrister not bowed his head at the moment, the Queen's Bench would have lost one of its most eloquent practitioners.

Fips stood as straight as he could; his cheek was pale with wrath. "M-m-ister Go-gortz," he said, "I always heard you were a blackguard; now I can pr-pr-peperove it. Flapper, your pistols! every ge-ge-genlmn knows what I mean."

Young Mr. Flapper had a small pair of pocket-pistols, which the tipsy barrister had suddenly remembered, and with which he proposed to sacrifice the West Indian. Gortz was nothing loath, but was quite as valorous as the lawyer.

Attwood, who, in spite of his potations, seemed the soberest man of the party, had much enjoyed the scene, until this sudden demand for the weapons. "Pshaw!" said he, eagerly, "don't give these men the means of murdering each other; sit down and let us have another song." But they would not be still; and Flapper forthwith produced his pistol-case, and opened it, in order that the duel might take place on the spot. There were no pistols there! "I beg your pardon," said Attwood, looking much confused; "I—I took the pistols home with me to clean them!"

I don't know what there was in his tone, or in the words, but we were sobered all of a sudden. Attwood was conscious of the singular effect produced by him, for he blushed, and endeavoured to speak of other things, but we could not bring our spirits back to the mark again, and soon separated for the night. As we issued into the street Jack took me aside, and whispered, "Have you a napoleon, Titmarsh, in your purse?" Alas! I was not so rich. My reply was, that I was coming to Jack, only in the morning, to borrow a similar sum.

He did not make any reply, but turned away homeward: I never heard him speak another word.

Two mornings after (for none of our party met on the day succeeding the supper), I was awakened by my porter, who brought a pressing letter from Mr. Gortz:—

律师当时没有低下头，王座法庭将会损失掉他们最雄辩的一个律师了。

菲浦斯尽可能地站直了，他的两颊因为愤怒而变得苍白。“高兹先生，”他说，“我经常听人说你是个恶棍。现在我可以证、证、证实了。弗拉普，你的手枪！每个绅、绅、绅士都知道我的意思是什么。”

这个喝醉的律师忽然想起来年轻的弗拉普先生有一对小型手枪，他打算用他的手枪和那个西印第安人决斗。高兹也很乐意，他和律师一样都无所畏惧。

阿特伍德尽管喝了许多酒，但看起来却是宴会上最清醒的人，他正津津有味地欣赏着这一幕，听到他们突然要武器，就急切地说：“哼！不要给这些人武器让他们互相残杀。坐下来，让我们再唱另一首歌。”但是他们都不愿意安静下来。弗拉普即刻把他的手枪盒子拿了出来，把它打开，以使决斗能当场进行。可是盒子里面没有手枪！阿特伍德看起来很慌乱地说：“对不起，我把手枪带回家清洗了！”

我不知道是他的语气还是话语里的某些东西让我们猛得都清醒了。阿特伍德意识到这是他所造成的效果，因此他脸红了，尽力去说些别的话题，但是我们都不能再回到常态，那天晚上很快就散场了。当我们出来走到街上时，杰克把我拉到一边小声说：“蒂特马舍，你的钱包里有一块金币吗？”哎呀！我没有这么多钱。我的回答是，我还打算明天早上去他那里借一块金币呢！

他没做任何回答，只是往回家的方向走去了。我没听到他再说一句话。

两天后的早晨（从那天晚上散了之后我们彼此都没有见过面），我被门房叫醒了，他带来一封高兹先生的急信：

亲爱的蒂特马舍——我希望你会到这里来吃早餐。阿特伍德出事了。

您忠实的

所罗门·高兹

"DEAR T. ,—I wish you would come over here to breakfast. There's a row about Attwood.—

Yours truly,
SOLOMON GORTZ."

I immediately set forward to Gortz's; he lived in the Rue du Helder, a few doors from Attwood's new lodging. If the reader is curious to know the house in which the catastrophe of this history took place, he has but to march some twenty doors down from the Boulevard des Italiens, when he will see a fine door, with a naked Cupid shooting at him from the hall, and a Venus beckoning him up the stairs. On arriving at the West Indian's, at about mid-day (it was a Sunday morning), I found that gentleman in his dressing-gown, discussing, in the company of Mr. Fips, a large plate of bifteck aux pommes.

"Here's a pretty row!" said Gortz, quoting from his letter;—"Attwood's off—have a bit of beefsteak?"

"What do you mean?" exclaimed I, adopting the familiar phraseology of my acquaintances:—"Attwood off? —has he cut his stick?"

"Not bad," said the feeling and elegant Fips—"not such a bad guess, my boy; but he has not exactly CUT HIS STICK."

"What then?"

"WHY, HIS THROAT." The man's mouth was full of bleeding beef as he uttered this gentlemanly witticism.

I wish I could say that I was myself in the least affected by the news. I did not joke about it like my friend Fips; this was more for propriety's sake than for feeling's: but for my old school acquaintance, the friend of my early days, the merry associate of the last few months, I own, with shame, that I had not a tear or a pang. In some German tale there is an account of a creature most beautiful and bewitching, whom all men admire and follow; but this charming and fantastic spirit only leads them, one by one, into ruin, and then leaves them. The novelist, who describes her beauty, says that his heroine is a fairy, and HAS NO HEART. I think the intimacy which is begotten over the wine-bottle, is a spirit of this nature; I never knew a good feeling come from it, or an honest friendship made by it; it only entices men and ruins them; it is only a phantom of friendship and feeling, called up by the delirious blood, and the wicked spells of the wine.

我即刻前往高兹家。他住在海尔德街，离阿特伍德的新住所只有几户远。如果读者很想知道这个故事的结局发生在哪里，他只要顺着意大利大道走二十幢房屋，就会看到一扇精致的大门，门厅里有一个裸着身子的丘比特正向进来的人射箭，一个维纳斯在召唤人们上台阶。到那个西印第安人家里时，已大约中午了（是一个星期天的早晨），我看到他穿着睡袍正和菲浦斯在议论着，旁边还有一大盘苹果牛排。

“这里出事了！”高兹引用他信里的话说，“阿特伍德走了——你来点牛排吗？”

“你是什么意思？”我用熟人之间的那种随便的口气叫道，“阿特伍德走了？——他自己离去了？”

“不错，”富于同情心且优雅的菲浦斯说，“没有比这更糟糕的猜测了，我的朋友。但他不是逃走的。”

“那怎么？”

“怎么，他咽气了。”当菲浦斯说出这句绅士妙语时，他嘴里塞满了血淋淋的牛排。可以说只有我自己被这个消息给震动了。我没有像我的朋友菲浦斯那样对此事开玩笑，虽然我更多的是出于礼貌，而不是感情。但是我羞愧地承认，对我的老同学、我以前的朋友、最近几个月的快乐朋友——阿特伍德的死，我没有一滴眼泪和一丝悲痛。在一些德国小说中，经常有一个非常漂亮和迷人的姑娘，而所有的男人都崇拜她、追求她的故事。但是这种娇媚和幻想的美人只会引导他们一个一个地走向毁灭，然后又抛弃他们。描述这种美人的小说家说他的女主角是一个仙女，无心的仙女。我认为在酒桌上所产生的亲密关系也是这种性质的。我从来不相信在酒瓶里能产生任何一种美好的感情或通过酒瓶能建立起任何一种忠实的友谊。它只会诱惑男人，毁灭男人。这种关系只是被兴奋的血液、酒精激发的邪恶魔力所唤起的一种友谊和感情的幻象。

但是放弃这种道德说教吧！（作家不打算再说下去了，在这里要插入最可怜的人物）对可怜的阿特伍德的品质，我们经过一番议论，对他的死亡

But to drop this strain of moralizing (in which the writer is not too anxious to proceed, for he cuts in it a most pitiful figure), we passed sundry criticisms upon poor Attwood's character, expressed our horror at his death—which sentiment was fully proved by Mr. Fips, who declared that the notion of it made him feel quite faint, and was obliged to drink a large glass of brandy; and, finally, we agreed that we would go and see the poor fellow's corpse, and witness, if necessary, his burial.

Flapper, who had joined us, was the first to propose this visit: he said he did not mind the fifteen francs which Jack owed him for billiards, but he was anxious to GET BACK HIS PISTOL. Accordingly, we sallied forth, and speedily arrived at the hotel which Attwood inhabited still. He had occupied, for a time, very fine apartments in this house: and it was only on arriving there that day that we found he had been gradually driven from his magnificent suite of rooms au premier, to a little chamber in the fifth story:—we mounted, and found him. It was a little shabby room, with a few articles of rickety furniture, and a bed in an alcove; the light from the one window was falling full upon the bed and the body. Jack was dressed in a fine lawn shirt; he had kept it, poor fellow, TO DIE IN; for in all his drawers and cupboards there was not a single article of clothing; he had pawned everything by which he could raise a penny—desk, books, dressing-case, and clothes; and not a single halfpenny was found in his possession. [1]

He was lying as I have drawn him, one hand on his breast, the other falling towards the ground. There was an expression of perfect calm on the face, and no mark of blood to stain the side towards the light. On the other side, however, there was a great pool of black blood, and in it the pistol; it looked more like a toy than a weapon to take away the life of this vigourous young man. In his forehead, at the side, was a small black wound; Jack's life had passed through it; it was little bigger than a mole.

"Regardez un peu," said the landlady, "messieurs, il m'a gâté trois matelas, et il me doit quarante quatre francs."

This was all his epitaph: he had spoiled three mattresses, and owed the landlady four-and-forty francs. In the whole world there was not a soul to love him or lament him. We, his friends, were looking at his body more as an object of curiosity, watching it with a kind of interest with which one follows the

表示出我们的惊骇——这种感情在菲浦斯身上得到最好的证明，他宣称这个消息差点让他晕过去，以至于他不得不喝一大杯白兰地酒镇静下来。最后我们都同意去看看那个可怜的家伙的尸体，如果必要的话，就参加他的葬礼。

弗拉普也加入进来，他是第一个提出去看看阿特伍德的。他说他不在乎杰克玩弹子戏欠了他十五法郎。但他急着要拿回他的手枪。接着我们出发了，很快就到了阿特伍德住的旅馆。他一度住的都是旅馆里很好的房间。到了那里，我们才发现他已逐渐从一楼豪华的房间被驱赶到了五楼的小房间。——我们上楼找到了他的房间，那是一间破旧的小房间，里面有几件东倒西歪的家具，在凹进去的地方放着一张床。从一扇窗户里透过来的阳光洒在了床上和尸体上。躺在床上的杰克穿着一件上等细麻布的衬衫。可怜的人儿，他就是穿着它死去的。因为在他所有的抽屉和小橱子里都找不到一条布丝了。他把所有的只要能换来一便士的东西都当掉了——桌子、书、衣箱和衣服。在他遗留下来的东西中连半个便士都找不到。[1]

我走近他，他的一只手放在胸上，另一只手垂向地面。脸上的表情非常平静，朝着日光的这一边没有被血玷污的痕迹。而在另一边，有一大摊黑色的血迹，血迹中有把手枪。看起来更像是一件玩具而不是一件武器夺走了这个精力充沛的年轻人的性命。在他额头的一侧有一个黑色的小伤口。杰克的性命就是从这个伤口里失去的。它只比一颗痣大一点。

“看一会儿吧，”女房东说，“先生们，他弄坏了我三个床垫，还欠我四十四法郎。”

这是他所有的墓志铭。他弄坏了三个床垫，欠女房东四十四法郎。在整个世界上没有一个灵魂是爱着他、为他哀悼的。作为他的朋友，我们看着他的尸体更像是在观看一件好奇的物体，怀着一种观看悲剧第五幕［欧洲传统悲剧一般是五幕剧。——译注］的兴趣来观看眼前的这一幕，离开时的心情也像戏剧结束、大幕拉上、离开剧院的心情。

在杰克的床旁边有一个小桌，桌上放着他最后一餐的残余物和一封拆

fifth act of a tragedy, and leaving it with the same feeling with which one leaves the theatre when the play is over and the curtain is down.

Beside Jack's bed, on his little "table de nuit," lay the remains of his last meal, and an open letter, which we read. It was from one of his suspicious acquaintances of former days, and ran thus:—

"Où es tu, cher Jack? why you not come and see me—tu me dois de l'argent, entends tu? —un chapeau, une cachemire, a box of the Play. Viens demain soir, je t'attendrai at eight o'clock, Passage des Panoramas. My Sir is at his country.

"Adieu *à* demain.

Fifine.

Samedi."

I shuddered as I walked through this very Passage des Panoramas, in the evening. The girl was there, pacing to and fro, and looking in the countenance of every passer-by, to recognize Attwood. "ADIEU À DEMAIN!"—there was a dreadful meaning in the words, which the writer of them little knew. "Adieu *à* demain!"—the morrow was come, and the soul of the poor suicide was now in the presence of God. I dare not think of his fate; for, except in the fact of his poverty and desperation, was he worse than any of us, his companions, who had shared his debauches, and marched with him up to the very brink of the grave?

There is but one more circumstance to relate regarding poor Jack—his burial; it was of a piece with his death.

He was nailed into a paltry coffin and buried, at the expense of the arrondissement, in a nook of the burial-place beyond the Barrière de l'Etoile. They buried him at six o'clock, of a bitter winter's morning, and it was with difficulty that an English clergyman could be found to read a service over his grave. The three men who have figured in this history acted as Jack's mourners; and as the ceremony was to take place so early in the morning, these men sat up the night through, AND WERE ALMOST DRUNK as they followed his coffin to its resting-place.

开的信，我们看了这封信。它是前些日子他的一个可疑的相识者写来的：

你在哪里，亲爱的杰克？你为什么不来看我——你欠着我的钱，你明白吗？——一顶帽子、一件开司米服装和一场戏剧的包厢。明晚过来，我八点等着你，在全景图走廊。我先生在乡下。

明天见。

菲菲

星期六

当我晚上经过那条全景图走廊［餐馆、艺廊交集的场所。——译注］时，我浑身发抖。——那个女人在那里了，她来回地踱步，看着每一个过路人的面孔好认出阿特伍德。“明天见！”——这句话里有种可怕的意味，而写这句话的菲菲却意识不到。“明天见！”——次日到了，这个可怜的自杀者的灵魂出现在上帝的面前。我不敢想象他的命运。因为除了他贫穷和绝望的事实，难道他比我们这些分享他放荡的生活、与他一起走上坟墓边缘的朋友中的任何一个还要更坏吗？

对于可怜的杰克来说，只有一件事情是和他有关的了——埋葬。它与死亡是一体的。

是区里出的钱把他钉进一个廉价的棺材，埋葬在埃托瓦勒［是一个广场。——译注］栅栏外墓地的一个隐蔽角落。他们是在冬天一个严寒的早晨六点埋葬他的，也找不到一位能在他墓穴上读祈祷文的英国牧师。前面提到的三个人都作为杰克的送葬者出席。因葬礼那么早举行，这些人整夜都没睡。当他们跟随着棺材来到安息地时几乎都喝醉了。

MORAL

"When we turned out in our great-coats," said one of them afterwards, "reeking of cigars and brandy-and-water, d—e, sir, we quitefrightened the old buck of a parson; he did not much like our company." After the ceremony was concluded, these gentlemen were very happy to get home to a warm and comfortable breakfast, and finished the day royally at Frascati's.

NOTES:

[1] In order to account for these trivial details, the reader must be told that the story is, for the chief part, a fact; and that the little sketch in this page was TAKEN FROM NATURE. The letter was likewise a copy from one found in the manner described.

道德教训

“当我们穿着大衣出现的时候，”后来他们其中的一个说，“身上发出了香烟和白兰地酒的味道，这可把一位老教区牧师给吓坏了。他不太喜欢我们几个人。”葬礼结束后，这些绅士很高兴地回家去吃温热可口的早餐去了，他们在朋友弗拉斯卡蒂家里度过了快乐的一天。

注释：

[1] 为了说明这些琐碎的细节，一定要告诉读者，故事的主要部分都是事实。这一页的一小部分是自由的发挥。后半部分也是以同样的方式摹写的。

Napoleon and His System

On Prince Louis Napoleon's Work

Any person who recollects the history of the absurd outbreak of Strasburg, in which Prince Louis Napoleon Bonaparte figured, three years ago, must remember that, however silly the revolt was, however, foolish its pretext, however doubtful its aim, and inexperienced its leader, there was, nevertheless, a party, and a considerable one in France, that were not unwilling to lend the new projectors their aid. The troops who declared against the Prince, were, it was said, all but willing to declare for him; and it was certain that, in many of the regiments of the army, there existed a strong spirit of disaffection, and an eager wish for the return of the imperial system and family.

As to the good that was to be derived from the change, that is another question. Why the Emperor of the French should be better than the King of the French, or the King of the French better than the King of France and Navarre, it is not our business to inquire; but all the three monarchs have no lack of supporters; republicanism has no lack of supporters; St. Simonianism was followed by a respectable body of admirers; Robespierrism has a select party of friends. If, in a country where so many quacks have had their day, Prince Louis Napoleon thought he might renew the imperial quackery, why should he not? It has recollections with it that must always be dear to a gallant nation; it has certain claptraps in its vocabulary that can never fail to inflame a vain, restless, grasping, disappointed one.

In the first place, and don't let us endeavour to disguise it, they hate us. Not all the protestations of friendship, not all the wisdom of Lord Palmer-

拿破仑与他的体制

——论路易·拿破仑王子的著作

任何人只要回忆起三年前路易·拿破仑［拿破仑三世（NapoleonⅢ，1808—1873）即路易·拿破仑·波拿巴。路易·波拿巴之子，拿破仑一世之侄。法兰西第二共和国总统（1848—1851 年）、第二帝国皇帝（1852—1870 年）。著有《政治沉思录》、《拿破仑观念》等。——译注］所发动的斯特拉斯堡暴动，就一定会意识到不管那次叛乱多么愚蠢，借口多么荒谬，目的多么可疑，领导者多么缺乏经验，然而在法国还是有一个政党和一个重要的人物乐意实施这种计划的。据说那些公开对抗王子的军队差一点要表态支持王子。可以确定的是，在许多军团内部都存在着一种强烈的不满情绪以及要恢复帝国体制及帝国家族的强烈渴望。

至于从这场变动中将会得到的好处，那就是另一个问题了。为什么法国的皇帝要强于法国的国王，法国的国王要强于法兰西纳瓦尔国王［波旁家族的纳瓦尔国王。——译注］，这些都不是我们要探究的问题。但是这三类帝王都不缺乏支持者：共和主义不缺乏拥护者；圣西门主义也有一大批的赞同者；罗伯斯比尔有一批杰出的支持者。在一个国家内如果有这么多的政治骗子走运，路易·拿破仑王子为什么不能想当然地认为他也能重建帝国体制呢？这个国家的历史记忆让它热心于塑造一个勇敢的民族，法语中还包含着某些华而不实的言语，对于一个空虚、焦虑、贪婪和失望的人

ston, not all the diplomacy of our distinguished plenipotentiary, Mr. Henry Lytton Bulwer—and let us add, not all the benefit which both countries would derive from the alliance—can make it, in our times at least, permanent and cordial. They hate us. The Carlist organs revile us with a querulous fury that never sleeps; the moderate party, if they admit the utility of our alliance, are continually pointing out our treachery, our insolence, and our monstrous infractions of it; and for the Republicans, as sure as the morning comes, the columns of their journals thunder out volleys of fierce denunciations against our unfortunate country. They live by feeding the natural hatred against England, by keeping old wounds open, by recurring ceaselessly to the history of old quarrels, and as in these we, by God's help, by land and by sea, in old times and late, have had the uppermost, they perpetuate the shame and mortification of the losing party, the bitterness of past defeats, and the eager desire to avenge them. A party which knows how to exploiter this hatred will always be popular to a certain extent; and the imperial scheme has this, at least, among its conditions.

Then there is the favourite claptrap of the "natural frontier." The Frenchman yearns to be bounded by the Rhine and the Alps; and next follows the cry, "Let France take her place among nations, and direct, as she ought to do, the affairs of Europe." These are the two chief articles contained in the new imperial programme, if we may credit the journal which has been established to advocate the cause. A natural boundary—stand among the nations—popular development—Russian alliance, and a reduction of la perfide Albion to its proper insignificance. As yet we know little more of the plan: and yet such foundations are sufficient to build a party upon, and with such windy weapons a substantial Government is to be overthrown!

In order to give these doctrines, such as they are, a chance of finding favour with his countrymen, Prince Louis has the advantage of being able to refer to a former great professor of them—his uncle Napoleon. His attempt is at once pious and prudent; it exalts the memory of the uncle, and furthers the interests of the nephew, who attempts to show what Napoleon's ideas really were; what good had already resulted from the practice of them; how cruelly

来说，这些言语总能激发起他的斗志。

首先，我们不要试图去掩饰这个事实即法国仇视我们英国。不是所有的友好主张、不是帕麦斯顿［Palmerston，英国外相。——译注］的所有智能、不是我们杰出的全权大使亨利·李顿·布尔威先生的所有交际手腕，还有，不是两个国家的联盟就能让两国之间的友谊在我们这个时代变得牢固而亲密的。他们仇视我们。西班牙国王查理一世支持者的报刊总是带着抱怨和怒气辱骂我们；中间稳健派政党，即使他们承认了我们结盟的利益，也在不断地挑剔我们的背叛、傲慢和可笑的违规行为；至于共和党，像早晨会到来一样可以确定，他们报纸的专栏会用猛烈的痛斥言辞来轰击和对抗我们不幸的国家。他们通过助长人们对英国本能的憎恨心理来生存，把旧日的创伤公布于众，持续不断地重提旧日两国纷争的历史，因为我们靠着上帝、陆地和海洋的帮助，在以前和现在都达到了一个最高峰，他们把以前失去国土的屈辱、以前失败的痛苦，还有要求报复的热切都持久地保留下来。知道怎样去利用这种憎恨情绪的政党经常会得到民众一定程度的欢迎。至少他们的帝国体制在当时的情势下采取了这种做法。

然后就有了“自然边界”这种异想天开的说法。法国人渴望他们的边界以莱茵河和阿尔卑斯山为限。接着又有了另一种喊声：“让法国在众国家中取得它应有的地位，既而掌管欧洲事务。”如果我们相信报纸的这番言论，那它就是新帝国方案中的两项主要条款。一个自然的边界——在众国家中居于领导地位——积极发展与俄国的联盟，把背信弃义的阿尔比恩排挤到边缘。我们目前为止对这个计划都知之不多。而这些计划提倡者也足够在其基础上建立一个政党了，然后用这种无形的武器去推翻当权政府！

为了提出这样的主张，利用时机讨好民众，路易王子因自己能够求助于前任伟大的领袖——他的叔父拿破仑而独具优势。他努力向人们展示拿破仑的观念到底是怎样的，以及拿破仑观念的实施已给人们带来了什么好处。他的这种努力既虔诚又审慎，既提升了他叔父的影响力，又加强了他本人的势力。可是多么让人痛心啊！拿破仑的观念竟被外国战争和困境所

they had been thwarted by foreign wars and difficulties; and what vast benefits WOULD have resulted from them; aye, and (it is reasonable to conclude) might still, if the French nation would be wise enough to pitch upon a governor that would continue the interrupted scheme. It is, however, to be borne in mind that the Emperor Napoleon had certain arguments in favour of his opinions for the time being, which his nephew has not employed. On the 13th Vendémiaire, when General Bonaparte believed in the excellence of a Directory, it may be remembered that he aided his opinions by forty pieces of artillery, and by Colonel Murat at the head of his dragoons. There was no resisting such a philosopher; the Directory was established forthwith, and the sacred cause of the minority triumphed. In like manner, when the General was convinced of the weakness of the Directory, and saw fully the necessity of establishing a Consulate, what were his arguments? Moreau, Lannes, Murat, Berthier, Leclerc, Lefebvre—gentle apostles of the truth! —marched to St. Cloud, and there, with fixed bayonets, caused it to prevail. Error vanished in an instant. At once five hundred of its high-priests tumbled out of windows, and lo! three Consuls appeared to guide the destinies of France! How much more expeditious, reasonable, and clinching was this argument of the 18th Brumaire, than any one that can be found in any pamphlet! A fig for your duodecimos and octavos! Talk about points, there are none like those at the end of a bayonet; and the most powerful of styles is a good rattling "article" from a nine-pounder.

At least this is our interpretation of the manner in which were always propagated the Idées Napoléoniennes. Not such, however, is Prince Louis's belief; and, if you wish to go along with him in opinion, you will discover that a more liberal, peaceable, prudent Prince never existed: you will read that "the mission of Napoleon" was to be the "testamentary executor of the revolution;" and the Prince should have added the legatee; or, more justly still, as well as the EXECUTOR, he should be called the EXECUTIONER, and then his title would be complete. In Vendémiaire, the military Tartuffe, he threw aside the Revolution's natural heirs, and made her, as it were, ALTER HER WILL; on the 18th of Brumaire he strangled her, and on the 19th seized on

挫败，否则人们会从中得到很多收益的。当然（很合理地得出结论）还有，如果法国人足够明智的话，就该选定一位统治者来继续拿破仑的被中断的事业。然而在人们思想中根深蒂固的却是眼下就是否支持皇帝拿破仑还存在一定的争议，拿破仑的侄子还无暇顾及这一点。在葡月 13 日（法兰西共和国的一月，相当于公历 9 月 22 日、23 日、24 日到 10 月 20 日、21 日、22 日——译注），当波拿巴将军认识到督政府［法国 1795—1799 年的政府。——译注］的好处的时候，人们或许还记得他是通过四十门大炮和以穆哈为首的龙骑兵来支持他的行为的，没人敢对此进行抵抗。督政府即刻成立了，少数派的神圣事业胜利了，同样，当这位将军意识到督政府的缺陷和建立一个执政府［1799—1804 年间法国的一个政府。——译注］的必要性的时候，他又是依靠什么来推行自己的方案呢？莫罗、拉纳、穆莱特、贝尔蒂埃、勒克莱尔、勒费弗尔［都是拿破仑手下的将领。——译注］——他们才是改革方案的具体执行人！——他们进军到圣克洛德区，在那里用配备的刺刀迫使政府改革成功。在刺刀的威胁下，异议马上就消失了。五百个高级神甫立刻匆匆地翻过窗户逃跑了。瞧!! 支配法国命运的三位执政官［1799—1804 年间法国的三位执政官。——译注］出现了！雾月 18 日政变［法兰西共和历的第二月，相当于公历 10 月 22、23、24 日到 11 月 20、21、22 日。——译注］的证据比在任何小册子里所能找到的论据都要合理明确！去你的十二开本和八开本吧！小册子中的任何观点都抵不上刺刀的锋利，最强有力的文体也抵不上轰轰作响的大炮。

这只是我们对拿破仑实施自己观念所经常采用的手段所作出的解释。然而这并不是路易王子的观点。如果你愿意认同他的观点，你将会发现一个更为开明、平和、审慎的王子是从来也不存在的。你将会得知“拿破仑的使命”变成了“革命遗嘱执行人”。王子还应再加上遗产继承人的称号；或者更公正地说，他还应该被称做刽子手，这样他的称号就全面了。在葡月，这个军队里的答丢夫［莫里哀同名戏剧中的主人公，伪善者。——译注］把革命的合理继承人抛在一边，使她改变了自己的意志。在雾月 18 日

her property, and kept it until force deprived him of it. Illustrations, to be sure, are no arguments, but the example is the Prince's, not ours.

In the Prince's eyes, then, his uncle is a god; of all monarchs, the most wise, upright, and merciful. Thirty years ago the opinion had millions of supporters; while millions again were ready to avouch the exact contrary. It is curious to think of the former difference of opinion concerning Napoleon; and, in reading his nephew's rapturous encomiums of him, one goes back to the days when we ourselves were as loud and mad in his dispraise. Who does not remember his own personal hatred and horror, twenty-five years ago, for the man whom we used to call the "bloody Corsican upstart and assassin?" What stories did we not believe of him? —what murders, rapes, robberies, not lay to his charge? —we who were living within a few miles of his territory, and might, by books and newspapers, be made as well acquainted with his merits or demerits as any of his own countrymen.

Then was the age when the Idées Napoléoniennes might have passed through many editions; for while we were thus outrageously bitter, our neighbours were as extravagantly attached to him by a strange infatuation—adoredhim like a god, whom we chose to consider as a fiend; and vowed that, under his government, their nation had attained its highest pitch of grandeur and glory. In revenge there existed in England (as is proved by a thousand authentic documents) a monster so hideous, a tyrant so ruthless and bloody, that the world's history cannot show his parallel. This ruffian's name was, during the early part of the French revolution, Pittetcobourg. Pittetcobourg's emissaries were in every corner of France; Pittetcobourg's gold chinked in the pockets of every traitor in Europe; it menaced the life of the godlike Robespierre; it drove into cellars and fits of delirium even the gentle philanthropist Marat; it fourteen times caused the dagger to be lifted against the bosom of the First Consul, Emperor, and King,—that first, great, glorious, irresistible, cowardly, contemptible, bloody hero and fiend, Bonaparte, before mentioned.

On our side of the Channel we have had leisure, long since, to re-consider our verdict against Napoleon; though, to be sure, we have not changed our

他勒死了她，在19日占有了她的财产，一直保留在身边直到被军队剥夺。这都是毫无争议的例证，拿破仑是王子的榜样，不是我们的。

在王子的眼中，他的叔父是一个神，一个最明智、正直、仁慈的君主。三十年前这种观点能有数以百万计的支持者，当然也会有数百万人对此持反对态度。想想以前人们对于拿破仑所持的不同看法真是让人感到好奇。在读到他侄子对他热情颂扬的赞词时，我们仿佛又回到了大声而疯狂地对他进行指责的日子。二十五年前，对于拿破仑，我们一直不是都持憎恨和厌恶的态度、称他为“残忍的科西嘉发迹者和暗杀者”吗？他什么样的事情没有做过？——谋杀、抢夺的行为不都归于他的名下吗？——我们国家离他的领土只有几英里之隔，人们可以通过书刊报纸像他自己的国民一样认识他的功绩和过失。

接着拿破仑的观念又经过了多次翻版。当我们因法国的威胁而如此愤怒痛苦的时候，我们的邻居法国人却狂热地赞美他——把他当做神灵来崇拜，而我们只认为他是个恶魔。但我们要承认的是，在他的统治下，他们国家达到了光荣和伟大的顶峰。相反在英国出现的是（许多可靠的资料证实）一个如此可怕、如此无情的暴君，世界历史上也找不出类似他这样的人物。这个恶棍的名字叫皮特考伯格。皮特考伯格的间谍出没在法国的各个角落，皮特考伯格的黄金在欧洲每个卖国贼的口袋里叮当作响。它威胁到神圣的罗伯斯比尔的生命，它闯入精神错乱者的地窖和房间，甚至连温和的革命领袖马拉也不放过，它曾经十四次把匕首举到了第一执政官、皇帝和国王的胸口前——即那个伟大、光荣、不可抵抗、懦弱、卑鄙、血腥的英雄和魔鬼波拿巴。

在英吉利海峡的这一边，很久以来我们就有时间去重新认识我们对拿破仑的判断。可以确定的是，对于皮特考伯格，我们并没有改变原来的看法。但在皮特考伯格死后，几乎所有的党派在说到拿破仑的爱国主义、才华和他个人的优点时都充满深切的敬意。然而在法国，至少在一些法国党派中，观点上还没有发生这样的改变。在共和党看来，皮特考伯格仍然是

opinion about Pittetcobourg. After five-and-thirty years all parties bear witness to his honesty, and speak with affectionate reverence of his patriotism, his genius, and his private virtue. In France, however, or, at least among certain parties in France, there has been no such modification of opinion. With the Republicans, Pittetcobourg is Pittetcobourg still,—crafty, bloody, seeking whom he may devour; and perfide Albion more perfidious than ever. This hatred is the point of union between the Republic and the Empire; it has been fostered ever since, and must be continued by Prince Louis, if he would hope to conciliate both parties.

With regard to the Emperor, then, Prince Louis erects to his memory as fine a monument as his wits can raise. One need not say that the imperial apologist's opinion should be received with the utmost caution; for a man who has such a hero for an uncle may naturally be proud of and partial to him; and when this nephew of the great man would be his heir likewise, and, hearing his name, step also into his imperial shoes, one may reasonably look for much affectionate panegyric. "The empire was the best of empires," cries the Prince; and possibly it was; undoubtedly, the Prince thinks it was; but he is the very last person who would convince a man with the proper suspicious impartiality. One remembers a certain consultation of politicians which is recorded in the Spelling-book; and the opinion of that patriotic sage who avowed that, for a real blameless constitution, an impenetrable shield for liberty, and cheap defence of nations, there was nothing like leather.

Let us examine some of the Prince's article. If we may be allowed humbly to express an opinion, his leather is not only quite insufficient for those vast public purposes for which he destines it, but is, moreover, and in itself, very BAD LEATHER. The hides are poor, small, unsound slips of skin; or, to drop this cobbling metaphor, the style is not particularly brilliant, the facts not very startling, and, as for the conclusions, one may differ with almost every one of them. Here is an extract from his first chapter, "*on Governments in general*":—

"I speak it with regret, I can see but two governments, at this day, which

皮特考伯格——一个狡诈、残忍的人，不忠的阿尔比恩比以前更狡猾了。这种憎恨是把共和国和帝国联合起来的基点。从那时起一直到现在，他们都在助长这种仇视情绪，如果路易王子将来希望调和两个党派的话，他也一定要把这种仇视情绪继续维持下去。

对于拿破仑皇帝，路易王子用他力所能及的智慧在自己的记忆中树立了一个雄伟的纪念碑。人们没必要认为这个帝国辩护士的观点就应受到高度的重视。因为有一个英雄做叔父的人自然会以他为荣并偏袒他。当这位伟人的侄子同样也是他的继承人、听着他的名字要接替他的位置时，在他的书中能找到许多充满深情的颂词也是必然的了。王子叫喊道："法兰西第一帝国是最好的帝国。"或许它是，但这无疑只是王子的看法。愿意带着适度可疑的公正来确信拿破仑的最后一个人也就是他了。人们都记得在拼写课本中所收录的某些政治家的会议记录。那位爱国伟人拿破仑公开承认，为了一个真正的无可责难的政体、一个维护自由的不可侵犯的防护体系以及经济合理的国家防御体制，还是自己的帝国体制最好。

让我们仔细看看王子的一些文章。请允许我们谦逊地表达这样一个观点，即他的那套理论不仅不投合广大公众的意愿，而且就它自身来说，也是非常低劣的货色。它的外壳是粗劣、细小、腐烂的皮肤。抛开这种粗俗的隐喻来说，就是文体不吸引人，所引用的事实也不令人感兴趣。至于结论，人们或许对其中的任何一个都是持异议的。这里有从他第一章中抽取出来的一部分——《论一般性政府》。

> 我很遗憾地说，到目前为止，我只看到有两个政府完成了上帝所委托给他们的任务。他们是位于世界两端的两个巨人。一个在古老世界的一端，一个在崭新世界的一端。然而，我们古老的欧洲就像是一座喷口日趋衰竭的火山，东西两端的那两个国家正向着完美的体制坚定地前进。一个是在个人意志的领导下前进，另一个则是在自由的领导下前进。

fulfil the mission that Providence has confided to them; they are the two colossi at the end of the world; one at the extremity of the old world, the other at the extremity of the new. Whilst our old European centre is as a volcano, consuming itself in its crater, the two nations of the East and the West, march without hesitation, towards perfection; the one under the will of a single individual, the other under liberty.

"Providence has confided to the United States of North America the task of peopling and civilizing that immense territory which stretches from the Atlantic to the South Sea, and from the North Pole to the Equator. The Government, which is only a simple administration, has only hitherto been called upon to put in practice the old adage, Laissez faire, laissez passer, in order to favour that irresistible instinct which pushes the people of America to the west.

In Russia it is to the imperial dynasty that is owing all the vast progress which, in a century and a half, has rescued that empire from barbarism. The imperial power must contend against all the ancient prejudices of our old Europe: it must centralize, as far as possible, all the powers of the state in the hands of one person, in order to destroy the abuses which the feudal and communal franchises have served to perpetuate. The last alone can hope to receive from it the improvements which it expects.

"But thou, France of Henry IV, of Louis XIV, of Carnot, of Napoleon—thou, who wert always for the west of Europe the source of progress, who possessest in thyself the two great pillars of empire, the genius for the arts of peace and the genius of war—hast thou no further mission to fulfil? Wilt thou never cease to waste thy force and energies in intestine struggles? No; such cannot be thy destiny: the day will soon come, when, to govern thee, it will be necessary to understand that thy part is to place in all treaties thy sword of Brennus on the side of civilization."

These are the conclusions of the Prince's remarks upon governments in general; and it must be supposed that the reader is very little wiser at the end than at the beginning. But two governments in the world fulfil their mission: the one government, which is no government; the other, which is a despotism. The duty of France is IN ALL TREATIES to place her sword of Brennus in the scale of civilization. Without quarrelling with the somewhat confused

上帝把一片广袤领土的移民和文明化任务委托给了美国北部的共和国，这片宽阔的领土从大西洋延伸到南部海域，从北极延伸到赤道。他们的政府只是一个简单的行政机关，到目前为止，还只是在实践着这句古老的谚语——“任凭别人干什么，任凭别人怎么过”以支持美国人不可抗拒的西部大移民行动。

在俄国则要归功于帝国政府，正是帝国政府使其在一百五十年来取得了很大的进步，把俄国从野蛮的状态中拯救了出来。我们欧洲以往对帝王权力都有着古老的偏见，俄国的这种政府体制无疑是对我们偏见的驳斥。它必须要尽可能地把政府所有的权力都集中在一个人的手中，以消除封建特权和共和制对选举权的滥用。只有帝王体制能取得它所期望的进步。

但是你，亨利四世、路易十四、卡诺［Carnot，数学家，国民公会代表，公安委员会委员，共和国十四军的创编者，1794 年参加热月 9 日反革命政变。——译注］、拿破仑统治下的法兰西——你一直都是西欧发展的源头，你自身又具备帝国的两大支柱即和平艺术的天赋与战争的天赋——难道你就没有更进一步的使命要去履行吗？你就不会停止把精力浪费在内部斗争上吗？不。这不是你的命运。这天会很快到来的，你要克制住自己，有必要意识到你的职责就是在所有的条约中既要扮演文明的角色又要时刻把布雷努斯［Brennus，古高卢首领，公元前 390 年入侵意大利，攻占罗马。——译注］之剑放在身边。

这些都是王子在对一般性政府进行评论之后所得出的结论。我们一定能想象得出读者在结尾并不比开始要明白多少。但是就那两个履行使命的政府来说，其中一个是无政府，另一个是专制政府。法国的责任就是在所有的协议谈判中都要把布雷努斯之剑放在身边。不用挑剔文章后半部分有些混乱的语言，我们倒要以上帝的名义问问这三个问题：布雷努斯之剑是什么东西？法国怎样去使用它？难道沿着美国共和主义这条溪流和另一条

language of the latter proposition, may we ask what, in Heaven's name, is the meaning of all the three? What is this épée de Brennus? and how is France to use it? Where is the great source of political truth, from which, flowing pure, we trace American republicanism in one stream, Russian despotism in another? Vastly prosperous is the great republic, if you will: if dollars and cents constitute happiness, there is plenty for all: but can any one, who has read of the American doings in the late frontier troubles, and the daily disputes on the slave question, praise the GOVERNMENT of the States? —a Government which dares not punish homicide or arson performed before its very eyes, and which the pirates of Texas and the pirates of Canada can brave at their will? There is no government, but a prosperous anarchy; as the Prince's other favourite government is a prosperous slavery. What, then, is to be the épée de Brennus government? Is it to be a mixture of the two? "Society," writes the Prince, axiomatically, "contains in itself two principles—the one of progress and immortality, the other of disease and disorganization." No doubt; and as the one tends towards liberty, so the other is only to be cured by order: and then, with a singular felicity, Prince Louis picks us out a couple of governments, in one of which the common regulating power is as notoriously too weak, as it is in the other too strong, and talks in rapturous terms of the manner in which they fulfil their "providential mission!"

From these considerations on things in general, the Prince conducts us to Napoleon in particular, and enters largely into a discussion of the merits of the imperial system. Our author speaks of the Emperor's advent in the following grandiose way:—

> "Napoleon, on arriving at the public stage, saw that his part was to be the TESTAMENTARY EXECUTOR of the Revolution. The destructive fire of parties was extinct; and when the Revolution, dying, but not vanquished, delegated to Napoleon the accomplishment of her last will, she said to him, 'Establish upon solid bases the principal result of my efforts. Unite divided Frenchmen. Defeat feudal Europe that is leagued against me. Cicatrize my wounds. Enlighten the nations. Execute that in width, which I have had to perform in depth. Be for Europe what I have been for France. And, even if you must wa-

俄国专制主义的溪流，我们就能找到政治真理的伟大源头在哪里吗？如果你会说，广阔富裕的国家就是伟大的共和国，金钱就能构筑快乐，那美国确实有很多的金钱。但是人们如果知道美国最近在边境纠纷问题上的所作所为和在奴隶问题上的持久争议，他还会赞扬这个国家的制度吗？——不正是因为那个政府不敢惩罚在它眼前所发生的杀人和纵火案件的罪犯，得克萨斯的海盗和加拿大的海盗才敢任意妄为的吗？那里没有政府，只是极端的无政府状态。而王子所倾心的另一个政府同样也是一个极端的奴隶制政府。那么，布雷努斯政府之剑会是什么呢？它会是两者的混合体吗？王子引用格言写道，“人类社会本来具有两种倾向性——一种是倾向于进步和完善，另一种是倾向于无秩序和混乱”。无疑当一方倾向于自由的时候，另一方就要受到制度的管制。接着，路易王子就非常幸运地给我们挑出了这两个政府，其中一个的管理能力是声名狼藉、太差劲了，而另一个则是太专制了，但王子却用一种兴高采烈的语气说他们完成了“上帝的使命”！

从这些对一般性政府的考虑出发，王子又特意把我们引到了拿破仑身上，用很多篇幅讨论了帝国体制的优点。我们的作者在讲到皇帝出现的时候是用下面夸张的方式来讲述的：

> 拿破仑一到了公众舞台上就明白他的角色将是革命遗嘱执行人。党派纷争已得到平息。当革命行将完结，但是还没有取得胜利的时候，她就授权拿破仑来完成她最后的遗愿，她对他说：“在我努力奠定的坚实革命基础上建立一个政府。把分散的法国人联合起来。打败那些联合起来反对我的欧洲封建联盟。让我的伤口得到愈合。启蒙民众。广泛深入地把革命进行下去，我已经让这场革命深入人心了。这是为欧洲也是为法国。还有，甚至你还必须要用自己的血来灌溉文明之树——即便你会看到你的计划遭到误解，你的后代无处安身，在地球上到处流浪，也永远不要放弃法国人神圣的事业。用天才所能发现得到的并且得到人们赞同的方法来确保她的胜利。”

ter the tree of civilization with your blood—if you must see your projects misunderstood, and your sons without a country, wandering over the face of the earth, never abandon the sacred cause of the French people. Insure its triumph by all the means which genius can discover and humanity approve.'

"This grand mission Napoleon performed to the end. His task was difficult. He had to place upon new principles a society still boiling with hatred and revenge; and to use, for building up, the same instruments which had been employed for pulling down.

"The common lot of every new truth that arises, is to wound rather than to convince—rather than to gain proselytes, to awaken fear. For, oppressed as it long has been, it rushes forward with additional force; having to encounter obstacles, it is compelled to combat them, and overthrow them; until, at length, comprehended and adopted by the generality, it becomes the basis of new social order.

"Liberty will follow the same march as the Christian religion. Armed with death from the ancient society of Rome, it for a long while excited the hatred and fear of the people. At last, by force of martyrdoms and persecutions, the religion of Christ penetrated into the conscience and the soul; it soon had kings and armies at its orders, and Constantine and Charlemagne bore it triumphant throughout Europe. Religion then laid down her arms of war. It laid open to all the principles of peace and order which it contained; it became the prop of Government, as it was the organizing element of society. Thus will it be with liberty. In 1793 it frightened people and sovereigns alike; then, having clothed itself in a milder garb, IT INSINUATED ITSELF EVERYWHERE IN THE TRAIN OF OUR BATTALIONS. In 1815 all parties adopted its flag, and armed themselves with its moral force—covered themselves with its colours. The adoption was not sincere, and liberty was soon obliged to reassume its warlike accoutrements. With the contest their fears returned. Let us hope that they will soon cease, and that liberty will soon resume her peaceful standards, to quit them no more.

"The Emperor Napoleon contributed more than any one else towards accelerating the reign of liberty, by saving the moral influence of the revolution, and diminishing the fears which it imposed. Without the Consulate and the Empire, the revolution would have been only a grand drama, leaving grand revolutions but no traces: the revolution would have been drowned in the counter-revolu-

拿破仑把这个宏伟的使命执行到底。他的任务是艰巨的。他不得不在一个为憎恨和复仇而激动的社会中推行新的政策。为了建立，他使用了推翻旧制度时所采用的革命暴力手段。

每个新的真理出现的时候，它的运气通常是不尽如人意的，它所面对的指责要多于信任，多于所赢得的支持和在人们心中所唤起的恐惧。由于它被压抑得太久了，它就以一种超强的力量向前猛冲。它不得不面对阻碍的力量并与其搏斗直至打倒它们。最后它被大多数人理解和接受并构成了新社会秩序的基础。

自由将会像基督教一样沿着相同的步伐前进。从罗马的古代社会开始，基督教就是以死亡来作为代价的，有很长一段时间它在人们心中所激起的都是憎恨和恐惧。最后，通过殉难和迫害的力量，基督教渗透到人们的意识和灵魂之中。它很快就有了执行命令的国王和军队，君士坦丁一世［君士坦丁一世（约公元 280—337），古罗马帝国皇帝（公元 306—337 年），史称君士坦丁大帝。——译注］和查理曼大帝［查理曼大帝（公元 742—814），768—814 年为法兰克王，公元 800—814 年为西罗马帝国皇帝。——译注］推动它在整个欧洲取得了胜利。宗教就放下了它战争的武器。它敞开胸怀吸纳所有和平与秩序的原则。它成了政府的支柱，也成了社会的重要组织部分。这也是自由所要经历的步骤。在 1793 年［法国粉碎欧洲君主国家的武装干涉。——译注］它同样吓坏了人们和统治者。然后，它自己穿上了温和的外衣在我们军队的秩序下把自己暗暗隐藏起来。在 1815 年［拿破仑退位。——译注］所有的党派都采用了它的旗帜，用它的道德力量来武装他们自己——戴着它的徽章。这种行为并不是表里一致的，很快自由又不得不再次拿起它的战争装备。伴随着斗争，人们的恐惧又回来了。让我们希望战争很快就会停止，自由将很快恢复她平静的状态，并再也不要离开人们了。

拿破仑皇帝通过保全革命的精神影响力、减少它给人们所带来的

tion. The contrary, however, was the case. Napoleon rooted the revolution in France, and introduced, throughout Europe, the principal benefits of the crisis of 1789. To use his own words, 'He purified the revolution, he confirmed kings, and ennobled people.' He purified the revolution, in separating the truths which it contained from the passions that, during its delirium, disfigured it. He ennobled the people in giving them the consciousness of their force, and those institutions which raise men in their own eyes. The Emperor may be considered as the Messiah of the new ideas; for—and we must confess it—in the moments immediately succeeding a social revolution, it is not so essential to put rigidly into practice all the propositions resulting from the new theory, but to become master of the regenerative genius, to identify one's self with the sentiments of the people, and boldly to direct them towards the desired point. To accomplish such a task YOUR FIBRE SHOULD RESPOND TO THAT OF THE PEOPLE, as the Emperor said; you should feel like it, your interests should be so intimately raised with its own, that you should vanquish or fall together."

Let us take breath after these big phrases,—grand round figures of speech,—which, when put together, amount like certain other combinations of round figures to exactly 0. We shall not stop to argue the merits and demerits of Prince Louis's notable comparison between the Christian religion and the Imperial-revolutionary system. There are many blunders in the above extract as we read it; blundering metaphors, blundering arguments, and blundering assertions; but this is surely thc grandest blunder of all; and one wonders at the blindness of the legislator and historian who can advance such a parallel. And what are we to say of the legacy of the dying revolution to Napoleon? Revolutions do not die, and, on their death-beds, making fine speeches, hand over their property to young officers of artillery. We have all read the history of his rise. The constitution of the year Ⅲ. was carried. Old men of the Montagne, disguised royalists, Paris sections, PITTETCOBOURG, above all, with his money-bags, thought that here was a fine opportunity for a revolt, and opposed the new constitution in arms: the new constitution had knowledge of a young officer who would not hesitate to defend its cause, and who effectually beat the majority. The tale may be found in every account of

恐惧而加速了自由的统治，在这方面他的作用要超过其他任何人。没有执政府和帝国，革命只能是一场壮观的戏剧，除了上演壮观的革命场面之外而没遗留下来任何痕迹。革命也早在反革命潮流中被淹没掉了。然而事实是相反的。拿破仑在法国巩固了革命，把1789年革命的原则推广到欧洲各地。用他自己的话说，是“他净化了这场革命，巩固了王权，使人们的尊严得到了提高”。他净化了这场革命，把革命中的真理成分从激情之中抽取出来，在人们为革命而发狂的时候，这种激情曾损害了革命的真理。他让人们意识到自身的力量、提高他们的地位，那些公共机构都从它们自己的角度来选拔人才。皇帝或许还被认为是新思想的救世主。因为——我们必须承认——在突然成功的社会变革中，要把从新思想中获得的所有提议都严格地付诸实践并不重要，重要的是成为新一代领导人，就要使自己得到民众的认同，大胆地带领他们向着期望的目标前进。如同这位皇帝说的那样，要完成这样一件任务，你必须要得到人民的响应，得到他们的支持，你的利益要和他们的利益紧密联系在一起，那样你才能完全征服或击败他们。

让我们看完这些大段的句子后先喘口气——王子一副庄重率直的演讲形象——但是把这种形象和演讲的内容放在一起，就一点价值也没有了。对于路易王子把基督教和帝国革命体制相比的是非功过我们用不着停下来争论。仅在我们抽取的上面一部分中就存在许多明显的错误——错误的隐喻、错误的辩论和错误的断言，但这个比喻确实是整篇文章中最大的错误。人们对一个竟能提出如此比喻的立法者和历史学家的无知而感到奇怪。对于垂死的革命传授给拿破仑的遗嘱我们能说些什么呢？革命没有消亡，而是在它临死之际发表了一番精彩的言论，把他们的遗产移交给年轻的炮兵军官（拿破仑）。我们都知道拿破仑崛起的历史。共和三年宪法付诸实施了。山区的老人们伪装成保皇主义者，同时在巴黎地区，皮特考伯格首先凭借他的钱袋认为这是一个反叛的大好机会，可以用武力反对新宪法：新

the revolution, and the rest of his story need not be told. We know every step that he took: we know how, by doses of cannon-balls promptly administered, he cured the fever of the sections—that fever which another camp-physician (Menou) declined to prescribe for; we know how he abolished the Directory; and how the Consulship came; and then the Empire; and then the disgrace, exile, and lonely death. Has not all this been written by historians in all tongues? —by memoir-writing pages, chamberlains, marshals, lackeys, secretaries, contemporaries, and ladies of honour? Not a word of miracle is there in all this narration; not a word of celestial missions, or political Messiahs. From Napoleon's rise to his fall, the bayonet marches alongside of him: now he points it at the tails of the scampering "five hundred,"—now he charges with it across the bloody planks of Arcola—now he flies before it over the fatal plain of Waterloo.

Unwilling, however, as he may be to grant that there are any spots in the character of his hero's government, the Prince is, nevertheless, obliged to allow that such existed; that the Emperor's manner of rule was a little more abrupt and dictatorial than might possibly be agreeable. For this the Prince has always an answer ready—it is the same poor one that Napoleon uttered a million of times to his companions in exile—the excuse of necessity. He WOULD have been very liberal, but that the people were not fit for it; or that the cursed war prevented him—or any other reason why. His first duty, however, says his apologist, was to form a general union of Frenchmen, and he set about his plan in this wise:—

"Let us not forget, that all which Napoleon undertook, in order to create a general fusion, he performed without renouncing the principles of the revolution. He recalled the émigrés, without touching upon the law by which their goods had been confiscated and sold as public property. He reestablished the Catholic religion at the same time that he proclaimed the liberty of conscience, and endowed equally the ministers of all sects. He caused himself to be consecrated by the Sovereign Pontiff, without conceding to the Pope's demand any of the liberties of the Gallican church. He married a daughter of the Emperor of Austria, without abandoning any of the rights of France to the conquests

宪法知道一个年轻的军官会毫不犹豫地去维护他的事业，会有效地打击大多数反叛者。在每篇法国革命的报道文章中都能找到这个故事，故事的剩余部分就不用讲了。我们知道拿破仑走过的每一步。我们知道他是怎样果断地用炮弹这种药剂治疗了巴黎各区的反叛激情——另一个军营医师梅努[梅努（Menou）国民大会常备军的无能统帅。——译注]则拒绝开这种药方。我们知道他是怎样废除了督政府；又是怎样取得了终身执政官的职位；接着又建立了帝国；然后就是耻辱、放逐和孤独的死亡。这些不都已被历史学家用各种语言写过——被回忆录、侍从、元帅、仆人、荣誉秘书和同时代的人讲过了吗？在所有这类的叙述中都没有奇迹、神圣的使命或政治救世主这样的词语。从拿破仑的崛起到失败，他都离不开武力。他用武力指挥军队穿过布满血迹的阿尔科拉桥[阿尔科拉是意大利的一个村子，1796 年拿破仑在那里打败了人数比他多的奥国军队。攻占阿尔科拉桥的战斗持续了三天，打得非常艰难。——译注]——并用武力结束了惨败的滑铁卢战役。

虽然王子可能不愿意承认在拿破仑的政体中存在着任何缺陷，但他又不得不承认缺陷还是有的，即皇帝统治的方式有些粗鲁和独裁，不是很让人满意。对于这点，王子也有备好的答案——即拿破仑在放逐时对他的同伴说过一百万次的理由。他原本会很开明大度的，但人们不需要这种大度，是该死的战争或其他的原因妨碍了他那样做。路易王子为他辩护说，拿破仑的第一职责就是形成一个法国人的统一联盟，他是这样着手实施他的计划的：

> 我们不要忘记拿破仑所做的一切都是为了建立一个统一的联盟，他在执行这一任务的时候并没有弃绝革命的原则。他召回了流亡贵族，并没有触动他们已经被法律没收或作为公共财产变卖的财物。他在重建天主教的同时又宣告信仰的自由，还给所有教派的教长捐赠了物品。后来他成了神圣罗马帝国皇帝，但他并没有牺牲法国天主教徒的自由

she had made. He reestablished noble titles, without attaching to them any privileges or prerogatives, and these titles were conferred on all ranks, on all services, on all professions. Under the empire all idea of caste was destroyed; no man ever thought of vaunting his pedigree—no man ever was asked how he was born, but what he had done.

"The first quality of a people which aspires to liberal government, is respect to the law. Now, a law has no other power than lies in the interest which each citizen has to defend or to contravene it. In order to make a people respect the law, it was necessary that it should be executed in the interest of all, and should consecrate the principle of equality in all its extension. It was necessary to restore the prestige with which the Government had been formerly invested, and to make the principles of the revolution take root in the public manners. At the commencement of a new society, it is the legislator who makes or corrects the manners; later, it is the manners which make the law, or preserve it from age to age intact."

Some of these fusions are amusing. No man in the empire was asked how he was born, but what he had done; and, accordingly, as a man's actions were sufficient to illustrate him, the Emperor took care to make a host of new title-bearers, princes, dukes, barons, and what not, whose rank has descended to their children. He married a princess of Austria; but, for all that, did not abandon his conquests—perhaps not actually; but he abandoned his allies, and, eventually, his whole kingdom. Who does not recollect his answer to the Poles, at the commencement of the Russian campaign? But for Napoleon's imperial father-in-law, Poland would have been a kingdom, and his race, perhaps, imperial still. Why was he to fetch this princess out of Austria to make heirs for his throne? Why did not the man of the people marry a girl of the people? Why must he have a Pope to crown him—half a dozen kings for brothers, and a bevy of aides-de-camp dressed out like so many mountebanks from Astley's, with dukes' coronets, and grand blue velvet marshals' bâtons? We have repeatedly his words for it. He wanted to create an aristocracy—another acknowledgment on his part of the Republican dilemma—another apology for the revolutionary blunder. To keep the republic within bounds, a despotism is necessary; to rally round the despotism, an aristocracy must be created; and for what have we

权利而屈从于罗马教皇的要求。他娶了奥地利皇帝的一个女儿，但并没有放弃法国作为战胜国的任何权利。他重建了贵族的称号，但没有给他们附加任何特权，所有等级、所有机构人员、所有行业都被赠予这些称号。在帝国的统治下，拿破仑的这种做法打破了世袭的思想。再也没有人去吹嘘他的家族系谱——再也没有人被问及他的出身是怎样的，取而代之的是他做过什么。

对于每一个渴望开明政府的公民来说，最重要的品质就是尊重法律。现在，法律关系到每个公民的切身利益，他不得不去维护或触犯法律。为了让每个公民尊重法律，很有必要让法律关切到全体人民的利益，在广泛的领域内使平等的原则神圣化。恢复以前政府所具有的威望也是必要的，让革命的原则在公众行为中扎根。在一个新社会的开始阶段都是立法者规定或纠正人们的行为，后来就是人们的行为演变成法律或保护法律完整无缺地一代一代往下传。

有些话还是挺有趣的。在帝国里没有人会被问及他的出身，人们只会问他做过什么。因此一个人的行动就足以证明他的为人，皇帝喜欢结交许多有新头衔的人物，王子、公爵、男爵等等，他们的身份已传给了他们的后代。他娶了一个奥地利的公主，虽然如此，他也没有放弃他的征服地盘——好像事实不是这样的。他背弃了他的盟友，最后又背弃了他整个王国。谁不记得在俄国战役开始时他对波兰人的答复呢？要不是拿破仑帝王的岳父，波兰早就变成他的一个王国［波兰当时被奥地利、俄国、普鲁士所瓜分。——译注］，也是帝制的了。他为什么要从奥地利接来这位公主为他的王权生育继承人呢？为什么这个同所有人一样平等的男人不娶一个普通的少女呢？他让罗马教皇为自己加冕——让许多兄弟做国王，身边一群副官的穿着打扮就像来自爱司特垒［英格兰的地名。——译注］的江湖骗子一样，他们带着公爵的王冠，穿着华丽的蓝色天鹅绒衣服，拿着将军的官杖，他为什么要这样做呢？很明显，他想建立一个贵族统治的国家——

been labouring all this while? for what have bastilles been battered down, and king's heads hurled, as a gage of battle, in the face of armed Europe? To have a Duke of Otranto instead of a Duke de la Tremoille, and Emperor Stork in place of King Log. O, lame conclusion! Is the blessed revolution which is prophesied for us in England only to end in establishing a Prince Fergus O'Connor, or a Cardinal Wade, or a Duke Daniel Whittle Harvey? Great as those patriots are, we love them better under their simple family names, and scorn titles and coronets.

At present, in France, the delicate matter of titles seems to be better arranged, any gentleman, since the Revolution, being free to adopt any one he may fix upon; and it appears that the Crown no longer confers any patents of nobility, but contents itself with saying, as in the case of M. de Pontois, the other day, "Le Roi trouve convenable that you take the title of," &c.

To execute the legacy of the revolution, then; to fulfil his providential mission; to keep his place,—in other words, for the simplest are always the best,—to keep his place, and to keep his Government in decent order, the Emperor was obliged to establish a military despotism, to re-establish honours and titles; it was necessary, as the Prince confesses, to restore the old prestige of the Government, in order to make the people respect it; and he adds—a truth which one hardly would expect from him,—"At the commencement of a new society, it is the legislator who makes and corrects the manners; later, it is the manners which preserve the laws." Of course, and here is the great risk that all revolutionizing people run—they must tend to despotism; "they must personify themselves in a man," is the Prince's phrase; and, according as is his temperament or disposition—according as he is a Cromwell, a Washington, or a Napoleon—the revolution becomes tyranny or freedom, prospers or falls.

Somewhere in *the St. Helena memorials*, Napoleon reports a message of his to the Pope. "Tell the Pope," he says to an archbishop, "to remember that I have six hundred thousand armed Frenchmen, qui marcheront avec moi, pour moi, et comme moi." And this is the legacy of the revolution, the advancement of freedom! A hundred volumes of imperial special pleading will

他不可能建立共和制——不可能把大革命彻底进行下去。为了让共和国受到约束，专制是必要的；要防止专制，贵族统治是必要的。我们为什么要详尽阐释这些呢？摧毁巴士底狱、砍掉国王的头、与武装的欧洲同盟作战是为了什么呢？就是为了让奥特朗公爵取代代穆叶公爵，斯多克皇帝取代罗格国王。哦，多么无用的结局啊！难道这场神圣的革命就预示着我们在英国只是不再有一个叫福格斯·奥康纳的王子，或一个叫维德的红衣主教，或一个叫丹尼尔·怀特·哈维的公爵吗？尽管那些爱国者很伟大，但是我们更喜欢他们原来的简单的名字，嘲笑那些所谓的头衔和王冠。

目前在法国，关于头衔这件棘手的事情似乎得到了较好的处理，自革命以来，每个绅士都可以自由选定他所喜欢的头衔。看来君王不再会授予人们任何贵族的特权，他只是口头上过过瘾而已。以德·庞特瓦先生为例，在不久前的某天，“国王发现你用这个头衔是合适的”等等。

接着就要把革命的遗训贯彻下去，完成上帝所托付的使命，巩固他自己的地位——换句简单的话来说，就是为了巩固他的地位，使他的政府能有效而体面地运转，皇帝不得不实行军事专制，重新设立荣誉和头衔制度。如同王子所供认的那样，恢复政府旧日的威望是必要的，是为了让人们能尊重它。他又补充道：人们不要期望从他那里得到什么真理——“在一个新社会的开始阶段是立法者规定或纠正人们的行为；后来就是人们的行为维护法律。”当然，这里所有正在革命的人都要冒很大的风险——即他们必然会进入一个专制主义的社会。“他们必须要使自己表现得像一个男子汉那样”，这是王子所说的。根据革命者的性情或气质——根据克伦威尔、华盛顿或拿破仑的性格特点——革命会变成专制或自由，成功或失败。

在《圣赫勒拿岛回忆录》[拿破仑所著。——译注]中，拿破仑对罗马教皇报告了这样一个信息，他对一位大主教说：“告诉罗马教皇，要记住我有六十万武装的法国人，他们跟着我前进、服从我、信任我。”这就是革命的遗训、自由的进步！一百卷有关帝国体制的辩护词也无法对这样的言论作出解释——这个既傲慢又羞耻的人无意之中就把帝王的优势、能力和缺

not avail against such a speech as this—one so insolent, and at the same time so humiliating, which gives unwittingly the whole of the Emperor's progress, strength, and weakness. The six hundred thousand armed Frenchmen were used up, and the whole fabric falls; the six hundred thousand are reduced to sixty thousand, and straightway all the rest of the fine imperial scheme vanishes: the miserable senate, so crawling and abject but now, becomes of a sudden endowed with a wondrous independence; the miserable sham nobles, sham empress, sham Kings, dukes, princes, chamberlains, pack up their plumes and embroideries, pounce upon what money and plate they can lay their hands on, and when the allies appear before Paris, when for courage and manliness there is yet hope, when with fierce marches hastening to the relief of his capital, bursting through ranks upon ranks of the enemy, and crushing or scattering them from the path of his swift and victorious despair, the Emperor at last is at home,—where are the great dignitaries and the lieutenant-generals of the empire? Where is Maria Louisa, the Empress Eagle, with her little callow King of Rome? Is she going to defend her nest and her eaglet? Not she. Empress-queen, lieutenant-general, and court dignitaries, are off on the wings of all the winds—profligati sunt, they are away with the money-bags, and Louis Stanislaus Xavier rolls into the palace of his fathers.

With regard to Napoleon's excellences as an administrator, a legislator, a constructor of public works, and a skilful financier, his nephew speaks with much diffuse praise, and few persons, we suppose, will be disposed to contradict him. Whether the Emperor composed his famous code, or borrowed it, is of little importance; but he established it, and made the law equal for every man in France except one. His vast public works and vaster wars were carried on without new loans or exorbitant taxes; it was only the blood and liberty of the people that were taxed, and we shall want a better advocate than Prince Louis to show us that these were not most unnecessarily and lavishly thrown away. As for the former and material improvements, it is not necessary to confess here that a despotic energy can effect such far more readily than a Government of which the strength is diffused in many conflicting parties. No doubt, if we could create a despotical governing machine, a steam autocrat,—

陷都给暴露了出来，六十万法国人被驱使得筋疲力尽，整个组织体制都垮了。六十万的人马后来缩减到六万，很快帝国的其他宏伟方案也破产了。——曾经如此可怜、没有地位的参议院现在突然被赋予了独立性。可怜的假贵族、假皇后、假国王和公爵、王子、侍从们把他们漂亮的衣服和刺绣品都打了包，家里的钱和餐具都被他们随手一扫而光。当拿破仑集结部队在巴黎出现的时候，他们除了勇气和雄赳赳的气概之外还存有一丝希望，他们加紧步伐立即对首都进行援救，冲破层层敌军的阻挠，皇帝最后终于到家了。[1815 年 3 月，拿破仑一世由厄尔巴岛逃回法国，迅速聚集旧部，进军巴黎，重新称帝，并立即组建军队。——译注]——那些显要的贵族、帝国的将军到哪里去了？皇后玛丽亚·路易莎和她的小罗马国王在哪里呢？她将会保护她的巢穴和她的小鹰[鹰，是拿破仑的徽志。——译注]吗？她不会。皇后、将军和宫廷显要在关键时刻都逃走了——荒淫的他们是带着钱袋子走的。路易十八又回到了波旁家族的王宫。

对于拿破仑作为一个行政官员、一个立法者、公共事务的创立人和精明的财政人员的优点，他的侄子用了大段大段的篇幅来予以赞颂，很少有人会就这些问题故意去反驳他。是皇帝本人编写了他那部著名的法典还是从别人那里借鉴来的，这都不重要。但是他确立了这部法典，宣称在法国法律对每个人都是平等的，只有他除外。他大量的公众事务和大量的战争都是在没有借债或征收过高赋税的条件下进行的，只不过人民要付出鲜血和自由的代价。我们将需要一个比路易王子更高明的拥护者来向我们说明这些不是不必要的浪费。至于拿破仑在位期间所取得的进步，一个专制的政府必然比一个把力量分散在许多党派纷争上的政府能更快地产生作用，这点是用不着解释的。毋庸置疑，如果我们可以制造一个专制的统治机器——一个精力旺盛、冷淡、不知疲倦、杰出的独裁者，我们应该比以前更进步，比在任何形式的政府统治下生活得更加轻松。部长们可以惬意地享受他们的退休金，实现自己的规划，约翰勋爵可以在空闲时创作他的故事或悲剧，帕默斯顿勋爵[英国外相。——译注]就不用绞尽脑汁地给

passionless, untiring, and supreme,—we should advance further, and live more at ease than under any other form of government. Ministers might enjoy their pensions and follow their own devices; Lord John might compose histories or tragedies at his leisure, and Lord Palmerston, instead of racking his brains to write leading articles for *Cupid*, might crown his locks with flowers, and sing ερωτα μουνον, his natural Anacreontics; but alas! not so: if the despotic Government has its good side, Prince Louis Napoleon must acknowledge that it has its bad, and it is for this that the civilized world is compelled to substitute for it something more orderly and less capricious. Good as the Imperial Government might have been, it must be recollected, too, that since its first fall, both the Emperor and his admirer and would-be successor have had their chance of reestablishing it. "Fly from steeple to steeple" the eagles of the former did actually, and according to promise perch for a while on the towers of Nôtre Dame. We know the event: if the fate of war declared against the Emperor, the country declared against him too; and, with old Lafayette for a mouthpiece, the representatives of the nation did, in a neat speech, pronounce themselves in permanence, but spoke no more of the Emperor than if he had never been. Thereupon the Emperor proclaimed his son the Emperor Napoleon II. "L'Empereur est mort, vive l'Empereur!" shouted Prince Lucien. Psha! not a soul echoed the words: the play was played, and as for old Lafayette and his "permanent" representatives, a corporal with a hammer nailed up the door of their spouting-club, and once more Louis Stanislas Xavier rolled back to the bosom of his people.

In like manner Napoleon III. returned from exile, and made his appearance on the frontier. His eagle appeared at Strasburg, and from Strasburg advanced to the capital; but it arrived at Paris with a keeper, and in a post-chaise; whence, by the orders of the sovereign, it was removed to the American shores, and there magnanimously let loose. Who knows, however, how soon it may be on the wing again, and what a flight it will take?

《爱神》写文章了，他可以在自己的大衣上别上花朵，吟唱阿那克里翁［古希腊的抒情诗人。——译注］的诗歌。唉！但一切并不是这样的。如果专制政府有它好的一面，路易·拿破仑王子一定承认它也有坏的一面，就是因为这个原因，“文明”的世界才不得不转换成为一个更有秩序和更为稳定的世界。虽然帝制政体曾经是好的政体，但人们还必须要记住，从它首次被击垮之后，皇帝和他的崇拜者及将来的继任者都有重建它的机会。先前的拿破仑这只鹰确实做到了“从一个尖塔飞到另一个尖塔，”还根据承诺在圣母院的塔尖上停歇了一会儿。我们知道事情发展的过程。他战败了，民众也公开反对他。以老拉斐德为首的国会议员代表们在演讲中继续发表他们自己的言论，但是不再提起皇帝，仿佛他从来没有存在过。随即拿破仑一世宣布他的儿子为皇帝拿破仑二世。当吕西安·波拿巴［Lucien Bonaparte（1775—1840），法国政治家，拿破仑之大弟，五百人院议长。——译注］王子喊道“拿破仑一世驾崩，拿破仑一世万岁”的时候，没有一个人会作出回应。戏剧结束了，至于老拉斐德和议员代表，一位带着锤子的下士把他们演讲俱乐部的门给钉死了，路易十八［1814 年拿破仑一世的统治垮台，反法联军进入巴黎，决定波旁王朝的路易十八复辟。1824 年路易十八死，由路易十六的弟弟查理十世继位。1830 年七月革命中被推翻，波旁复辟王朝告终。——译注］复辟。

同样，拿破仑三世结束了放逐生活又回来了，他在边境出现了。他的势力军队在斯特拉斯堡出现，并从斯特拉斯堡前进到首都。但他是带着一个坐在轻便马车里的监护人到达巴黎的。在那里，在统治者的命令下它被移交到美国海岸，在那里获得释放。然而谁知道，这只鹰可能会很快再次展开翅膀做一次怎样的飞行呢？

The Story of Mary Ancel

"GO, my nephew," said old Father Jacob to me, "and complete thy studies at Strasburg: Heaven surely hath ordained thee for the ministry in these times of trouble, and my excellent friend Schneider will work out the divine intention."

Schneider was an old college friend of uncle Jacob's, was a Benedictine monk, and a man famous for his learning; as for me, I was at that time my uncle's chorister, clerk, and sacristan; I swept the church, chanted the prayers with my shrill treble, and swung the great copper incense-pot on Sundays and feasts; and I toiled over the Fathers for the other days of the week.

The old gentleman said that my progress was prodigious, and, without vanity, I believe he was right, for I then verily considered that praying was my vocation, and not fighting, as I have found since.

You would hardly conceive (said the Captain, swearing a great oath) how devout and how learned I was in those days; I talked Latin faster than my own beautiful patois of Alsatian French; I could utterly overthrow in argument every Protestant (heretics we called them) parson in the neighbourhood, and there was a confounded sprinkling of these unbelievers in our part of the country. I prayed half a dozen times a day; I fasted thrice in a week; and, as for penance, I used to scourge my little sides, till they had no more feeling than a peg-top: such was the godly life I led at my uncle Jacob's in the village of Steinbach.

Our family had long dwelt in this place, and a large farm and a pleasant house were then in the possession of another uncle—uncle Edward. He was the youngest of the three sons of my grandfather; but Jacob, the elder, had shown a decided vocation for the church, from, I believe, the age of three, and now was by no means tired of it at sixty. My father, who was to have in-

玛丽·昂塞勒的故事

“去吧！我的侄子，”老神甫雅各布对我说，“去斯特拉斯堡［位于德法边境的法国城市斯特拉斯堡。——译注］完成你的学业。上天注定你要在这段困难时期做一个牧师，我有一个很优秀的朋友叫施耐德，他会为你做出神圣的安排。”

施耐德是雅各布叔父旧日的一个大学朋友，一个本笃会的修道士，他因博学而有名。至于我，我那段时间是我叔父唱诗班的歌手、他的教会文书和圣器看管人。我打扫教堂，用尖锐刺耳的声音唱祈祷歌，在周日和节日里摇晃巨大的铜制香炉，其余的时间我为神甫们辛勤地干活。

老神甫说我的进步是惊人的。他并没有虚夸，我相信他说的是正确的，因为我一直都认为祈祷而不是争斗才是我的天职。

你很难想象（上尉很庄重地说）在那些日子里我是多么虔诚和博学。我讲拉丁文的速度比说自己国家美丽的阿尔萨斯方言的速度都要快。在争辩中我可以把附近教区的每个新教徒牧师都给打败（我们叫他们异教徒），因为在我们国家的部分地区还有一些该受诅咒的少量异教徒。我每天祈祷六次，一周斋戒三次，至于苦修，我常常是用鞭子鞭打我身体的一侧，直到它们像陀螺一样失去了任何感觉。这就是我在史坦巴哈乡村雅各布叔父家里所过的敬神生活。

我们家族在这个地方已居住了很长时间。一个大的农场和一幢舒适的房子都是我另一位叔父——爱德华叔父的财产。他是我祖父三个儿子当中

herited the paternal property, was, as I hear, a terrible scamp and scapegrace, quarrelled with his family, and disappeared altogether, living and dying at Paris; so far we knew through my mother, who came, poor woman, with me, a child of six months, on her bosom, was refused all shelter by my grandfather, but was housed and kindly cared for by my good uncle Jacob.

Here she lived for about seven years, and the old gentleman, when she died, wept over her grave a great deal more than I did, who was then too young to mind anything but toys or sweetmeats.

During this time my grandfather was likewise carried off: he left, as I said, the property to his son Edward, with a small proviso in his will that something should be done for me, his grandson.

Edward was himself a widower, with one daughter, Mary, about three years older than I, and certainly she was the dearest little treasure with which Providence ever blessed a miserly father; by the time she was fifteen, five farmers, three lawyers, twelve Protestant parsons, and a lieutenant of Dragoons had made her offers: it must not be denied that she was an heiress as well as a beauty, which, perhaps, had something to do with the love of these gentlemen. However, Mary declared that she intended to live single, turned away her lovers one after another, and devoted herself to the care of her father.

Uncle Jacob was as fond of her as he was of any saint or martyr. As for me, at the mature age of twelve I had made a kind of divinity of her, and when we sang "*Ave Maria*" on Sundays I could not refrain from turning to her, where she knelt, blushing and praying and looking like an angel, as she was. Besides her beauty, Mary had a thousand good qualities; she could play better on the harpsichord, she could dance more lightly, she could make better pickles and puddings, than any girl in Alsace; there was not a want or a fancy of the old hunks her father, or a wish of mine or my uncle's, that she would not gratify if she could; as for herself, the sweet soul had neither wants nor wishes except to see us happy.

I could talk to you for a year of all the pretty kindnesses that she would do for me; how, when she found me of early mornings among my books, her presence "would cast a light upon the day;" how she used to smooth and fold my little surplice, and embroider me caps and gowns for high feast-days; how

最小的。雅各布排行第二，但是他从三岁起就表示要在教堂中履行自己的天职。我相信，直到现在的六十岁，他对教堂也没有任何厌倦。我听说，我的父亲，就是那个要继承祖父财产的人，是一个可怕的坏蛋和无赖，他和家里人吵了一架之后就完全消失了，在巴黎过活直至死去。迄今为止我们从我母亲那里就只知道这些。我母亲，这个可怜的女人怀里抱着六个月大的我就回到了这里，我祖父拒绝对她提供食宿，但是好心的雅各布叔父给了我们房子住并仁慈地照顾我们。

我母亲在这里大约居住了七年。当她死去的时候，雅各布叔父对着她的墓穴痛哭，他的悲痛远远超过了我，我那时还很小，所关心的只是玩具和糖果。

在这段时间我祖父也去世了。他把财产都留给了他的儿子爱德华，但在他的遗嘱里还有一个小的附带条件，即应该为我——他的孙子做点什么。

爱德华自己是一个鳏夫，他有一个女儿名叫玛丽，大约比我年长三岁，她当然是上帝赐给这个可怜父亲的最可贵的财富了。到她十五岁的时候，就已经有五个农场主、三个律师、十二个新教徒牧师和一个龙骑兵中尉向她求过婚了。不可否认的是她既是一位继承人又是一位美人，也许它们都和那些绅士的爱情有某种关系。然而玛丽宣称她喜欢独自生活，陆续地拒绝了那些求婚者，全心全意照顾她父亲。

雅各布叔父是以自己作为一个圣徒或殉教者的身份喜欢玛丽的。至于我，在到了十二岁的成熟年龄时就已经把她神圣化了。当我们在周日唱《万福玛利亚》的时候，我禁不住把眼睛转向她，她在那里跪着，脸微微发红，正在祈祷，看起来就像是一个天使。除了她的美貌，玛丽身上还有许多优点。她的拨弦古钢琴弹得很好，会跳轻盈的舞蹈，她还会做很好的泡菜和布丁，比阿尔萨斯任何一个女孩做的都要好。在她身上没有她那位守财奴父亲的贪婪和吝啬，也没有我和叔父对于神秘天国的渴望，这些都不能让她感到满足。对于她自己来说，这个温柔的姑娘唯一期望的就是看到我们快乐。

she used to bring flowers for the altar, and who could deck it so well as she? But sentiment does not come glibly from under a grizzled moustache, so I will drop it, if you please.

Amongst other favours she showed me, Mary used to be particularly fond of kissing me: it was a thing I did not so much value in those days, but I found that the more I grew alive to the extent of the benefit, the less she would condescend to confer it on me; till at last, when I was about fourteen, she discontinued it altogether, of her own wish at least; only sometimes I used to be rude, and take what she had now become so mighty unwilling to give.

I was engaged in a contest of this sort one day with Mary, when, just as I was about to carry off a kiss from her cheek, I was saluted with a staggering slap on my own, which was bestowed by uncle Edward, and sent me reeling some yards down the garden.

The old gentleman, whose tongue was generally as close as his purse, now poured forth a flood of eloquence which quite astonished me. I did not think that so much was to be said on any subject as he managed to utter on one, and that was abuse of me; he stamped, he swore, he screamed; and then, from complimenting me, he turned to Mary, and saluted her in a manner equally forcible and significant; she, who was very much frightened at the commencement of the scene, grew very angry at the coarse words he used, and the wicked motives he imputed to her.

"The child is but fourteen," she said; "he is your own nephew, and a candidate for holy orders:—father, it is a shame that you should thus speak of me, your daughter, or of one of his holy profession."

I did not particularly admire this speech myself, but it had an effect on my uncle, and was the cause of the words with which this history commences. The old gentleman persuaded his brother that I must be sent to Strasburg, and there kept until my studies for the church were concluded. I was furnished with a letter to my uncle's old college chum, Professor Schneider, who was to instruct me in theology and Greek.

I was not sorry to see Strasburg, of the wonders of which I had heard so much; but felt very loath as the time drew near when I must quit my pretty cousin, and my good old uncle. Mary and I managed, however, a parting

谈到她为我付出的一切好意，我可以给你说上一年的时间。在早晨，当她发现埋在书堆里的我的时候，她的出现能给我的一天都投上光彩。她常常把我的小白色法衣熨好叠好，到重大节日的时候给我的帽子和长袍绣上花。她经常把花带到祭坛上来，还有谁能像她那样把祭坛打扮得如此漂亮呢？但感情并不是随随便便就从嘴上得来的，如果你乐意的话，我就不说这些了。

在玛丽给予我的其他恩惠中还有一条，那就是她过去还特别喜欢吻我。在那些日子里我觉不出它有什么价值。但是当我发现自己对这种恩惠变得越来越敏感时，她却越来越少地授予我这种恩惠了。直到最后，在我大约十四岁的时候，她就完全停止吻我了，这只是她自己的打算。只不过有时我常常是粗鲁的，硬要她很不情愿地吻我。

有一天我和玛丽为这种事情争论，当我就要从她脸颊上获得一个吻的时候，我自己脸上突然被回敬了一扇令人吃惊的耳光，这是叔父爱德华赐予我的，他一巴掌打得我在院子里后退了好几步。

这个老绅士，他的嘴巴平常都像他的钱包一样严实，现在却滔滔不绝地骂了起来，着实让我吃了一惊。我并不认为他在其他话题上或对其他人所说的话要超过这次对我的辱骂所说的话。他跺脚、咒骂、尖叫。后来又从讥讽我转向对玛丽的斥责，用的也是同样严厉而暗含讽刺的话。玛丽刚开始是被吓坏了，现在听到他父亲使用的粗俗语言以及强加在她身上的邪恶动机，她变得非常生气。

“这个孩子只有十四岁，”她说，“他是你自己的侄子，牧师的候选人。——父亲，你这样说我——你的女儿，说一个神职人员是耻辱的。”

我自己并不是特别喜欢这句话，但它却对我叔父产生了作用，并由此导致了故事开头的那段话。爱德华叔父劝说他哥哥一定要把我送到斯特拉斯堡，在那里完成我的神职学业。雅各布叔父给了我一封写给他旧日同学施耐德教授的信，施耐德教授将指导我的神学和希腊语。

我并不是不愿意去看看斯特拉斯堡、去见识见识我所听过的奇闻逸事，

walk, in which a number of tender things were said on both sides. I am told that you Englishmen consider it cowardly to cry; as for me, I wept and roared incessantly: when Mary squeezed me, for the last time, the tears came out of me as if I had been neither more nor less than a great wet sponge. My cousin's eyes were stoically dry; her ladyship had a part to play, and it would have been wrong for her to be in love with a young chit of fourteen—so she carried herself with perfect coolness, as if there was nothing the matter. I should not have known that she cared for me, had it not been for a letter which she wrote me a month afterwards—THEN, nobody was by, and the consequence was that the letter was half washed away with her weeping; if she had used a watering-pot the thing could not have been better done.

Well, I arrived at Strasburg—a dismal, old-fashioned, rickety town in those days—and straightway presented myself and letter at Schneider's door; over it was written—COMITÉ DE SALUT PUBLIC.

Would you believe it? I was so ignorant a young fellow, that I had no idea of the meaning of the words; however, I entered the citizen's room without fear, and sat down in his ante-chamber until I could be admitted to see him.

Here I found very few indications of his reverence's profession; the walls were hung round with portraits of Robespierre, Marat, and the like; a great bust of Mirabeau, mutilated, with the word Traître underneath; lists and republican proclamations, tobacco-pipes and fire-arms. At a deal-table, stained with grease and wine, sat a gentleman, with a huge pigtail dangling down to that part of his person which immediately succeeds his back, and a red nightcap, containing a TRICOLOUR cockade as large as a pancake. He was smoking a short pipe, reading a little book, and sobbing as if his heart would break. Every now and then he would make brief remarks upon the personages or the incidents of his book, by which I could judge that he was a man of the very keenest sensibilities "Ah, brigand! " "O, malheureuse! " "O, Charlotte, Charlotte! " The work which this gentleman was perusing is called "*The Sorrows of Werter*;" it was all the rage, in those days, and my friend was only following the fashion. I asked him if I could see Father Schneider? he turned towards me a hideous, pimpled face, which I dream of now at forty years' distance.

"Father who?" said he. "Do you imagine that citizen Schneider has not

但是当离别的日期临近，我必须要离开我的堂姐、我好心的雅各布叔父的时候，我就很不高兴了。临走之前，玛丽和我最后一次出去散步，两人都说了许多体贴亲切的话。我知道你们英国人认为哭是懦弱的表现。但我却抑制不住地哭泣和喊叫。当玛丽最后一次紧紧拥抱我的时候，泪水从我的眼睛里喷涌而出，我仿佛就是一块大大的湿海绵。我堂姐的眼睛却是无动于衷、干燥的。这位小姐还要去参加一个聚会，像她这样对一个十四岁的小孩产生爱情是不正常的——因此她的表情非常的冷静，仿佛一切都无所谓。要不是一个月后收到了她写给我的一封信，我还真不知道她其实是在乎我的。她写信的时候一定没有人在旁边，因为信纸上的一半字迹都被她的泪水给打湿了，一个水罐也盛不了她那么多的泪水。

就这样，我到了斯特拉斯堡——一个沉闷、古老、破旧不堪的城镇——我马上就带着信件来到施耐德的门口，门上面写着——国家安全委员会。

你会相信吗？我那时是一个如此无知的年轻人，以至于我都不知道这些字的含义。我无所畏惧地走进这个市民的房间，先是坐在前厅里，后来才被允许进去看他。

在他的房间里，我几乎发现不了他所从事的牧师职业的任何迹象。墙壁周围挂着些罗伯斯比尔、马拉这类人物的肖像；一件很大的米拉波[Mirabeau（1749—1791)，法国政治家、演说家，法国大革命初期国民议会的议长。——译注]的半身塑像，它是残缺不全的，下面有些“过激”的文字；还有很多表格和共和党的公告、烟斗和武器。在一张被油和酒弄脏了的松木桌子旁边站着一位先生，他留着长长的过肩的辫子，一顶红色的帽子，帽子上有一个像煎饼那么大的三色帽章。他正抽着一个短烟斗，读着一本小书，不断啜泣着，仿佛他的心都要碎了。他还不时地对书中的人物或故事做简单的评论，通过他的评论可以看出他是一个很热心的人——“啊，坏蛋!”“哦，不幸啊!”“哦，夏绿蒂，夏绿蒂!”这位绅士正在阅读的书的名字是《少年维特之烦恼》，这本书在当时正风行一时，这位

thrown off the absurd mummery of priesthood? If you were a little older you would go to prison for calling him Father Schneider—many a man has died for less;" and he pointed to a picture of a guillotine, which was hanging in the room.

I was in amazement.

"What is he? Is he not a teacher of Greek, an abbé, a monk, until monasteries were abolished, the learned editor of the songs of 'Anacreon?'"

"He WAS all this," replied my grim friend; "he is now a Member of the Committee of Public Safety, and would think no more of ordering your head off than of drinking this tumbler of beer."

He swallowed, himself, the frothy liquid, and then proceeded to give me the history of the man to whom my uncle had sent me for instruction.

Schneider was born in 1756: was a student at Würzburg, and afterwards entered a convent, where he remained nine years. He here became distinguished for his learning and his talents as a preacher, and became chaplain to Duke Charles of Würtemberg. The doctrines of the Illuminati began about this time to spread in Germany, and Schneider speedily joined the sect. He had been a professor of Greek at Cologne; and being compelled, on account of his irregularity, to give up his chair, he came to Strasburg at the commencement of the French Revolution, and acted for some time a principal part as a revolutionary agent at Strasburg.

["Heaven knows what would have happened to me had I continued long under his tuition!" said the Captain. "I owe the preservation of my morals entirely to my entering the army. A man, sir, who is a soldier, has very little time to be wicked; except in the case of a siege and the sack of a town, when a little license can offend nobody."]

By the time that my friend had concluded Schneider's biography, we had grown tolerably intimate, and I imparted to him (with that experience so remarkable in youth) my whole history—my course of studies, my pleasant country life, the names and qualities of my dear relations, and my occupations in the vestry before religion was abolished by order of the Republic. In the course of my speech I recurred so often to the name of my cousin Mary, that the gentleman could not fail to perceive what a tender place she had in my heart.

朋友也只不过是在赶时髦。我问他能否见见施耐德神甫？他向我转过脸来，是一张丑陋长有丘疹的面孔，我猜他大约有四十岁的年龄。

“神甫？”他说，“你以为市民施耐德还没有甩掉那个荒谬可笑的教士身份啊？如果你年龄再大一些，你会因叫他施耐德神甫而坐牢的——许多人就因为这个送了命。”他指了指挂在房间里的一张断头台的画。

我很惊讶。

“那他是做什么的啊？直到修道院被取消的时候，他不都应是一位希腊语教师、一位神甫、一个修道士、阿那克瑞翁［公元前6世纪的希腊抒情诗人。——译注］诗歌的学者编辑吗？”

“他全部都是，”这位严厉的朋友说，“他现在是国家安全委员会的一个成员，想让你的人头落地并不比喝这酒杯里的啤酒更难。”

他自己吞下了那瓶泛着泡沫的液体，然后就给我讲施耐德——即我叔父要我找的那个人——的历史。

施耐德1756年出生，曾是伍茨堡的一名学生，后来进入一所修道院，在那里待了九年。他因具备一个传道士的博学和才能而很有名气，后来成为符腾堡查尔斯公爵的牧师。启蒙主义大约就是在这个时候传入德国的，施耐德很快加入了这个派别。他曾是科隆的希腊语教授，考虑到启蒙工作的无规律性，不得不放弃了教职。他在法国大革命开始时来到斯特拉斯堡，作为在斯特拉斯堡的一个革命负责人，他有段时间在革命中扮演了主要的角色。

［“如果我长时间听从他的教诲，上帝知道在我身上还会发生什么事情！”上尉说，“我自己的德行要完全归功于我服役军队的那段经历。先生，作为一个士兵的男人几乎是没有机会去变坏的，除非是在围攻或洗劫一座城镇的情况下，那时才能得到一点许可，可以去冒犯小人物。”］

在这位朋友讲完施耐德历史的时候，我们已变得挺亲密了，我把自己全部的历史也都告诉他了（年轻人奇怪的心理）——我学习的课程，我愉快的乡村生活，我亲爱的亲戚们的名字和品质，还有在共和国下命令取消

Then we reverted to "*The Sorrows of Werter*," and discussed the merits of that sublime performance. Although I had before felt some misgivings about my new acquaintance, my heart now quite yearned towards him. He talked about love and sentiment in a manner which made me recollect that I was in love myself; and you know that when a man is in that condition, his taste is not very refined, any maudlin trash of prose or verse appearing sublime to him, provided it correspond, in some degree, with his own situation.

"Candid youth!" cried my unknown, "I love to hear thy innocent story and look on thy guileless face. There is, alas! so much of the contrary in this world, so much terror and crime and blood, that we who mingle with it are only too glad to forget it. Would that we could shake off our cares as men, and be boys, as thou art, again!"

Here my friend began to weep once more, and fondly shook my hand. I blessed my stars that I had, at the very outset of my career, met with one who was so likely to aid me. What a slanderous world it is, thought I; the people in our village call these Republicans wicked and bloody-minded; a lamb could not be more tender than this sentimental bottle-nosed gentleman! The worthy man then gave me to understand that he held a place under Government. I was busy in endeavouring to discover what his situation might be, when the door of the next apartment opened, and Schneider made his appearance.

At first he did not notice me, but he advanced to my new acquaintance, and gave him, to my astonishment, something very like a blow.

"You drunken, talking fool," he said, "you are always after your time. Fourteen people are cooling their heels yonder, waiting until you have finished your beer and your sentiment!"

My friend slunk muttering out of the room.

"That fellow," said Schneider, turning to me, "is our public executioner: a capital hand too, if he would but keep decent time; but the brute is always drunk, and blubbering over '*The Sorrows of Werter*!'"

I know not whether it was his old friendship for my uncle, or my proper merits, which won the heart of this sternest ruffian of Robespierre's crew; but certain it is, that he became strangely attached to me, and kept me constantly about his person. As for the priesthood and the Greek, they were of

宗教之前我在教堂法衣室所从事的职业。在我讲述的过程中我多次都提到了我堂姐玛丽的名字，他一定可以感觉到玛丽在我心中所占据的是一个多么温柔的位置。

然后我们又回到《少年维特之烦恼》这本书上来，讨论这部杰作的优点。虽然我刚开始时对这位新结识的人还有些疑虑，可现在我的心都倾向到他那一边去了。他谈到爱情和感情时的态度都让我想起了自己的爱情。你知道当一个人处在那种处境中的时候，他的鉴赏水平不会很高的，任何伤感的拙劣散文或诗句对于他来说都是卓越的，只要它在某种程度上能与他所处的境况正好相契。

“坦率的年轻人!”这个陌生人叫道，“我喜欢听你单纯的故事，看你天真的面庞。唉！在这个世界上有太多反面的事情了，这么多的恐怖、罪行和流血，生活于其中的我们庆幸的是还能把它们忘却。希望我们可以摆脱掉成年人的烦心事，再次成为像你这样的男孩!”

我的朋友又开始哭泣起来，他亲热地和我握手。我感谢自己的命运，让我在刚出来经历世事的时候能遇到一个乐意帮助我的人。我想，这是一个多么造谣中伤的世界啊！我们村子里的人都把这些共和党人称做邪恶和血腥的人。可是一只羔羊也不会比这个感伤、酒糟鼻的绅士更温和的了！这位令人尊敬的人向我透露说他在政府部门有一个职位。我正要力图查问出他的职位会是什么的时候，隔壁房间的门开了，施耐德出现了。

起先他没有注意到我，但是他向前走到我新相识的这位朋友身边，让我惊讶的是，施耐德打了他一下子。

“你这个醉鬼，还多嘴,”他说，“你常常迟到。十四个人都在那里久等了，一直等到你喝完啤酒，发泄完情绪为止!”

我的朋友咕哝着从房间里溜走了。

“那个家伙,”施耐德转向我说，“是我们公众的刽子手。如果他能守时的话，现在也是一个上尉了，但这个畜生经常喝醉，为《少年维特之烦恼》哭泣!”

course very soon out of the question. The Austrians were on our frontier; every day brought us accounts of battles won; and the youth of Strasburg, and of all France, indeed, were bursting with military ardor. As for me, I shared the general mania, and speedily mounted a cockade as large as that of my friend, the executioner.

The occupations of this worthy were unremitting. Saint Just, who had come down from Paris to preside over our town, executed the laws and the aristocrats with terrible punctuality; and Schneider used to make country excursions in search of offenders with this fellow, as a provost-marshal, at his back. In the meantime, having entered my sixteenth year, and being a proper lad of my age, I had joined a regiment of cavalry, and was scampering now after the Austrians who menaced us, and now threatening the Emigrés, who were banded at Coblentz. My love for my dear cousin increased as my whiskers grew; and when I was scarcely seventeen, I thought myself man enough to marry her, and to cut the throat of any one who should venture to say me nay.

I need not tell you that during my absence at Strasburg, great changes had occurred in our little village, and somewhat of the revolutionary rage had penetrated even to that quiet and distant place. The hideous "Fête of the Supreme Being" had been celebrated at Paris; the practice of our ancient religion was forbidden; its professors were most of them in concealment, or in exile, or had expiated on the scaffold their crime of Christianity. In our poor village my uncle's church was closed, and he, himself, an inmate in my brother's house, only owing his safety to his great popularity among his former flock, and the influence of Edward Ancel.

The latter had taken in the Revolution a somewhat prominent part; that is, he had engaged in many contracts for the army, attended the clubs regularly, corresponded with the authorities of his department, and was loud in his denunciations of the aristocrats in his neighbourhood. But owing, perhaps, to the German origin of the peasantry, and their quiet and rustic lives, the revolutionary fury which prevailed in the cities had hardly reached the country people. The occasional visit of a commissary from Paris or Strasburg served to keep the flame alive, and to remind the rural swains of the existence of a Republic in France.

我不知道是因为我叔父与他往日的友谊还是我本人的某些优点赢得了这位罗伯斯比尔团伙中的严厉暴徒的心。不过可以肯定的是，他开始喜欢我了，经常把我留在他身边。至于神学和希腊语，很快就不必谈了。奥地利人正威胁我们的边境，每天我们都能得到战争胜利的消息。斯特拉斯堡和所有法国的年轻人都充满了对于军事的热情。至于我，我也分享了这份狂热，很快也戴上了一块像我的朋友——刽子手戴的那样大的帽章。

这位杰出人物的工作一直是不间断的。圣·鞠斯特［罗伯斯比尔忠实的同志。——译注］从巴黎来到我们这个城镇负责工作，用可怕而严格的标准来执行法律、处死贵族。施耐德作为一个拥护他的宪兵主任，过去常常和这个家伙为了抓捕罪犯在国内做短途旅行。这时我已到了十六岁，成为那个年龄段的一个帅小伙了，我加入了一个骑兵团，有时跑来跑去地追逐那些威胁我们的奥地利人，有时去威胁那些在科布伦茨［德国城名，1792年法国逃亡贵族曾在那里组织反革命军队。——译注］的联合逃亡者。我对亲爱的堂姐的爱情也随着我身体的发育而不断加深。当我刚刚十七岁的时候，我认为自己完全可以和她结婚了，谁胆敢说不，我会和他拼命的。

在我离开斯特拉斯堡的那段时间我们那个小村庄也发生了很大的变化，革命的某些狂热也渗透到了那个安静、遥远的地方。革命的最高权威已在巴黎设立机构。我们古老的宗教习俗也受到禁止。宗教的公开信仰者大部分都藏了起来，或离开本国，或因为基督教徒的罪名而在断头台上赎罪。在我们可怜的村子里，我叔父的教堂被关闭了，他自己住在他兄弟的房子里，他的安全还要归功于以前信徒们对他的爱戴，还有爱德华·昂塞勒的势力。

从表面上看，爱德华·昂塞勒是参加了革命。这表现在，他忙着和军队签了许多契约，定期参加俱乐部，与他部门的主管当局保持联系，大声地谴责周边的贵族。或许要归因于这些农民的德国血统和他们安静质朴的生活，才使得村民们没有陷入在城市里流行的革命狂热情绪中去。巴黎或

Now and then, when I could gain a week's leave of absence, I returned to the village, and was received with tolerable politeness by my uncle, and with a warmer feeling by his daughter.

I won't describe to you the progress of our love, or the wrath of my uncle Edward, when he discovered that it still continued. He swore and he stormed; he locked Mary into her chamber, and vowed that he would withdraw the allowance he made me, if ever I ventured near her. His daughter, he said, should never marry a hopeless, penniless subaltern; and Mary declared she would not marry without his consent. What had I to do? —to despair and to leave her. As for my poor uncle Jacob, he had no counsel to give me, and, indeed, no spirit left: his little church was turned into a stable, his surplice torn off his shoulders, and he was only too lucky in keeping HIS HEAD on them. A bright thought struck him: suppose you were to ask the advice of my old friend Schneider regarding this marriage? he has ever been your friend, and may help you now as before.

(Here the Captain paused a little.) You may fancy (continued he) that it was droll advice of a reverend gentleman like uncle Jacob to counsel me in this manner, and to bid me make friends with such a murderous cut-throat as Schneider; but we thought nothing of it in those days; guillotining was as common as dancing, and a man was only thought the better patriot the more severe he might be. I departed forthwith to Strasburg, and requested the vote and interest of the Citizen President of the Committee of Public Safety.

He heard me with a great deal of attention. I described to him most minutely the circumstance, expatiated upon the charms of my dear Mary, and painted her to him from head to foot. Her golden hair and her bright blushing cheeks, her slim waist and her tripping tiny feet; and furthermore, I added that she possessed a fortune which ought, by rights, to be mine, but for the miserly old father. "Curse him for an aristocrat!" concluded I, in my wrath.

As I had been discoursing about Mary's charms Schneider listened with much complacency and attention: when I spoke about her fortune, his interest redoubled; and when I called her father an aristocrat, the worthy ex-Jesuit gave a grin of satisfaction, which was really quite terrible. O, fool that I was to trust him so far!

The very same evening an officer waited upon me with the following note

斯特拉斯堡的代表偶尔也到这里来拜访，负责维持革命的火焰继续燃烧下去，提醒乡村的少年要知道法国共和国的存在。

偶尔，当我可以得到一个星期的休假时，我就回到村庄，得到我叔父还算过得去的接待，还有他女儿温暖的体贴。

对于我和玛丽的爱情进展情况，还有叔父爱德华发现我们两人仍在继续发展时的愤怒，我就不再向你描述了。他咒骂、大发雷霆，把玛丽锁进她的房间里，发誓说如果我胆敢靠近她，他就要收回对我的资助费用。他说，他的女儿不会嫁给一个没有希望、身无分文的副官。而玛丽也宣布没有父亲的同意，她不会结婚。我该怎么做呢？——是绝望地离开她吗？至于我可怜的叔父雅各布，他也给我提不出什么建议。实际上，他也没有多余的精力了。他的小教堂已变成了一个马厩，他的白色法衣被人从肩膀上扯掉了，唯一幸运的是他的脑袋还能保得住。他忽然有了个聪明的想法，告诉我说，你可以就这件婚事征求我的老朋友施耐德的意见啊？他曾是你的朋友，现在也会像以前那样帮你的。

（说到这里上尉暂停了一会儿）你可以想象（他继续说），像雅各布叔父这样一位牧师提供给我这种建议是多么滑稽可笑啊！居然吩咐我去和施耐德这样凶恶的凶手结交朋友。但是在那些日子里我们都想不了这么多了。断头台上的斩决像舞会一样平常，人们认为只要一个人越严肃他就越爱国。我即刻就离开村子去斯特拉斯堡请求国家安全委员会公民主席施耐德的支持和帮助。

施耐德很专注地听我讲。我把事情很详细地向他描述了，还详述了我亲爱的玛丽从头到脚的魅力。她的金发和她明亮的白里透红的脸颊，她纤细的腰肢和她轻盈的小脚。此外，我又补充道，她拥有一份本该属于我的财产——要不是她那个守财奴的老父亲，财产应该是我的。“诅咒他这个贵族！”出于愤怒，我说出了这样的话来作为结语。

当我讲玛丽的迷人之处的时候，施耐德就非常自满而专注地听着。当我讲到她的财产的时候，他的兴趣更浓了。当我称她的父亲是一个贵族的

from Saint Just:—

"STRASBURG, Fifth year of the Republic, one and indivisible,

11 Ventôse.

"The citizen Pierre Ancel is to leave Strasburg within two hours, and to carry the enclosed despatches to the President of the Committee of Public Safety at Paris. The necessary leave of absence from his military duties has been provided. Instant punishment will follow the slightest delay on the road.

Salut et Fraternité. "

There was no choice but obedience, and off I sped on my weary way to the capital.

As I was riding out of the Paris gate, I met an equipage which I knew to be that of Schneider. The ruffian smiled at me as I passed, and wished me a bon voyage. Behind his chariot came a curious machine, or cart; a great basket, three stout poles, and several planks, all painted red, were lying in this vehicle, on the top of which was seated my friend with the big cockade. It was the PORTABLE GUILLOTINE which Schneider always carried with him on his travels. The bourreau was reading "The Sorrows of Werter," and looked as sentimental as usual.

I will not speak of my voyage in order to relate to you Schneider's. My story had awakened the wretch's curiosity and avarice, and he was determined that such a prize as I had shown my cousin to be should fall into no hands but his own. No sooner, in fact, had I quitted his room than he procured the order for my absence, and was on the way to Steinbach as I met him.

The journey is not a very long one; and on the next day my uncle Jacob was surprised by receiving a message that the citizen Schneider was in the village, and was coming to greet his old friend. Old Jacob was in an ecstasy, for he longed to see his college acquaintance, and he hoped also that Schneider had come into that part of the country upon the marriage-business of your humble servant. Of course Mary was summoned to give her best dinner, and wear her best frock; and her father made ready to receive the new State dignitary.

Schneider's carriage speedily rolled into the court-yard, and Schneider's

时候，这位尊敬的前任耶稣会信徒露出了满意的微笑，真是很可怕。我真是愚蠢，竟那么信任他！

当天傍晚，一个官员带着一张圣·鞠斯特的便条来拜访我，上面写着——

斯特拉斯堡，共和国五年，风月（法国的月份）11号

市民皮埃尔·昂塞勒要在两小时内离开斯特拉斯堡，负责把密封急件送给巴黎的国家安全委员会主席。他在军队的请假许可已得到批准。路上稍有延迟即要受到处罚。

友好致敬。

除了服从之外没有选择，我即刻踏上了前往巴黎的令人厌烦的路途。

当我骑马从城门出去的时候遇见了一辆马车，我知道那是施耐德的。我从马车旁边经过的时候，这个恶棍还朝我微笑，祝我旅途顺利。在他四轮马车后面还跟着一辆二轮马车，有一个大大的篮子、三根牢固的杆子和几块厚木板，它们都被漆成了红色，平放在马车上面，在这些东西上面坐着我那位戴着大帽章的朋友。这些东西可是施耐德在旅行的时候经常携带的移动式断头台。那个刽子手正读着《少年维特之烦恼》，他看起来和平时一样感伤。

为了给你讲施耐德的事情，我就不说自己的旅行了。我的故事已唤起了那个卑鄙小人的好奇心和贪婪欲。像我堂姐这样的美人，他觉得应该归自己所有。实际上，我刚一离开他的房间，他就为我拟好了命令让我暂时离开。当我遇到他的时候，他正在去往史坦巴赫［石溪之意，德国的一个边镇。——译注］的路上。

路程不是很长。次日我的雅各布叔父就很惊讶地听到一个消息，说是市民施耐德到村子里向他的老朋友致意来了。老雅各布高兴得都出神了，因为他太想见到他的同学了，他还希望施耐德是为他侄子的婚事到这个村

CART followed, as a matter of course. The ex-priest only entered the house; his companion remaining with the horses to dine in private. There was a most touching meeting between him and Jacob. They talked over their old college pranks and successes; they capped Greek verses, and quoted ancient epigrams upon their tutors, who had been dead since the Seven Years' War. Mary declared it was quite touching to listen to the merry friendly talk of these two old gentlemen.

After the conversation had continued for a time in this strain, Schneider drew up all of a sudden, and said quietly, that he had come on particular and unpleasant business—hinting about troublesome times, spies, evil reports, and so forth. Then he called uncle Edward aside, and had with him a long and earnest conversation: so Jacob went out and talked with Schneider's FRIEND; they speedily became very intimate, for the ruffian detailed all the circumstances of his interview with me. When he returned into the house, some time after this pleasing colloquy, he found the tone of the society strangely altered. Edward Ancel, pale as a sheet, trembling, and crying for mercy; poor Mary weeping; and Schneider pacing energetically about the apartment, raging about the rights of man, the punishment of traitors, and the one and indivisible republic.

"Jacob," he said, as my uncle entered the room, "I was willing, for the sake of our old friendship, to forget the crimes of your brother. He is a known and dangerous aristocrat; he holds communications with the enemy on the frontier; he is a possessor of great and ill-gotten wealth, of which he has plundered the Republic. Do you know," said he, turning to Edward Ancel, "where the least of these crimes, or the mere suspicion of them, would lead you?"

Poor Edward sat trembling in his chair, and answered not a word. He knew full well how quickly, in this dreadful time, punishment followed suspicion; and, though guiltless of all treason with the enemy, perhaps he was aware that, in certain contracts with the Government, he had taken to himself a more than patriotic share of profit.

"Do you know," resumed Schneider, in a voice of thunder, "for what purpose I came hither, and by whom I am accompanied? I am the administrator of the justice of the Republic. The life of yourself and your family is in my

子里来的。当然，玛丽也穿上她最好的罩袍，被叫过来准备丰盛的晚餐。她父亲已做好准备迎接这位新的显贵了。施耐德的四轮马车快速地驶进了院子，后面的二轮马车理所当然的也跟进来了。只有这位前任牧师走进了房间，他的刽子手朋友则留下来和马在一起，单独吃晚饭。这里就有了施耐德和雅各布相见的感人一幕。他们谈起了以前在学校里的恶作剧和取得的胜利，还用希腊诗联句，引用古老的警句来议论他们的导师，而这位导师在七年战争后就已死去了。玛丽也表示，听着这两个老先生友好而快乐的谈话太让人感动了。

在这种气氛下的谈话只持续了一段时间，施耐德就忽然停住了，平静地说，他是为了某件特别不愉快的事情到这里来的——暗示这件事情和困难时期、间谍、不祥的报告诸如此类的东西有关。然后他把爱德华叔父叫到一边和他展开了一番长时间的热切的谈话。因此雅各布就出去和施耐德的刽子手朋友谈话，他们很快就变得非常亲密了，因为那个刽子手向他详述了接见我的所有情形。当雅各布回到房间的时候，施耐德和爱德华叔父的会谈才刚结束了一会儿，他发现屋里的气氛奇怪地发生了变化。爱德华·昂塞勒的脸色像白纸一样白，他颤抖着请求宽恕；可怜的玛丽正在哭泣；施耐德正用力地在房间里踱着步，就人权、叛逆者的处罚和不可分割的共和国愤怒地大发议论。

当雅各布叔父进入房间时，施耐德说："雅各布，看在我们旧日的友情上，我是愿意忽略你弟弟的罪过的。但他是一个众所周知、危险的贵族；他和边境上的敌人保持联系；他还拥有许多非法占有的财富，这些都是他掠夺的共和国的财富。你知道吗?"他转向爱德华·昂塞勒说，"是什么罪过或者猜疑诱使你这样做的?"

可怜的爱德华坐在他的椅子上发抖，一言不发。他完全知道在这段可怕的时期内，猜疑后面紧随而来的就是惩罚；即使是没有通敌，他或许也明白，在与政府打交道的过程中，他关心自己的程度要超过关注国家的利益。

hands: yonder man, who follows me, is the executor of the law; he has rid the nation of hundreds of wretches like yourself. A single word from me, and your doom is sealed without hope, and your last hour is come. Ho! Gregoire!" shouted he; "is all ready?"

Gregoire replied from the court, "I can put up the machine in half an hour. Shall I go down to the village and call the troops and the law people?"

"Do you hear him?" said Schneider. "The guillotine is in your court-yard; your name is on my list, and I have witnesses to prove your crime. Have you a word in your defence?"

Not a word came; the old gentleman was dumb; but his daughter, who did not give way to his terror, spoke for him.

"You cannot, sir," said she, "although you say it, FEEL that my father is guilty; you would not have entered our house thus alone if you had thought it. You threaten him in this manner because you have something to ask and to gain from us: what is it, citizen? —tell us how much you value our lives, and what sum we are to pay for our ransom?"

"Sum!" said uncle Jacob; "he does not want money of us: my old friend, my college chum, does not come hither to drive bargains with anybody belonging to Jacob Ancel?"

"Oh, no, sir, no, you can't want money of us," shrieked Edward; "we are the poorest people of the village: ruined, Monsieur Schneider, ruined in the cause of the Republic."

"Silence, father," said my brave Mary; "this man wants a PRICE: he comes, with his worthy friend yonder, to frighten us, not to kill us. If we die, he cannot touch a sou of our money; it is confiscated to the State. Tell us, sir, what is the price of our safety?"

Schneider smiled, and bowed with perfect politeness.

"Mademoiselle Marie," he said, "is perfectly correct in her surmise. I do not want the life of this poor drivelling old man: my intentions are much more peaceable, be assured. It rests entirely with this accomplished young lady (whose spirit I like, and whose ready wit I admire), whether the business between us shall be a matter of love or death. I humbly offer myself, citizen Ancel, as a candidate for the hand of your charming daughter. Her goodness, her beauty, and the large fortune which I know you intend to give her, would

施耐德用一种恐吓的语气继续说道：“你知道我到这里来的目的是什么吗？是谁陪我一块儿来的吗？我是共和国的治安行政官员。你自己和你家庭成员的性命就掌握在我手中。在那边跟随我来的人就是法律的执行者。他已经除掉了成百个像你这样卑鄙的人。我只要说一句话，你的命运就没有任何希望地被决定了，你最后的时刻到来了。嗬！格瑞奥！”他喊道，“准备好了吗？”

格瑞奥在院子里答道：“我半小时内就把机械组装好。需要我到村子里把部队和治安人员叫来吗？”

“你听到他的话了吗？”施耐德说，“断头台就在院子里。你的名字可是写在我的名单上的，而且我有证人来证明你的罪行。你还要为自己辩护吗？”

爱德华·昂塞勒沉默无语。但是他的女儿在施耐德的恐吓面前并没有屈服。

“先生，你不能这样做，”她说，“虽然你说你认为我父亲有罪，但是如果你真的那样以为的话，你就不会这样单独来到我们家。你用这种方式威胁我父亲是因为你想从我们这儿得到或索要什么东西。你到底要什么？——告诉我，你认为我们生命的价值是多少，我们需要付多少数目的赎金？”

“钱！”雅各布叔父说，“他不想要我们的钱。我的老朋友，我的大学同学不是到这里来和雅各布·昂塞勒家的人讨价还价的？”

“哦，不，先生，不，你不能要我们的钱，”爱德华尖叫道，“我们是村子里最贫穷的人。我们破产了，施耐德先生，因共和国而破产了。”

“父亲，安静下来，”勇敢的玛丽说，“这个人想要我们付出代价。他和院子里的那位尊敬的朋友是来恐吓我们的，不是要杀我们。如果我们死了，他得不到我们的一个子儿。我们的钱会让政府没收的。告诉我们，先生，我们安全的代价是什么？”

施耐德微笑着，很有礼貌地弯腰鞠了个躬。

render her a desirable match for the proudest man in the republic, and, I am sure, would make me the happiest."

"This must be a jest, Monsieur Schneider," said Mary, trembling, and turning deadly pale: "you cannot mean this; you do not know me: you never heard of me until to-day."

"Pardon me, belle dame," replied he; "your cousin Pierre has often talked to me of your virtues; indeed, it was by his special suggestion that I made the visit."

"It is false! —it is a base and cowardly lie!" exclaimed she (for the young lady's courage was up),—"Pierre never could have forgotten himself and me so as to offer me to one like you. You come here with a lie on your lips—a lie against my father, to swear his life away, against my dear cousin's honour and love. It is useless now to deny it: father, I love Pierre Ancel; I will marry no other but him—no, though our last penny were paid to this man as the price of our freedom."

Schneider's only reply to this was a call to his friend Gregoire.

"Send down to the village for the maire and some gendarmes; and tell your people to make ready."

"Shall I put THE MACHINE up?" shouted he of the sentimental turn.

"You hear him," said Schneider; "Marie Ancel, you may decide the fate of your father. I shall return in a few hours," concluded he, "and will then beg to know your decision."

The advocate of the rights of man then left the apartment, and left the family, as you may imagine, in no very pleasant mood.

Old uncle Jacob, during the few minutes which had elapsed in the enactment of this strange scene, sat staring wildly at Schneider, and holding Mary on his knees: the poor little thing had fled to him for protection, and not to her father, who was kneeling almost senseless at the window, gazing at the executioner and his hideous preparations. The instinct of the poor girl had not failed her; she knew that Jacob was her only protector, if not of her life—Heaven bless him! —of her honour. "Indeed," the old man said, in a stout voice, "this must never be, my dearest child—you must not marry this man. If it be the will of Providence that we fall, we shall have at least the thought to console us that we die innocent. Any man in France at a time like this,

他说："玛丽小姐的猜测是完全正确的。我并不想要这个可怜的胡言乱语的老人的性命。我的目的非常平和，你们放心。它取决于这位出色的年轻姑娘（我喜欢她的气质，欣赏她机灵的才智），我们的这笔交易能否达成将关系到爱情和死亡。公民昂塞勒，我谦逊地代表我自己向你这位迷人的女儿求婚。她的德行、她的美貌，还有我所知道的您将留给她的一笔可观的财产都使得她可以和共和国最荣耀的人相配，我确定，她会让我成为世界上最幸福的人。"

"这一定是个玩笑，施耐德先生，"玛丽脸色变得煞白，颤抖着说，"你不能这样打算。你不了解我。直到今天为止你还从没听说过我。"

"对不起，美人，"他回答道，"你的堂弟皮埃尔经常对我说起你的优点。实际上，正是由于他特别的建议，我才到这里来的。"

"这是假的！——是卑鄙、懦弱的谎言！"她大声地说（因为这位年轻姑娘的勇气被激发出来了），"皮埃尔从来也不可能忘记他和我的感情，把我献给像你这样的人。你满嘴谎言地到这里来——对我父亲撒谎，要夺走他的性命，还撒谎来攻击我亲爱的堂弟的名誉和爱情。现在要否认也是没用的了。父亲，我爱皮埃尔·昂塞勒。我只能嫁给他——即使是把我们的钱都给他来换取我们的自由也在所不惜。"

施耐德的反应是叫喊他的朋友格瑞奥。

"去村子里把镇长和一些宪兵叫来，告诉你手下的人准备好。"

"需要我把机械装好吗？"他用感伤的音调喊道。

"你听到他的话了，"施耐德说，"玛丽·昂塞勒，你可以决定你父亲的命运。我会在几个小时后再回来看你的决定。"

然后，这位人权拥护者就离开了，留下这三个人在房间，你可以想象得到，他们的心情都糟透了。

老雅各布叔父在这奇怪的一幕已过去的几分钟里一直坐在那儿愤怒地盯着施耐德，抓住趴在他膝上的玛丽的手。可怜的玛丽逃到他这里来寻求保护，而不是她父亲那里，她父亲几乎是没有任何知觉的在窗口跪着，注

would be a coward and traitor if he feared to meet the fate of the thousand brave and good who have preceded us."

"Who speaks of dying?" said Edward. "You, Brother Jacob? —you would not lay that poor girl's head on the scaffold, or mine, your dear brother's. You will not let us die, Mary; you will not, for a small sacrifice, bring your poor old father into danger?"

Mary made no answer. "Perhaps," she said, "there is time for escape: he is to be here but in two hours; in two hours we may be safe, in concealment, or on the frontier." And she rushed to the door of the chamber, as if she would have instantly made the attempt: two gendarmes were at the door. "We have orders, Mademoiselle," they said, "to allow no one to leave this apartment until the return of the citizen Schneider."

Alas! all hope of escape was impossible. Mary became quite silent for a while; she would not speak to uncle Jacob; and, in reply to her father's eager questions, she only replied, coldly, that she would answer Schneider when he arrived.

The two dreadful hours passed away only too quickly; and, punctual to his appointment, the ex-monk appeared. Directly he entered, Mary advanced to him, and said, calmly,—

"Sir, I could not deceive you if I said that I freely accepted the offer which you have made me. I will be your wife; but I tell you that I love another; and that it is only to save the lives of those two old men that I yield my person up to you."

Schneider bowed, and said,—

"It is bravely spoken. I like your candor—your beauty. As for the love, excuse me for saying that is a matter of total indifference. I have no doubt, however, that it will come as soon as your feelings in favour of the young gentleman, your cousin, have lost their present fervour. That engaging young man has, at present, another mistress—Glory. He occupies, I believe, the distinguished post of corporal in a regiment which is about to march to—Perpignan, I believe."

It was, in fact, Monsieur Schneider's polite intention to banish me as far as possible from the place of my birth; and he had, accordingly, selected the Spanish frontier as the spot where I was to display my future military talents.

视着刽子手和他那套可怕的设备。这一幕还没有把可怜的玛丽给击垮。她知道雅各布是她唯一的保护人，她也愿以自己的性命和荣誉来祈求上帝保佑他！老雅各布叔父用坚定的语气说："一定不要答应他，我最亲爱的孩子——你不能和这个男人结婚。如果这是上帝要我们承担的命运，我们至少应该用这样的想法来安慰自己，那就是我们是无辜死去的。每一个处在这种情境下的法国人，如果他惧怕接受这种勇敢而善良的人们的命运，那他就是一个懦夫和叛徒。"

"谁在说死?"爱德华说，"你，雅各布哥哥？——你不能把这个可怜的女孩的头放在断头台上，还有我的，你亲爱的兄弟的头。你不能让我们死，玛丽，你就不愿意作出一点小小的牺牲，忍心让你可怜的老父亲陷入危险之中吗?"

玛丽没有回答。过了一会儿，她说："也许还有逃走的时间。他会在两小时后回来。在这两小时里我们可能会安全地藏起来或逃到边境上。"她冲到房间的门口，仿佛她立即就要逃出去。两个宪兵在门口把守着，他们说："我们有命令，小姐，任何人不准离开这个房间直到施耐德公民回来。"

唉！不存在任何逃出去的希望。玛丽有一会儿变得非常沉默，她不跟雅各布叔父说话。对于她父亲急切的询问，她只是冷淡地回答说，当施耐德回来的时候她会给他答复的。

可怕的两个小时很快就过去了。那位前任修道士施耐德准时出现了。他直接走进房间，玛丽走上前去平静地说：

"先生，即使我说我愿意接受你对我的求婚，我也不能欺骗你。我将会成为你的妻子。但我要告诉你我爱的是另外一个人，而且我把我的人交给你只是为了挽救那两个老人的性命。"

施耐德鞠了一躬说：

"终于勇敢地讲出来了。我喜欢你的坦率，美人。至于爱情，请原谅我说它是无关紧要的。然而，我不怀疑，它会像你喜欢那个年轻的小伙子的感情一样很快就会到来的，你的堂弟已经失去了以往的热情。那位可爱的

Mary gave no answer to this sneer: she seemed perfectly resigned and calm: she only said,—

"I must make, however, some conditions regarding our proposed marriage, which a gentleman of Monsieur Schneider's gallantry cannot refuse."

"Pray command me," replied the husband elect. "Fair lady, you know I am your slave."

"You occupy a distinguished political rank, citizen representative," aid she; "and we in our village are likewise known and beloved. I should be ashamed, I confess, to wed you here; for our people would wonder at the sudden marriage, and imply that it was only by compulsion that I gave you my hand. Let us, then, perform this ceremony at Strasburg, before the public authorities of the city, with the state and solemnity which befits the marriage of one of the chief men of the Republic."

"Be it so, madam," he answered, and gallantly proceeded to embrace his bride.

Mary did not shrink from this ruffian's kiss; nor did she reply when poor old Jacob, who sat sobbing in a corner, burst out, and said,—

"O Mary, Mary, I did not think this of thee!"

"Silence, brother!" hastily said Edward; "my good son-in-law will pardon your ill-humour."

I believe uncle Edward in his heart was pleased at the notion of the marriage; he only cared for money and rank, and was little scrupulous as to the means of obtaining them.

The matter then was finally arranged; and presently, after Schneider had transacted the affairs which brought him into that part of the country, the happy bridal party set forward for Strasburg. Uncles Jacob and Edward occupied the back seat of the old family carriage, and the young bride and bridegroom (he was nearly Jacob's age) were seated majestically in front. Mary has often since talked to me of this dreadful journey. She said she wondered at the scrupulous politeness of Schneider during the route; nay, that at another period she could have listened to and admired the singular talent of this man, his great learning, his fancy, and wit; but her mind was bent upon other things, and the poor girl firmly thought that her last day was come.

In the meantime, by a blessed chance, I had not ridden three leagues

年轻人现在已有了另一个情人——荣誉。我相信，他现在军团里所担任的下士职务会永远持续下去的。”

事实上，施耐德先生的卑鄙意图是要把我驱除到离我出生之地尽可能远的地方。因此，他选择了西班牙的边境作为让我施展未来军事才能的地方。

玛丽对这种讥笑没有什么反应。她看起来十分的顺从和平静，她只是说：

“然而，至于我们的婚姻计划，我必须要提出一些条件，像施耐德这样豪侠的绅士是不能拒绝的。”

“请吩咐我吧！”这位被选定的丈夫回答道，“美丽的女士，你知道我就是你的奴仆。”

“你作为公民代表拥有显要的政治地位，”她说，“而我们家在村子里也同样是有名声，受到村民爱戴的。我承认在这里和你结婚会让我感到羞愧。因为我们的村民会对这么突然的婚事感到怀疑，暗示我是被迫嫁给你的。那么，就让我们在斯特拉斯堡，在市里的公众当局面前举行仪式，那种尊严和庄重的场合才适合共和国重要人物的婚礼。

“就这样，女士。”施耐德回答说，殷勤地走上前来拥抱他的新娘。

在这个恶棍亲吻她的时候，她没有退缩。她也没有回答可怜的老雅各布，他坐在角落里啜泣着突然说：

“哦，玛丽，玛丽，我不认为这就是你想要的！”

爱德华急忙说：“安静，兄弟！我的好女婿会原谅你的坏脾气的。”

我相信爱德华叔父内心对这件婚姻还是感到高兴的。他只在乎金钱和地位，至于用什么方式得到它们，他根本就不在乎。

然后，事情就解决了。在施耐德处理完这件事情之后，这个快乐的结婚团体就向斯特拉斯堡前进了。老雅各布叔父和爱德华坐在老式家庭马车的后座上，年轻的新娘和新郎（他和雅各布差不多大）庄严地坐在前面。后来玛丽时常跟我说起这次可怕的旅程。她说在路途上对于施耐德的小心

from Strasburg, when the officer of a passing troop of a cavalry regiment, looking at the beast on which I was mounted, was pleased to take a fancy to it, and ordered me, in an authoritative tone, to descend, and to give up my steed for the benefit of the Republic. I represented to him, in vain, that I was a soldier, like himself, and the bearer of despatches to Paris. "Fool!" he said; "do you think they would send despatches by a man who can ride at best but ten leagues a day?" And the honest soldier was so wroth at my supposed duplicity, that he not only confiscated my horse, but my saddle, and the little portmanteau which contained the chief part of my worldly goods and treasure. I had nothing for it but to dismount, and take my way on foot back again to Strasburg. I arrived there in the evening, determining the next morning to make my case known to the citizen St. Just; and though I made my entry without a sou, I don't know what secret exultation I felt at again being able to return.

The ante-chamber of such a great man as St. Just was, in those days, too crowded for an unprotected boy to obtain an early audience; two days passed before I could obtain a sight of the friend of Robespierre. On the third day, as I was still waiting for the interview, I heard a great bustle in the courtyard of the house, and looked out with many others at the spectacle.

A number of men and women, singing epithalamiums, and dressed in some absurd imitation of Roman costume, a troop of soldiers and gendarmerie, and an immense crowd of the badauds of Strasburg, were surrounding a carriage which then entered the court of the mayoralty. In this carriage, great God! I saw my dear Mary, and Schneider by her side. The truth instantly came upon me: the reason for Schneider's keen inquiries and my abrupt dismissal; but I could not believe that Mary was false to me. I had only to look in her face, white and rigid as marble, to see that this proposed marriage was not with her consent.

I fell back in the crowd as the procession entered the great room in which I was, and hid my face in my hands: I could not look upon her as the wife of another,—upon her so long loved and truly—the saint of my childhood—the pride and hope of my youth—torn from me for ever, and delivered over to the unholy arms of the murderer who stood before me.

The door of St. Just's private apartment opened, and he took his seat at

谨慎的礼貌感到很惊讶。如果是在另一个时期，她或许会倾听并赞美这个男人的非凡才能，他丰富的学识，他的想象力和机智。但是她的思想却在别的事情上，这个可怜的姑娘坚定地认为她的末日到了。

同时，非常幸运的是，当我离开斯特拉斯堡还不到三英里的时候，一个从我身边经过的骑兵团的军官看着我骑的马，就很高兴地喜欢上了，他用命令的口气让我下来，为了共和国的利益让我放弃这匹马。我徒劳地向他解释说我也像他自己的士兵一样是去巴黎送急信的带信人。“傻瓜!”他说，“你认为他们会让一个人骑着一天最多只能跑十英里的马去送急件吗?”这个诚实的军人以为我说的是谎言，因此十分愤怒，他不仅没收了我的马，还把那个装着我在世间主要财物的小旅行箱给没收了。我只好下了马，徒步走回斯特拉斯堡。我晚上就到了斯特拉斯堡，决定第二天早晨把我的事情向公民圣·鞠斯特报告。尽管我身无分文地回去了，但我那时还不知道自己应该为这次回来而暗自窃喜。

那时像圣·鞠斯特这样的大人物的接待室，通常都是很拥挤的，人们都挤着要得到早点的接见。在我得到允许可以见到罗伯斯比尔这位朋友之前，两天过去了。第三天，当我正等着会面的时候，我听到这个房间所处的院子里传来了喧闹声，因此就和许多人一起去看院子里的场面。

许多男人和女人唱着祝婚诗，穿着奇怪的模仿罗马人装束的衣服，一对士兵和宪兵，还有一大群斯特拉斯堡马路上爱看热闹的人，他们都簇拥着一辆驶进市长院子里来的马车。在这个马车里，天哪！我看到了我亲爱的玛丽和她身边的施耐德。我突然明白了事情的真相，知道施耐德的热切询问，以及我突然被打发走的原因是什么了。但我不相信玛丽对我的背叛。我只是看到她的脸色像大理石一样发白，表情僵硬，可以看出这件婚姻并不合她心意。

当队列进入我所在的大房子的时候，我被人群挤到了后面，我用手遮住我的脸。我不能看到她成为别人的妻子，这么长时间真诚爱慕的她——我童年的天使——我青年时期的骄傲和希望——就要永远地离开我，被送

the table of mayoralty just as Schneider and his cortége arrived before it.

Schneider then said that he came in before the authorities of the Republic to espouse the citoyenne Marie Ancel.

"Is she a minor?" asked St. Just.

"She is a minor, but her father is here to give her away."

"I am here," said uncle Edward, coming eagerly forward and bowing. "Edward Ancel, so please you, citizen representative. The worthy citizen Schneider has done me the honour of marrying into my family."

"But my father has not told you the terms of the marriage," said Mary, interrupting him, in a loud, clear voice.

Here Schneider seized her hand, and endeavoured to prevent her from speaking. Her father turned pale, and cried, "Stop, Mary, stop! For Heaven's sake, remember your poor old father's danger!"

"Sir, may I speak?"

"Let the young woman speak," said St. Just, "if she have a desire to talk." He did not suspect what would be the purport of her story.

"Sir," she said, "two days since the citizen Schneider entered for the first time our house; and you will fancy that it must be a love of very sudden growth which has brought either him or me before you today. He had heard from a person who is now unhappily not present, of my name and of the wealth which my family was said to possess; and hence arose this mad design concerning me. He came into our village with supreme power, an executioner at his heels, and the soldiery and authorities of the district entirely under his orders. He threatened my father with death if he refused to give up his daughter; and I, who knew that there was no chance of escape, except here before you, consented to become his wife. My father I know to be innocent, for all his transactions with the State have passed through my hands. Citizen representative, I demand to be freed from this marriage; and I charge Schneider as a traitor to the Republic, as a man who would have murdered an innocent citizen for the sake of private gain."

During the delivery of this little speech, uncle Jacob had been sobbing and panting like a broken-winded horse; and when Mary had done, he rushed up to her and kissed her, and held her tight in his arms. "Bless thee, my child!" he cried, "for having had the courage to speak the truth, and shame

到站在我前面的那个凶手的可怕臂膀中。

圣·鞠斯特私人房间的门打开了，当施耐德和他的随从们走到市长桌子前面的时候，圣·鞠斯特也在桌子边坐下了。

然后，施耐德说他到共和国的主管当局面前来娶公民玛丽·昂塞勒。

“她一个未成年人吗?”圣·鞠斯特问。

“她是一个未成年人，但她的父亲在这里负责把新娘交给新郎。”

“我在这里。”爱德华叔父鞠着躬说，急切地向前面走来。“爱德华·昂塞勒，很高兴见到您，公民代表。杰出的公民施耐德能够成为我们家庭中的成员让我感到非常的荣耀。”

“但是我父亲没有告诉你这桩婚事的条件。”玛丽打断他，大声而清楚地说。

施耐德抓住了她的手，竭力不让她说话。她父亲脸色变得苍白，喊道：“不要说了，玛丽，不要说了！看在上帝的分上，想想你可怜的老父亲的危险吧!”

“先生，我可以说吗?”玛丽说。

圣·鞠斯特说：“如果这位年轻的女士很想说，就让她说。”他猜不出她将会说些什么。

玛丽说：“先生，两天前公民施耐德第一次到了我们家。您可以想象得到，那一定是非常快速发展的爱情才在今天把他和我带到您的面前来。他从一个人那里听说了我的名字和据说我家庭所占有的财富后——不幸的是那个人现在不在场，他就对我起了歹意。他大摇大摆地来到我们村庄，后面跟着一个刽子手，还有听从他命令的军队和地区政府人员。如果我父亲拒绝交出他的女儿，他就用死亡来威胁他。我知道当时没有机会逃跑，除非是在您的面前才能澄清事实，因此就答应做他的妻子。我知道我的父亲是无辜的，因为他与政府的所有交易都是我亲自处理的。公民代表，我要求解除这桩婚姻。我以一个共和国叛徒的罪名控告施耐德，他为了个人利益企图谋害无辜的公民。”

thy old father and me, who dared not say a word."

"The girl amazes me," said Schneider, with a look of astonishment. "I never saw her, it is true, till yesterday; but I used no force: her father gave her to me with his free consent, and she yielded as gladly. Speak, Edward Ancel, was it not so?"

"It was, indeed, by my free consent," said Edward, trembling.

"For shame, brother!" cried old Jacob. "Sir, it was by Edward's free consent and my niece's; but the guillotine was in the court-yard! Question Schneider's famulus, the man Gregoire, him who reads '*The Sorrows of Werter.*'"

Gregoire stepped forward, and looked hesitatingly at Schneider, as he said, "I know not what took place within doors; but I was ordered to put up the scaffold without; and I was told to get soldiers, and let no one leave the house."

"Citizen St. Just," cried Schneider, "you will not allow the testimony of a ruffian like this, of a foolish girl, and a mad ex-priest, to weigh against the word of one who has done such service to the Republic: it is a base conspiracy to betray me; the whole family is known to favour the interest of the émigrés."

"And therefore you would marry a member of the family, and allow the others to escape; you must make a better defence, citizen Schneider," said St. Just, sternly.

Here I came forward, and said that, three days since, I had received an order to quit Strasburg for Paris immediately after a conversation with Schneider, in which I had asked him his aid in promoting my marriage with my cousin, Mary Ancel; that he had heard from me full accounts regarding her father's wealth; and that he had abruptly caused my dismissal, in order to carry on his scheme against her.

"You are in the uniform of a regiment in this town; who sent you from it?" said St. Just.

I produced the order, signed by himself, and the despatches which Schneider had sent me.

"The signature is mine, but the despatches did not come from my office. Can you prove in any way your conversation with Schneider?"

在玛丽简短陈述的时候，雅各布叔父一直在啜泣，像一匹马似的喘息。当玛丽讲完后，他冲上前去亲吻了她，用双臂紧紧抱住她。“祝福你，我的孩子!”他喊道，“你有勇气把事实真相讲出来，让你的老父亲和我感到羞愧啊！我们不敢说一句话。”

“这个姑娘真是让我感到吃惊，”施耐德带着惊异的表情说，“两天前我还从来没有见过她，这是真的。但是我并没有强迫他们。他父亲是自愿把她交给我的，她也是很高兴答应的。说啊！爱德华·昂塞勒，不是这样吗?”

“的确是这样，是我自愿的。”爱德华颤抖着说。

“耻辱啊，兄弟!”雅各布喊道，“先生，婚事是经过爱德华和我侄女同意的。但是断头台就在院子里啊！问一下施耐德的随从格瑞奥，就是那个读《少年维特之烦恼》的人，事情就清楚了。”

格瑞奥向前慢慢走过来，犹豫地看着施耐德，他说:“我不知道房间里发生了什么事。但我得到命令要在外面搭起断头台，他还告诉我去叫士兵过来，不让任何一个人离开房间。”

“公民圣·鞠斯特，”施耐德喊道，“你不能听信这个恶棍，还有那个愚蠢的姑娘、那个疯狂的前任牧师的证言，他们诽谤我这个为共和国做了许多工作的人啊！这是一个要出卖我的卑鄙阴谋。人们都知道他们全家支持流亡者的势力。”

“因此你就要和这个家庭的成员结婚，允许流亡者逃跑。你需要找个好点的理由，公民施耐德。”圣·鞠斯特严厉地说。

这时我挺身而出说，三天前我去请求施耐德帮忙促成我和我堂姐玛丽·昂塞勒的婚事，在我和他的谈话结束后，我就收到了立即离开斯特拉斯堡去巴黎的命令。他从我这里听到了关于玛丽父亲的财富的全部消息。他就突然把我打发走，以执行他抢夺玛丽的计划。

“你穿着这个城镇的军团制服，是谁派你走的?”圣·鞠斯特问。

我把便条拿出来，是他签的字，施耐德送给我的快信。

"Why," said my sentimental friend Gregoire, "for the matter of that, I can answer that the lad was always talking about this young woman: he told me the whole story himself, and many a good laugh I had with citizen Schneider as we talked about it."

"The charge against Edward Ancel must be examined into," said St. Just. "The marriage cannot take place. But if I had ratified it, Mary Ancel, what then would have been your course?"

Mary felt for a moment in her bosom, and said—"He would have died to-night—I would have stabbed him with this dagger."[1]

The rain was beating down the streets, and yet they were thronged; all the world was hastening to the market-place, where the worthy Gregoire was about to perform some of the pleasant duties of his office. On this occasion, it was not death that he was to inflict; he was only to expose a criminal who was to be sent on afterwards to Paris. St. Just had ordered that Schneider should stand for six hours in the public place of Strasburg, and then be sent on to the capital to be dealt with as the authorities might think fit.

The people followed with execrations the villain to his place of punishment; and Gregoire grinned as he fixed up to the post the man whose orders he had obeyed so often—who had delivered over to disgrace and punishment so many who merited it not.

Schneider was left for several hours exposed to the mockery and insults of the mob; he was then, according to his sentence, marched on to Paris, where it is probable that he would have escaped death, but for his own fault. He was left for some time in prison, quite unnoticed, perhaps forgotten: day by day fresh victims were carried to the scaffold, and yet the Alsatian tribune remained alive; at last, by the mediation of one of his friends, a long petition was presented to Robespierre, stating his services and his innocence, and demanding his freedom. The reply to this was an order for his instant execution: the wretch died in the last days of Robespierre's reign. His comrade, St. Just, followed him, as you know; but Edward Ancel had been released before this, for the action of my brave Mary had created a strong feeling in his favour.

"And Mary?" said I.

Here a stout and smiling old lady entered the Captain's little room: she

“是我的签字，但是这封快信不是我办公室的，你能用什么方法证明施耐德和你的谈话吗？”

我感伤的朋友格瑞奥说：“就这件事情我可以作证。这个青年人经常谈论这位年轻的姑娘。他告诉了我他自己全部的故事，当公民施耐德和我说起这些的时候，我们还感到很好笑。”

“对爱德华·昂塞勒的指控还要详细调查，”圣·鞠斯特说，“婚礼不能举行了。但是如果我认可了这件婚事，玛丽·昂塞勒，你会采取什么方法呢？”

玛丽在她的怀中摸索了一会儿说：“他会在今晚死去——我会用这把匕首刺死他的。”[1]

天空劈里啪啦地下着雨，但是街道上仍挤满了人。所有的人都赶紧涌向市场，在那里尊敬的格瑞奥正要履行一项愉快的使命。这次，他要面对的不是死亡，而是揭发一个随后就要被送到巴黎的罪犯施耐德。圣·鞠斯特已命令施耐德在斯特拉斯堡的公共场所站立六小时，然后被送到首都接受当局政府的处置。

人们咒骂着这个坏蛋，来到他接受惩罚的地方。当格瑞奥被安顿在他以前经常听从命令的那个人的职位上时，他微笑了——那个人让他受了那么多他不该受的耻辱和惩罚。

施耐德被留下来几个小时面对民众的嘲弄和侮辱。然后，根据宣判结果被送往巴黎，在那里要不是他自己的失误，他或许就逃过一死了。他在监狱里有段时间都被人遗忘了，不被注意。一天又一天新的罪犯被带上断头台，而这个阿尔萨斯的民众领袖仍活着。最后经过他一位朋友的调停，一封长长的请愿书送到了罗伯斯比尔面前，书上陈述了他的贡献和他的无辜，要求恢复自由。他得到的答复却是立即执行的命令。这个卑鄙的小人是在罗伯斯比尔执政的最后一天死去的。你知道，圣·鞠斯特在施耐德死后不久也死去了。爱德华·昂塞勒因为我勇敢的玛丽的行为给他帮了大忙，在这之前就已被赦免了罪过。

was leaning on the arm of a military-looking man of some forty years, and followed by a number of noisy, rosy children.

"This is Mary Ancel," said the Captain, "and I am Captain Pierre, and yonder is the Colonel, my son; and you see us here assembled in force, for it is the fête of little Jacob yonder, whose brothers and sisters have all come from their schools to dance at his birthday."

NOTES:

[1] This reply, and, indeed, the whole of the story, is historical. An account, by Charles Nodier, in the Revue de Paris, suggested it to the writer.

“那么，玛丽呢?”我说。

这时一个矮胖带着微笑的老女士进了上尉的小房间。她正靠在一个军人模样、大约四十岁的男子的臂膀上，后面还跟着许多吵闹、脸色红润的小孩。

“这是玛丽·昂塞勒,”上尉说，“我就是皮埃尔上尉，那位是上校，我的儿子。你看到我们这么多人聚集在一起，是因为今天是那边的小雅各布的生日，他的兄弟姐妹们都从学校里赶来要在他的生日宴会上跳舞。”

注释:

[1] 这句答复的话和整个故事情节都是真实的。它是查尔斯·那迪耶向作者推荐的巴黎杂志上的一篇文章。

Beatrice Merger

BEATRICE MERGER, whose name might figure at the head of one of Mr. Colburn's politest romances—so smooth and aristocratic does it sound—is no heroine, except of her own simple history; she is not a fashionable French Countess, nor even a victim of the Revolution.

She is a stout, sturdy girl of two-and-twenty, with a face beaming with good nature, and marked dreadfully by smallpox; and a pair of black eyes, which might have done some execution had they been placed in a smoother face. Beatrice's station in society is not very exalted; she is a servant of all-work: she will dress your wife, your dinner, your children; she does beef-steaks and plain work; she makes beds, blacks boots, and waits at table;—such, at least, were the offices which she performed in the fashionable establishment of the writer of this book: perhaps her history may not inaptly occupy a few pages of it.

"My father died," said Beatrice, "about six years since, and left my poor mother with little else but a small cottage and a strip of land, and four children too young to work. It was hard enough in my father's time to supply so many little mouths with food; and how was a poor widowed woman to provide for them now, who had neither the strength nor the opportunity for labour?

"Besides us, to be sure, there was my old aunt; and she would have helped us, but she could not, for the old woman is bed-ridden; so she did nothing but occupy our best room, and grumble from morning till night: Heaven knows, poor old soul, that she had no great reason to be very happy; for you know, sir, that it frets the temper to be sick; and that it is worse still to be sick and hungry too.

"At that time, in the country where we lived (in Picardy, not very far

贝阿特里斯·麦琪

贝阿特里斯·麦琪这个名字很容易让人想到浪漫小说的开头——它听起来是如此的悦耳和贵族化——不过我们这位贝阿特里斯只拥有自己简单的故事，她并不是小说中的女主人公。她不是一个时髦的法国伯爵夫人，因此也就不是大革命的受害者了。

她是一个二十二岁的矮胖、结实的姑娘，脸上带着自然的善意的微笑和可怕的天花印记，还有一双黑色的眼睛，如果这双眼睛长在一张平滑的脸上或许还会有些吸引力。贝阿特里斯的社会地位也不高。她是一个干各种工作的用人。她会给你的妻子穿衣，准备你的晚餐，照顾你的孩子；她会做牛排和普通的工作；她收拾床铺，擦黑色的长靴，在饭桌旁边服侍。就这样，在本书作者时髦的住宅里她至少是尽了一个用人的职责的。作者在这里要用几页篇幅来讲述她的故事。

贝阿特里斯说："大约是六年前，我父亲死了，他给我可怜的母亲只留下一间小屋，一小块地，还有四个年幼、没有工作能力的孩子。我父亲在世的时候就很难让这么多的孩子吃饱，现在一个可怜的、既没有力气也没有机会去劳动的寡妇又能给他们提供什么呢？

"除我们之外，还有我的老姨妈。她也可能会帮帮我们的，但是她不能，因为她只能卧在床上，除了占着我们最好的房间之外，她从早到晚地抱怨，什么也不做。可怜的老人，她没有什么快乐的理由。先生，你知道疾病会让人的脾气变坏，既有病又挨饿就更糟糕了。

from Boulogne), times were so bad that the best workman could hardly find employ; and when he did, he was happy if he could earn a matter of twelve sous a day. Mother, work as she would, could not gain more than six; and it was a hard job, out of this, to put meat into six bellies, and clothing on six backs. Old aunt Bridget would scold, as she got her portion of black bread; and my little brothers used to cry if theirs did not come in time. I, too, used to cry when I got my share; for mother kept only a little, little piece for herself, and said that she had dined in the fields,—God pardon her for the lie! And bless her, as I am sure He did; for, but for Him, no working man or woman could subsist upon such a wretched morsel as my dear mother took.

"I was a thin, ragged, barefooted girl, then, and sickly and weak for want of food; but I think I felt mother's hunger more than my own: and many and many a bitter night I lay awake, crying, and praying to God to give me means of working for myself and aiding her. And He has, indeed, been good to me," said pious Beatrice, "for He has given me all this!

"Well, time rolled on, and matters grew worse than ever: winter came, and was colder to us than any other winter, for our clothes were thinner and more torn; mother sometimes could find no work, for the fields in which she laboured were hidden under the snow; so that when we wanted them most we had them least—warmth, work, or food.

"I knew that, do what I would, mother would never let me leave her, because I looked to my little brothers and my old cripple of an aunt; but still, bread was better for us than all my service; and when I left them the six would have a slice more; so I determined to bid good-bye to nobody, but to go away, and look for work elsewhere. One Sunday, when mother and the little ones were at church, I went in to Aunt Bridget, and said, 'Tell mother, when she comes back, that Beatrice is gone.' I spoke quite stoutly, as if I did not care about it.

"'Gone! gone where?' said she. 'You ain't going to leave me alone, you nasty thing; you ain't going to the village to dance, you ragged, barefooted slut: you're all of a piece in this house—your mother, your brothers, and you. I know you've got meat in the kitchen, and you only give me black bread;' and here the old lady began to scream as if her heart would break; but

“那时在我们住的乡村（在毕加，法国的一个地区，离布洛涅不是很远），情势是非常糟糕的，以至于最好的工人也很难找到工作。即使是有工作，一天能挣十二个苏就让人很高兴了。妈妈如果去工作，一天所挣的钱也超不过六个苏。工作非常辛苦，除了这些，还要供六个人的吃穿。当老姨妈布里吉特拿到她那份黑面包时，她会责骂我们不好好待她；而我年幼的弟弟在没有及时吃到东西时，还会常常哭闹。我在得到自己那份食物时也常常哭泣，因为我母亲只留下一点、很少的一点食物给她自己，她说自己已经在田地里吃过了——上帝饶恕她的谎言吧！我确信上帝会祝福她的。要不是上帝的保佑，没有人会像我亲爱的母亲那样靠这么可怜的一点点食物生存下去的。

“我是一个瘦弱、衣衫褴褛、光着脚的女孩，因缺少食物，身体多病、虚弱。但我认为母亲的饥饿程度要远远超过我。在许多许多个痛苦的夜晚，我睡不着，哭泣着，祈求上帝给我工作的机会，为了我自己，也为了帮助母亲。上帝确实对我是仁慈的，”虔诚的贝阿特里斯说，“因为他把这些都赐予了我！”

“就这样，随着时间的流逝，生活境况变得比以前更糟糕了。冬天到了，对我们来说它比任何一个冬天都要寒冷，因为我们的衣服都越来越单薄和破旧。母亲有时找不到工作，因为她劳作的田地都被白雪覆盖着。当我们最需要温暖、工作和食物的时候，我们得到的却最少。

“我知道，不管我自己怎么乐意，我母亲也不会让我离开她的，因为我还要照顾我的小弟弟和残废的老姨妈。但是，我们更需要的是面包而不是照顾。我离开家，他们五口人还能多分得一点食物。因此我决定不向任何人告别，离家去别处寻找工作。一个星期天，母亲和弟妹们都去教堂了，我走进布里吉特姨妈的房间说：‘妈妈回来的时候，告诉她贝阿特里斯走了。’我很坚决地说，仿佛我一点儿都不在乎。

“‘走！去哪里？’她说，‘你不能把我一个人留在这儿，你这个讨厌的东西，你不要去村子里跳舞，你这个衣服破烂、光着脚的荡妇。这个房子

we did not mind it, we were so used to it.

"'Aunt,' said I, 'I'm going, and took this very opportunity because you WERE alone: tell mother I am too old now to eat her bread, and do no work for it: I am going, please God, where work and bread can be found:' and so I kissed her: she was so astonished that she could not move or speak; and I walked away through the old room, and the little garden, God knows whither!

"I heard the old woman screaming after me, but I did not stop nor turn round. I don't think I could, for my heart was very full; and if I had gone back again, I should never have had the courage to go away. So I walked a long, long way, until night fell; and I thought of poor mother coming home from mass, and not finding me; and little Pierre shouting out, in his clear voice, for Beatrice to bring him his supper. I think I should like to have died that night, and I thought I should too; for when I was obliged to throw myself on the cold, hard ground, my feet were too torn and weary to bear me any further.

"Just then the moon got up; and do you know I felt a comfort in looking at it, for I knew it was shining on our little cottage, and it seemed like an old friend's face? A little way on, as I saw by the moon, was a village: and I saw, too, that a man was coming towards me; he must have heard me crying, I suppose.

"Was not God good to me? This man was a farmer, who had need of a girl in his house; he made me tell him why I was alone, and I told him the same story I have told you, and he believed me and took me home. I had walked six long leagues from our village that day, asking everywhere for work in vain; and here, at bedtime, I found a bed and a supper!

"Here I lived very well for some months; my master was very good and kind to me; but, unluckily, too poor to give me any wages; so that I could save nothing to send to my poor mother. My mistress used to scold; but I was used to that at home, from Aunt Bridget: and she beat me sometimes, but I did not mind it; for your hardy country girl is not like your tender town lasses, who cry if a pin pricks them, and give warning to their mistresses at the first hard word. The only drawback to my comfort was, that I had no news of

里的你们都是一伙儿的——你母亲，你弟弟，还有你。我知道你们厨房里有肉，却只给我黑面包吃。’说到这里，这个老女人又开始尖叫了，仿佛她的心都碎了。但我们都不介意，因为我们都习惯了。

“我说：‘姨妈，趁只有你一个人在家的机会，我要走了。告诉母亲，我已足够大了，不能什么也不做，吃她的面包了。我要走了，请求上帝能让我找到工作和面包。’我吻了她，她惊讶得呆住了。穿过这个旧的房间和小花园我就走了，上帝知道我要到哪里去！

“我听到姨妈在我后面尖叫，但是我没有停下来也没有回头。我觉得自己不能那样做，因为我的心情很激动。如果我回去，就没有勇气再离开了。我走了很长很长的一段路，直到天黑。我想到可怜的妈妈做完弥撒回到家里，找不到我；小皮埃尔用他嘹亮的嗓音叫喊贝阿特里斯给他吃晚饭。我以为自己那晚就要死去了，我想我会的，因为当我行走在冰冷、坚硬的土地上的时候，我的脚裂开了口子，疲倦得不能再向前走了。

“然后月亮升起来了。你知道吗？看着月亮的时候，我感到了一些安慰，因为我知道它也照在我们的小屋上面，难道它不像一位老朋友的面庞吗？又走了一会儿，借着月光我看到有一个村子，一个男人正向我走来，我想他一定听到了我的哭声。

“上帝对我难道不好吗？这个男人是一个农民，他家里正需要一个女孩干活。他问我为什么单独一个人，我告诉了他自己的故事，他相信我，就把我带回家了。那天离开我们的村子之后，我已经走了六英里，徒劳地各处打听工作。在这会儿要睡觉的时候，我竟找到了一张床和一份晚餐！

“在那个农民家里，我住了几个月，过得很好。我的主人对我很好，不幸的是，他太穷了，不能给我任何工钱。因此我什么也积攒不下来送给我可怜的母亲。我的女主人经常责骂我，但我在家里就已经习惯布里吉特姨妈的责骂了。她有时还打我，但我也不介意。因为吃苦耐劳的乡下女孩不像娇弱的城里女孩，如果一根针刺伤了她们，她们就会哭喊，如果女主人对她们说些严厉的话，她们就会向她提出警告。在这里唯一的缺陷就是我

my mother; I could not write to her, nor could she have read my letter, if I had; so there I was, at only six leagues' distance from home, as far off as if I had been to Paris or to 'Merica.

"However, in a few months I grew so listless and homesick, that my mistress said she would keep me no longer; and though I went away as poor as I came, I was still too glad to go back to the old village again, and see dear mother, if it were but for a day. I knew she would share her crust with me, as she had done for so long a time before; and hoped that, now, as I was taller and stronger, I might find work more easily in the neighbourhood.

"You may fancy what a fête it was when I came back; though I'm sure we cried as much as if it had been a funeral. Mother got into a fit, which frightened us all; and as for Aunt Bridget, she SKREELED away for hours together, and did not scold for two days at least. Little Pierre offered me the whole of his sup-per; poor little man! his slice of bread was no bigger than before I went away.

"Well, I got a little work here and a little there; but still I was a burden at home rather than a bread-winner; and, at the closing-in of the winter, was very glad to hear of a place at two leagues' distance, where work, they said, was to be had. Off I set, one morning, to find it, but missed my way, somehow, until it was night-time before I arrived. Night-time and snow again; it seemed as if all my journeys were to be made in this bitter weather.

"When I came to the farmer's door, his house was shut up, and his people all a-bed; I knocked for a long while in vain; at last he made his appearance at a window up-stairs, and seemed so frightened, and looked so angry that I suppose he took me for a thief. I told him how I had come for work. 'Who comes for work at such an hour?' said he. 'Go home, you impudent baggage, and do not disturb honest people out of their sleep.' He banged the window to; and so I was left alone to shift for myself as I might. There was no shed, no cow-house, where I could find a bed; so I got under a cart, on some straw; it was no very warm berth. I could not sleep for the cold: and the hours passed so slowly, that it seemed as if I had been there a week instead of a night; but still it was not so bad as the first night when I left home, and when the good farmer found me.

没有妈妈的消息。我不能给她写信，当然她也就读不到我的信了。虽然这里离家只有六英里远，但我好像是到了巴黎或美加一样。

“然而，才过了几个月，我就变得无精打采，开始想家了，我女主人说她也不能再留我了。尽管我走时像刚来一样贫穷，但我仍很高兴能回到老家，去看看我亲爱的母亲，哪怕是只有一天。我知道她会和我一起分享面包皮，就像她很长时间以前所做的那样。我还希望，随着我长得越来越高，越来越强壮，我可以在附近比较容易地找到工作。

“你可以想象得到，当我回去的时候，家里就像过节一样，虽然我们那天哭了很多，就像以前在葬礼上哭得那么多。妈妈都昏倒过去了，当时可吓坏了我们。至于布里吉特姨妈，她沉默了几个小时，后来至少有两天都没有责骂我们。小皮埃尔把他全部的晚饭都给我了。可怜的孩子！他的那片面包并不比我走之前大。

“就这样，我时不时地在各处找点工作。但是对于家里来说，我仍然是一个负担，而不是个能挣得面包的劳动力。在冬天就要结束的时候，我很高兴听到人们说起，在两英里远的一个地方可以找到工作。我就立即在一个早晨出发去找那个地方了，但是我迷了路，直到晚上才到那里。又是夜晚和下雪，似乎我所有的旅程都是在这样严寒的天气里进行的。

“当我到那个农场主家门口的时候，他家里已经关上门，所有的人都上床睡觉了，我徒劳地敲了很长时间。后来主人在楼上一扇窗户后面出现了，看起来他被吓坏了，也很生气，我猜想他是把我当成小偷了。我告诉他我是来找工作的。‘谁在这个点儿来找工作啊?’他说，‘回家吧！你这个无礼的姑娘，不要打扰别人的睡眠。’他砰地就把窗户关上了，留下我一个人去找地方安身。那里没有小屋，也没有牛舍，找不到睡觉的地方。因此我就在一个两轮马车下面铺了些稻草过夜，也不暖和。因为太冷了，我不可能睡着。时间过得很慢，我好像是在那儿过了一周而不是一夜。但它比我第一次离家出走的那个晚上还要好些。

“到了早晨天还没亮的时候，农场主的仆人出来了，他们看到我蜷缩在

"In the morning, before it was light, the farmer's people came out, and saw me crouching under the cart: they told me to get up; but I was so cold that I could not: at last the man himself came, and recognized me as the girl who had disturbed him the night before. When he heard my name, and the purpose for which I came, this good man took me into the house, and put me into one of the beds out of which his sons had just got; and, if I was cold before, you may be sure I was warm and comfortable now! such a bed as this I had never slept in, nor ever did I have such good milk-soup as he gave me out of his own breakfast. Well, he agreed to hire me; and what do you think he gave me? —six sous a day! and let me sleep in the cow-house besides: you may fancy how happy I was now, at the prospect of earning so much money.

"There was an old woman among the labourers who used to sell us soup: I got a cupful every day for a half-penny, with a bit of bread in it; and might eat as much beet-root besides as I liked; not a very wholesome meal, to be sure, but God took care that it should not disagree with me.

"So, every Saturday, when work was over, I had thirty sous to carry home to mother; and tired though I was, I walked merrily the two leagues to our village, to see her again. On the road there was a great wood to pass through, and this frightened me; for if a thief should come and rob me of my whole week's earnings, what could a poor lone girl do to help herself? But I found a remedy for this too, and no thieves ever came near me; I used to begin saying my prayers as I entered the forest, and never stopped until I was safe at home; and safe I always arrived, with my thirty sous in my pocket. Ah! you may be sure, Sunday was a merry day for us all."

This is the whole of Beatrice's history which is worthy of publication; the rest of it only relates to her arrival in Paris, and the various masters and mistresses whom she there had the honour to serve. As soon as she enters the capital the romance disappears, and the poor girl's sufferings and privations luckily vanish with it. Beatrice has got now warm gowns, and stout shoes, and plenty of good food. She has had her little brother from Picardy; clothed, fed, and educated him: that young gentleman is now a carpenter, and an honour to his profession. Madame Merger is in easy circumstances, and receives, yearly, fifty francs from her daughter. To crown all, Mademoiselle Beatrice

两轮马车下面，就叫我起来。但是我太冷了，起不来。后来农场主出来了，他认出我就是昨晚打扰他的那个女孩。当他听到我的名字和我来的意图时，这个好心人就把我带进房里，让我躺在他儿子刚刚起来的床上。因为在这之前我很冷，你可以想象得到现在我是多么的温暖和舒适！我从来没有睡过这样舒适的床，也从来没有喝过那么好的牛奶，牛奶是农场主从自己的早餐中分出来给我的。就这样，他同意雇用我了。你知道他给我多少报酬吗？——一天六个苏！此外还让我睡在牛舍里，你可以想象得到我当时是多么高兴啊！我能够挣到这么多的钱。

“在这些干活的人之中有一个老妇人经常卖汤给我们，我每天花半个便士喝满满一杯，里面还有一点面包。此外，还可以吃到很多我喜欢的甜菜根，当然它们并不是些非常有益于健康的食物，但上帝还是很眷顾我的，没有让我感到难以下咽。

“就这样，在每个星期六工作结束的时候，我就可以把三十个苏带回家里给妈妈。虽然我很疲乏，但是走两英里路回到家里还是让我感到非常快乐。在回家的路上要穿过一片树林，这片树林让我感到很害怕。因为如果有一个小偷出来抢我一个星期的工钱的话，我一个可怜的女孩又能怎样保护自己呢？但我找到一个补救的方法，也没有小偷靠近过我。当走进树林的时候，我就开始做祷告，直到我安全回到家里才停下来。我总是口袋里装着三十苏安全地回到家里。啊！你可以想象得到，星期日对于我们全家人来说都是一个快乐的日子。”

这就是贝阿特里斯能够公开的全部故事，其余的就涉及她来巴黎后的事情了。她有幸服侍了各种各样的男主人和女主人。她一来到首都就没有什么离奇的遭遇了，这个可怜女孩的苦难和贫困也幸运地随之消失了。贝阿特里斯现在已有了温暖的外套和结实的鞋子，还有很多可口的食物。她已把她的小弟弟从毕加带了出来，给他穿衣、吃饭，让他接受教育，那个年轻的小伙子现在已是一个木匠了，在那个行业里干得还很不错。麦琪太太现在也过着闲适的生活，每年能从她女儿这里收到五十法郎。除此之外，

herself is a funded proprietor, and consulted the writer of this biography as to the best method of laying out a capital of two hundred francs, which is the present amount of her fortune.

God bless her! she is richer than his Grace the Duke of Devonshire; and, I dare say, has, in her humble walk, been more virtuous and more happy than all the dukes in the realm.

It is, indeed, for the benefit of dukes and such great people (who, I make no doubt, have long since ordered copies of these Sketches), that poor little Beatrice's story has been indited. Certain it is, that the young woman would never have been immortalized in this way, but for the good which her betters may derive from her example. If your ladyship will but reflect a little, after boasting of the sums which you spend in charity; the beef and blankets which you dole out at Christmas; the poonah-painting which you execute for fancy fairs; the long, long sermons which you listen to at St. George's, the whole year through;—your ladyship, I say, will allow that, although perfectly meritorious in your line, as a patroness of the Church of England, of Almack's, and of the Lying-in Asylum, yours is but a paltry sphere of virtue, a pitiful attempt at benevolence, and that this honest servant-girl puts you to shame! And you, my Lord Bishop: do you, out of your six sous a day, give away five to support your flock and family? Would you drop a single coach-horse (I do not say, A DINNER, for such a notion is monstrous, in one of your lordship's degree), to feed any one of the starving children of your lordship's mother—the Church?

I pause for a reply. His lordship took too much turtle and cold punch for dinner yesterday, and cannot speak just now: but we have, by this ingenious question, silenced him altogether: let the world wag as it will, and poor Christians and curates starve as they may, my lord's footmen must have their new liveries, and his horses their four feeds a day.

When we recollect his speech about the Catholics—when we remember his last charity sermon,—but I say nothing. Here is a poor benighted superstitious creature, worshipping images, without a rag to her tail, who has as much faith, and humility, and charity as all the reverend bench.

This angel is without a place; and for this reason (besides the pleasure of

贝阿特里斯自己还是一个有固定利息长期借款的业主，她还和本书的作者商量怎样用最好的方法把二百法郎的资本投资出去，这二百法郎是她现在的积蓄。

上帝祝福她！她比德文郡［英国郡名。——译注］的公爵还要富有。而且我敢说她这种谦卑的生活比这个国家里所有公爵的生活都要坦诚和快乐。

我的确是把这个可怜的小贝阿特里斯的故事写给公爵和此类大人物看的（这些人很长时间以来就在要这些速写的副本了），可以确定的是，这位贝阿特里斯不会因为这种方式而获得不朽，但人们却可以以她为榜样，从她那儿学到一些好的品行。如果夫人您会做些善事，也不过是自夸您在慈善事业上花了多少钱；您在圣诞节时发放出多少牛肉和毛毯；您给圣母做了红木画像；整整一年您都在听圣·乔治牧师做长长的布道。夫人，我承认虽然作为英国教会、阿耳马克［阿耳马克的聚会处在圣詹姆士皇宫附近的大王街，18—19世纪上流社会的大宴会在此地举行。——译注］、救济院的一个赞助人，您的行为是值得称赞的，但是您的行为也只是微不足道的一点儿德行、一点儿慈善的尝试，与贝阿特里斯这个坦诚谦逊的女佣相比你会感到羞耻的！还有您，我的主教大人，您可以从每天的六个苏中拿出五个苏来支援您的亲人和家庭吗？您会从一个单人马车上下来（我不说是一顿晚餐，因为在您的地位看来这是太离奇了）给任何一个教会的饥饿的孩子东西吃吗？

我停下来等着您的答复。主教大人昨晚吃了太多的甲鱼肉，喝了太多的冷饮料，现在不能说话，但是我们用这个巧妙的问题让他完全安静了下来。他说，让世界任它的意愿去发展吧！任可怜的基督徒和副牧师们怎样去挨饿吧！但我的男仆们一定要有他们的新制服，他们的马一天也要喂四次。

回想起他有关天主教徒的演讲——回想起他最后的慈善布道——我什么也说不出。这里有一个可怜的无知的迷信的人，她崇拜上帝，即使身无

composing the above slap at episcopacy)—I have indited her history. If the Bishop is going to Paris, and wants a good honest maid-of-all-work, he can have her, I have no doubt; or if he chooses to give a few pounds to her mother, they can be sent to Mr. Titmarsh, at the publisher's.

Here is Miss Merger's last letter and autograph. The note was evidently composed by an Écrivain public:—

> "Madame,—Ayant apris par ce Monsieur, que vous vous portiez bien, ainsi que Monsieur, ayant su aussi que vous parliez de moi dans votre lettre cette nouvelle m'a fait bien plaisir Je profite de l'occasion pour vous faire passer ce petit billet où Je voudrais pouvoir m'enveloper pour aller vous voir et pour vous dire que Je suis encore sans place Je m'ennuye toujours de ne pas vous voir ainsi que Minette (Minette is a cat) qui semble m'interroger tour a tour et demander où vous êtes. Je vous envoye aussi la note du linge a blanchir—ah, Madame! Je vais cesser de vous ecrire mais non de vous regretter."
>
> Beatrice Merger.

分文她也像所有值得尊敬的主教一样有许多信心、谦逊和仁慈。

这位天使目前还没有住所，这也是我写她的故事的原因（所写的以上指责主教管区的乐趣除外）。如果主教准备去巴黎，需要一个善良忠实做各种工作的女仆的话，他可以雇用她。或者，如果他要选择送给她母亲几镑钱的话，可以把钱送到作者蒂特马舍先生的家里来。

这里是麦琪小姐最近的信和亲笔签名。这封短信很明显是代写书信的人给她写的：

> 太太——我已经从这位先生这里收到您的问好了，还有先生，我也知道您在信里提到了我，这个消息让我很高兴，我找了机会给您写这封短信，我真希望自己也能随着这封信被寄过去看看您，还要告诉您我现在还没有找到住所。我经常为不能去看您和米奈（一只猫）而感到烦恼，米奈以前常常一圈一圈地围着我“问”您去哪里了。我还要寄给您这张浆洗衣服的账单——啊，太太！就写到这里，我要停下笔了，但我不会忘记您的。
>
> 贝阿特里斯·麦琪

Caricatures and Lithography in Paris

FIFTY years ago, there lived, at Munich, a poor fellow, by name Aloys Senefelder, who was in so little repute as an author and artist, that printers and engravers refused to publish his works at their own charges, and so set him upon some plan for doing without their aid. In the first place, Aloys invented a certain kind of ink, which would resist the action of the acid that is usually employed by engravers, and with this he made his experiments upon copper-plates, as long as he could afford to purchase them. He found that to write upon the plates backwards, after the manner of engravers, required much skill and many trials; and he thought that, were he to practise upon any other polished surface—a smooth stone, for instance, the least costly article imaginable—he might spare the expense of the copper until he had sufficient skill to use it.

One day, it is said, that Aloys was called upon to write—rather a humble composition for an author and artist—a washing-bill. He had no paper at hand, and so he wrote out the bill with some of his newly-invented ink, upon one of his Kilheim stones. Some time afterwards he thought he would try and take an IMPRESSION of his washing-bill: he did, and succeeded. Such is the story, which the reader most likely knows very well; and having alluded to the origin of the art, we shall not follow the stream through its windings and enlargement after it issued from the little parent rock, or fill our pages with the rest of the pedigree. Senefelder invented Lithography. His invention has not made so much noise and larum in the world as some others, which have an origin quite as humble and unromantic; but it is one to which we owe no small profit, and a great deal of pleasure; and, as such, we are bound to speak of it

巴黎的石版讽刺画

大约五十年前在慕尼黑住着一位穷小伙子，他的名字叫亚洛依·逊纳菲尔德［逊纳菲尔德（1771—1834，Senefelder，Aloys），捷裔德国平版印刷术发明者。1771年11月6日生于布拉格，1834年2月26日卒于慕尼黑。自1792年起从事音乐乐谱创作与戏剧的写作。1796年，偶将湿衣放在一块用油脂笔写过字的石板上，再上油墨，只有字迹部分吸墨，其余部分不吸。从中得到启发，随即利用水油相拒原理，用油墨在石板上书写、绘画后，润水印刷，这就是原始的石印术。1797—1798年，首先采用石印术印刷文件、乐谱和图画等。1800年在德国奥芬巴赫创办印刷所。1805年和1817年，先后制造出木制和铁制石印机。他还研制了制版转写墨，并创造了转写制版法。1818年编写出版《石版印刷教科书》。——译注］，作为一名作家和艺术家他并没有什么名气，因此印刷工和镌板工人都拒绝在他们的印刷社里出版他的作品，这些都促使他萌发出了一个计划，要发明一种方法，即使没有印刷工和镌板工人的帮助也能印刷自己的作品。首先，亚洛依发明了一种墨水，它能抵制镌板工人经常使用的酸性物质的腐蚀，一开始，只要能支付得起，他就用这种墨水在铜制的碟子上做实验。他发现模仿镌板工人的方法在碟子的背面书写需要很高的技巧以及做许多的试验。他想，如果他在其他光滑的物体表面上练习——例如一块平滑的石头；这是可以想象得到的最廉价的物品了——他就可以省去铜的费用而练习掌握这门技术。

with all gratitude and respect. The schoolmaster, who is now abroad, has taught us, in our youth, how the cultivation of art "emollit mores nec sinit esse"—(it is needless to finish the quotation); and Lithography has been, to our thinking, the very best ally that art ever had; the best friend of the artist, allowing him to produce rapidly-multiplied and authentic copies of his own works (without trusting to the tedious and expensive assistance of the engraver); and the best friend to the people likewise, who have means of purchasing these cheap and beautiful productions, and thus having their ideas "mollified" and their manners "feros" no more.

With ourselves, among whom money is plenty, enterprise so great, and everything matter of commercial speculation, Lithography has not been so much practised as wood or steel engraving; which, by the aid of great original capital and spread of sale, are able more than to compete with the art of drawing on stone. The two former may be called art done by MACHINERY. We confess to a prejudice in favour of the honest work of HAND, in matters of art, and prefer the rough workmanship of the painter to the smooth copies of his performances which are produced, for the most part, on the wood-block or the steel-plate.

The theory will possibly be objected to by many of our readers; the best proof in its favour, we think, is, that the state of art amongst the people in France and Germany, where publishers are not so wealthy or enterprising as with us,[1] and where Lithography is more practised, is infinitely higher than in England, and the appreciation more correct. As draughtsmen, the French and German painters are incomparably superior to our own; and with art, as with any other commodity, the demand will be found pretty equal to the supply: with us, the general demand is for neatness, prettiness, and what is called EFFECT in pictures, and these can be rendered completely, nay, improved, by the engraver's conventional manner of copying the artist's performances. But to copy fine expression and fine drawing, the engraver himself must be a fine artist; and let anybody examine the host of picture-books which appear every Christmas, and say whether, for the most part, painters or engravers possess any artistic merit? We boast, nevertheless, of some of the

据说有一天，亚洛依被叫去书写——可不是作家或画家的作品——一张洗衣传单。他手边没纸，因此就用他新发明的墨水写在了一块克尔海姆［巴伐利亚州一县城，位于阿尔特米尔河注入多瑙河处。——译注］的石头上。过了一会儿，他想可以试着用这种石板印一张洗衣传单，结果他真的成功了。读者或许都已经听说了这个故事。这个故事也交代了石版印刷术的起源，在这块小小的石头上后来又发展出许多新的印刷技巧，印刷内容的表现领域也得到了扩展，关于这些内容，我们就不谈了。亚洛依发明了石版印刷术。石版印刷术的发明不像世界上其他的发明一样会制造许多噪音和垃圾，它的起源非常的简单和普通，但是我们却能从中得到很多益处和快乐。就因为这个原因，谈到它的时候我们都怀着一种感激和尊敬的心情。现移居国外的校长曾教导我们说，在我们的青年时代，艺术是怎样"修养文明品德，反对粗野不驯（拉丁语）"的。我们认为石版印刷术是艺术曾经拥有过的最好的助手、艺术家的最好的朋友，它能让艺术家快速地复印出他大量真实作品的副本（没必要再去依赖镌刻工人费时而昂贵的帮助），对普通人来说它也是最好的朋友，人们可以买得起这些价廉物美的作品。

在那些资本雄厚、生意兴旺的商业投机人看来，石版印刷术并不像木版或钢版印刷术那样实用。木版或钢版印刷术有大量的原始资本作底，销路也得到普及，与石版印刷术相竞争时也更具实力。前两种艺术可以被称做机器制作。我们承认在艺术领域人们对于手工制作的作品还存有偏见。大多数人还是喜欢把画家手艺的复制品刻在木印版或钢版的平滑表面上。

这种看法可能会招致许多读者的反对，而他们反对的理由就是在法国人和德国人的心目中艺术的地位是很高的。德国和法国的印刷者不像我们英国的印刷者那么富有和商业化[1]，因此在他们那里石版印刷术就更加实用，比在英国的地位要高，也能得到人们恰当的赏识。至于制图员，无可争议，法国和德国的画家都要比我们英国的画家具备优势；至于艺术品，它和其他的商品一样都需要满足消费者的需求。我们英国人对艺术品一般

best engravers and painters in Europe. Here, again, the supply is accounted for by the demand; our highest class is richer than any other aristocracy, quite as well instructed, and can judge and pay for fine pictures and engravings. But these costly productions are for the few, and not for the many, who have not yet certainly arrived at properly appreciating fine art.

Take the standard "Album" for instance—that unfortunate collection of deformed Zuleikas and Medoras (from the "Byron Beauties", the Flowers, Gems, Souvenirs, Caskets of Loveliness, Beauty, as they may be called); glaring caricatures of flowers, singly, in groups, in flower-pots, or with hideous deformed little Cupids sporting among them; of what are called "mezzotinto," pencil-drawings, "poonah-paintings," and what not. "The Album" is to be found invariably upon the round rosewood brass-inlaid drawing-room table of the middle classes, and with a couple of "Annuals" besides, which flank it on the same table, represents the art of the house; perhaps there is a portrait of the master of the house in the dining-room, grim-glancing from above the mantel-piece; and of the mistress over the piano upstairs; add to these some odious miniatures of the sons and daughters, on each side of the chimney-glass; and here, commonly (we appeal to the reader if this is an overcharged picture), the collection ends. The family goes to the Exhibition once a year, to the National Gallery once in ten years: to the former place they have an inducement to go; there are their own portraits, or the portraits of their friends, or the portraits of public characters; and you will see them infallibly wondering over No. 2645 in the catalogue, representing "*The Portrait of a Lady*," or of the "*First Mayor of Little Pedlington since the passing of the Reform Bill*;" or else bustling and squeezing among the miniatures, where lies the chief attraction of the Gallery. England has produced, owing to the effects of this class of admirers of art, two admirable, and five hundred very clever, portrait painters. How many ARTISTS? Let the reader count upon his five fingers, and see if, living at the present moment, he can name one for each.

If, from this examination of our own worthy middle classes, we look to the same class in France, what a difference do we find! Humble cafés in coun-

的要求就是整洁、漂亮，看重的是这些外观之类的因素，这些都能通过镌版工人对于艺术家作品的传统复制方法得以实现，并且还能得到改进。但是要临摹好的作品和绘画，镌版工人本人还必须是一位很好的艺术家。每年圣诞节期间，印刷厂都会印出一堆画册，让任何一个仔细看过这些画册的人说说，是否绝大部分的画家或镌刻工人具有艺术的天赋呢？然而我们却自恃有着欧洲最好的镌刻工人和画家。在这里，供应也是随着需求变化的。我们的上流社会阶层比任何贵族都要富有和有教养，他们能够鉴别好的绘画和版画作品，并具有购买能力。但是这些昂贵的作品只是为少数人生产的，不适合那些不具备艺术鉴赏能力的大多数人。

以一般性的“画像”为例——不恰当地会集了变形的祖雷克哈和美多拉（来自于“拜伦作品中的美人”）、花朵、珠宝、纪念品、可爱的首饰盒等，鲜艳的花朵成束地插在花盆里，或者还有丑陋的变形的小丘比特在花丛中游戏。它们都是些金属版印刷品、铅笔绘画或红木绘画等等。我们经常能在中产阶级会客室的青龙木桌子上发现这类“画像”，此外还有两幅“年历”挂在桌子的两侧，它们都体现了这个家庭的艺术品味；或在餐厅壁炉台的上面还挂着一幅家中男主人的肖像，他正用严肃的目光扫视着房间；楼上摆放钢琴的墙壁上方还挂着女主人的肖像；除此之外在烟囱通道的两侧还有些令人作呕的孩子的小画像。到这儿，通常我们要问读者这幅是否要价过高，然后画像的展览就结束了。一家人每年去看一次展览会，每十年去一次国家画廊。展览会对他们来说还是有些诱惑的。那里会有他们自己的肖像或他们朋友的肖像或公众人物的肖像。你会看到他们总是拥挤在《一位女士的肖像》或《改革法案通过后小贝德林顿市第一任市长》或诸如此类的其他小画像面前，这也是画廊里最吸引人的地方。在中产阶层这种审美趣味的带动下，英国至今已产生了两位杰出的肖像画家、五百位手艺精湛的肖像画家。但是能有多少艺术家呢？让读者数数他的五根手指头，看看目前他能否数出五个艺术家的名字。

如果从英国的中产阶层转到法国的中产阶层来看，我们会发现两者之

try towns have their walls covered with pleasing picture papers, representing "*Les Gloires de l'Armée Française*," the "*Seasons*," the "*Four Quarters of the World*," "*Cupid and Psyche*," or some other allegory, landscape or history, rudely painted, as papers for walls usually are; but the figures are all tolerably well drawn; and the common taste, which has caused a demand for such things, is undeniable. In Paris, the manner in which the cafés and houses of the restaurateurs are ornamented, is, of course, a thousand times richer, and nothing can be more beautiful, or more exquisitely finished and correct, than the designs which adorn many of them. We are not prepared to say what sums were expended upon the painting of "Véry's" or "Véfour's," of the "Salle Musard," or of numberless other places of public resort in the capital. There is many a shop-keeper whose sign is a very tolerable picture; and often have we stopped to admire (the reader will give us credit for having remained OUTSIDE) the excellent workmanship of the grapes and vine-leaves over the door of some very humble, dirty, inodorous shop of a marchand de vin.

These, however, serve only to educate the public taste, and are ornaments for the most part much too costly for the people. But the same love of ornament which is shown in their public places of resort, appears in their houses likewise; and every one of our readers who has lived in Paris, in any lodging, magnificent or humble, with any family, however poor, may bear witness how profusely the walls of his smart salon in the English quarter, or of his little room au sixième in the Pays-Latin, has been decorated with prints of all kinds. In the first, probably, with bad engravings on copper from the bad and tawdry pictures of the artists of the time of the Empire; in the latter, with gay caricatures of Granville or Monnier; military pieces, such as are dashed off by Raffet, Charlet, Vernet (one can hardly say which of the three designers has the greatest merit, or the most vigorous hand); or clever pictures from the crayon of the Deverias, the admirable Roqueplan, or Decamp. We have named here, we believe, the principal lithographic artists in Paris; and those—as doubtless there are many—of our readers who have looked over Monsieur Aubert's portfolios, or gazed at that famous caricature-shop window in the Rue de Coq, or are even acquainted with the exterior of Monsieur

间存在着多么大的差异啊！就法国乡村城镇中一家简朴的咖啡馆来说，咖啡馆主人也会在房间的墙壁上挂满令人愉悦的绘画作品，如《法国军队的荣耀》、《四季》、《世界的四方》、《丘比特和普赛克》或其他类似的作品等等，在纸张上风景或历史都得到了逼真的描绘，这些画都画得还不错。不可否认，这些画也体现了公众的审美趣味。在巴黎，咖啡馆和饭店房屋的装饰方式也有很多，而且没有什么能比它们的装饰设计更漂亮、更精致的了。我们不打算讨论威利、威福（两者皆为巴黎大饭店的名字——译注），穆萨德大厅和首都其他无数的公共休闲场所在绘画方面所付出的开销。甚至许多小店店主的招牌都是不错的绘画作品。我们经常在一些简朴、肮脏、没有气味的酒店门口不由自主地停下来赞美（读者会为我们驻留在外面而称赞我们的）门口招牌上的葡萄和葡萄藤叶子的杰出手艺。

然而这些只适合于去培养公众的审美趣味，对于大多数人来说这种装饰还是太昂贵了。但是他们把在公共场所中所体现的对于装饰的喜爱也移入了自己的家庭之中。每一个在巴黎居住过的读者，不管他是住在高档还是下等的公寓里，不论他是和什么样的家庭在一起，他都可以看到富人家漂亮的会客室的墙上挂满了绘画作品，即使在拉丁区六楼的小房间里都装饰着各种各样的印刷制品。前者的房间里或许还挂着些帝国时代艺术家的拙劣而俗气的铜版绘画作品。后者的房间里则挂着些格兰维尔［Granville (1803—1847)，法国讽刺画家。——译注］或莫尼埃［Monnier (1805—1877)，讽刺漫画家。——译注］的鲜明的讽刺画；拉费［Denis Auguste Marie Raffet (1804—1860)，法国画家。——译注］、查勒特［Charlet (1792—1845)，法国画家。——译注］、约瑟夫·凡内［Joseph Vernet (1714—1789)，法国著名的浪漫主义画家。——译注］（这三个画家可以说是不分上下的）的军事题材的绘画作品或来自德维尔亚（Deverias）、罗克普雷（Roqueplan）、德坎普（Decamp）的活泼的蜡笔画。我们在这里已提到了巴黎主要的石版画家。对于那些已浏览过欧博［Aubert，法国漫画家。——译注］先生的代表作选或注视过德坷克街著名漫画商店的橱窗，

Delaporte's little emporium in the Burlington Arcade, need not be told how excellent the productions of all these artists are in their genre. We get in these engravings the loisirs of men of genius, not the finikin performances of laboured mediocrity, as with us: all these artists are good painters, as well as good designers; a design from them is worth a whole gross of Books of Beauty; and if we might raise a humble supplication to the artists in our own country of similar merit—to such men as Leslie, Maclise, Herbert, Cattermole, and others—it would be, that they should, after the example of their French brethren and of the English landscape painters, take chalk in hand, produce their own copies of their own sketches, and never more draw a single "Forsaken One," "Rejected One," "Dejected One" at the entreaty of any publisher or for the pages of any Book of Beauty, Royalty, or Loveliness, whatever.

Can there be a more pleasing walk in the whole world than a stroll through the Gallery of the Louvre on a fête-day; not to look so much at the pictures as at the lookers-on? Thousands of the poorer classes are there: mechanics in their Sunday clothes, smiling grisettes, smart dapper soldiers of the line, with bronzed wondering faces, marching together in little companies of six or seven, and stopping every now and then at Napoleon or Leonidas as they appear in proper vulgar heroics in the pictures of David or Gros. The taste of these people will hardly be approved by the connoisseur, but they have a taste for art. Can the same be said of our lower classes, who, if they are inclined to be sociable and amused in their holidays, have no place of resort but the tap-room or tea-garden, and no food for conversation except such as can be built upon the politics or the police reports of the last *Sunday paper*? So much has Church and State puritanism done for us—so well has it succeeded in materializing and binding down to the earth the imagination of men, for which God has made another world (which certain statesmen take but too little into account)—that fair and beautiful world of art, in which there CAN be nothing selfish or sordid, of which Dulness has forgotten the existence, and which Bigotry has endeavoured to shut out from sight—

"On a banni les démons et les fées,

甚至对于伯林顿街道上德拉波特先生的小商场外部也很熟悉的读者来说，就没必要再告诉他们这些石版画家的作品是多么出色的了。我们所得到的这些版画作品都是天才艺术家的业余作品，而不是平庸画家吃力创作的、过分润饰的作品。这些石版艺术家既是优秀的画家，又是出色的构图设计者。他们的一个构图设计能够传达出一整本美术书所蕴含的知识。如果我们要在自己的国家中谦逊地列出具有同样成就的艺术家——如莱斯利［Leslie（1802—1873），英国画家、雕塑家。——译注］，麦克列斯［Maclise，19世纪英国著名画家皇家科学院的艺术家。——译注］，赫伯特，凯特摩尔等等——如果他们能以法国同行和英国的风景画画家做榜样的话，他们就应该手里拿着粉笔去创作他们自己的素描摹本，而不是在任何出版者的请求下，在美术书籍、皇室画册或其他书页中画那些“被淘汰的作品”、“被拒绝的作品”和“沮丧的作品”了。

只要别把太多的注意力放在看画上还有周围的观看者身上，还能有什么比节日里漫步在罗浮宫让人愉快的呢？数以千计的穷人阶层都在那里：穿着星期日服装的机械工人、微笑的青年劳动妇女，还有潇洒整洁的部队军人，他们的脸都是青铜色的，六七个人走在一起，带着惊讶的表情不时地在拿破仑或列奥尼达［Leonidas，斯巴达国王。——译注］的画像前停下，他们在大卫或格罗［Gros（1771—1835），法国画家。——译注］的绘画中得到恰当的粗俗英勇的表现。这些人的审美趣味是很难得到鉴赏家的认同的，但他们对艺术有自己的兴趣。难道社会下层的人们如果想在假日里娱乐和交际的话就只能去酒吧间或有茶室的公园，谈话的话题就只能围绕着最近《星期日报》的政治和警方报道吗？基督教和清教主义已为我们做了很多——它很成功地把人类的想象力世俗化并束缚在现实生活中，因为上帝已创造了另一个世界——那个公平而美丽的艺术世界，在那里没有自私和卑鄙，也不存在沉闷，固执已尽力从人们的视线中退出——

人们已摒弃了魔鬼和仙女，

Le raisonneur tristement s'accrédite;
On court, hélas! apres la verité;
Ah! croyez moi, l'erreur a son mérite!"

We are not putting in a plea, here for demons and fairies, as Voltaire does in the above exquisite lines; nor about to expatiate on the beauties of error, for it is none; but the clank of steam-engines, and the shouts of politicians, and the struggle for gain or bread, and the loud denunciations of stupid bigots, have wellnigh smothered poor Fancy among us. We boast of our science, and vaunt our superior morality. Does the latter exist? In spite of all the forms which our policy has invented to secure it—in spite of all the preachers, all the meeting-houses, and all the legislative enactments—if any person will take upon himself the painful labour of purchasing and perusing some of the cheap periodical prints which form the people's library of amusement, and contain what may be presumed to be their standard in matters of imagination and fancy, he will see how false the claim is that we bring forward of superior morality. The aristocracy who are so eager to maintain, were, of course, not the last to feel, the annoyance of the legislative restrictions on the Sabbath, and eagerly seized upon that happy invention for dissipating the gloom and ennui ordered by Act of Parliament to prevail on that day—*the Sunday paper*. It might be read in a club-room, where the poor could not see how their betters ordained one thing for the vulgar, and another for themselves; or in an easy-chair, in the study, whither my lord retires every Sunday for his devotions. It dealt in private scandal and ribaldry, only the more piquant for its pretty flimsy veil of double-entendre. It was a fortune to the publisher, and it became a necessary to the reader, which he could not do without, any more than without his snuff-box, his opera-box, or his chasse after coffee. The delightful novelty could not for any time be kept exclusively for the haut ton; and from my lord it descended to his valet or tradesmen, and from Grosvenor Square it spread all the town through; so that now the lower classes have their scandal and ribaldry organs, as well as their betters (the rogues, they WILL imitate them!) and as their tastes are somewhat coarser than my lord's, and their numbers a thousand to one, why of course the prints have increased, and the

思维着的理性受到推崇。

人们竞相追逐真理，

啊！相信我，即使错误也是有价值的！

就如伏尔泰在上面那首雅致的诗中所说的那样，我们在这里不再祈求魔鬼和仙女，也不准备去详述错误的妙处，因为它没有什么价值可言。但是蒸汽机的当啷声、政客的呼喊声、争夺利益和面包的吵闹声、对愚蠢执拗的人的大声斥责声，把我们的鉴赏力几乎都给抑制住了。我们夸耀自己的科学，吹嘘我们高尚的道德，但是后者存在吗？尽管我们制定了所有方针政策——尽管所有的传道士、所有的聚会场所、所有立法条例都是为了维护高尚的道德——但人们还是乐意去购买和阅读那些粗俗廉价的刊物来娱乐自己，在这些刊物中读者会发现我们所提出的高尚道德是多么的虚伪。贵族们也体会到了法定安息日的烦恼，所以他们热切地抓住了这个快乐的发明——《星期日报》来驱散法定安息日的阴郁和无聊。他们或许是在一个俱乐部聚会室里读报，或许是每个周日专心致志地坐在书房里的安乐椅上读报，穷人就不明白那些富人怎么会读这些被他们自己称做粗俗的东西。这些报刊传播的都是私人丑闻和下流事件，并运用许多虚夸的修饰语来作为掩饰。它在给出版者带来财富的同时也成了读者必不可少的业余消遣，就像不能没有鼻烟盒、歌剧包厢和喝完咖啡后的过嘴酒一样。这种刊物又不是专为上流人物发行，因此从贵族到仆从和店主，从格罗夫那广场到整个城镇，下等阶层的人们也开始读丑闻报刊了，虽然他们的喜好（这些下层民众，他们会模仿上流人物的！）和审美品味与贵族相比还是有些粗糙，但是他们之间的人数比例却是一千比一，因此随着印刷术的提高和发展，刊物也开始大批量地生产，直至蔓延到整个城镇，这会让杜布瓦神甫为此脸红，让路易四世［以举止庄重而著称的法国国王。——译注］大喊羞耻的。但是法国在君主政体衰落时期的放肆与我们这个保持着安息日制度国家的堕落简直是不能相提并论的。

profligacy has been diffused in a ratio exactly proportionable to the demand, until the town is infested with such a number of monstrous publications of the kind as would have put Abbé Dubois to the blush, or made Louis XV cry shame. Talk of English morality! —the worst licentiousness, in the worst period of the French monarchy, scarcely equalled the wickedness of this Sabbath-keeping country of ours.

The reader will be glad, at last, to come to the conclusion that we would fain draw from all these descriptions—why does this immorality exist? Because the people MUST be amused, and have not been taught HOW; because the upper classes, frightened by stupid cant, or absorbed in material wants, have not as yet learned the refinement which only the cultivation of art can give; and when their intellects are uneducated, and their tastes are coarse, the tastes and amusements of classes still more ignorant must be coarse and vicious likewise, in an increased proportion.

Such discussions and violent attacks upon high and low, Sabbath Bills, politicians, and what not, may appear, perhaps, out of place in a few pages which purport only to give an account of some French drawings: all we would urge is, that, in France, these prints are made because they are liked and appreciated; with us they are not made, because they are not liked and appreciated: and the more is the pity. Nothing merely intellectual will be popular among us: we do not love beauty for beauty's sake, as Germans; or wit, for wit's sake, as the French: for abstract art we have no appreciation. We admire H. B.'s caricatures, because they are the caricatures of well-known political characters, not because they are witty; and Boz, because he writes us good palpable stories (if we may use such a word to a story); and Madame Vestris, because she has the most beautifully shaped legs;—the ART of the designer, the writer, the actress (each admirable in its way,) is a very minor consideration; each might have ten times the wit, and would be quite unsuccessful without their substantial points of popularity.

In France such matters are far better managed, and the love of art is a thousand times more keen; and (from this feeling, surely) how much superiority is there in French SOCIETY over our own; how much better is social

读者将会从我们上述的描述中得出结论——那为什么这种刊物还要存在下去呢？因为人们需要娱乐，但是还没有人教给他们怎样去娱乐。上流阶层要么被愚蠢的假话吓怕了，要么沉醉于物质财富的追求，他们还没有认识到只有艺术的教化才能赋予人们文雅的魅力。当人们的智力没有受到开发和培育，他们的审美趣味就是粗糙的。如果一个阶层的审美趣味和娱乐仍未受到重视的话，他们的审美趣味和娱乐活动也同样会变得越来越粗糙和堕落。

对于上流阶层和下等阶层进行如此的讨论和攻击，还有安息日、政客等诸如此类的东西出现在描述法国绘画的文章里可能都是不恰当的，我们提到这一切无非是想说明，在法国，这些印刷品被生产出来是因为它们能得到读者的喜爱和欣赏。在我们国家，非常遗憾，它们没有被生产出来是因为没有得到英国人的喜爱和欣赏。只有理性才能在我们国家得到流行。我们不像德国人那样为美而美或像法国人那样为诙谐而诙谐，对于抽象的艺术我们没有什么鉴赏能力。我们赞美 H. B. 的漫画是因为它们画的都是些众所周知的政治人物的漫画，不是因为它们的诙谐；我们喜欢博兹［狄更斯早期的笔名 Boz。——译注］是因为他能给我们写很好看的故事；喜欢维丝德丽［Lucia Elizabeth Vestris（1797—1856），当时最有名的女低音。——译注］是因为她有着一双漂亮的长腿；至于画家、作家、女演员的才艺（都具有各自令人钦佩的特长），我们则考虑得很少，如果他们本身没有现实性的东西讨人喜欢的话，那他们就不会有现在这么大的名声。

在法国这类事情就处理得很好，因为人们对于艺术的热爱非常强烈。（当然，正是由于这种热爱）艺术在法国社会中的地位要远远高于我们国家，它也能得到人们正确的赏识和理解。比起我们国家中的贫富差距，法国人与人之间的生活状况要平等得多，虽然我们拥有占据优势的财富、教育和政治自由！在谦逊、快乐、文雅和庄重方面，没有哪个国家的阶层能与英国人相比，它们不仅是英国人假日的性格品质，也是工作日的性格品质，它们能给人们的生活增添许多欢乐，就像好的衣服、好的牛肉或更高

happiness understood; how much more manly equality is there between Frenchman and Frenchman, than between rich and poor in our own country, with all our superior wealth, instruction, and political freedom! There is, amongst the humblest, a gayety, cheerfulness, politeness, and sobriety, to which, in England, no class can show a parallel: and these, be it remembered, are not only qualities for holidays, but for working-days too, and add to the enjoyment of human life as much as good clothes, good beef, or good wages. If, to our freedom, we could but add a little of their happiness! —it is one, after all, of the cheapest commodities in the world, and in the power of every man (with means of gaining decent bread) who has the will or the skill to use it.

We are not going to trace the history of the rise and progress of art in France; our business, at present, is only to speak of one branch of art in that country—lithographic designs, and those chiefly of a humourous character. A history of French caricature was published in Paris, two or three years back, illustrated by numerous copies of designs, from the time of Henry III to our own day. We can only speak of this work from memory, having been unable, in London, to procure the sight of a copy; but our impression, at the time we saw the collection, was as unfavourable as could possibly be: nothing could be more meagre than the wit, or poorer than the execution, of the whole set of drawings. Under the Empire, art, as may be imagined, was at a very low ebb; and, aping the Government of the day, and catering to the national taste and vanity, it was a kind of tawdry caricature of the sublime; of which the pictures of David and Girodet, and almost the entire collection now at the Luxembourg Palace, will give pretty fair examples. Swollen, distorted, unnatural, the painting was something like the politics of those days; with force in it, nevertheless, and something of grandeur, that will exist in spite of taste, and is born of energetic will. A man, disposed to write comparisons of characters, might, for instance, find some striking analogies between Mountebank Murat, with his irresistible bravery and horsemanship, who was a kind of mixture of Duguesclin and Ducrow, and Mountebank David, a fierce, powerful painter and genius, whose idea of beauty and sublimity seemed to have

的报酬一样。至于自由，它只能给我们增添一点有限的快乐！——自由毕竟是世界上最廉价的商品，它掌握在每一个拥有意志或权利来使用它的人手中。

我们就不再去追溯法国艺术兴起和发展的历史了。目前我们要谈谈在法国的一个艺术流派——石版画。大部分石版画都具有幽默的特点。两三年前在法国巴黎出版了一本漫画史的书，书中印有从亨利三世到今天的许多插图摹本。这部著作现在只能留存在我们的记忆中，因为伦敦已找不到这本书的版本了。但是这部书中所收集的图画并没有给我们留下很好的印象，整本绘画作品都才智贫乏、制作粗糙。可想而知，帝国体制下的艺术是处于低潮状态的，它们要奉承当朝政府，迎合民众的审美趣味和虚荣心，对严肃崇高的题材做俗气而拙劣的模仿。大卫和吉洛底的绘画作品，还有现在卢森堡宫殿中所收藏的绝大部分作品都会给我们做出最好的证明。它们夸张、扭曲、做作的风格就像当时的政治形势一样，虽然里面也有一些庄严的力量，但它们更多的是源于画家本人精力充沛的意志而不是大众的审美趣味。如果要把人物形象做个比较的话，它们都像极了那个英勇无畏、具有高超骑马术的江湖骗子穆莱特[拿破仑皇帝手下的一个著名的将领 Murat。——译注]。还有江湖骗子大卫，一位狂热、权威的画家和天才，他对于美和崇高的观念似乎都是来源于林荫大道上的血腥情节剧。然而他们两者在各自的领域内都很杰出，在那个虚伪、英雄崇拜的不信教的年代里像上帝一样受到人们的崇敬。

至于可怜的漫画和出版自由，他们就像神话故事中的合法公主一样，公主与她的随从们即快乐奇异的小矮子都完全处于巨人的权力统治下。公主般的出版界就这样受到当局严密的监视和看守（虽然，也对其尊贵的地位表示出一点尊敬），她不敢表达自己的真实想法。至于可怜的漫画，它被塞住了口扔在一边，就像囚禁在小玻璃瓶中的魔鬼。

出版界在接下来的君主统治时期是如何生存的就不言而喻了。拿破仑

been gained from the bloody melodramas on the Boulevard. Both, however, were great in their way, and were worshipped as gods, in those heathen times of false belief and hero-worship.

As for poor caricature and freedom of the press, they, like the rightful princess in a fairy tale, with the merry fantastic dwarf, her attendant, were entirely in the power of the giant who ruled the land. The Princess Press was so closely watched and guarded (with some little show, nevertheless, of respect for her rank), that she dared not utter a word of her own thoughts; and, for poor Caricature, he was gagged, and put out of the way altogether: imprisoned as completely as ever Asmodeus was in his phial.

How the Press and her attendant fared in succeeding reigns, is well known; their condition was little bettered by the downfall of Napoleon: with the accession of Charles X they were more oppressed even than before—more than they could bear; for so hard were they pressed, that, as one has seen when sailors are working a capstan, back of a sudden the bars flew, knocking to the earth the men who were endeavouring to work them. The Revolution came, and up sprung Caricature in France; all sorts of fierce epigrams were discharged at the flying monarch, and speedily were prepared, too, for the new one.

About this time there lived at Paris (if our information be correct) a certain M. Philipon, an indifferent artist (painting was his profession), a tolerable designer, and an admirable wit. M. Philipon designed many caricatures himself, married the sister of an eminent publisher of prints (M. Aubert), and the two, gathering about them a body of wits and artists like themselves, set up journals of their own:—*La Caricature*, first published once a week; and *the Charivari* afterwards, a daily paper, in which a design also appears daily.

At first the caricatures inserted in the *Charivari* were chiefly political; and a most curious contest speedily commenced between the State and M. Philipon's little army in the Galérie Véro-Dodat. Half a dozen poor artists on the one side, and his Majesty Louis Philippe, his august family, and the numberless placemen and supporters of the monarchy, on the other; it was some-

的倒台，查理十世的就任并没有让它们从中得到什么好处，而它们受到的压制比以前更严重了——甚至超过了它们所能忍受的限度。它们受到的压制是如此痛苦，就像人们看到水手们正在操作一个绞盘，突然后面支撑的杆子断裂了，绞盘就砸到了地面上正努力工作的人。大革命来了，法国的漫画也得以破土而出，各种各样的讽刺短诗把讽刺矛头都指向了频繁更替王位的君主。

大约就是这个时候，在巴黎（如果我们的消息是正确的话）有一位名字叫菲利庞的先生，他是一位讽刺艺术家（绘画是他的职业）、一位出色的制图员、一位令人钦佩的才子。菲利庞先生自己画了许多漫画，并娶了一位著名的报刊发行者奥贝尔的妹妹为妻，他们两人又发动了周围的一些才子和艺术家创立了他们自己的杂志——《讽刺漫画》，开始是每周出版一期，过后叫《逗闹》，变成了日报，每天里面都会有插图。

起先，《逗闹》中所插入的漫画主要是政治题材的。很快政府和菲利庞先生的小群体之间就发生了一场极为荒谬的争论。半打的穷艺术家站在一方，路易斯·菲力浦陛下、他威严的家族、无数的官吏和君主政体的支持者则站在另一方。有点像特耳西特斯［荷马史诗中最丑陋、最会骂人的男子，因嘲笑阿喀琉斯而被杀。——译注］嘲笑阿喀琉斯，他那轻蔑的嘲笑像毒箭一样穿透了多层的圆盾。必须要承认，我们法国的特耳西特斯并不是一个普通的对手，他所攻击的对象多是懦弱、虚伪、恶毒、庞大的敌人。但我们看到的却是怪物在毒箭的作用下扭曲着——对他矮小的对手回报以粗野的愤怒并给予盲目的一击！——既然他们能画得出来，可以想象得到，他们已足够凶猛到能消灭对手的程度了。

抛开巨人和矮子的隐喻，简单地说，法国的国王遭受了这么多的痛苦，他的部长们受到如此冷酷的嘲笑，国王的家族成员和他自己卓越的形象都被漫画家画成了如此可憎怪诞的肖像，而且还总是处于一种怪诞的表情、环境和伪装的面目之中。如此荒谬可笑的形象又是如此生动传神，以至于国王不得不屈尊来到战场上和荒谬可笑的敌人进行战斗。起诉、捕获、罚

thing like Thersites girding at Ajax, and piercing through the folds of the clypei septemplicis with the poisonous shafts of his scorn. Our French Thersites was not always an honest opponent, it must be confessed; and many an attack was made upon the gigantic enemy, which was cowardly, false, and malignant. But to see the monster writhing under the effects of the arrow—to see his uncouth fury in return, and the blind blows that he dealt at his diminutive opponent! —not one of these told in a hundred; when they DID tell, it may be imagined that they were fierce enough in all conscience, and served almost to annihilate the adversary.

To speak more plainly, and to drop the metaphor of giant and dwarf, the King of the French suffered so much, his Ministers were so mercilessly ridiculed, his family and his own remarkable figure drawn with such odious and grotesque resemblance, in fanciful attitudes, circumstances, and disguises, so ludicrously mean, and often so appropriate, that the King was obliged to descend into the lists and battle this ridiculous enemy in form. Prosecutions, seizures, fines, regiments of furious legal officials, were first brought into play against poor M. Philipon and his little dauntless troop of malicious artists; some few were bribed out of his ranks; and if they did not, like Gilray in England, turn their weapons upon their old friends, at least laid down their arms, and would fight no more. The bribes, fines, indictments, and loud-tongued avocats du roi made no impression; Philipon repaired the defeat of a fine by some fresh and furious attack upon his great enemy; if his epigrams were more covert, they were no less bitter; if he was beaten a dozen times before a jury, he had eighty or ninety victories to show in the same field of battle, and every victory and every defeat brought him new sympathy. Every one who was at Paris a few years since must recollect the famous "poire" which was chalked upon all the walls of the city, and which bore so ludicrous a resemblance to Louis Philippe. The poire became an object of prosecution, and M. Philipon appeared before a jury to answer for the crime of inciting to contempt against the King's person, by giving such a ludicrous version of his face. Philipon, for defence, produced a sheet of paper, and drew a poire, a real large Burgundy pear: in the lower parts round and capacious, narrower

款，一大群狂怒的执法官员首先站出来与贫穷的菲利庞先生和他那群无所畏惧的“心怀恶意”的艺术家作战，其中有少数人受到贿赂离开了菲利庞的队伍，即使他们没有把武器对准他们的老朋友，他们至少是放下武器，不再战斗了。贿赂、罚款、起诉和王权拥护者的大声斥责对菲利庞都没有什么作用，菲利庞对强大的敌人回报以更为生动而猛烈的攻击。他的讽刺作品虽然变得含蓄了但依然锋芒毕露。即使他在陪审团面前被打败了十二次，他也要争取更多的机会来反败为胜，而每次胜利和失败他都能赢来别人更多的同情。几年前凡是在巴黎住过的人都一定会记得当时在城市的所有墙壁上用粉笔画的著名的“梨子”，它是如此的荒谬，与路易·菲力浦又是如此的相像。这个“梨子”就成了起诉菲利庞的一个证据，因为这个荒谬可笑的脸部特写，菲利庞先生被传唤到陪审团面前，就煽动人们对于国王本人的轻视情绪这一罪行做出答复。被告菲利庞拿出一张纸，在纸上画了一个梨，一个真正的大大的勃艮第［法国东南部地方的地名。——译注］的梨，梨的下半部分圆圆的很宽大，靠近梨梗的地方就变狭小了，梨梗上还带有两三片树叶。他对陪审团说：“这里可没有什么叛逆罪，人们会反对这样一个无害的植物果实吗?”然后，他又画了第二个梨子，和前一个差不多，只不过在梨子的中间乱涂了一两道线，看起来有些像一个著名人物的眼睛、鼻子和嘴，最后他画出了路易·菲力浦的精确肖像：众所周知的小绺顶发、繁茂的连鬓胡子和下巴，既没有诋毁也没有恶意的嘲讽。他说：“那么，陪审团的先生们，我可以说陛下的脸像一个梨子吗？你们自己说，尊敬的市民们，它到底像不像一个梨子?”这样的辩解还是有效果的。菲利庞因此被宣判无罪，而这个梨子就成了不朽的了。

后来著名的九月法律颁布了。从1830年8月起，“从今以后成为一条真理”的出版界的自由［七月革命后路易·菲力浦上台。——译注］就被自以为得到民众拥护的新上任国王厚颜无耻地扼杀了。路易·菲力浦是在部长们的支持下取得王位的，其中有很多人在几年前还曾是顽固的共和党员，还有议院的支持，议院是法国人选举的神圣组织，它能以任何一种方

near the stalk, and crowned with two or three careless leaves. "There was no treason in THAT," he said to the jury; "could any one object to such a harmless botanical representation?" Then he drew a second pear, exactly like the former, except that one or two lines were scrawled in the midst of it, which bore somehow a ludicrous resemblance to the eyes, nose, and mouth of a celebrated personage; and, lastly, he drew the exact portrait of Louis Philippe; the well-known toupet, the ample whiskers and jowl were there, neither extenuated nor set down in malice. "Can I help it, gentlemen of the jury, then," said he, "if his Majesty's face is like a pear? Say yourselves, respectable citizens, is it, or is it not, like a pear?" Such eloquence could not fail of its effect; the artist was acquitted, and La poire is immortal.

At last came the famous September laws: the freedom of the Press, which, from August, 1830, was to be "désormais une vérité," was calmly strangled by the Monarch who had gained his crown for his supposed championship of it; by his Ministers, some of whom had been stout Republicans on paper but a few years before; and by the Chamber, which, such is the blessed constitution of French elections, will generally vote, unvote, revote in any way the Government wishes. With a wondrous union, and happy forgetfulness of principle, monarch, ministers, and deputies issued the restriction laws; the Press was sent to prison; as for the poor dear Caricature, it was fairly murdered. No more political satires appear now, and "through the eye, correct the heart;" no more poires ripen on the walls of the metropolis; Philipon's political occupation is gone.

But there is always food for satire; and the French caricaturists, being no longer allowed to hold up to ridicule and reprobation the King and the deputies, have found no lack of subjects for the pencil in the ridicules and rascalities of common life. We have said that public decency is greater amongst the French than amongst us, which, to some of our readers, may appear paradoxical; but we shall not attempt to argue that, in private roguery, our neighbours are not our equals. The procès of Gisquet, which has appeared lately in the papers, shows how deep the demoralization must be, and how a Government, based itself on dishonesty (a tyranny, that is, under the title and fic-

式赞成、否决或重审政府的命令。有了这些联盟的支持以及对原则问题的疏忽，国王、部长和下院议员们很快就颁布了严格的法律。报刊受到监制，可怜的漫画也遭到了封杀。现在政治题材的讽刺作品不见了，“通过眼睛，矫正心灵”，城市的墙上也不再有成熟的梨子，菲利庞的政治漫画就这样告一段落。

但是讽刺作品总会找到讽刺题材的。虽然法国的讽刺画家不被允许去继续嘲笑、斥责国王和议院，然而在日常生活的堕落和卑劣行径方面，他们的画笔并不缺少题材。我们已经说过，法国人比我们更注重公众的体面，这或许会让一些读者感到矛盾。但我们不会在这个问题上展开争论了，在个人的无赖行为方面，我们的邻居与我们并不能相提并论。最近报纸上刊登的吉斯凯［Gisquet，七月王朝时期大金融家，1831 年曾任警署署长。——译注］诉讼案件就显示出人们的道德败坏已达到了多么深的程度，一个建立在欺诈（在民主的称号下伪装的专制）基础上的政府也一定会在它自身内部和处理国家事务的机关中实践和容纳腐败。因此，欺骗性的契约、挪用资金或在不正当的特权和垄断许可下获得非法利益的部长们——营私舞弊的治安特权都在破坏着自由和商业的整体性——和那些喜欢调查这类细节的人物可以在法国历史中找到许多这样的事例。从路易王朝、法制时代到现在，整个法国的财政体制都是一场骗局。在高层权威部门的示范带领下，政府欺诈公众，小商人欺诈他们的顾客。因此，在高层权威的庇护下，诈骗的诡计在法国始终能维持一种厚颜无耻的高贵外表和大胆的直率，我们国家的诈骗则不具备这种外在的特征。

在法国的讽刺艺术家为了自我娱乐而描绘的形形色色的流氓形象之中，有一个远远超越其他所有人的非常杰出（借用江奈生·魏尔德所赋予这个词的意义）的形象。在这个人物形象身上几乎体现了所有流氓人物的特点，他被认为是典型的骗子代表。就像所有的政治讽刺短文都是从帕斯金［Pasquin（1761—1818），原名为 John Williams，帕斯金是他的笔名，英国的讽刺作家。——译注］嘴里说出来的一样，所有流行的假话、欺诈和骗

tion of a democracy,) must practise and admit corruption in its own and in its agents' dealings with the nation. Accordingly, of cheating contracts, of ministers dabbling with the funds, or extracting underhand profits for the granting of unjust privileges and monopolies,—of grasping, envious police restrictions, which destroy the freedom, and, with it, the integrity of commerce,—those who like to examine such details may find plenty in French history: the whole French finance system has been a swindle from the days of Louvois, or Law, down to the present time. The Government swindles the public, and the small traders swindle their customers, on the authority and example of the superior powers. Hence the art of roguery, under such high patronage, maintains in France a noble front of impudence, and a fine audacious openness, which it does not wear in our country.

Among the various characters of roguery which the French satirists have amused themselves by depicting, there is one of which the GREATNESS (using the word in the sense which Mr. Jonathan Wild gave to it) so far exceeds that of all others, embracing, as it does, all in turn, that it has come to be considered the type of roguery in general; and now, just as all the political squibs were made to come of old from the lips of Pasquin, all the reflections on the prevailing cant, knavery, quackery, humbug, are put into the mouth of Monsieur Robert Macaire.

A play was written, some twenty years since, called the "*Auberge des Adrets*," in which the characters of two robbers escaped from the galleys were introduced—Robert Macaire, the clever rogue above mentioned, and Bertrand, the stupid rogue, his friend, accomplice, butt, and scapegoat, on all occasions of danger. It is needless to describe the play—a witless performance enough, of which the joke was Macaire's exaggerated style of conversation, a farrago of all sorts of high-flown sentiments such as the French love to indulge in—contrasted with his actions, which were philosophically unscrupulous, and his appearance, which was most picturesquely sordid. The play had been acted, we believe, and forgotten, when a very clever actor, M. Frederick Lemaitre, took upon himself the performance of the character of Robert Macaire, and looked, spoke, and acted it to such admirable perfection, that

术都是从罗伯尔·玛盖尔的形象上体现出来的。

二十年前有一部名叫《向阳山坡的小旅店》的戏剧。在这部戏剧里介绍了两个从帆船上逃亡的强盗人物——罗伯尔·玛盖尔（前面提到的聪明的无赖）和伯特兰（一个愚蠢的无赖，罗伯尔·玛盖尔的朋友、共犯、对头，还是所有危险场合中的替罪羊）。这里就没必要再去描述这部戏剧了——它是一场足够滑稽的戏剧表演，其中的笑料就是罗伯尔·玛盖尔谈话时的夸张语调和表情与他镇静无耻的行为，都与他惨不忍睹的外表形成了鲜明的对比。人们或许已遗忘了这出已上演过的戏剧，当时是一个非常聪明伶俐的演员弗雷德里克·勒梅特先生扮演罗伯尔·玛盖尔这个角色，他的扮相、谈吐和动作是如此完美，以至于整个城镇的观众对他的表演都回报以热烈的掌声，而讽刺画家们也很乐意在作品中去模仿他独特的形象和服饰。罗伯尔·玛盖尔先生穿着一件非常别致的绿色外套，上面有很多破裂的地方和补丁，一条深红色的裤子也装饰着同样的裂缝和补丁，浓密的连鬓胡子和长卷发，巨大的宽领巾和衬衫褶边都很肮脏、破烂，一顶破帽子歪戴在头上，遮住了他的一只眼睛，帽子上还有一块补丁很吸引人的注意力——除了这些服饰之外，他还有一个像吱吱嘎嘎的暖炉一样的鼻烟盒，还有一条不知道用什么方法系在身上的手帕，一条像男人的大腿一样粗的鞭子，这就是罗伯尔·玛盖尔的全部装饰。他是菲尔丁笔下的“布鲁斯金”和哥尔德斯密斯笔下的“比乌·蒂波斯”的综合体。他既邋遢又虚荣，还兼有许多无耻的恶行。罗伯尔·玛盖尔经常去欺诈别人，如果他能得到多于一个先令的钱，他就会毫无顾忌地杀掉那个人。他以温和而冷静的态度上演了一幕又一幕（或者它们之间也有些区别），与他的行为相伴的是非常镇静达观的评论，这是我们可以从一个拥有像他那样的才智、精力、亲切个性的人身上所期望得到的。

伯特兰即是罗伯尔·玛盖尔开玩笑的嘲弄对象，又要为玛盖尔的罪过和行为做替罪羊。实际上这个傻瓜在这场哑剧中的角色完全是受小丑玛盖

the whole town rung with applauses of the performance, and the caricaturists delighted to copy his singular figure and costume. M. Robert Macaire appears in a most picturesque green coat, with a variety of rents and patches, a pair of crimson pantaloons ornamented in the same way, enormous whiskers and ringlets, an enormous stock and shirt-frill, as dirty and ragged as stock and shirt-frill can be, the relic of a hat very gayly cocked over one eye, and a patch to take away somewhat from the brightness of the other—these are the principal pièces of his costume—a snuff-box like a creaking warming-pan, a handkerchief hanging together by a miracle, and a switch of about the thickness of a man's thigh, formed the ornaments of this exquisite personage. He is a compound of Fielding's "Blueskin"and Goldsmith's "Beau Tibbs." He has the dirt and dandyism of the one, with the ferocity of the other: sometimes he is made to swindle, but where he can get a shilling more, M. Macaire will murder without scruple: he performs one and the other act (or any in the scale between them) with a similar bland imperturbability, and accompanies his actions with such philosophical remarks as may be expected from a person of his talents, his energies, his amiable life and character.

Bertrand is the simple recipient of Macaire's jokes, and makes vicarious atonement for his crimes, acting, in fact, the part which pantaloon performs in the pantomime, who is entirely under the fatal influence of clown. He is quite as much a rogue as that gentleman, but he has not his genius and courage. So, in pantomimes, (it may, doubtless, have been remarked by the reader,) clown always leaps first, pantaloon following after, more clumsily and timidly than his bold and accomplished friend and guide. Whatever blows are destined for clown, fall, by some means of ill-luck, upon the pate of pantaloon: whenever the clown robs, the stolen articles are sure to be found in his companion's pocket; and thus exactly Robert Macaire and his companion Bertrand are made to go through the world; both swindlers, but the one more accomplished than the other. Both robbing all the world, and Robert robbing his friend, and, in the event of danger, leaving him faithfully in the lurch. There is, in the two characters, some grotesque good for the spectator—a kind of "*Beggars' Opera*"moral.

尔的支配和控制的。他像玛盖尔一样是个恶棍，但是他没有玛盖尔的才智和勇气。因此在这场哑剧中小丑总是最先跳出来，后面跟着傻瓜伯特兰，他看起来可要比那位大胆、成功的朋友和向导玛盖尔笨拙和胆怯多了。无论先前怎样注定为小丑所承担的灾祸，最终都会以某种不幸的方式落到傻瓜的头顶上。每当小丑偷盗别人的财物时，偷盗的物品必定会跑到他同伴伯特兰的口袋中去。就这样罗伯尔·玛盖尔和他的朋友伯特兰游历了整个世界。两个人都是骗子，但一个比另一个具有才智。两个人都偷盗财物，但罗伯尔会抢劫他的朋友，并且在危险的时候总是撇下他朋友一个人，自己逃跑。对于观众来说，这两个形象都有些《乞丐的歌剧》[18 世纪 20 年代末在伦敦上演的一部针砭时弊的歌剧，它取材于日常生活，采用通俗幽默的对白和流行的曲调，赢得了市民的广泛好评。——译注] 的寓意。

自从罗伯尔穿着他那套破烂衣服、带着手杖和鼻烟盒，伯特兰穿着破旧的外套、带着个什么都能装得下的口袋在舞台上出现以来，他们就受到了巴黎人民的热烈欢迎。凭借着这两个典型的欺诈形象，菲利庞先生和他的朋友杜米埃 [Daumier (1808—1879)，法国画家及讽刺漫画家。他生前最主要是以政治和社会讽刺家著称。——译注] 在针砭时弊的基础上又创造了许多令人愉悦的讽刺作品。

这些大胆的讽刺画家敢于描绘的第一个人物形象就是带有政治性讽刺意味的。玛盖尔的红色裤子和破烂的外套看起来就和国王本人一样——一个“成熟的梨子”——他能在一个充斥着欺诈和骗子的国家中做国王，说明他要比他国家中的所有恶棍都狡猾。伯特兰则恰恰相反，他经常是带着一种愉悦和尊敬的神情倾听真正的王室欺诈故事，并会用最为强烈的赞赏表情和声音叫喊道：“啊！够狡猾！好！”——法语中的“欺诈”这个词是很难译的——它的意思是指法国的骗子和其他国家的骗子截然不同。只有那些知道法国讽刺短诗价值的人才能想象得到这个词语的魅力。讽刺短诗的内容非常精彩，包罗万象，里面有很多词语只可意会不可言传。讽刺短诗打击并动摇了整个王朝。特耳西特斯已经嘲弄了阿喀琉斯，就是全身武

Ever since Robert, with his dandified rags and airs, his cane and snuff-box, and Bertrand with torn surtout and all-absorbing pocket, have appeared on the stage, they have been popular with the Parisians; and with these two types of clever and stupid knavery, M. Philipon and his companion Daumier have created a world of pleasant satire upon all the prevailing abuses of the day.

Almost the first figure that these audacious caricaturists dared to depict was a political one: in Macaire's red breeches and tattered coat appeared no less a personage than the King himself—the old Poire—in a country of humbugs and swindlers the facile princeps; fit to govern, as he is deeper than all the rogues in his dominions. Bertrand was opposite to him, and having listened with delight and reverence to some tale of knavery truly royal, was exclaiming with a look and voice expressive of the most intense admiration, "AH VIEUX BLAGUEUR! va!" the word blague is untranslatable—it means FRENCH humbug as distinct from all other; and only those who know the value of an epigram in France, an epigram so wonderfully just, a little word so curiously comprehensive, can fancy the kind of rage and rapture with which it was received. It was a blow that shook the whole dynasty. Thersites had there given such a wound to Ajax, as Hector in arms could scarcely have inflicted: a blow sufficient almost to create the madness to which the fabulous hero of Homer and Ovid fell a prey.

Not long, however, was French caricature allowed to attack personages so illustrious: the September laws came, and henceforth no more epigrams were launched against politics; but the caricaturists were compelled to confine their satire to subjects and characters that had nothing to do with the State. The Duke of Orleans was no longer to figure in lithography as the fantastic Prince Rosolin; no longer were multitudes (in chalk) to shelter under the enormous shadow of M. d'Argout's nose: Marshal Lobau's squirt was hung up in peace, and M. Thiers's pigmy figure and round spectacled face were no more to appear in print. [2] Robert Macaire was driven out of the Chambers and the Palace—his remarks were a great deal too appropriate and too severe for the ears of the great men who congregated in those places.

装的赫克托耳也承受不了这种嘲弄。这种打击几乎足以让荷马和奥维德作品中的英雄变得疯狂。

然而法国讽刺画家被允许去攻击著名人士的时间并不长。很快九月法律就颁布了，因此政治上反动的讽刺短诗就消失了。讽刺画家不得不把他们的讽刺对象限制在与政府没有任何关系的主题和人物形象上。在石版印刷画中，读者们就看不到以罗瑟林王子形象出现的奥尔良公爵；也没有人群躲在阿尔古［Argout，法国海军大臣。——译注］鼻子的巨大阴影下寻求庇护；也没有和平收缴的洛班将军的水枪、梯也尔先生的侏儒身材和戴着眼镜的圆脸。[2]罗伯尔·玛盖尔被逐出了议院和宫廷——他的言论对于聚集在这些地方的显贵人物的耳朵来说是太犀利、太尖锐了。

议院和宫廷对罗伯尔·玛盖尔关上了大门，但是这个恶棍被逐出恶棍的乐园之后，看到"他面前还有整个世界可以去选择"，他发现在这个世界中并不缺乏机会来运用他的才智。法庭里有无赖的律师、卑鄙的代理人、愚蠢的陪审团和发伪誓的法官；还有证券交易所，里面充斥着赌博和欺诈；医药这个行业则被庸医们轮流统治着；戏剧舞台上流行的是伪善之言；风行一时的事物都是夸张的愚笨和奢侈。罗伯尔·玛盖尔变成剥削者来欺诈所有的人。在整个帝国中，他可以任意嘲笑所有人的等级、职业、谎言和罪行，但只有特权阶层除外。就像蓝胡子的妻子一样，他可以看到任何事情，但是一定要提防那个蓝色的房间。罗伯尔比蓝胡子的妻子更明智，他知道如果进了那个蓝房间，他的脑袋就保不住了。因此，罗伯尔暂时远离那个房间。他的牺牲会有任何用处吗？蓝胡子不会永远活着；或许，直到现在，那些人还正在（人们有些疑惑）试图消灭他。

罗伯尔和他的朋友同时还给我们提供了一幅生活图景，也许读者能从这幅图景的简明描述中得到启发。我们并不是要通过罗伯尔·玛盖尔这个形象来判断法国的民族道德，如同我们不会根据上个世纪的《乞丐的歌剧》来判断我们自己民族的道德一样。但是就道德和民族风俗来说，讽刺作品可以给我们提供更多的启发，这是我们从正规的历史著作

The Chambers and the Palace were shut to him; but the rogue, driven out of this rogue's paradise, saw "that the world was all before him where to choose," and found no lack of opportunities for exercising his wit. There was the Bar, with its roguish practitioners, rascally attorneys, stupid juries, and forsworn judges; there was the Bourse, with all its gambling, swindling, and hoaxing, its cheats and its dupes; the Medical Profession, and the quacks who ruled it, alternately; the Stage, and the cant that was prevalent there; the Fashion, and its thousand follies and extravagances. Robert Macaire had all these to exploiter. Of all the empire, through all the ranks, professions, the lies, crimes, and absurdities of men, he may make sport at will; of all except of a certain class. Like Bluebeard's wife, he may see everything, but is bidden TO BEWARE OF THE BLUE CHAMBER. Robert is more wise than Bluebeard's wife, and knows that it would cost him his head to enter it. Robert, therefore, keeps aloof for the moment. Would there be any use in his martyrdom? Bluebeard cannot live for ever; perhaps, even now, those are on their way (one sees a suspicious cloud of dust or two) that are to destroy him.

In the meantime Robert and his friend have been furnishing the designs that we have before us, and of which perhaps the reader will be edified by a brief description. We are not, to be sure, to judge of the French nation by M. Macaire, any more than we are to judge of our own national morals in the last century by such a book as the "*Beggars' Opera*;" but upon the morals and the national manners, works of satire afford a world of light that one would in vain look for in regular books of history. Doctor Smollett would have blushed to devote any considerable portion of his pages to a discussion of the acts and character of Mr. Jonathan Wild, such a figure being hardly admissible among the dignified personages who usually push all others out from the possession of the historical page; but a chapter of that gentleman's memoirs, as they are recorded in that exemplary recueil—the "*Newgate Calendar*;" nay, a canto of the great comic epic (involving many fables, and containing much exaggeration, but still having the seeds of truth) which the satirical poet of those days wrote in celebration of him—we mean Fielding's "*History of Jonathan Wild the Great*" does seem to us to give a more curious picture of the manners of

中找不到的。斯摩莱特博士［斯摩莱特（1721—1771），英国小说家，代表作《蓝登传》。——译注］、如果把他作品中的很多篇幅都用来探讨江奈生·魏尔德［菲尔丁（1707—1754），18世纪英国杰出的小说家，《大伟人江奈生·魏尔德传》是他的一部重要作品，这部小说是以当时一个有名的强盗首领魏尔德的事迹为根据而创作的。——译注］的个性和行为的话，他会为此而感到脸红的，江奈生·魏尔德这样的人物几乎是上层人士所接受不了的，他们经常会收存一些历史著作而排斥其他的一切作品。但是江奈生·魏尔德的事迹不仅被记录在他那本典型的文集——《监狱日历》中；而且还构成了伟大的滑稽史诗的一个篇章（包括许多寓言和夸张，但仍有事实的根据），那是讽刺诗人为了纪念他而写的——我们是指菲尔丁的《大伟人江奈生·魏尔德传》——这本小说确实是给我们更多地提供了那个时代的生活风俗的奇异画卷，而不仅是对于当时历史的认识。在他的乔治二世（1727—1760）史书的结尾，斯摩莱特谦逊地对于文学和生活风俗做了一章简短的评论。他谈约翰·葛洛佛［John Glover（1767—1849），英国风景画家。——译注］的《列奥尼达》，西伯［Cibber，Theophilus（1703—1758），英国演员兼剧作家。英国戏剧界中一个被普遍看做声名狼藉的人物。——译注］的《粗心丈夫》，梅逊（Mason，1792—1872）、格雷（Thomas Gray，1716－1771）这两个感伤诗人的诗歌，“简练的文体，广博的学识和科尔克的优越感觉，雅致的审美趣味，优美的沉思和利特尔顿所特有的柔情”。他说：“乔治二世国王在雄辩术方面是无与伦比的，国内的女性也以她们自身的审美趣味和独创性而驰名。卡特小姐在学识和批评知识方面比得上著名的达西耶［Anne Dacier（1654－1720），法国的古典文学评论家、翻译家和编辑。——译注］；兰诺克斯太太因在诗歌和散文领域的努力而使自己名声突出；雷德小姐在肖像画方面，不管是袖珍画还是大幅绘画，不管是油画还是蜡笔画，都胜过驰名的罗萨尔巴［罗萨尔巴（1675—1757），意大利肖像女画家。——译注］。塞万提斯［16世纪西

those times than any recognized history of them. At the close of his history of George II, Smollett condescends to give a short chapter on Literature and Manners. He speaks of Glover's "*Leonidas*," Cibber's "*Careless Husband*," the poems of Mason, Gray, the two Whiteheads, "the nervous style, extensive erudition, and superior sense of a Corke; the delicate taste, the polished muse, and tender feeling of a Lyttelton." "King," he says, "shone unrivalled in Roman eloquence, the female sex distinguished themselves by their taste and ingenuity. Miss Carter rivalled the celebrated Dacier in learning and critical knowledge; Mrs. Lennox signalized herself by many successful efforts of genius both in poetry and prose; and Miss Reid excelled the celebrated Rosalba in portrait-painting, both in miniature and at large, in oil as well as in crayons. The genius of Cervantes was transferred into the novels of Fielding, who painted the characters and ridiculed the follies of life with equal strength, humour, and propriety. The field of history and biography was cultivated by many writers of ability, among whom we distinguish the copious Guthrie, the circumstantial Ralph, the labourious Carte, the learned and elegant Robertson, and above all, the ingenious, penetrating, and comprehensive Hume," &c. &c. We will quote no more of the passage. Could a man in the best humour sit down to write a graver satire? Who cares for the tender muse of Lyttelton? Who knows the signal efforts of Mrs. Lennox's genius? Who has seen the admirable performances, in miniature and at large, in oil as well as in crayons, of Miss Reid? Labourious Carte, and circumstantial Ralph, and copious Guthrie, where are they, their works, and their reputation? Mrs. Lennox's name is just as clean wiped out of the list of worthies as if she had never been born; and Miss Reid, though she was once actual flesh and blood, "rival in miniature and at large" of the celebrated Rosalba, she is as if she had never been at all; her little farthing rushlight of a soul and reputation having burnt out, and left neither wick nor tallow. Death, too, has overtaken copious Guthrie and circumstantial Ralph. Only a few know whereabouts is the grave where lies labourious Carte; and yet, O wondrous power of genius! Fielding's men and women are alive, though History's are not. The progenitors of circumstantial Ralph sent forth, after much labour and pains of mak-

班牙著名的现实主义作家，代表作《堂吉诃德》。——译注］的才华体现在菲尔丁的小说中，菲尔丁用同样的讽刺幽默手法来描述人物形象并嘲讽生活中的愚蠢行为。历史和传记领域已被许多有才能的作家所占据了，在他们当中，我们知道有满腹经纶的葛斯瑞［William Guthrie（1708—1770），英国的大将兼历史学家，以善描写战争出名。——译注］，描述详尽的拉尔夫（Ralph），矫揉造作的卡特（Carte），学识渊博、文笔雅致的罗伯逊，还有他们当中最为机智、深刻、包罗万象的休谟［Hume（1711—1776），英国哲学家、历史学家、经济学家。——译注］”等等。我们就不再引用更多的人名了。一个人在心情好的时候会坐下来写一篇沉重的讽刺文章吗？谁关心诗人的感伤沉思？谁知道兰诺克斯太太杰出的成就？谁曾看到过雷德小姐在袖珍画、大幅绘画、油画和蜡笔画中的出色表现？矫揉造作的卡特，描述详尽的拉尔夫，满腹经纶的葛斯瑞，他们的作品和名誉都在哪里呢？兰诺克斯太太的名字已从杰出人物的目录册中被清除了出去，仿佛从来没有出生过这个人似的；雷德小姐虽然曾是真实的血肉之躯，但在袖珍画和大幅绘画方面，她好像最终也没有胜过著名的罗萨尔巴，她灵魂的最后一点微光都已燃尽，既没有留下灯芯也没有留下蜡脂。死亡也埋没了满腹经纶的葛斯瑞和描述详尽的拉尔夫。只有很少人知道矫揉造作的卡特的墓穴在哪里。然而，天才却具有令人惊奇的力量！菲尔丁笔下的男人和女人是充满生气的，尽管历史上并不存在这些人物。那些历史学家在付出了大量的心血和汗水后，塑造出来的都是些行尸走肉的人物，他们到死也不过获得个描述详尽的称号。但是，瞧！菲尔丁就不用费那么大的力，在最舒适、最快乐的写作生活方式中，菲尔丁创作了这么多的人物形象，他们要比拉尔夫或雷德小姐更有趣，更生动，更具有活力。阿米莉亚［阿米莉亚，1751年菲尔丁最后一本小说中的女主人公。——译注］没给她的丈夫准备简单的晚餐吗？斯奈普·查斯戴莱小姐没有阻止费尔布兰德先生的罪行吗？亚当牧师［《汤姆·琼斯》中的主要人物形象。——译注］

ing, educating, feeding, clothing, a real man child, a great palpable mass of flesh, bones, and blood (we say nothing about the spirit), which was to move through the world, ponderous, writing histories, and to die, having achieved the title of circumstantial Ralph; and lo! without any of the trouble that the parents of Ralph had undergone, alone perhaps in a watch or spunging-house, fuddled most likely, in the blandest, easiest, and most good-humoured way in the world, Henry Fielding makes a number of men and women on so many sheets of paper, not only more amusing than Ralph or Miss Reid, but more like flesh and blood, and more alive now than they. Is not Amelia preparing her husband's little supper? Is not Miss Snapp chastely preventing the crime of Mr. Firebrand? Is not Parson Adams in the midst of his family, and Mr. Wild taking his last bowl of punch with the Newgate Ordinary? Is not every one of them a real substantial HAVE-been personage now—more real than Reid or Ralph? For our parts, we will not take upon ourselves to say that they do not exist somewhere else: that the actions attributed to them have not really taken place; certain we are that they are more worthy of credence than Ralph, who may or may not have been circumstantial; who may or may not even have existed, a point unworthy of disputation. As for Miss Reid, we will take an affidavit that neither in miniature nor at large did she excel the celebrated Rosalba; and with regard to Mrs. Lennox, we consider her to be a mere figment, like Narcissa, Miss Tabitha Bramble, or any hero or heroine depicted by the historian of "*Peregrine Pickle.*"

In like manner, after viewing nearly ninety portraits of Robert Macaire and his friend Bertrand, all strongly resembling each other, we are inclined to believe in them as historical personages, and to canvass gravely the circumstances of their lives. Why should we not? Have we not their portraits? Are not they sufficient proofs? If not, we must discredit Napoleon (as Archbishop Whately teaches), for about his figure and himself we have no more authentic testimony.

Let the reality of M. Robert Macaire and his friend M. Bertrand be granted, if but to gratify our own fondness for those exquisite characters: we find the worthy pair in the French capital, mingling with all grades of its society,

不是在他的家族成员中吗？魏尔德先生不是在监狱里接受了命运的最后一击吗？他们中的每一个人不都比雷德或拉尔夫还要真实吗？对于我们来说，我们要确定的不是他们存在不存在，他们的行为有没有发生过，我们要确定的是他们是否比拉尔夫更可信。至于他们有没有得到详尽的描述，有没有存在过，这点并不重要。对于雷德小姐，我们拿出一份宣誓书来证明在袖珍画和大幅绘画作品中她并没有胜过著名的罗萨尔巴·卡列拉；对于兰诺克斯太太，我们只认为她是个虚构的人物，就像那喀索斯［希腊神话里变成水仙的人物。——译注］，塔见莎·布兰布尔小姐或历史学家斯摩莱特在《流浪的皮克勒》［斯摩莱特的小说。——译注］中所描写的任何主人公一样。

同样，在看过将近九十幅罗伯尔·玛盖尔和他朋友伯特兰的画像之后，它们每张都非常相像，我们更愿意去相信他们就是真实的人物，愿意严肃地去讨论他们的生活环境。为什么我们会这样认为呢？难道我们没有他们的肖像吗？而它们不就是最充分的证据吗？如果它们不是证据的话，那我们一定也不会相信拿破仑存在了（正像大主教所教导的那样），因为对于他的外形和本人，我们确实也拿不出可靠的证据。

既然我们那么喜欢罗伯尔·玛盖尔和伯特兰这两个人物形象，就让我们认可他们的真实性吧！在法国的首都巴黎，我们会发现这“高尚”的一对混入了社会所有的阶层，在巴黎进行由他们主演的阴谋、放荡、纠纷、恶作剧、投机买卖，这些就像在我们英国的主要城市所上演的那些骗局一样。人们都知道诈骗是不分国界，不分地方的，即使是在民风好的地方也避免不了，而在法国人当中它更能找到适合它生长的土壤。

那些没有祖传财富可继承的人不得不运用他们自己的才智去获得荣誉，甚至有时只是为了生存。我们看到伯特兰和罗伯尔·玛盖尔先生轮流选定各行各业来施展他们自己独特的机智。作为公众人物，我们已经介绍了他们两个人的外表特征，也交代过政府已开始嫉妒他们，把他们从政府机关逐了出去，如同辉格党［自由党前身。——译注］对布鲁厄姆勋爵

pars magna in the intrigues, pleasures, perplexities, rogueries, speculations, which are carried on in Paris, as in our own chief city; for it need not be said that roguery is of no country nor clime, but finds ὡς πανταχου γε πατρις ἡ βοσκουσα γη, is a citizen of all countries where the quarters are good; among our merry neighbours it finds itself very much at its ease.

Not being endowed, then, with patrimonial wealth, but compelled to exercise their genius to obtain distinction, or even subsistence, we see Messrs. Bertrand and Macaire, by turns, adopting all trades and professions, and exercising each with their own peculiar ingenuity. As public men, we have spoken already of their appearance in one or two important characters, and stated that the Government grew fairly jealous of them, excluding them from office, as the Whigs did Lord Brougham. As private individuals, they are made to distinguish themselves as the founders of journals, sociétés en commandite (companies of which the members are irresponsible beyond the amount of their shares), and all sorts of commercial speculations, requiring intelligence and honesty on the part of the directors, confidence and liberal disbursements from the shareholders.

These are, among the French, so numerous, and have been of late years (in the shape of Newspaper Companies, Bitumen Companies, Galvanized-Iron Companies, Railroad Companies, &c.) pursued with such a blind FUROR and lust of gain, by that easily excited and imaginative people, that, as may be imagined, the satirist has found plenty of occasion for remark, and M. Macaire and his friend innumerable opportunities for exercising their talents.

We know nothing of M. Emile de Girardin, except that, in a duel, he shot the best man in France, Armand Carrel; and in Girardin's favour it must be said, that he had no other alternative; but was right in provoking the duel, seeing that the whole Republican party had vowed his destruction, and that he fought and killed their champion, as it were. We know nothing of M. Girardin's private character: but, as far as we can judge from the French public prints, he seems to be the most speculative of speculators, and, of course, a fair butt for the malice of the caricaturists. His one great crime, in the eyes of the French Republicans and Republican newspaper proprietors, was, that

[Henry Peter Brougham（1778—1868），英国律师、辉格党政治家、改革家、英国大法官兼上院议长（1830－1834 年）。在任大法官前后曾主持多次重大的法律改革。——译注] 所做的那样。作为民间人物形象，他们又摇身变成了著名报刊、两合公司（在公司中业务如果超过成员股份的数目，成员一概不负责任。）的创办人，所有的商业投机都需要董事这一方的机智诚实，还有股东们的信任和慷慨支出。

最近几年，在法国有很多人（以报业公司、沥青公司、镀锌铁公司、铁路公司等形式）狂热而贪婪地追求金钱。可以想象得到，讽刺画家就在这些人中发现了他们所要寻求的创作素材。在这种社会背景下，罗伯尔·玛盖尔和他的朋友也拥有很多的机会来施展他们的才能。

对于埃米尔·德·吉拉丁先生，我们只知道他在一次决斗中击毙了法国大名鼎鼎的阿蒙德·卡雷尔。从吉拉丁的角度出发，我们必须要说的是，除此之外他没有别的选择。但是就挑起决斗这件事来说，他的做法是对的。看到整个共和党都发誓要消灭他，他不得不起来斗争并杀死了他们的带头人。我们对于吉拉丁先生本人一点儿也不了解。但是，我们至少能够从法国的一些公共刊物中来了解他，他似乎是最敢于冒险的一位投机者，因此他也就成了讽刺画家们恶意嘲讽的目标。在法国共和党及其报业业主的眼里，吉拉丁先生的一个显著罪行就是创办了一份称做《完全君主制》的刊物——一份由君主政体投资的刊物——它每年的订阅费用只需四十法郎，而国家报的费用是它的两倍；《逗闹》的费用是它的一半。尽管所有的报纸、所有的党派都在“斥责”可怜的吉拉丁先生和他的刊物，但是共和党的出版刊物对他的攻击是最强烈的，它们每天都轮番轰炸地对他进行谴责和人身攻击。我们也不知道这些辱骂是好意还是恶意。总之，后来就导致了吉拉丁和卡雷尔的决斗。在决斗结束后，吉拉丁拿着手枪彬彬有礼地发誓，以后要阻止更多流血事件的发生。吉拉丁除了创办刊物之外，还是其他许多投机行业的开创人。这些投机行业的资本和创办刊物的资本一样都是由股份和股东们筹款建立起

Girardin set up a journal, as he called it, "*franchement monarchique*," a journal in the pay of the monarchy, that is,—and a journal that cost only forty francs by the year. The National costs twice as much; the *Charivari* itself costs half as much again; and though all newspapers, of all parties, concurred in "snubbing" poor M. Girardin and his journal, the Republican prints, were by far the most bitter against him, thundering daily accusations and personalities; whether the abuse was well or ill founded, we know not. Hence arose the duel with Carrel; after the termination of which, Girardin put by his pistol, and vowed, very properly, to assist in the shedding of no more blood. Girardin had been the originator of numerous other speculations besides the journal: the capital of these, like that of the journal, was raised by shares, and the shareholders, by some fatality, have found themselves woefully in the lurch; while Girardin carries on the war gayly, is, or was, a member of the Chamber of Deputies, has money, goes to Court, and possesses a certain kind of reputation. He invented, we believe, the "Institution Agronome de Coetbo,"[3] the "Physionotype," the "Journal des Connoissances Utiles," the "Panthéon Littéraire," and the system of "Primes"—premiums, that is—to be given, by lottery, to certain subscribers in these institutions. Could Robert Macaire see such things going on, and have no hand in them?

Accordingly Messrs. Macaire and Bertrand are made the heroes of many speculations of the kind. In almost the first print of our collection, Robert discourses to Bertrand of his projects. "Bertrand," says the disinterested admirer of talent and enterprise, "J'adore l'industrie. Si tu veux nous creons une banque, mais la, une vraie banque: capital cent millions de millions, cent milliards de milliards d'actions. Nous enfonçons la banque de France, les banquiers, les banquistes; nous enfonçons tout le monde." "Oui," says Bertrand, very calm and stupid, "mais les gendarmes??" "Que tu es bête, Bertrand: est-ce qu'on arrête un millionnaire?" Such is the key to M. Macaire's philosophy; and a wise creed too, as times go.

Acting on these principles, Robert appears soon after; he has not created a bank, but a journal. He sits in a chair of state, and discourses to a shareholder. Bertrand, calm and stupid as before, stands humbly behind. "Sir,"

来的，不幸的是，股东们很快就发现自己受骗上当了。但吉拉丁仍乐此不疲地实施这种战略，他一直都是国民议会的议员，既有钱去打官司，也拥有一定的社会名誉。我们认为是他发明了“农学家机构联合会”[3]、“人像描摹”、“鉴赏家刊物”、“文学圣殿”和“奖金”制度——即通过抽彩给奖法赠给在这些机构中工作的某个人员。罗伯尔·玛盖尔看到这样的事情能不去插手吗？

因此罗伯尔·玛盖尔和伯特兰先生在石版讽刺画中就变成了许多投机行业中的主人公。在第一张图版罗伯尔就对伯特兰讲到他的计划，这位想创办企业的罗伯尔说：“伯特兰，我喜欢产业。你知道吗？我们要开办一家银行，一家真正的银行，有上百亿的资本、上千亿的股票。我们要击败法国的银行和银行家，击败所有的人。”伯特兰非常平静和愚蠢地说：“是。但是警察呢？”“伯特兰你这个傻瓜呀！——无论做什么事情，人们会阻止一个百万富翁吗？”这就是罗伯尔·玛盖尔人生观的核心思想，而以后的事实也证明了他这种认识是明智的。

罗伯尔很快就按照这种原则来行动了。他还没有开办银行，而是创办了一个刊物。他坐在一把豪华的椅子上对一个股东讲话。伯特兰像以前一样平静而愚蠢，谦逊地站在椅子后面。期刊杂志《谎话》的编辑说：“先生，在新的股份制组合中《谎言》的利润提升了。这份刊物值二十法郎，我们卖二十三点五法郎。一百万个订阅者就会给我们带来三百五十万法郎的利润。这是我的统计数字，如果不属实，我会因欺诈罪而受到起诉的。”读者可能会想象到这幕场景发生在英国，因为在英国有许多这样的诈骗计划书在此之前还得到了人们的信任。在第三十三张图版，罗伯尔仍是一个报界人士，他交给编辑一篇自己写的猛烈攻击法律的文章。编辑说：“亲爱的玛盖尔先生，这篇文章一定要改动，因为我们必须要歌颂法律。”多才多艺的玛盖尔说：“好，好！我会修改的，会给您写一篇吹嘘法律的文章。”

有这样的事情吗？法国新闻记者会这样作践他们自己吗？这群流氓！他们应该到英国来学学言行一致。在英国新闻媒体的诚实就像我们呼吸的

says the editor of *La Blague*, journal quotidienne, "our profits arise from a new combination. The journal costs twenty francs; we sell it for twenty-three and a half. A million subscribers make three millions and a half of profits; there are my figures; contradict me by figures, or I will bring an action for libel." The reader may fancy the scene takes place in England, where many such a swindling prospectus has obtained credit ere now. At Plate 33, Robert is still a journalist; he brings to the editor of a paper an article of his composition, a violent attack on a law. "My dear M. Macaire," says the editor, "this must be changed; we must PRAISE this law." "Bon, bon!" says our versatile Macaire. "Je vais rétoucher ça, et je vous fais en faveur de la loi UN ARTICLE MOUSSEUX."

Can such things be? Is it possible that French journalists can so forget themselves? The rogues! they should come to England and learn consistency. The honesty of the Press in England is like the air we breathe, without it we die. No, no! in France, the satire may do very well; but for England it is too monstrous. Call the press stupid, call it vulgar, call it violent,—but honest it is. Who ever heard of a journal changing its politics? O tempora! O mores! as Robert Macaire says, this would be carrying the joke too far.

When he has done with newspapers, Robert Macaire begins to distinguish himself on "Change",[4] as a creator of companies, a vender of shares, or a dabbler in foreign stock. "Buy my coal-mine shares," shouts Robert; "gold mines, silver mines, diamond mines, 'sont de la pot-bouille de la ratatouille en comparaison de ma houille.'" "Look," says he, on another occasion, to a very timid, open-countenanced client, "you have a property to sell! I have found the very man, a rich capitalist, a fellow whose bills are better than bank-notes." His client sells; the bills are taken in payment, and signed by that respectable capitalist, Monsieur de Saint Bertrand. At Plate 81, we find him inditing a circular letter to all the world, running thus: "Sir,—I regret to say that your application for shares in the Consolidated European Incombustible Blacking Association cannot be complied with, as all the shares of the C. E. I. B. A. were disposed of on the day they were issued. I have, nevertheless, registered your name, and in case a second series should be put forth, I shall have the honour of immediately giving you notice. I am, sir,

空气一样，如果缺少了它，我们会窒息而死。不，法国的讽刺作品却做得很好，但这点对英国来说就太难了。不管杂志报纸是怎样的愚蠢、粗俗和偏激，它最重要的本质就是忠实于现实。谁曾听说过一份报纸总是变换它的政治策略的？就像罗伯尔·玛盖尔说的那样，这种社会习俗会使玩笑越开越大的。

当罗伯尔·玛盖尔脱离报界之后，他又开始“变化”了[4]，这次他是以一个公司创立人、股份出售者、涉猎国外证券的人员出现的。罗伯尔喊道：“买我的煤矿股份，金矿、银矿、钻石矿‘与我的煤矿相比，就是混杂的一锅焖菜’。”在另一个场合中，他对一个胆怯、想要投资的顾客说：“看！你有笔财产要转让出去！而我已经找到了合适的人选，他是一个富有的资本家，他的账单比钞票还要赢利。”这位顾客就把财产出售了，而作为抵偿的账单是由尊敬的资本家——圣·伯特兰先生签署的。在第八十一页图版，我们会看到罗伯尔正在写一份通知，内容是这样的：“先生，我很遗憾地告诉您，您在联合欧洲不燃物炭粉协会所申请的股份不能照计划给您了，因为在E. I. B. A.（公司缩写——译注）发行股份的当天，所有的股份就被转让了。但是我记下了您的名字，如果第二批股份被放出来的话，我会立即通知您的。先生，我是您的理事罗伯尔·玛盖尔。”他对伯特兰说：“把这个通知印出三十万份来，用它们来毒害整个法国。”愚蠢的伯特兰像平常一样规劝道：“但是我们没有卖出一个股份，你口袋里没有一便士，还有——”“伯特兰，你这个蠢驴。照我吩咐的做。”

这类讽刺也适用于英国吗？我们有联合欧洲不燃物炭粉协会吗？我们有身无分文的理事发行高架铁道的计划书，利用市场诈骗股东股份的吗？关于这方面的信息，读者还需求助于报纸来了解。经常到城市、熟悉商业的人就能说出是否所有出现在规划公司通告首页名单上的人物都会像罗特希尔德一样富有或像人们所期望的那样忠实。

当玛盖尔已经充分剥削了股票交易所之后，不管是作为一个欺诈公众

yours, &c., the Director, Robert Macaire."—"Print 300,000 of these," he says to Bertrand, "and poison all France with them." As usual, the stupid Bertrand remonstrates—"But we have not sold a single share; you have not a penny in your pocket, and"—"Bertrand, you are an ass; do as I bid you."

Will this satire apply anywhere in England? Have we any Consolidated European Blacking Associations amongst us? Have we penniless directors issuing El Dorado prospectuses, and jockeying their shares through the market? For information on this head, we must refer the reader to the newspapers; or if he be connected with the city, and acquainted with commercial men, he will be able to say whether ALL the persons whose names figure at the head of announcements of projected companies are as rich as Rothschild, or quite as honest as heart could desire.

When Macaire has sufficiently exploité the Bourse, whether as a gambler in the public funds or other companies, he sagely perceives that it is time to turn to some other profession, and, providing himself with a black gown, proposes blandly to Bertrand to set up a new religion. "Mon ami," says the repentant sinner, "le temps de la commandite va passer, MAIS LES BADAUDS NE PASSERONT PAS." (O rare sentence! it should be written in letters of gold!) "OCCUPONS NOUS DE CE QUI EST ÉTERNEL. Si nous fassions une réligion?" On which M. Bertrand remarks, "A religion! what the devil—a religion is not an easy thing to make." But Macaire's receipt is easy. "Get a gown, take a shop," he says, "borrow some chairs, preach about Napoleon, or the discovery of America, or Molière—and there's a religion for you."

We have quoted this sentence more for the contrast it offers with our own manners, than for its merits. After the noble paragraph, "Les badauds ne passeront pas. Occupons nous de ce qui est éternel," one would have expected better satire upon cant than the words that follow. We are not in a condition to say whether the subjects chosen are those that had been selected by Pére Enfantin, or Chatel, or Lacordaire; but the words are curious, we think, for the very reason that the satire is so poor. The fact is, there is no religion in Paris; even clever M. Philipon, who satirizes everything, and must know, therefore, some little about the subject which he ridicules, has nothing to say but, "Preach a sermon, and that makes a religion; anything will do."

基金的赌徒还是欺诈其他公司的赌徒，他都明智地认识到是该转向其他行业的时候了，他自己穿上一件黑色的长袍，并温和地建议伯特兰去创立一种新的宗教。这个忏悔的罪人说：“我的朋友，两合公司的时代就要过去了，但是马路上爱看热闹的人还没有散去。(哦，珍贵的句子！它应该用金色的信纸来写）如果我们要从事宗教行业的话，就让我们专注于不朽的人物吧”伯特兰说：“宗教究竟是什么啊？——创立一个宗教并不是件容易的事情。”但玛盖尔的回答很容易，他说：“拿件长袍，租家店铺，借一些椅子，宣扬一些关于拿破仑或发现美洲或莫里哀的言论——那就是你要寻求的宗教。”

我们引述这段话主要是为了把它和我们英国的社会风俗做比较，而不是分析它的意义。在这句话即“马路上爱看热闹的人还没有散去，让我们专注于不朽的人物吧”之后，读者会期待作者就这句伪善的话做出更妙的讽刺，而不是期待着看下面的句子。我们也不知道这些主题是否都经过了安凡丹神甫或沙泰尔或拉科代尔［Lacordaire（1802—1861），法国天主教传道士，以口才好著称。——译注］的审查，但这句话是很让人难以理解的，我们认为其原因就在于这种讽刺是无意义的。事实上在巴黎已没有宗教了。甚至聪明的菲利庞先生在讽刺了任何世事之后也一定知道，关于他嘲笑的这个宗教主题，除了这句——“宣讲一篇布道文，就能创立一个宗教，宣讲什么事情都可以”，就没什么可说的了。如果宣讲什么事情都可以，人们就会明白，那里的人们并不是很需要宗教的。答丢夫在他那个时代还有很多机会来发表伪善的言论，因为那时的宗教信念是存在的。现在的法国却没有讽刺性的宗教伪善之言了，因为它的对立面——真的宗教完全消失了，没有了实物，当然也就没有了投影。如果一个讽刺诗人要讽刺当今英国的宗教伪君子——上层教会的伪君子、下层教会的伪君子、混杂的不信国教的伪君子、不信罗马天主教的伪君子——他会找到足够充分的主题。而在法国，宗教伪君子和波旁家族都一起消失了。在法国（或者主要是首都巴黎。）那些对宗教仍然虔诚的人同样也没有受到什么影响，因为

If ANYTHING will do, it is clear that the religious commodity is not in much demand. Tartuffe had better things to say about hypocrisy in his time; but then Faith was alive; now, there is no satirizing religious cant in France, for its contrary, true religion, has disappeared altogether; and having no substance, can cast no shadow. If a satirist would lash the religious hypocrites in ENGLAND now—the High Church hypocrites, the Low Church hypocrites, the promiscuous Dissenting hypocrites, the No Popery hypocrites—he would have ample subject enough. In France, the religious hypocrites went out with the Bourbons. Those who remain pious in that country (or, rather, we should say, in the capital, for of that we speak,) are unaffectedly so, for they have no worldly benefit to hope for from their piety; the great majority have no religion at all, and do not scoff at the few, for scoffing is the minority's weapon, and is passed always to the weaker side, whatever that may be. Thus H. B. caricatures the Ministers: if by any accident that body of men should be dismissed from their situations, and be succeeded by H. B.'s friends, theTories,—what must the poor artist do? He must pine away and die, if he be not converted; he cannot always be paying compliments; for caricature has a spice of Goethe's Devil in it, and is "der Geist der stets verneint," the Spirit that is always denying.

With one or two of the French writers and painters of caricatures, the King tried the experiment of bribery; which succeeded occasionally in buying off the enemy, and bringing him from the republican to the royal camp; but when there, the deserter was never of any use. Figaro, when so treated, grew fat and desponding, and lost all his sprightly VERVE; and Nemesis became as gentle as a Quakeress. But these instances of "ratting" were not many. Some few poets were bought over; but, among men following the profession of the press, a change of politics is an infringement of the point of honour, and a man must FIGHT as well as apostatize. A very curious table might be made, signalizing the difference of the moral standard between us and the French. Why is the grossness and indelicacy, publicly permitted in England, unknown in France, where private morality is certainly at a lower ebb? Why is the point of private honour now more rigidly maintained among the French? Why is it, as it should be, a moral disgrace for a Frenchman to go into debt, and no disgrace for him to cheat his customer? Why is there more honesty and

他们并不希望从他们的虔诚中得到什么世俗利益。而大多数人没有宗教信仰，他们也不嘲笑少数的信仰者，因为嘲笑是少数派的武器，无论什么样的嘲笑，经常是被弱者这一方所利用的。因而 H. B. 会嘲笑政府部长们，如果有任何机会的话，它会把那批人从所在的职位上开除掉，让 H. B. 的朋友——保守党成员们继任。——可怜的艺术家该怎样做呢？如果他不找些对立面来攻击的话，他一定会憔悴下去、死去的，因为他不能总是在作品里歌功颂德，因为漫画里面有歌德的魔鬼这种调味料，有一种总是要否认的精神。

对于法国一两个杰出的作家和讽刺画家，国王曾试着用贿赂的方法来收买他们。在收买敌人方面，这种方法偶尔也会成功，会把敌人从共和党派收买到皇室的阵营中去。但是收买了之后，这些叛离者也就没什么用处了。当费加罗［博马舍《费加罗》三部曲中的人物形象。——译注］被收买之后，他变胖了也沮丧了，失去了原有的生机勃勃的活力，即使复仇女神也会变得像贵格会教徒［基督教的一个教派。——译注］一样温和。但是在作家和讽刺画家中这种“叛变”的例子并不是很多，很少有人被收买过去。而且，在从事出版行业的人群中，一个人在政治立场上的变化会对其荣誉观念构成威胁，他一定要对此进行抵制。就以下的一些问题，人们可以创作一套版画来表明英国人和法国人之间的道德标准有怎样的不同。为什么在英国，人们会允许下流和粗俗公开存在，而在法国这个个人道德明显处于衰落趋势的国度却没有这种情况？为什么现在法国人的心目中仍严格维护着个人荣誉的观念？为什么对于一个法国人来说，陷入债务会让他感到道德上的羞耻，而当他去欺骗自己的顾客时却没有什么羞耻感？为什么那里会有这样的忠实和那样的忠实——这样的礼貌和那样的礼貌？——我们该怎样去解释在各个民族中所存在的独特德行和恶习呢？

上述内容是玛盖尔牧师作为一个精神骗子的个人行为。当玛盖尔律师到法院时，他就成了刑事被告的辩护人和诉讼代理人（一个更加谦卑的职

less—more propriety and less? —and how are we to account for the particular vices or virtues which belong to each nation in its turn?

The above is the Reverend M. Macaire's solitary exploit as a spiritual swindler: as MAÎTRE Macaire in the courts of law, as avocat, avoué—in a humbler capacity even, as a prisoner at the bar, he distinguishes himself greatly, as may be imagined. On one occasion we find the learned gentleman humanely visiting an unfortunate détenu—no other person, in fact, than his friend M. Bertrand, who has fallen into some trouble, and is awaiting the sentence of the law. He begins—

"Mon cher Bertrand, donne moi cent écus, je te fais acquitter d'emblée."

"J'ai pas d'argent."

"Hé bien, donne moi cent francs."

"Pas le sou."

"Tu n'as pas dix francs?"

"Pas un liard."

"Alors donne moi tes bottes, je plaiderai la circonstance atténuante."

The manner in which Maître Macaire soars from the cent écus (a high point already) to the sublime of the boots, is in the best comic style. In another instance he pleads before a judge, and, mistaking his client, pleads for defendant, instead of plaintiff. "The infamy of the plaintiff's character, my LUDS, renders his testimony on such a charge as this wholly unavailing." "M. Macaire, M. Macaire," cries the attorney, in a fright, "you are for the plaintiff!" "This, my lords, is what the defendant WILL SAY. This is the line of defence which the opposite party intend to pursue; as if slanders like these could weigh with an enlightened jury, or injure the spotless reputation of my client!" In this story and expedient M. Macaire has been indebted to the English bar. If there be an occupation for the English satirist in the exposing of the cant and knavery of the pretenders to religion, what room is there for him to lash the infamies of the law? On this point the French are babes in iniquity compared to us—a counsel prostituting himself for money is a matter with us so stale, that it is hardly food for satire: which, to be popular, must find some much more complicated and interesting knavery whereon to exercise its skill.

M. Macaire is more skilful in love than in law, and appears once or twice

位）。可以想象得到，他会做得更加出色。在一个场合中，我们发现这位博学的先生正充满仁慈地探访一个不幸的犯人，这个犯人不是别人，正是陷入困境之中的伯特兰先生，伯特兰正在等待法律的判决。玛盖尔开始说话了——

“我亲爱的伯特兰，给我一百埃居［法国的古金币，古银币。——译注］，我会立即让你宣告无罪。”

“我没有钱。”

“唉！好吧，给我一百法郎。”

“一个苏也没有。”

“你连十法郎都没有吗？”

“一个里亚［法国古铜币名，相当于四分之一苏。——译注］也没有。”

“那就把你的靴子给我，我会用减轻罪行的情节给你辩护的。”

玛盖尔律师的要价从一百埃居（一个顶点）跌到靴子这个极点构成了最好的喜剧效果。在另一个案例中，他是在一个法官面前辩护，但他把自己的当事人弄错了，不是为原告辩护，而成了为被告辩护了。“法官大人，原告本人的臭名昭著使得他指控的证据完全无效。”代理人惊骇地喊道：“玛盖尔先生，玛盖尔先生，你是为原告辩护啊！”玛盖尔先生立即使用权宜之计，说道：“我的老爷，这是被告将要说的话，这是对方打算实行的辩护路线。仿佛这些诽谤会得到一个开明陪审团的重视或者会损害我当事人清白的名誉似的！”这种故事在英国法庭是很普遍的。对于暴露宗教冒牌者的伪善之言和恶棍行为的英国讽刺诗人来说，还有什么空余之地让他去痛斥法律的丑恶吗？在这点上，法国人与我们相比还是缺乏经验的——一个律师为了钱出卖自己对我们来说是很陈旧的事情，几乎不能构成讽刺的素材，为了让作品受到欢迎，一定要找一些更为复杂、更有趣的恶棍行为来进行讽刺。

玛盖尔先生在爱情上要比法庭上表现得更为机智，在温柔情感的影响下，他有一两次都是以非常亲切的模样出现在我们面前的。我们发现他出

in a very amiable light while under the influence of the tender passion. We find him at the head of one of those useful establishments unknown in our country—a Bureau de Mariage: half a dozen of such places are daily advertised in the journals: and "une veuve de trente ans ayant une fortune de deux cent mille francs," or "une demoiselle de quinze ans, jolie, d'une famille très distinguée, qui possède trente mille livres de rentes,"—continually, in this kind-hearted way, are offering themselves to the public: sometimes it is a gentleman, with a "physique agréable,—des talens de societé"—and a place under Government, who makes a sacrifice of himself in a similar manner. In our little historical gallery we find this philanthropic anti-Malthusian at the head of an establishment of this kind, introducing a very meek, simple-looking bachelor to some distinguished ladies of his connoissance. "Let me present you, sir, to Madame de St. Bertrand "(it is our old friend), "veuve de la grande armée, et Mdlle. Eloa de Wormspire. Ces dames brulent de l'envie de faire vôtre connoissance. Je les ai invitées *à* diner chez vous ce soir: vous nous menerez *à* l'opéra, et nous ferons une petite partie d'écarté. Tenez vous bien, M. Gobard! ces dames ont des projets sur vous!"

Happy Gobard! happy system, which can thus bring the pure and loving together, and acts as the best ally of Hymen! The announcement of the rank and titles of Madame de St. Bertrand—"veuve de la grande armée "—is very happy. "La grande armée" has been a father to more orphans, and a husband to more widows, than it ever made. Mistresses of cafés, old governesses, keepers of boarding-houses, genteel beggars, and ladies of lower rank still, have this favourite pedigree. They have all had malheurs (what kind it is needless to particularize), they are all connected with the grand homme, and their fathers were all colonels. This title exactly answers to the "clergyman's daughter " in England—as, "A young lady, the daughter of a clergyman, is desirous to teach," &c. "A clergyman's widow receives into her house a few select," and so forth. "Appeal to the benevolent. —By a series of unheard-of calamities, a young lady, daughter of a clergyman in the west of England, has been plunged," &c. &c. The difference is curious, as indicating the standard of respectability.

The male beggar of fashion is not so well known among us as in Paris, where street-doors are open; six or eight families live in a house; and the gentleman who

现在婚姻所前，婚姻所是一个在我们国家还不为人所知、但在法国已显示出其实用价值的机构。报纸上每天都会刊登半打这类婚姻所的广告：“一位拥有二十万法郎财产的三十岁寡妇”或“一个十五岁的漂亮小姐，出身于一个非常高贵的家庭，拥有三万法郎的年金”，她们就以这种方式把自己推销出去；有时是一个先生，具有“令人满意的外表、社交的才能和政府机构的一个职位”，他也以同样的方式推销自己。在石版画册里，我们发现这位慈善的玛盖尔先生也出现在婚姻所前，他正把一位脾气温顺、相貌普通的单身汉介绍给他所认识的杰出女士：“先生，让我把您介绍给圣·伯特兰夫人吧！（伯特兰可是我们的老朋友了）”，“还有大军［拿破仑一世指挥的大军。——译注］将领的寡妇穆黛勒·艾劳尔·德·沃姆斯贝尔。这些夫人都很渴望认识您。我已邀她们今晚到您家里吃晚餐，您再把我们带到歌剧院，最后还有一小场埃卡泰牌戏。好好把握住机会，高巴先生！这些夫人都在打您的主意呢！”

高巴会多么快乐啊！玛盖尔先生就像婚姻之神最好的助手一样利用这个巧妙的方法把欺诈和爱情联系在一起！圣·伯特兰夫人的身份和称号是“大军将领的寡妇”，这个说法很有意思。这段时间以来，许多孤儿的父亲和许多寡妇的丈夫都是“拿破仑大军将领”。咖啡馆的女主人、老保姆、寄宿处的看守人、有教养的穷人、较低阶层的女士都有这种令人羡慕的高贵血统。她们都有不幸的命运（是什么样的不幸就没必要说了），她们都和某个大人物有关系，她们的父亲都是上校。这种称号就相当于英国的“牧师的女儿”——如“一位年轻的女士——牧师的女儿求聘教师的职位”，“一位牧师的寡妇在她住宅内举办沙龙”，“一位年轻的女士——英国西部一个牧师的女儿陷入了空前的灾难，呼吁各界人士的慈善帮助”等等。这种差异真是很奇怪，它显示出我们两个国家的习俗规范是很不一样的。

上流社会的男性乞丐在我们国家并不像在巴黎那样广为人知。在巴黎，临街的大门都是开着的。一幢大房子里通常住着六个或八个家庭。通过乞讨来谋生的先生不用挨家挨户地敲门就可以拜访六个家庭，而且

earns his livelihood by this profession can make half a dozen visits without the trouble of knocking from house to house, and the pain of being observed by the whole street, while the footman is examining him from the area. Some few may be seen in England about the inns of court, where the locality is favourable (where, however, the owners of the chambers are not proverbially soft of heart, so that the harvest must be poor); but Paris is full of such adventurers,—fat, smooth-tongued, and well dressed, with gloves and gilt-headed canes, who would be insulted almost by the offer of silver, and expect your gold as their right. Among these, of course, our friend Robert plays his part; and an excellent engraving represents him, snuff-box in hand, advancing to an old gentleman, whom, by his poodle, his powdered head, and his drivelling, stupid look, one knows to be a Carlist of the old régime. "I beg pardon," says Robert; "is it really yourself to whom I have the honour of speaking?"—"It is." "Do you take snuff?"—"I thank you."—"Sir, I have had misfortunes—I want assistance. I am a Vendéan of illustrious birth. You know the family of Macairbec—we are of Brest. My grandfather served the King in his galleys; my father and I belong, also, to the marine. Unfortunate suits at law have plunged us into difficulties, and I do not hesitate to ask you for the succor of ten francs."—"Sir, I never give to those I don't know."—"Right, sir, perfectly right. Perhaps you will have the kindness to LEND me ten francs?"

The adventures of Doctor Macaire need not be described, because the different degrees in quackery which are taken by that learned physician are all well known in England, where we have the advantage of many higher degrees in the science, which our neighbours know nothing about. We have not Hahnemann, but we have his disciples; we have not Broussais, but we have the College of Health; and surely a dose of Morrison's pills is a sublimer discovery than a draught of hot water. We had St. John Long, too—where is his science? —and we are credibly informed that some important cures have been effected by the inspired dignitaries of "the church" in Newman Street which, if it continue to practise, will sadly interfere with the profits of the regular physicians, and where the miracles of the Abbé of Paris are about to be acted over again.

In speaking of M. Macaire and his adventures, we have managed so entirely to convince ourselves of the reality of the personage, that we have quite forgotten to speak of Messrs. Philipon and Daumier, who are, the one the in-

也不会招致整条街上人们的注视目光以及这个地区步兵们的监视。在英国法院旅馆的周围可以看到少数的这类乞丐，那可是个有利的地方（然而房间的老板并不是软心肠，因此他们得到的东西一定很少）。但在巴黎这类冒险家就有很多——他们都胖乎乎的，油嘴滑舌，穿着讲究，戴着手套，有镀金的手杖，如果给他们银子，就会受到辱骂，因为他们所期望的是金子。在这些人群之中，我们的朋友罗伯尔也扮演了其中的一个角色。有一幅出色的版画是这样描绘他的：他手里拿着鼻烟盒，走到一位老绅士面前，这个老绅士带着长卷毛狗，头发上扑了粉，以一种愚蠢的表情喋喋不休地说话，通过这些外貌特征，人们就知道他是一个旧的保王党成员。罗伯尔说："对不起！是您本人在和我讲话吗？""是的。""您吸鼻烟吗？""谢谢。""先生，我很不幸——我需要帮助。我是一个旺代人［法国西部保皇党人。——译注］，出身于显贵的家庭。您知道迈凯尔白克家族吗？——我们都是布勒斯特的［法国港市。——译注］。我的祖父曾在军舰上为国王效忠，我父亲和我也属于海军。一场法律上的不幸诉讼让我们陷入了困境之中，我不得不向您请求十法郎的援助。"——"先生，我从来不把钱给陌生人"。——"对，先生，完全正确。但你或许会行行好借给我十法郎吗？"

罗伯尔作为医生的冒险经历就不需要再作描述了，因为在英国，人们对医生所采用的骗术已司空见惯，英国的医学发展很快，而法国人对此还不是很了解。虽然我们没有哈尼曼［哈尼曼（1755—1843），德国医生，最早提出顺势疗法，意为激发人体固有的自愈能力战胜疾病。——译注］，但我们有他的信徒；虽然我们没有布鲁塞［Francois Broussais（1772—1838），法国医学家。——译注］，但是我们有卫生学院；莫里森一份剂量的药丸与饮热水相比确实是一个更为崇高的发现。我们也有圣徒约翰［行医布道的圣徒。——译注］——但他的医术在哪里呢？——我们被确切地告知许多重要的治愈方法都是受到上帝启示而有的，如果这种启示继续进行下去的话，它必定会妨碍普通医生的利

ventor, the other the designer, of the Macaire Picture Gallery. As works of esprit, these drawings are not more remarkable than they are as works of art, and we never recollect to have seen a series of sketches possessing more extraordinary cleverness and variety. The countenance and figure of Macaire and the dear stupid Bertrand are preserved, of course, with great fidelity throughout; but the admirable way in which each fresh character is conceived, the grotesque appropriateness of Robert's every successive attitude and gesticulation, and the variety of Bertrand's postures of invariable repose, the exquisite fitness of all the other characters, who act their little part and disappear from the scene, cannot be described on paper, or too highly lauded. The figures are very carelessly drawn; but, if the reader can understand us, all the attitudes and limbs are perfectly CONCEIVED, and wonderfully natural and various. After pondering over these drawings for some hours, as we have been while compiling this notice of them, we have grown to believe that the personages are real, and the scenes remain imprinted on the brain as if we had absolutely been present at their acting. Perhaps the clever way in which the plates are coloured, and the excellent effect which is put into each, may add to this illusion. Now, in looking, for instance, at H. B.'s slim vapoury figures, they have struck us as excellent LIKENESSES of men and women, but no more: the bodies want spirit, action, and individuality. George Cruikshank, as a humourist, has quite as much genius, but he does not know the art of "effect" so well as Monsieur Daumier; and, if we might venture to give a word of advice to another humourous designer, whose works are extensively circulated—the illustrator of "*Pickwick*" and "*Nicholas Nickleby*,"—it would be to study well these caricatures of Monsieur Daumier; who, though he executes very carelessly, knows very well what he would express, indicates perfectly the attitude and identity of his figure, and is quite aware, beforehand, of the effect which he intends to produce. The one we should fancy to be a practised artist, taking his ease; the other, a young one, somewhat bewildered: a very clever one, however, who, if he would think more, and exaggerate less, would add not a little to his reputation.

Having pursued, all through these remarks, the comparison between English art and French art, English and French humour, manners, and morals, perhaps we should endeavour, also, to write an analytical essay on Eng-

益，到那时巴黎的神甫也不得不出来予以调停了。

谈到罗伯尔先生和他的冒险经历，我们都倾向于相信这个人物是真实存在的，以至于完全忘记了作者菲利庞和杜米埃先生：菲利庞是罗伯尔故事的编写者，杜米埃是罗伯尔画册的绘画者。虽然这部作品不是纯艺术作品，但我们从来也没预料得到能在这一系列的素描画中看到这么多出色机智的表现和变化。罗伯尔与傻瓜伯特兰的面部表情和外形自始至终都保持着一种极为逼真的效果。作者在构思每个鲜明的人物形象时都采用了巧妙的手法，罗伯尔每个连续的表情和姿势都恰如其分、荒唐可笑；伯特兰一律平静的姿态也有所变化；还有其他一些扮演小角色的人物形象都得到了微妙的处理，而这些是语言所描述不出来的，因此也无法对它们进行高度的赞美。人物外形画得都很随意，如果读者能正确理解的话，就是说所有的姿势和四肢都得到完美的设计，非常自然又变化多端。在对这些绘画作品沉思了几个小时，汇编了相关的短评之后，我们不得不相信这些人物是真实的，因为画中的一幕幕场景都印在了我们的脑海里，仿佛我们亲眼目睹过他们的行为一样。或许还有在图版上色方面所采用的巧妙手法使得每张图版都具备了逼真的效果，它们都加深了我们的幻觉。举个例子，看看 H. B. 里面细长模糊的人物外形，它们只是因为酷似男人和女人而给我们留下印象，除此之外就没有别的了。人物需要精神、行动和个性。乔治·克鲁仙柯［克鲁仙柯（1792—1878）是英国艺术家和佻戏漫画家。——译注］作为一个幽默家是有很多天赋的，但他不像杜米埃先生那样能够很好地了解艺术的“真实”。这位幽默插图画家的作品也非常流行——他是《匹克威克》和《尼古拉斯·尼古贝》的插图画家，如果我们敢于给他提句建议的话，那就是去好好学习学习杜米埃先生的讽刺漫画。杜米埃先生虽然画得很随意，但他清楚地知道自己要表达的是什么，要显示出他笔下人物形象的精神态度和社会身份，这样才能创造出逼真的艺术效果。我们认为杜米埃是一位熟练自如的艺术家，而乔治·克鲁仙柯还是一位未成熟的艺术家。如

lish cant or humbug, as distinguished from French. It might be shown that the latter was more picturesque and startling, the former more substantial and positive. It has none of the poetic flights of the French genius, but advances steadily, and gains more ground in the end than its sprightlier compeer. But such a discussion would carry us through the whole range of French and English history, and the reader has probably read quite enough of the subject in this and the foregoing pages.

We shall, therefore, say no more of French and English caricatures generally, or of Mr. Macaire's particular accomplishments and adventures. They are far better understood by examining the original pictures, by which Philipon and Daumier have illustrated them, than by translations first into print and afterwards into English. They form a very curious and instructive commentary upon the present state of society in Paris, and a hundred years hence, when the whole of this struggling, noisy, busy, merry race shall have exchanged their pleasures or occupations for a quiet coffin (and a tawdry lying epitaph) at Montmartre, or Père la Chaise; when the follies here recorded shall have been superseded by new ones, and the fools now so active shall have given up the inheritance of the world to their children: the latter will, at least, have the advantage of knowing, intimately and exactly, the manners of life and being of their grandsires, and calling up, when they so choose it, our ghosts from the grave, to live, love, quarrel, swindle, suffer, and struggle on blindly as of yore. And when the amused speculator shall have laughed sufficiently at the immensity of our follies, and the paltriness of our aims, smiled at our exploded superstitions, wondered how this man should be considered great, who is now clean forgotten (as copious Guthrie before mentioned); how this should have been thought a patriot who is but a knave spouting commonplace; or how that should have been dubbed a philosopher who is but a dull fool, blinking solemn, and pretending to see in the dark; when he shall have examined all these at his leisure, smiling in a pleasant contempt and good-humoured superiority, and thanking Heaven for his increased lights, he will shut the book, and be a fool as his fathers were before him. It runs in the blood. Well hast thou said, O ragged Macaire,—"Le jour va passer, MAIS LES BADAUDS NE PASSERONT PAS."

果他能多想想，少点夸张，将来还是会取得很大名声的。

通过这些评论，我们已经把英国和法国的艺术、幽默、风俗和道德做了一番比较，或许我们也应该就英国的伪善之言或欺骗尝试着写一篇分析性的随笔，与法国人相区别。这篇随笔或许能显示出法国人的作品更为生动和令人惊讶，而英国人的作品则更加内容充实和明确。虽然英国人没有法国天才人物的奔放想象力，但却能够平稳地前进，最终取得更大的发展。但是这样的一场讨论将会涉猎法国和英国的整个历史范畴，而读者或许已在这里和前文中对这个主题了解得够多了。

因此我们就不再泛泛地讨论法国、英国漫画或玛盖尔先生出色的成就和冒险了。只有仔细观看菲利庞和杜米埃插图的原作，而不是首印的译本和后来译成英文的版本，读者才能更好地理解它们。它们对于当今的法国社会状况作了奇妙的启发性注解，一百年以后，当整个喧嚣、忙碌、快乐的民族都躺在蒙马特或拉雪兹公墓的棺材（拥有一个俗气的假的墓志铭）中的时刻，当时事讽刺剧被新的事物所取代的时候，现在如此活跃的愚人将会给他们的后代留下一份文化遗产，而后代也可以从这些文艺作品中去了解他们祖先的生活和风俗，他们还会把我们的鬼魂从墓穴里召唤出来，去生活、爱、争吵、欺骗、遭受苦难和盲目的奋斗。当后代的读者在充分嘲笑了我们大量的愚蠢行为、我们为之奋斗的可鄙目标和我们被戳穿的迷信之后，他们将会感到疑惑，这个应该被认为是伟大人物的人现在却被忘记了（如前面提到的满腹经纶的葛斯瑞）；这个曾被认为是爱国者的人物只不过是个喋喋不休地讲谎话的无赖；或者是曾被授予哲学家称号的人物只不过是个迟钝的愚人，他还一本正经地假装能在黑暗中看见事物。当他在空闲时细细地看了全部作品，带着愉快的轻蔑和优越感笑了起来，为他增长的智能感谢上帝的时候，他会合上书本，像他以前的祖先一样做一个愚人。人的本性遗传了下来。哦，衣衫褴褛的玛盖尔不是说过吗？——“这天就要过去了，但是马路上爱看热闹的人还没散去。”

NOTES:

[1] These countries are, to be sure, inundated with the productions of our market, in the shape of Byron Beauties, reprints from the "*Keepsakes*," "*Books of Beauty*," and such trash; but these are only of late years, and their original schools of art are still flourishing.

[2] Almost all the principal public men had been most ludicrously caricatured in *the Charivari*: those mentioned above were usually depicted with the distinctive attributes mentioned by us.

[3] It is not necessary to enter into descriptions of these various inventions.

[4] We have given a description of a genteel Macaire in the account of M. de Bernard's novels.

注释：

［1］这些国家的艺术市场也充斥着我们国家的艺术产品，以《纪念品》、《美术册》这类垃圾刊物那里再版的“拜伦作品中的美人”（19世纪早期以拜伦作品中的美人为题材的绘画非常流行。——译注）的形式出现。但这只是最近几年的事情，他们本国的艺术流派仍很兴盛。

［2］几乎所有主要的公众人物都在《逗闹》中受到可笑的讽刺，就我们上面所提到的人物来说，他们的显著特点都得到了逼真的描绘。

［3］没必要再去详细描述这些各种各样的发明了。

［4］我们在叙述德·贝尔纳的小说中已经描述过装做绅士派头的玛盖尔了。

Little Poinsinet

ABOUT the year 1760, there lived, at Paris, a little fellow, who was the darling of all the wags of his acquaintance. Nature seemed, in the formation of this little man, to have amused herself, by giving loose to half a hundred of her most comical caprices. He had some wit and drollery of his own, which sometimes rendered his sallies very amusing; but, where his friends laughed with him once, they laughed at him a thousand times, for he had a fund of absurdity in himself that was more pleasant than all the wit in the world. He was as proud as a peacock, as wicked as an ape, and as silly as a goose. He did not possess one single grain of common sense; but, in revenge, his pretensions were enormous, his ignorance vast, and his credulity more extensive still. From his youth upwards, he had read nothing but the new novels, and the verses in the almanacs, which helped him not a little in making, what he called, poetry of his own; for, of course, our little hero was a poet. All the common usages of life, all the ways of the world, and all the customs of society, seemed to be quite unknown to him; add to these good qualities, a magnificent conceit, a cowardice inconceivable, and a face so irresistibly comic, that every one who first beheld it was compelled to burst out a-laughing, and you will have some notion of this strange little gentleman. He was very proud of his voice, and uttered all his sentences in the richest tragic tone. He was little better than a dwarf; but he elevated his eyebrows, held up his neck, walked on the tips of his toes, and gave himself the airs of a giant. He had a little pair of bandy legs, which seemed much too short to support anything like a human body; but, by the help of these crooked supporters, he thought he could dance like a Grace; and, indeed, fancied all the graces possible were to be found in his person. His goggle eyes were always rolling about wildly, as if in correspondence with the disorder of his little brain and his countenance

矮个儿的普万斯奈

大约是1760年左右，在巴黎住着一个矮个儿的小伙子，他的名字叫普万斯奈。他是一个非常受人欢迎的滑稽小丑。自然之神似乎也慷慨地赋予了他许多滑稽的特性。他有一些自己独特的小聪明和滑稽，这些有时会使得他的俏皮话显得非常有趣。但是普万斯奈的朋友们经常为此嘲笑他，因为普万斯奈的荒唐行为比世界上所有的滑稽小丑都要令人捧腹大笑。他像孔雀一样骄傲，像人猿一样邪恶，像鹅一样愚蠢。他一点儿生活常识也不具备，却很自负，非常无知和容易轻信。从青年时代起，他除了新小说和年历中的韵文之外就什么也没有读过，据他说，他读的这些东西对于自己做诗是很有用的，毋庸置疑，我们的这个小主人公当然也是个诗人了。对于所有日常生活中的惯例、人们的生活习惯和社会习俗，他都一无所知。除了这些令人好笑的特点之外，他还严重自负、非常胆小，加上那张滑稽的面孔，让每个第一眼看到它的人都会忍俊不禁地笑起来，并希望对这个矮个儿的小先生有所了解。普万斯奈对自己的声音感到非常自豪，他经常用低沉而悲惨的语调讲话。并不比一个侏儒高多少的他时常扬起自己的眉毛，挺直自己的脖子，踮着脚尖走路，让他自己看起来仿佛是个巨人一样。他还长着一对罗圈腿，腿看起来那么短以至于都无法想象它们是怎样支撑一个人的身体的，但是，靠着两条罗圈腿的支撑，普万斯奈认为自己也可以像一个优雅的绅士那样跳舞。他还自负地认为他本人具有非常优雅的风度。他的眼睛总是急切地四处转动，仿佛要和他不断摇晃的小脑袋和带着

thus wore an expression of perpetual wonder. With such happy natural gifts, he not only fell into all traps that were laid for him, but seemed almost to go out of his way to seek them; although, to be sure, his friends did not give him much trouble in that search, for they prepared hoaxes for him incessantly.

One day the wags introduced him to a company of ladies, who, though not countesses and princesses exactly, took, nevertheless, those titles upon themselves for the nonce; and were all, for the same reason, violently smitten with Master Poinsinet's person. One of them, the lady of the house, was especially tender; and, seating him by her side at supper, so plied him with smiles, ogles, and champagne, that our little hero grew crazed with ecstasy, and wild with love. In the midst of his happiness, a cruel knock was heard below, accompanied by quick loud talking, swearing, and shuffling of feet: you would have thought a regiment was at the door. "Oh Heavens!" cried the marchioness, starting up, and giving to the hand of Poinsinet one parting squeeze; "fly—fly, my Poinsinet: 'tis the colonel—my husband!" At this, each gentleman of the party rose, and, drawing his rapier, vowed to cut his way through the colonel and all his mousquetaires, or die, if need be, by the side of Poinsinet.

The little fellow was obliged to lug out his sword too, and went shuddering down stairs, heartily repenting of his passion for marchionesses. When the party arrived in the street, they found, sure enough, a dreadful company of mousquetaires, as they seemed, ready to oppose their passage. Swords crossed,—torches blazed; and, with the most dreadful shouts and imprecations, the contending parties rushed upon one another; the friends of Poinsinet surrounding and supporting that little warrior, as the French knights did King Francis at Pavia, otherwise the poor fellow certainly would have fallen down in the gutter from fright.

But the combat was suddenly interrupted; for the neighbours, who knew nothing of the trick going on, and thought the brawl was real, had been screaming with all their might for the police, who began about this time to arrive. Directly they appeared, friends and enemies of Poinsinet at once took to their heels; and, in THIS part of the transaction, at least, our hero himself showed that he was equal to the longest-legged grenadier that ever ran away.

When, at last, those little bandy legs of his had borne him safely to his

永远的惊讶表情的面部协调起来。带着如此滑稽的天赋，他不仅经常陷入别人为自己设置的圈套之中，似乎还故意自投罗网。当然，可以确定的是，他的朋友们不会让他费力去找圈套的，因为他们总是持续不断地给他设置了各种各样的骗局。

有一天，他的一群爱开玩笑的朋友把他介绍给一群女士，虽然那些女士不是真正的伯爵夫人和亲王夫人，但也并不妨碍她们目前采用这些称号。所有的人都被普万斯奈滑稽的容貌给迷住了。有一位女士，也就是他们聚会场所的女主人，表现得尤其温和。她让普万斯奈吃晚餐的时候坐在她旁边，不断地向他施以微笑，眉目传情，还给他倒香槟酒，以至于我们的小主人公变得心醉神迷，因为爱情而激动不已。就在他正快乐享受的时候，突然听到楼梯下面传来了粗鲁的敲门声，还有急促的大声讲话的声音、诅咒声和拖着脚步的声音，听起来好像是有一个军团来到了门口。“哦，上帝!”这位侯爵夫人叫道，她站起身来，紧紧握了握普万斯奈的手以示告别，“快走，快走，普万斯奈，是上校——我的丈夫!”这时，房间里的每个先生都站了起来，抽出他们的轻剑，发誓要从上校和他的火枪手队伍中冲出去，如果必要的话，为了普万斯奈牺牲性命也在所不惜。

普万斯奈也不得不拔出了自己的剑，浑身战栗着下了楼，衷心地为自己刚才对侯爵夫人所产生的爱情感到后悔不迭。当他们这伙人到了街上的时候才发现，确实是一群可怕的火枪手来了，这些火枪手看起来似乎是已准备好要截住他们的道路了。在火把的照耀下，这两伙人都刀剑相对，伴随着可怕的喊叫声和诅咒声，双方都向彼此冲了过去。普万斯奈的朋友们都围住了他对他进行支援，就像法国骑士在帕维亚为法兰西国王所做的那样，否则这个可怜的家伙一定会受惊掉进街沟里去的。

但是这场战斗很快就被中止了。因为街上的邻居不知道这是一场恶作剧，还以为是真正的打仗，他们就大声喊叫，把警察叫了过来。警察一出现，普万斯奈的朋友和敌人立即逃窜了。在逃跑过程中，我们主人公的表现和长腿掷弹兵没什么两样。

lodgings, all Poinsinet's friends crowded round him, to congratulate him on his escape and his valor.

"Egad, how he pinked that great red-haired fellow!" said one.

"No; did I?" said Poinsinet.

"Did you? Psha! don't try to play the modest, and humbug US; you know you did. I suppose you will say, next, that you were not for three minutes point to point with Cartentierce himself, the most dreadful swordsman of the army."

"Why, you see," says Poinsinet, quite delighted, "it was so dark that I did not know with whom I was engaged; although, corbleu, I DID FOR one or two of the fellows." And after a little more of such conversation, during which he was fully persuaded that he had done for a dozen of the enemy at least, Poinsinet went to bed, his little person trembling with fright and pleasure; and he fell asleep, and dreamed of rescuing ladies, and destroying monsters, like a second Amadis de Gaul.

When he awoke in the morning, he found a party of his friends in his room: one was examining his coat and waistcoat; another was casting many curious glances at his inexpressibles. "Look here!" said this gentleman, holding up the garment to the light; "one—two—three gashes! I am hanged if the cowards did not aim at Poinsinet's legs! There are four holes in the sword arm of his coat, and seven have gone right through coat and waistcoat. Good Heaven! Poinsinet, have you had a surgeon to your wounds?"

"Wounds!" said the little man, springing up, "I don't know—that is, I hope—that is—O, Lord! O , Lord! I hope I'm not wounded!" and, after a proper examination, he discovered he was not.

"Thank Heaven! thank Heaven!" said one of the wags (who, indeed, during the slumbers of Poinsinet had been occupied in making these very holes through the garments of that individual), "if you have escaped, it is by a miracle. Alas! alas! all your enemies have not been so lucky."

"How! is anybody wounded?" said Poinsinet.

"My dearest friend, prepare yourself; that unhappy man who came to revenge his menaced honour—that gallant officer—that injured husband, Colonel Count de Cartentierce—"

"Well?"

最后靠着两条罗圈腿，他安全地返回了住所，普万斯奈的朋友们都聚集到他周围，庆贺他的逃脱和英勇。

“天哪！他是怎样刺伤了那个高大的红头发的家伙啊！”一个人说。

“没有啊！是我干的吗？”普万斯奈说。

“是你干的吗？哼！不要假装谦虚了，欺骗我们。你知道是你干的。我猜你将要说的下一句是，你没用三分钟就和卡腾第耶尔本人刀剑相接了，他可是军队里最可怕的剑客。”

“怎么，你看到了，”普万斯奈很高兴地说，“天太黑了，我不知道和我交战的是谁。尽管如此，我还是打败了一两个家伙。”经过一番这样的谈论之后，普万斯奈相信自己至少打败了一打的敌人，由于惊吓和快乐这个小家伙一直都兴奋得发抖，最后他上床睡觉去了，在睡梦中他梦见自己像第二个高卢的阿马迪斯［Amadis of Gaul，中世纪西班牙骑士传奇中的人物。——译注］一样在消灭怪物，拯救贵妇人。

当他第二天早晨醒来的时候，他发现有一群朋友正在自己的房间里。一个正检查他的外套和背心，另一个则很好奇地扫视着他的裤子。“看这儿！”一位先生把他的一件外衣提到有光亮的地方说，“一个——两个——三个裂缝！那些该死的混蛋肯定是瞄准了普万斯奈的腿！外套的手臂处有四个窟窿，前身还有七个窟窿是径直穿过外套和背心的。上帝啊！普万斯奈，你找外科医生看过你的伤口了吗？”

“伤口！”这个小家伙跳了起来说，“我不知道啊——但愿——但愿，哦，上帝！哦，上帝！但愿我没有受伤！”经过一番彻底的检查之后，他发现自己没有受伤。

“感谢上帝！感谢上帝！”一个人说道（其实就是他在普万斯奈睡觉的时候忙着在衣服上弄了这些洞），“你逃脱掉了，真是个奇迹。哎呀！可你的敌人并不都是这么幸运的。”

“怎么！有人受伤吗？”普万斯奈说。

“我亲爱的朋友，你可要做好心理准备。那个为了受损的荣誉来报复的

"IS NO MORE! he died this morning, pierced through with nineteen wounds from your hand, and calling upon his country to revenge his murder."

When this awful sentence was pronounced, all the auditory gave a pathetic and simultaneous sob; and as for Poinsinet, he sank back on his bed with a howl of terror, which would have melted a Visigoth to tears, or to laughter. As soon as his terror and remorse had, in some degree, subsided, his comrades spoke to him of the necessity of making his escape; and, huddling on his clothes, and bidding them all a tender adieu, he set off, incontinently, without his breakfast, for England, America, or Russia, not knowing exactly which.

One of his companions agreed to accompany him on a part of this journey,—that is, as far as the barrier of St. Denis, which is, as everybody knows, on the high road to Dover; and there, being tolerably secure, they entered a tavern for breakfast; which meal, the last that he ever was to take, perhaps, in his native city, Poinsinet was just about to discuss, when, behold! a gentleman entered the apartment where Poinsinet and his friend were seated, and, drawing from his pocket a paper, with "AU NOM DU ROY" flourished on the top, read from it, or rather from Poinsinet's own figure, his exact signalement, laid his hand on his shoulder, and arrested him in the name of the King, and of the provost-marshal of Paris. "I arrest you, sir," said he, gravely, "with regret; you have slain, with seventeen wounds, in single combat, Colonel Count de Cartentierce, one of his Majesty's household; and, as his murderer, you fall under the immediate authority of the provost-marshal, and die without trial or benefit of clergy."

You may fancy how the poor little man's appetite fell when he heard this speech. "In the provost-marshal's hands?" said his friend: "then it is all over, indeed! When does my poor friend suffer, sir?"

"At half-past six o'clock, the day after tomorrow," said the officer, sitting down, and helping himself to wine. "But stop," said he, suddenly; "sure I can't mistake? Yes—no—yes, it is. My dear friend, my dear Durand! don't you recollect your old schoolfellow, Antoine?" And herewith the officer flung himself into the arms of Durand, Poinsinet's comrade, and they performed a most affecting scene of friendship.

"This may be of some service to you," whispered Durand to Poinsinet;

人，那个英勇的军官，那个受伤害的丈夫，德·卡腾第耶尔伯爵上校——”

“怎么了?”

“不在了！他今天早上死了，身上被你刺了十九处，死前号召他的部下给他报仇。”

当这个可怕的句子被说出来后，所有的听众都同时发出了悲哀的啜泣声，而普万斯奈在发出了一声恐怖的嚎叫后，就仰倒在床上，一个西哥特人也会被此时的他感化得苦笑不得。等他稍稍平息了一下惊骇和懊悔的情绪之后，同伴们就劝他要立即逃跑，他们把他的衣服卷作一团，向他亲切地告别。普万斯奈没有吃早餐，就即刻出发了，他也不知道自己到底是该去英国、美国还是俄国。

有一个朋友愿意陪他走一段路程，他们两个就走到圣丹尼斯关卡那个地方，人人都知道，那里正是通往多佛尔的大路，还算安全，他们进了一家酒菜馆吃早餐，这或许就是他在自己家乡吃的最后一顿早餐了，普万斯奈正打算津津有味地吃一顿，这时，看！一位先生走进了普万斯奈和他的朋友入座的房间，他从衣兜里抽出一张纸，纸上有“以国王的名义”的花体字，并且宣读它。与其说是那张纸上的确切描述，倒不如说是普万斯奈本人的外表引起了那位先生的注意，他发现自己要找的人就近在眼前，他把手压在普万斯奈的肩膀上，以国王和巴黎宪兵主任的名义逮捕他。他严肃地说：“抱歉，先生，我要拘捕你。因为你在一场争斗中杀死了德·卡腾第耶尔伯爵上校，上校身上有十七处伤口［原文如此。——译注］，他是陛下的家族成员之一，作为杀害他的凶手，宪兵主任得到命令要即刻判决你死刑，无须法庭审问或牧师的祈祷恩惠。”

你可以想象得到当这个可怜的小矮人听到这个消息的时候，他立即就没了胃口。“落到宪兵主任的手中?”他的朋友说，“那么，确实是一切都完了！先生，我这个可怜的朋友什么时候受刑啊?”

“后天六点半。”那个官员说，他坐了下来给自己倒酒喝。“但是等等，”他突然说，“我真的不会弄错吧？是的——不——是的，就是你。我亲爱的

and, after some further parley, he asked the officer when he was bound to deliver up his prisoner; and, hearing that he was not called upon to appear at the Marshalsea before six o'clock at night, Monsieur Durand prevailed upon Monsieur Antoine to wait until that hour, and in the meantime to allow his prisoner to walk about the town in his company. This request was, with a little difficulty, granted; and poor Poinsinet begged to be carried to the houses of his various friends, and bid them farewell. Some were aware of the trick that had been played upon him: others were not; but the poor little man's credulity was so great, that it was impossible to undeceive him; and he went from house to house bewailing his fate, and followed by the complainant marshal's officer.

The news of his death he received with much more meekness than could have been expected; but what he could not reconcile to himself was, the idea of dissection afterwards. "What can they want with me?" cried the poor wretch, in an unusual fit of candour. "I am very small and ugly; it would be different if I were a tall fine-looking fellow." But he was given to understand that beauty made very little difference to the surgeons, who, on the contrary, would, on certain occasions, prefer a deformed man to a handsome one; for science was much advanced by the study of such monstrosities. With this reason Poinsinet was obliged to be content; and so paid his rounds of visits, and repeated his dismal adieux.

The officer of the provost-marshal, however amusing Poinsinet's woes might have been, began, by this time, to grow very weary of them, and gave him more than one opportunity to escape. He would stop at shop-windows, loiter round corners, and look up in the sky, but all in vain: Poinsinet would not escape, do what the other would. At length, luckily, about dinner-time, the officer met one of Poinsinet's friends and his own: and the three agreed to dine at a tavern, as they had breakfasted; and there the officer, who vowed that he had been up for five weeks incessantly, fell suddenly asleep, in the profoundest fatigue; and Poinsinet was persuaded, after much hesitation on his part, to take leave of him.

And now, this danger overcome, another was to be avoided. Beyond a doubt the police were after him, and how was he to avoid them? He must be disguised, of course; and one of his friends, a tall, gaunt lawyer's clerk, agreed to provide him with habits.

朋友，我亲爱的杜昂！你不记得你的老同学安东尼吗?”这位官员说着就紧紧抱住了杜昂，普万斯奈的同伴和这位官员上演了一幕感人的友谊场景。

杜昂对普万斯奈小声说，“这或许会对你有些帮助”，他们经过一番深入的谈话之后，杜昂问这位官员决定什么时候把囚犯移交给当局，在得知他没有被命令于晚上六点之前送到宪兵主任那里之后，杜昂先生就劝说安东尼一直等到六点，同时能允许犯人在他的陪同下到城镇四处走走。这个请求虽然有点让人为难，但最终还是得到许可了。可怜的普万斯奈请求官员能带他去他的朋友家里，向他们告别。有些人知道这是玩弄他的一场恶作剧，有的还不知道。但是这个可怜的小矮人非常轻信，要想让他不受骗那几乎是不可能的。在那位官员的跟随下，他挨家挨户地向他的朋友告别，并为自己的命运悲叹。

他用人们所预料不到的非常顺从的态度接受了死亡的消息，但他不能让自己安心，一直琢磨分析的是：“他们到底想从我这里得到什么呢?”这个可怜的不幸的人忽然叫道：“我很矮，也很丑。如果我是一个高个儿、相貌英俊的人，那结果就不一样了。”但他又知道，对于外科医生来说，外貌俊美的人和丑陋的人并没什么区别，相反在某些场合，他们喜欢一个丑陋的人要甚于英俊的人。通过对畸形人物的研究，科学才取得了很大的进步。想到这个理由，普万斯奈不由得感到有些满意。他就这样一圈圈地拜访他的朋友，重复进行他忧郁的告别。

那位宪兵主任的官员起初被普万斯奈的苦恼给逗乐了，然而过了些时候他开始变得有点厌倦了，因此就给普万斯奈制造了许多机会让他逃跑。这位官员要么在商店橱窗那里停下来，要么在角落处四处闲逛，要么抬头看着天空，但这一切都是徒劳的，普万斯奈不会像别的犯人那样逃跑。最后，幸运的是，大约在吃晚餐的时间，官员遇到了普万斯奈的一个朋友，那也是他的朋友，三个人就一起到酒菜馆吃饭，饭馆还是他们吃早餐的那家。到了饭馆之后，官员发誓说他已经连续忙碌五个星期了，然后就带着极度的疲惫睡着了。普万斯奈经过一番犹豫之后，终于禁不住那个朋友的

So little Poinsinet dressed himself out in the clerk's dingy black suit, of which the knee-breeches hung down to his heels, and the waist of the coat reached to the calves of his legs; and, furthermore, he blacked his eyebrows, and wore a huge black periwig, in which his friend vowed that no one could recognize him. But the most painful incident, with regard to the periwig, was, that Poinsinet, whose solitary beauty—if beauty it might be called—was a head of copious, curling, yellow hair, was compelled to snip off every one of his golden locks, and to rub the bristles with a black dye; "for if your wig were to come off," said the lawyer, "and your fair hair to tumble over your shoulders, every man would know, or at least suspect you." So off the locks were cut, and in his black suit and periwig little Poinsinet went abroad.

His friends had their cue; and when he appeared amongst them, not one seemed to know him. He was taken into companies where his character was discussed before him, and his wonderful escape spoken of. At last he was introduced to the very officer of the provost-marshal who had taken him into custody, and who told him that he had been dismissed the provost's service, in consequence of the escape of the prisoner. Now, for the first time, poor Poinsinet thought himself tolerably safe, and blessed his kind friends who had procured for him such a complete disguise. How this affair ended I know not,—whether some new lie was coined to account for his release, or whether he was simply told that he had been hoaxed: it mattered little; for the little man was quite as ready to be hoaxed the next day.

Poinsinet was one day invited to dine with one of the servants of the Tuileries; and, before his arrival, a person in company had been decorated with a knot of lace and a gold key, such as chamberlains wear; he was introduced to Poinsinet as the Count de Truchses, chamberlain to the King of Prussia. After dinner the conversation fell upon the Count's visit to Paris; when his Excellency, with a mysterious air, vowed that he had only come for pleasure. "It is mighty well," said a third person, "and, of course, we can't cross-question your Lordship too closely;" but at the same time it was hinted to Poinsinet that a person of such consequence did not travel for NOTHING, with which opinion Poinsinet solemnly agreed; and, indeed, it was borne out by a subsequent declaration of the Count, who condescended, at last, to tell the company, in confidence, that he HAD a mission, and a most important one—to find, namely, among the literary men of France, a governor for the Prince

劝说，逃走了。

现在，这个危险是克服掉了，但是还有另外一种危险要避免碰到。毫无疑问，警察正在追踪他，他要怎样才能避免警察的注意呢？当然，他一定要伪装起来。他的一个朋友——一个高个儿、瘦削的律师所职员答应给他提供衣服。

矮个儿的普万斯奈就穿上了这个职员的一套脏兮兮的黑色服装，这套衣服的短裤垂到了他的脚踝，上衣的腰部到了他的小腿处。他还把眉毛染黑了，头上戴着一顶大大的黑色假发，这样装扮之后，他朋友发誓说，再也没有人能认出他来了。但最痛苦的事情是，普万斯奈唯一的美丽之处——或许能被称做美丽——就是他那一头浓密、卷曲的金发，为了戴假发，他不得不剪去金发，在头发茬上涂些黑色的染料。那位律师所职员说："如果你的假发脱落了，金发垂到你的肩膀上，人们就会注意你或怀疑你的。"因此剪掉了头发之后，矮个儿的普万斯奈就穿着黑色的衣服戴着假发准备出国了。

他的朋友们都得到了暗示，即当普万斯奈在他们中间出现的时候，他们都要假装不认识他。他还被带到那些议论他本人的人群中去。最后，他还被介绍给那个要拘留他的官员，那个官员说他因为囚犯逃跑已经被宪兵司令解雇了。现在，可怜的普万斯奈终于认为自己是安全的了，他感谢好心的朋友让他拥有了一个完全不同的假面目。我不知道这件事情是怎样结束的——是他的朋友又想出了别的谎言使他的罪行得到赦免，还是只简单地告诉了普万斯奈他上当被骗了，这些都无关紧要，因为这个小矮人总是免不了再次上当受骗的。

有一次，普万斯奈受邀请和一位杜伊勒里宫的仆人一起用餐。这个人在来之前，就在衣服上装饰了花边和金色的钥匙，像国王内侍的穿着一样。他是以德·图克斯伯爵，普鲁士国王侍从的身份被介绍给普万斯奈的。晚餐后，谈论的话题就转到了伯爵到巴黎旅行这件事上。当这位阁下以一种神秘的态度发誓说他只是为了消遣而来巴黎的时候，一个人说，"很好，当

Royal of Prussia. The company seemed astonished that the King had not made choice of Voltaire or D'Alembert, and mentioned a dozen other distinguished men who might be competent to this important duty; but the Count, as may be imagined, found objections to every one of them; and, at last, one of the guests said, that, if his Prussian Majesty was not particular as to age, he knew a person more fitted for the place than any other who could be found,—his honourable friend, M. Poinsinet, was the individual to whom he alluded.

"Good Heavens!" cried the Count, "is it possible that the celebrated Poinsinet would take such a place? I would give the world to see him!" And you may fancy how Poinsinet simpered and blushed when the introduction immediately took place.

The Count protested to him that the King would be charmed to know him; and added, that one of his operas (for it must be told that our little friend was a vaudeville-maker by trade) had been acted seven-and-twenty times at the theatre at Potsdam. His Excellency then detailed to him all the honours and privileges which the governor of the Prince Royal might expect; and all the guests encouraged the little man's vanity, by asking him for his protection and favour. In a short time our hero grew so inflated with pride and vanity, that he was for patronizing the chamberlain himself, who proceeded to inform him that he was furnished with all the necessary powers by his sovereign, who had specially enjoined him to confer upon the future governor of his son the royal order of the Black Eagle.

Poinsinet, delighted, was ordered to kneel down; and the Count produced a large yellow ribbon, which he hung over his shoulder, and which was, he declared, the grand cordon of the order. You must fancy Poinsinet's face, and excessive delight at this; for as for describing them, nobody can. For four-and-twenty hours the happy chevalier paraded through Paris with this flaring yellow ribbon; and he was not undeceived until his friends had another trick in store for him.

He dined one day in the company of a man who understood a little of the noble art of conjuring, and performed some clever tricks on the cards. Poinsinet's organ of wonder was enormous; he looked on with the gravity and awe of a child, and thought the man's tricks sheer miracles. It wanted no more to set his companions to work.

"Who is this wonderful man?" said he to his neighbour.

然我们也不会太仔细盘问大人您的”，同时普万斯奈也得到暗示，像这样一个举足轻重的人物不会无缘无故来旅行的，对于这个猜测，普万斯奈严肃地表示赞同。实际上伯爵后来的声明也证实了这一猜测，最后他屈尊地告诉这些人，他私底下有一个任务，一个非常重要的任务——即要在法国的文人之中给普鲁士的王子殿下寻找一个管理人。让这些人都感到吃惊的是国王没有选择伏尔泰或达兰贝尔［D'Alembert（1717—1783），法国著名的物理学家、数学家和天文学家。——译注］，他们还提出了许多其他有能力承担这个责任的杰出人物，但是这些人物也都遭到了伯爵的反对。最后，一个客人说，如果普鲁士陛下不在乎年龄的话，他知道有一个人比其他任何人都更加适合这个职位——他所暗示的这个人就是他尊敬的朋友普万斯奈先生。

“天哪！”伯爵叫道，“杰出的普万斯奈愿意接受这个职位吗？为了能见到他，我愿付出一切！”你可以想象得到，这个突如其来的推荐会让普万斯奈怎样傻笑和脸红啊！

伯爵向普万斯奈断言，普鲁士国王非常渴望能认识他，另外普万斯奈的一个歌剧（必须要说明的是，我们的小普万斯奈还是一个职业的轻歌舞剧演员）已经在德国北方都市的戏院上演了二十七场。这位阁下向他详述了作为王子殿下的管理人所能期望得到的荣誉和特权，在座的所有客人也都借此机会来恭维和巴结普万斯奈，普万斯奈的虚荣心进一步膨胀了起来。我们的主人公很快就因为骄傲和虚荣心而飘飘然了，他请求这位国王侍从能照应他，这位侍从告诉他，国王赋予了他所有必要的权力，还特别嘱咐说，国王要把黑鹰王室勋章赠给他儿子将来的管理人。

普万斯奈很高兴地跪了下去接受命令，伯爵拿出一条大的黄色绶带，把绶带挂在普万斯奈的肩上，他宣布，这是勋章里面最高等级的绶带。你一定能想象得到普万斯奈的面部表情，那可是极度的兴奋，以至于任何人都无法用语言来描述。在整整一天的时间里，这位快乐的骑士普万斯奈就一直带着这条闪耀的黄色绶带在巴黎四处游行，这场骗局一直持续到他的

"Why," said the other, mysteriously, "one hardly knows who he is; or, at least, one does not like to say to such an indiscreet fellow as you are." Poinsinet at once swore to be secret. "Well, then," said his friend, "you will hear that man—that wonderful man—called by a name which is not his: his real name is Acosta: he is a Portuguese Jew, a Rosicrucian, and Cabalist of the first order, and compelled to leave Lisbon for fear of the Inquisition. He performs here, as you see, some extraordinary things, occasionally; but the master of the house, who loves him excessively, would not, for the world, that his name should be made public."

"Ah, bah!" said Poinsinet, who affected the bel esprit; "you don't mean to say that you believe in magic, and cabalas, and such trash?"

"Do I not? You shall judge for yourself." And, accordingly, Poinsinet was presented to the magician, who pretended to take a vast liking for him, and declared that he saw in him certain marks which would infallibly lead him to great eminence in the magic art, if he chose to study it.

Dinner was served, and Poinsinet placed by the side of the miracle-worker, who became very confidential with him, and promised him—aye, before dinner was over—a remarkable instance of his power. Nobody, on this occasion, ventured to cut a single joke against poor Poinsinet; nor could he fancy that any trick was intended against him, for the demeanor of the society towards him was perfectly grave and respectful, and the conversation serious. On a sudden, however, somebody exclaimed, "Where is Poinsinet? Did any one see him leave the room?"

All the company exclaimed how singular the disappearance was; and Poinsinet himself, growing alarmed, turned round to his neighbour, and was about to explain.

"Hush!" said the magician, in a whisper; "I told you that you should see what I could do. I HAVE MADE YOU INVISIBLE; be quiet, and you shall see some more tricks that I shall play with these fellows."

Poinsinet remained then silent, and listened to his neighbours, who agreed, at last, that he was a quiet, orderly personage, and had left the table early, being unwilling to drink too much. Presently they ceased to talk about him, and resumed their conversation upon other matters.

At first it was very quiet and grave, but the master of the house brought back the talk to the subject of Poinsinet, and uttered all sorts of abuse con-

朋友们又想出新花样来捉弄他为止。

还有一次，他是和一位懂些魔法技艺的人在一起用餐，这个人用扑克牌表演了一些巧妙的戏法。普万斯奈对此感到非常惊异，他带着孩子般的认真和敬畏观看表演，认为这个人的魔法简直就是奇迹。它应该不会再让同伴们来哄骗自己了。

“这个奇妙的人是谁啊?”普万斯奈问旁边的一个朋友。

“噢,”那个朋友神秘地说，“人们都不太清楚他到底是谁。即使知道，人们也不愿意告诉像你这样轻率的人的。”普万斯奈立刻发誓说他会保密。“那么，好吧,”他的朋友说，“你会听到别人用另一个名字称呼他——即那个奇妙的人，但那不是他的真名，他的真名是阿科斯塔。他是一个葡萄牙的犹太人，一个罗齐克鲁斯派［17—18世纪一种自称有各种秘传的知识和力量的秘密宗教结社。——译注］成员，一流的魔法家，他是为了逃避宗教法庭的审判被迫离开里斯本的。你也看到了，他有时会在这里表演一些奇异的魔法，但这里的房东太溺爱他了，无论如何也不愿公开他的名字。

普万斯奈装做才子的样子说：“啊，呸！你不是要说你信仰魔术、戏法和这些垃圾吧?”

“我没有啊？你还是自己判断吧!”因此，这位朋友就把普万斯奈引见给魔法家，魔法家装做很喜欢他的样子，他还断言说看到普万斯奈身上有魔法师的天赋，如果他选择学习这门技艺的话，肯定会在魔法这个领域取得杰出的成就。

晚餐准备好了，普万斯奈被安置在魔法师的身边，魔法师和普万斯奈已经很亲密了，他向普万斯奈保证——在晚餐结束前——会让他看到奇异的魔法显示。这时，饭桌旁没有人敢开普万斯奈的玩笑了，普万斯奈也想象不到其中会有什么诡计，因为周围的人对他的行为举止都很严肃尊敬，谈论的话题也很严肃。忽然有一个人叫道：“普万斯奈到哪里去了？有人看到他离开房间了吗?”

所有的仆人和朋友都叫了起来，普万斯奈的消失是多么奇怪啊！普万

cerning him. He begged the gentleman, who had introduced such a little scamp into his house, to bring him thither no more: whereupon the other took up, warmly, Poinsinet's defence; declared that he was a man of the greatest merit, frequenting the best society, and remarkable for his talents as well as his virtues.

"Ah!" said Poinsinet to the magician, quite charmed at what he heard, "how ever shall I thank you, my dear sir, for thus showing me who my true friends are?"

The magician promised him still further favours in prospect; and told him to look out now, for he was about to throw all the company into a temporary fit of madness, which, no doubt, would be very amusing.

In consequence, all the company, who had heard every syllable of the conversation, began to perform the most extraordinary antics, much to the delight of Poinsinet. One asked a nonsensical question, and the other delivered an answer not at all to the purpose. If a man asked for a drink, they poured him out a pepper-box or a napkin: they took a pinch of snuff, and swore it was excellent wine; and vowed that the bread was the most delicious mutton ever tasted. The little man was delighted.

"Ah!" said he, "these fellows are prettily punished for their rascally backbiting of me!"

"Gentlemen," said the host, "I shall now give you some celebrated champagne," and he poured out to each a glass of water.

"Good Heavens!" said one, spitting it out, with the most horrible grimacc, "whcrc did you get this detestable claret?"

"Ah, faugh!" said a second, "I never tasted such vile corked burgundy in all my days!" and he threw the glass of water into Poinsinet's face, as did half a dozen of the other guests, drenching the poor wretch to the skin. To complete this pleasant illusion, two of the guests fell to boxing across Poinsinet, who received a number of the blows, and received them with the patience of a fakir, feeling himself more flattered by the precious privilege of beholding this scene invisible, than hurt by the blows and buffets which the mad company bestowed upon him.

The fame of this adventure spread quickly over Paris, and all the world longed to have at their houses the representation of Poinsinet the Invisible. The servants and the whole company used to be put up to the trick; and Poin-

斯奈自己也惊慌了，转向他身边的人，正要做出解释。

魔法家对他耳语说："别作声！我告诉过你，你该看我做什么。我已经把你变没了。安静，你还会看到我在这些家伙身上施展的其他魔法。"

普万斯奈就保持沉默听他旁边的人说话。他的朋友们最后都一致认为，普万斯奈是一个安分守己的人，他早早地离开饭桌是因为不想喝太多的酒。现在他们又停止谈论他了，重新开始谈论其他的话题。

开始，人们的谈话是非常安静和严肃的，但是房东又把话题扯到普万斯奈身上，对他大加辱骂。他请求这些先生不要再把这个小坏蛋介绍到他房里来，不要再带他过来了，于是其他的人就开始热心地为他辩护，称他是一个具有良好德行的人，经常光顾上流社会，他的才能和他的德行一样卓越。

普万斯奈为他所听到的话感到陶醉，他对魔术家说："啊！我该怎样谢您呢？我亲爱的先生，因为这样就能看出谁才是我真正的朋友。"

魔术家告诉他好戏还在后头，让他现在注意了，因为他要让所有的人都陷入暂时的疯狂，这无疑会很有趣的。

因此所有的人在听到谈话的只言片语后就开始做一些非常离奇的滑稽动作，这可把普万斯奈给逗乐了。一个人问了一个毫无意义的问题，而另一个人答非所问。一个人要喝点东西，别人倒给他的却是胡椒粉或餐巾。他们吸了口鼻烟就发誓说这是最好的酒，还发誓说面包是他们所尝过的最美味的羊肉。这些可把小矮人给逗乐了。

他说："啊！这些在背后说我坏话的人可遭受到惩罚了！"

房东说："先生们，我要给你们喝著名的香槟酒"。说着他就在每个杯子里都倒上了水。

"天哪！"一个人吐了出来，并做了一个很可怕的扮相说，"你是从哪儿弄到这些可恶的红葡萄酒的？"

"啊，呸！"另一个说，"我从来也没尝过这么讨厌的有塞子气味的勃艮第葡萄酒！"他把这杯水泼到了普万斯奈的脸上，其他的六个客人也照做不

sinet, who believed in his invisibility as much as he did in his existence, went about with his friend and protector the magician. People, of course, never pretended to see him, and would very often not talk of him at all for some time, but hold sober conversation about anything else in the world. When dinner was served, of course there was no cover laid for Poinsinet, who carried about a little stool, on which he sat by the side of the magician, and always ate off his plate. Everybody was astonished at the magician's appetite and at the quantity of wine he drank; as for little Poinsinet, he never once suspected any trick, and had such a confidence in his magician, that, I do believe, if the latter had told him to fling himself out of window, he would have done so, without the slightest trepidation.

Among other mystifications in which the Portuguese enchanter plunged him, was one which used to afford always a good deal of amusement. He informed Poinsinet, with great mystery, that HE WAS NOT HIMSELF; he was not, that is to say, that ugly, deformed little monster, called Poinsinet; but that his birth was most illustrious, and his real name Polycarte. He was, in fact, the son of a celebrated magician; but other magicians, enemies of his father, had changed him in his cradle, altering his features into their present hideous shape, in order that a silly old fellow, called Poinsinet, might take him to be his own son, which little monster the magician had likewise spirited away.

The poor wretch was sadly cast down at this; for he tried to fancy that his person was agreeable to the ladies, of whom he was one of the warmest little admirers possible; and to console him somewhat, the magician told him that his real shape was exquisitely beautiful, and as soon as he should appear in it, all the beauties in Paris would be at his feet. But how to regain it? "Oh, for one minute of that beauty!" cried the little man; "what would he not give to appear under that enchanting form!" The magician hereupon waved his stick over his head, pronounced some awful magical words, and twisted him round three times; at the third twist, the men in company seemed struck with astonishment and envy, the ladies clasped their hands, and some of them kissed his. Everybody declared his beauty to be supernatural.

Poinsinet, enchanted, rushed to a glass. "Fool!" said the magician, "do you suppose that YOU can see the change? My power to render you invisible, beautiful, or ten times more hideous even than you are, extends only to oth-

误，可怜的普万斯奈全身都湿透了。为了圆满地制造这个假象，两个客人还在普万斯奈的对面打了起来，普万斯奈身上无缘无故挨了很多拳头，但他用僧者的耐心接受了这一切。他为自己能有这个宝贵的特权，能看到别人看不见的场景而高兴，这些疯狂的人给予他的拳头和殴打就算不了什么了。

这个奇闻很快就传遍了巴黎，所有的人都希望在他们的家里能上演普万斯奈不见了的魔法。所有的仆人和朋友都被唆使加入这场骗局中来。普万斯奈如同相信自己的存在一样，也相信别人是看不见他的。他和朋友、保护人魔法家一起四处走动。当然，人们都假装看不到他，也不经常谈论他，而是说些别的严肃话题。当晚饭准备好的时候，当然也就没有普万斯奈的餐具了，普万斯奈总是携带着一个小凳子，坐在魔法师的旁边，魔法师盘子里的东西经常都被他给吃掉了。人人都为魔法家的胃口和酒量感到吃惊。至于矮个儿的普万斯奈，他从来也没怀疑过这是一场骗局，而是对他的魔法家充满了信任，我相信，即使后者让他从窗户上跳出去，他也不会有丝毫恐惧的。

在这个葡萄牙的巫师给他设置的其他幻象中，有一个也非常有趣。他很神秘地告诉普万斯奈说，他并不是他本人，也就是说，他不是那个叫做普万斯奈的丑陋、畸形、矮个的怪物。他的出身非常显贵，他的真名叫波利卡特。他实际上是一个著名魔法家的儿子，但是其他的魔法家是他父亲的敌人，因此那些敌人就在摇篮中把他的外形变成了现在丑陋的样子，以使那个愚蠢的叫普万斯奈的老家伙能代替他做他父亲的儿子，他们后来又把这个小怪物给偷走了。

这样说着，可怜的人儿很悲哀地沮丧起来，因为他总是设想自己的外表是讨女士喜欢的，在她们之中，他可能是最热情的小情人之一。为了稍微安慰安慰他，魔法家告诉他说，他真正的外形是很优雅很英俊的，以这样的外形一出现，巴黎所有的美人都会拜倒在他脚下。但是怎样才能恢复以前的外形呢？“哦，就一分钟也可以！”这个小矮人叫道，“只要能以那样

ers, not to you. You may look a thousand times in the glass, and you will only see those deformed limbs and disgusting features with which devilish malice has disguised you." Poor little Poinsinet looked, and came back in tears. "But," resumed the magician,—"ha, ha, ha! —I know a way in which to disappoint the machinations of these fiendish magi."

"Oh, my benefactor! —my great master! —for Heaven's sake tell it!" gasped Poinsinet.

"Look you—it is this. A prey to enchantment and demoniac art all your life long, you have lived until your present age perfectly satisfied; nay, absolutely vain of a person the most singularly hideous that ever walked the earth!"

"Is it?" whispered Poinsinet. "Indeed and indeed I didn't think it so bad!"

"He acknowledges it! he acknowledges it!" roared the magician. "Wretch, dotard, owl, mole, miserable buzzard! I have no reason to tell thee now that thy form is monstrous, that children cry, that cowards turn pale, that teeming matrons shudder to behold it. It is not thy fault that thou art thus ungainly: but wherefore so blind? wherefore so conceited of thyself? I tell thee, Poinsinet, that over every fresh instance of thy vanity the hostile enchanters rejoice and triumph. As long as thou art blindly satisfied with thyself; as long as thou pretendest, in thy present odious shape, to win the love of aught above a negress; nay, further still, until thou hast learned to regard that face, as others do, with the most intolerable horror and disgust, to abuse it when thou seest it, to despise it, in short, and treat that miserable disguise in which the enchanters have wrapped thee with the strongest, hatred and scorn, so long art thou destined to wear it."

Such speeches as these, continually repeated, caused Poinsinet to be fully convinced of his ugliness; he used to go about in companies, and take every opportunity of inveighing against himself; he made verses and epigrams against himself; he talked about "that dwarf, Poinsinet;" "that buffoon, Poinsinet;" "that conceited, hump-backed Poinsinet;" and he would spend hours before the glass, abusing his own face as he saw it reflected there, and vowing that he grew handsomer at every fresh epithet that he uttered.

Of course the wags, from time to time, used to give him every possible encouragement, and declared that since this exercise, his person was amazing-

迷人的外表出现，我什么都不在乎!”于是魔术家把他的手杖举到头顶上摇晃起来，嘴里发出一些威严的神秘咒语，拉着普万斯奈绕了三圈，在第三圈的时候，所有的先生都带着惊异和嫉妒的表情看着他，女士们则紧握十指异常激动，有的人还亲吻了他的手。每个人都声称他的美丽让人不可思议。

普万斯奈陶醉了，立即冲到一个镜子前面。魔法家说:“傻瓜!你以为你能看到变化吗?我让你隐形、变得英俊或变得十分丑陋，都是给别人看的，不是给你看的。你在镜子前看一千次，所看到的也只是那些畸形的四肢和令人作呕的外形，这都是可恶的怨恨带给你的乔装打扮。”可怜的普万斯奈看着魔术家，含着眼泪从镜子前退了回来。“但是,”魔术家又说道,“哈哈!——我知道有一个方法可以让这些残忍的魔术家的阴谋无法得逞。”

“哦，我的恩人!——我伟大的主人!——看在上帝的分上，告诉我吧!”普万斯奈急切地说。

“看看你这个样子!你甘愿自己的一生都要被魔法和恶魔所折磨，直到现在你都活得很自足，你甚至还为这个世界上最丑陋的外表而自负。

“是吗?”普万斯奈嘀咕说，“实际上，实际上，我没有想到它会这样糟糕!”

“他承认了!他承认了!”魔术家吼叫道，“可怜的人儿、老耄、猫头鹰、鼹鼠、贪婪的人!我现在要告诉你，你的外表是可怕的，以至于会把孩子吓哭，让胆小的人面色苍白，使成群的主妇战栗。你这么难看不是你的过错，但是为何如此视而不见?为何对自己如此自负?我告诉你，普万斯奈，你的虚荣心每次占了上风的时候，怀有敌意的巫师就会高兴得意。只要你盲目对自己感到满意，你目前可憎的外形就不会消失。直到你学会了像别人一样，带着无法忍受的惊骇和厌恶看这张脸，并去辱骂它轻视它，简而言之，就是用最强烈的憎恨和轻蔑来对待这些巫师给你伪装的糟糕外形，他们的阴谋就不会得逞。”

这些不断重复的言语使得普万斯奈完全确信自己是丑陋的了。他经常

ly improved. The ladies, too, began to be so excessively fond of him, that the little fellow was obliged to caution them at last—for the good, as he said, of society; he recommended them to draw lots, for he could not gratify them all; but promised when his metamorphosis was complete, that the one chosen should become the happy Mrs. Poinsinet; or, to speak more correctly, Mrs. Polycarte.

I am sorry to say, however, that, on the score of gallantry, Poinsinet was never quite convinced of the hideousness of his appearance. He had a number of adventures, accordingly, with the ladies, but strange to say, the husbands or fathers were always interrupting him. On one occasion he was made to pass the night in a slipper-bath full of water; where, although he had all his clothes on, he declared that he nearly caught his death of cold. Another night, in revenge, the poor fellow—""dans le simple appareil D'une beauté, qu'on vient d'arracher au sommeil." spent a number of hours contemplating the beauty of the moon on the tiles. These adventures are pretty numerous in the memoirs of M. Poinsinet; but the fact is, that people in France were a great deal more philosophical in those days than the English are now, so that Poinsinet's loves must be passed over, as not being to our taste. His magician was a great diver, and told Poinsinet the most wonderful tales of his two minutes' absence under water. These two minutes, he said, lasted through a year, at least, which he spent in the company of a naiad, more beautiful than Venus, in a palace more splendid than even Versailles. Fired by the description, Poinsinet used to dip, and dip, but he never was known to make any mermaid acquaintances, although he fully believed that one day he should find such.

The invisible joke was brought to an end by Poinsinet's too great reliance on it; for being, as we have said, of a very tender and sanguine disposition, he one day fell in love with a lady in whose company he dined, and whom he actually proposed to embrace; but the fair lady, in the hurry of the moment, forgot to act up to the joke; and instead of receiving Poinsinet's salute with calmness, grew indignant, called him an impudent little scoundrel, and lent him a sound box on the ear. With this slap the invisibility of Poinsinet disappeared, the gnomes and genii left him, and he settled down into common life again, and was hoaxed only by vulgar means.

A vast number of pages might be filled with narratives of the tricks that

和魔术家一起走动，并利用每个机会来痛骂自己。他创作了讽刺短诗来嘲讽自己；他嘴里经常说着“那个矮子，普万斯奈”、“那个小丑角，普万斯奈”、“那个自负、驼背的普万斯奈”；他还会对着镜子辱骂里面的影子，发誓说在每次咒骂之后，他就变得更英俊了。

当然那些爱开玩笑的人也不时地给他打气，声称自从他开始这种练习之后，他的外表令人惊奇地得到了改善。女士们也开始越来越喜欢他了，以至于这个矮个儿的家伙不得不在最后告诫她们说，为了大家的利益，他建议她们去抽签，因为他不能满足所有的人。但是他向大家允诺，当他的魔术变形结束的时候，他会选择那个抽中签的人做快乐的普万斯奈太太，更准确地说，应该是波利卡特太太。

然而遗憾的是，在对女子献殷勤这点上，普万斯奈从来也认识不到自己外表的丑陋。因此，他和女士们有过许多奇遇，但是说也奇怪，这些女士的丈夫或父亲经常对他的艳遇构成了阻碍。有一次他跑到一个澡堂里度过了一夜，在那里尽管他把所有的衣服都穿上了，他还宣称自己几乎要被冻死了。在另一个晚上，这个可怜的家伙为了看“一个刚从睡眠中挣脱出来的裸体美人”花了几个小时在屋顶的砖瓦上注视美丽的月光。在普万斯奈先生的传记中像这样的奇遇还有很多。事实上那时的法国人比现在的英国人要开放得多，因此这里必须要省略掉普万斯奈的爱情了，因为它不合我们英国人的口味。他跟随的魔法家还是一个出色的潜水员，他告诉了普万斯奈他在水下两分钟的奇遇。他说，这两分钟至少持续了一年的时间，他是在一位仙女的陪伴下度过了这段时间，那位仙女比维纳斯还要漂亮，她住在一个比凡尔赛宫还要壮观的宫殿里。魔术家的这番描述激起了普万斯奈的兴趣，他经常去潜水、潜水，但人们从来也没听说他结识过任何美人鱼，尽管他坚信自己终有一天会找到她们。

由于普万斯奈太信任魔法家的谎话，这个隐形的笑话终于宣告结束了。我们曾说过，他具有温柔而自信的性情，有一天他在和一群人吃饭的时候，爱上了其中的一位女士，他竟然打算去拥抱她，但是那位漂亮的女士在匆

were played upon him; but they resemble each other a good deal, as may be imagined, and the chief point remarkable about them is the wondrous faith of Poinsinet. After being introduced to the Prussian ambassador at the Tuileries, he was presented to the Turkish envoy at the Place Vendôme, who received him in state, surrounded by the officers of his establishment, all dressed in the smartest dresses that the wardrobe of the Opéra Comique could furnish.

As the greatest honour that could be done to him, Poinsinet was invited to eat, and a tray was produced, on which was a delicate dish prepared in the Turkish manner. This consisted of a reasonable quantity of mustard, salt, cinnamon and ginger, nutmegs and cloves, with a couple of tablespoonfuls of cayenne pepper, to give the whole a flavor; and Poinsinet's countenance may be imagined when he introduced into his mouth a quantity of this exquisite compound.

"The best of the joke was," says the author who records so many of the pitiless tricks practised upon poor Poinsinet, "that the little man used to laugh at them afterwards himself with perfect good humour; and lived in the daily hope that, from being the sufferer, he should become the agent in these hoaxes, and do to others as he had been done by." Passing, therefore, one day, on the Pont Neuf, with a friend, who had been one of the greatest performers, the latter said to him, "Poinsinet, my good fellow, thou hast suffered enough, and thy sufferings have made thee so wise and cunning, that thou art worthy of entering among the initiated, and hoaxing in thy turn." Poinsinet was charmed; he asked when he should be initiated, and how? It was told him that a moment would suffice, and that the ceremony might be performed on the spot. At this news, and according to order, Poinsinet flung himself straightway on his knees in the kennel; and the other, drawing his sword, solemnly initiated him into the sacred order of jokers. From that day the little man believed himself received into the society; and to this having brought him, let us bid him a respectful adieu.

忙之中，忘记了在这场玩笑中她应扮演的角色，没有平静地接受普万斯奈的爱意，而是变得愤怒起来，称他是一个鲁莽的小恶棍，还给了他一个响亮的耳光。伴随着这一巴掌，普万斯奈的隐形笑剧就结束了，妖魔鬼怪离开了他，他又回到日常生活中来，现在只有世俗的手段才能哄骗他。

人们在普万斯奈身上所要弄的诡计还有很多，要把它们记下来可是需要很多纸张的。但是这些诡计大部分都是相似的，可以想象得到，这些诡计能够得逞的关键之处就在于普万斯奈惊人的轻信。在杜伊勒里宫被介绍给普鲁士的大使后，他又在旺多姆广场被介绍给土耳其的外交使节，那个外交使节正式地接见了他，周围还有行政官员的陪同，他们都穿着最漂亮时髦的服装，那些服装只有喜剧院才能提供的。

让普万斯奈感到荣幸的是，他还被邀请吃东西。侍者端出了一个盘子，上面有一道精美的菜，是按照土耳其的方式调制的。这道菜是由一定数量的芥末、盐、肉桂和姜、肉豆蔻、丁香所组成，还有两大汤匙的辣椒粉作调味料。当普万斯奈把这些特殊的混合物放进嘴里的时候，你可以想象得到他的表情会是怎样。

记录下这么多要弄普万斯奈的诡计的作者说："最好笑的是那个矮个儿的家伙经常在事后很幽默地嘲笑自己，每天都希望自己能从骗局中的受害者变成施骗者，以其人之道还治其人之身。"因此，有一天他和一个朋友从奈夫桥上经过，这个朋友一直是最好的表演者之一，他告诉普万斯奈说："普万斯奈，我的好朋友，你遭受的陷害够多了，这些遭遇已让你变得很聪明和狡猾了，因此你有资格加入到我们的团体中来，轮到你欺骗别人了。"普万斯奈陶醉了，他问什么时候才能加入，怎样加入？那个人告诉他片刻就足够了，可以当场举行仪式。听到这个消息后，普万斯奈立刻就依照命令猛地跪在下水道里，那个人抽出刀来，庄严地宣告要招收他加入神圣的诙谐者团体。从那天起，这个小矮人就相信他自己被团体接受了。写到这里，也让我们向他致意告别吧。

The Devil 's Wager

IT was the hour of the night when there be none stirring save churchyard ghosts—when all doors are closed except the gates of graves, and all eyes shut but the eyes of wicked men.

When there is no sound on the earth except the ticking of the grasshopper, or the croaking of obscene frogs in the poole.

And no light except that of the blinking starres, and the wicked and devilish wills-o'-the-wisp, as they gambol among the marshes, and lead good men astraye.

When there is nothing moving in heaven except the owle, as he flappeth along lazily; or the magician, as he rides on his infernal broomsticke, whistling through the aire like the arrowes of a Yorkshire archere.

It was at this hour (namely, at twelve o'clock of the night,) that two beings went winging through the black clouds, and holding converse with each other. Now the first was Mercurius, the messenger, not of gods (as the heathens feigned), but of daemons; and the second, with whom he held company, was the soul of Sir Roger de Rollo, the brave knight. Sir Roger was Count of Chauchigny, in Champagne; Seigneur of Santerre, Villacerf and aultre lieux. But the great die as well as the humble; and nothing remained of brave Rodger now, but his coffin and his deathless soul.

And Mercurius, in order to keep fast the soul, his companion, had bound him round the neck with his tail; which, when the soul was stubborn, he would draw so tight as to strangle him well-nigh, sticking into him the barbed point thereof; whereat the poor soul, Sir Rollo, would groan and roar lustily.

Now they two had come together from the gates of purgatorie, being

魔鬼的赌赛

在晚上的这个时刻，除了墓地的鬼魂之外所有的人都休息了；除了墓穴的门之外，所有的门都关上了；除了恶人的眼睛之外，所有的眼睛都闭上了。

除了昆虫的啾啾声或池塘里可憎的青蛙的呱呱声之外，在这个地球上就没有别的声音了。

除了星星闪烁的微光和邪恶的鬼火之外，就没有别的光亮了，当鬼火在沼泽之中跳跃时，会把好人也引入歧途。

天空中除了猫头鹰懒洋洋地拍翅飞行，巫师骑着地狱的扫帚柄像约克郡弓箭手的箭一样划过天空之外就没有别的东西在移动了。

在这个时候（即晚上十二点钟），有两个生灵互相交谈着穿过黑色的云层。一个是地狱里的恶魔使者——而不是神的（正如由异教徒佯装的神），另一个是勇敢的骑士罗杰·德·罗尔洛先生的灵魂。罗杰先生是法国香槟区的一位伯爵，桑泰尔和维拉塞尔夫领地的封建主。现在的罗杰除了他的棺材和不死的灵魂之外，什么也没留下来。

恶魔使者为了牢牢地看守住他的同伴罗杰这个灵魂，就用自己的尾巴把他系在脖子上。当这个灵魂执拗不听话的时候，他会紧紧地拉扯他以至于几乎要把他勒死，还用他的尖角刺他，可怜的罗尔洛先生的灵魂则起劲地呻吟和吼叫。

现在他们两个已经从炼狱的大门一起出来了，注定要到那个可怜的灵

bound to those regions of fire and flame where poor sinners fry and roast in saecula saeculorum.

"It is hard," said the poor Sir Rollo, as they went gliding through the clouds, "that I should thus be condemned for ever, and all for want of a single ave."

"How, Sir Soul?" said the daemon, "you were on earth so wicked, that not one, or a million of aves, could suffice to keep from hell-flame a creature like thee; but cheer up and be merry; thou wilt be but a subject of our lord the Devil, as am I; and, perhaps, thou wilt be advanced to posts of honour, as am I also:" and to show his authoritie, he lashed with his tail the ribbes of the wretched Rollo.

"Nevertheless, sinner as I am, one more ave would have saved me; for my sister, who was Abbess of St. Mary of Chauchigny, did so prevail, by her prayer and good works, for my lost and wretched soul, that every day I felt the pains of purgatory decrease; the pitchforks which, on my first entry, had never ceased to vex and torment my poor carcass, were now not applied above once a week; the roasting had ceased, the boiling had discontinued; only a certain warmth was kept up, to remind me of my situation."

"A gentle stewe," said the daemon.

"Yea, truly, I was but in a stew, and all from the effects of the prayers of my blessed sister. But yesterday, he who watched me in purgatory told me, that yet another prayer from my sister, and my bonds should be unloosed, and I, who am now a devil, should have been a blessed angel."

"And the other ave?" said the daemon.

"She died, sir—my sister died—death choked her in the middle of the prayer." And hereat the wretched spirit began to weepe and whine piteously; his salt tears falling over his beard, and scalding the tail of Mercurius the devil.

"It is, in truth, a hard case," said the daemon; "but I know of no remedy save patience, and for that you will have an excellent opportunity in your lodgings below."

"But I have relations," said the Earl; "my kinsman Randal, who has in-

魂要经受永生煎熬的地狱中去。

当他们滑行着穿过云层的时候，可怜的罗尔洛先生说："地狱是让人难以忍受的，我将会永远受刑，现在我最想要的就是一个祈福。"

"什么，先生？"恶魔说，"你在世上如此邪恶，以至于一百万个祈福也不能让你这样的人物避免地狱烈火的惩罚。高兴快乐起来吧！你将会像我一样成为魔鬼王国的臣民。或许，你也会像我一样被提升到一个可敬的职位上的。"为了显示他的权威，恶魔用自己的尾巴鞭打着可怜的罗尔洛。

"尽管我是个罪人，但是再有一个祈福就能挽救我了。因为我的姐姐是圣玛丽修道院的院长，她对我的祈福就非常奏效，由于她为我迷失而可怜的灵魂所做的祈祷和善行，每天我都能感觉到自己在炼狱中所受的苦难在一点点减少。在我刚进去的时候，魔鬼的叉子从来也没停止过折磨我可怜的尸体，但是现在一周都不超过一次了。炙烤的刑罚停止了，烹煮的刑罚也中断了。只有炼狱中保持的一定热度才使我想起自己的处境。"

"像温和的热水浴。"魔鬼说。

"确实像是在一个温热的浴室里，所有这些都是我神圣的姐姐祈祷的作用。昨天，在炼狱中看守我的那个魔鬼告诉我，只要我姐姐再给我祈祷一次，我就能被释放了，现在是魔鬼的我，就会变成一个神圣的天使。"

"那个祈祷呢？"魔鬼说。

"先生，她死了——我的姐姐死了——死亡之神在她祈祷的中途扼住了她的咽喉。"说到这里，这个可怜的灵魂开始悲哀地哭泣起来，他辛酸的泪水顺着他的胡须流了下来，烫伤了魔鬼使者的尾巴。

魔鬼说："事实上，这是一件很难办的事情。但我知道除了耐心之外没有别的补救方法，这样你才会在下面的住所中拥有一个不错的机会。"

"但是我有亲属，"伯爵说，"我的侄子兰德尔，他继承了我的土地，难道他不会为他的叔父做一个祈祷吗？"

"在你活着的时候，你可是憎恨并且压制他的。"

"这倒是真的。但是一个祈福也并不过分啊！还有他的姐姐，我的侄女

herited my lands, will he not say a prayer for his uncle?"

"Thou didst hate and oppress him when living."

"It is true; but an ave is not much; his sister, my niece, Matilda—"

"You shut her in a convent, and hanged her lover."

"Had I not reason? besides, has she not others?"

"A dozen, without doubt."

"And my brother, the prior?"

"A liege subject of my lord the Devil: he never opens his mouth, except to utter an oath, or to swallow a cup of wine."

"And yet, if but one of these would but say an ave for me, I should be saved."

"Aves with them are rarae aves," replied Mercurius, wagging his tail right waggishly; "and, what is more, I will lay thee any wager that not one of these will say a prayer to save thee."

"I would wager willingly," responded he of Chauchigny; "but what has a poor soul like me to stake?"

"Every evening, after the day's roasting, my lord Satan giveth a cup of cold water to his servants; I will bet thee thy water for a year, that none of the three will pray for thee."

"Done!" said Rollo.

"Done!" said the daemon; "and here, if I mistake not, is thy castle of Chauchigny."

Indeed, it was true. The soul, on looking down, perceived the tall towers, the courts, the stables, and the fair gardens of the castle. Although it was past midnight, there was a blaze of light in the banqueting-hall, and a lamp burning in the open window of the Lady Matilda.

"With whom shall we begin?" said the daemon: "with the baron or the lady?"

"With the lady, if you will."

"Be it so; her window is open, let us enter."

So they descended, and entered silently into Matilda's chamber.

The young lady's eyes were fixed so intently on a little clock, that it was

玛蒂尔达——”

“你把她关在一所修道院里，绞死了她的爱人。”

“难道我是故意的吗？难道她还没找到其他的爱人吗？”

“毫无疑问，会有一打的。”

“还有我的兄弟，修道院的院长？”

“他可是我们魔鬼王国中的一个忠诚臣民，除了发誓或喝酒之外，他从来不张口。”

“然而，只要他们中的一个愿为我做一个祈祷，我就能得救了。”

“让他们做祈祷是很难的，”恶魔使者恶作剧地摇摆着它的尾巴回答道，“而且，我愿意和你打赌，在他们当中不会有人做祈祷来解救你。”

“我也愿意打赌，”伯爵回应说，“但是像我这样一个可怜的灵魂拿什么做赌注呢？”

“每个晚上，在一天的炙烤结束后，撒旦主人会给他的下人一杯冷水。如果他们三个人没有一个人为你祈祷的话，就以你一年的冷水做赌注吧！”

“好！”罗尔洛说。

“好！”魔鬼说：“如果我没弄错的话，这里就是你在香槟区的城堡。”

确实是。罗尔洛的灵魂向下一看，看到了高高的城楼、院子、马厩和城堡内美丽的花园。尽管现在已过了午夜，宴会厅里还有一道明亮的强光，从玛蒂尔达的房间敞开的窗户中可以看到有一盏点燃的灯。

“我们从谁开始呢？”魔鬼说，“男爵还是女士？”

“如果你愿意的话，就从这个女士开始吧！”

“好，她的窗户是开着的，我们进去吧！”

因此他们从云层中降了下来，悄无声息地进入了玛蒂尔达的房间。

这位年轻的女士正目不转睛地盯着一个小钟表，显然她没有察觉到有两个访客进了房间。她坐在一个大椅子上，美丽的脸颊靠着白色的手臂，白色的手臂支撑在椅子的坐垫上。她正愉悦地沉浸在甜蜜的思念和诗意的遐想之中。在她旁边有一架鲁特琴，桌子下面放着一本祈祷书（虔诚总是

no wonder that she did not perceive the entrance of her two visitors. Her fair cheek rested on her white arm, and her white arm on the cushion of a great chair in which she sat, pleasantly supported by sweet thoughts and swan's down; a lute was at her side, and a book of prayers lay under the table (for piety is always modest). Like the amorous Alexander, she sighed and looked (at the clock)—and sighed for ten minutes or more, when she softly breathed the word "Edward!"

At this the soul of the Baron was wroth. "The jade is at her old pranks," said he to the devil; and then addressing Matilda: "I pray thee, sweet niece, turn thy thoughts for a moment from that villainous page, Edward, and give them to thine affectionate uncle."

When she heard the voice, and saw the awful apparition of her uncle (for a year's sojourn in purgatory had not increased the comeliness of his appearance), she started, screamed, and of course fainted.

But the devil Mercurius soon restored her to herself. "What's o'clock?" said she, as soon as she had recovered from her fit: "is he come?"

"Not thy lover, Maude, but thine uncle—that is, his soul. For the love of Heaven, listen to me: I have been frying in purgatory for a year past, and should have been in heaven but for the want of a single ave."

"I will say it for thee to-morrow, uncle."

"To night, or never."

"Well, to night be it:" and she requested the devil Mercurius to give her the prayer-book from under the table; but he had no sooner touched the holy book than he dropped it with a shriek and a yell. "It was hotter," he said, "than his master Sir Lucifer's own particular pitchfork." And the lady was forced to begin her ave without the aid of her missal.

At the commencement of her devotions the daemon retired, and carried with him the anxious soul of poor Sir Roger de Rollo.

The lady knelt down—she sighed deeply; she looked again at the clock, and began—

"Ave Maria."

When a lute was heard under the window, and a sweet voice singing—

谦虚的)。她像多情的亚历山大一样看着钟表叹息——十分钟或更长的时间之后，她温柔地低声说："爱德华!"

男爵的灵魂听到之后变得极为愤怒，他对魔鬼说："这个轻佻的女人对情人还念念不忘。"然后又对玛蒂尔达说："我请求你，亲爱的侄女，把你对那个讨厌的小侍从爱德华的思念分一点给你亲爱的叔父。"

当她听到声音的时候，也看到了她叔父可怕的幽灵（在炼狱中住了一年也没有让他的外表变得更标致一点)，她尖叫着跳了起来，当场就吓昏了。

但是魔鬼使者很快就让她恢复过来。她刚清醒过来，就问道："几点钟了，他来了吗?"

"不是你的爱人，玛蒂尔达，而是你的叔父——是他的灵魂。看在上帝的分上，听我说，过去的一年里，我都在炼狱里接受煎烤的惩罚，现在只需要一个祈福就能升入天堂了。"

"我明天会为你祈祷，叔父。"

"就今晚，要不就没机会了。"

"好吧！就今晚。"她请求魔鬼使者把桌子下面的祈祷书递给她。但是当恶魔刚碰到那本圣书的时候，就尖叫着把它扔在了地上，他说："太热了，比主人路西弗［魔鬼撒旦堕落前的名字。——译注］自己专用的叉子还要热。"因此，玛蒂尔达不得不在没有祈祷书的帮助下开始祈祷。

在她开始祈祷的时候，魔鬼带着焦急不安的罗杰退到一边。

玛蒂尔达跪下——她深深地叹息，又看了一眼时钟，开始祈祷——

"圣母玛利亚。"

这时从窗户下面传来了鲁特琴弹奏的声音，还有一个悦耳的嗓音歌唱着——

"听!"玛蒂尔达说。

现在白日的辛劳结束了，

"Hark!" said Matilda.

"Now the toils of day are over,
And the sun hath sunk to rest,
Seeking, like a fiery lover,
The bosom of the blushing west—

"The faithful night keeps watch and ward,
Raising the moon, her silver shield,
And summoning the stars to guard
The slumbers of my fair Mathilde!"

"For mercy's sake!" said Sir Rollo, "the ave first, and next the song."

So Matilda again dutifully betook her to her devotions, and began—

"Ave Maria gratia plena!" but the music began again, and the prayer ceased of course.

"The faithful night! Now all things lie
Hid by her mantle dark and dim,
In pious hope I hither hie,
And humbly chant mine ev'ning hymn.

"Thou art my prayer, my saint, my shrine!
(For never holy pilgrim kneel'd,
Or wept at feet more pure than thine),
My virgin love, my sweet Mathilde!"

"Virgin love!" said the Baron. "upon my soul, this is too bad!" and he thought of the lady's lover whom he had caused to be hanged.

But SHE only thought of him who stood singing at her window.

"Niece Matilda!" cried Sir Roger, agonizedly, "wilt thou listen to the lies of an impudent page, whilst thine uncle is waiting but a dozen words to make him happy?"

太阳也沉下去休息，
像一个炽热的爱人，投入
羞涩的西方的怀抱——

忠实的夜晚像守护神一样，
升起月亮，她银色的盾牌，
召唤星星去守卫我美丽的玛蒂尔达的睡眠！

“看在上帝面上！”罗尔洛说，“先祈祷，再听歌。”

因此玛蒂尔达又顺从地开始祈祷了——

“圣母玛利亚，仁慈无比！”但是音乐又响起来了，祈祷也随之停了下来。

忠实的夜晚！现在所有的事物
都笼罩在她黑暗的幕布中，
带着虔诚的希望，我赶到这里，
恭顺地吟唱我的夜晚赞歌。

你是我的祈祷，我的圣人，我的圣地！
（跪着或哭泣的朝圣者也不会比你更纯洁）
我纯洁的爱情，我温柔的玛蒂尔达！

“纯洁的爱情！”伯爵说，“对我的灵魂而言，这太糟糕了！”他想起了玛蒂尔达的爱人正是被他绞死的。

玛蒂尔达现在心里所想的只有那个站在她窗户旁边唱歌的爱人。

“玛蒂尔达侄女！”罗杰先生极度痛苦地叫道，“你要听一个鲁莽的侍从的谎言吗？而你的叔父还在等着你的祈祷，让他幸福呢？”

At this Matilda grew angry: "Edward is neither impudent nor a liar, Sir Uncle, and I will listen to the end of the song."

"Come away," said Mercurius; "he hath yet got wield, field, sealed, congealed, and a dozen other rhymes beside; and after the song will come the supper."

So the poor soul was obliged to go; while the lady listened, and the page sung away till morning.

"My virtues have been my ruin," said poor Sir Rollo, as he and Mercurius slunk silently out of the window. "Had I hanged that knave Edward, as I did the page his predecessor, my niece would have sung mine ave, and I should have been by this time an angel in heaven."

"He is reserved for wiser purposes," responded the devil: "he will assassinate your successor, the lady Mathilde's brother; and, in consequence, will be hanged. In the love of the lady he will be succeeded by a gardener, who will be replaced by a monk, who will give way to an ostler, who will be deposed by a Jew pedler, who shall, finally, yield to a noble earl, the future husband of the fair Mathilde. So that, you see, instead of having one poor soul a-frying, we may now look forward to a goodly harvest for our lord the Devil."

The soul of the Baron began to think that his companion knew too much for one who would make fair bets; but there was no help for it; he would not, and he could not, cry off: and he prayed inwardly that the brother might be found more pious than the sister.

But there seemed little chance of this. As they crossed the court, lackeys, with smoking dishes and, full jugs, passed and repassed continually, although it was long past midnight. On entering the hall, they found Sir Randal at the head of a vast table, surrounded by a fiercer and more motley collection of individuals than had congregated there even in the time of Sir Rollo. The lord of the castle had signified that "it was his royal pleasure to be drunk," and the gentlemen of his train had obsequiously followed their master. Mercurius was delighted with the scene, and relaxed his usually rigid countenance into a bland and benevolent smile, which became him wonderfully.

这时的玛蒂尔达生气了："爱德华既不鲁莽也不是一个说谎的人，叔父，我要把这首歌听完。"

"走吧！"恶魔使者说，"他还有十二首其他的歌曲没唱呢？等他唱完天就亮了。"

罗杰这个可怜的灵魂不得不离开，而玛蒂尔达一直听到那个侍从唱到早晨离去为止。

当可怜的罗杰和恶魔使者从窗户中悄悄溜走的时候，罗杰说："是我的德行导致了我的失败，如果我像以前绞死爱德华的前身一样杀死现在的那个恶棍爱德华，我的侄女就会给我祈福，我现在就是天堂里的天使了。"

"主人让他留下来还有更明智的目的，"魔鬼说，"他将会暗杀你的继承者即玛蒂尔达的弟弟。然后他就会被绞死。在玛蒂尔达的爱情世界中，他将会被一个园林工人所接替，园林工人又被一个修道士所代替，修道士又将会让位给一个旅店中看马的侍从，侍从又会被一个犹太商贩排挤掉，犹太商贩最后会把她交给一个高贵的伯爵，他就是玛蒂尔达女士未来的丈夫。因此你可以看到，我们的撒旦主人可以让我们有很好的收获的，而不是只会让一个可怜的灵魂去接受煎烤。"

伯爵的幽灵想，他的这位同伴知道的事情太多了，这不利于赌赛的公正。但现在也无济于事了，他不愿意也不能取消这个赌赛。他内心里祈求玛蒂尔达的弟弟会比他姐姐要孝顺些。

但是这个机会看起来也不太可能。尽管现在已过午夜很长时间了，当他们穿过院子的时候，却看到一些男仆端着热气腾腾的饭菜，扛着满满的罐子出出进进。走进门厅，他们发现兰德尔先生正坐在一张大桌子的首位上，一群人聚集在他四周，这些人要比罗杰先生所生活的那个时期更精力旺盛和混杂。城堡的主人已表明"被灌醉是他无上的快乐"，一长列的先生跟在他们主人后面巴结奉承。这一幕把恶魔使者给逗乐了，他一贯严肃的表情缓和了下来，竟露出了温和仁慈的微笑。

已经死去一年的罗杰先生和一个有着爪子、尖角和尾巴的怪物的出现

The entrance of Sir Roger, who had been dead about a year, and a person with hoofs, horns, and a tail, rather disturbed the hilarity of the company. Sir Randal dropped his cup of wine; and Father Peter, the confessor, incontinently paused in the midst of a profane song, with which he was amusing the society.

"Holy Mother!" cried he, "it is Sir Roger."

"Alive!" screamed Sir Randal.

"No, my lord," Mercurius said; "Sir Roger is dead, but cometh on a matter of business; and I have the honour to act as his counsellor and attendant."

"Nephew," said Sir Roger, "the daemon saith justly; I am come on a trifling affair, in which thy service is essential."

"I will do anything, uncle, in my power."

"Thou canst give me life, if thou wilt?" But Sir Randal looked very blank at this proposition. "I mean life spiritual, Randal," said Sir Roger; and thereupon he explained to him the nature of the wager.

Whilst he was telling his story, his companion Mercurius was playing all sorts of antics in the hall; and, by his wit and fun, became so popular with this godless crew, that they lost all the fear which his first appearance had given them. The friar was wonderfully taken with him, and used his utmost eloquence and endeavours to convert the devil; the knights stopped drinking to listen to the argument; the men-at-arms forbore brawling; and the wicked little pages crowded round the two strange disputants, to hear their edifying discourse. The ghostly man, however, had little chance in the controversy, and certainly little learning to carry it on. Sir Randal interrupted him. "Father Peter," said he, "our kinsman is condemned for ever, for want of a single ave: wilt thou say it for him?" "Willingly, my lord," said the monk, "with my book;" and accordingly he produced his missal to read, without which aid it appeared that the holy father could not manage the desired prayer. But the crafty Mercurius had, by his devilish art, inserted a song in the place of the ave, so that Father Peter, instead of chanting an hymn, sang the following irreverent ditty—

扰乱了欢闹的人群。兰德尔手中的酒杯跌落在地上。彼得这个忏悔神甫正唱着一首世俗的歌曲来娱乐大家，正唱到中途，也即刻停了下来。

“圣母啊！”他叫道，“是罗杰先生。”

“活着的！”兰德尔尖叫道。

“不，我的主人，”恶魔使者说，“罗杰先生死了，但我们是为一件事情而来的。我很荣幸做他的顾问和随从。”

“侄子，”罗杰先生说，“魔鬼说得没错。我是为一件微不足道的小事来的，在这件事情上你的帮助对我来说很重要。”

“我会尽我的力量做任何事情，叔父。”

“如果你愿意的话，你能给我生命？”但是兰德尔看起来对这件事情很茫然，“我是指灵魂的生命，兰德尔。”罗杰说，他又把打赌的事情向兰德尔解释了一遍。

当他正讲述自己的故事的时候，他的同伴魔鬼使者正在门厅中做出各种各样的滑稽动作。凭借着他的机智和玩笑，他受到了那些信仰无神论的人群的欢迎，他们刚见到魔鬼时的恐惧之情也消失了。彼得神甫也很好奇地对他发生了兴趣，他用最善辩的口才努力劝说魔鬼叛依宗教；骑士们也不喝酒了，都停下来听他们的争论；武装的士兵则力图避免两方吵起架来；淘气的小侍从们挤在这两群奇怪的争论者周围，听他们那些带有教训意味的谈话。然而，魔鬼使者很少有争论的机会，当然也几乎没有什么学识能把这场争论进行下去。兰德尔先生打断了他们，他说：“彼得神甫，我的叔父就因为缺少一次祈福而要永远地接受惩罚，你愿意为他祈祷吗?”“愿意，我的主人。”彼得神甫说。他拿出他的祈祷书读了起来，没有这本书的帮助，看来这个神甫还不能完成这个祈祷。但是狡猾的恶魔使出了魔鬼般的行径，他在祈祷文的页码中插入了一首歌曲，因此彼得神甫没有唱赞美诗，反而唱起了下面这首轻浮的小曲——

"Some love the matin-chimes, which toll
The hour of prayer to sinner:
But better far's the mid-day bell,
Which speaks the hour of dinner;
For when I see a smoking fish,
Or capon drown'd in gravy,
Or noble haunch on silver dish,
Full glad I sing mine ave.
"My pulpit is an ale-house bench,
Whereon I sit so jolly;
A smiling rosy country wench
My saint and patron holy.
I kiss her cheek so red and sleek,
I press her ringlets wavy;
And in her willing ear I speak
A most religious ave.
"And if I'm blind, yet heaven is kind,
And holy saints forgiving;
For sure he leads a right good life
Who thus admires good living.
Above, they say, our flesh is air,
Our blood celestial ichor:
Oh, grant! mid all the changes there,
They may not change our liquor!"

And with this pious wish the holy confessor tumbled under the table in an agony of devout drunkenness; whilst the knights, the men-at-arms, and the wicked little pages, rang out the last verse with a most melodious and emphatic glee. "I am sorry, fair uncle," hiccupped Sir Randal, "that, in the matter of the ave, we could not oblige thee in a more orthodox manner; but the holy father has failed, and there is not another man in the hall who hath an idea of a prayer."

有人喜爱早晨的钟声，敲响的钟声
告诉罪人祈祷的时间到了。
但我更喜欢的还是中午的钟声，
它告诉人们午餐的时间到了。
当我看见一条热气腾腾的鱼，
或一只浸在肉汁中的阉鸡，
或银制盘子上的大片羊肉，
我就满心欢喜地唱起我的赞美诗。
我的布道坛是酒馆里的一条长凳，
我非常快活地坐在凳子上面。
一个微笑的涨红脸的乡村姑娘，
是我神圣的圣徒和恩主。
我亲吻她如此红润和光滑的脸颊，
抚摸她波浪状的长卷发；
在她心甘情愿的耳朵旁边
我最虔诚地祈祷。
虽然我是蒙昧的，但天堂是仁慈的，
神圣的圣徒是仁慈的；
是他引导着一个正直善良的生命，
而这个生命如此羡慕愉快的生活，
在天上，他们说，我们的肉体是空气，
我们的血是灵液：
哦，承认吧！在所有的事物中，
我们最喜爱的还是美酒！

伴随着这个虔诚的祝愿，忏悔神甫因醉到了极点而跌倒在桌子下面。与此同时，骑士们、武装的士兵们和捣蛋的小侍从们也用最悦耳的音调，

"It is my own fault," said Sir Rollo; "for I hanged the last confessor." And he wished his nephew a surly good-night, as he prepared to quit the room.

"Au revoir, gentlemen," said the devil Mercurius; and once more fixed his tail round the neck of his disappointed companion.

The spirit of poor Rollo was sadly cast down; the devil, on the contrary, was in high good humour. He wagged his tail with the most satisfied air in the world, and cut a hundred jokes at the expense of his poor associate. On they sped, cleaving swiftly through the cold night winds, frightening the birds that were roosting in the woods, and the owls who were watching in the towers.

In the twinkling of an eye, as it is known, devils can fly hundreds of miles: so that almost the same beat of the clock which left these two in Champagne, found them hovering over Paris. They dropped into the court of the Lazarist Convent, and winded their way, through passage and cloister, until they reached the door of the prior's cell.

Now the prior, Rollo's brother, was a wicked and malignant sorcerer; his time was spent in conjuring devils and doing wicked deeds, instead of fasting, scourging, and singing holy psalms: this Mercurius knew; and he, therefore, was fully at ease as to the final result of his wager with poor Sir Roger.

"You seem to be well acquainted with the road," said the knight.

"I have reason," answered Mercurius, "having, for a long period, had the acquaintance of his reverence, your brother; but you have little chance with him."

"And why?" said Sir Rollo.

"He is under a bond to my master, never to say a prayer, or else his soul and his body are forfeited at once."

"Why, thou false and traitorous devil!" said the enraged knight; "and thou knewest this when we made our wager?"

"Undoubtedly: do you suppose I would have done so had there been any chance of losing?"

And with this they arrived at Father Ignatius's door.

"Thy cursed presence threw a spell on my niece, and stopped the tongue

欢天喜地地重复着小曲的最后一句。兰德尔打着嗝儿说："对不起，亲爱的叔父，对于祈祷这件事情，我们不能用正统的方式让您满意。但神甫失败了，在这个大厅中就没有其他的人可以做祈祷了。"

"是我自己的过失，"罗杰说，"因为我绞死了最后一个忏悔神甫。"在他要离开房间的时候，他阴郁地祝他侄子晚安。

魔鬼使者说："先生们，再见!"他又再一次用尾巴缠住他失望的同伴的脖子。

可怜的罗杰很沮丧，相反，魔鬼却很高兴，他非常得意地摇摆着他的尾巴，开玩笑打趣他可怜的同伴。他们飞快地穿过寒冷的夜空，惊起了栖息在树林中的鸟群和看守着钟塔的猫头鹰。

众所周知，一眨眼的功夫，魔鬼就能飞几百英里，因此当他们两个刚离开香槟区不一会儿，就出现在巴黎的上空。他们降落到拉扎尔修道院的院子里，然后穿过小径和回廊，径直来到院长房间的门前。

罗杰的兄弟现在是一个邪恶的巫师，他把时间都用在召鬼和做恶事上，而不是斋戒、苦修和唱赞美诗。对于这些，魔鬼使者都知道，因此对于他和罗杰先生的这场赌赛，他很有把握能赢。

"你好像很熟悉这条路。"罗杰说。

魔鬼使者回答说："那是因为我已经认识你的弟弟很长时间了。在他身上，你几乎没什么机会能赢了。"

"为什么?"罗杰说。

"他和我的主人有个契约，就是从不做祈祷，否则他的灵魂和躯体会立即消失。"

"你这个虚伪、奸诈的魔鬼!"愤怒的罗杰说，"当我们打赌的时候，你就知道这些了?"

"当然，你以为我没有十足的把握就会和你打赌吗?"

这样说着，他们就到了以革那提神甫的门前。

"你可恶的在场迷惑了我的侄女，还不让我侄子的牧师说话，我相信如

of my nephew's chaplain; I do believe that had I seen either of them alone, my wager had been won."

"Certainly; therefore, I took good care to go with thee: however, thou mayest see the prior alone, if thou wilt; and lo! his door is open. I will stand without for five minutes, when it will be time to commence our journey."

It was the poor Baron's last chance: and he entered his brother's room more for the five minutes' respite than from any hope of success.

Father Ignatius, the prior, was absorbed in magic calculations: he stood in the middle of a circle of skulls, with no garment except his long white beard, which reached to his knees; he was waving a silver rod, and muttering imprecations in some horrible tongue.

But Sir Rollo came forward and interrupted his incantation. "I am," said he, "the shade of thy brother Roger de Rollo; and have come, from pure brotherly love, to warn thee of thy fate."

"Whence camest thou?"

"From the abode of the blessed in Paradise," replied Sir Roger, who was inspired with a sudden thought; "it was but five minutes ago that the Patron Saint of thy church told me of thy danger, and of thy wicked compact with the fiend. 'Go,' said he, 'to thy miserable brother, and tell him there is but one way by which he may escape from paying the awful forfeit of his bond.'"

"And how may that be?" said the prior; "the false fiend hath deceived me; I have given him my soul, but have received no worldly benefit in return. Brother! dear brother! how may I escape?"

"I will tell thee. As soon as I heard the voice of blessed St. Mary Lazarus (the worthy Earl had, at a pinch, coined the name of a saint), I left the clouds, where, with other angels, I was seated, and sped hither to save thee. 'Thy brother,' said the Saint, 'hath but one day more to live, when he will become for all eternity the subject of Satan; if he would escape, he must boldly break his bond, by saying an ave.'"

"It is the express condition of the agreement," said the unhappy monk, "I must say no prayer, or that instant I become Satan's, body and soul."

"It is the express condition of the Saint," answered Roger, fiercely;

果让我单独见他们，我就会赢这场赌赛。”

“当然可以，和你在一起我会很小心的。如果你乐意，你可以单独去见院长。瞧！他的门开着。我会在外面等你五分钟，五分钟后我们就要启程离开了。”

这是可怜的伯爵最后的机会。他走进他兄弟的房间更多的是为了这五分钟的延期，而对结果他几乎不抱有什么成功的希望了。

以革那提神甫也是修道院的院长，他正专心致志地做巫术预测，他站在一圈头盖骨中间，除了长长的白色胡须之外，没穿任何衣服，胡须垂到了他的膝盖那里，他正摇动着一根镀银的杆子，嘴里咕哝着一些可怕的词语。

罗尔洛走上前去，打断了他的巫术。他说：“我是你的兄弟罗杰·德·罗尔洛的幽灵，我纯粹是为了兄弟情谊来到这里的，向你提出命运的警告。”

“你从哪里来？”

“从天堂神圣的住所中来，”罗杰先生答道，他这时突然有了一个想法，“在五分钟之前，你的教堂守护神把你的危险告诉了我，还有你和魔鬼签订的邪恶契约。他说：‘去，到你那个可怜的兄弟那儿去，告诉他只有一个办法才能让他免于可怕的违约所带来的惩罚。’”

“那会怎么样呢？”院长说，“虚伪的魔鬼欺骗了我，我已经把我的灵魂给他了，但是没有收到任何尘世的回报。兄弟！亲爱的兄弟！我怎样才能逃脱惩罚？”

“我会告诉你的。我一听到神圣的玛丽·拉扎尔的告诫（尊敬的伯爵在紧要关头捏造了一个圣徒的名字），我就离开了云层，在那里我是和天使们在一起的，我快速来到这里拯救你。圣徒说：‘如果你的兄弟愿意永远做撒旦臣民的话，他还有一天的生命；如果他想避免这个不幸，他必须要大胆地做一个祈祷来违背契约。’”

不幸的修道士说：“协议上明确规定，我不能做祈祷，否则我的躯体和

"pray, brother, pray, or thou art lost for ever."

So the foolish monk knelt down, and devoutly sung out an ave. "Amen!" said Sir Roger, devoutly.

"Amen!" said Mercurius, as, suddenly, coming behind, he seized Ignatius by his long beard, and flew up with him to the top of the church-steeple.

The monk roared, and screamed, and swore against his brother; but it was of no avail: Sir Roger smiled kindly on him, and said, "Do not fret, brother; it must have come to this in a year or two."

And he flew alongside of Mercurius to the steeple-top: BUT THIS TIME THE DEVIL HAD NOT HIS TAIL ROUND HIS NECK. "I will let thee off thy bet," said he to the daemon; for he could afford, now, to be generous.

"I believe, my lord," said the daemon, politely, "that our ways separate here." Sir Roger sailed gayly upwards: while Mercurius having bound the miserable monk faster than ever, he sunk downwards to earth, and perhaps lower. Ignatius was heard roaring and screaming as the devil dashed him against the iron spikes and buttresses of the church.

灵魂就归撒旦所有了。”

“这是圣徒的明确表示，”罗杰坚决地回答说，“祈祷吧！兄弟，祈祷吧！否则你要永远被遗弃了。”

因此，这个愚蠢的修道士就跪下了，虔诚地祈福。罗杰终于松了一口气，虔诚地说道：“阿门!”

魔鬼使者这时突然从后面走了进来说：“阿门!”他抓住以革那提的长胡须把他扔到了教堂尖塔的顶端上。

修道士在吼叫、诅咒他的兄弟，但一切都无济于事。罗杰先生温和地对他微笑说：“不要苦恼，兄弟，在一两年之内你迟早会有这个结果的。”

他和恶魔使者并肩飞到教堂的尖塔上，但是这次使者没有用尾巴缠住他的脖子。“我会让你取消你的赌注的。”他对魔鬼说，因为他现在赢了，就变得大方了。

“我相信，我的主人，”魔鬼有礼貌地说，“我们要在这里分开了。”罗杰快乐地向上飞去，而恶魔使者把可怜的以革那提修道士绑得比以前更紧了，他们向地面坠落下去，或许还要更往下去。当魔鬼把他往教堂的铁钉和拱壁上撞击时，可以听得到以革那提的嚎叫声和尖叫声。

Madame Sand and the New Apocalypse

I don't know an impression more curious than that which is formed in a foreigner's mind, who has been absent from this place for two or three years, returns to it, and beholds the change which has taken place, in the meantime, in French fashions and ways of thinking. Two years ago, for instance, when I left the capital, I left the young gentlemen of France with their hair brushed en toupet in front, and the toes of their boots round; now the boot-toes are pointed, and the hair combed flat, and, parted in the middle, falls in ringlets on the fashionable shoulders; and, in like manner, with books as with boots, the fashion has changed considerably, and it is not a little curious to contrast the old modes with the new. Absurd as was the literary dandyism of those days, it is not a whit less absurd now: only the manner is changed, and our versatile Frenchmen have passed from one caricature to another.

The revolution may be called a caricature of freedom, as the empire was of glory; and what they borrow from foreigners undergoes the same process. They take top-boots and mackintoshes from across the water, and caricature our fashions; they read a little, very little, Shakespeare, and caricature our poetry: and while in David's time art and religion were only a caricature of Heathenism, now, on the contrary, these two commodities are imported from Germany; and distorted caricatures originally, are still farther distorted on passing the frontier.

I trust in heaven that German art and religion will take no hold in our country (where there is a fund of roast-beef that will expel any such humbug in the end); but these sprightly Frenchmen have relished the mystical doctrines mightily; and having watched the Germans, with their sanctified looks,

乔治桑女士与新的启示

对于一个刚离开法国两三年又回到法国的外国人来说，看到这两三年中法国人在社会风气和思想方式上所发生的变化，一定会让他感到好奇。例如两年前，当我离开巴黎的时候，法国年轻先生们的发式是在前面梳成小绺的顶发，脚上穿着圆头的靴子，而现在的靴子成了尖头的，发式是中分的卷发，一直垂到肩膀上。书籍也和靴子、社会风尚一样有着流行的变化，这没什么可奇怪的。以前的文学有着矫揉做作的荒谬，但现在其荒谬性也没有得到丝毫的减弱，只是风格变了，多才多艺的法国人已从一种滑稽模仿转向另一种滑稽模仿。

法国大革命可被称做对自由的一种讽刺，如同帝国是对荣誉的讽刺一样。从外国所借鉴的一切也得到了法国人的改造加工。他们穿着防水的长统靴和雨衣，讽刺我们英国的社会风气；他们很少读莎士比亚的作品，却敢于讽刺我们的诗歌。在大卫的时代，艺术和宗教还只是对异教进行讽刺，现在却恰恰相反，从德国输入的这两件商品改变了原来的讽刺倾向，并且在进入法国后又得到进一步的曲解。

我确信德国的艺术和宗教不会在我们国家流行起来（在我们国家丰盛的烤牛肉最终会把这些骗人的东西给驱逐出去的），但这些思想活跃的法国人已强烈地迷上了神秘主义的学说，他们用神圣化的目光来观察德国人及其稀奇古怪的仿古作品和神秘的先验论谈话，模仿他们的流行风尚。他们做这些事情的时候都尽可能地投入和严肃。上帝才知道，这是不是真正的

and quaint imitations of the old times, and mysterious transcendental talk, are aping many of their fashions; as well and solemnly as they can: not very solemnly, God wot; for I think one should always prepare to grin when a Frenchman looks particularly grave, being sure that there is something false and ridiculous lurking under the owl-like solemnity.

When last in Paris, we were in the midst of what was called a Catholic reaction. Artists talked of faith in poems and pictures; churches were built here and there; old missals were copied and purchased; and numberless portraits of saints, with as much gilding about them as ever was used in the fifteenth century, appeared in churches, ladies' boudoirs, and picture-shops. One or two fashionable preachers rose, and were eagerly followed; the very youth of the schools gave up their pipes and billiards for some time, and flocked in crowds to Nôtre Dame, to sit under the feet of Lacordaire. I went to visit the Church of Nôtre Dame de Lorette yesterday, which was finished in the heat of this Catholic rage, and was not a little struck by the similarity of the place to the worship celebrated in it, and the admirable manner in which the architect has caused his work to express the public feeling of the moment. It is a pretty little bijou of a church: it is supported by sham marble pillars; it has a gaudy ceiling of blue and gold, which will look very well for some time; and is filled with gaudy pictures and carvings, in the very pink of the mode. The congregation did not offer a bad illustration of the present state of Catholic reaction. Two or three stray people were at prayers; there was no service; a few countrymen and idlers were staring about at the pictures; and the Swiss, the paid guardian of the place, was comfortably and appropriately asleep on his bench at the door. I am inclined to think the famous reaction is over: the students have taken to their Sunday pipes and billiards again; and one or two cafés have been established, within the last year, that are ten times handsomer than Nôtre Dame de Lorette.

However, if the immortal Görres and the German mystics have had their day, there is the immortal Goethe, and the Pantheists; and I incline to think that the fashion has set very strongly in their favour. Voltaire and the Encyclopaedians are voted, now, barbares, and there is no term of reprobation

严肃。当一个法国人看起来非常严肃的时候，可以确定在这种猫头鹰似的严肃下必定隐藏着某种虚伪和荒谬的东西，让人们不由得感到好笑。

最近我们在巴黎正赶上天主教在法国流行。艺术家们谈论诗歌和绘画作品中的宗教信仰；各地兴建教堂；旧的祈祷书被再版和出售；许多圣徒的肖像也都像15世纪时那样被镀了金摆放在教堂、女士闺房和画店里。巴黎还出现了一两个受民众欢迎的传道士，他们受到人们的竞相追随；有一段时间，学校里的年轻人还放弃了他们的烟斗和弹子戏，成群结队地去圣母院，聆听拉科代尔的布道。我昨天去参观了洛荷特圣母院教堂，它就是在这股天主教的流行热潮中建好的，这个教堂没有受到周围教堂建筑物的影响，建筑师也没有用令人赞美的建筑样式传达公众的信仰热情。它是一个小巧雅致的教堂，支撑物是一些劣等的大理石柱子；它有着华丽的用蓝色和金色装饰的天花板，这种漂亮的颜色会持续一段时间；教堂里面摆满了非常流行且华丽的绘画和雕塑。教堂里的人也并没有给反动的天主教抹黑。有两三个人正在祈祷，没有服务的神职人员；一些同胞和游手好闲的人散落在四处注视着画像；教堂雇用的一个瑞士卫兵在门口的长椅上舒服地睡着了。我认为这场天主教运动就要结束了，因为学生们在周日已重新拿起烟斗，玩弹子戏了。去年也有一两家咖啡馆开始营业了，它们的室内装饰要比洛荷特圣母院漂亮十倍。

然而，如果不朽的格雷斯［Josef Görres（1776—1848）是德国政治民族主义的奠基人，在某种程度也可以说是欧洲政治民族主义的开山鼻祖。——译注］和德国的神秘主义者，还有不朽的歌德和泛神论者仍然在世的话，我认为他们还是很赞同这种社会风气的。伏尔泰和百科全书派现在被公认为是野蛮人，没人再去强烈指责无情的休谟和爱尔维修［Helvetiuses（1715—1771），法国启蒙思想家，哲学家。——译注］，他们两个活着就是要破坏和怀疑。虽然伏尔泰的嘲讽和双关语修辞都让人不舒服，但我认为在他的作品中还含有比现在混乱的法国先验论更为果断和诚挚的思想。泛神论现在还只是一个名词。无论是个人还是群体都已经开始认识到

strong enough for heartless Humes and Helvetiuses, who lived but to destroy, and who only thought to doubt. Wretched as Voltaire's sneers and puns are, I think there is something more manly and earnest even in them, than in the present muddy French transcendentalism. Pantheism is the word now; one and all have begun to éprouver the besoin of a religious sentiment; and we are deluged with a host of gods accordingly. Monsieur de Balzac feels himself to be inspired; Victor Hugo is a god; Madame Sand is a god; that tawdry man of genius, Jules Janin, who writes theatrical reviews for the *Débats*, has divine intimations; and there is scarce a beggarly, beardless scribbler of poems and prose, but tells you, in his preface, of the sainteté of the sacerdoce littéraire; or a dirty student, sucking tobacco and beer, and reeling home with a grisette from the chaumiére, who is not convinced of the necessity of a new "Messianism," and will hiccup, to such as will listen, chapters of his own drunken Apocalypse. Surely, the negatives of the old days were far less dangerous than the assertions of the present; and you may fancy what a religion that must be, which has such high priests.

There is no reason to trouble the reader with details of the lives of many of these prophets and expounders of new revelations. Madame Sand, for instance, I do not know personally, and can only speak of her from report. True or false, the history, at any rate, is not very edifying; and so may be passed over: but, as a certain great philosopher told us, in very humble and simple words, that we are not to expect to gather grapes from thorns, or figs from thistles, we may, at least, demand, in all persons assuming the character of moralist or philosopher—order, soberness, and regularity of life; for we are apt to distrust the intellect that we fancy can be swayed by circumstance or passion; and we know how circumstance and passion WILL sway the intellect: how mortified vanity will form excuses for itself; and how temper turns angrily upon conscience, that reproves it. How often have we called our judge our enemy, because he has given sentence against us! —How often have we called the right wrong, because the right condemns us! And in the lives of many of the bitter foes of the Christian doctrine, can we find no personal reason for their hostility? The men in Athens said it was out of regard for religion that they murdered Socrates; but we have had time, since then, to reconsider the verdict; and Socrates' character is pretty pure now, in spite of the sen-

宗教情感是不可缺少的，因此我们就被淹没在一群偶像之中。巴尔扎克觉得自己受到了激励；维克多·雨果是一个偶像；乔治桑是一个偶像；那个为《辩论》[法国的思想学术杂志。——译注]专栏写戏剧评论的庸才于勒·若南[Jules Janin (1804—1874)，法国浪漫主义作家和批评家。——译注]说他的写作受到了神的启示；生活富裕、留着胡须的文人会在他们的作品序言里告诉你说文学是个神圣的职业；而年轻的一代则抽着烟、喝着啤酒，同一个来自乡村的青年劳动妇女摇摇晃晃回家过夜，他们还认识不到一个新救世主降临的必要性，因此他们会打着嗝、醉醺醺地听启示录的章节。的确，否定以往远远不如维持现状困难，你可以想象得到有这样高层次牧师的宗教会是个什么样子。

这里就没有必要罗列一些新预言家和宗教阐释者的生活来烦扰读者了。我们就以乔治桑为例，我不认识她本人，只能以报刊报道为据来谈论她。过去是真是假都没什么启发意义了，因此我们就可以忽略掉乔治桑的过去。但是有一个伟大的哲学家用非常谦逊而简洁的话语告诉过我们，虽然我们不能期望从荆棘上收获葡萄或从蓟属植物上收获无花果，但我们至少可以要求所有的人都具备道德主义者或哲学家的品质——即理性、克制、规律地生活。我们知道外部的环境和激情会怎样地支配和动摇理智；人的虚荣心会怎样为自己寻找借口；人的情绪又会怎样地违背良心。我们经常去指责我们的敌人，原因就是他们和我们相对抗！——我们经常把对的称为错的，因为对的一方谴责了我们！对基督教教义的许多死敌的仇恨，其中难道就没有私人原因吗？雅典人说苏格拉底不尊重宗教，就把他给杀害了。不管以前的判决是怎样，我们现在却认为苏格拉底的品质是非常高尚的。

巴黎的哲学家会力图向你解释在乔治桑女士的思想中所经历的一些变化——她在经历了最初的考验、努力和痛苦之后终于达到了现在的精神启蒙的愉悦状态。乔治桑的个人才智都体现在她的作品中，她的作品大多都是上下两册。她最初是在那本迷人的小说《印第安娜》中强烈地攻击婚姻。她叫喊道：“怜悯那些不幸婚姻中的女性吧！婚姻把她们束缚在一个男人身

tence and the jury of those days.

The Parisian philosophers will attempt to explain to you the changes through which Madame Sand's mind has passed,—the initiatory trials, labours, and sufferings which she has had to go through,—before she reached her present happy state of mental illumination. She teaches her wisdom in parables, that are, mostly, a couple of volumes long; and began, first, by an eloquent attack on marriage, in the charming novel of "*Indiana.*" "Pity," cried she, "for the poor woman who, united to a being whose brute force makes him her superior, should venture to break the bondage which is imposed on her, and allow her heart to be free."

In support of this claim of pity, she writes two volumes of the most exquisite prose. What a tender, suffering creature is Indiana; how little her husband appreciates that gentleness which he is crushing by his tyranny and brutal scorn; how natural it is that, in the absence of his sympathy, she, poor clinging confiding creature, should seek elsewhere for shelter; how cautious should we be, to call criminal—to visit with too heavy a censure—an act which is one of the natural impulses of a tender heart, that seeks but for a worthy object of love. But why attempt to tell the tale of beautiful Indiana? Madame Sand has written it so well, that not the hardest-hearted husband in Christendom can fail to be touched by her sorrows, though he may refuse to listen to her argument. Let us grant, for argument's sake, that the laws of marriage, especially the French laws of marriage, press very cruelly upon unfortunate women.

But if one wants to have a question of this, or any nature, honestly argued, it is, better, surely, to apply to an indifferent person for an umpire. For instance, the stealing of pocket-handkerchiefs or snuff-boxes may or may not be vicious; but if we, who have not the wit, or will not take the trouble to decide the question ourselves, want to hear the real rights of the matter, we should not, surely, apply to a pickpocket to know what he thought on the point. It might naturally be presumed that he would be rather a prejudiced person—particularly as his reasoning, if successful, might get him OUT OF GAOL. This is a homely illustration, no doubt; all we would urge by it is, that Madame Sand having, according to the French newspapers, had a stern husband, and also having, according to the newspapers, sought "sympathy" elsewhere, her arguments may be considered to be somewhat partial, and received with some little caution.

上，而那个男人只是靠着蛮力来支配她，她们应该敢于挣脱这种婚姻的束缚，让心灵获得自由。”

乔治桑写了两册非常优美的小说来支持这种同情女性的观点。印第安娜是一个多么温柔痛苦的人儿啊！她的丈夫对这个文雅的人儿又是多么的不了解啊！他用专制的行为和残忍的轻蔑来压制自己妻子。没有了丈夫的同情，印第安娜这个可怜的具有依赖性、易于轻信的人儿自然会去别处寻求庇护。我们不忍心把她称做可耻的人——因为要对她做出谴责真是太难了——一颗温柔的心灵只是凭着自然的冲动行事，只是为了寻求一个值得爱的人。但我们在这里就没必要讲述美丽的印第安娜的故事了，因为乔治桑已经把这个故事写得很好了，即使是作为基督教徒的铁石心肠的丈夫也会被印第安娜的悲伤所打动，尽管他或许会拒绝听她的辩论。我们要承认的是，婚姻律法，尤其是法国的婚姻律法对不幸的女人是非常残忍而不公的。

如果有人对这个看法有所质疑或想认真地予以争论，他最好去请一个中立人做仲裁。举例来说，偷窃别人口袋中的手帕或鼻烟盒可能被判为有罪，也可能被判为无罪。无论我们有没有才智，还是不愿意自己费力去判断问题，要想了解事情的真相，我们都不会去询问一个扒手，从他那儿了解他对此事的看法。人们自然就能推测出，扒手是一个怀有偏见的人物——尤其是他的推论，如果推论成立的话，他就不会被逮进监狱了。无疑这只是个简单的例子。我们由此想推出的就是乔治桑也曾有过一个严厉的丈夫，根据法国报纸的报道，她也曾在别处寻求过“同情”，人们据此也会认为她的论据存在某些偏见，因而得不到足够的重视。

谁才是社会的改革者呢？——是那些对现存社会体制不满的人。谁会认为我们这个生活、恋爱、结婚、生小孩、养育儿女的生活体制是完美的呢？我相信没有一个人会认为它是完美的。当一个人抨击这个世界及人们的生活作风时，当他大声激昂地向人们宣讲信仰、习俗和法律的暴政时，只要我们仔细研究一下这个布道者的品质，我们就能非常清晰地了解其思

And tell us who have been the social reformers? —the haters, that is, of the present system, according to which we live, love, marry, have children, educate them, and endow them—ARE THEY PURE THEMSELVES? I do believe not one; and directly a man begins to quarrel with the world and its ways, and to lift up, as he calls it, the voice of his despair, and preach passionately to mankind about this tyranny of faith, customs, laws; if we examine what the personal character of the preacher is, we begin pretty clearly to understand the value of the doctrine. Any one can see why Rousseau should be such a whimpering reformer, and Byron such a free and easy misanthropist, and why our accomplished Madame Sand, who has a genius and eloquence inferior to neither, should take the present condition of mankind (French-kind) so much to heart, and labour so hotly to set it right.

After "*Indiana*" (which, we presume, contains the lady's notions upon wives and husbands) came "*Valentine*," which may be said to exhibit her doctrine, in regard of young men and maidens, to whom the author would accord, as we fancy, the same tender license. "*Valentine*" was followed by "*Lelia*," a wonderful book indeed, gorgeous in eloquence, and rich in magnificent poetry: a regular topsyturvyfication of morality, a 'thieves' and 'prostitutes' apotheosis. This book has received some late enlargements and emendations by the writer; it contains her notions on morals, which, as we have said, are so peculiar, that, alas! they only can be mentioned here, not particularized: but of "*Spiridion*" we may write a few pages, as it is her religious manifesto.

In this work, the lady asserts her pantheistical doctrine, and openly attacks the received Christian creed. She declares it to be useless now, and unfitted to the exigencies and the degree of culture of the actual world; and, though it would be hardly worth while to combat her opinions in due form, it is, at least, worth while to notice them, not merely from the extraordinary eloquence and genius of the woman herself, but because they express the opinions of a great number of people besides: for she not only produces her own thoughts, but imitates those of others very eagerly; and one finds in her writings so much similarity with others, or, in others, so much resemblance to her, that the book before us may pass for the expression of the sentiments of a certain French party.

"Dieu est mort," says another writer of the same class, and of great genius too. —"Dieu est mort," writes Mr. Henry Heine, speaking of the Christian God; and he adds, in a daring figure of speech;—"N'entendez-vous pas

想的价值意义。人们都明白为什么卢梭会是一个牢骚抱怨的改革者，拜伦是一个无拘无束的愤世嫉俗者，为什么天赋和口才都不如卢梭和拜伦的乔治桑会为人类现在的状况如此忧虑、会如此热情地努力把它调整到正确的方向。

乔治桑在《印第安娜》之后（我们认为，这本书包含了这位女士对于妻子和丈夫的看法）又出版了《瓦朗蒂娜》，这本书呈现了她自己的一套学说，对于年轻的男士和女士，作者同样都给予了温和的宽容。《瓦朗蒂娜》之后又出版了《莱莉亚》，这也是一本杰作，修辞华丽，充满了美好的诗意，并颠覆了传统的道德观念，把小偷和妓女予以神化。这本书后来又得到作者的扩展和修订，书中所体现的道德观念很特别，但我们只能在这里提一下，不再详细阐述了。我们要围绕着《斯宾利地安》（1839 年——译注）写上几页，因为这本书是她的宗教宣言。

在这部作品中，乔治桑女士维护她的泛神论学说，公开攻击被人们普遍接受的基督教教义。她宣布，现在的基督教教义是无价值的，不适合现实世界文化的迫切需要和发展水平。虽然她的这个观点不值得人们去反对，但至少值得人们去注意，它不仅仅是这位女士个人的看法，而且表达了大多数人的观点。因为她不仅提出了自己的想法，还非常热心地再现了其他人的想法，所以人们就能在她的作品中找到许多相似的感受以及与她相似的地方。《斯宾利地安》这本书表达了法国某个特定群体的真实感想。

一位伟大的天才说过“上帝死了”，亨利·海涅［海涅（1797—1856），德国诗人。——译注］在谈到基督教的上帝时也写道“上帝死了”，他还做着一个大胆的演讲手势说：“你们没有听到敲响的钟声吗？——那是人们在给一个垂死的上帝做圣礼！”另一个泛神论的诗人哲学家埃德加尔基内［Edgar Quinet（1803—1875），法国的历史学家，哲学家。——译注］有一首诗，在诗中基督和圣母玛利亚都死了，基督被归类为普罗米修斯式的人物。《斯宾利地安》就是对这个主题的延续，或许你能从中听到作者对于这个主题的一些见解。

sonner la Clochette? —on porte les sacremens à un Dieu qui se meurt!?" Another of the pantheist poetical philosophers, Mr. Edgar Quinet, has a poem, in which Christ and the Virgin Mary are made to die similarly, and the former is classed with Prometheus. This book of "*Spiridion*" is a continuation of the theme, and perhaps you will listen to some of the author's expositions of it.

It must be confessed that the controversialists of the present day have an eminent advantage over their predecessors in the days of folios; it required some learning then to write a book, and some time, at least—for the very labour of writing out a thousand such vast pages would demand a considerable period. But now, in the age of duodecimos, the system is reformed altogether: a male or female controversialist draws upon his imagination, and not his learning; makes a story instead of an argument, and, in the course of 150 pages (where the preacher has it all his own way) will prove or disprove you anything. And, to our shame be it said, we Protestants have set the example of this kind of proselytism—those detestable mixtures of truth, lies, false sentiment, false reasoning, bad grammar, correct and genuine philanthropy and piety—I mean our religious tracts, which any woman or man, be he ever so silly, can take upon himself to write, and sell for a penny, as if religious instruction were the easiest thing in the world. We, I say, have set the example in this kind of composition, and all the sects of the earth will, doubtless, speedily follow it. I can point you out blasphemies in famous pious tracts that are as dreadful as those above mentioned; but this is no place for such discussions, and we had better return to Madame Sand. As Mrs. Sherwood expounds, by means of many touching histories and anecdotes of little boys and girls, her notions of church history, church catechism, church doctrine;—as the author of "*Father Clement, a Roman Catholic Story*," demolishes the stately structure of eighteen centuries, the mighty and beautiful Roman Catholic faith, in whose bosom repose so many saints and sages,—by the means of a three-and-sixpenny duodecimo volume, which tumbles over the vast fabric, as David's pebble-stone did Goliath;—as, again, the Roman Catholic author of "*Geraldine*" falls foul of Luther and Calvin, and drowns the awful echoes of their tremendous protest by the sounds of her little half-crown trumpet: in like manner, by means of pretty sentimental tales, and cheap apologues, Mrs. Sand proclaims HER truth—that we need a new Messiah, and that the Christian religion is no more! O awful, awful name of God! Light unbearable! Mystery unfathomable! Vastness immeasurable! —Who are these who come

当今的辩论者可要比对开本书籍流行时代的前辈幸运多了。在对开本书籍流行的时代写一本书不仅要求作者具有很多的学识，还要占用很多的时间——写满一千张这样大的纸张需要付出大量的劳动和相当长的一段时间。在当今十二开本的时代，作者的写作方法也完全改变了，无论是男性还是女性作者所依靠的是他们的想象力，而不是他们的学识；他们是去编造一个故事而不是就一个话题展开争论，在一百五十页的篇幅中，作者（说教者用他自己的方式）就会向你证明些什么或驳斥些什么。但让我们羞愧的是，英国的新教徒已经树立了这种改变宗教信仰的榜样。——那些事实、谎言、虚伪的感情、虚伪的推理、糟糕的语法、真正的博爱和可恶的虔诚的混合物——我是指我们的宗教传单，无论是男是女都曾愚蠢地写过这些能卖一便士的东西，仿佛宗教教诲是世界上最容易的东西。我们已确立了这种作品的范例，而地球上其他的宗教无疑也会迅速地对其进行效仿。在虔诚的宗教传单中我可以给你指出一些亵渎神明的言辞，它们像我上面所提到的那些事物一样可怕，但是这里没有篇幅去讨论这个问题了，还是让我们回到乔治桑这个话题上来。就像舍伍德太太通过少男少女的动人故事和逸事来详细阐释她对于教会历史、教义问答手册、教会教义的看法一样，就像《仁慈的神甫，一个罗马天主教的故事》的作者通过许多圣徒和圣人的事迹，通过九便士十二开本的小册子把强大的罗马天主教组织搞得一团混乱一样，就像大卫用石子对付歌利亚（旧约中的非利士巨人——译注）一样；就像《杰拉尔丁》的罗马天主教作者同路德和加尔文相对抗，遭到他们吹喇叭抗议一样，乔治桑也是通过极为感伤的故事和简单的寓言来表明自己的想法——即我们需要一个新的救世主，基督教已经不适合我们了！哦，可怕的上帝的名字！无法忍受的灵光！深不可测的神秘！无边无际的广阔！——这些挺身而出解释玄义，闭着眼睛注视灵光的深度，测量无边无际的广阔的人是谁呢？哦，以前上帝的信徒不敢说出上帝的名字！哦，灵光，如果上帝的预言者看到了就会即刻死去！那现在信奉它的人是谁呢？——当然是女人，而且大部分是脆弱的女人——虽然理智薄弱，在

forward to explain the mystery, and gaze unblinking into the depths of the light, and measure the immeasurable vastness to a hair? O, name, that God's people of old did fear to utter! O, light, that God's prophet would have perished had he seen! Who are these that are now so familiar with it? —Women, truly; for the most part weak women—weak in intellect, weak mayhap in spelling and grammar, but marvellously strong in faith:—women, who step down to the people with stately step and voice of authority, and deliver their twopenny tablets, as if there were some Divine authority for the wretched nonsense recorded there!

With regard to the spelling and grammar, our Parisian Pythoness stands, in the goodly fellowship, remarkable. Her style is a noble, and, as far as a foreigner can judge, a strange tongue, beautifully rich and pure. She has a very exuberant imagination, and, with it, a very chaste style of expression. She never scarcely indulges in declamation, as other modern prophets do, and yet her sentences are exquisitely melodious and full. She seldom runs a thought to death (after the manner of some prophets, who, when they catch a little one, toy with it until they kill it), but she leaves you at the end of one of her brief, rich, melancholy sentences, with plenty of food for future cogitation. I can't express to you the charm of them; they seem to me like the sound of country bells—provoking I don't know what vein of musing and meditation, and falling sweetly and sadly on the ear.

This wonderful power of language must have been felt by most people who read Madame Sand's first books, "*Valentine*" and "*Indiana*": in "*Spiridion*" it is greater, I think, than ever; and for those who are not afraid of the matter of the novel, the manner will be found most delightful. The author's intention, I presume, is to describe, in a parable, her notions of the downfall of the Catholic church; and, indeed, of the whole Christian scheme: she places her hero in a monastery in Italy, where, among the characters about him, and the events which occur, the particular tenets of Madame Dudevant's doctrine are not inaptly laid down. Innocent, faithful, tender-hearted, a young monk, by name Angel, finds himself, when he has pronounced his vows, an object of aversion and hatred to the godly men whose lives he so much respects, and whose love he would make any sacrifice to win. After enduring much, he flings himself at the feet of his confessor, and begs for his sympathy and counsel; but the confessor spurns him away, and accuses him, fiercely, of some unknown and terrible crime—bids him never return to the

拼写和语法方面也很差劲，但她们在信仰上却是异常的坚定。这些女人迈着庄严的步伐，用权威的语调说着话走向人们身边，递给他们两便士的小册子，仿佛在那堆胡言乱语中有着某种神圣的东西！

在文字的拼写和语法方面，我们这位巴黎的女预言者在她同辈当中应是很杰出的。她的语言风格典雅，即使是一个外国人也能判断出来，她的语言很特别，句式多变且完美。她拥有丰富的想象力，语言表达方式也简洁朴实。像现代其他预言者所做的那样，她经常沉浸于慷慨激昂的演说中，但她的句子精致，音韵和谐。她很少有关于死亡的想法（仿照一些预言者的态度——当他们抓住一个小东西，会玩弄它直到把它杀死），但她在简洁、多变、伤感的句子背后却给读者留下了丰富的遐想空间。我无法用语言向你描述它们的优美，我感觉它们就像是乡村的钟声——让人忘却了沉思，只是听到耳边传来一阵悦耳悲伤的声音。

对于大多数读过乔治桑的《瓦朗蒂娜》和《印第安娜》的读者而言，他们一定能够从作品中感觉到她的语言的神奇力量。我认为《斯宾利地安》的语言要比前两部小说更加精彩。对于那些不厌烦小说的人来说，他们会发现这部作品的风格更讨人喜欢。我猜想，作者的意图是要在一个寓言中描述她对于天主教衰落的看法，实际上也是对整个基督教体制衰落的看法。她把主人公设置在一个意大利的修道院中，在那里，围绕着他周围的人物和所发生的事件，巧妙地传达了杜德望夫人（即乔治桑——译注）独特的教义学说。主人公是一个叫安琪儿的年轻修道士，他天真、诚实、心地善良，在发过誓言要忠实于上帝之后，却发现他自己深为尊敬的神甫们是厌恶和憎恨他的，而他愿意付出任何代价来赢得神甫们的关爱和好感。在忍耐了一段时间之后，他终于跪倒在他的忏悔神甫脚下，请求他的怜悯和忠告，但是忏悔神甫一脚把他踢开，严厉指责他所犯下的罪行，这些罪行都是安琪儿所不知道的，都是些可怕的罪行。——神甫命令他再也不要回来忏悔了，直到他的心灵真正悔悟，用诚挚的忏悔洗刷掉玷污他灵魂的污点为止。

confessional until contrition has touched his heart, and the stains which sully his spirit are, by sincere repentance, washed away.

"Thus speaking," says Angel, "Father Hegesippus tore away his robe, which I was holding in my supplicating hands. In a sort of wildness I still grasped it tighter; he pushed me fiercely from him, and I fell with my face towards the ground. He quitted me, closing violently after him the door of the sacristy, in which this scene had passed. I was left alone in the darkness. Either from the violence of my fall, or the excess of my grief, a vein had burst in my throat, and a haemorrhage ensued. I had not the force to rise; I felt my senses rapidly sinking, and, presently, I lay stretched on the pavement, unconscious, and bathed in my blood."

[Now the wonderful part of the story begins.]

"I know not how much time I passed in this way. As I came to myself I felt an agreeable coolness. It seemed as if some harmonious air was playing round about me, stirring gently in my hair, and drying the drops of perspiration on my brow. It seemed to approach, and then again to withdraw, breathing now softly and sweetly in the distance, and now returning, as if to give me strength and courage to rise.

"I would not, however, do so as yet; for I felt myself, as I lay, under the influence of a pleasure quite new to me; and listened, in a kind of peaceful aberration, to the gentle murmurs of the summer wind, as it breathed on me through the closed window-blinds above me. Then I fancied I heard a voice that spoke to me from the end of the sacristy: it whispered so low that I could not catch the words. I remained motionless, and gave it my whole attention. At last I heard, distinctly, the following sentence:—'Spirit of Truth, raise up these victims of ignorance and imposture.' 'Father Hegesippus,' said I, in a weak voice, 'is that you who are returning to me?' But no one answered. I lifted myself on my hands and knees, I listened again, but I heard nothing. I got up completely, and looked about me: I had fallen so near to the only door in this little room, that none, after the departure of the confessor, could have entered it without passing over me; besides, the door was shut, and only opened from the inside by a strong lock of the ancient shape. I touched it, and assured myself that it was closed. I was seized with terror, and, for some moments, did not dare to move. Leaning against the door, I looked round, and endeavoured to see into the gloom in which the angles of the room were enveloped. A pale light, which came from an upper window, half closed, was seen

“这样说着，”安琪儿说，“希格士乌神甫撕破了我哀求的双手抓住的长袍。我仍然疯狂地紧紧抓住它，他猛地把我推开，我就脸朝下摔倒在地板上。他离开我，在他身后砰地把圣器收藏室的门给关上了，这一幕就发生在圣器收藏室里。我独自一个人被遗弃在黑暗中。要么是我摔得太猛烈了，要么是我悲伤过度，我咽喉中的一条血管爆裂了，接着流出了鲜血。我没有力气站起来，呼吸也很快变得微弱起来，我伸展四肢躺在地上，浸在血泊中失去了任何意识。”

[现在故事的精彩部分开始了]

“我不知道自己这样过了多长时间。当我苏醒过来的时候，我感觉到有一股令人惬意的凉爽空气正向我吹来，仿佛是一些和谐的空气在我周围嬉戏，在我的头发上忙碌，它们吹干了我额头上的汗珠，好像是要走近我，但接着又离开了，一会儿是在远处柔和亲切地呼吸，一会儿又回到我的身边，仿佛是要给我站起来的力量和勇气。

“然而，我仍站不起来。当我躺着的时候，我感觉自己心旷神怡，异常平静地聆听夏风温柔的低语声，夏日的风是从上面关着的百叶窗缝隙中吹到我身上来的。然后，我想自己是听到了在圣器收藏室的一端有一个声音在对我说话。它的声音是如此微弱，以至于我听不清它在说些什么。我保持静默，全神贯注地倾听。终于我听清楚了下面的句子——‘真理之神，扶起这些无知受骗的受害者。’‘希格士乌神甫，’我用微弱的声音说，‘是你回到我身边了吗?’但是没有人回答。我用双手和膝盖支撑起自己，又听了一遍，但是什么也没听到。我完全站起来了，看看我的四周。我跌倒的地方离门口很近，这个小房间只有这一个门，在神甫离开后，没人会绕过我走进房间，而且，门是关着的，只能通过里边那把老式结实的锁才能把门打开。我摸了摸锁，确信它是锁着的。我的心有一阵被恐惧攫住了，我不敢移动。靠在门上，我环顾四周，尽力去看清这个包裹在黑暗中的房间的各个角落。一盏微弱的灯光从上面的一扇窗户中透射了进来，窗户是半掩着的，可以看到灯光在房子中间摇曳着。风吹打着百叶窗开开合合，把

to be trembling in the midst of the apartment. The wind beat the shutter to and fro, and enlarged or diminished the space through which the light issued. The objects which were in this half light—the praying-desk, surmounted by its skull—a few books lying on the benches—a surplice hanging against the wall—seemed to move with the shadow of the foliage that the air agitated behind the window. When I thought I was alone, I felt ashamed of my former timidity; I made the sign of the cross, and was about to move forward in order to open the shutter altogether, but a deep sigh came from the praying-desk, and kept me nailed to my place. And yet I saw the desk distinctly enough to be sure that no person was near it. Then I had an idea which gave me courage. Some person, I thought, is behind the shutter, and has been saying his prayers outside without thinking of me. But who would be so bold as to express such wishes and utter such a prayer as I had just heard?

"Curiosity, the only passion and amusement permitted in a cloister, now entirely possessed me, and I advanced towards the window. But I had not made a step when a black shadow, as it seemed to me, detaching itself from the praying-desk, traversed the room, directing itself towards the window, and passed swiftly by me. The movement was so rapid that I had not time to avoid what seemed a body advancing towards me, and my fright was so great that I thought I should faint a second time. But I felt nothing, and, as if the shadow had passed through me, I saw it suddenly disappear to my left.

"I rushed to the window, I pushed back the blind with precipitation, and looked round the sacristy: I was there, entirely alone. I looked into the garden—it was deserted, and the mid-day wind was wandering among the flowers. I took courage, I examined all thecorners of the room; I looked behind the praying-desk, which was very large, and I shook all the sacerdotal vestments which were hanging on the walls, everything was in its natural condition, and could give me no explanation of what had just occurred. The sight of all the blood I had lost led me to fancy that my brain had, probably, been weakened by the haemorrhage, and that I had been a prey to some delusion. I retired to my cell, and remained shut up there until the next day."

I don't know whether the reader has been as much struck with the above mysterious scene as the writer has; but the fancy of it strikes me as very fine; and the natural SUPERNATURALNESS is kept up in the best style. The shutter swaying to and fro, the fitful LIGHT APPEARING over the furniture of the room, and giving it an air of strange motion—the awful shadow which

灯光所照射的地方一会儿变大，一会儿变小。在这半明半暗的灯光中——有一张被头盖骨覆盖着的祈祷桌——长椅上平放着几本书——宽大的白色法衣挂在墙上——它们像是在和窗后摇动的树影一起移动。当我发现只有我一个人时，我不由得为我先前的胆怯而羞愧。我正打算走上前去把百叶窗全部打开，但是从祈祷桌那里传来一阵深深的叹息声，吓得我立即钉住不动了。但我十分清楚地看到祈祷桌旁边并没有人。我又鼓足勇气想，或许是窗户后面有个人在做祈祷，他没有注意到我。但是谁会表达那样的愿望，做我刚才听到的那样的祈祷呢？

"在修道院里唯一被允许的爱好和娱乐就是好奇，现在我的心也完全被好奇所占据了，我向前走到窗户旁边。但我还没迈出一步，就看到一个黑影离开了祈祷桌，它穿过房间，直奔窗户，迅速地从我身边闪过。这些动作太迅速了，以至于当这个身影向我奔来的时候，我都来不及躲避，我当时是如此恐惧以至于我以为自己会再次晕倒。但是我没有，当影子从我身边经过的时候，我看到它迅速地从我左侧消失了。

"我冲向窗户那里，猛地把百叶窗向后推开，看看圣器收藏室的周围，确实是我一个人在那里。我又向花园里面张望——那是一处荒废的花园，只有午间的风还在花丛中徘徊。我鼓起勇气，检查了房间里所有的角落，我还看了大大的祈祷桌的后面，我把所有挂在墙上的僧侣的法衣都摇了一遍，每件东西还都是原来的样子，它们不能向我解释刚才所发生的一切。看到地上我流出的血，我想，或许是我的大脑因流血而变得虚弱，刚才只不过是我的幻觉。我又回到我的小房间，把自己关在里面，直到第二天。"

我不知道上述神秘场景是否给读者也留下了深刻的印象，但它们确实是给我留下了很好的印象。作者在非常优美的文体中再现了超自然的神秘。来回摇动的百叶窗、照在房间家具上的忽明忽暗的灯光都给奇怪的动静提供了背景空间——可怕的阴影从那个胆怯的年轻见习修道士的身边经过——这一幕被很好地描绘了出来："我冲向窗户那里，猛地把百叶窗向后推开。圣器储藏室里并没有别人。我向花园里张望，那是一所废弃的花园，

passed through the body of the timid young novice—are surely very finely painted. "I rushed to the shutter, and flung it back: there was no one in the sacristy. I looked into the garden; it was deserted, and the mid-day wind was roaming among the flowers." The dreariness is wonderfully described: only the poor pale boy looking eagerly out from the window of the sacristy, and the hot mid-day wind walking in the solitary garden. How skilfully is each of these little strokes dashed in, and how well do all together combine to make a picture! But we must have a little more about Spiridion's wonderful visitant.

"As I entered into the garden, I stepped a little on one side, to make way for a person whom I saw before me. He was a young man of surprising beauty, and attired in a foreign costume. Although dressed in the large black robe which the superiors of our order wear, he had, underneath, a short jacket of fine cloth, fastened round the waist by a leathern belt, and a buckle of silver, after the manner of the old German students. Like them, he wore, instead of the sandals of our monks, short tight boots; and over the collar of his shirt, which fell on his shoulders, and was as white as snow, hung, in rich golden curls, the most beautiful hair I ever saw. He was tall, and his elegant posture seemed to reveal to me that he was in the habit of commanding. With much respect, and yet uncertain, I half saluted him. He did not return my salute; but he smiled on me with so benevolent an air, and at the same time, his eyes severe and blue, looked towards me with an expression of such compassionate tenderness, that his features have never since then passed away from my recollection. I stopped, hoping he would speak to me, and persuading myself, from the majesty of his aspect, that he had the power to protect me; but the monk, who was walking behind me, and who did not seem to remark him in the least, forced him brutally to step aside from the walk, and pushed me so rudely as almost to cause me to fall. Not wishing to engage in a quarrel with this coarse monk, I moved away; but, after having taken a few steps in the garden, I looked back, and saw the unknown still gazing on me with looks of the tenderest solicitude. The sun shone full upon him, and made his hair look radiant. He sighed, and lifted his fine eyes to heaven, as if to invoke its justice in my favour, and to call it to bear witness to my misery; he turned slowly towards the sanctuary, entered into the choir, and was lost, presently, in the shade. I longed to return, spite of the monk, to follow this noble stranger, and to tell him my afflictions; but who was he, that I imagined he would listen to them, and cause them to cease? I felt, even while his softness drew

只有午间的风还在花丛中徘徊。”阴郁的场景被精彩地描绘出来，只有一个可怜的苍白的男孩急切地从圣器储藏室的窗户处向外张望，夏日的热风在荒凉的花园里游荡。每一处描写都是那么的巧妙，而把所有的描写放在一起将会是一幅多么好的图画啊！但我们下面必须要多了解了解斯宾利地安的杰出贵宾了。

“当我走进花园的时候，我稍微向路边靠了靠，以给那个向我迎面走来的人让出道来。他是一个有着惊人美貌的年轻男子，一副外国人的装扮。尽管他外面穿着我们普通院长所穿的大大的黑色长袍，但是在长袍里面他穿着上等布料做的短上衣，腰上系着一条皮带，银制的皮扣，他是在仿效以前德国学生的样子，他没有穿我们修道士的便鞋，而是结实的短统靴，他衬衫的领子像雪一样白。他留着浓密卷曲的金发，那是我曾见过的最美丽的头发。他个子挺高，其优雅的姿势表明他是习惯于指挥别人的。我非常尊敬又有些局促地向他行了个礼。他没有回应，只是很慈善地朝我微笑，同时他的眼神严肃而忧郁，用一种怜悯和善的表情看着我，自此以后他的形象就留存在我的记忆之中。我停住脚步，希望他会和我说话，并说服自己相信像他这样尊贵的人会有能力来保护我的。但是一个走在我后面的修道士，他看起来好像是一点儿也没有注意到这个尊贵的人，蛮横地把他挤到道路的一侧，还非常粗鲁地推挤我，差点让我跌倒。我不想和这个粗俗的修道士吵架，因此就离开了。但是在花园里走了几步后，我向后一看，看到那个陌生人仍然用温和关心的表情注视着我。太阳照在他身上，他的头发闪闪发光。他叹息着，抬起头看着天空，仿佛是为了我而唤起它的正义，请求它目睹我的悲惨处境。他慢慢地转身走向教堂，加入唱诗班，他的身影很快就消失了。我渴望去报复那个修道士的恶意，渴望能跟随这个高贵的陌生人，把我的痛苦告诉他，我想象着他会听我的倾诉、不再让我受苦，但他是谁呢？甚至当他的温和仁慈把我的心拉向他时，我仍能感觉到他在我心中激起了一种恐惧，因为我在他的相貌中也看出了严厉的表情。”

me towards him, that he still inspired me with a kind of fear; for I saw in his physiognomy as much austerity as sweetness."

Who was he? —we shall see that. He was somebody very mysterious indeed; but our author has taken care, after the manner of her sex, to make a very pretty fellow of him, and to dress him in the most becoming costumes possible.

The individual in tight boots and a rolling collar, with the copious golden locks, and the solemn blue eyes, who had just gazed on Spiridion, and inspired him with such a feeling of tender awe, is a much more important personage than the reader might suppose at first sight. This beautiful, mysterious, dandy ghost, whose costume, with a true woman's coquetry, Madame Dudevant has so rejoiced to describe—is her religious type, a mystical representation of Faith struggling up towards Truth, through superstition, doubt, fear, reason,—in tight inexpressibles, with "a belt such as is worn by the old German students." You will pardon me for treating such an awful person as this somewhat lightly; but there is always, I think, such a dash of the ridiculous in the French sublime, that the critic should try and do justice to both, or he may fail in giving a fair account of either. This character of Hebronius, the type of Mrs. Sand's convictions—if convictions they may be called—or, at least, the allegory under which her doubts are represented, is, in parts, very finely drawn; contains many passages of truth, very deep and touching, by the side of others so entirely absurd and unreasonable, that the reader's feelings are continually swaying between admiration and something very like contempt—always in a kind of wonder at the strange mixture before him. But let us hear Madame Sand:—

"Peter Hebronius," says our author, "was not originally so named. His real name was Samuel. He was a Jew, and born in a little village in the neighbourhood of Innsprück. His family, which possessed a considerable fortune, left him, in his early youth, completely free to his own pursuits. From infancy he had shown that these were serious. He loved to be alone and passed his days, and sometimes his nights, wandering among the mountains and valleys in the neighbourhood of his birthplace. He would often sit by the brink of torrents, listening to the voice of their waters, and endeavouring to penetrate the meaning which Nature had hidden in those sounds. As he advanced in years, his inquiries became more curious and more grave. It was necessary that he should receive a solid education, and his parents sent him to study in the Ger-

他是谁呢？——我们等会儿就会知道。他的确是一个非常神秘的人。我们的作者仿效女人的样子创造了一个非常漂亮的男性人物，让他穿上了尽可能合适的服装。

穿着结实靴子和翻领服装的那个人有着浓密的金色卷发和严肃的蓝眼睛，他刚才还注视着斯宾利地安，激起了斯宾利地安内心中的敬畏和好感，这个人物比读者第一眼看到他的时候所猜想的还要重要。对于这个美丽、神秘、服装华丽的人物的装束，杜德望夫人是带着女人般的卖俏心情欢喜地进行描述的——这个人物是她的宗教形象代表，代表着一种神秘的信仰，而这个信仰正穿过迷信、怀疑、恐惧和理智向着真理奋斗前进——在紧身裤子上有“一条以前德国学生束的腰带”，请原谅我用这种轻率的态度来对待这样一个令人崇敬的人物。我认为，在法国式的严肃中经常存有这种可笑的炫耀，批评家应力图公平地对待这点，否则他不会对作品作出公正的评论。希伯纽斯这个人物是乔治桑定罪的人物代表——如果它们可以被称做定罪的话——或者，至少是她笔下的一个寓言性人物，围绕着这个人物有许多真实、深刻而动人的篇章，还有一些非常荒谬不合理的内容，以至于读者不断地在赞赏和类似轻蔑的态度中来回摇摆——总是对他面前这个奇怪的混合物感到好奇。让我们听听乔治桑是怎么说的：

“彼得·希伯纽斯不是他的原名。他的真名是塞缪尔。他是一个犹太人，出生在因斯普鲁克［德国地名。——译注］附近的一个小村庄。他的家庭拥有一份可观的财产，在他少年时期，父母就让他完全自由地追求自己的生活目标。从幼年起，他就显示出其性格严肃的一面。他喜欢独自一个人度过白天和夜晚，喜欢在他家乡附近的山谷中徘徊。他经常会坐在山涧激流的边缘聆听流水的声音，努力要参透在这声音中所隐藏的自然奥秘。长大一些的时候，他对自然的探究变得越来越好奇和认真。他父母看来很有必要让他接受一套完整的教育了，就把他送到德国的大学去学习。当时路德刚死去一百年，他的言论和名声仍存活在他信徒的内心。新的信仰正在巩固它所取得的地位。宗教改革者虽然还像刚开始时一样热情，但他们

man universities. Luther had been dead only a century, and his words and his memory still lived in the enthusiasm of his disciples. The new faith was strengthening the conquests it had made; the Reformers were as ardent as in the first days, but their ardour was more enlightened and more measured. Proselytism was still carried on with zeal, and new converts were made every day. In listening to the morality and to the dogmas which Lutheranism had taken from Catholicism, Samuel was filled with admiration. His bold and sincere spirit instantly compared the doctrines which were now submitted to him, with those in the belief of which he had been bred; and, enlightened by the comparison, was not slow to acknowledge the inferiority of Judaism. He said to himself, that a religion made for a single people, to the exclusion of all others,—which only offered a barbarous justice for rule of conduct,—which neither rendered the present intelligible nor satisfactory, and left the future uncertain,—could not be that of noble souls and lofty intellects; and that he could not be the God of truth who had dictated, in the midst of thunder, his vacillating will, and had called to the performance of his narrow wishes the slaves of a vulgar terror. Always conversant with himself, Samuel, who had spoken what he thought, now performed what he had spoken; and, a year after his arrival in Germany, solemnly abjured Judaism, and entered into the bosom of the Reformed Church. As he did not wish to do things by halves, and desired as much as was in him to put off the old man and lead a new life, he changed his name of Samuel to that of Peter. Some time passed, during which he strengthened and instructed himself in his new religion. Very soon he arrived at the point of searching for objections to refute, and adversaries to overthrow. Bold and enterprising, he went at once to the strongest, and Bossuet was the first Catholic author that he set himself to read. He commenced with a kind of disdain; believing that the faith which he had just embraced contained the pure truth. He despised all the attacks which could be made against it, and laughed already at the irresistible arguments which he was to find in the works of the Eagle of Meaux. But his mistrust and irony soon gave place to wonder first, and then to admiration: he thought that the cause pleaded by such an advocate must, at least, be respectable; and, by a natural transition, came to think that great geniuses would only devote themselves to that which was great. He then studied Catholicism with the same ardour and impartiality which he had bestowed on Lutheranism. He went into France to gain instruction from the professors of the Mother Church, as he

的热情已变得更加理智和有分寸了。宗教改革这一运动仍在狂热地进行，每天都会有人改变信仰。在谛听路德教从天主教中所吸取的道德训诫和教义时，塞缪尔的心中就充满了赞赏之情。这位大胆而真诚的塞缪尔立即把呈现在他面前的教义和他从小就被灌输的信仰做了一番比较，受到比较的启发，他很快就认识到犹太教是个劣等的宗教。他对自己说，只有利于一个人而排斥其他所有人的宗教——只能对人类行为的准则进行残暴的审判，它既不能使现在的一切得到理解，也不能让人满意，只能留下不确定的未来——这样的宗教塑造不出崇高的灵魂和有才智的人物，他不能在威吓中、在粗俗而恐怖的奴役下成为口述的真理之神，他踌躇满志地希望并呼吁实践他的真实愿望。深为了解自己的塞缪尔，以前总是说出他的想法，现在则开始实践他所说出的想法。在他到德国一年后，就庄严地发誓放弃犹太教，加入了新教。由于他不希望做事情半途而废，一定要摆脱以往的自己开始全新的生活，他就把塞缪尔的名字改成彼得。在过去的一段时间里，他在新的宗教信仰中不断提高和完善自己。很快，他就发展到了要驳斥异议、击败对手的程度。凭着自己的胆量和魄力，他立即找到了一个最强有力的对手即博须埃［Bossuet（1627—1704），法国天主教的护卫者，是最有声望的主教之一。——译注］，这是他获悉的第一位天主教作者。他开始是带着轻蔑读博须埃的书，相信他刚接受的信仰包含着正确的真理。对于新教的所有攻击他都持对抗和轻视的态度，在博须埃的作品中他对于自己要找的不可避免的争论早已持嘲笑的态度了。但是他的怀疑和冷嘲很快就被惊奇所代替，接着就是赞赏，他认为博须埃这样的一位辩护者所辩护的理由是值得尊敬的，在经历了自然的转变之后，他开始认为，那些伟大的天才只会把自己献给伟大的事业。后来，他就用以前研究路德教的热情和诚意来研究天主教。他去法国接受圣母院的神学教授的指导，就像他以前在德国从神学博士那里接受新教教义一样。他见到了阿尔诺·费纳隆那济安生的格列高理二世（公元4世纪的神学家、教父）、博须埃等人。这些大师的指导和德行让他更为赏识他们的才能，他很快就深入到天主教的教义

had from the Doctors of the reformed creed in Germany. He saw Arnauld Fénelon, that second Gregory of Nazianzen, and Bossuet himself. Guided by these masters, whose virtues made him appreciate their talents the more, he rapidly penetrated to the depth of the mysteries of the Catholic doctrine and morality. He found, in this religion, all that had for him constituted the grandeur and beauty of Protestantism,—the dogmas of the Unity and Eternity of God, which the two religions had borrowed from Judaism; and, what seemed the natural consequence of the last doctrine—a doctrine, however, to which the Jews had not arrived—the doctrine of the immortality of the soul; free will in this life; in the next, recompense for the good, and punishment for the evil. He found, more pure, perhaps, and more elevated in Catholicism than in Protestantism, that sublime morality which preaches equality to man, fraternity, love, charity, renouncement of self, devotion to your neighbour; Catholicism, in a word, seemed to possess that vast formula, and that vigourous unity, which Lutheranism wanted. The latter had, indeed, in its favour, the liberty of inquiry, which is also a want of the human mind; and had proclaimed the authority of individual reason: but it had so lost that which is the necessary basis and vital condition of all revealed religion—the principle of infallibility; because nothing can live except in virtue of the laws that presided at its birth; and, in consequence, one revelation cannot be continued and confirmed without another. Now, infallibility is nothing but revelation continued by God, or the Word, in the person of his vicars.

"At last, after much reflection, Hebronius acknowledged himself entirely and sincerely convinced, and received baptism from the hands of Bossuet. He added the name of *Spiridion* to that of Peter, to signify that he had been twice enlightened by the Spirit. Resolved thenceforward to consecrate his life to the worship of the new God who had called him to Him, and to the study of His doctrines, he passed into Italy, and, with the aid of a large fortune, which one of his uncles, a Catholic like himself, had left to him, he built this convent where we now are."

A friend of mine, who has just come from Italy, says that he has there left Messrs. Sp—r, P—l, and W. Dr—d, who were the lights of the great church in Newman Street, who were themselves apostles, and declared and believed that every word of nonsense which fell from their lips was a direct spiritual intervention. These gentlemen have become Puseyites already, and are, my friend states, in the high way to Catholicism. Madame Sand herself

和训诫学说的玄学内部。他在天主教中发现了构成新教的所有伟大和美妙之处——上帝的团结和永恒的教义，这两个宗教（天主教和新教）都是从犹太教那里借鉴来的，还有看起来是最终教义的自然结果——然而，犹太人没有达到这个教义的要求——灵魂不朽的教义；生命中的自由意志；好人得到报偿，恶人得到惩罚。他发现，天主教可能比新教要更正确、更高尚，它对人们宣扬的高尚美德有平等、博爱、仁慈、热爱你的邻人等。总而言之，天主教似乎是拥有更为广阔的宗教准则，还有路德教所缺乏的那种强有力的团结性。路德教受人欢迎的一点就在于它具有探究［新教的主要特点是专一信奉《圣经》，拒绝接受罗马教会添加的教义，并主张废除繁文缛节、崇尚个人信仰和思辨，抑制教会的规模和势力，建立严明的个人道德。——译注］的自由，但也缺乏人类的理智。在宣布了个人理智的权威之后，它却丢失了所有天启教（自然教之对）必备的基础和极其重要的条件——即确实可靠的法则。只有在刚开始就指挥一切的律法的效力中，一切才能正常运转。因此，单独一个启示是得不到延续和证实的。现在，确实可靠的就是上帝所延续的启示或他的代表作——《圣经》。

“最后，经过很多思索之后，希伯纽斯真诚而投入地信奉了天主教，接受了博须埃对他的洗礼。他在‘彼得’的前面又加上了斯宾利地安这个名字来象征他已经从圣灵那里受到了两次启发。从那时起，他就下定决心要把他的生命献给召唤他的神圣上帝和上帝教义的研究工作。他去了意大利，在那里，他有一个叔父也是个天主教徒，叔父留给他一大笔财产，在这笔财产的帮助下，他建造了我们身边的这个修道院。

我的一个朋友刚刚从意大利回来，说他在那里也遇到了像斯宾利地安那样的传道士，他们都是教会名人，也是宗教信仰的鼓吹者，他们宣称并相信自己说出的每个无意义的字都是神灵启示的结果。这些人已变成溥西派［19世纪英国强硬赞成倾向天主教的圣礼观的宗教派别。——译注］的成员了，我朋友声称，他们必然都会叛依天主教的。乔治桑本人也曾是个天主教徒，在著名的拉姆泰神甫［拉姆泰（1782—1854），法国神甫、作

was a Catholic sometime since: having been converted to that faith along with M. N—, of the Academy of Music; Mr. L—, the pianoforte player; and one or two other chosen individuals, by the famous Abbé de la M—. Abbé de la M— (so told me in the Diligence, a priest, who read his breviary and gossiped alternately very curiously and pleasantly) is himself an âme perdue: the man spoke of his brother clergyman with actual horror; and it certainly appears that the Abbé's works of conversion have not prospered; for Madame Sand, having brought her hero (and herself, as we may presume) to the point of Catholicism, proceeds directly to dispose of that as she has done of Judaism and Protestantism, and will not leave, of the whole fabric of Christianity, a single stone standing.

I think the fate of our English Newman Street apostles, and of M. de la M—, the mad priest, and his congregation of mad converts, should be a warning to such of us as are inclined to dabble in religious speculations; for, in them, as in all others, our flighty brains soon lose themselves, and we find our reason speedily lying prostrated at the mercy of our passions; and I think that Madame Sand's novel of Spiridion may do a vast deal of good, and bears a good moral with it; though not such an one, perhaps, as our fair philosopher intended. For anything he learned, Samuel-Peter-Spiridion-Hebronius might have remained a Jew from the beginning to the end. Wherefore be in such a hurry to set up new faiths? Wherefore, Madame Sand, try and be so preternaturally wise? Wherefore be so eager to jump out of one religion, for the purpose of jumping into another? See what good this philosophical friskiness has done you, and on what sort of ground you are come at last. You are so wonderfully sagacious, that you flounder in mud at every step; so amazingly clear-sighted, that your eyes cannot see an inch before you, having put out, with that extinguishing genius of yours, every one of the lights that are sufficient for the conduct of common men. And for what? Let our friend Spiridion speak for himself. After setting up his convent, and filling it with monks, who entertain an immense respect for his wealth and genius, Father Hebronius, unanimously elected prior, gives himself up to further studies, and leaves his monks to themselves. Industrious and sober as they were, originally, they grow quickly intemperate and idle; and Hebronius, who does not appear among his flock until he has freed himself of the Catholic religion, as he has of the Jewish and the Protestant, sees, with dismay, the evil condition of his disciples, and regrets, too late, the precipitancy by which he renounced, then

家，鼓吹天主教社会主义，被罗马教廷开除教籍。——译注］的影响下，她是和音乐学院的M.N.弗朗兹·李斯特［李斯特（Franz Liszt，1811—1886），著名的匈牙利作曲家、钢琴家、指挥家，伟大的浪漫主义大师。——译注］，以及由神甫本人挑选的一两个人一起叛依的。（一个好奇而愉快的一边读着每日祈祷书一边闲谈的牧师在马车里这样告诉我）拉姆奈神甫（神甫是对天主教教士的称呼。——译注）是一个疯狂的人，这个牧师说起他兄弟的时候用的是一种非常厌恶的口气。看来拉姆奈神甫还没有成功彻底地叛依宗教。而乔治桑则让她的主人公（我们可以想象是她自己）彻底叛依了天主教并让他直接去攻击犹太教和新教，不让基督教的整个大厦留下一块完整的瓦片。

我认为，我们英国的宗教鼓吹者和疯狂皈依宗教信仰的全体教徒的命运对我们这些想要去涉猎宗教思考的人来说是个警告。因为在他们身上，我们看到的是理智失去了控制而变得反复无常，任凭情感摆布。我认为乔治桑的小说《斯宾利地安》对人还是很有益的，作品中具有很好的道德精神，尽管它不可能是女哲学家的有意为之。不管塞缪尔一彼得一斯宾利地安—希伯纽斯信奉什么，他从头到尾始终都是个犹太人。为什么他要如此匆忙地创立一种新的信仰呢？为什么乔治桑要如此安排呢？为什么主人公要如此热切地从一个宗教转入另一个宗教呢？看看这种思维的活跃给他带来了什么好处以及他最后能得出什么结论。虽然他有着惊人的洞察力，但结果却是每走一步都要陷入泥泞中去；他有着锐利的目光，但结果却是眼睛一点儿也看不见前面的东西，即使是用尽了所有的精力。为什么呢？让我们的朋友斯宾利地安自己说吧！希伯纽斯神甫在建立了自己的修道院后，又在修道院里招满了修道士，这些修道士都非常崇敬他的地位和才能，一致推选他为院长，但他却沉迷于深入的宗教研究工作中去，听任他的修道士们自行其是。尽管那些修道士本来是勤奋和认真的，但没有了管制，他们很快就变得放纵和懒散了。如同放弃犹太教和新教一样，希伯纽斯又再一次放弃了天主教信仰。当他再次出现在全体教徒面前的时候，他沮丧地

and for ever, Christianity. "But, as he had no new religion to adopt in its place, and as, grown more prudent and calm, he did not wish to accuse himself unnecessarily, once more, of inconstancy and apostasy, he still maintained all the exterior forms of the worship which inwardly he had abjured. But it was not enough for him to have quitted error, it was necessary to discover truth. But Hebronius had well looked round to discover it; he could not find anything that resembled it. Then commenced for him a series of sufferings, unknown and terrible. Placed face to face with doubt, this sincere and religious spirit was frightened at its own solitude; and as it had no other desire nor aim on earth than truth, and nothing else here below interested it, he lived absorbed in his own sad contemplations, looked ceaselessly into the vague that surrounded him like an ocean without bounds, and seeing the horizon retreat and retreat as ever he wished to near it. Lost in this immense uncertainty, he felt as if attacked by vertigo, and his thoughts whirled within his brain. Then, fatigued with his vain toils and hopeless endeavours, he would sink down depressed, unmanned, life-wearied, only living in the sensation of that silent grief which he felt and could not comprehend."

It is a pity that this hapless Spiridion, so eager in his passage from one creed to another, and so loud in his profession of the truth, wherever he fancied that he had found it, had not waited a little, before he avowed himself either Catholic or Protestant, and implicated others in errors and follies which might, at least, have been confined to his own bosom, and there have lain comparatively harmless. In what a pretty state, for instance, will Messrs. Dr—d and P—l have left their Newman Street congregation, who are still plunged in their old superstitions, from which their spiritual pastors and masters have been set free! In what a state, too, do Mrs. Sand and her brother and sister philosophers, Templars, Saint Simonians, Fourierites, Lerouxites, or whatever the sect may be, leave the unfortunate people who have listened to their doctrines, and who have not the opportunity, or the fiery versatility of belief, which carries their teachers from one creed to another, leaving only exploded lies and useless recantations behind them! I wish the state would make a law that one individual should not be allowed to preach more than one doctrine in his life, or, at any rate, should be soundly corrected for every change of creed. How many charlatans would have been silenced,—how much conceit would have been kept within bounds,—how many fools, who are dazzled by fine sentences, and made drunk by declamation, would have remained, quiet

看到自己的信徒们已堕落到邪恶的状态，他后悔自己当时仓促而永远地放弃了基督教，但一切都为时已晚。“由于他没有新的宗教信仰可以选择，由于他变得越来越谨慎和平静，他不愿意去过多地谴责自己了，在又一次的叛教之后，他表面上仍对宗教保持着尊敬的态度，而在内心里已发誓要断绝了。对于他来说，仅完善自身是远远不够的，他还需要去发现真理。希伯纽斯开始努力地去四处寻求真理，但他没有发现类似真理的东西。接着他又经受了一系列未知的和可怕的苦难。在独自质疑的时候，这个诚恳和严谨的灵魂被自身的孤独给吓坏了，由于它在世界上除了真理之外没有别的欲望和目标，也没有别的兴趣和爱好，他只能全神贯注地陷入悲哀的沉思中去，不停地去探究他周围未知的一切，他就像是漂浮在没有边际的海上，在他要靠近地平线的时候，却看着地平线向后慢慢地退下去、退下去。迷失在这种无边的不确定状态中，他自己被弄得晕头转向。在被徒劳的辛苦和无望的努力弄得身心疲惫之后，他沮丧地消沉了下去，失去了男子汉的气概，对生命感到厌倦，只好生活在静穆而悲伤的感觉中，他能感觉到悲伤却无法领会其意义。”

这个不幸的斯宾利地安在他的一生中是如此热切地从一个信仰转向另一个信仰，如此执著地追求真理，无论他是在哪里认为自己找到了真理，他都会毫不犹豫地公开宣称自己是天主教徒或新教教徒，尽管其中可能包含着一些错误和愚笨的因素，但它们都被他兼收并蓄地收纳于自己心中，相比较而言，这些东西放在原处倒是无害的。举例来说，Dr-dand p-l 先生会让那些仍沉迷于自己旧有迷信中的纽曼街的全体教徒陷入一种怎样不妙的状态，而他们的精神牧师和导师已经从中获得了解脱！教堂的神甫们会让他们的全体教徒背弃原有的宗教信仰和灵魂牧师吗？乔治桑和她的哲学家群体如圣殿派、圣西门［圣西门（1760—1825），法国 19 世纪上半叶第一位空想社会主义者。——译注］、傅立叶［傅立叶（1772—1837），法国空想社会主义者。——译注］、勒鲁［勒鲁（1797—1871），法国记者、作家，鼓吹天主教社会主义。——译注］或无论什么派别的哲学家让那些聆

and sober, in that quiet and sober way of faith which their fathers held before them. However, the reader will be glad to learn that, after all his doubts and sorrows, Spiridion does discover the truth (THE truth, what a wise Spiridion!) and some discretion with it; for, having found among his monks, who are dissolute, superstitious—and all hate him—one only being, Fulgentius, who is loving, candid, and pious, he says to him, "If you were like myself, if the first want of your nature were, like mine, to know, I would, without hesitation, lay bare to you my entire thoughts. I would make you drink the cup of truth, which I myself have filled with so many tears, at the risk of intoxicating you with the draught. But it is not so, alas! you are made to love rather than to know, and your heart is stronger than your intellect. You are attached to Catholicism,—I believe so, at least,—by bonds of sentiment which you could not break without pain, and which, if you were to break, the truth which I could lay bare to you in return would not repay you for what you had sacrificed. Instead of exalting, it would crush you, very likely. It is a food too strong for ordinary men, and which, when it does not revivify, smothers. I will not, then, reveal to you this doctrine, which is the triumph of my life, and the consolation of my last days; because it might, perhaps, be for you only a cause of mourning and despair... Of all the works which my long studies have produced, there is one alone which I have not given to the flames; for it alone is complete. In that you will find me entire, and there LIES THE TRUTH. And, as the sage has said you must not bury your treasures in a well, I will not confide mine to the brutal stupidity of these monks. But as this volume should only pass into hands worthy to touch it, and be laid open for eyes that are capable of comprehending its mysteries, I shall exact from the reader one condition, which, at the same time, shall be a proof: I shall carry it with me to the tomb, in order that he who one day shall read it, may have courage enough to brave the vain terrors of the grave, in searching for it amid the dust of my sepulchre. As soon as I am dead, therefore, place this writing on my breast... Ah! when the time comes for reading it, I think my withered heart will spring up again, as the frozen grass at the return of the sun, and that, from the midst of its infinite transformations, my spirit will enter into immediate communication with thine!"

Does not the reader long to be at this precious manuscript, which contains THE TRUTH; and ought he not to be very much obliged to Mrs. Sand, for being so good as to print it for him? We leave all the story aside: how Ful-

听他们教义的不幸的人和没机会倾听的人都陷入了怎样的状态呢？他们本人在多种狂热的信仰中就摇摆不定，只会在他们身后留下被戳穿的谎言，最终宣告放弃信仰！我希望政府会制定一条法律，不允许一个人在他的一生中信奉一种以上的信仰，或者，无论如何，人们每次改变信仰都应该全面而彻底。这样会有多少骗子为此沉默——多少想法受到限制——多少被优美的句子所迷惑、雄辩的气势所陶醉的愚人会在他们的神甫面前保持住清醒和平静啊！但读者后来会得知，斯宾利地安在经历了所有的怀疑和悲伤之后，他终于发现了真理。（多么聪明的斯宾利地安啊！）在修道士中，除一人之外，其余的人都堕落、迷信并仇恨斯宾利地安，那唯一的人就是傅箴修，他仁爱、坦率并且虔诚，斯宾利地安就对他说："如果你像我本人一样活着的目的就是要去探究世界，我会毫不犹豫地把我全部的思想都袒露给你。我会冒着让你中毒的危险，让你饮真理之酒，酒杯里盛满了我那么多的眼泪。但现实不会是这样的。唉！你被创造出来是为了爱，而不是为了探究世界，你的情感要胜于你的理智。你附属于天主教——我相信——你不会轻易挣脱情感的束缚，如果你要挣脱的话，作为回报我向你所展示的真理也不能弥补你所牺牲的一切。它不会对你有所帮助，反而很有可能会压垮你。当它受到窒息、无法复活的时候，它对普通人来说就是难以消化的食物。因此，我不会向你泄露这个教义，这是我生命的胜利，是我在世界上最后时日的安慰。它对你来说或许只是个哀悼和绝望的理由……在我漫长的研究岁月所创作的全部作品中，只有一本我没有烧掉，因为只有它是圆满的。在这本书里，你会发现一个纯粹的我，还有其中所潜藏的真理。如同圣人说过的那样，你不能把财宝藏在一口井中，因此我不会把我的财宝交托给那些蛮横愚蠢的修道士。由于这本书要传到一个有资格接受它的人手中，要在一双能理解它玄义的眼睛面前打开，因此我要给读者提一个条件，同时，这也是一个考验。我要把这本书带到我的坟墓中，以便于那个人有一天会找到它，他需要有足够的胆量，不畏惧墓穴的恐怖，在我坟墓的尘土中找到它。因此，当我死了之后，把这部作品放在

gentius had not the spirit to read the manuscript, but left the secret to Alexis; how Alexis, a stern old philosophical unbelieving monk as ever was, tried in vain to lift up the gravestone, but was taken with fever, and obliged to forego the discovery; and how, finally, Angel, his disciple, a youth amiable and innocent as his name, was the destined person who brought the long-buried treasure to light. Trembling and delighted, the pair read this tremendous MANUSCRIPT OF SPIRIDION.

Will it be believed, that of all the dull, vague, windy documents that mortal ever set eyes on, this is the dullest? If this be absolute truth, *à quoi bon* search for it, since we have long, long had the jewel in our possession, or since, at least, it has been held up as such by every sham philosopher who has had a mind to pass off his wares on the public? Hear Spiridion:—

"How much have I wept, how much have I suffered, how much have I prayed, how much have I laboured, before I understood the cause and the aim of my passage on this earth! After many incertitudes, after much remorse, after many scruples, I HAVE COMPREHENDED THAT I WAS A MARTYR! —But why my martyrdom? said I; what crimne did I commit before I was born, thus to be condemned to labour and groaning, from the hour when I first saw the day up to that when I am about to enter into the night of the tomb?

"At last, by dint of imploring God—by dint of inquiry into the history of man, a ray of the truth has descended on my brow, and the shadows of the past have melted from before my eyes. I have lifted a corner of the curtain: I have seen enough to know that my life, like that of the rest of the human race, has been a series of necessary errors, yet, to speak more correctly, of incomplete truths, conducting, more or less slowly and directly, to absolute truth and ideal perfection. But when will they rise on the face of the earth—when will they issue from the bosom of the Divinity—those generations who shall salute the august countenance of Truth, and proclaim the reign of the ideal on earth? I see well how humanity marches, but I neither can see its cradle nor its apotheosis. Man seems to me a transitory race, between the beast and the angel; but I know not how many centuries have been required, that he might pass from the state of brute to the state of man, and I cannot tell how many ages are necessary that he may pass from the state of man to the state of angel!

"Yet I hope, and I feel within me, at the approach of death, that which

我的胸膛上……啊！当它重见天日的时候，我想，那时我枯萎的心脏也会再次跳动起来，就像冰冻的草地会在阳光的照射下再次复苏一样，等那个人打开这本书时，我的灵魂就开始直接与他的灵魂对话了。”

难道读者不渴望看到这份包含着真理的宝贵手稿吗？难道他不应该感激乔治桑女士如此好心地给他印出来吗？我们就把故事粗略地交代一下。傅箴修没有胆量去读这份手稿，但是他把这个秘密传给了艾勒克斯。艾勒克斯曾是一个严厉的哲学怀疑论者，一个老修道士，他试图抬起斯宾利地安坟墓的墓碑去寻找手稿，但他患了热病，还没发现手稿就去世了。最后是他的信徒安琪儿，人如其名的一个亲切而单纯的年轻人成了注定人选，他让这份久埋地下的手稿得以重见天日。他双手颤抖着高兴地阅读这份厚厚的斯宾利地安的手稿。

你相不相信，在凡人所看过的所有单调、含糊、空谈的文献中这份手稿是最乏味的呢？如果这是绝对的真理，那找到它又有什么用呢？难道就是为了让它被每个虚伪的哲学家当做珠宝一样展示吗？听听斯宾利地安是怎么说的——

“在我懂得我人生道路的事业和目标之前，我流过多少眼泪，遭受过多少苦难，做过多少祈祷，付出过多少辛劳啊！在经历了许多怀疑、懊悔和踌躇之后，我终于意识到自己是一个殉道者！——我问上帝，为什么要我殉道呢？在我出生之前，我犯了什么罪过，为什么让我从刚出生的那天起直到我就要步入坟墓的那一时刻都要接受辛劳和痛苦的惩罚呢？

“最后，由于哀求上帝和探究人类的历史进程，一线真理之光终于照射在我的额头上，我眼前过去的阴影被驱散了。我揭开了人生舞台上幕布的一角。我充分地了解到，我的生活就像其他人的生活一样，是由一系列不可避免的罪过构成的，说得更准确些，是不完善的人生在或多或少慢慢地、执著地向着绝对的真理和理想的圆满前进。但圆满的真理何时才会在地球上出现——何时才会从上帝那里传授给我们——那些世世代代的人会迎接尊严的真理出现，期盼理想国度的降临吗？我深知人类是怎样前进发展的，

warns me that great destinies await humanity. In this life all is over for me. Much have I striven, to advance but little: I have laboured without ceasing, and have done almost nothing. Yet, after pains immeasurable, I die content, for I know that I have done all I could, and am sure that the little I have done will not be lost.

"What, then, have I done? this wilt thou demand of me, man of a future age, who will seek for truth in the testaments of the past. Thou who wilt be no more Catholic—no more Christian, thou wilt ask of the poor monk, lying in the dust, an account of his life and death. Thou wouldst know wherefore were his vows, why his austerities, his labours, his retreat, his prayers?

"You who turn back to me, in order that I may guide you on your road, and that you may arrive more quickly at the goal which it has not been my lot to attain, pause, yet, for a moment, and look upon the past history of humanity. You will see that its fate has been ever to choose between the least of two evils, and ever to commit great faults in order to avoid others still greater. You will see... on one side, the heathen mythology, that debased the spirit, in its efforts to deify the flesh; on the other, the austere Christian principle, that debased the flesh too much, in order to raise the worship of the spirit. You will see, afterwards, how the religion of Christ embodies itself in a church, and raises itself a generous democratic power against the tyranny of princes. Later still, you will see how that power has attained its end, and passed beyond it. You will see it, having chained and conquered princes, league itself with them, in order to oppress the people, and seize on temporal power. Schism, then, raises up against it the standard of revolt, and preaches the bold and legitimate principle of liberty of conscience: but, also, you will see how this liberty of conscience brings religious anarchy in its train; or, worse still, religious indifference and disgust. And if your soul, shattered in the tempestuous changes which you behold humanity undergoing, would strike out for itself a passage through the rocks, amidst which, like a frail bark, lies tossing trembling truth, you will be embarrassed to choose between the new philosophers—who, in preaching tolerance, destroy religious and social unity—and the last Christians, who, to preserve society, that is, religion and philosophy, are obliged to brave the principle of toleration. Man of truth! to whom I address, at once, my instruction and my justification, at the time when you shall live, the science of truth no doubt will have advanced a step. Think, then, of all your fathers have suffered, as, bending beneath the weight of

但我既看不到它的原始起源状态，也看不到它将来的神化状态。对我来说，人就是介于野兽和天使之间的转瞬即逝的种族。我不知道需要多少个世纪，这个种族才能从野蛮的状态前进到人类的状态；我也不知道需要多少年，人才能从人类的状态前进到天使的状态！

“然而我希望，在接近死亡的时候我能感知到死神对我的告诫，即伟大的命运女神在等候着人类。在我就要结束的全部生活中，我奋斗了很多，却几乎没有取得什么进步。我从未停止过劳作，但几乎什么也没有做成。然而，在无边无际的痛苦之后，我满意地死去，因为我知道我已尽我所能，确信我所做的微不足道的事情不会随着我的死亡而消逝。

“那么，我做过什么呢？这将会是未来的你，在过去的经书中寻找真理的你要问我的问题。你将不再是天主教徒——也不是基督教徒，你会要求这个躺在灰尘中的可怜的修道士来叙述自己的一生。你将会知道他为什么会有誓约，会苦行、静修和祈祷？

“跟我来，我可以在你的人生道路上引导你，让你较快地达到目标，这些都是我生前没有机会来实现的。但是让我们暂停一会儿，来看看人类以往的历史，你就会明白人类曾在两种邪恶的命运缝隙之间做出选择，一方面在避免过失，一方面又犯下严重的过失。你会看到……异教徒的信仰是贬低精神，努力把肉体神圣化的；基督教教义则是极力贬低肉体，来提升对精神的崇拜。接着，你会看到，基督教是怎样在教堂中使自己的教义得到普及，把自己提升到一个神圣的民主权威的高度来对抗君主专制。再往后，你会看到基督教的政权是怎样达到了自己的目的并逾越了它的权限范围。你还会看到，基督教已经控制并征服了君主，同他们相结盟以压制人民，掌握世俗的权力。接着，教会分立，人们又提出了反叛的主张，宣扬大胆而合法的道德自由的原则，但是，你也会看到这种道德的自由是怎样给社会秩序带来了混乱，更坏的是，它导致了人们对宗教的淡漠和厌恶情绪。如果你的灵魂被人类所经历的这场剧烈变化给弄垮了，它会为自己寻找一条道路来度过灾难，在这场灾难中，真理潜藏了起来，要在新哲学家

their ignorance and uncertainty, they have traversed the desert across which, with so much pain, they have conducted thee! And if the pride of thy young learning shall make thee contemplate the petty strifes in which our life has been consumed, pause and tremble, as you think of that which is still unknown to yourself, and of the judgment that your descendants will pass on you. Think of this, and learn to respect all those who, seeking their way in all sincerity, have wandered from the path, frightened by the storm, and sorely tried by the severe hand of the All-Powerful. Think of this, and prostrate yourself; for all these, even the most mistaken among them, are saints and martyrs.

"Without their conquests and their defeats, thou wert in darkness still. Yes, their failures, their errors even, have a right to your respect; for man is weak . . . Weep then, for us obscure travellers—unknown victims, who, by our mortal sufferings and unheard-of labours, have prepared the way before you. Pity me, who have passionately loved justice, and perseveringly sought for truth, only opened my eyes to shut them again for ever, and saw that I had been in vain endeavouring to support a ruin, to take refuge in a vault of which the foundations were worn away."...

The rest of the book of *Spiridion* is made up of a history of the rise, progress, and (what our philosopher is pleased to call) decay of Christianity—of an assertion, that the "doctrine of Christ is incomplete;" that "Christ may, nevertheless, take his place in the Pantheon of divine men!" and of a long, disgusting, absurd, and impious vision, in which the Saviour, Moses, David, and Elijah are represented, and in which Christ is made to say—"WE ARE ALL MESSIAHS, when we wish to bring the reign of truth upon earth; we are all Christs, when we suffer for it!"

And this is the ultimatum, the supreme secret, the absolute truth! and it has been published by Mrs. Sand, for so many napoleons per sheet, in the Revue des *Deux Mondes*: and *the Deux Mondes* are to abide by it for the future. After having attained it, are we a whit wiser? "Man is between an angel and a beast: I don't know how long it is since he was a brute—I can't say how long it will be before he is an angel." Think of people living by their wits, and living by such a wit as this! Think of the state of mental debauch and disease which must have been passed through, ere such words could be written, and could be popular!

When a man leaves our dismal, smoky London atmosphere, and

和新基督徒的身份中做出抉择会让你感到很为难。新哲学家宣扬信仰自由，但这种信仰自由破坏了宗教和社会的统一性；新基督徒要保护社会与宗教的统一性，因此他们不得不去挑战信仰自由的原则。相信真理的人啊！我要向你传授我的教诲。在你所生活的未来时代，科学无疑会前进一大步。但是想想你的祖先在屈从于无知和未知力量的统治下所遭受的苦难，他们痛苦地穿越沙漠，引导着人类！具有学识的年轻人应该反思一下我们在生活中所消耗、踌躇和担忧的微不足道的竞争，你要想想那些对我们来说仍然未知的事物和将来后代对你们的评价。要学着去尊敬那些真诚寻找人生道路的人，他们迷了路，受到暴风雨的惊吓，痛苦地承受所有世俗力量的严峻考验。想想这些，让自己拜倒在他们脚下吧！因为所有这些人（他们当中即使犯有重大错误的人）都是圣人和殉道者。

“没有他们的胜利和失败，你仍然会生活在黑暗中。他们的失败甚至他们的错误都值得你去尊敬，因为人是脆弱的……为我们无名的跋涉者、未知的牺牲者哭泣吧！他们通过承受凡人致命的苦难和闻所未闻的辛劳已为你们铺平了道路。怜悯我吧！我曾强烈地热爱正义、不屈不挠地寻求真理，但我所做的一切都是徒劳和逃避，我一直是徒劳地去支撑一个已倒毁的东西，在一个地基已经动摇的地下室里避难。”……

《斯宾利地安》这本书的其余部分是由基督教兴起、发展和衰退（我们的哲学家宣称的）的历史所构成的——另外还有一个断言，即“基督的教义是不完善的”、“但基督或许可以取代先贤祠中的圣人们的位置”，还有很长篇幅的，令人厌恶、荒谬、虚伪的幻想，在作者的幻想中，救世主、摩西、大卫和以利亚都是救世主的代表，作者让耶稣基督发言——“当我们希望能给地球上带来真理的统治时，我们都是救世主；当我们为此而遭受苦难的时候，我们都是基督！”

这是最终的结论、最重要的秘密、最绝对的真理！这部手稿被乔治桑女士以每张几个金币的价格印在《两世界评论》杂志中，《两世界评论》要带着这部手稿走向未来了。但是在得到这部手稿之后，我们有没有变得更

breathes, instead of coal-smoke and yellow fog, this bright, clear, French air, he is quite intoxicated by it at first, and feels a glow in his blood, and a joy in his spirits, which scarcely thrice a year, and then only at a distance from London, he can attain in England. Is the intoxication, I wonder, permanent among the natives? And may we not account for the ten thousand frantic freaks of these people by the peculiar influence of French air and sun? The philosophers are from night to morning drunk, the politicians are drunk, the literary men reel and stagger from one absurdity to another, and how shall we understand their vagaries? Let us suppose, charitably, that Madame Sand had inhaled a more than ordinary quantity of this laughing gas when she wrote for us this precious manuscript of *Spiridion.* That great destinies are in prospect for the human race we may fancy, without her ladyship's word for it: but more liberal than she, and having a little retrospective charity, as well as that easy prospective benevolence which Mrs. Sand adopts, let us try and think there is some hope for our fathers (who were nearer brutality than ourselves, according to the Sandean creed), or else there is a very poor chance for us, who, great philosophers as we are, are yet, alas! far removed from that angelic consummation which all must wish for so devoutly. She cannot say—is it not extraordinary? —how many centuries have been necessary before man could pass from the brutal state to his present condition, or how many ages will be required ere we may pass from the state of man to the state of angels? What the deuce is the use of chronology or philosophy? We were beasts, and we can't tell when our tails dropped off: we shall be angels; but when our wings are to begin to sprout, who knows? In the meantime, O, man of genius, follow our counsel: lead an easy life, don't stick at trifles; never mind about DUTY, it is only made for slaves; if the world reproach you, reproach the world in return, you have a good loud tongue in your head: if your strait-laced morals injure your mental respiration, fling off the old-fashioned stays, and leave your free limbs to rise and fall as Nature pleases; and when you have grown pretty sick of your liberty, and yet unfit to return to restraint, curse the world, and scorn it, and be miserable, like my Lord Byron and other philosophers of his kidney; or else mount a step higher, and, with conceit still more monstrous, and mental vision still more wretchedly debauched and weak, begin suddenly to find yourself afflicted with a maudlin compassion for the human race, and a desire to set them right after your own fashion. There is the quarrelsome stage of drunkenness, when a man can as yet walk and

聪明一些呢？“人介于天使和野兽之间。我不知道他作为野兽要持续多少时间——我也说不出他还需要多少时间才能变成天使。”人们难道就是靠这样的智慧生存的！想想人类必然要经历的精神上的堕落和不健全的状态，这就是他所写的、受人们喜爱的句子！

当人们远离伦敦阴沉、烟雾弥漫的空气，不再吸入煤烟和黄雾而是明亮清新的法国空气时，他一定会被这种空气给陶醉了，感觉到精神焕发。在伦敦，一年之中很少能呼吸到这样清新的空气，只有离开伦敦一段距离，才能享受得到。我想知道，法国本地人会长久地陶醉于这种空气中吗？可不可以说，是因为受法国空气和阳光的特别影响，才有了这些人的怪诞行为呢？哲学家从早到晚都是醉醺醺的；政治家也醉了；文人兴奋地蹒跚摇晃着从一种谬论转向另一种谬论。我们应该怎样去了解他们的古怪行为呢？我们可以猜想，当乔治桑给我们写这篇宝贵的《斯宾利地安》的手稿时，她已经吸入了过量的这种可笑的气体。命运女神对于人类的期待我们可以想象得到，不需要乔治桑女士把它写出来。但她又慈善地回顾了人类的历史，对人类做了善意的展望，让我们试着去想象，我们的祖先还是有希望升入天堂的（虽然根据乔治桑的信条，他们比现在的我们还要残忍），否则我们就没有什么机会了，即使我们是伟大的哲学家。然而，唉！我们离人们所期望的天使般的完美状态还有很大的距离。乔治桑说不出还需多长时间——难道这不奇怪吗？——在这之前，人类从野蛮状态过渡到目前的状态需要多少个世纪呢？年表或哲学的用处到底是什么呢？我们是野兽，我们不知何时我们的尾巴才会进化掉？我们将会是天使，但是何时我们才会长出翅膀呢？哦，天才人物还是听从我们的劝告吧！过轻松的生活，不为琐事而纷争；不必介意有关责任的事，它只是为奴隶而设的；如果世人责备你，作为回报，你也要责备世人，只要你具备很好的口才。如果你的极端严谨的道德观念损害了你的精神自由，那就甩掉老式的做派，让你的身体顺其自然地自由发展；当你已经变得对自由极为厌倦，但又不适合再回到以前束缚的状态，那就像拜伦勋爵或他那种性格的哲学家一样去诅咒世

speak, when he can call names, and fling plates and wine-glasses at his neighbour's head with a pretty good aim; after this comes the pathetic stage, when the patient becomes wondrous philanthropic, and weeps wildly, as he lies in the gutter, and fancies he is at home in bed—where he ought to be; but this is an allegory.

I don't wish to carry this any farther, or to say a word in defence of the doctrine which Mrs. Dudevant has found "incomplete";—here, at least, is not the place for discussing its merits, any more than Mrs. Sand's book was the place for exposing, forsooth, its errors: our business is only with the day and the new novels, and the clever or silly people who write them. Oh! if they but knew their places, and would keep to them, and drop their absurd philosophical jargon! Not all the big words in the world can make Mrs. Sand talk like a philosopher: when will she go back to her old trade, of which she was the very ablest practitioner in France?

I should have been glad to give some extracts from the dramatic and descriptive parts of the novel, that cannot, in point of style and beauty, be praised too highly. One must suffice,—it is the descent of Alexis to seek that unlucky manuscript, *Spiridion.*

"It seemed to me," he begins, "that the descent was eternal; and that I was burying myself in the depths of Erebus: at last, I reached a level place,—and I heard a mournful voice deliver these words, as it were, to the secret centre of the earth—'He will mount that ascent no more!'—Immediately I heard arise towards me, from the depth of invisible abysses, a myriad of formidable voices united in a strange chant—'Let us destroy him! Let him be destroyed! What does he here among the dead? Let him be delivered back to torture! Let him be given again to life!'""Then a feeble light began to pierce the darkness, and I perceived that I stood on the lowest step of a staircase, vast as the foot of a mountain. Behind me were thousands of steps of lurid iron; before me, nothing but a void—an abyss, and ether; the blue gloom of midnight beneath my feet, as above my head. I became delirious, and quitting that staircase, which methought it was impossible for me to reascend, I sprung forth into the void with an execration. But, immediately, when I had uttered the curse, the void began to be filled with forms and colours, and I presently perceived that I was in a vast gallery, along which I advanced, trembling. There was still darkness round me; but the hollows of the vaults gleamed with a red light, and showed me the strange and hideous forms of

人、蔑视他们。你将会发现那些更高层次的人虽然很自负，但精神境界也很低俗，看到这些，你会禁不住为整个人类而忧虑，渴望以你个人的方式把他们改造过来。这就到了喝醉酒好闹事的阶段，这时候人还能正常行走说话，能称呼别人的姓名，把盘子和酒杯准确地扔向邻人的头部；然后就到了悲哀的阶段，醉酒的人开始良心发现，大声哭泣，当他躺在街沟里的时候还以为是躺在家里的床上呢。但这是个比喻。

我不想再进一步探讨这个话题或为杜德望夫人已发现的“不完善”的教义说一句辩护的话。——这里不是讨论教义价值的地方，但在乔治桑的书里确实是暴露了教义的缺陷。我们的事情只是关心时事和新的小说，关心是聪明或愚蠢的人写的小说。哦！如果他们知道自己的地位，想要保住地位，那就放弃他们抽象的哲学术语吧！并不是世界上所有的大话都能让乔治桑像一个哲学家似的大发议论。她何时会回到以前写小说的老本行中去呢？在写小说方面，她可是法国的一个很有才华的作家。

我很高兴能从这本小说中抽取一些戏剧性和描述性的段落，虽然它们的文体和语言并不是非常的优美。这一段是艾勒克斯进入坟墓里去寻找《斯宾利地安》那本手稿的段落。

他是这样开始的，“在我看来，坟墓里的路好像没有尽头一样。我穿过阳世与阴世之间的黑暗区域。最后我到了一个平地上——我听到有一个悲痛的嗓音把下面这几句话传到了地球隐秘的中心——‘他不再爬那个斜坡了！’——很快，我听到有一个声音从看不见的深渊深处向我传来，它与许多可怕的声音掺合在一起，组成了一首奇怪的歌——‘让我们消灭他！让我们毁掉他！他在死人这里做什么？把他送回阳世去接受折磨！再次给予他生命！’”

“然后有一道微弱的光线穿透了周围的黑暗，我发觉自己站在一个梯子的最低一级上，梯子像一个山脚那么大，在我身后是几千级火红的铁梯。我的面前则空空荡荡——只有脚下的深渊和头顶的苍天，在我的脚下是午夜阴郁的一团黑暗，它和我头上的色彩是一样的。我变得神志昏迷，离开

their building . . . I did not distinguish the nearest objects; but those towards which I advanced assumed an appearance more and more ominous, and my terror increased with every step I took. The enormous pillars which supported the vault, and the tracery thereof itself, were figures of men, of supernatural stature, delivered to tortures without a name. Some hung by their feet, and, locked in the coils of monstrous serpents, clenched their teeth in the marble of the pavement; others, fastened by their waists, were dragged upwards, these by their feet, those by their heads, towards capitals, where other figures stooped towards them, eager to torment them. Other pillars, again, represented a struggling mass of figures devouring one another; each of which only offered a trunk severed to the knees or to the shoulders, the fierce heads whereof retained life enough to seize and devour that which was near them. There were some who, half hanging down, agonized themselves by attempting, with their upper limbs, to flay the lower moiety of their bodies, which drooped from the columns, or were attached to the pedestals; and others, who, in their fight with each other, were dragged along by morsels of flesh,—grasping which, they clung to each other with a countenance of unspeakable hate and agony. Along, or rather in place of, the frieze, there were on either side a range of unclean beings, wearing the human form, but of a loathsome ugliness, busied in tearing human corpses to pieces—in feasting upon their limbs and entrails. From the vault, instead of bosses and pendants, hung the crushed and wounded forms of children; as if to escape these eaters of man's flesh, they would throw themselves downwards, and be dashed to pieces on the pavement. . . The silence and motionlessness of the whole added to its awfulness. I became so faint with terror, that I stopped, and would fain have returned. But at that moment I heard, from the depths of the gloom through which I had passed, confused noises, like those of a multitude on its march. And the sounds soon became more distinct, and the clamour fiercer, and the steps came hurrying on tumultuously—at every new burst nearer, more violent, more threatening. I thought that I was pursued by this disorderly crowd; and I strove to advance, hurrying into the midst of those dismal sculptures. Then it seemed as if those figures began to heave,—and to sweat blood,—and their beady eyes to move in their sockets. At once I beheld that they were all looking upon me, that they were all leaning towards me,—some with frightful derision, others with furious aversion. Every arm was raised against me, and they made as though they would crush me with the quivering

了那个梯子，我想我不可能再爬上那个梯子了，我诅咒着向前走进那片空洞之中。但是在我诅咒完之后，那个空荡的空间立刻就充满了形状和色彩，我即刻发觉到自己是在一个巨大的花园里，我浑身颤抖，沿着花园向前走。我身边仍是一团黑暗，但是在地下室的洞穴里闪烁着一道红光，这道红光向我展现了里面建筑物的奇怪而丑陋的样式……我连最近的物体也分辨不出，但是在我向前走的时候，面前所呈现的东西越来越有种不祥的预感，我每走一步，恐惧就增加一分。支撑着地下室的巨大柱子和它的窗花格都是人形的，他们都具有不可思议的高度，正要被送去接受无名的拷打。有些人是被吊着脚挂了起来，身上紧紧缠着蟒蛇，这些蟒蛇在大理石铺就的路面上咬紧了牙齿；另一些人是被缠住腰部在向上拖动；一些人是脚朝向柱顶；另一些人是头朝向柱顶；其余的人朝他们弯着腰，急于要折磨他们。一些柱子还显示了一群挣扎着的人在吞吃其他的人。每个人都被切断了膝盖或肩膀，但他们凶猛的头部还保持着足够的生命力来抓食旁边的人；还有一些掉着一半身子的人，努力用他们的上肢去剥他们下半身的皮，而他们的下半身或是从柱子上垂下来，或是被缚在柱脚上；其他互相打斗的人则带着一种说不出的憎恨和痛苦的表情互相缠绕着抓住对方。再向前，就是柱子的中楣那个地方，两侧都有一排模糊的东西扮成了人的外形，但是非常丑陋，它们在忙着把人的尸体撕成碎片——津津有味地吃着尸体的上肢和内脏。离开地下室，就不是凸饰和垂饰了，而是吊着一些被压碎或受伤的孩子外形的东西，他们仿佛是要逃避这些吃尸体的怪物，他们向下跳，结果撞在地面上成了碎块……整个场景的沉默和肃静更增加了它的恐怖气氛。我吓得就要晕倒了，我停下来，想回去。这时我听到从我经过的黑暗深处传来了混杂的噪音，就像许多人在行进。声音很快就变得更加清晰起来，吵闹声也变得更加强烈了，脚步声越来越急了——越近一步，就越强烈，越具有威胁性。我认为自己是被这些混乱的人群所追赶，我努力向前走，赶紧窜入那些忧郁的雕塑群中。接着，那些雕像看起来仿佛是肿胀了起来，流出了血——它们小而亮的眼睛随着它们的底座一起移动。我看到

limbs they had torn one from the other."...

It is, indeed, a pity that the poor fellow gave himself the trouble to go down into damp, unwholesome graves, for the purpose of fetching up a few trumpery sheets of manuscript; and if the public has been rather tired with their contents, and is disposed to ask why Mrs. Sand's religious or irreligious notions are to be brought forward to people who are quite satisfied with their own, we can only say that this lady is the representative of a vast class of her countrymen, whom the wits and philosophers of the eighteenth century have brought to this condition. The leaves of the Diderot and Rousseau tree have produced this goodly fruit: here it is, ripe, bursting, and ready to fall;—and how to fall? Heaven send that it may drop easily, for all can see that the time is come.

它们都在注视着我，都在向我倾斜——有的带着可怕的嘲笑，有的带着强烈的厌恶，每只手臂都朝我举起，它们的姿势仿佛是要用它们颤抖的四肢把我挤碎。”

的确很可怜，这个可怜的家伙为了拿出手稿那些无用的纸张，就进入了潮湿阴暗的墓穴。如果民众已经厌倦了作品内容，他们就想问问乔治桑女士为什么要给那些很满意自身生活的人提出宗教和无宗教信仰的观念，我们只能说，这位女士是很大一部分法国国民的代表，18 世纪的理性和哲学家造就了这种状况。狄德罗的叶子和卢梭的树已经培育出了这样的果实。它就在这里，成熟了、胀破了皮，就要落地了。——怎样落地呢？是上帝让它轻松地落地，因为所有人都能看出它到了落地的时间了。

The Case of Peytel

In a Letter to Edward Briefless, Esquire, of Pump Court, Temple

Paris, November, 1839.

MY DEAR BRIEFLESS,—Two months since, when the act of accusation first appeared, containing the sum of the charges against Sebastian Peytel, all Paris was in a fevour on the subject. The man's trial speedily followed, and kept for three days the public interest wound up to a painful point. He was found guilty of double murder at the beginning of September; and, since that time, what with Maroto's disaffection and Turkish news, we have had leisure to forget Monsieur Peytel, and to occupy ourselves with τι νέον. Perhaps Monsieur de Balzac helped to smother what little sparks of interest might still have remained for the murderous notary. Balzac put forward a letter in his favour, so very long, so very dull, so very pompous, promising so much, and performing so little, that the Parisian public gave up Peytel and his casc altogether; nor was it until to day that some small feeling was raised concerning him, when the newspapers brought the account how Peytel's head had been cut off at Bourg.

He had gone through the usual miserable ceremonies and delays which attend what is called, in this country, the march of justice. He had made his appeal to the Court of Cassation, which had taken time to consider the verdict of the Provincial Court, and had confirmed it. He had made his appeal for mercy; his poor sister coming up all the way from Bourg (a sad journey, poor thing!) to have an interview with the King, who had refused to see her. Last Monday morning, at nine o'clock, an hour before Peytel's breakfast, the Greffier of Assize Court, in company with the Curé of Bourg, waited on him, and informed him that he had only three hours to live. At twelve o'clock,

柏伊特尔案件

——给无人委聘的爱德华律师的一封信

巴黎，1839 年 11 月

亲爱的爱德华律师，两个月前，当法庭刚刚起诉塞巴斯蒂安·柏伊特尔时，整个巴黎都对这个案子寄予了热切的关注。法庭对柏伊特尔的审判很快就开始了，而公众的兴趣也持续了三天。柏伊特尔在 9 月初被判定是犯有两起谋杀罪。从那时起马洛托的不忠和土耳其的新闻转移了我们的兴趣，我们就把柏伊特尔的案子给抛在了一边。或许巴尔扎克［法国小说家。——译注］也帮人们把心中所存留的对于柏伊特尔的一点点兴趣给掩盖住了。巴尔扎克写了一封为柏伊特尔辩护的信，信是那么的冗长、单调和浮夸，允诺了那么多，而实际做的那么少，以至于让巴黎的公众完全忘记了柏伊特尔和他的案子。直到今天，当报纸上报道了柏伊特尔在市镇断头台被处以死刑的消息时，它也没有引起人们的特别关注。

柏伊特尔在正常的法律程序安排下经历了法国司法拖沓进展的过程。他曾向最高上诉法院上诉，最高上诉法院在从容地考虑了省级法院的判决后批准其判决。他也曾呼吁法庭对其进行宽恕；他可怜的姐姐从市镇一路走来（可怜的人，悲伤的旅程），要见国王，但是国王拒绝接见她。上个星期一早晨的九点钟，即柏伊特尔早餐前的一个小时，在教区牧师陪伴下的立法法院公证人就已等候柏伊特尔了，他们告诉柏伊特尔他只有三个小时

Peytel's head was off his body: an executioner from Lyons had come over the night before, to assist the professional throat-cutter of Bourg.

I am not going to entertain you with any sentimental lamentations for this scoundrel's fate, or to declare my belief in his innocence, as Monsieur de Balzac has done. As far as moral conviction can go, the man's guilt is pretty clearly brought home to him. But any man who has read the "Causes Célèbres," knows that men have been convicted and executed upon evidence ten times more powerful than that which was brought against Peytel. His own account of his horrible case may be true; there is nothing adduced in the evidence which is strong enough to overthrow it. It is a serious privilege, God knows, that society takes upon itself, at any time, to deprive one of God's creatures of existence. But when the slightest doubt remains, what a tremendous risk does it incur! In England, thank Heaven, the law is more wise and more merciful: an English jury would never have taken a man's blood upon such testimony: an English judge and Crown advocate would never have acted as these Frenchmen have done; the latter inflaming the public mind by exaggerated appeals to their passions: the former seeking, in every way, to draw confessions from the prisoner, to perplex and confound him, to do away, by fierce cross-questioning and bitter remarks from the bench, with any effect that his testimony might have on the jury. I don't mean to say that judges and lawyers have been more violent and inquisitorial against the unhappy Peytel than against any one else; it is the fashion of the country: a man is guilty until he proves himself to be innocent; and to batter down his defence, if he have any, there are the lawyers, with all their horrible ingenuity, and their captivating passionate eloquence. It is hard thus to set the skilful and tried champions of the law against men unused to this kind of combat; nay, give a man all the legal aid that he can purchase or procure, still, by this plan, you take him at a cruel, unmanly disadvantage; he has to fight against the law, clogged with the dreadful weight of his presupposed guilt. Thank God that, in England, things are not managed so.

However, I am not about to entertain you with ignorant disquisitions about the law. Peytel's case may, nevertheless, interest you; forthe tale is a very stirring and mysterious one; and you may see how easy a thing it is for a man's life to be talked away in France, if ever he should happen to fall under

的时间了。在十二点，柏伊特尔就会人头落地：一个里昂的刽子手昨晚就赶到这里来帮助布尔格的执行刽子手了。

我不打算向你表述我对柏伊特尔这个罪犯命运的感伤哀悼，也不愿像巴尔扎克先生一样宣布自己相信他是无辜的。只要人们仍坚信道德，那么柏伊特尔所犯的罪行必须要得到确实的证明。任何一个了解这个“著名案件”的人都知道，对柏伊特尔的审判和执刑所依据的证据资料都不足以对他构成指控。柏伊特尔自己对案件的陈述或许是真实的，在证据中也没有充分的资料能强有力地对其进行反驳。生命是一个人最重要的权利，而法庭却可以在任何时候剥夺创造物的这一生存权利。在案件仍存有一丝疑点的时候，如果匆忙做出判决就会冒很大的风险！感谢上帝，在英国，法律要更为明智和宽大一些。英国陪审团从来也不会根据这样的证据去剥夺一个人的生命，英国的法官和刑事律师从来也不会像法国的法官和律师那样行事，后者主要是通过夸张的言论煽动公众的情绪，而前者则利用各种方法使犯人招供，折磨犯人并挫败他，通过严厉的盘问和法官言辞激烈的陈述，排除掉犯人的证言将会给陪审团所带来的任何影响。我不是说法官和律师针对不幸的柏伊特尔的审判要比其他人更为残酷，这是法国的社会风气，人是有罪的除非他能拿出证据证明自己的无辜。法庭辩护律师具有巧舌如簧的辩论能力来击败被告。对不习惯法庭辩论的人来说，让他们与受过专门训练、有经验的律师进行辩论是很难占上风的。即使是给了被告方以尽可能的法律援助，但法庭律师还是会根据其推测的犯罪嫌疑来对被告进行残忍而卑鄙的攻击。感谢上帝，在英国，事情不是这样处理的。

然而，我不打算就法律的话题展开讨论。柏伊特尔的案件或许会让你发生兴趣的，因为这个故事非常激动人心和不可思议。你可以看到，在法国如果一个人被怀疑有犯罪行为的话，那么法庭要剥夺一个人的生命是一件多么容易的事情。这个案子是这样开始的：

最近在安省发生的所有事件中，没有比安省贝莱的公证人塞巴斯

the suspicion of a crime. The French "Acte d'accusation" begins in the following manner:—

"Of all the events which, in these latter times, have afflicted the department of the Ain, there is none which has caused a more profound and lively sensation than the tragical death of the lady, Félicité Alcazar, wife of Sebastian Benedict Peytel, notary, at Belley. At the end of October, 1838, Madame Peytel quitted that town, with her husband, and their servant Louis Rey, in order to pass a few days at Macon: at midnight, the inhabitants of Belley were suddenly awakened by the arrival of Monsieur Peytel, by his cries, and by the signs which he exhibited of the most lively agitation: he implored the succours of all the physicians in the town; knocked violently at their doors; rung at the bells of their houses with a sort of frenzy, and announced that his wife, stretched out, and dying, in his carriage, had just been shot, on the Lyons road, by his domestic, whose life Peytel himself had taken.

"At this recital a number of persons assembled, and what a spectacle was presented to their eyes.

"A young woman lay at the bottom of a carriage, deprived of life; her whole body was wet, and seemed as if it had just been plunged into the water. She appeared to be severely wounded in the face; and her garments, which were raised up, in spite of the cold and rainy weather, left the upper part of her knees almost entirely exposed. At the sight of this half-naked and inanimate body, all the spectators were affected. People said that the first duty to pay to a dying woman was, to preserve her from the cold, to cover her. A physician examined the body; he declared that all remedies were useless; that Madame Peytel was dead and cold.

"The entreaties of Peytel were redoubled; he demanded fresh succors, and, giving no heed to the fatal assurance which had just been given him, required that all the physicians in the place should be sent for. A scene so strange and so melancholy; the incoherent account given by Peytel of the murder of his wife; his extraordinary movements; and the avowal which he continued to make, that he had despatched the murderer, Rey, with strokes of his hammer, excited the attention of Lieutenant Wolf, commandant of gendarmes: that officer gave orders for the immediate arrest of Peytel; but the latter threw himself into the arms of a friend, who interceded for him, and begged the police not immediately to seize upon his person.

蒂安·柏伊特尔的妻子费利西特·阿尔卡萨尔的惨死更轰动一时的事件了。在1838年10月底，柏伊特尔夫人和她丈夫，还有他们的仆人路易·雷离开贝莱去玛孔住些日子。在午夜，贝莱的居民突然被返回的柏伊特尔给叫醒了，他叫喊着并焦虑不安地向他们示意动作，他请求城镇里所有医生的援助，他猛烈地敲医生家的门，疯狂地按他们的门铃，说他的妻子在马车里躺着，她就要死去了，她在通往里昂的道路上被用人打了一枪，柏伊特尔已杀死了用人。

这样说着，许多人聚集到马车旁边，呈现在他们眼前的是怎样一种场面啊！

一个年轻的女人躺在马车的一端，被夺去了生命。她浑身都是湿的，好像刚从水里捞出来的一样。她看起来是脸部严重受了伤。虽然是寒冷下雨的天气，她的外套却被拉了上去，膝盖以上的部分几乎是全裸的。看到这个半裸的、没有生命的身体，所有的旁观者都震动了。人们说首先要给这个垂死的女人盖上衣服，以免她受冻。一个医生在检查了她的身体之后声称所有的治疗方法都没用了，柏伊特尔夫人已死了，浑身冰凉。

柏伊特尔的恳求越来越强烈，他不顾医生的死亡通告，请求进一步的救援，要这个地方所有的医生都过来帮忙。这是一幕多么奇怪而忧郁的场景啊！柏伊特尔语无伦次的陈述，他奇异的举动，还有他所做的供认，即说他用锤子打死了凶手雷，这些都引起了宪兵司令伍尔夫中卫的注意，这个军官下令要立即逮捕柏伊特尔，但是柏伊特尔得到了一位朋友的保护，他朋友为他说情，请求警察不要立即抓人。

柏伊特尔夫人的尸体被运送到公寓里。躺在路上仍流着血的用人尸体也被移开了。柏伊特尔要对此案做出解释，就这样。……

现在有必要告诉读者的是，当一个英国律师不得不起诉一个刑事罪犯的时候，他会用最恰当的法律术语写出他的起诉条款，尤其警告陪审团根

"The corpse of Madame Peytel was transported to her apartment; the bleeding body of the domestic was likewise brought from the road, where it lay; and Peytel, asked to explain the circumstances, did so."...

Now, as there is little reason to tell the reader, when an English counsel has to prosecute a prisoner on the part of the Crown for a capital offence, he produces the articles of his accusation in the most moderate terms, and especially warns the jury to give the accused person the benefit of every possible doubt that the evidence may give, or may leave. See how these things are managed in France, and how differently the French counsel for the Crown sets about his work.

He first prepares his act of accusation, the opening of which we have just read; it is published six days before the trial, so that an unimpassioned, unprejudiced jury has ample time to study it, and to form its opinions accordingly, and to go into court with a happy, just prepossession against the prisoner.

Read the first part of the Peytel act of accusation; it is as turgid and declamatory as a bad romance; and as inflated as a newspaper document, by an unlimited penny-a-liner:—"The department of the Ain is in a dreadful state of excitement; the inhabitants of Belley come trooping from their beds,—and what a sight do they behold;—a young woman at the bottom of a carriage, toute ruisselante, just out of a river; her garments, in spite of the cold and rain, raised, so as to leave the upper part of her knees entirely exposed, at which all the beholders were affected, and cried, that the FIRST DUTY was to cover her from the cold." This settles the case at once; the first duty of a man is to cover the legs of the sufferer; the second to call for help. The eloquent "Substitut du Procureur du Roi" has prejudged the case, in the course of a few sentences. He is putting his readers, among whom his future jury is to be found, into a proper state of mind; he works on them with pathetic description, just as a romance-writer would: the rain pours in torrents; it is a dreary evening in November; the young creature's situation is neatly described; the distrust which entered into the breast of the keen old officer of gendarmes strongly painted, the suspicions which might, or might not, have been entertained by the inhabitants, eloquently argued. How did the advocate know that the people had such? Did all the bystanders say aloud, "I suspect

据证据所提供的或遗漏的事实对被告人持有任何一种怀疑。让我们看看这些事情在法国是怎样被处理的，法国刑事律师的起诉条例与我们英国律师是多么的不一样。

律师首先准备他的起诉条例，我们刚才已读过了条例的开始部分。它在法庭审判的前六天就被印制了出来，以使公正的陪审团能有充分的时间去研究它，从而形成自己的看法，带着对罪犯的恰当公正的印象走进法院。

对柏伊特尔的起诉条例的第一部分就像一篇拙劣的小说那样浮夸做作，像穷酸的文人写的报纸文章一样言过其实："贝莱处于一种可怕的骚动状态之中。那里的居民匆忙地从床上爬起来，到了现场。——他们看到的是怎样的一幕啊！一个年轻的女子躺在马车的一端，全身都湿了，像是从河里捞出来一样。虽然是寒冷下雨的天气，她的外套却被拉了上去，膝盖以上的部分几乎是全裸的。看到这里，所有的旁观者都震动了。人们说首先要给这个垂死的女人盖上衣服，以免她受冻。"这就开始进入案件了。人们首先要做的是给受害者盖上衣服，其次才是请求帮助。雄辩的律师在开始的这几句话中就已经为案子定下了基调。他使读者，其中包括未来的陪审团，形成一种特定的思想观念。他就像一位写小说的作者一样用哀婉动人的描述来对读者施加影响：大雨倾盆，在 11 月的一个沉闷的傍晚，柏伊特尔所处的状况得到了简洁的描述，而那个热心的老宪兵官员内心中的怀疑却得到了重点描绘，有所怀疑的居民与无所怀疑的居民也在起诉条例中雄辩地展开了争论。律师是怎么知道居民观点的呢？难道所有的旁观者大声说"我怀疑这是柏伊特尔先生的谋杀，他讲的关于那个用人的故事是骗人的"吗？或者是那些居民去见过市长，把他们的疑虑上报给了政府？或者是那里的律师听到了居民们的谈话？都没有。但是这位律师却向你描述了整个场景，仿佛它确实存在过，并提供了全面的怀疑报道，仿佛它们就是事实，确定、公开、明显，每个人都可以看到并予以保证。

律师已经给听众事先提供了案发资料，也为他们准备了被告方的陈述，他用一种相当公正的态度说，"现在，让我们听听柏伊特尔先生的陈述"。

that this is a case of murder by Monsieur Peytel, and that his story about the domestic is all deception?" or did they go off to the mayor, and register their suspicion? or was the advocate there to hear them? Not he; but he paints you the whole scene, as though it had existed, and gives full accounts of suspicions, as if they had been facts, positive, patent, staring, that everybody could see and swear to.

Having thus primed his audience, and prepared them for the testimony of the accused party, "Now," says he, with a fine show of justice, "let us hear Monsieur Peytel;" and that worthy's narrative is given as follows:—

> "He said that he had left Mâcon on the 31st October, at eleven o'clock in the morning, in order to return to Belley, with his wife and servant. The latter drove, or led, an open car; he himself was driving his wife in a four-wheeled carriage, drawn by one horse: they reached Bourg at five o'clock in the evening; left it at seven, to sleep at Pont d'Ain, where they did not arrive before midnight. During the journey, Peytel thought he remarked that Rey had slackened his horse's pace. When they alighted at the inn, Peytel bade him deposit in his chamber 7,500 francs, which he carried with him; but the domestic refused to do so, saying that the inn gates were secure, and there was no danger. Peytel was, therefore, obliged to carry his money upstairs himself. The next day, the 1st November, they set out on their journey again, at nine o'clock in the morning; Louis did not come, according to custom, to take his master's orders. They arrived at Tenay about three, stopped there a couple of hours to dine, and it was eight o'clock when they reached the bourg of Rossillon, where they waited half an hour to bait the horses.
>
> "As they left Rossillon, the weather became bad, and the rain began to fall: Peytel told his domestic to get a covering for the articles in the open chariot; but Rey refused to do so, adding, in an ironical tone, that the weather was fine. For some days past, Peytel had remarked that his servant was gloomy, and scarcely spoke at all.
>
> "After they had gone about 500 paces beyond the bridge of Andert, that crosses the river Furans, and ascended to the least steep part of the hill of Darde, Peytel cried out to his servant, who was seated in the car, to come down from it, and finish the ascent on foot.
>
> "At this moment a violent wind was blowing from the south, and the rain was falling heavily: Peytel was seated back in the right corner of the carriage,

柏伊特尔的叙述是这样记录的：

他说他是在10月31日上午十一点钟离开了玛孔，他和他的妻子还有用人要返回贝莱。用人驾着一辆敞篷马车，他自己和妻子坐着一辆一匹马拉着的四轮马车，他们在晚上五点到了布尔格。七点离开，去安桥过夜，他们午夜之前没有赶到那里。在旅程中，柏伊特尔注意到雷减慢了马车的速度。当他们从马车上下来，在旅馆落脚的时候，柏伊特尔吩咐用人把带的七千五百法郎存放到他房间里去。但是用人拒绝这样做，说旅馆的大门是安全的，没有危险。因此，柏伊特尔不得不自己带着钱上楼了。第二天，11月1日，他们在早上九点又开始启程了。路易没有像往常那样听从主人的命令。他们大约是下午三点到了特奈，在那里停留了两个小时来用餐，他们到罗斯庸镇时候已是晚上八点了，在那里他们用了半个小时来喂马。

当他们离开罗斯庸的时候，天气就变坏了，下起了雨。柏伊特尔让他的用人把敞篷马车上的物品用东西给盖上，但是雷拒绝那么做，还用挖苦的语调说天气很好。在过去的几天里，柏伊特尔已经注意到他的用人非常郁闷，几乎不说话。

在他们离开横跨伏兰河的安德顿桥大约五百步之后，他们开始爬塔德山的一个有点陡的峭壁，柏伊特尔叫他坐在车里的用人下来，好步行爬坡。

这时一阵猛烈的风从南方吹来，雨也下大了，柏伊特尔坐在马车后座的右侧，他的妻子在他旁边睡着了，头靠在他的左肩上。忽然，他听到一阵枪声（他已经在几步远的距离之外看到了亮光)，柏伊特尔夫人被惊醒了，叫道：‘我可怜的丈夫，快把枪拿出来。’马也受到了惊吓，开始一路小跑。柏伊特尔很快就拔出了枪，朝马车外面在路边奔跑的一个人开火。

直到目前为止，他还不知道自己的妻子已经中弹了，他从马车的

and his wife, who was close to him, was asleep, with her head on his left shoulder. All of a sudden he heard the report of a fire-arm (he had seen the light of it at some paces' distance), and Madame Peytel cried out, 'My poor husband, take your pistols;' the horse was frightened, and began to trot. Peytel immediately drew the pistol, and fired, from the interior of the carriage, upon an individual whom he saw running by the side of the road.

"Not knowing, as yet, that his wife had been hit, he jumped out on one side of the carriage, while Madame Peytel descended from the other; and he fired a second pistol at his domestic, Louis Rey, whom he had just recognized. Redoubling his pace, he came up with Rey, and struck him, from behind, a blow with the hammer. Rey turned at this, and raised up his arm to strike his master with the pistol which he had just discharged at him; but Peytel, more quick than he, gave the domestic a blow with the hammer, which felled him to the ground (he fell his face forwards), and then Peytel, bestriding the body, despatched him, although the brigand asked for mercy.

"He now began to think of his wife and ran back, calling out her name repeatedly, and seeking for her, in vain, on both sides of the road. Arrived at the bridge of Andert, he recognized his wife, stretched in a field, covered with water, which bordered the Furans. This horrible discovery had so much the more astonished him, because he had no idea, until now, that his wife had been wounded: he endeavoured to draw her from the water; and it was only after considerable exertions that he was enabled to do so, and to place her, with her face towards the ground, on the side of the road. Supposing that, here, she would be sheltered from any further danger, and believing, as yet, that she was only wounded, he determined to ask for help at a lone house, situated on the road towards Rossillon; and at this instant he perceived, without at all being able to explain how, that his horse had followed him back to the spot, having turned back of its own accord, from the road to Belley.

"The house at which he knocked was inhabited by two men, of the name of Thannet, father and son, who opened the door to him, and whom he entreated to come to his aid, saying that his wife had just been assassinated by his servant. The elder Thannet approached to, and examined the body, and told Peytel that it was quite dead; he and his son took up the corpse, and placed it in the bottom of the carriage, which they all mounted themselves, and pursued their route to Belley. In order to do so, they had to pass by Rey's body, on the road, which Peytel wished to crush under the wheels of his carriage. It was to rob him of 7,500 francs, said Peytel, that the attack had been made."

一侧跳了出去，而柏伊特尔夫人却从另一侧下去了。他这才认出奔跑的那个人是他的用人路易·雷，他又朝用人开了第二枪，并加快步伐追上了雷，从后面用锤子敲了雷一下，这时雷回过身来，举起胳膊要用刚才射击的手枪打他的主人，但是柏伊特尔的动作更快，用锤子敲了他头部一下，他便脸朝下摔倒在地上。接着，柏伊特尔骑在他身上，尽管这个强盗请求饶恕，但柏伊特尔还是杀死了他。

他这时想起了自己的妻子，就往回跑，并重复喊他妻子的名字，但是在道路的两边都没有找到她。到了安德耐桥那里，他才发现了自己的妻子，她躺在一块田地里，身上都被伏兰河的水给浸透了。这个可怕的发现让他大吃一惊，因为他现在还不知道妻子已受伤了。他努力把妻子从水里拖出来，费了好大的劲，终于把妻子放在了路边。他想，在这里他妻子就不会再遇到危险了，他仍然以为她只是受了伤，没有生命危险。他决定去路边请求帮助，那里有幢房屋。这时，他发现他的马也独自从通往贝莱的路上折了回来跟随他来到这里。

他敲门的那幢房子里住着两个男人，是父子两个，姓桑奈，他们开了门，柏伊特尔请求他们的帮助，说他的妻子刚刚遭到仆人的暗杀。于是，老桑奈就跟随他来到妻子旁边，检查了身体，他告诉柏伊特尔，他妻子已经死了。他和他儿子把尸体搬起来，放到马车的一端，他们一起上了马车，继续前往贝莱。路上，他们必须要从雷的尸体旁经过，柏伊特尔希望他的马车轮子能把雷的尸体压碎。他说，就为了抢劫他的七千五百法郎，才导致了这场事故。

我们的起诉律师在这里完全放弃了雄辩、忧郁的语调，而是用不加虚饰、毫无想象力的语调来叙述那个不幸犯人的案件。陪审团要怎样来听这个人的话呢？他们应该为这篇无聊的陈述文字而惩罚这位律师。为什么不用起诉条例开头部分那种浮夸的文风来帮帮可怜的柏伊特尔呢？如果那样，他就会这样写道：

Our friend, the Procureur's Substitut, has dropped, here, the eloquent and pathetic style altogether, and only gives the unlucky prisoner's narrative in the baldest and most unimaginative style. How is a jury to listen to such a fellow? they ought to condemn him, if but for making such an uninteresting statement. Why not have helped poor Peytel with some of those rhetorical graces which have been so plentifully bestowed in the opening part of the act of accusation? He might have said:—

"Monsieur Peytel is an eminent notary at Belley; he is a man distinguished for his literary and scientific acquirements; he has lived long in the best society of the capital; he had been but a few months married to that young and unfortunate lady, whose loss has plunged her bereaved husband into despair—almost into madness. Some early differences had marked, it is true, the commencement of their union; but these, which, as can be proved by evidence, were almost all the unhappy lady's fault,—had happily ceased, to give place to sentiments far more delightful and tender. Gentlemen, Madame Peytel bore in her bosom a sweet pledge of future concord between herself and her husband: in three brief months she was to become a mother.

"In the exercise of his honourable profession,—in which, to succeed, a man must not only have high talents, but undoubted probity,—and, gentlemen, Monsieur Peytel DID succeed—DID inspire respect and confidence, as you, his neighbours, well know;—in the exercise, I say, of his high calling, Monsieur Peytel, towards the end of October last, had occasion to make a journey in the neighbourhood, and visit some of his many clients.

"He travelled in his own carriage, his young wife beside him. Does this look like want of affection, gentlemen? or is it not a mark of love—of love and paternal care on his part towards the being with whom his lot in life was linked,—the mother of his coming child,—the young girl, who had everything to gain from the union with a man of his attainments of intellect, his kind temper, his great experience, and his high position? In this manner they travelled, side by side, lovingly together. Monsieur Peytel was not a lawyer merely, but a man of letters and varied learning; of the noble and sublime science of geology he was, especially, an ardent devotee."

(Suppose, here, a short panegyric upon geology. Allude to the creation

柏伊特尔先生是贝莱一个有名的公证人。他以自己在文学和科学方面的学识而有名。他曾在首都的上流社会中生活过很长一段时间。他和那位年轻、不幸的女士结婚才几个月，她的离去让她的丈夫陷入了绝望——几乎是疯狂之中。在他们结合的早期，两人确实是有些争论，但是有证据可以证明，这些主要都是不幸的女士的过失——不再乐意付出更真诚、更温柔的感情。先生们，柏伊特尔夫人内心里有个美妙的誓言，那就是要保证她和她丈夫之间的未来能够和谐，还有三个月她就要做母亲了。

在他高尚的职业领域中，要取得成功，一个男人不仅要有很杰出的才能，还要正直、诚实。——先生们，柏伊特尔先生是成功的，他得到了人们的尊敬和信任，关于这一点，你们和他的邻居都是很了解的。——在履行工作任务的时候，由于他具有很强的号召力，柏伊特尔先生在最近10月底，就有机会去附近做一次旅行，拜访他的一些客户。

他坐着自己的马车旅行，他年轻的妻子坐在他旁边。先生们，难道这看起来像是缺乏感情吗？难道这不是爱情的标志吗？还有他对那个与他的命运紧密相连的女子的爱情和父亲般的关照——那个他未来孩子的母亲——年轻的女孩，她能从这个有才智、好脾气、具有出色工作经验和较高地位的人身上得到所有的一切，不是吗？就这样他们肩并肩一起旅行。柏伊特尔先生不仅仅是个法学家，还是个具有丰富学识的文人，他也是个伟大的地质学爱好者，尤其要提到的是，他还是个热情的宗教教徒。

(假如这里有一篇关于地质的简短颂词。间接提到这个伟大世界的创造，然后自然地提到造物主。想象一下柏伊特尔这个笃信宗教的人[1]和他年轻的妻子关于这个话题的谈话。)

of this mighty world, and then, naturally, to the Creator. Fancy the conversations which Peytel, a religious man,[1] might have with his young wife upon the subject.)

"Monsieur Peytel had lately taken into his service a man named Louis Rey. Rey was a foundling, and had passed many years in a regiment—a school, gentlemen, where much besides bravery, alas! is taught; nay, where the spirit which familiarizes one with notions of battle and death, I fear, may familiarize one with ideas, too, of murder. Rey, a dashing reckless fellow, from the army, had lately entered Peytel's service, was treated by him with the most singular kindness; accompanied him (having charge of another vehicle) upon the journey before alluded to; and KNEW THAT HIS MASTER CARRIED WITH HIM A CONSIDERABLE SUM OF MONEY; for a man like Rey an enormous sum, 7,500 francs. At midnight on the 1st of November, as Madame Peytel and her husband were returning home, an attack was made upon their carriage. Remember, gentlemen, the hour at which the attack was made; remember the sum of money that was in the carriage; and remember that the Savoy frontier IS WITHIN A LEAGUE OF THE SPOT where the desperate deed was done."

Now, my dear Briefless, ought not Monsieur Procureur, in common justice to Peytel, after he had so eloquently proclaimed, not the facts, but the suspicions, which weighed against that worthy, to have given a similar florid account of the prisoner's case? Instead of this, you will remark, that it is the advocate's endeavour to make Peytel's statements as uninteresting in style as possible; and then he demolishes them in the following way:—

"Scarcely was Peytel's statement known, when the common sense of the public rose against it. Peytel had commenced his story upon the bridge of Andert, over the cold body of his wife. On the 2nd November he had developed it in detail, in the presence of the physicians, in the presence of the assembled neighbours—of the persons who, on the day previous only, were his friends. Finally, he had completed it in his interrogatories, his conversations, his writings, and letters to the magistrates and everywhere these words, repeated so often, were only received with a painful incredulity. The fact was that, besides the singular character which Peytel's appearance, attitude, and talk had worn ever since the event, there was in his narrative an inexplicable enigma; its con-

柏伊特尔先生最近雇用了一个叫路易·雷的男仆。雷是一个弃儿，而且已经在军团里度过了许多年——在这所学校里，唉！传授最多的就是勇敢；而且，在那里除了让一个人熟悉战争和死亡的观念之外，恐怕，还会让一个人熟悉谋杀的念头。这个鲁莽、冲劲很足的小伙子后来离开了军队，被柏伊特尔雇用，他得到主人非常仁慈的对待，陪伴主人（驾着另一辆马车）开始了前面提到的旅程。他知道主人身上带了一笔钱。对于像雷这样的人来说，七千五百法郎是一个大数目。在11月1日的午夜，在柏伊特尔夫人和她丈夫回家的路途中，雷就有了攻击他们马车的打算。先生们，记住雷攻击马车的时间；记住马车里钱的数目；记住案发现场离萨沃伊边界只有一里格。

现在，法庭起诉律师在没有事实根据的情况下就如此果断地宣布了他对柏伊特尔的猜疑，这猜疑对柏伊特尔是很不利的，在这之后，他还能对柏伊特尔做出公正的判决和报道吗？你将会注意到，律师不但没有这样做，反而在努力使柏伊特尔的陈述尽可能的无趣，然后他就会用下面的辩词来驳倒它们：

当围观的群众对此案已愤愤不平的时候，柏伊特尔还没做任何交代。他后来是从安德耐桥上他妻子冰冷的身体开始讲述事发经历的。11月2日，在医生、聚集的旁观者和他以前的朋友面前，他已详细地交代了事实。最后，他在回复地方行政官的讯问、谈话和信件中又不断重复着相同的话，但人们从中得到的只是怀疑。事实是，除了柏伊特尔在事发之后他的表现、态度和谈话特征之外，他的叙述中始终存在着一个让人费解的谜，这个谜是如此的自相矛盾和不现实，以至于镇静沉着的人也会对此反感，甚至连朋友也不会相信。

因为起诉律师不是代表他个人而是代表整个法国公众讲话，他当然了

tradictions and impossibilities were such, that calm persons were revolted at it, and that even friendship itself refused to believe it."

Thus Mr. Attorney speaks, not for himself alone, but for the whole French public; whose opinions, of course, he knows. Peytel's statement is discredited EVERYWHERE; the statement which he had made over the cold body of his wife—the monster! It is not enough simply to prove that the man committed the murder, but to make the jury violently angry against him, and cause them to shudder in the jury-box, as he exposes the horrid details of the crime.

"Justice," goes on Mr. Substitute (who answers for the feelings of everybody), "DISTURBED BY THE PRE-OCCUPATIONS OF PUBLIC OPINION, commenced, without delay, the most active researches. The bodies of the victims were submitted to the investigations of men of art; the wounds and projectiles were examined; the place where the event took place explored with care. The morality of the author of this frightful scene became the object of rigorous examination; the exigeances of the prisoner, the forms affected by him, his calculating silence, and his answers, coldly insulting, were feeble obstacles; and justice at length arrived, by its prudence, and by the discoveries it made, to the most cruel point of certainty."

You see that a man's demeanour is here made a crime against him; and that Mr. Substitute wishes to consider him guilty, because he has actually the audacity to hold his tongue. Now follows a touching description of the domestic, Louis Rey:—

"Louis Rey, a child of the Hospital at Lyons, was confided, at a very early age, to some honest country people, with whom he stayed until he entered the army. At their house, and during this long period of time, his conduct, his intelligence, and the sweetness of his manners were such, that the family of his guardians became to him as an adopted family; and his departure caused them the most sincere affliction. When Louis quitted the army, he returned to his benefactors, and was received as a son. They found him just as they had ever known him (I acknowledge that this pathos beats my humble defence of Peytel entirely), except that he had learned to read and write; and the certificates of his commanders proved him to be a good and gallant soldier.

解公众的看法。柏伊特尔的陈述处处都受到怀疑，他对于其妻子冰冷的身体所做的陈述——是多么残忍啊！它不仅足以证明柏伊特尔犯了谋杀罪，而且还使得陪审团对他极为反感，当柏伊特尔把罪行的可怕细节暴露出来的时候，陪审席中的陪审团成员都会因此而发抖。

起诉律师（为了回应公众的看法）继续说道："正义虽然受到公众先入为主的偏见的干扰，但积极的调查工作还是没有受到耽搁就立即开始了。受害者的尸体已移交给专业人士检查；对伤口和子弹也进行了检查；事发地点也得到仔细的勘察。案发人员的品行成为严格调查的目标；犯人的无礼要求、沉默、答复和冷淡都不会对案件调查构成什么障碍。真相一定会水落石出，而正义最终会取得胜利。"

在这里，你将看到一个人的品行会成为他罪行的重要依据。那位起诉律师想判柏伊特尔有罪，而他也确实有能力让柏伊特尔保持缄默。接下来就是关于用人路易·雷的感人描述：

> 路易·雷是一个在里昂医院出生的弃儿，他很小的时候就被委托给善良的村民抚养，一直到他加入军队。他在村民家里度过了一段很长的时期，他的品行、才智和温和的举止都博得了村民的喜爱，他的一个保护人还主动收养了他。他的离去使村民们感到很痛苦。当路易离开军队的时候，他又回到他恩人那里，被恩人认做儿子。他们发现雷还像以前一样，（我承认这种怜悯完全战胜了我为柏伊特尔谦恭的辩护之意）只不过学会读书写字了。军队指挥官的证书也证明他是一个善良英勇的士兵。
>
> 雷觉得自己有必要创一番事业，因此他离开了朋友们，为宪兵队的一个中尉德·蒙特里夏尔先生帮佣，从他那里我们又得到了关于雷的品行的新证据。确实，路易喜欢女人和酒。但他曾是一名士兵，这些人性的弱点也是正常的，根据证人的言论，他的所作所为、他的才智和他令人愉快的举止完全可以被弥补这些过失。在1839年7月，雷

"The necessity of creating some resources for himself, obliged him to quit his friends, and to enter the service of Monsieur de Montrichard, a lieutenant of gendarmerie, from whom he received fresh testimonials of regard. Louis, it is true, might have a fondness for wine and a passion for women; but he had been a soldier, and these faults were, according to the witnesses, amply compensated for by his activity, his intelligence, and the agreeable manner in which he performed his service. In the month of July, 1839, Rey quitted, voluntarily, the service of M. de Montrichard; and Peytel, about this period, meeting him at Lyons, did not hesitate to attach him to his service. Whatever may be the prisoner's present language, it is certain that up to the day of Louis's death, he served Peytel with diligence and fidelity.

"More than once his master and mistress spoke well of him. EVERYBODY who has worked, or been at the house of Madame Peytel, has spoken in praise of his character; and, indeed, it may be said, that these testimonials were general.

"On the very night of the 1st of November, and immediately after the catastrophe, we remark how Peytel begins to make insinuations against his servant; and how artfully, in order to render them more sure, he disseminates them through the different parts of his narrative. But, in the course of the proceeding, these charges have met with a most complete denial. Thus we find the disobedient servant who, at Pont d'Ain, refused to carry the money-chest to his master's room, under the pretext that the gates of the inn were closed securely, occupied with tending the horses after their long journey: meanwhile Peytel was standing by, and neither master nor servant exchanged a word, and the witnesses who beheld them both have borne testimony to the zeal and care of the domestic.

"In like manner, we find that the servant, who was so remiss in the morning as to neglect to go to his master for orders, was ready for departure before seven o'clock, and had eagerly informed himself whether Monsieur and Madame Peytel were awake; learning from the maid of the inn, that they had ordered nothing for their breakfast. This man, who refused to carry with him a covering for the car, was, on the contrary, ready to take off his own cloak, and with it shelter articles of small value; this man, who had been for many days so silent and gloomy, gave, on the contrary, many proofs of his gayety—almost of his indiscretion, speaking, at all the inns, in terms of praise of his master and mistress. The waiter at the inn at Dauphin, says he was a tall young fellow, mild and good-natured; 'we talked for some time about horses, and

自愿离开了德·蒙特里夏尔先生。大约就在这个时期，柏伊特尔在里昂遇到了他，很快就毫不犹豫地雇用他服侍自己。不管柏伊特尔现在是怎么说的，但可以肯定的是直到路易死亡那天，他一直都是勤恳忠实服侍柏伊特尔的。

他的男主人和女主人都不止一次说过他的好话。曾在柏伊特尔夫人家里工作过或住过的其他人也都赞扬过他的品质。这种看法的确是很普遍的。

在11月1日的晚上，灾难刚刚发生之后，我们注意到柏伊特尔是怎样开始含沙射影地攻击他的用人。为了让谎言显得更加真实，他是多么狡猾啊！他通过不同的叙述内容来散布谣言。但是在诉讼过程中，这些控告却遭到绝大部分的否定。我们发现在安桥这个不服从主人的用人拒绝把钱匣子送到主人房里的前提是旅馆的大门已安全地关上了。在经过一段长途旅程之后，他当时正忙着照管马匹，柏伊特尔则正站在一边，主人和用人之间没说一句话，看到他们的证人还可以证明这个用人的热心和谨慎。

同样我们也发现那个在早晨如此怠慢、不去听从主人吩咐的用人，其实是在七点钟之前就做好离开的准备了，他急切地想知道柏伊特尔先生和夫人是否睡醒了，他还是从旅馆的女仆那里得知主人没有吩咐任何早餐。他没有拒绝给马车盖上东西，恰恰相反，他还准备用自己的斗篷遮盖马车里不是很值钱的物品；这个用人在那几天之内也没有沉默忧郁，相反，有很多证人证明他是快乐的——在所有的旅店中，甚至他轻率的谈话也都是赞扬他主人的。多凡旅馆的侍者说雷是一个高个儿的年轻小伙子，脾气和善，‘我们谈论了一会儿马匹，还有其他的一些事情。他看起来很自然，并不是心事重重’。在安桥，他对别人说起自己是个弃儿，还有他被养大的地方和他帮佣过的地方。最后在罗斯庸镇，他死前的一个小时，他还和港口的港务长谈论一些话题，彼此都很熟悉了。

such things; he seemed to be perfectly natural, and not pre-occupied at all. ' At Pont d'Ain, he talked of his being a foundling; of the place where he had been brought up, and where he had served; and finally, at Rossillon, an hour before his death, he conversed familiarly with the master of the port, and spoke on indifferent subjects.

"All Peytel's insinuations against his servant had no other end than to show, in every point of Rey's conduct, the behaviour of a man who was premeditating attack. Of what, in fact, does he accuse him? Of wishing to rob him of 7,500 francs, and of having had recourse to assassination, in order to effect the robbery. But, for a premeditated crime, consider what singular improvidence the person showed who had determined on committing it; what folly and what weakness there is in the execution of it.

"How many insurmountable obstacles are there in the way of committing and profiting by crime! On leaving Belley, Louis Rey, according to Peytel's statement, knowing that his master would return with money, provided himself with a holster pistol, which Madame Peytel had once before perceived among his effects. In Peytel's cabinet there were some balls; four of these were found in Rey's trunk, on the 6th of November. And, in order to commit the crime, this domestic had brought away with him a pistol, and no ammunition; for Peytel has informed us that Rey, an hour before his departure from Mâcon, purchased six balls at a gunsmith's. To gain his point, the assassin must immolate his victims; for this, he has only one pistol, knowing, perfectly well, that Peytel, in all his travels, had two on his person; knowing that, at a late hour of the night, his shot might fail of effect; and that, in this case, he would be left to the mercy of his opponent.

"The execution of the crime is, according to Peytel's account, still more singular. Louis does not get off the carriage, until Peytel tells him to descend. He does not think of taking his master's life until he is sure that the latter has his eyes open. It is dark, and the pair are covered in one cloak; and Rey only fires at them at six paces' distance: he fires at hazard, without disquieting himself as to the choice of his victim; and the soldier, who was bold enough to undertake this double murder, has not force nor courage to consummate it. He flies, carrying in his hand a useless whip, with a heavy mantle on his shoulders, in spite of the detonation of two pistols at his ears, and the rapid steps of an angry master in pursuit, which ought to have set him upon some better means of escape. And we find this man, full of youth and vigour, lying with his face to the ground, in the midst of a public road, falling without a struggle, or resist-

柏伊特尔对他用人的所有含沙射影的攻击都是为了显示雷的任何一种行为都是有预谋的。实际上，柏伊特尔控告他什么呢？雷想抢夺他的七千五百法郎，为了实施这个抢劫计划，他不得不采用谋杀这种方法。但是，作为一个有预谋的犯罪行为，我们可以看到这个决定犯罪的人是多么奇怪地不计后果，而且在实施犯罪行为的时候又是多么的愚蠢和软弱。

在他实施犯罪行为的过程中会有多少难以克服的障碍啊！根据柏伊特尔的陈述，在他们离开贝莱去玛孔的时候，由于路易·雷知道他的主人将会带着钱回家，他就自备了一把带皮套的手枪，柏伊特尔夫人在此之前曾看到过这把手枪。在柏伊特尔的私人房间里我们找到一些子弹，它们同11月6日在雷身上所发现的四颗子弹都是一样的。为了实施犯罪行为，这个用人自己带了一把手枪，但是没有子弹。柏伊特尔告诉我们说，雷在离开玛孔前的一小时到一个军械工人那里买了六颗子弹。为了达到他的目的，这次暗杀一定要消灭掉他的主人。我们知道，要做到这些，他只有一把手枪，而柏伊特尔在整个旅途中都随身携带两把手枪。我们也知道，在深夜他的射击有可能是失败的，假如是那样的话，他就会任对手任意摆布了。

根据柏伊特尔的叙述，在犯罪行为的实施过程中还有许多奇怪的地方。路易是一直等到柏伊特尔让他下车的时候才从马车上下来的。他也是一直等到确定主人已注意他时，才想到结束主人性命的。天已经黑了，那对夫妇一起盖着一个斗篷，雷只是在六步远的地方朝他们射击，他是在危急之中开的火，也没有费力去选择受害者。这个有足够胆量犯双重谋杀罪的士兵在最后却没有力量或勇气来完成罪行了。他手里拿着一条无用的鞭子，肩上披着一个沉重的斗篷逃走了，也顾不上耳边两支手枪的开火声和愤怒的主人快速追赶的脚步声，在这种情况下他应该采取一种更好的逃跑方式的。我们发现这个充满活力的年轻人脸朝下躺在了马路中央，在主人锤子的敲击下他没有一点挣扎

ance, under the blows of a hammer!

"And suppose the murderer had succeeded in his criminal projects, what fruit could he have drawn from them? —Leaving, on the road, the two bleeding bodies; obliged to lead two carriages at a time, for fear of discovery; not able to return himself, after all the pains he had taken to speak, at every place at which they had stopped, of the money which his master was carrying with him; too prudent to appear alone at Belley; arrested at the frontier, by the excise officers, who would present an impassable barrier to him till morning, what could he do, or hope to do? The examination of the car has shown that Rey, at the moment of the crime, had neither linen, nor clothes, nor effects of any kind. There was found in his pockets, when the body was examined, no passport, nor certificate; one of his pockets contained a ball, of large calibre, which he had shown, in play, to a girl, at the inn at Mâcon, a little horn-handled knife, a snuff-box, a little packet of gunpowder, and a purse, containing only a half-penny and some string. Here is all the baggage, with which, after the execution of his homicidal plan, Louis Rey intended to take refuge in a foreign country.[2] Beside these absurd contradictions, there is another remarkable fact, which must not be passed over; it is this:—the pistol found by Rey is of antique form, and the original owner of it has been found. He is a curiosity-merchant at Lyons; and, though he cannot affirm that Peytel was the person who bought this pistol of him, he perfectly recognizes Peytel as having been a frequent customer at his shop!

"No, we may fearlessly affirm that Louis Rey was not guilty of the crime which Peytel lays to his charge. If, to those who knew him, his mild and open disposition, his military career, modest and without a stain, the touching regrets of his employers, are sufficient proofs of his innocence,—the calm and candid observer, who considers how the crime was conceived, was executed, and what consequences would have resulted from it, will likewise acquit him, and free him of the odious imputation which Peytel endeavours to cast upon his memory.

"But justice has removed the veil, with which an impious hand endeavoured to cover itself. Already, on the night of the 1st of November, suspicion was awakened by the extraordinary agitation of Peytel; by those excessive attentions towards his wife, which came so late; by that excessive and noisy grief, and by those calculated bursts of sorrow, which are such as Nature does not exhibit. The criminal, whom the public conscience had fixed upon; the man whose frightful combinations have been laid bare, and whose falsehoods, step by step,

和反抗就倒下了。

假如凶手的犯罪计划成功了，他会因此得到什么下场呢？——在马路上扔下两具流着血的尸体，因害怕被人发现，他不得不同时驾着两辆马车逃走；他还不能自己往回走，因为在他们每一处停留的地方他还要费心地向人们做出解释；他要很小心，不能单独在贝莱出现；他还有可能会被边境检察官员逮捕，一直到早晨，这些在场的边境检察官员都是他不可逾越的障碍，他能做什么或者想做什么呢？对马车的检查已显示出，雷在犯罪的时候既没有带衣物也没有任何的财物。当检查尸体的时候，在他的口袋里没有发现护照，也没有证书。他的一个口袋里装着一颗子弹，是颗宽口径手枪使用的子弹，他曾在玛孔的旅馆里开玩笑地向一个女孩展示过，还有一把小的牛角柄匕首、一个鼻烟盒、一小包火药和一个钱包，钱包里只有半个便士和一些线头。这就是路易·雷在完成杀人计划后，想要去国外避难所带的全部东西。[2]除了这些荒谬的自相矛盾之处，还有另一个明显的事实不能被我们忽略掉，那就是——在雷身边找到的手枪是把老式的手枪，我们已经找到了手枪原来的主人，他是里昂的一个古玩商人，虽然他不能确定是柏伊特尔买了他的那把手枪，但他却能很快地认出柏伊特尔是一位经常光顾他商店的顾客！

我们可以大胆地断言路易·雷不是柏伊特尔所控告的罪人。那些了解他温和开朗性情的人，他那谦逊、没有污点的军人生涯，他的雇主们对他的感人哀悼都足以证明他的无辜——而冷静正直的旁观者在考虑了犯罪行为的计划和实施过程以及由此带来的结果后，同样会宣判他无罪，使他从柏伊特尔尽力转嫁给他的罪责中得到解脱。

尽管有一只邪恶的手尽力去掩盖真相，但是正义已经掀开了真相的面纱。早在11月1日的夜晚，柏伊特尔异常的不安就已经引起人们的怀疑，他对他妻子过度的关心来得太迟了。那过度渲染的伤心与故意做出的悲伤喊叫都不是自然呈现出来的。在审判前的诉讼过程中，

have been exposed, during the proceedings previous to the trial; the murderer, at whose hands a heart-stricken family, and society at large, demands an account of the blood of a wife;—that murderer is Peytel."

When, my dear Briefless, you are a judge (as I make no doubt you will be, when you have left off the club all night, cigar-smoking of mornings, and reading novels in bed), will you ever find it in your heart to order a fellow-sinner's head off upon such evidence as this? Because a romantic Substitut du Procureur de Roi chooses to compose and recite a little drama, and draw tears from juries, let us hope that severe Rhadamanthine judges are not to be melted by such trumpery. One wants but the description of the characters to render the piece complete, as thus:—

<table>
<tr><th>Personnages</th><th>Costumes</th></tr>
<tr><td>Sebastien Peytel, Meurtrier</td><td>Habillement complet de notaire perfide: figure pâle, barbe noire, cheveux noirs.</td></tr>
<tr><td>Louis Rey, Soldat rétiré, bon, brave, franc, jovial aimant le vin, les femmes, la gaieté, ses maîtres surtout; vrai Français, enfin.</td><td>Costume ordinaire; il porte sur ses épaules une couverture de cheval.</td></tr>
<tr><td colspan="2">Wolff, Lieutenant de gendarmerie.</td></tr>
<tr><td colspan="2">Felicité d'Alcazar Femme et victime de Peytel.</td></tr>
<tr><td colspan="2">Médecins, Villageois, Filles d'Auberge, Garçons d'Ecurie, &c., &c.</td></tr>
<tr><td colspan="2">La scène se passe sur le pont d'Andert, entre Mâcon et Belley. Il est minuit. La pluie tombe: les tonnerres grondent. Le ciel est couvert de nuages, et sillonné d'éclairs.</td></tr>
</table>

All these personages are brought into play in the Procureur's drama; the villagers come in with their chorus; the old lieutenant of gendarmes with his suspicions; Rey's frankness and gayety, the romantic circumstances of his birth, his gallantry and fidelity, are all introduced, in order to form a contrast with Peytel, and to call down the jury's indignation against the latter. But are these proofs? or anything like proofs? And the suspicions, that are to serve instead of proofs, what are they?

"My servant, Louis Rey, was very sombre and reserved," says Peytel;

这个罪犯可怕的罪行被一点点地暴露了出来，他的谎言也一步一步地被揭穿。凶手一手制造了他的家庭悲剧，他要对自己妻子的死亡做出解释；那个凶手就是柏伊特尔。

我亲爱的爱德华律师，如果你是一个法官（无疑，我相信你将会是一个法官的，只要你晚上能离开俱乐部，早晨不再抽雪茄，不再躺在床上读小说），你会根据这样的证据判决一个犯人的死刑吗？这个不注重事实的起诉律师创作并朗诵了一个小剧本来获取陪审团的眼泪，让我们希望严峻公正的法官们不要被这种虚有其表的东西所感化。其实只要人物的描述能使戏剧片断完整就可以了，像这样：

人物	服装
塞巴斯蒂安·柏伊特尔　凶手	穿着一套公证人的服装，脸色苍白，黑色的胡子，黑色的头发
路易·雷　退职的士兵，善良、勇敢、直率、开朗，喜欢酒和女人，愉快、真正的法国人	平常的衣服，肩上扛着马匹用的毯子
伍尔夫　宪兵队中尉	
费利西特·阿尔卡萨尔　柏伊特尔的女人和受害者	
医生，村民，客栈的女仆，马房的伙计等等	
故事发生在玛孔和贝莱之间的安德耐桥上。时间是午夜，大雨倾盆，雷声轰鸣。天空布满了阴云和纵横交错的闪电。	

所有上述人物都出现在起诉律师的戏剧中。村民是说着合唱台词上场的；宪兵队的老中尉则是带着怀疑的神情上场；雷的直率和快乐、他的传奇身世、他的勇气和忠诚都在戏剧中得到了介绍，与柏伊特尔形成对比，使陪审团对柏伊特尔持反感态度。但这些就是证据吗？或者有任何一件事情是真正的证据吗？我们能用怀疑代替证据吗？

"he refused to call me in the morning, to carry my money-chest to my room, to cover the open car when it rained." The Prosecutor disproves this by stating that Rey talked with the inn maids and servants, asked if his master was up, and stood in the inn-yard, grooming the horses, with his master by his side, neither speaking to the other. Might he not have talked to the maids, and yet been sombre when speaking to his master? Might he not have neglected to call his master, and yet have asked whether he was awake? Might he not have said that the inn-gates were safe, out of hearing of the ostler witness? Mr. Substitute's answers to Peytel's statements are no answer at all. Every word Peytel said might be true, and yet Louis Rey might not have committed the murder; or every word might have been false, and yet Louis Rey might have committed the murder.

> "Then," says Mr. Substitute, "how many obstacles are there to the commission of the crime? And these are—
>
> "1. Rey provided himself with ONE holster pistol, to kill two people, knowing well that one of them had always a brace of pistols about him.
>
> "2. He does not think of firing until his master's eyes are open: fires at six paces, not caring at whom he fires, and then runs away.
>
> "3. He could not have intended to kill his master, because he had no passport in his pocket, and no clothes; and because he must have been detained at the frontier until morning; and because he would have had to drive two carriages, in order to avoid suspicion.
>
> "4. And, a most singular circumstance, the very pistol which was found by his side had been bought at the shop of a man at Lyons, who perfectly recognized Peytel as one of his customers, though he could not say he had sold that particular weapon to Peytel."

Does it follow, from this, that Louis Rey is not the murderer, much more, that Peytel is? Look at argument No. 1. Rey had no need to kill two people: he wanted the money, and not the blood. Suppose he had killed Peytel, would he not have mastered Madame Peytel easily? —a weak woman, in an excessively delicate situation, incapable of much energy, at the best of times.

2. "He does not fire till he knows his master's eyes are open." Why, on a stormy night, does a man driving a carriage go to sleep? Was Rey to wait until his master snored? "He fires at six paces, not caring whom he hits;"—and might not this happen too? The night is not so dark but that he can see his master, in HIS USUAL PLACE, driving. He fires and hits—whom? Madame Peytel, who had left her place, AND WAS WRAPPED UP WITH PEYTEL IN HIS CLOAK. She screams out, "Husband, take your pistols." Rey

"我的仆人路易·雷是非常忧郁和冷淡的，"柏伊特尔说，"他拒绝在早晨叫我，拒绝把我的钱匣放到我的房间里，下雨的时候拒绝给马车盖上东西。"起诉律师通过雷和旅馆女佣、仆人谈话的陈述驳斥了这点，雷问过女佣他的主人是否起床了，还有雷站在旅馆的院子里喂马，他的主人就在他身边，两人没有说话。难道雷不会和女仆说完话后，在他主人面前是忧郁的吗？难道他不会是忘记了叫他主人，却还记得询问主人是否起床了吗？难道他不会是听旅店中马夫说旅馆的大门是安全的吗？起诉律师对于柏伊特尔的陈述所作的答复根本就不是答案。或许柏伊特尔说的每个字都是真的，但路易·雷却没有犯谋杀罪；或许柏伊特尔说的每个字都是假的，但路易·雷却有可能犯了谋杀罪。

起诉律师说：

> 后来在实施犯罪的过程中有多少阻碍呢？这就是——
>
> 1. 雷只自备了一把带皮套的手枪来杀两个人，但他很清楚地知道主人身上经常带着两把手枪。
>
> 2. 直到主人睁开眼睛，他才想到开火。在六步远的距离处开火，没有注意到他是对着谁开火，然后就跑掉了。
>
> 3. 他并没有打算杀他的主人，因为他的口袋里没有护照，也没有带衣物；因为他不得不在边界被扣留到早晨；还有为了避免人们的怀疑，他不得不驾驶两辆马车。
>
> 4. 而一个最奇异的细节是，在雷旁边找到的那把手枪是在里昂的一个商店里买的，商店的主人很快就能认出柏伊特尔是他的一个顾客，虽然他不能确定那把枪就是卖给了柏伊特尔。

从这些理由就能得出路易·雷不是凶手而柏伊特尔就是凶手吗？看看第一条，雷虽然带着一把手枪但他没必要杀两个人。他想要的是钱，而不是人的性命。假如他杀了柏伊特尔，难道他不会轻而易举地控制柏伊特尔

knows that his master has a brace, thinks that he has hit the wrong person, and, as Peytel fires on him, runs away. Peytel follows, hammer in hand; as he comes up with the fugitive, he deals him a blow on the back of the head, and Rey falls—his face to the ground. Is there anything unnatural in this story? —anything so monstrously unnatural, that is, that it might not be true?

3. These objections are absurd. Why need a man have change of linen? If he had taken none for the journey, why should he want any for the escape? Why need he drive two carriages? —He might have driven both into the river, and Mrs. Peytel in one. Why is he to go to the douane, and thrust himself into the very jaws of danger? Are there not a thousand ways for a man to pass a frontier? Do smugglers, when they have to pass from one country to another, choose exactly those spots where a police is placed?

And, finally, the gunsmith of Lyons, who knows Peytel quite well, cannot say that he sold the pistol to him; that is, he did NOT sell the pistol to him; for you have only one man's word, in this case (Peytel's), to the contrary; and the testimony, as far as it goes, is in his favour. I say, my lud, and gentlemen of the jury, that these objections of my learned friend, who is engaged for the Crown, are absurd, frivolous, monstrous; that to SUSPECT away the life of a man upon such suppositions as these, is wicked, illegal, and inhuman; and, what is more, that Louis Rey, if he wanted to commit the crime—if he wanted to possess himself of a large sum of money, chose the best time and spot for so doing; and, no doubt, would have succeeded, if Fate had not, in a wonderful manner, caused Madame Peytel TO TAKE HER HUSBAND'S PLACE, and receive the ball intended for him in her own head.

But whether these suspicions are absurd or not, hit or miss, it is the advocate's duty, as it appears, to urge them. He wants to make as unfavourable an impression as possible with regard to Peytel's character; he, therefore, must, for contrast's sake, give all sorts of praise to his victim, and awaken every sympathy in the poor fellow's favour. Having done this, as far as lies in his power, having exaggerated every circumstance that can be unfavourable to Peytel, and given his own tale in the baldest manner possible—having declared that Peytel is the murderer of his wife and servant, the Crown now proceeds to back this assertion, by showing what interested motives he had, and by relating, after its own fashion, the circumstances of his marriage.

They may be told briefly here. Peytel was of a good family, of Mâcon,

夫人吗？——在非常危险的处境下，一个柔弱的女人没什么能力来反抗，这可是最好的时机。

第二条，“直到雷知道他的主人睁开了眼睛，他才开枪”。在一个暴风雨的夜晚，驾着马车的人还会睡觉吗？难道雷要等到主人打鼾吗？“他在六步远的地方开的枪，没注意到他射击的对象是谁”——也不可能发生这种事啊？夜晚并不是那么漆黑，他还是能看到他主人坐在平常的位子上驾着马车。他开枪击中的是谁呢？是柏伊特尔夫人，她离开了自己的座位，围着她丈夫柏伊特尔的斗篷。她叫道：“丈夫，拿出你的手枪。”雷知道他的主人有两把手枪，认识到自己刚才打错人了，当柏伊特尔朝他开枪的时候，他就跑了。柏伊特尔手里拿着锤子追他，当他追上这个逃亡者的时候，他在雷的后脑敲了一下，雷就脸朝下倒在了地上。难道这个故事就没有什么奇异之处吗？——这么荒谬的事情难道是真实的吗？

第三条，反驳的理由也是荒谬的。为什么一个人在逃亡的时候需要更换衣服呢？如果他旅程中都没有带任何东西，那么在逃亡的时候为什么就该带东西呢？为什么他需要驾驶两辆马车呢？——他可以把两辆马车都赶到河里，包括柏伊特尔的那辆。为什么他要去海关把自己往虎口里送呢？对于一个男人来说，难道过边界没有别的方法吗？难道那些不得不从一个国家转到另一个国家的走私犯会选择那些设置警察的地点吗？

还有里昂卖枪械的商人，他很熟悉柏伊特尔却不能确定他是把那支手枪卖给了他，也就是说，他没有把那支手枪卖给他。在这种情况下，你只有把一个人的话反过来理解才会对柏伊特尔有利。我说，法官大人和陪审团的先生们，这位受王权雇佣的律师所提的异议是荒谬的、轻浮的、可怕的，根据这样的推测来怀疑并剥夺一个人的生命是邪恶、违法和残忍的行为。在他们看来，那个路易·雷如果想犯罪——如果想自己拥有一大笔钱，那就应该选择一个最好的时机和地点去作案，这样才会取得成功，如果命运没有令人奇怪地安排柏伊特尔夫人坐在她丈夫的位置上，那颗本来要射向她丈夫的子弹没有射到她头部的话，路易·雷的罪行就会圆满成立了。

and entitled, at his mother's death, to a considerable property. He had been educated as a notary, and had lately purchased a business, in that line, in Belley, for which he had paid a large sum of money; part of the sum, 15,000 francs, for which he had given bills, was still due.

Near Belley, Peytel first met Felicité Alcazar, who was residing with her brother-in-law, Monsieur de Montrichard; and, knowing that the young lady's fortune was considerable, he made an offer of marriage to the brother-in-law, who thought the match advantageous, and communicated on the subject with Felicité's mother, Madame Alcazar, at Paris. After a time Peytel went to Paris, to press his suit, and was accepted. There seems to have been no affectation of love on his side; and some little repugnance on the part of the lady, who yielded, however, to the wishes of her parents, and was married. The parties began to quarrel on the very day of the marriage, and continued their disputes almost to the close of the unhappy connection. Felicité was half blind, passionate, sarcastic, clumsy in her person and manners, and ill educated; Peytel, a man of considerable intellect and pretensions, who had lived for some time at Paris, where he had mingled with good literary society. The lady was, in fact, as disagreeable a person as could well be, and the evidence describes some scenes which took place between her and her husband, showing how deeply she must have mortified and enraged him.

A charge very clearly made out against Peytel, is that of dishonesty; he procured from the notary of whom he bought his place an acquittance in full, whereas there were 15,000 francs owing, as we have seen. He also, in the contract of marriage, which was to have resembled, in all respects, that between Monsieur Broussais and another Demoiselle Alcazar, caused an alteration to be made in his favour, which gave him command over his wife's funded property, without furnishing the guarantees by which the other son-in-law was bound. And, almost immediately after his marriage, Peytel sold out of the funds a sum of 50,000 francs, that belonged to his wife, and used it for his own purposes.

About two months after his marriage, PEYTEL PRESSED HIS WIFE TO MAKE HER WILL. He had made his, he said, leaving everything to her, in case of his death: after some parley, the poor thing consented. [3] This is a cruel suspicion against him; and Mr. Substitute has no need to enlarge

但无论这些猜疑是荒谬还是合理，正确还是错误，要使任何一方成立，这都是律师的责任。对于柏伊特尔的品性，律师想尽可能地给陪审团制造出一种不好的印象。因此，为了形成对比，他就把所有的赞美都用在了他的受害者身上，以唤起陪审团的同情。做到了这点之后，只要他还有能力，他就会把对柏伊特尔不利的种种因素都予以夸大，用尽可能不加虚饰的方式来讲述柏伊特尔的故事——已宣称柏伊特尔是杀害他妻子和用人的凶手后，现在法庭要通过呈现柏伊特尔的作案动机、联系他的婚姻状况来进一步支持这个观点。

这里就简单地介绍一下。柏伊特尔出生于玛孔一个有教养的家庭，在他母亲死后，继承了一笔可观的财产。他被培养成一个公证人，后来在贝莱从事工作，并购置了一笔产业，为了这笔产业，他付出了一大笔钱，其中有一万五千法郎的账单还未付现金。

在贝莱附近，柏伊特尔初次遇到了费利西特·阿尔卡萨尔，她当时正住在她姐夫蒙特里夏尔先生家里。在了解到这位年轻的女士拥有一笔相当可观的财产之后，柏伊特尔就向她的姐夫提出要和费利西特·阿尔卡萨尔结婚的请求，她姐夫认为这门婚姻还是很不错的，就和在巴黎的费利西特的母亲商量这门婚事。过了一段时间，柏伊特尔去了巴黎，坚持向费利西特求婚，被费利西特的母亲接受了。从柏伊特尔这边来看，他好像对费利西特没有爱情。而费利西特女士这边也有些抵触，但她最后还是顺从了她亲人的意愿，结婚了。两个人从结婚的当天就开始吵架，一直延续到这场不幸的婚姻结束为止。费利西特在为人和举止方面有些轻率、性情暴躁、好挖苦人，并且愚笨、缺乏教养。柏伊特尔是个有才华有抱负的人，他在巴黎住过一段时间，在那里他曾加入过有素养的文学团体。实际上，费利西特是个很难相处的女人，有证据描述了发生在费利西特和她丈夫之间的争吵，显示出她曾经多么深深地伤害、激怒过柏伊特尔。

对柏伊特尔的一项重要的指控就是欺诈。他从他收买的公证人那里获得了一张清欠收据，但我们知道，他仍欠有一万五千法郎的债务。他还在

upon it. As for the previous fact, the dishonest statement about the 15,000 francs, there is nothing murderous in that—nothing which a man very eager to make a good marriage might not do. The same may be said of the suppression, in Peytel's marriage contract, of the clause to be found in Broussais', placing restrictions upon the use of the wife's money. Mademoiselle d'Alcazar's friends read the contract before they signed it, and might have refused it, had they so pleased.

After some disputes, which took place between Peytel and his wife (there were continual quarrels, and continual letters passing between them from room to room), the latter was induced to write him a couple of exaggerated letters, swearing "by the ashes of her father" that she would be an obedient wife to him, and entreating him to counsel and direct her. These letters were seen by members of the lady's family, who, in the quarrels between the couple, always took the husband's part. They were found in Peytel's cabinet, after he had been arrested for the murder, and after he had had full access to all his papers, of which he destroyed or left as many as he pleased. The accusation makes it a matter of suspicion against Peytel, that he should have left these letters of his wife's in a conspicuous situation.

"All these circumstances," says the accusation, "throw a frightful light upon Peytel's plans. The letters and will of Madame Peytel are in the hands of her husband. Three months pass away, and this poor woman is brought to her home, in the middle of the night, with two balls in her head, stretched at the bottom of her carriage, by the side of a peasant."

"What other than Sebastian Peytel could have committed this murder? —whom could it profit? —who but himself had an odious chain to break, and an inheritance to receive? Why speak of the servant's projected robbery? The pistols found by the side of Louis's body, the balls bought by him at Mâcon, and those discovered at Belley among his effects, were only the result of a perfidious combination. The pistol, indeed, which was found on the hill of Darde, on the night of the 1st of November, could only have belonged to Peytel, and must have been thrown by him, near the body of his domestic, with the paper which had before enveloped it. Who had seen this pistol in the hands of Louis? Among all the gendarmes, work-women, domestics, employed by Peytel and his brother-in-law, is there one single witness

布鲁塞先生和另一位阿尔卡萨尔女士（费利西特的姐姐）的公证下，在婚约以及其他的契约中做了有利于自己的一些改动，使他自己能控制妻子的带有固定利息的财产，而无须像另一位女婿那样必须要提供担保人。几乎是在刚结婚之后，柏伊特尔就为了个人目的，取出了本属于他妻子的五万法郎。

大约是在他婚后两个月，柏伊特尔就强迫他妻子写她的遗嘱。他说他已写了自己的遗嘱，如果他死了，会把一切东西都留给她。两人在做了一些交涉之后，可怜的费利西特答应了他的要求。[3]这是柏伊特尔身上的一个最大疑点，诉讼代理人没必要再详述它了。至于先前的事实，关于欺诈一万五千法郎的陈述，那里面并没有什么杀人的因素——一个渴望拥有美好婚姻的男子不会那样做的。同样受到怀疑的还有在柏伊特尔的婚约中，隐瞒了在布鲁塞公证的文件中发现的条款，这个条款限制了他对妻子金钱的使用权利。阿尔卡萨尔女士的朋友在他们签署这个契约之前就读过它，如果他们愿意的话会对此予以拒绝的。

在柏伊特尔和他的妻子之间发生了一些争论之后（他们在所有地方持续不断地吵架），柏伊特尔夫人受到丈夫的诱使写了两封言过其实的信件，以“她父亲的骨灰发誓”，她会做柏伊特尔的顺从的妻子，请求他来告诫和指引自己。这些信被夫人的家庭成员看到了，他们在这对夫妻吵架的时候总是站在丈夫的立场上。在柏伊特尔因谋杀罪被逮捕后，在他的私人小房间里发现，凡是柏伊特尔所能接触到的文件，都被他尽可能地毁坏和扔掉了。法庭起诉就把这件事作为怀疑柏伊特尔犯罪的指控，即他应该把他妻子的信件保留在一个公开明显的地方，不应该藏起来。

法庭起诉人说：“所有这些事件都显露出柏伊特尔可怕的作案计划。柏伊特尔夫人的信件和遗嘱都在她丈夫的手中。三个月过去了，这个可怜的女人被丈夫带回娘家，在午夜的时候，头部中了两颗子弹，躺在马车的一端、一个农民的旁边。”

“除了塞巴斯蒂安·柏伊特尔，还有谁会实施这场谋杀呢？——这场谋

who had seen this weapon in Louis's possession? It is true that Madame Peytel did, on one occasion, speak to M. de Montrichard of a pistol; which had nothing to do, however, with that found near Louis Rey."

Is this justice, or good reason? Just reverse the argument, and apply it to Rey. "Who but Rey could have committed this murder? —who but Rey had a large sum of money to seize upon? —a pistol is found by his side, balls and powder in his pocket, other balls in his trunks at home. The pistol found near his body could not, indeed, have belonged to Peytel: did any man ever see it in his possession? The very gunsmith who sold it, and who knew Peytel, would he not have known that he had sold him this pistol? At his own house, Peytel has a collection of weapons of all kinds; everybody has seen them—a man who makes such collections is anxious to display them. Did any one ever see this weapon? —Not one. And Madame Peytel did, in her lifetime, remark a pistol in the valet's possession. She was short-sighted, and could not particularize what kind of pistol it was; but she spoke of it to her husband and her brother-in-law." This is not satisfactory, if you please; but, at least, it is as satisfactory as the other set of suppositions. It is the very chain of argument which would have been brought against Louis Rey by this very same compiler of the act of accusation, had Rey survived, instead of Peytel, and had he, as most undoubtedly would have been the case, been tried for the murder.

This argument was shortly put by Peytel's counsel:—"if Peytel had been killed by Rey in the struggle, would you not have found Rey guilty of the murder of his master and mistress?" It is such a dreadful dilemma, that I wonder how judges and lawyers could have dared to persecute Peytel in the manner which they did.

After the act of accusation, which lays down all the suppositions against Peytel as facts, which will not admit the truth of one of the prisoner's allegations in his own defence, comes the trial. The judge is quite as impartial as the preparer of the indictment, as will be seen by the following specimens of his interrogatories:—

Judge. "The act of accusation finds in your statement contradictions, improbabilities, impossibilities. Thus your domestic, who had determined to assassinate you, in order to rob you, and who MUST HAVE CALCULATED

杀的受益者会是谁呢？——难道不是柏伊特尔自己要挣脱可怕的婚姻束缚，继承一笔遗产吗？为什么说是用人预先计划的抢劫呢？在路易尸体旁找到的那把手枪以及路易在玛孔买的子弹还有在贝莱发现的路易的财物都不能证明他是谋杀凶手。手枪确实是 11 月 1 日晚上在塔德山上找到的，但它只能是柏伊特尔的手枪，一定是他把手枪扔在了用人的尸体旁，枪上还带着先前的包装纸。谁曾看到过路易手中有这把枪呢？在柏伊特尔和他的姐夫所雇用的所有宪兵、女仆和用人之中，有没有一个证人看到过路易手中拿过这件武器呢？有一次，柏伊特尔夫人确实曾对蒙特里夏尔先生提到过一把手枪，因为但它和路易·雷身边所发现的这把手枪没有任何关系。”

这公平吗？理由充分吗？法庭只不过是否定了被告方的理由，然后再为雷开脱。“谁说不会是雷犯了谋杀罪呢？谁说雷不会抢劫那笔钱呢？——在他旁边发现的一把手枪、他口袋里的子弹和火药，还有家中他衣箱里的其他子弹都可以作证。在他身边发现的那把手枪也不可能是柏伊特尔的，又有谁见过柏伊特尔拿过这把枪呢？那个认识柏伊特尔的军械商人难道还不知道自己有没有把这支手枪卖给柏伊特尔吗？在柏伊特尔自己家里，他收集了各种各样的武器，很多人都见到过——收集东西的人总会急着向众人炫耀它们的，但是有没有人看到过这把手枪呢？——没有。柏伊特尔夫人活着的时候曾注意到这个男仆有一把手枪，因为她近视，所以辨别不出是哪一种手枪，但是她向她的丈夫和她姐夫提到过这把手枪。”你看看，这种解释虽然并不一定充分，但作为一种猜测，它还是很有可能的。控诉条例的作者同样也会根据这些猜测来驳斥路易·雷的。如果活着的不是柏伊特尔，而是雷，无疑他也会成为因谋杀罪而被审判的对象。

柏伊特尔的律师立刻就提出这个反对理由——“如果柏伊特尔在争斗中被雷杀死了，难道你们不会判决雷有谋杀罪吗？”这是如此可怕的设想啊！我想知道法官和律师为何敢用这种方式来迫害柏伊特尔。

在控诉条例把所有的推测当做事实来攻击柏伊特尔之后，法庭就不再允许柏伊特尔为自己做任何事实的辩解，接着就是审判。法官像起诉书的

UPON THE CONSEQUENCE OF A FAILURE, had neither passport nor money upon him. This is very unlikely; because he could not have gone far with only a single halfpenny, which was all he had."

Prisoner. "My servant was known, and often passed the frontier without a passport."

Judge. "YOUR DOMESTIC HAD TO ASSASSINATE TWO PERSONS, and had no weapon but a single pistol. He had no dagger; and the only thing found on him was a knife."

Prisoner. "In the car there were several turner's implements, which he might have used."

Judge. "But he had not those arms upon him, because you pursued him immediately. He had, according to you, only this old pistol."

Prisoner. "I have nothing to say."

Judge. "Your domestic, instead of flying into woods, which skirt the road, ran straight forward on the road itself: THIS, AGAIN, IS VERY UNLIKELY."

Prisoner. "This is a conjecture I could answer by another conjecture; I can only reason on the facts."

Judge. "How far did you pursue him?"

Prisoner. "I don't know exactly."

Judge. "You said 'two hundred paces.'"

No answer from the prisoner.

Judge. "Your domestic was young, active, robust, and tall. He was ahead of you. You were in a carriage, from which you had to descend: you had to take your pistols from a cushion, and THEN your hammer;—how are we to believe that you could have caught him, if he ran? It is IMPOSSIBLE."

Prisoner. "I can't explain it: I think that Rey had some defect in one leg. I, for my part, run tolerably fast."

Judge. "At what distance from him did you fire your first shot?"

Prisoner. "I can't tell."

Judge. "Perhaps he was not running when you fired."

Prisoner. "I saw him running."

Judge. "In what position was your wife?"

Prisoner. "She was leaning on my left arm, and the man was on the right

筹备人一样相当“公正”，这点我们可以从下面抽取的一部分审问中了解到：

法官：“控诉条例发现你的陈述中有很多自相矛盾和不可能成立的地方。比如，你的用人为了抢劫，决定要暗杀你，他也一定会考虑到暗杀失败后的结果，但是他既没带护照也没带钱。这是不太可能的，因为身上只有半个便士是跑不了多远的。”

被告：“我的仆人知道可以不带，也经常不带护照通过边境。”

法官：“你的用人不得不暗杀两个人，但是他只有一把手枪。他没有匕首，在他身上找到的只有一把小刀。”

被告：“在马车里有一些车工的工具，他也可以使用。”

法官：“但是他身上没有这些工具，因为你立刻就追上他了，据你所说，他只有这把旧式的手枪。”

被告：“我无话可说。”

法官：“你的用人没有跑进马路旁边的树林，反而是在马路上向前跑，这又是不太可能的。”

被告：“这只是一个推测，我不能回答。我只能根据事实来推理。”

法官：“你追了他多远？”

被告：“我不是很清楚。”

法官：“你说过是‘两百步’。”

被告没有回答。

法官：“你的用人年轻、灵敏、强壮，个子也高。他跑在你的前面。你要从马车上下来，从垫子下面拿出手枪，还有锤子。——我们怎么能相信，如果他跑了，你会抓住他？这是不可能的。”

被告：“我无法解释。我想是因为雷的一条腿有点缺陷，而我跑得还算是快的。”

法官：“你开第一枪的时候离他有多远？”

被告：“我不知道。”

side of the carriage."

Judge. "The shot must have been fired *à bout portant*, because it burned the eyebrows and lashes entirely. The assassin must have passed his pistol across your breast."

Prisoner. "The shot was not fired so close; I am convinced of it: professional gentlemen will prove it."

Judge. "That is what you pretend, because you understand perfectly the consequences of admitting the fact. Your wife was hit with two balls—one striking downwards, to the right, by the nose, the other going horizontally through the cheek, to the left."

Prisoner. "The contrary will be shown by the witnesses called for the purpose."

Judge. "IT IS A VERY UNLUCKY COMBINATION FOR YOU that these balls, which went, you say, from the same pistol, should have taken two different directions."

Prisoner. "I can't dispute about the various combinations of fire-arms—professional persons will be heard."

Judge. "According to your statement, your wife said to you, 'My poor husband, take your pistols.'"

Prisoner. "She did."

Judge. "In a manner quite distinct?"

Prisoner. "Yes."

Judge. "So distinct that you did not fancy she was hit?"

Prisoner. "Yes; that is the fact."

Judge. "HERE, AGAIN, IS AN IMPOSSIBILITY; and nothing is more precise than the declaration of the medical men. They affirm that your wife could not have spoken—their report is unanimous."

Prisoner. "I can only oppose to it quite contrary opinions from professional men, also: you must hear them."

Judge. "What did your wife do next?"

……

Judge. "You deny the statements of the witnesses:" (they related to Peytel's demeanour and behaviour, which the judge wishes to show were very unusual;—and what if they were?) "Here, however, are some mute witnes-

法官："当你开枪的时候，或许他还没有跑。"

被告："我看见他跑了。"

法官："你妻子在什么位置？"

被告："她正靠在我的左臂上，那个用人在马车的右侧。"

法官："一定是顶着枪口开的枪，因为子弹把眉毛和睫毛全部都烧着了。暗杀者一定是在你对面开的枪。"

被告："并不是很近距离地开枪。我确信这一点，专业人士也可以证明。"

法官："那是你假装的，因为你完全知道承认事实的后果。你妻子中了两弹——一颗是向下的，在鼻子的右侧穿过，另一颗是水平的，向左穿过脸颊。"

被告："相关证人所显示的结果将会是相反的。"

法官："对你来说非常不幸的是，这些据你所说是从同一把手枪所射出的子弹，竟然是两种不同的方向。"

被告："对于手枪不同的组合方式，我无法辩解——专业人员会解释的。"

法官："依照你的陈述，你妻子对你说：'我可怜的丈夫，拿出你的手枪。'"

被告："是的。"

法官："以一种非常特别的语气？"

被告："是的。"

法官："如此特别，以至于你想象不到她已中枪了吗？"

被告："是的。确实是。"

法官："这又是不可能的。没有什么会比医生的陈述更准确的了。他们证实你的妻子当时已不可能说话——他们的报告都是一致的。"

被告："我只能提出反对，它们与从专业人士那里得来的鉴定恰恰相反，您必须听听他们的观点。"

ses, whose testimony, you will not perhaps refuse. Near Louis Rey's body was found a horse-cloth, a pistol, and a whip. . . Your domestic must have had this cloth upon him when he went to assassinate you: it was wet and heavy. An assassin disencumbers himself of anything that is likely to impede him, especially when he is going to struggle with a man as young as himself."

Prisoner. "My servant had, I believe, this covering on his body; it might be useful to him to keep the priming of his pistol dry."

The president caused the cloth to be opened, and showed that there was no hook, or tie, by which it could be held together; and that Rey must have held it with one hand, and, in the other, his whip, and the pistol with which he intended to commit the crime; which was impossible.

Prisoner. "These are only conjectures."

And what conjectures, my God! upon which to take away the life of a man. Jefferies, or Fouquier Tinville, could scarcely have dared to make such. Such prejudice, such bitter persecution, such priming of the jury, such monstrous assumptions and unreason—fancy them coming from an impartial judge! The man is worse than the public accuser.

"Rey," says the Judge, "could not have committed the murder, BECAUSE HE HAD NO MONEY IN HIS POCKET, TO FLY. IN CASE OF FAILURE." And what is the precise sum that his lordship thinks necessary for a gentleman to have, before he makes such an attempt? Are the men who murder for money, usually in possession of a certain independence before they begin? How much money was Rey, a servant, who loved wine and women, had been stopping at a score of inns on the road, and had, probably, an annual income of 400 francs,—how much money was Rey likely to have?

"Your servant had to assassinate two persons." This I have mentioned before. Why had he to assassinate two persons,[4] when one was enough? If he had killed Peytel, could he not have seized and gagged his wife immediately?

"Your domestic ran straight forward, instead of taking to the woods, by the side of the rood: this is very unlikely." How does his worship know? Can any judge, however enlightened, tell the exact road that a man will take, who has just missed a coup of murder, and is pursued by a man who is firing pistols at him? And has a judge a right to instruct a jury in this way, as to what

法官："你的妻子接着又做了什么？"

……

法官："你否认了证人的陈述。"（他们联系到柏伊特尔的举止和行为，法官想显示出它们是异常的。——即使是那样，又有什么关系呢？）"然而这里还有些无言的证据，你或许是不会否认的。在路易·雷尸体旁边发现了一件马衣［盖在马身上或装饰马用的。——译注］、一把手枪和一条鞭子……当你的用人去暗杀你的时候，一定是穿着这件又湿又沉的衣服。一个暗杀者会摆脱掉任何有可能妨碍他行为的东西，尤其是当他将要同一个势均力敌的人斗争的时候。"

被告："我相信，我的用人是穿着这件衣服的，或许它对作案是有用的，可以让手枪的火药不被淋湿。"

法庭庭长把那件衣服打开，可以看出它既没有挂钩也没有带子，无法系在一起。那么雷一定是一手抓住衣服，另一只手拿着鞭子和要实施犯罪的手枪，这是不可能的。

被告："这些只是猜测。"

我的上帝，这是什么样的猜测啊！根据这样的猜测去剥夺一个人的生命。即使是杰弗瑞或富基埃·坦维尔［坦维尔（1746—1795），法国律师，法国大革命时期的政治家，任革命法庭检察官，在恐怖时代曾批准处决过几百人，后来自己也被送上断头台。——译注］也不敢这样做的。这样的偏见、这样的迫害、这样荒谬的假设和猜测竟出现在一个公正法官的审讯过程中——简直让人无法想象！这个法官比公开的起诉者还要坏。

法官说："雷不可能犯谋杀罪，因为万一失败了就要逃跑，但他身上却没带钱。"这位法官大人认为一个先生在作案时需要带多少钱呢？难道为了钱财而谋杀的罪犯都要带有一定的钱财吗？雷作为一个喜欢酒色的用人曾在马路边的小酒店里欠了多少账呢？或许他每年会有四百法郎的收入——但雷到底能有多少钱呢？

"你的仆人不得不暗杀两个人。"我前面已提到了这句话。为什么杀一

they shall, or shall not, believe?

"You have to run after an active man, who has the start of you: to jump out of a carriage; to take your pistols; and THEN, your hammer. THIS IS IMPOSSIBLE." By heavens! does it not make a man's blood boil, to read such blundering, blood-seeking sophistry? This man, when it suits him, shows that Rey would be slow in his motions; and when it suits him, declares that Rey ought to be quick; declares ex cathedra, what pace Rey should go, and what direction he should take; shows, in a breath, that he must have run faster than Peytel; and then, that he could not run fast, because the cloak clogged him; settles how he is to be dressed when he commits a murder, and what money he is to have in his pocket; gives these impossible suppositions to the jury, and tells them that the previous statements are impossible; and, finally, informs them of the precise manner in which Rey must have stood holding his horse-cloth in one hand, his whip and pistol in the other, when he made the supposed attempt at murder. Now, what is the size of a horse-cloth? Is it as big as a pocket-handkerchief? Is there no possibility that it might hang over one shoulder; that the whip should be held under that very arm? Did you never see a carter so carry it, his hands in his pockets all the while? Is it monstrous, abhorrent to nature, that a man should fire a pistol from under a cloak on a rainy day? —that he should, after firing the shot, be frightened, and run; run straight before him, with the cloak on his shoulders, and the weapon in his hand? Peytel's story is possible, and very possible; it is almost probable. Allow that Rey had the cloth on, and you allow that he must have been clogged in his motions; that Peytel may have come up with him—felled him with a blow of the hammer; the doctors say that he would have so fallen by one blow—he would have fallen on his face, as he was found: the paper might have been thrust into his breast, and tumbled out as he fell. Circumstances far more impossible have occurred ere this; and men have been hanged for them, who were as innocent of the crime laid to their charge as the judge on the bench, who convicted them.

In like manner, Peytel may not have committed the crime charged to him; and Mr. Judge, with his arguments as to possibilities and impossibilities,—Mr. Public Prosecutor, with his romantic narrative and inflammatory harangues to the jury,—may have used all these powers to bring to death an

个人就已足够的时候，他必须要杀两个人呢？[4]假如他杀了柏伊特尔，难道他不会即刻就抓住柏伊特尔的妻子，塞住她的口吗？

“你的用人没有跑进路边的树林，而是直着向前跑，这是不可能的。”法官大人是怎么知道的呢？不管是多么有见识的法官，他能告诉一个因谋杀失败、被开枪人所追赶的罪犯应该走哪条路吗？难道一个法官能用这种方式向陪审团提供现场消息、左右陪审团的看法吗？

“你不得不追赶那个行动灵敏的用人，他在你的前面。你要从马车里跳出来，拿出你的手枪，还有你的锤子，这是不可能的。”老天在上！读到这样的诡辩难道不让人愤怒吗？这个法官在适当的时候就会辩护说，雷的动作有些慢，而在另一个适当的时候，就会辩护说雷应该是跑得快的。他还能权威地宣布雷应该采用什么速度，走哪个方向，说明雷一定会比柏伊特尔跑得快，如果他跑不快，那也是因为斗篷妨碍了他。他还会安排雷在谋杀的时候应该怎样穿衣服，口袋里带多少钱。他把这些没有事实根据的猜测都提供给陪审团，最后告诉他们，假定雷要谋杀，他会怎样一只手抓着马衣，另一只手拿着鞭子和手枪。一件马衣又不会像手帕那样小，难道雷不会把马衣扛在肩上，胳膊下夹着鞭子吗？你见到过驾驶马车的人始终把手放在口袋里携带东西的吗？在下雨天，一个人从斗篷下开枪又有什么奇怪的呢？在开枪后，他会受到惊吓逃跑，肩上扛着马衣，手里拿着手枪向前直跑，也完全可能啊？柏伊特尔对案件的描述是可能的，非常可能，几乎完全可能。雷既然穿着马衣，那么他的行动必然会受到阻碍，因此柏伊特尔就可以追上他，用锤子给他一击。医生说雷会因这一击而倒下的——我们也发现雷正是脸朝下倒地的。然而，法官却迟迟不能做出判定，宣布柏伊特尔是无辜的。他们坚信柏伊特尔犯有指控的罪行。

柏伊特尔有可能没犯下被指控的罪行，但法官大人用他的猜测来进行推理、起诉律师在陪审团面前的虚构夸张的叙述——这些都足以给一个无辜的人带来死亡。案子从开始到结束都被这种敌意所引导着，人们很容易就能看到它的结果是什么。下面是外省报纸的消息：

innocent man. From the animus with which the case had been conducted from beginning to end, it was easy to see the result. Here it is, in the words of the provincial paper:—

BOURG, 28 October, 1839.

"The condemned Peytel has just undergone his punishment, which took place four days before the anniversary of his crime. The terrible drama of the bridge of Andert, which cost the life of two persons, has just terminated on the scaffold. Mid day had just sounded on the clock of the Palais: the same clock tolled midnight when, on the 30th of August, his sentence was pronounced.

"Since the rejection of his appeal in Cassation, on which his principal hopes were founded, Peytel spoke little of his petition to the King. The notion of transportation was that which he seemed to cherish most. However, he made several inquiries from the gaoler of the prison, when he saw him at meal-time, with regard to the place of execution, the usual hour, and other details on the subject. From that period, the words 'Champ de Foire' (the fair-field, where the execution was to be held), were frequently used by him in conversation.

"Yesterday, the idea that the time had arrived seemed to be more strongly than ever impressed upon him; especially after the departure of the curate, who latterly has been with him every day. The documents connected with the trial had arrived in the morning. He was ignorant of this circumstance, but sought to discover from his guardians what they tried to hide from him; and to find out whether his petition was rejected, and when he was to die.

"Yesterday, also, he had written to demand the presence of his counsel, M. Margerand, in order that he might have some conversation with him, and regulate his affairs, before he …; he did not write down the word, but left in its place a few points of the pen.

"In the evening, whilst he was at supper, he begged earnestly to be allowed a little wax-candle, to finish what he was writing: otherwise, he said, TIME MIGHT FAIL. This was a new, indirect manner of repeating his ordinary question. As light, up to that evening, had been refused him, it was thought best to deny him in this, as in former instances; otherwise his suspicions might have been confirmed. The keeper refused his demand.

"This morning, Monday, at nine o'clock, the Greffier of the Assize Court, in fulfilment of the painful duty which the law imposes upon him, came to the prison, in company with the curé of Bourg, and announced to the convict that

布尔格，1839 年 10 月 28 日

法庭刚刚宣判了对柏伊特尔的裁决，还有四天就是案发一周年的时间了。发生在安德耐桥上的惨剧夺去了两个人的生命，这一案件将在断头台上画上句号。正午的时钟刚刚在王宫敲响，同样当 8 月 30 日对柏伊特尔执刑时，钟声也敲响了。

他把自己的希望主要都寄托在了上诉书上，由于他向上诉法院提出的上诉被驳回，他不再去请求国王。他强烈渴望自己能被判处流放。但是在吃饭时间，他向监狱看守打听了一些关于行刑地方的消息、平常行刑的时间以及其他一些细节问题。从那时起，他在谈话中就经常提到“集市场”(处死刑的地方)。

昨天，他越来越强烈地感到死亡的时间就要到来了，尤其是在教区牧师离开之后，这个牧师近来每天都和他在一起。有关审判的文件在早晨已被送到监狱。他还不知道这件事情，但他试图从监护人那里查问出他们在尽力瞒着他什么，想弄清楚他的上诉是否被驳回了，他什么时候死。

昨天，他写了封信要求和他的律师玛尔热朗先生见面，就是为了和他谈谈话，在他（死）之前，安排一下他的个人事务。但他没有写下那个（死）字，而是在那个地方用钢笔点了几个点。

傍晚，在吃晚餐的时候，他急切地向监护人提出请求，能否允许他晚上点一小根蜡烛，以写完他要写的东西，他说，否则就没有时间了。这次与以往所提请求的方式很不一样是新的、间接的。他的请求没有得到许可，监护人认为还是像以往的先例一样最好是拒绝他，以免使他的怀疑得到确证。

今天早上即星期一的九点钟，巡回法院的公证人在布尔格牧师的陪同下来履行法律职责，向罪犯宣布其上诉已被驳回，他还有三个小时可活了。柏伊特尔非常平静地接受了这个不幸的消息，他本人看起来没有受到很大影响，就像当初在审判席上一样。“我准备好了，但我

his petition was rejected, and that he had only three hours to live. He received this fatal news with a great deal of calmness, and showed himself to be no more affected than he had been on the trial. 'I am ready; but I wish they had given me four-and-twenty hours' notice,'—were all the words he used.

"The Greffier now retired, leaving Peytel alone with the curé, who did not thenceforth quit him. Peytel breakfasted at ten o'clock.

"At eleven, a picquet of mounted gendarmerie and infantry took their station upon the place before the prison, where a great concourse of people had already assembled. An open car was at the door. Before he went out Peytel asked the gaoler for a looking-glass; and having examined his face for a moment, said, 'At least, the inhabitants of Bourg will see that I have not grown thin.'

"As twelve o'clock sounded, the prison gates opened, an aide appeared, followed by Peytel, leaning on the arm of the curate. Peytel's face was pale, he had a long black beard, a blue cap on his head, and his great-coat flung over his shoulders, and buttoned at the neck.

"He looked about at the place and the crowd; he asked if the carriage would go at a trot; and on being told that that would be difficult, he said he would prefer walking, and asked what the road was. He immediately set out, walking at a firm and rapid pace. He was not bound at all.

"An immense crowd of people encumbered the two streets through which he had to pass to the place of execution. He cast his eyes alternately upon them and upon the guillotine, which was before him.

"Arrived at the foot of the scaffold, Peytel embraced the curé, and bade him adieu. He then embraced him again; perhaps, for his mother and sister. He then mounted the steps rapidly, and gave himself into the hands of the executioner, who removed his coat and cap. He asked how he was to place himself, and on a sign being made, he flung himself briskly on the plank, and stretched his neck. In another moment he was no more.

"The crowd, which had been quite silent, retired, profoundly moved by the sight it had witnessed. As at all executions, there was a very great number of women present.

"Under the scaffold there had been, ever since the morning, a coffin. The family had asked for his remains, and had them immediately buried, privately: and thus the unfortunate man's head escaped the modellers in wax, several of whom had arrived to take an impression of it."

Down goes the axe; the poor wretch's head rolls gasping into the basket;

希望他们最好还是在二十四小时之前通知我。”他就说了这些。

公证人退下了，只留下牧师和柏伊特尔在一起，牧师就一直陪伴到他被处以死刑为止。柏伊特尔在十点吃了早餐。

十一点，设岗的宪兵队和步兵团成员都在监狱前站好自己的位置，那里早就聚集了一大群人。在门口有一辆敞篷马车。柏伊特尔在出去之前问监狱看守要了一面镜子，仔细地看了一会儿他的脸说：“至少，布尔格的居民将会看到我没有变瘦。”

十二点的钟声敲响了，监狱的大门打开了，柏伊特尔靠在牧师的手臂上，跟在一个助手的后面。柏伊特尔的脸色是苍白的，留着长长的黑色胡须，头上戴着一顶蓝色的帽子，肩上披着他的大外套，在脖颈处系着扣子。

他向四处看了看广场和人群，问马车能否小跑着过去，驾车的人告诉他很困难，他说他还是步行走过去为好，问是哪条路。他即刻就出发了，步伐坚定而快速，但毕竟还没有跑起来。

在他去执行死刑的广场所经过的两条街上都挤满了人。他轮流地瞧了瞧人群和前面的断头台。

到了断头台下面，柏伊特尔拥抱了牧师，向他说再见。接着，他又拥抱了牧师一次，或许是把牧师当做他的母亲和姐姐来告别吧。他快速地走上台阶，把自己交给刽子手，刽子手把他的帽子和外套脱掉。他问刽子手自己该怎样做，刽子手给他做了个示意动作，他自己就灵活地躺在了木板上，伸出脖子。再等一会儿，他就不在这个世上了。

人群一直是非常静默的，但是看到这一幕，他们也很受震动，退了下去。在整个行刑过程中，还有不少的女观众在场。

在早晨，断头台下面就摆放着一副棺材。罪犯家人要求保留其遗体，以便于让他们能私下里即刻安葬，这样柏伊特尔的人头就能避免落到蜡像制作人的手里，虽然已有一些做蜡像模型的人赶到这里来一睹为快。

the spectators go home, pondering; and Mr. Executioner and his aides have, in half an hour, removed all traces of the august sacrifice, and of the altar on which it had been performed. Say, Mr. Briefless, do you think that any single person, meditating murder, would be deterred therefrom by beholding this—nay, a thousand more executions? It is not for moral improvement, as I take it, nor for opportunity to make appropriate remarks upon the punishment of crime, that people make a holiday of a killing-day, and leave their homes and occupations, to flock and witness the cutting off of a head. Do we crowd to see Mr. Macready in the new tragedy, or Mademoiselle Elssler in her last new ballet and flesh-coloured stockinnet pantaloons, out of a pure love of abstract poetry and beauty; or from a strong notion that we shall be excited, in different ways, by the actor and the dancer? And so, as we go to have a meal of fictitious terror at the tragedy, of something more questionable in the ballet, we go for a glut of blood to the execution. The lust is in every man's nature, more or less. Did you ever witness a wrestling or boxing match? The first clatter of the kick on the shins, or the first drawing of blood, makes the stranger shudder a little; but soon the blood is his chief enjoyment, and he thirsts for it with a fierce delight. It is a fine grim pleasure that we have in seeing a man killed; and I make no doubt that the organs of destructiveness must begin to throb and swell as we witness the delightful savage spectacle.

Three or four years back, when Fieschi and Lacenaire were executed, I made attempts to see the execution of both; but was disappointed in both cases. In the first instance, the day for Fieschi's death was, purposely, kept secret; and he was, if I remember rightly, executed at some remote quarter of the town. But it would have done a philanthropist good, to witness the scene which we saw on the morning when his execution did NOT take place.

It was carnival time, and the rumour had pretty generally been carried abroad that he was to die on that morning. A friend, who accompanied me, came many miles, through the mud and dark, in order to be in at the death. We set out before light, floundering through the muddy Champs Elysées; where, besides, were many other persons floundering, and all bent upon the same errand. We passed by the Concert of Musard, then held in the Rue St. Honoré; and round this, in the wet, a number of coaches were collected. The ball was just up, and a crowd of people in hideous masquerade, drunk, tired,

斧子砍了下来，可怜的柏伊特尔的人头顺势滚到了一个篮子里。围观者若有所思地回家了，剩下刽子手和他的助手在半个小时之内就把一切行刑的痕迹给清除掉了。爱德华律师，你认为任何一个策划谋杀的人在这里看到一千来遍这样的情境会受到感动、不再犯罪吗？我认为，它不是为了提升人们的道德水平，也不是提供一个机会让人们对罪行的惩罚做出适当的议论，相反，处死刑的日子被人们当成了节日，他们抛下手中的工作，离开自己的家，聚集到一起来目睹人头落地的场面。出于对抽象的艺术和美的纯粹热爱，我们拥挤着去看过麦克里迪的新悲剧或艾勒塞勒女士最新的芭蕾舞剧吗？我们能从演员和舞蹈家那里受到强烈的激励吗？同人们在悲剧中去享受虚构的恐怖或在芭蕾舞剧中享受艺术之美一样，人们也去处死刑的地方享受流血给他们带来的快感。在每个人的本性中都有着或多或少的这种欲望。你曾目睹过摔跤或拳击比赛吗？第一次看到被人踢在胫骨上或看到流出鲜血，会让人因恐怖而战栗。但是很快，人就找到了嗜血的快乐，并且能从中体会到一种强烈的愉悦。目睹一个人被杀死是种非常残忍的快乐。我毫不怀疑，当我们目睹这一野蛮场面时，我们的破坏欲一定会因此而兴奋膨胀。

三四年前，当费埃希和拉色内尔［一个在 1836 年被处死刑的杀人犯。——译注］被处决的时候，我还准备去现场观看，但都没有看成。先说费埃希，他处死刑的日期是特意保密的。如果我没记错，他应该是在城里某个偏僻的地方被处决的。对于我们来说，没能在早晨看到他的处决，也算是法院做的一件善事。

那时正是狂欢节时期，谣言已传到国外，说费埃希要在某日早晨被处决。陪我去看的还有一个朋友，他在黑暗中走了许多泥路，就是为了能亲眼见到费埃希被处死。我们在天亮之前就出发了，踉跄着穿过泥泞的爱丽舍宫街，在这里还有许多和我们抱同样目的的人在踉跄着前进。我们从缪萨特音乐厅旁经过，在圣奥诺雷街就被挡住了，这条街上聚集了许多马车，天还下着雨。舞会刚刚结束，穿着丑陋的舞会服装的男人都醉醺醺的，疲

dirty, dressed in horrible old frippery, and daubed with filthy rouge, were trooping out of the place: tipsy women and men, shrieking, jabbering, gesticulating, as French will do; parties swaggering, staggering forwards, arm in arm, reeling to and fro across the street, and yelling songs in chorus: hundreds of these were bound for the show, and we thought ourselves lucky in finding a vehicle to the execution place, at the Barrière d'Enfer. As we crossed the river and entered the Enfer Street, crowds of students, black workmen, and more drunken devils from more carnival balls, were filling it; and on the grand place there were thousands of these assembled, looking out for Fieschi and his cortège. We waited and waited; but alas! no fun for us that morning: no throat-cutting; no august spectacle of satisfied justice; and the eager spectators were obliged to return, disappointed of their expected breakfast of blood. It would have been a fine scene, that execution, could it but have taken place in the midst of the mad mountebanks and tipsy strumpets who had flocked so far to witness it, wishing to wind up the delights of their carnival by a bonnebouche of a murder.

The other attempt was equally unfortunate. We arrived too late on the ground to be present at the execution of Lacenaire and his co-mate in murder, Avril. But as we came to the ground (a gloomy round space, within the barrier—three roads lead to it; and, outside, you see the wine-shops and restaurateurs of the barrier looking gay and inviting,)—as we came to the ground, we only found, in the midst of it, a little pool of ice, just partially tinged with red. Two or three idle street-boys were dancing and stamping about this pool; and when I asked one of them whether the execution had taken place, he began dancing more madly than ever, and shrieked out with a loud fantastical, theatrical voice, "Venez tous Messieurs et Dames, voyez ici le sang du monstre Lacenaire, et de son compagnon le traitre Avril," or words to that effect; and straightway all the other gamins screamed out the words in chorus, and took hands and danced round the little puddle.

O, august Justice, your meal was followed by a pretty appropriate grace! Was any man, who saw the show, deterred, or frightened, or moralized in any way? He had gratified his appetite for blood, and this was all. There is something singularly pleasing, both in the amusement of execution-seeing, and in the results. You are not only delightfully excited at the time, but most

龛肮脏；还有穿着可憎的老式俗艳服装的女人，脸上涂抹着脏兮兮的胭脂，都成群地散了出来。摇摇晃晃的女人和男人都尖叫着，叽叽喳喳地做手势，一副法国人的做派；一群群的人臂挽臂，前后摇摆地向前走，一齐大声地唱着歌。这么多人一定是去看死刑的，我们认为自己还是很幸运的，能找到一辆马车去执刑广场。我们穿过塞纳河，来到了广场入口的街上，街上挤满了多从狂欢舞会里出来的成群的学生、黑人劳工和醉醺醺的恶棍。广场那里已聚集了成千的人，都在等着看费埃希和他的送葬人行列。我们等啊！等啊！但是，唉，那天早上并没有什么死刑，也没有法官审判的威严场面。热切的观众不得不失望地离开对他们所期盼的“鲜血早餐”很失望。否则在远道而来的江湖骗子和醉醺醺的妓女之中执行死刑将会是很精彩的一幕，他们聚集在一起就是想目睹一个谋杀犯的死亡，并从他人的死亡中得到振奋和快乐。

我们去看拉色内尔的死刑也同样的倒霉，因为我们去得太迟，拉色内尔和他的同伴艾维已被处死了。当我们到达执刑地点（一块阴暗的用栅栏围起来的圆形空地——有三条道路通向空地，栅栏外面，你会看到快乐而诱人的酒店，以及酒店的老板）的时候，只看到地面上有一小汪冰水，一部分被染红了。两三个街头闲逛的男孩正围着这汪水跳舞和跺脚。我问他们其中的一个是否已经处决罪犯了，他比刚才跳得更加疯狂了，用一种很大的、夸张的声音尖叫着，“女士们，先生们都过来看啊！这里是残忍的拉色内尔和他阴险的同伴艾维的血”，还有一些诸如此类的话。很快，其他的顽童也一齐尖叫起来，手拉着手围着这摊水跳舞。

哦！威严的审判啊！紧随其后的竟是如此滑稽的表演！任何一个看到这一幕的人会因此受到惊吓而提高德行吗？他只会使自己嗜血的爱好得到满足，无论是在目睹执刑过程中还是执刑后，人们都能从中找到独特的愉悦。你不仅当时快乐、兴奋，在事后你还会感到更加的放松。人的思想在经历了那紧张的一刻后，会变得非常的自满和放松。正如哲学家告诉我们的那样，我们总能从别人的不幸中得到些许安慰。想想我们在看完死刑后

pleasingly relaxed afterwards; the mind, which has been wound up painfully until now, becomes quite complacent and easy. There is something agreeable in the misfortunes of others, as the philosopher has told us. Remark what a good breakfast you eat after an execution; how pleasant it is to cut jokes after it, and upon it. This merry, pleasant mood is brought on by the blood tonic.

But, for God's sake, if we are to enjoy this, let us do so in moderation; and let us, at least, be sure of a man's guilt before we murder him. To kill him, even with the full assurance that he is guilty is hazardous enough. Who gave you the right to do so? —you, who cry out against suicides, as impious and contrary to Christian law? What use is there in killing him? You deter no one else from committing the crime by so doing: you give us, to be sure, half an hour's pleasant entertainment; but it is a great question whether we derive much moral profit from the sight. If you want to keep a murderer from farther inroads upon society, are there not plenty of hulks and prisons, God wot; treadmills, galleys, and houses of correction? Above all, as in the case of Sebastian Peytel and his family, there have been two deaths already; was a third death absolutely necessary? and, taking the fallibility of judges and lawyers into his heart, and remembering the thousand instances of unmerited punishment that have been suffered, upon similar and stronger evidence before, can any man declare, positively and upon his oath, that Peytel was guilty, and that this was not THE THIRD MURDER IN THE FAMILY?

NOTES:

[1] He always went to mass; it is in the evidence.

[2] This sentence is taken from another part of the "Acte d'accusation."

[3] "Peytel," says the act of accusation, "did not fail to see the danger which would menace him, if this will (which had escaped the magistrates in their search of Peytel's papers) was discovered. He, therefore, instructed his agent to take possession of it, which he did, and the fact was not mentioned for several months afterwards. Peytel and his agent were called upon to explain the circumstance, but refused, and their silence for a long time interrupted the 'instruction'" (getting up of the evidence). "All that could be obtained from them was an avowal, that such a will existed, constituting Peytel his wife's sole legatee; and a promise, on their parts, to produce it before the

吃着多么丰盛的早餐，会多么愉快地开玩笑，这种快乐的心情就是别人的血所换来的。

但是，看在上帝面上，当我们享受这些的时候，让我们有所节制吧！至少，我们应该在杀害一个人之前明确他的罪行。在还没有完全确证一个人的罪行之前就把他杀掉是危险的，这样的权利谁能拥有呢？那些叫喊着反对自杀的人，难道就因为自杀违背了基督教律法，是不虔诚的吗？杀了犯人又有什么用呢？这样做不会阻止人们犯罪，而只是带给人们半个小时的娱乐。问题的关键在于我们能否从中得到更多的道德教益。如果想要坏人不再危害社会，我们不是有很多的囚船、监狱，还有囚犯用的踏车、帆船和改造所吗？就塞巴斯蒂安·柏伊特尔和他的家庭来说，已经死了两个人了，第三个人的死亡还有必要吗？想想成千的人就因为这些带有偏见的证据而被处以不当的惩罚，真是让人为法官和律师的失误而忧虑啊！有没有人敢以类似的甚至更为确切的证据证明发誓断言柏伊特尔是有罪的，这不是他家里的第三起谋杀呢？

注释：

[1] 他经常去做弥撒，这是有证据的。

[2] 这是控诉条例另一部分中的句子。

[3] 控诉条例说："如果这个遗嘱（在搜寻柏伊特尔的文件时，地方法官没有注意到）被发现了，柏伊特尔肯定会预料得到他所面临的危险。因此，他让他的代理人拿着这份遗嘱，在后来的几个月中都没有提到这个事实。柏伊特尔和他的代理人被传唤到法庭来解释这件事情的详情，但遭到了他们的拒绝，他们很长一段时间都保持沉默，干扰了法庭'指令'的进行。""从他们那儿得到的只有一个供认，那就是存在这么一个遗嘱，指定柏伊特尔作为他妻子唯一的遗产继承人。他们也允诺在法庭宣判之前会把这份遗嘱交出来。"但是为什么要秘密保存这份遗嘱呢？对这份遗嘱的焦虑

court gave its sentence." But why keep the will secret? The anxiety about it was surely absurd and unnecessary: the whole of Madame Peytel's family knew that such a will was made. She had consulted her sister concerning it, who said—"If there is no other way of satisfying him, make the will;" and the mother, when she heard of it, cried out—"Does he intend to poison her?"

[4] M. Balzac's theory of the case is, that Rey had intrigued with Madame Peytel; having known her previous to her marriage, when she was staying in the house of her brother-in-law, Monsieur de Montrichard, where Rey had been a servant.

确实是奇怪和没必要的。柏伊特尔夫人的全部家人都知道制定了这么一个遗嘱。柏伊特尔夫人还就这件事情和她的姐姐商量，她姐姐说——“如果没有别的方法使他满足，那就立下这个遗嘱”，而她母亲在听说了这件事后哭喊道——“难道他想毒害我的女儿吗?”

[4] 巴尔扎克对这件案子的推测是，雷和柏伊特尔夫人私通。在费利西特结婚之前住在她姐夫蒙特里夏尔家的时候，雷就是她姐夫家里的用人。

Four Imitations of Béranger

Le Roi D'yvetot

Il était un roi d'Yvetot,
Peu connu dans l'histoire;
Se levant tard, se couchant tôt,
Dormant fort bien sans gloire,
Et couronné par Jeanneton
D'un simple bonnet de coton,
Dit-on.
Oh! oh! oh! oh! ah! ah! ah! ah!
Quel bon petit roi c'était là!
La, la.

Il fesait ses quatre repas
Dans son palais de chaume,
Et sur un âne, pas à pas,
Parcourait son royaume.
Joyeux, simple et croyant le bien,
Pour toute garde il n'avait rien
Qu'un chien.
Oh! oh! oh! oh! ah! ah! ah! ah! &c.
La, la.

仿贝朗瑞[1]的四首歌谣

Le Roi D'yvetot（《意弗托国王》法语原作——译注）

Il était un roi　d'Yvetot，
Peu connu dans　l'histoire；
Se levant tard，se couchant tôt，
Dormant fort bien sans gloire，
Et couronné par Jeanneton
D'un simple bonnet de coton，
Dit－on.
Oh！oh！oh！oh！ah！ah！ah！ah！
Quel bon petit roi c' était　là！
La，la.
Il fesait ses quatre repas
Dans son palais de chaume，
Et sur un âne，pas à pas，
Parcourait son royaume.
Joyeux，simple et croyant le bien，
Pour toute garde il n' avait rien

Il n'avait de goût onéreux
Qu'une soif un peu vive;
Mais, en rendant son peuple heureux,
Il faux bien qu'un roi vive.
Lui-même *à* table, et sans suppôt,
Sur chaque muid levait un pot
D'impôt.
Oh! oh! oh! oh! ah! ah! ah! ah! &c.
La, la.

Aux filles de bonnes maisons
Comme il avait su plaire,
Ses sujets avaient cent raisons
De le nommer leur père:
D'ailleurs il ne levait de ban
Que pour tirer quatre fois l'an
Au blanc.
Oh! oh! oh! oh! ah! ah! ah! ah! &c.
La, la.

Il n'agrandit point ses états,
Fut un voisin commode,
Et, modèle des potentats,
Prit le plaisir pour code.
Ce n'est que lorsqu'il expira,
Que le peuple qui l'enterra
Pleura.
Oh! oh! oh! oh! ah! ah! ah! ah! &c.
La, la.

Qu'un chien.

Oh! oh! oh! oh! ah! ah! ah! ah! &c.

La, la.

Il n'avait de goût onéreux

Qu'une soif un peu vive;

Mais, en rendant son peuple heureux,

Il faux bien qu'un roi vive.

Lui-mê me *à* table, et sans suppôt,

Sur chaque muid levait un pot

D'impôt.

Oh! oh! oh! oh! ah! ah! ah! ah! &c.

La, la.

Aux filles de bonnes maisons

Comme il avait su plaire,

Ses sujets avaient cent raisons

De le nommer leur père:

D'ailleurs il ne levait de ban

Que pour tirer quatre fois l'an

Au blanc.

Oh! oh! oh! oh! ah! ah! ah! ah! &c.

La, la.

Il n'agrandit point ses états,

Fut un voisin commode,

Et, modèle des potentats,

On conserve encor le portrait
De ce digne et bon prince;
C'est l'enseigne d'un cabaret
Fameux dans la province.
Les jours de fête, bien souvent,
La foule s'écrie en buvant
Devant:
Oh! oh! oh! oh! ah! ah! ah! ah!
Quel bon petit roi c'était *là*!
La, la.

The King of Yvetot

There was a king of Yvetot,
Of whom renown hath little said,
Who let all thoughts of glory go,
And dawdled half his days a-bed;
And every night, as night came round,
By Jenny, with a nightcap crowned,
Slept very sound:
Sing ho, ho, ho! and he, he, he!
That's the kind of king for me.

And every day it came to pass,
That four lusty meals made he;
And, step by step, upon an ass,
Rode abroad, his realms to see;
And wherever he did stir,

Prit le plaisir pour code.
Ce n'est que lorsqu'il expira,
Que le peuple qui l'enterra
Pleura.
Oh! oh! oh! oh! ah! ah! ah! ah! &c.
La, la.

On conserve encor le portrait
De ce digne et bon prince;
C'est l'enseigne d'un cabaret
Fameux dans la province.
Les jours de fête, bien souvent,
La foule s'écrie en buvant
Devant:
Oh! oh! oh! oh! ah! ah! ah! ah!
Quel bon petit roi c'était là!
La, la.

意弗托国王

有一个国王叫意弗托，
他的名声很少有人知道，
他把所有的荣耀观念都抛在一边，
在自己的床上消耗了半生。
每当夜晚来临的时候，
珍妮给他带上睡帽，

What think you was his escort, sir?
Why, an old cur.
Sing ho, ho, ho! &c.

If e'er he went into excess,
'Twas from a somewhat lively thirst;
But he who would his subjects bless,
Odd's fish! —must wet his whistle first;
And so from every cask they got,
Our king did to himself allot,
At least a pot.
Sing ho, ho! &c.

To all the ladies of the land,
A courteous king, and kind, was he;
The reason why you'll understand,
They named him Pater Patriae.
Each year he called his fighting men,
And marched a league from home, and then
Marched back again.
Sing ho, ho! &c.

Neither by force nor false pretence,
He sought to make his kingdom great,
And made (O princes, learn from hence),—
"Live and let live," his rule of state.
'Twas only when he came to die,
That his people who stood by,
Were known to cry.
Sing ho, ho! &c.

他就酣然入睡了。
唱嗬，嗬，嗬！他，他，他！
正是人们爱戴的那种国王。

每天他要吃四餐饭；
还骑在毛驴上一步一步，
到处视察他的王国。
无论他到哪里，
先生，你猜他的护卫是谁？
就是一条杂种狗。
唱嗬，嗬，嗬！

他无所节制的嗜好，
就是贪饮美酒。
为他的臣民祈神赐福，
这个奇怪的家伙！——一定要事先喝酒。
因此在臣民们得到的每桶酒中，
我们国王只分给自己一罐。
唱嗬，嗬，嗬！

对于国内所有的女士来说，
他是个仁慈而谦恭的国王。
这样你就会理解为何
这里的人们会称他为他们的父亲。
每年他让他的战士们
从家乡出发前进一里格，
接着再返回来。

The portrait of this best of kings
Is extant still, upon a sign
That on a village tavern swings,
Famed in the country for good wine.
The people in their Sunday trim,
Filling their glasses to the brim,
Look up to him,
Singing ha, ha, ha! and he, he, he!
That's the sort of king for me.

The King of Brentford (Another Version)

There was a king in Brentford,—of whom no legends tell,
But who, without his glory,—could eat and sleep right well.
His Polly's cotton nightcap,—it was his crown of state,
He slept of evenings early,—and rose of mornings late.

All in a fine mud palace,—each day he took four meals,
And for a guard of honour,—a dog ran at his heels,
Sometimes, to view his kingdoms,—rode forth this monarch good,
And then a prancing jackass—he royally bestrode.

There were no costly habits—with which this king was curst,
Except (and where's the harm on't?)—a somewhat lively thirst;
But people must pay taxes,—and kings must have their sport,
So out of every gallon—His Grace he took a quart.
He pleased the ladies round him,—with manners soft and bland;
With reason good, they named him,—the father of his land.

唱嗬，嗬，嗬！

他既非靠武力也非靠欺诈，
努力使自己的国家变得强大，
他治理国家的原则是“自己活也让别人活”。
当他死了的时候，
送葬的人民都为他哭泣。
唱嗬，嗬，嗬！

在一家乡村酒馆悬挂的招牌上，
仍然保留着这个好国王的画像，
这个酒馆的酒远近驰名。
在这里，人们穿着节日的服装，
仰望着他的画像，斟满酒杯。
唱嗬，嗬，嗬！他，他，他！
正是人们爱戴的那种国王。

布伦特福德国王（另一个版本）

在布伦特福德有一个国王——关于他没有什么传奇性的经历可讲，
但是没有光荣事迹的他——却吃得香，睡得甜。
一顶棉睡帽——就是他的王冠，
他晚上睡得早——早上起得晚。

在一个简朴的宫殿中——他每天吃四餐饭，
那位荣幸的守卫——就是紧跟着他的一条狗，

Each year his mighty armies—marched forth in gallant show;
Their enemies were targets—their bullets they were tow.

He vexed no quiet neighbour,—no useless conquest made,
But by the laws of pleasure,—his peaceful realm he swayed.
And in the years he reigned,—through all this country wide,
There was no cause for weeping,—save when the good man died.

The faithful men of Brentford,—do still their king deplore,
His portrait yet is swinging,—beside an alehouse door.
And topers, tender-hearted,—regard his honest phiz,
And envy times departed—that knew a reign like his.

Le Grenier

Je viens revoir l'asile où ma jeunesse
De la misère a subi les leçons.
J'avais vingt ans, une folle maîtresse,
De francs amis et l'amour des chansons.
Bravant le monde et les sots et les sages,
Sans avenir, riche de mon printemps,
Leste et joyeux je montais six étages.
Dans un grenier qu'on est bien *à* vingt ans!

C'est un grenier, point ne veux qu'on l'ignore.
Là fut mon lit, bien chétif et bien dur;
Là fut ma table; et je retrouve encore
Trois pieds d'un vers charbonnés sur le mur.
Apparaissez, plaisirs de mon bel âge,

有时，这个善良的国王去视察他的王国，
他快活地骑着毛驴庄严地巡视。

他没有什么奢侈的生活做派——对于这些他都是诅咒的，
但是——他有强烈的酒瘾；
人们必须要交税——国王必须得到他们的支持，
因此在每加仑酒中——他只收一夸脱的酒税。

他温和的举止——很讨周围女士们的喜欢。
因此，人们称他为——他们的父亲。
每年他强大的军队——都要盛装游行。
他们的敌人才是——他们炮弹的攻击目标。

他为动乱的邻国——进行的无益争战而烦恼，
他用快乐的法则——统治着自己的和平王国。
在他统治的年代里——整个国家
都没有人哭泣——只有他死的时候除外。

布伦特福德的忠实民众——仍哀悼着他们的国王，
他的画像还悬挂在——一家酒馆的门旁。
这里的酒徒和善良的人们——看着他诚实坦率的面孔，
怀念以往——他执政的岁月。

Le Grenier（《阁楼》法语原作——译注）

Je viens revoir l'asile où ma jeunesse
De la misère a subi les leçons.

Que d'un coup d'aile a fustigés le temps,
Vingt fois pour vous j'ai mis ma montre en gage.
Dans un grenier qu'on est bien *à* vingt ans!

Lisette ici doit surtout apparaître,
Vive, jolie, avec un frais chapeau;
Déj*à* sa main *à* l'étroite fenêtre
Suspend son schal, en guise de rideau.
Sa robe aussi va parer ma couchette;
Respecte, Amour, ses plis longs et flottans.
J'ai su depuis qui payait sa toilette.
Dans un grenier qu'on est bien *à* vingt ans!

A table un jour, jour de grande richesse,
De mes amis les voix brillaient en choeur,
Quand jusqu'ici monte un cri d'allégresse:
A Marengo Bonaparte est vainqueur.
Le canon gronde; un autre chant commence;
Nous célébrons tant de faits éclatans.
Les rois jamais n'envahiront la France.
Dans un grenier qu'on est bien *à* vingt ans!

Quittons ce toit où ma raison s'enivre.
Oh! qu'ils sont loin ces jours si regrettés!
J'échangerais ce qu'il me reste *à* vivre
Contre un des mois qu'ici Dieu m'a comptés,
Pour rêver gloire, amour, plaisir, folie,
Pour dépenser sa vie en peu d'instans,
D'un long espoir pour la voir embellie,
Dans un grenier qu'on est bien *à* vingt ans!

J'avais vingt ans, une folle maîtresse,
De francs amis et l'amour des chansons.
Bravant le monde et les sots et les sages,
Sans avenir, riche de mon printemps,
Leste et joyeux je montais six étages.
Dans un grenier qu'on est bien *à* vingt ans!
C'est un grenier, point ne veux qu'on l'ignore.
L*à* fut mon lit, bien chétif et bien dur;
L*à* fut ma table; et je retrouve encore
Trois pieds d'un vers charbonnés sur le mur.
Apparaissez, plaisirs de mon bel âge,
Que d'un coup d'aile a fustigés le temps,
Vingt fois pour vous j'ai mis ma montre en gage.
Dans un grenier qu'on est bien *à* vingt ans!

Lisette ici doit surtout apparaître,
Vive, jolie, avec un frais chapeau;
Déj*à* sa main *à* l'étroite fenêtre
Suspend son schal, en guise de rideau.
Sa robe aussi va parer ma couchette;
Respecte, Amour, ses plis longs et flottans.
J'ai su depuis qui payait sa toilette.
Dans un grenier qu'on est bien *à* vingt ans!

A table un jour, jour de grande richesse,
De mes amis les voix brillaient en choeur,
Quand jusqu'ici monte un cri d'allégresse:

The Garret

With pensive eyes the little room I view,
Where, in my youth, I weathered it so long;
With a wild mistress, a stanch friend or two,
And a light heart still breaking into song:
Making a mock of life, and all its cares,
Rich in the glory of my rising sun,
Lightly I vaulted up four pair of stairs,
In the brave days when I was twenty-one.

Yes; 'tis a garret—let him know't who will—
There was my bed—full hard it was and small.
My table there—and I decipher still
Half a lame couplet charcoaled on the wall.
Ye joys, that Time hath swept with him away,
Come to mine eyes, ye dreams of love and fun;
For you I pawned my watch how many a day,
In the brave days when I was twenty-one.
And see my little Jessy, first of all;
She comes with pouting lips and sparkling eyes:
Behold, how roguishly she pins her shawl
Across the narrow casement, curtain-wise;
Now by the bed her petticoat glides down,
And when did woman look the worse in none?
I have heard since who paid for many a gown,
In the brave days when I was twenty-one.

A Marengo Bonaparte est vainqueur.
Le canon gronde; un autre chant commence;
Nous célébrons tant de faits éclatans.
Les rois jamais n'envahiront la France.
Dans un grenier qu'on est bien *à* vingt ans!
Quittons ce toit où ma raison s'enivre.
Oh! qu'ils sont loin ces jours si regrettés!
J' échangerais ce qu'il me reste *à* vivre
Contre un des mois qu'ici Dieu m'a comptés,
Pour rêver gloire, amour, plaisir, folie,
Pour dépenser sa vie en peu d'instans,
D'un long espoir pour la voir embellie,
Dans un grenier qu' on est bien *à* vingt ans!

阁 楼

我用忧郁的眼睛来观察这个小房间，
在这里，我度过了我的青年时代，
与一个粗暴的女房东和一两个忠诚的朋友在一起，
有着总是想歌唱的轻松愉快的心情，
嘲弄生活和人世间所有的烦恼，
有着无敌的青春岁月，
能轻快地跃上四级台阶，
在我二十一岁勇敢的日子里。

它是一个阁楼——
那里有我的床——很小很硬，

One jolly evening, when my friends and I
Made happy music with our songs and cheers,
A shout of triumph mounted up thus high,
And distant cannon opened on our ears:
We rise,—we join in the triumphant strain,—
Napoleon conquers—Austerlitz is won—
Tyrants shall never tread us down again,
In the brave days when I was twenty-one.

Let us be gone—the place is sad and strange—
Now far, far off, these happy times appear;
All that I have to live I'd gladly change
For one such month as I have wasted here—
To draw long dreams of beauty, love, and power,
From founts of hope that never will outrun,
And drink all life's quintessence in an hour,
Give me the days when I was twenty-one!

Roger-Bontemps

Aux gens atrabilaires
Pour exemple donné,
En un temps de misères
Roger-Bontemps est né.
Vivre obscur *à* sa guise,
Narguer les mécontens:
Eh gai! c'est la devise
Du gros Roger-Bontemps.

还有我的桌子——我仍然能从墙上的炭笔画中
辨认出那两行不合诗韵的诗。
欢乐已随时光而去，
我眼前还能浮现出关于爱情和生活的梦想。
我用不了几天就会把手表当掉一次，
在我二十一岁勇敢的日子里。

我看到可爱的杰西
撅着嘴、两眼发光地进来了。
看，她多么调皮啊！
把披肩钉在窗户上，像个窗帘一样；
在床边她的裙子滑了下来，
女人还会有不穿衣服而难看的时候吗？
虽然我知道是谁给她买了许多睡衣，
在我二十一岁勇敢的日子里。

一个有趣的夜晚，我和朋友们在一起快乐地唱歌，
忽然听到了一阵凯旋的欢呼，
远处的炮声在我们耳边轰轰作响，
我们站了起来——加入胜利的队伍中——
拿破仑胜了，奥斯特里茨［在捷克境内，1805 年，拿破仑在此战胜奥俄联军。——译注］赢了——
暴君不会再压迫我们了！
在我二十一岁勇敢的日子里。

我们走吧！——离开这个让人伤感的地方——
那些快乐的时光已远去了。

Du chapeau de son père
Coiffé dans le grands jours,
De roses ou de lierre
Le rajeunir toujours;
Mettre un manteau de bure,
Vieil ami de vingt ans;
Eh gai! c'est la pa ure
Du gros Roger-Bontemps.

Posséder dans sa hutte
Une table, un vieux lit,
Des cartes, une flûte,

Un broc que Dieu remplit;
Un portrait de maîtresse,
Un coffre ét rien dedans;
Eh gai! c'est la richesse
Du gros Roger-Bontemps.

Aux enfans de la ville
Montrer de petits jeux;
Etre fesseur habile
De contes graveleux;
Ne parler que de danse
Et d'almanachs chantans;
Eh gai! c'est la science
Du gros Roger-Bontemps.

Faute de vins d'élite,
Sabler ceux du canton:

我愿意用我剩下的时日来换取
在这里度过的一个月——
从永不枯竭的希望源泉中
来获取关于美人、爱情和权力的梦想，
给我二十一岁的时光
让我停留在这一刻！

罗杰－伯特普斯

给郁郁寡欢的人提供一个榜样，
他就是苦难时代出生的罗杰－伯特普斯。
他随心所欲、默默无闻地生活，
嘲弄那些对生活不满的人。
啊！快乐是胖胖的罗杰－伯特普斯的人生格言。

他在重要的日子里会戴着他父亲的帽子，
帽子上经常变换着玫瑰或常青藤；
他穿着一件棕色的粗呢大衣，
它可是他二十年的老朋友了。
啊！快乐是胖胖的罗杰－伯特普斯的装饰品。

在他的茅屋里，他拥有
一张桌子、一张旧床、
一些纸牌、一支长笛、
一个总是空空如也的瓦罐，
一幅女主人的画像，
和一个空空如也的箱子。

Préférer Marguerite
Aux dames du grand ton:
De joie et de tendresse
Remplir tous ses instans;
Eh gai! c'est la sagesse
Du gros Roger-Bontemps.

Dire au ciel: Je me fie,
Mon père, *à* ta bonté;
De ma philosophie
Pardonne la gaîté
Que ma saison dernière
Soit encore un printemps;
Eh gai! c'est la prière
Du gros Roger-Bontemps.

Vous, pauvres pleins d'envie,
Vous, riches désireux,
Vous, dont le char dévie
Après un cours heureux;
Vous, qui perdrez peut-être
Des titres éclatans,
Eh gai! prenez pour maître
Le gros Roger-Bontemps.

Jolly Jack

When fierce political debate
Throughout the isle was storming,
And Rads attacked the throne and state,

啊！快乐就是胖胖的罗杰一伯特普斯的财产。

给城市的孩子表演小游戏；
因讲下流的故事常被打屁股；
还会谈论舞曲和历书中的歌曲。
啊！快乐就是胖胖的罗杰一伯特普斯的学识。

由于没有杰出人物的熏陶，
只是在区里长大。
他喜欢给贵妇人雏菊，
而她们心中立即就会充满了快乐和温存。
啊，快乐就是胖胖的罗杰一伯特普斯的智慧。

对上帝说，我相信你的仁慈，我的圣父，
请饶恕我的快乐
让我的下一个季节仍是春天。
啊！快乐就是胖胖的罗杰一伯特普斯的祈祷。

充满嫉妒的穷人，
贪婪的富人，
偏离幸福轨道的人，
失去荣誉地位的人，
啊！像这个胖胖的罗杰一伯特普斯一样快乐起来吧！

快乐的杰克

当激烈的政治辩论在整个不列颠岛上爆发开来的时候，

And Tories the reforming,
To calm the furious rage of each,
And right the land demented,
Heaven sent us Jolly Jack, to teach
The way to be contented.

Jack's bed was straw, 'twas warm and soft,
His chair, a three-legged stool;
His broken jug was emptied oft,
Yet, somehow, always full.
His mistress' portrait decked the wall,
His mirror had a crack;
Yet, gay and glad, though this was all
His wealth, lived Jolly Jack.

To give advice to avarice,
Teach pride its mean condition,
And preach good sense to dull pretence,
Was honest Jack's high mission.
Our simple statesman found his rule
Of moral in the flagon,
And held his philosophic school
Beneath the "George and Dragon."

When village Solons cursed the Lords,
And called the malt-tax sinful,
Jack heeded not their angry words,
But smiled and drank his skin full.
And when men wasted health and life,
In search of rank and riches,

激进派攻击王权和政府，
保守党要进行改革，
为了平息每个派别强烈的愤怒情绪，
使这个发狂的国家恢复正常，
上帝送给我们快乐的杰克，
教给我们自足的方法。

杰克的床是稻草铺成的，它温暖柔软，
他的椅子是一个三条腿的凳子，
他破碎的水罐常常是空的，
然而，不知何故，还能盛满水。
墙上挂着他女主人的画像，
他的镜子有个裂缝。
然而，快乐就是杰克生活中的全部财富。

给贪婪的人以忠告，
向骄傲的人传授谦虚的观念，
向虚伪的人宣讲乐于助人的观念，
这些都是忠实的杰克崇高的使命。
而我们愚蠢的政治家只知道在酒壶里创立道德原则，
在“乔治和龙骑兵”的名义下压制哲学派别。

当乡下的梭伦［古雅典政治改革家和诗人，传为古希腊“七贤”之一。——译注］诅咒贵族，
称麦芽税不道德的时候，
杰克没有在意他们愤怒的话语，
而是微笑着喝了一肚子的酒。

Jack marked, aloof, the paltry strife,
And wore his threadbare breeches.

"I enter not the church," he said,
"But I'll not seek to rob it;
So worthy Jack Joe Miller read,
While others studied Cobbett.
His talk it was of feast and fun;
His guide the Almanack;
From youth to age thus gayly run
The life of Jolly Jack."

And when Jack prayed, as oft he would,
He humbly thanked his Maker;
"I am," said he, "O Father good!
Nor Catholic nor Quaker:
Give each his creed, let each proclaim
His catalogue of curses;
I trust in Thee, and not in them,
In Thee, and in Thy mercies!

"Forgive me if, midst all Thy works,
No hint I see of damning;
And think there's faith among the Turks,
And hope for e'en the Brahmin.
Harmless my mind is, and my mirth,
And kindly is my laughter:
I cannot see the smiling earth,
And think there's hell hereafter."

当人们为了地位和财富而消耗健康和生命的时候，
杰克穿着他破旧的裤子，
冷眼瞧着这种无益的纷争。

他说："我不加入教会，
也不会试图抢劫教堂。"
当其他的人在研究科贝特［科贝特（1762—1835），英国著名散文家、政治活动家。——译注］时，
尊敬的杰克·乔·米勒却在读书。
他的谈话很有趣，对听者来说是种享受；
他的入门书是历书。
从青年到老年，快乐杰克的生活就这样快乐地度过。

当杰克祈祷的时候，他常常
会谦逊地感谢他的上帝。
他说："哦，仁慈的上帝！我既不是天主教徒也不是贵格会教徒，
请赋予每个人以信念，让他们放弃诅咒。
我信赖你，相信你的仁慈！"

"原谅我！因为我没有受到你的启示看到有罪的人；
我认为土耳其人也有信仰，
婆罗门也有希望。
我的思想是无害的，
我的欢笑和笑声也是友好的，
我看不到明媚人间的未来会有地狱。"

杰克死了。他没有留下遗产，

Jack died; he left no legacy,
Save that his story teaches:—
Content to peevish poverty;
Humility to riches.
Ye scornful great, ye envious small,
Come follow in his track;
We all were happier, if we all
Would copy JOLLY JACK.

只有他的训诫：

易怒的穷人要自足，

富人要谦逊。

嘲弄大人物，嫉妒小人物的你

要沿着他的轨迹前进；

如果我们全都效仿快乐的杰克，

我们都会更快乐的。

注释：

[1] 皮埃尔让·贝朗瑞（1780—1857），法国杰出的人民诗人和民众歌手。——译注

French Dramas and Melodramas

THERE are three kinds of drama in France, which you may subdivide as much as you please.

There is the old classical drama, well-nigh dead, and full time too: old tragedies, in which half a dozen characters appear, and spout sonorous Alexandrines for half a dozen hours. The fair Rachel has been trying to revive this genre, and to untomb Racine; but be not alarmed, Racine will never come to life again, and cause audiences to weep as of yore. Madame Rachel can only galvanize the corpse, not revivify it. Ancient French tragedy, red-heeled, patched, and be-periwigged, lies in the grave; and it is only the ghost of it that we see, which the fair Jewess has raised. There are classical comedies in verse, too, wherein the knavish valets, rakish heroes, stolid old guardians, and smart, free-spoken serving-women, discourse in Alexandrines, as loud as the Horaces or the Cid. An Englishman will seldom reconcile himself to the ronflement of the verses, and the painful recurrence of the rhymes; for my part, I had rather go to Madame Sagui's or see Deburau dancing on a rope: his lines are quite as natural and poetical.

Then there is the comedy of the day, of which Monsieur Scribe is the father. Good Heavens! with what a number of gay colonels, smart widows, and silly husbands has that gentleman peopled the play-books. How that unfortunate seventh commandment has been maltreated by him and his disciples. You will see four pieces, at the Gymnase, of a night; and so sure as you see them, four husbands shall be wickedly used. When is this joke to cease? Mon Dieu!

法国的戏剧与情节剧

在法国主要有三种类型的戏剧，如果你愿意的话，还可以把它们细分成更多的类型。

曾经盛极一时的旧式古典戏剧，现在几乎要名存实亡了。它分为三类：有旧式的悲剧，在这种悲剧中会有六个人物出场，声音洪亮、滔滔不绝地朗诵六个小时的亚历山大格式诗歌［古希腊后期，在埃及亚历山大地区发展的古希腊文化。——译注］。拉切尔女士曾试图复兴这种类型的戏剧，把拉辛从坟墓中发掘出来，但是不要惊慌，拉辛不会复生，也不会让观众像以前一样哭泣。拉切尔女士只能使尸体兴奋起来，却不能使它复活。有古老的法国悲剧，它已带着红色的鞋后跟、补丁和假发躺到墓穴中去了，我们看到的只是犹太女人所唤起的鬼魂。还有古典的诗体喜剧，里面有无赖的男仆、放荡的主人公、迟钝的老监护人和活泼直率的女仆，他们都用亚历山大诗体对话，声音像贺拉斯或熙德一样洪亮。一个英国人很难适应这种轮换交替的诗句和繁复的韵脚重复。至于我，我宁愿去煞纪太太［Madame Sagui（1786—1866），法国有名的走绳索玩杂耍的女艺人。——译注］那儿，或看德布劳走绳索，他的绳索更自然更具有想象力。

后来就有了当代的喜剧，它的创始人是斯克里布［Scribe（1791—1861），法国文学家。——译注］先生。上帝啊！这类剧本中出现了那么多放荡的上校、聪明的寡妇和愚蠢的丈夫。作者在剧本中放肆地滥用第七诫［第七诫，不可奸淫。——译注］。在体育馆你一个晚上能看到四出这样的

Play-writers have handled it for about two thousand years, and the public, like a great baby, must have the tale repeated to it over and over again.

Finally, there is the Drama, that great monster which has sprung into life of late years; and which is said, but I don't believe a word of it, to have Shakespeare for a father. If Monsieur Scribe's plays may be said to be so many ingenious examples how to break one commandment, the drame is a grand and general chaos of them all; nay, several crimes are added, not prohibited in the Decalogue, which was written before dramas were. Of the drama, Victor Hugo and Dumas are the well-known and respectable guardians. Every piece Victor Hugo has written, since "*Hernani*," has contained a monster—a delightful monster, saved by one virtue. There is Triboulet, a foolish monster; *Lucrèce Borgia*, a maternal monster; *Mary Tudor*, a religious monster; *Monsieur Quasimodo*, a humpback monster; and others, that might be named, whose monstrosities we are induced to pardon—nay, admiringly to witness—because they are agreeably mingled with some exquisite display of affection. And, as the great Hugo has one monster to each play, the great Dumas has, ordinarily, half a dozen, to whom murder is nothing; common intrigue, and simple breakage of the before-mentioned commandment, nothing; but who live and move in a vast, delightful complication of crime, that cannot be easily conceived in England, much less described.

When I think over the number of crimes that I have seen Mademoiselle Georges, for instance, commit, I am filled with wonder at her greatness, and the greatness of the poets who have conceived these charming horrors for her. I have seen her make love to, and murder, her sons, in the "*Tour de Nesle*." I have seen her poison a company of no less than nine gentlemen, at Ferrara, with an affectionate son in the number; I have seen her, as Madame de Brinvilliers, kill off numbers of respectable relations in the first four acts; and, at the last, be actually burned at the stake, to which she comes shuddering, ghastly, barefooted, and in a white sheet. Sweet excitement of tender sympathies! Such tragedies are not so good as a real, downright execution; but, in

戏剧，里面一定会出现四个上当受骗的丈夫。我的上帝啊！这种玩笑什么时候才会停止呢？这种题材已上演两千年之久了，而公众就像大小孩一样，任由这种故事一遍一遍地重复上演。

最近几年又出现了情节和人物怪异的戏剧即情节剧［一种不着重刻画人物，一味追求情节奇异，通常都有惩恶扬善结局的戏剧。——译注］。据说莎士比亚是这种戏剧的开创者，我可不相信这种说法。斯克里布先生的戏剧在如何打破戒律方面还是提供了许多具有独创性的范例，而这种情节剧就是一种大杂烩，里面加入了一些在十诫中没有被禁止的罪行［十诫是在戏剧产生之前被记载下来的。——译注］。在戏剧领域，维克多·雨果和大仲马都是众所周知、令人敬仰的代表人物。从《欧那尼》［雨果所作戏剧。1830年首次公演，曾引起古典派与浪漫派之间的激烈斗争。——译注］开始，维克多·雨果写下的每部作品都会出现一个怪物——被美德所拯救的、令人愉悦的怪物。有《国王寻乐》中的特里布耶［国王弗朗索瓦一世手下的弄臣。他因为驼背而经常被取笑，养成异常自卑与自尊的性格，因此在国王面前搞笑，帮着助纣为虐。——译注］这个愚蠢的怪物；《吕克莱斯·波尔吉》（1833年出版）中的一个充满母性的怪物；《玛丽·都铎尔》（Marie Tudor）中的一个信仰虔诚的怪物；《巴黎圣母院》中的加西莫多这个驼背怪物；还有其他的怪物等等。由于作者在这些怪物身上都掺入了一些动人的感情因素，因此我们不但能够接受他们的怪异——还能以赞赏的态度来看待他们。伟大的雨果能在每出戏剧中加入一个怪物，伟大的大仲马同样也会在他的作品中设置六个谋杀情节。虽然他作品里面出现的都是些普通的违反戒律的阴谋诡计，但人物的罪行却异常的复杂，扣人心弦。英国作家就很难构思出这样的作品，更谈不上去创作它们了。

例如，当我想到乔治夫人在大仲马的戏剧作品中所犯下的滔天罪行的时候，我不由得对大仲马所构思的数量奇多的罪行和惊人的恐怖而感到好奇。我曾看到过她在《内勒塔》［大仲马的通俗剧。内勒塔是塞纳河南岸的塔楼，保卫罗浮宫的一段城墙。相传有三个女人即勃艮第的玛格丽特，还

point of interest, the next thing to it: with what a number of moral emotions do they fill the breast; with what a hatred for vice, and yet a true pity and respect for that grain of virtue that is to be found in us all: our bloody, daughter-loving Brinvilliers; our warmhearted, poisonous Lucretia Borgia; above all, what a smart appetite for a cool supper afterwards, at the Café Anglais, when the horrors of the play act as a piquant sauce to the supper!

Or, to speak more seriously, and to come, at last, to the point. After having seen most of the grand dramas which have been produced at Paris for the last half-dozen years, and thinking over all that one has seen,—the fictitious murders, rapes, adulteries, and other crimes, by which one has been interested and excited,—a man may take leave to be heartily ashamed of the manner in which he has spent his time; and of the hideous kind of mental intoxication in which he has permitted himself to indulge.

Nor are simple society outrages the only sort of crime in which the spectator of Paris plays has permitted himself to indulge; he has recreated himself with a deal of blasphemy besides, and has passed many pleasant evenings in beholding religion defiled and ridiculed.

Allusion has been made, in a former paper, to a fashion that lately obtained in France, and which went by the name of Catholic reaction; and as, in this happy country, fashion is everything, we have had not merely Catholic pictures and quasi religious books, but a number of Catholic plays have been produced, very edifying to the frequenters of the theatres or the Boulevards, who have learned more about religion from these performances than they have acquired, no doubt, in the whole of their lives before. In the course of a very few years we have seen—"*The Wandering Jew*;" "*Belshazzar's Feast*;" "*Nebuchadnezzar*:" and the "*Massacre of the Innocents*;" "*Joseph and his Brethren*;" "*The Passage of the Red Sea*;" and "*The Deluge.*"

The great Dumas, like Madame Sand before mentioned, has brought a vast quantity of religion before the foot-lights. There was his famous tragedy of "*Caligula*," which, be it spoken to the shame of the Paris critics, was

有她的两个姊妹在那里过荒淫无耻的生活。——译注］中向自己的儿子表示爱意并谋害了他。我曾看到她在费拉拉［意大利城市。——译注］毒死了好几个先生，人数不少于九个，其中有一个就是她亲爱的儿子；还看到她以布林维里尔侯爵夫人的身份在最初的四幕中杀死了很多可敬的亲戚；最后一幕，她竟被绑在火刑柱上接受火刑，她浑身颤抖、赤着脚，裹着白色的裹尸布。这一幕激发了观众的怜悯之情！这样的悲剧还不如真实、直截了当的犯人处决精彩。但它们的好处就在于能激发起观众的道德情感，包括对邪恶的憎恨，对美德的赞赏等等。既残忍又深爱女儿的布林维里尔侯爵夫人，既热心又恶毒的鲁克蕾齐雅·博尔吉亚［罗马传说中的贞妇名。——译注］都给我们的晚餐增添了不错的开胃料！

简明扼要、严肃地来说，想想最近六年巴黎所上演的绝大多数壮观戏剧，我们都看到了什么呢？——都是些虚构的刺激人的谋杀、强奸、通奸和其他令观众感兴趣和刺激的罪行——观众在离去的时候或许会为他这样消遣时间、沉迷于这种可怕的精神陶醉而感到羞愧。

巴黎的戏剧观众不仅以社会犯罪行为还以许多亵渎神明的行为来作为消遣，他们在观看亵渎和嘲笑宗教的戏剧中度过了许多愉快的夜晚。

在前面我们已间接提到了法国最近的流行风气，天主教信仰在这里又得到盛行。在这个快乐的国度，风尚就是一切，除了天主教绘画和宗教书籍之外，许多天主教戏剧也被创作出来，它们对于剧院或林荫大道的戏剧常客来说是很有教诲意义的，因为这些常客更多地是从这些戏剧表演中来了解宗教，而不是从他们以前的生活中受到启发。在几年的时间内，我们就看到了——《流浪的犹太人》、《伯沙撒的宴会》、《尼布甲尼撒［圣经人物。——译注］》和《无辜的屠杀》、《约瑟和他的兄弟们》、《红海之路》、《大洪水》等宗教戏剧。

就像前面提到的乔治桑女士一样，著名的大仲马在他的戏剧中也加入了许多宗教因素。他著名的悲剧《卡利古拉［古罗马暴君。——译注］》——这部让巴黎评论家羞于提起的作品受到了观众的冷遇甚至遭到了

coldly received; nay, actually hissed, by them. And why? Because, says Dumas, it contained a great deal too much piety for the rogues. The public, he says, was much more religious, and understood him at once.

"As for the critics," says he, nobly, "let those who cried out against the immorality of Antony and Marguerite de Bourgogne, reproach me for THE CHASTITY OF MESSALINA." (This dear creature is the heroine of the play of "*Caligula.*") "It matters little to me. These people have but seen the form of my work: they have walked round the tent, but have not seen the arch which it covered; they have examined the vases and candles of the altar, but have not opened the tabernacle!"

"The public alone has, instinctively, comprehended that there was, beneath this outward sign, an inward and mysterious grace: it followed the action of the piece in all its serpentine windings; it listened for four hours, with pious attention (avec recueillement et religion), to the sound of this rolling river of thoughts, which may have appeared to it new and bold, perhaps, but chaste and grave; and it retired, with its head on its breast, like a man who had just perceived, in a dream, the solution of a problem which he has long and vainly sought in his waking hours."

You see that not only Saint Sand is an apostle, in her way; but Saint Dumas is another. We have people in England who write for bread, like Dumas and Sand, and are paid so much for their line; but they don't set up for prophets. Mrs. Trollope has never declared that her novels are inspired by Heaven; Mr. Buckstone has written a great number of farces, and never talked about the altar and the tabernacle. Even Sir Edward Bulwer (who, on a similar occasion, when the critics found fault with a play of his, answered them by a pretty decent declaration of his own merits,) never ventured to say that he had received a divine mission, and was uttering five-act revelations.

All things considered, the tragedy of "*Caligula*" is a decent tragedy; as decent as the decent characters of the hero and heroine can allow it to be; it may be almost said, provokingly decent: but this, it must be remembered, is

他们的嘘声反对。为什么呢？大仲马说，因为在这部作品中，他把许多反面人物塑造成了虔敬神灵的人物。他说，公众是非常虔诚的，他们很快就能理解他。

“至于评论家，”他豁达地说，“让那些抗议安东尼［大仲马戏剧《安东尼》中的主人公。——译注］和勃艮第玛格丽特［玛格丽特（1290—1315），法国王后，勃艮第国王罗贝尔二世的女儿，1305年嫁给未来的路易十世，1314年离弃，1315年被扼死。——译注］不道德的人因梅萨利纳［Messalina，罗马皇帝克劳狄的第三个妻子，以阴险和乱淫而出名。——译注］的贞洁而责备我吧！”（这个人物是戏剧《卡利古拉》中的女主人公）。“这对我来说无所谓。这些人只看到我作品的表面部分，他们绕着帐篷走，但是看不到它所遮掩的拱门，他们仔细观察了祭坛的瓶子和蜡烛，但是没有打开圣幕！”

“公众自然会了解到在这部戏剧的外表形式下所隐藏的内在的神秘魅力。观众跟随着迂回曲折的情节线索，专心致志地（聚精会神地、虔诚地）聆听思绪流动的声音，虽然这对他们来说有些新奇和大胆，它却是典雅庄重的。当他们离开剧院的时候就会豁然开朗，就像一个人在白天百思不得其解的问题忽然在梦中得到解决方案一样。

你看，不仅乔治桑是一个以自己的方式进行宗教预言的使徒，大仲马也是这样。在英国也有人像大仲马或乔治桑一样为面包而写作，他们的作品也能得到较高的报酬，但他们并不以预言者而自居。特罗洛普夫人从来也没有断言说她的小说是受到了上帝的启发而写出来的；布克斯通先生写了很多笑剧，但从来也没有谈到过祭坛和圣幕。甚至爱德华·布尔威先生（1803—1873，英国诗人。——译注）（在类似的场合，当评论界挑剔他的一部戏剧的时候，他通过描述一段自身的优点给以体面的答复和驳斥）也从来不敢说他已收到了上帝神圣的使命，要写出五幕启示剧来。

总的来看，《卡利古拉》这部悲剧还不错，它的男主人公和女主人公还都是很正派的，甚至可以说，正派得有些夸张。但必须要注意，它是现代

the characteristic of the modern French school (nay, of the English school too); and if the writer take the character of a remarkable scoundrel, it is ten to one but he turns out an amiable fellow, in whom we have all the warmest sympathy. "Caligula" is killed at the end of the performance; "Messalina" is comparatively well-behaved; and the sacred part of the performance, the tabernacle-characters apart from the mere "vase" and "candlestick" personages, may be said to be depicted in the person of a Christian convert, "Stella", who has had the good fortune to be converted by no less a person than Mary Magdalene, when she, Stella, was staying on a visit to her aunt, near Narbonne.

STELLA (Continuant.) Voilà

Que je vois s'avancer, sans pilote et sans rames,
Une barque portant deux hommes et deux femmes,
Et, spectacle inou? qui me ravit encor,
Tous quatre avaient au front une auréole d'or
D'où partaient des rayons de si vive lumière
Que je fus obligée *à* baisser la paupière;
Et, lorsque je rouvris les yeux avec effroi,
Les voyageurs divins étaient auprès de moi.
Un jour de chacun d'eux et dans toute sa gloire
Je te raconterai la merveilleuse histoire,
Et tu l'adoreras, j'espère; en ce moment,
Ma mère, il te suffit de savoir seulement
Que tous quatre venaient du fond de la Syrie:
Une édit les avait bannis de leur patrie,
Et, se faisant bourreaux, des hommes irrités,
Sans avirons, sans eau, sans pain et garrottés,
Sur une frêle barque échouée au rivage,
Les avaient *à* la mer poussés dans un orage.
Mais *à* peine l'esquif eut-il touché les flots
Qu'au cantique chanté par les saints matelots,

法国艺术流派的特点（在英国也是这样）。如果作家想写一个与众不同的坏蛋，十有八九这个坏蛋会变成一个善良亲切的家伙而博得观众的同情。“卡利古拉”在戏剧的最后一幕被杀死了；“梅萨利纳”还算品行端正；戏剧中最神圣的部分体现在叛依基督徒的“史黛拉”这个人物形象上面。“史黛拉”也是一个脱离了纯粹“花瓶”和“烛台”式的人物形象，在史黛拉去看望那邦尼附近居住的姨母的路途中，她像玛丽·玛德莱娜［《圣经》中的圣女。——译注］一样很幸运地叛依了基督教。

史黛拉（续篇）—— 那儿

我看到前面的那只小船上既没有领航员也没有船桨，
船上载着两男两女，
这个罕见的场面让我产生了兴趣，
他们四个人的额头上都有一圈金色的光环，
光线如此耀眼，以至于我不得不垂下眼皮。
当我惊恐地睁开双眼时，
这些神圣的游客已到我身边了。
我以天主的荣耀
向你讲述这个神奇的故事，
希望你会喜欢它，
我的母亲，你只知道这四个人都来自叙利亚偏僻的地方就足够了。
一道敕令把他们逐出了祖国，
那些恼怒的人担当了刽子手，
没有划船的人，没有水，没有面包和绞刑，
他们被驱逐到一个搁浅在海岸的破旧小船上，
暴风雨中的海浪推动着小船。
但是当小船刚触到海浪的时候，
这些神圣的人唱起了赞美歌，

L'ouragan replia ses ailes frémissantes,
Que la mer aplanit ses vagues mugissantes,
Et qu'un soleil plus pur, reparaissant aux cieux,
Enveloppa l'esquif d'un cercle radieux! . . .
JUNIA. —Mais c'était un prodige.
STELLA. — Un miracle, ma mère.
Leurs fers tombèrent seuls, l'eau cessa d'être amère,
Et deux fois chaque jour le bateau fut couvert
D'une manne pareille *à* celle du désert:
C'est ainsi que, poussés par une main céleste,
Je les vis aborder.
JUNIA. —Oh! dis vîte le reste!
STELLA. —A l'aube, trois d'entre eux quittèrent la maison:
Marthe prit le chemin qui mène *à* Tarascon,
Lazare et Maximin celui de Massilie,
Et celle qui resta... C'ÉTAIT LA PLUS JOLIE, (how truly French!)
Nous faisant appeler vers le milieu du jour,
Demanda si les monts ou les bois d'alentour
Cachaient quelque retraite inconnue et profonde,
Qui la pût séparer *à* tout jamais du monde...
Aquila se souvint qu'il avait pénétré
Dans un antre sauvage et de tous ignoré,
Grotte creusée aux flancs de ces Alpes sublimes,
Où l'aigle fait son aire au-dessus des abîmes.
Il offrit cet asile, et dès le lendemain
Tous deux, pour l'y guider, nous étions en chemin.
Le soir du second jour nous touchûmes sa base:
L*à*, tombant *à* genoux dans une sainte extase,
Elle pria long-temps, puis vers l'antre inconnu,
Dénouant sa chaussure, elle marcha pied nu.

飓风收拢了它颤动的双翼，

大海恢复了平静，

明亮的太阳在天空重新出现，

给小船罩上了一圈光晕！……

犹尼亚（使徒——译注）——这是一个奇观。

史黛拉——一个奇迹，我的母亲！

他们的手镣从手上脱落了下来，海水也不咸了，

每天船上会两次出现神所赐的食物，

就像上帝在沙漠中赐给希伯来的食物一样，

因此，也是上帝的手把这只船推到岸边的。

犹尼亚（使徒——译注）——哦！快说下面的事情！

史黛拉——在黎明的时候，他们当中有三个人离开了原地，

玛莎踏上了通向塔拉斯康的道路，

拉扎尔和马克西民去往梅西，

留下来的那个人……是最漂亮的，

在将近中午的时候，她召唤我们，

问附近是否有山或树林

或可以藏身的不为人所知的隐蔽处，

以使她能和所有的人都隔离开来……

亚居拉［圣经人物。——译注］记得他曾进过一个非常偏僻和陌生的洞穴，

洞穴在高高的阿尔卑斯山的凹陷的侧面，

鹰就在那儿的深渊下面筑它空中的巢穴。

他说出了这个隐蔽处，次日，

Nos prières, nos cris restèrent sans réponses:

Au milieu des cailloux, des épines, des ronces,

Nous la vîmes monter, un bâton *à* la main,

Et ce n'est qu'arrivée au terme du chemin,

Qu'enfin elle tomba sans force et sans haleine...

JUNIA.—Comment la nommait-on, ma fille?

STELLA.— Madeleine.

Walking, says Stella, by the sea-shore, "A bark drew near, that had nor sail nor oar; two women and two men the vessel bore: each of that crew, 'twas wondrous to behold, wore round his head a ring of blazing gold; from which such radiance glittered all around, that I was fain to look towards the ground. And when once more I raised my frightened eyne, before me stood the travellers divine; their rank, the glorious lot that each befell, at better season, mother, will I tell. Of this anon: the time will come when thou shalt learn to worship as I worship now. Suffice it, that from Syria's land they came; an edict from their country banished them. Fierce, angry men had seized upon the four, and launched them in that vessel from the shore. They launched these victims on the waters rude; nor rudder gave to steer, nor bread for food. As the doomed vessel cleaves the stormy main, that pious crew uplifts a sacred strain; the angry waves are silent as it sings; the storm, awe-stricken, folds its quivering wings. A purer sun appears the heavens to light, and wraps the little bark in radiance bright.

"**JUNIA.**—Sure, 'twas a prodigy.

"**STELLA.**—A miracle. Spontaneous from their hands the fetters fell. The salt sea-wave grew fresh, and, twice a day, manna (like that which on the desert lay) covered the bark and fed them on their way. Thus, hither led, at heaven's divine behest, I saw them land—

"**JUNIA.**—My daughter, tell the rest.

"**STELLA.**—Three of the four, our mansion left at dawn. One, Martha, took the road to Tarascon; Lazarus and Maximin to Massily; but one remained (the fairest of the three), who asked us, if i' the woods or mountains near, there chanced to be some cavern lone and drear; where she might hide,

为了给她带路，我们一起前往那个地方。
第二天晚上我们到了山脚下，
她在山脚下祈祷了很长时间，然后对着神秘的洞穴
脱下她的鞋子，赤脚前进。
对我们的恳求和叫喊，她都没有回应，
在碎石中、荆棘中、蔷薇中，
我们看着她手里拿根棍子努力地向上爬，
直到路的尽头，她才浑身无力、气喘吁吁地跌倒在地上……

犹尼亚（使徒——译注）——我的女儿，她的名字叫什么？

史黛拉——玛德莱娜。

史黛拉说她在海岸边行走的时候，看到“一只小船靠近了，船上既没有帆也没有桨，上面载着两男两女。让人惊奇的是，每个人的头上都环绕着一圈金色的光环，这些光环照得四处都闪闪发光，以至于我不得不闭上眼。当我再次睁开我惊恐的双眼时，这些神圣的游客已站在我面前了。母亲，我会在适当的时候告诉你他们的身份以及降临在他们身上的命运。不久以后，你也会像我现在一样来学着去崇拜他们。现在你只需知道他们来自叙利亚就足够了。一道敕令把他们逐出了祖国，残忍、愤怒的人们抓住了他们四个，把他们放在一只离开海岸的船上。他们让这些受害者在暴风雨的海面上漂流，船上既没有舵也没有食物。当小船在暴风雨的海面上乘风破浪前进的时候，虔诚的他们高声唱起了圣歌，愤怒的海浪平息了下来，暴风雨敬畏地收拢了它颤动的翅膀。明亮的太阳出现在天空中，给小船罩上了一圈明亮的光晕。

“犹尼亚——这确实是个奇迹。

“史黛拉——是奇迹。他们的手镣自动从手上脱落了下来，咸咸的海水也变淡了。一天有两次船上都会出现神赐的食物。就这样，在神圣上帝的

for ever, from all men. It chanced, my cousin knew of such a den; deep hidden in a mountain's hoary breast, on which the eagle builds his airy nest. And thither offered he the saint to guide. Next day upon the journey forth we hied; and came, at the second eve, with weary pace, unto the lonely mountain's rugged base. Here the worn traveller, falling on her knee, did pray awhile in sacred ecstasy; and, drawing off her sandals from her feet, marched, naked, towards that desolate retreat. No answer made she to our cries or groans; but walking midst the prickles and rude stones, a staff in hand, we saw her upwards toil; nor ever did she pause, nor rest the while, save at the entry of that savage den. Here, powerless and panting, fell she then.

"**JUNIA.** —What was her name, my daughter?

"**STELLA.** — MAGDALEN."

Here the translator must pause—having no inclination to enter "the tabernacle," in company with such a spotless high-priest as Monsieur Dumas.

Something "tabernacular" may be found in Dumas's famous piece of "*Don Juan de Marana.*" The poet has laid the scene of his play in a vast number of places: in heaven (where we have the Virgin Mary and little angels, in blue, swinging censers before her!)—on earth, under the earth, and in a place still lower, but not mentionable to ears polite; and the plot, as it appears from a dialogue between a good and a bad angel, with which the play commences, turns upon a contest between these two worthies for the possession of the soul of a member of the family of Marana.

"Don Juan de Marana" not only resembles his namesake, celebrated by Mozart and Molière, in his peculiar successes among the ladies, but possesses further qualities which render his character eminently fitting for stage representation: he unites the virtues of Lovelace and Lacenaire; he blasphemes upon all occasions; he murders, at the slightest provocation, and without the most trifling remorse; he overcomes ladies of rigid virtue, ladies of easy virtue, and ladies of no virtue at all; and the poet, inspired by the contemplation of such a character, has depicted his hero's adventures and conversation with wonderful feeling and truth.

The first act of the play contains a half-dozen of murders and intrigues;

指引下，我看到他们登陆了——

“犹尼亚——我的女儿，接着讲下面的事情！

“史黛拉——有三个人在黎明的时候离开了原地。玛莎踏上了通向塔拉斯康的道路；拉扎尔和马克西民去往梅西；还留下一个人（她是三个女人中最漂亮的）。她问我们，附近是否有山或树林，能否找到一个隐蔽的洞穴让她藏身以远离世人。碰巧，我的侄子知道有这样的一个洞穴，它藏在一座山峰的山腹深处，那里也是山鹰筑巢的地方。因此我们吩咐他带领这个圣徒前往那个洞穴。次日我们就出发了，在第二天的夜晚，我们迈着疲倦的步伐来到了那座荒山的山脚下。在那里，她筋疲力尽地跪在地上，专注祈祷了一会儿，然后从脚上脱下鞋子，赤脚向那个荒凉的洞穴走去。对我们的叫喊和恳求，她都没有回应，她手里拿着一根棍子在荆棘和粗糙的石头上前行，我们看到她艰难地向上跋涉，她一直坚持着走到洞穴那里，接着就浑身无力、气喘吁吁地跌倒在地。

“犹尼亚——我的女儿，她的名字叫什么？

“史黛拉——玛德莱娜。”

到这里，译者一定会停下来了——他可没兴趣再和仲马先生这样一位“圣洁的高级神甫”一起进入教堂聆听教义。

在大仲马著名的作品《唐璜·德·玛拉那》中也有这类宗教的成分。作家把戏剧场景设置在许多不同的地方：天堂（在那里有圣母玛利亚和在圣母面前摇晃香炉的忧郁小天使）、人间、地狱，还有地下更深的地方，但是就不说给文雅的耳朵听了。故事情节是从一个善良的天使和一个邪恶的天使之间的对话开始的，这两个精灵为拥有玛拉那家族一个成员的灵魂而展开了争夺。

在情场上，“唐璜·德·玛拉那”很像那位在莫扎特和莫里哀的作品中著名的同姓朋友“唐璜”，同时他还兼具其他的特点使得他的性格非常适合舞台表演。他综合了色鬼和拉色内尔这个恶棍的主要特点。他亵渎了所有的事物；他会因一次微不足道的挑衅就谋杀他人而对此没有丝毫悔恨；他

which would have sufficed humbler genius than M. Dumas's, for the completion of, at least, half a dozen tragedies. In the second act our hero flogs his elder brother, and runs away with his sister-in-law; in the third, he fights a duel with a rival, and kills him: whereupon the mistress of his victim takes poison, and dies, in great agonies, on the stage. In the fourth act, Don Juan, having entered a church for the purpose of carrying off a nun, with whom he is in love, is seized by the statue of one of the ladies whom he has previously victimized, and made to behold the ghosts of all those unfortunate persons whose deaths he has caused.

This is a most edifying spectacle. The ghosts rise solemnly, each in a white sheet, preceded by a wax-candle; and, having declared their names and qualities, call, in chorus, for vengeance upon Don Juan, as thus:—

DON SANDOVAL loquitur.

"I am Don Sandoval d'Ojedo. I played against Don Juan my fortune, the tomb of my fathers, and the heart of my mistress;—I lost all: I played against him my life, and I lost it. Vengeance against the murderer! vengeance!"—(The candle goes out.)

THE CANDLE GOES OUT, and an angel descends—a flaming sword in his hand—and asks: "Is there no voice in favour of Don Juan?" when lo! Don Juan's father (like one of those ingenious toys called "Jack-in-the-box,") jumps up from his coffin, and demands grace for his son.

When Martha the nun returns, having prepared all things for her elopement, she finds Don Juan fainting upon the ground.—"I am no longer your husband," says he, upon coming to himself; "I am no longer Don Juan; I am Brother Juan the Trappist. Sister Martha, recollect that you must die!"

This was a most cruel blow upon Sister Martha, who is no less a person than an angel, an angel in disguise—the good spirit of the house of Marana, who has gone to the length of losing her wings and forfeiting her place in heaven, in order to keep company with Don Juan on earth, and, if possible, to convert him. Already, in her angelic character, she had exhorted him to repentance, but in vain; for, while she stood at one elbow, pouring not merely hints, but long sermons, into his ear, at the other elbow stood a bad spirit,

还征服了具有德行的淑女、水性杨花的女人和全然没有德行的女人。这个人物激发了作家的创作灵感，作家用精彩的情感经历和事件描述了这位主人公的历险和对话。

戏剧的第一幕就包括六场谋杀和阴谋，看来这个人物足以完成大仲马的六部悲剧了。在第二幕我们的主人公鞭打了他的哥哥，和他的嫂子一起逃跑了。第三幕，他和一个对手决斗，杀死了对方，死者的情妇就在舞台上出于极度的痛苦而服毒自尽了。在第四幕，唐璜爱上一位修女，为带走她而进入一个教堂，结果被他以前欺骗过的一位女士的雕像抓住并让他目睹了他以前害死的不幸人们的鬼魂。

这一幕是最有教诲意义的场面。鬼魂严肃地出现在舞台上，每个鬼魂身上都裹着一条白色的被单，手里拿着一根蜡烛，在依次介绍完他们的名字和事迹之后，他们齐声要求向唐璜报复，就这样——

堂·桑德瓦说：

“我是堂·桑德瓦。我以我的财产、我父亲的坟墓、我情妇的爱情来抗议唐璜。——我失去了所有的一切，我用生命来反抗他，结果又失去了生命。向这个凶手复仇！复仇！”——（蜡烛熄灭。）

蜡烛熄灭，一个天使降落到舞台上——手里拿着一把燃烧的剑——他询问：“还有没有为唐璜辩护的？”这时，瞧！唐璜的父亲（就像是从玩偶匣里蹦出的玩具一样）从他的棺材里跳了出来，他请求赦免他的儿子。

当玛莎修女整理好私奔的东西返回来的时候，她发现唐璜晕倒在地上。——他苏醒后说：“我不再是你的丈夫了，我也不是唐璜了。我是特拉普［天主教西多会的一个支派，主张节食忏悔，坚守缄默，人称苦修派。——译注］的唐璜。玛莎修女，记住，你一定会死的！”

这是对玛莎修女的最残酷的打击，她正是一个伪装的天使——为了在人间和唐璜在一起，这个善良的姑娘丢弃了她的翅膀和在天堂中的位置。如果可能的话，她还要劝说他叛依宗教。她天使般的个性已使她规劝过唐璜悔改了，但是无济于事。因为当她站在一边苦口婆心地对唐璜说教的时

grinning and sneering at all her pious counsels, and obtaining by far the greater share of the Don's attention.

In spite, however, of the utter contempt with which Don Juan treats her,—in spite of his dissolute courses, which must shock her virtue,—and his impolite neglect, which must wound her vanity, the poor creature (who, from having been accustomed to better company, might have been presumed to have had better taste), the unfortunate angel feels a certain inclination for the Don, and actually flies up to heaven to ask permission to remain with him on earth.

And when the curtain draws up, to the sound of harps, and discovers white-robed angels walking in the clouds, we find the angel of Marana upon her knees, uttering the following address:—

LE BON ANGE

Vierge, à qui le calice à la liqueur amère
Fut si souvent offert,
Mère, que l'on nomma la douloureuse mère,
Tant vous avez souffert!

Vous, dont les yeux divins sur la terre des hommes
Ont versé plus de pleurs
Que vos pieds n'ont depuis, dans le ciel où nous sommes,
Fait éclore de fleurs.

Vase d'élection, étoile matinale,
Miroir de pureté,
Vous qui priez pour nous, d'une voix virginale,
La suprême bonté;

A mon tour, aujourd'hui, bienheureuse Marie,
Je tombe à vos genoux;
Daignez donc m'ècouter, car c'est vous que je prie,
Vous qui priez pour nous.

候，在另一边则站着一个邪恶的神灵，它龇牙咧嘴地嘲笑她虔诚的劝告，并分散了唐璜的许多注意力。

然而，不管唐璜怎样轻蔑地对待她——不管他放荡的行为怎样让她感到震惊——他无礼的轻视怎样伤害了她，这个可怜的人儿！这个不幸的天使确实是真心喜欢唐璜的，她还飞上天堂请求上帝允许她在人间和唐璜在一起。

当幕布拉上去后，观众听到了竖琴的声音，看到身穿白色长袍的天使们在云端中行走，我们发现玛莎跪在地上，说出下面的话——

善良的天使

（法语原作——译注）

经常饮用苦涩泪水的圣母啊！
您有那么多的忧伤，我们称您为忧伤的母亲！

您神圣的双眼流下的泪水，
更多地是从您的脚下流到人间的土地上，在我们的天空中
它流经的这些地方都盛开了花朵。

精致的圣器、闪烁的星星，
是您圣洁的化身，
您用圣洁的声音为我们祈祷
美好的祝愿。

今天，轮到我了，万福玛利亚，
我拜倒在你的脚下，
请您聆听
我真诚的祈祷！

Which may be thus interpreted:—

O Virgin blest! by whom the bitter draught
So often has been quaffed,
That, for thy sorrow, thou art named by us
The Mother Dolorous!

Thou, from whose eyes have fallen more tears of woe,
Upon the earth below,
Than 'neath thy footsteps, in this heaven of ours,
Have risen flowers!

O beaming morning star! O chosen vase!
O mirror of all grace!
Who, with thy virgin voice, dost ever pray
Man's sins away;

Bend down thine ear, and list, O blessed saint!
Unto my sad complaint;
Mother! to thee I kneel, on thee I call,
Who hearest all.

She proceeds to request that she may be allowed to return to earth, and follow the fortunes of Don Juan; and, as there is one difficulty, or, to use her own words,—

Mais, comme vous savez qu'aux voûtes éternelles,
Malgré moi, tend mon vol,
Soufflezsur mon étoile et détachez mes ailes,
Pour m'enchainer au sol;

Her request is granted, her star is BLOWN OUT (O poetic allusion!) and she descends to earth to love, and to go mad, and to die for Don Juan!

The reader will require no further explanation, in order to be satisfied as

可以这样翻译成英语：

哦，神圣的圣母！经常畅饮苦涩泪水的您，
因为您的忧伤，我们把您称做忧伤的母亲！

您神圣的双眼流下的泪水，
更多地是从您的脚下流到人间的土地上，
在我们的天空中它流经的这些地方长出了花朵。

哦，发光的晨星！哦，精致的圣器！
哦，是您仁慈的化身！
您用圣洁的声音，
祈祷人类远离罪恶。

哦，神圣的天使，垂下你的耳朵！
聆听我悲哀的诉苦。
圣母！我拜倒在您的脚下，
请求您的帮助。

接着她就请求圣母能允许她回到人间去追随唐璜，要翻译这几句有点困难，还是用她的原话合适——

您知道在天穹中，
我无意飞翔，
请吹灭我的星宿，卸下我的翅膀，
让我回到地面。

to the moral of this play: but is it not a very bitter satire upon the country, which calls itself the politest nation in the world, that the incidents, the indecency, the coarse blasphemy, and the vulgar wit of this piece, should find admirers among the public, and procure reputation for the author? Could not the Government, which has re-established, in a manner, the theatrical censorship, and forbids or alters plays which touch on politics, exert the same guardianship over public morals? The honest English reader, who has a faith in his clergyman, and is a regular attendant at Sunday worship, will not be a little surprised at the march of intellect among our neighbours across the Channel, and at the kind of consideration in which they hold their religion. Here is a man who seizes upon saints and angels, merely to put sentimentsin their mouths which might suit a nymph of Drury Lane. He shows heaven, in order that he may carry debauch into it; and avails himself of the most sacred and sublime parts of our creed as a vehicle for a scene-painter's skill, or an occasion for a handsome actress to wear a new dress.

M. Dumas's piece of "*Kean*" is not quite so sublime; it was brought out by the author as a satire upon the French critics, who, to their credit be it spoken, had generally attacked him, and was intended by him, and received by the public, as a faithful portraiture of English manners. As such, it merits special observation and praise. In the first act you find a Countess and an Ambassadress, whose conversation relates purely to the great actor. All the ladies in London are in love with him, especially the two present. As for the Ambassadress, she prefers him to her husband (a matter of course in all French plays), and to a more seducing person still—no less a person than the Prince of Wales! who presently waits on the ladies, and joins in their conversation concerning Kean. "This man," says his Royal Highness, "is the very pink of fashion. Brummell is nobody when compared to him; and I myself only an insignificant private gentleman. He has a reputation among ladies, for which I sigh in vain; and spends an income twice as great as mine." This admirable historic touch at once paints the actor and the Prince; the estimation in which the one was held, and the modest economy for which the other was so notorious.

她的请求得到应允，她的星宿被吹灭了（哦，浪漫的幻想），然后她降临到人间来爱恋唐璜，为他而死！

关于这部戏剧的道德意义，读者就不需要我再作进一步的解释了。这样的戏剧情节，这样下流、亵渎的言辞和粗俗的智慧却能受到民众的欢迎，为作者带来声誉，难道它不是对这个自认为是世界上最文雅的国度的辛辣讽刺吗？目前的法国政府已在一定程度上又重新建立了戏剧审查制度来禁止或改动那些触及政治问题的戏剧，难道它就不能对公众道德行使同样的监护权利吗？信任牧师、经常出席周日礼拜的英国读者对于我们邻人理智的进展以及他们对宗教所持的看法则一点儿也不感到奇怪。这个在戏剧中抓住圣徒和天使的人只是想通过他们来讨好特鲁里街［因特鲁里剧院而取名。——译注］美女的感情。他展现天堂是为了能在其中表现堕落，他利用我们宗教教义中最神圣和崇高的部分作为布景师的技术工具或许只是为了让一位漂亮的女演员有机会再穿一件新的服装。

大仲马先生的《凯恩》［凯恩（1787—1833），英国著名悲剧演员，以表演莎士比亚剧而闻名。——译注］就没有采用那么崇高的宗教题材，它是作者为讽刺法国评论界而作的。据说，那些经常攻击他的人跟着他沾了不少光，但他的创作意图却被公众理解为是对英国社会风俗如实生动的描绘，就因为这个原因，戏剧得到了观众的认可和赞扬。在第一幕出场的是一位伯爵夫人和一位大使夫人，她们谈论的话题都是关于这位杰出的演员凯恩。伦敦所有的女士都爱上了他，尤其是舞台上的这两位。至于大使夫人，她对凯恩的喜爱要甚于她的丈夫（在法国戏剧中这是理所当然的事情）和另一位更具魅力的先生——即威尔斯王子！现在正陪同这些女士的威尔斯王子也加入了她们关于凯恩的谈话，殿下说："这个人是个时髦的人物。布鲁梅尔［Brummell（1778—1840），乔治四世时的花花公子，为男子着时新服装之先驱。——译注］与他相比都算不了什么，我在他面前也只是个微不足道的绅士。他在女士中享有声誉，对于这个我只有徒然叹息。他的开销是我的两倍。"这几句赞美的话立即就把演员和王子的形象特点给勾勒

Then we have Kean, at a place called the Trou de Charbon, the "Coal Hole," where, to the edification of the public, he engages in a fisty combat with a notorious boxer. This scene was received by the audience with loud exclamations of delight, and commented on, by the journals, as a faultless picture of English manners. "The Coal Hole" being on the banks of the Thames, a nobleman—LORD MELBOURN! —has chosen the tavern as a rendezvous for a gang of pirates, who are to have their ship in waiting, in order to carry off a young lady with whom his lordship is enamoured. It need not be said that Kean arrives at the nick of time, saves the innocent Meess Anna, and exposes the infamy of the Peer. A violent tirade against noblemen ensues, and Lord Melbourn slinks away, disappointed, to meditate revenge. Kean's triumphs continue through all the acts: the Ambassadress falls madly in love with him; the Prince becomes furious at his ill success, and the Ambassador dreadfully jealous. They pursue Kean to his dressing-room at the theatre; where, unluckily, the Ambassadress herself has taken refuge. Dreadful quarrels ensue; the tragedian grows suddenly mad upon the stage, and so cruelly insults the Prince of Wales that his Royal Highness determines to send HIM TO BOTANY BAY. His sentence, however, is commuted to banishment to New York; whither, of course, Miss Anna accompanies him; rewarding him, previously, with her hand and twenty thousand a year!

This wonderful performance was gravely received and admired by the people of Paris: the piece was considered to be decidedly moral, because the popular candidate was made to triumph throughout, and to triumph in the most virtuous manner; for, according to the French code of morals, success among women is, at once, the proof and the reward of virtue.

The sacred personage introduced in Dumas's play behind a cloud, figures bodily in the piece of the *Massacre of the Innocents*, represented at Paris last year. She appears under a different name, but the costume is exactly that of Carlo Dolce's Madonna; and an ingenious fable is arranged, the interest of which hangs upon the grand Massacre of the Innocents, perpetrated in the fifth act. One of the chief characters is Jean le Précurseur, who threatens woe to Herod and his race, and is beheaded by orders of that sovereign.

出来了，即人们对凯恩的评价，还有众所周知的威尔斯王子的谦逊节制。

接着我们就看到凯恩出现在一个叫做“煤洞”的地方，在那里为了教诲民众，他卷入了一场拳击比赛，对手是一位臭名昭著的拳击手。这一幕作为对英国社会风俗的完美描绘不仅赢得了观众响亮的叫好声，报纸还对此展开了评论。“煤洞”是泰晤士河岸边的一家小旅馆，一个叫墨尔本的勋爵选择它作为一帮海盗的约会地点，这群海盗为了带走勋爵所迷恋的一位年轻姑娘，已在此备好了船。不言而喻，凯恩在关键时刻赶到了这里，救了这位无辜的安娜小姐，并把勋爵的丑事给抖搂了出来。接着又有了他驳斥勋爵的措辞激烈的长篇演说，墨尔本勋爵失望地溜走了，计划要报仇。在每一幕戏剧中凯恩都取得了一连串的胜利。大使夫人疯狂地爱上了他。威尔斯王子对他的成功感到恼怒，大使则嫉妒得发狂，他们追随凯恩来到他剧院中的化妆室，不幸的是，却发现了躲避在此的大使夫人。接着就发生了可怕的争吵，悲剧演员凯恩忽然在舞台上变疯了，他残酷地辱骂威尔斯王子，以至于王子殿下决定要遣送他到波特尼海湾［位于澳大利亚。——译注］，然而他又减轻了刑法，判他流放到纽约。当然，无论到哪里，拥有两万年金的安娜小姐都始终陪伴着他！

这出戏剧的精彩演出受到巴黎人的热烈欢迎，人们认为它是合乎道德的，因为这个讨人喜欢的主人公从始至终都是胜利的，而且还是以最为道德的方式取得了胜利。根据法国的道德习俗，能博得女士的爱情就是对德行的证明和奖赏。

在大仲马的戏剧中，神秘的圣徒主要都出现在《屠杀婴孩》这部戏剧中，去年在巴黎又再度上演这部戏剧。它换了另一个名字，但仍然披着圣母的宗教外衣。剧中安排了一个巧妙的情节，最吸引人的地方就是第五幕屠杀婴孩的场面。主要人物之一是先驱吉恩诅咒希律大帝［希律一世，公元前 40 年，被罗马议会册封为犹大王。他生性凶残多疑，甚至杀害自己的妻儿，并且因为喜好模仿罗马风俗，课税沉重，不得犹太人民心。在他执政最后一段时期，耶稣与施洗约翰诞生，也是他下令屠杀伯利恒城两岁以

In the Festin de Balthazar, we are similarly introduced to Daniel, and the first scene is laid by the waters of Babylon, where a certain number of captive Jews are seated in melancholy postures; a Babylonian officer enters, exclaiming, "Chantez nous quelques chansons de Jerusalem," and the request is refused in the language of the Psalm. Belshazzar's Feast is given in a grand tableau, after Martin's picture. That painter, in like manner, furnished scenes for the Deluge. Vast numbers of schoolboys and children are brought to see these pieces; the lower classes delight in them. The famous *Juif Errant*, at the theatre of the Porte St. Martin, was the first of the kind, and its prodigious success, no doubt, occasioned the number of imitations which the other theatres have produced.

The taste of such exhibitions, of course, every English person will question; but we must remember the manners of the people among whom they are popular; and, if I may be allowed to hazard such an opinion, there is in every one of these Boulevard mysteries, a kind of rude moral. The Boulevard writers don't pretend to "tabernacles"and divine gifts, like Madame Sand and Dumas before mentioned. If they take a story from the sacred books, they garble it without mercy, and take sad liberties with the text; but they do not deal in descriptions of the agreeably wicked, or ask pity and admiration for tenderhearted criminals and philanthropic murderers, as their betters do. Vice is vice on the Boulevard; and it is fine to hear the audience, as a tyrant king roars out cruel sentences of death,or a bereaved mother pleads for the life of her child, making their remarks on the circumstances of the scene. "Ah, le gredin!" growls an indignant countryman. "Quel monstre!" says a grisette, in a fury. You see very fat old men crying like babies, and, like babies, sucking enormous sticks of barley-sugar. Actors and audience enter warmly into the illusion of the piece; and so especially are the former affected, that at Franconi's, where the battles of the Empire are represented, there is as regular gradation in the ranks of the mimic army as in the real imperial legions. After a man has served, with credit, for a certain number of years in the line, he is promoted to be an officer—an acting officer. If he conducts himself well, he may rise to be a Colonel or a General of Division;if ill, he is degraded to the

下的男婴。——译注］和他的家族受难，被希律王下令斩首。

在巴尔达莎［Balthazar，是巴比伦的最后一个国王，他曾举办盛大丰富的宴会，招待一千位达官贵人。在宴会中，他把美酒装在他父亲从耶路撒冷圣殿中所偷出来的圣杯中给大家享用。而当晚，这亵渎圣物的人就受到了上帝的惩罚。——译注］的宴会上，我们又看到了但以理［犹太人的先知。——译注］。第一幕的布景为巴比伦的河水，在布景中有一些俘虏的犹太人以忧郁的姿势坐着。一个巴比伦的官员走了过来，他叫道："你们唱几首耶路撒冷的歌!"这个要求被犹太人庄严地拒绝了。巴尔达莎的盛宴被马丁［马丁·里诺，法国画家。——译注］的画像处理成一个很壮观的舞台造型，画家同样也提供了洪水的舞台布景。许多男生和小孩都被带到剧院里观看这出戏剧。较低阶层的人都能从这类戏剧中得到愉悦。在圣马丁城剧院上演的著名的《流浪的犹太人》开了这类戏剧的先河，它惊人的成功无疑引起了其他剧院的效仿。

当然，对于这类表演的审美趣味，每个英国人都会有所怀疑。但我们必须了解这是他们的社会风俗。我敢说，这种审美趣味在巴黎的神秘剧中已有所体现，它是一种粗俗的道德剧。但是神秘剧的作者不像前面提到的乔治桑女士和大仲马一样自称具有神赐的天赋。如果他们从圣书中抽取一个故事，他们会毫不留情地加以窜改，随意处理原文，但是他们不会把邪恶的人物描述成受人欢迎的形象，或者为软心肠的罪犯和慈善的凶手祈求观众的怜悯和赞美，坏蛋就是坏蛋。当一个专制国王吼叫着执行残忍的死刑或一个失去亲人的母亲为她的孩子请求赦免死刑的时候，听听现场观众的评论是很不错的。一个愤怒的乡下人咆哮道："这个无赖!"一个青年劳动妇女愤怒地说："多么残忍的人啊!"你会看到肥胖的老人像孩子一样哭泣，像孩子一样吮吸着巨大的麦芽糖棒。演员和观众们都很兴奋地沉迷于戏剧的幻觉中。在弗朗科尼剧院上演帝国战争的戏剧场面时，模仿表演的军队和真正的帝王军团一样都有着正规的等级之分。当一个士兵在军队忠诚服务几年之后，他会被提升为一个军官——一个代理军官。如果他表现

ranks again; or, worst degradation of all, drafted into a regiment of Cossacks or Austrians. Cossacks is the lowest depth, however; nay, it is said that the men who perform these Cossack parts receive higher wages than the mimic grenadiers and old guard. They will not consent to be beaten every night, even in play; to be pursued in hundreds, by a handful of French; to fight against their beloved Emperor. Surely there is fine hearty virtue in this, and pleasant child-like simplicity.

So that while the drama of Victor Hugo, Dumas, and the enlightened classes, is profoundly immoral and absurd, the DRAMA of the common people is absurd, if you will, but good and right-hearted. I have made notes of one or two of these pieces, which all have good feeling and kindness in them, and which turn, as the reader will see, upon one or two favourite points of popular morality. A drama that obtained a vast success at the Porte Saint Martin was "*La Duchesse de la Vauballière.*" The Duchess is the daughter of a poor farmer, who was carried off in the first place, and then married by M. le Duc de la Vauballière, a terrible roué, the farmer's landlord, and the intimate friend of Philippe d'Orléans, the Regent of France.

Now the Duke, in running away with the lady, intended to dispense altogether with ceremony, and make of Julie anything but his wife; but Georges, her father, and one Morisseau, a notary, discovered him in his dastardly act, and pursued him to the very feet of the Regent, who compelled the pair to marry and make it up.

Julie complies; but though she becomes a Duchess, her heart remains faithful to her old flame, Adrian, the doctor; and she declares that, beyond the ceremony, no sort of intimacy shall take place between her husband and herself.

Then the Duke begins to treat her in the most ungentleman-like manner: he abuses her in every possible way; he introduces improper characters into her house; and, finally, becomes so disgusted with her, that he determines to make away with her altogether.

For this purpose, he sends forth into the highways and seizes a doctor, bidding him, on pain of death, to write a poisonous prescription for Madame

得好，他可以再被提升到分队中的上校或将军；如果表现不好，他会被降级回到队伍；而最糟糕的降级就是被派遣到哥萨克或奥地利的军团中。哥萨克军团是最低级别。然而，据说表演哥萨克那一方的演员要比模仿掷弹兵和守卫的演员们报酬高。甚至在表演的时候，他们也不愿意每晚挨打，不愿意去反抗他们敬爱的国王，不愿意他们成百人的队伍被一小撮法国人追赶。当然在这里面也有些诚恳的美德和单纯的快乐。

维克多·雨果、大仲马和开明阶层的戏剧都道德败坏且荒谬可笑，普通人的戏剧虽然也荒唐可笑，但却是充满善意的。我记得有一两部这样的作品，它们都充满了善意和仁慈，读者将会看到，它们所表现出的公众道德观念都是令人称赞的。在圣马丁城剧院取得巨大成功的戏剧就是《德·拉·伏巴里耶尔公爵夫人》，公爵夫人朱丽是一个贫穷农夫的女儿，刚出场就被德·拉·伏巴里耶尔公爵先生抢走与之结婚。这个公爵是个可怕的浪荡子，是农夫的地主、法国摄政王菲利普·德·奥尔良的亲密朋友。

公爵带着这位女士私奔，想要省却婚礼仪式，不想娶朱丽做妻子。但是朱丽的父亲乔治和一位叫莫里斯的公证人发现了公爵的卑怯行为，追赶他到了摄政王那里，摄政王强迫公爵和朱丽结婚并从中予以调停。

朱丽同意了。虽然她成为了一个公爵夫人，她的心却仍旧忠实于她的旧情人阿德里安——阿德里安是一位医生。她宣布，除了日常礼仪之外，在她丈夫和她之间不能有任何亲密的行为。

然后公爵就开始用各种粗鄙的行为来对待她，他用各种方法虐待她，还把一些不正派的人物介绍到她房间里来。最后公爵变得非常厌恶她，决定要除掉她。

为了达到这个目的，他来到大路上抓住一个医生，用生命相威胁，命令他给公爵夫人开一个毒药的药方。公爵夫人吞下了毒药。哦，可怕啊！这个医生正是阿德里安。可以想象，当他发现是自己谋害了他心爱的情人时，他会多么悔恨啊！

然而，读者不必为女主角的命运担忧，因为没有一个悲剧的女主角会

la Duchesse. She swallows the potion; and O horror! the doctor turns out to be Dr. Adrian; whose woe may be imagined, upon finding that he has been thus committing murder on his true love!

Let not the reader, however, be alarmed as to the fate of the heroine; no heroine of a tragedy ever yet died in the third act; and, accordingly, the Duchess gets up perfectly well again in the fourth, through the instrumentality of Morisseau, the good lawyer.

And now it is that vice begins to be really punished. The Duke, who, after killing his wife, thinks it necessary to retreat, and take refuge in Spain, is tracked to the borders of that country by the virtuous notary, and there receives such a lesson as he will never forget to his dying day.

Morisseau, in the first instance, produces a deed (signed by his Holiness the Pope), which annuls the marriage of the Duke de la Vauballière; then another deed, by which it is proved that he was not the eldest son of old La Vauballière, the former Duke; then another deed, by which he shows that old La Vauballière (who seems to have been a disreputable old fellow) was a bigamist, and that, in consequence, the present man, styling himself Duke, is illegitimate; and finally, Morisseau brings forward another document, which proves that the REG'LAR Duke is no other than Adrian, the doctor!

Thus it is that love, law, and physic combined, triumph over the horrid machinations of this star-and-gartered libertine.

"*Hermann l'Ivrogne*" is another piece of the same order; and though not very refined, yet possesses considerable merit. As in the case of the celebrated Captain Smith of Halifax, who "took to drinking ratafia, and thought of poor Miss Bailey,"—a woman and the bottle have been the cause of Hermann's ruin. Deserted by his mistress, who has been seduced from him by a base Italian Count, Hermann, a German artist, gives himself entirely up to liquor and revenge: but when he finds that force, and not infidelity, have been the cause of his mistress's ruin, the reader can fancy the indignant ferocity with which he pursues the infâme ravisseur. A scene, which is really full of spirit, and excellently well acted, here ensues! Hermann proposes to the Count, on the eve of their duel, that the survivor should bind himself to es-

在第三幕死去的。因此，公爵夫人在第四幕靠好心的律师莫里斯的帮助，又完全恢复，能起床了。

现在是恶人受到惩罚的时候了。公爵在谋害他的妻子后，觉得自己必须要逃离这个地方，到西班牙避难，但是善良的公证人一直跟踪他到了边境，从那里把他给押了回来。

莫里斯在法庭诉讼中，出示了一张契约（上面有神圣罗马教皇的签名），这张契约宣告德·拉·伏巴里耶尔公爵的婚姻无效；接着他又出示了另一张契约，这个契约证明他并不是前任公爵老德·拉·伏巴里耶尔的长子；然后又拿出一份契约，这个契约证明老伏巴里耶尔（一个声名狼藉的老家伙）犯有重婚罪，因此这个自称为公爵的人是非法的公爵；最后莫里斯又拿出另一份文件，文件证明合法的公爵正是阿德里安医生！

戏剧就这样把爱情、法律和医术组合在一起，最后浪荡子的阴谋破产了，好人取得了胜利。

《酒鬼赫尔曼》是另一部同样类型的戏剧，虽然它不是很文雅，但也有可取之处。它是根据哈利法克斯［英国城市。——译注］著名的史密斯上尉事件改编的。主人公赫尔曼“喜欢喝苦杏仁酒，想念可怜的玛丽小姐”——酒和女人导致了他的堕落。赫尔曼被他的情妇所抛弃，因为一个卑鄙的意大利伯爵勾引了他的情妇。他是一个德国艺术家，却沉浸于酗酒和复仇之中，当他发现伯爵对他以前的情妇并不忠诚，只是玩弄他的情妇之后，读者可以想象他在追赶这个无耻流氓的时候是多么的愤怒。接着就上演了精彩的一幕！在他们决斗的那天晚上，赫尔曼向伯爵建议，幸存者应该立誓要娶不幸的玛丽，但伯爵宣称自己已结婚了，赫尔曼发现决斗并不能解决问题（他的目的是要挽回玛丽的荣誉），就只想报仇，他杀害了伯爵。不久，有两伙人来到赫尔曼的公寓，一伙是学生，他们告诉赫尔曼他已经获得了绘画奖金；另一伙是警察，他们来逮捕赫尔曼入狱以接受法律的处罚。

我还可以列举出许多这类表现大众道德的戏剧。戏剧中的诱奸者或恶

pouse the unhappy Marie; but the Count declares himself to be already married, and the student, finding a duel impossible (for his object was to restore, at all events, the honour of Marie), now only thinks of his revenge, and murders the Count. Presently, two parties of men enter Hermann's apartment: one is a company of students, who bring him the news that he has obtained the prize of painting; the other the policemen, who carry him to prison, to suffer the penalty of murder.

I could mention many more plays in which the popular morality is similiarly expressed. The seducer, or rascal of the piece, is always an aristocrat,—a wicked count, or licentious marquis, who is brought to condign punishment just before the fall of the curtain. And too good reason have the French people had to lay such crimes to the charge of the aristocracy, who are expiating now, on the stage, the wrongs which they did a hundred years since. The aristocracy is dead now; but the theatre lives upon traditions: and don't let us be too scornful at such simple legends as are handed down by the people from race to race. Vulgar prejudice against the great it may be; but prejudice against the great is only a rude expression of sympathy with the poor; long, therefore, may fat épiciers blubber over mimic woes, and honest proletaires shake their fists, shouting—"Gredin, scélérat, monstre de marquis!" and such republican cries.

Remark, too, another development of this same popular feeling of dislike against men in power. What a number of plays and legends have we (the writer has submitted to the public, in the prceeding pages, a couple of specimens; one of French, and the other of Polish origin,) in which that great and powerful aristocrat, the Devil, is made to be miserably tricked, humiliated, and disappointed? A play of this class, which, in the midst of all its absurdities and claptraps, had much of good in it, was called "*Le Maudit des Mers.*" Le Maudit is a Dutch captain, who, in the midst of a storm, while his crew were on their knees at prayers, blasphemed and drank punch; but what was his astonishment at beholding an archangel with a sword all covered with flaming resin, who told him that as he, in this hour of danger, was too daring, or too wicked, to utter a prayer, he never should cease roaming the seas until he

棍经常是一个贵族——一个邪恶的伯爵或一个放荡的侯爵，他会在落幕前接受应得的惩罚。法国人有很正当的理由来指控贵族的罪行，在舞台上贵族要为他们一百年前所犯下的罪过赎罪。贵族现在是灭亡了，但戏剧却要依靠历史而生存，我们也不要蔑视这种代代相传的浅薄的传奇。它可能是对大人物的粗俗偏见，但是对大人物的偏见只不过是同情穷人的拙劣表达。因此看了这类戏剧之后，肥胖的杂货商会悲哀地哭泣，忠实的无产者会摇晃着他们的拳头，喊道——“坏蛋、无赖、残忍的侯爵！”共和主义者也是这样叫喊的。

还要注意的是，现在民众对权势人物的厌恶感也在增强。我们不是在很多戏剧和传奇中（在前面的篇幅中，作者已提供给公众两个样本了，一个来自法国，一个来源于波兰）都看到大人物、有权势的贵族和恶棍受到悲惨的戏弄和羞辱吗？有一出这种类型的戏剧叫做《海上被诅咒的人》，虽然里面有许多荒唐的行为和华而不实的言行，但还是有很多优点的。被诅咒的人是一个荷兰的船长，在海上航行遇到暴风雨的时候，他的船员们都跪下祈祷，他却一边辱骂，一边喝着混合甜饮料。忽然，他惊奇地看到一个大天使拿着一把剑出现在他面前，那把剑上覆盖了一层燃烧的松脂。大天使告诉他，他在遇难的时候太鲁莽、太恶毒了，以至于连一个祈祷也不做，因此他将会受到诅咒，永远在海上漂游，直到他找到一个人愿意为他向上帝祈祷为止！

一百年只允许他登陆一次，来寻找为他祈祷的人。这个过程经历了四百年的时间，在戏剧中有许多情节就描述了这位不幸的荷兰人的愤怒和徒劳的尝试。为了找到为他祈祷的人，他竭尽全力。在第二幕，他把一位修女出卖给法兰西斯科·皮泽洛［16世纪西班牙的一位探险投机家。——译注］的一位随从；在第三幕，他暗杀了纳苏［美洲巴哈马的首都，后成为英国殖民地。——译注］英勇的威廉王子。但是每次在落幕前，拿着剑的天使就会出现——天使说：“叛逆不会减轻对你的惩罚——罪行不会让你得到赦免——到海上去！到海上去！”可怜的他又回到海上，再孤独地漂泊一

could find some being who would pray to Heaven for him!

Once only, in a hundred years, was the skipper allowed to land for this purpose; and this piece runs through four centuries, in as many acts, describing the agonies and unavailing attempts of the miserable Dutchman. Willing to go any lengths in order to obtain his prayer, he, in the second act, betrays a Virgin of the Sun to a follower of Pizarro: and, in the third, assassinates the heroic William of Nassau; but ever before the dropping of the curtain, the angel and sword make their appearance—"Treachery," says the spirit, "cannot lessen thy punishment;—crime will not obtain thy release—A la mer! *à* la mer!" and the poor devil returns to the ocean, to be lonely, and tempest-tossed, and sea-sick for a hundred years more.

But his woes are destined to end with the fourth act. Having landed in America, where the peasants on the sea-shore, all dressed in Italian costumes, are celebrating, in a quadrille, the victories of Washington, he is there lucky enough to find a young girl to pray for him. Then the curse is removed, the punishment is over, and a celestial vessel, with angels on the decks and "sweet little cherubs" fluttering about the shrouds and the poop, appear to receive him.

This piece was acted at Franconi's, where, for once, an angel-ship was introduced in place of the usual horsemanship.

One must not forget to mention here, how the English nation is satirized by our neighbours; who have some droll traditions regarding us. In one of the little Christmas pieces produced at the Palais Royal (satires upon the follies of the past twelve months, on which all the small theatres exhaust their wit), the celebrated flight of Messrs. Green and Monck Mason was parodied, and created a good deal of laughter at the expense of John Bull. Two English noblemen, Milor Cricri and Milor Hanneton, appear as descending from a balloon, and one of them communicates to the public the philosophic observations which were made in the course of his aerial tour.

"On leaving Vauxhall," says his lordship, "we drank a bottle of Madeira, as a health to the friends from whom we parted, and crunched a few biscuits to support nature during the hours before lunch. In two hours we arrived

百年，船在海上是动荡不定的，一百年的时间他又要在晕船中度过了。

但他的灾难注定会在第四幕结束。在美国登陆后，他看到海岸上有一些穿着意大利服装的农民，他们正跳着瓜德利尔舞［美洲的一种舞蹈。——译注］来庆祝华盛顿的胜利，他在那里很幸运地找到一位年轻的少女愿意为他祈祷。接着，咒语消失了，惩罚结束了，一艘天船出现了，甲板上有大天使和小天使，小天使围绕着船尾和甲板拍动着翅膀，看来是要迎接他的。

这场戏剧是在弗朗科尼剧院上演的，在那里，平常表演马术的地方第一次出现了一艘天使船。

写到这里，我们还要说说，法国人是怎样讽刺英国人的，他们总是认为英国人是有些滑稽可笑的。在王宫上演的一部小型圣诞节戏剧中（为讥刺过去一年所发生的蠢事，所有的小型戏剧都绞尽了脑汁），他们就拙劣地模仿了格林和蒙克·梅森［英国当时研究气球飞行的人。——译注］，在嘲讽约翰牛［代表英国。——译注］的飞行，制造了很多英国人的笑料。两个英国贵族克瑞克瑞和哈尼顿出现在舞台上，他们刚从气球上下来，其中的一个在向公众通告他们在空中旅行期间所做的观察。

他说："离开沃克斯豪尔［英国地名。——译注］的时候，我们喝了一瓶马德拉葡萄酒，与我们即将离开的朋友干杯，在午餐前嚼了几片饼干来维持体力。两个小时后，我们到了坎特伯雷，周围被层层云朵包裹着。午餐是瓶装的黑啤酒。在多佛尔港，有一阵气流带着我们走了几米远，很冷，喝了点樱桃白兰地酒。我们平安穿过英吉利海峡，想到那些在下面的汽船中晕船的人，不由得非常同情他们。我们又喝了一些瓶装的黑啤酒。在加来岛上空，我们吃了晚餐，即英国传统的烤牛肉。靠近敦刻尔克时——天已经黑了，有一轮新月挂在天空，我们喝了点白兰地和水。夜色很浓重了，我们的晚餐只是喝了点朗姆酒，然后就睡觉了。当我们在科隆［德国莱茵河畔城市。——译注］上空烧水、吃早餐的时候，太阳冲破了早晨的雾霭，明亮地照耀着我们。又过了几个小时，我们结束了这次值得纪念的旅行，

at Canterbury, enveloped in clouds: lunch, bottled porter: at Dover, carried several miles in a tide of air, bitter cold, cherry-brandy; crossed over the Channel safely, and thought with pity of the poor people who were sickening in the steamboats below: more bottled porter: over Calais, dinner, roast-beef of Old England; near Dunkirk,—night falling, lunar rainbow, brandy-and-water; night confoundedly thick; supper, nightcap of rum-punch, and so to bed. The sun broke beautifully through the morning mist, as we boiled the kettle and took our breakfast over Cologne. In a few more hours we concluded this memorable voyage, and landed safely at Weilburg, in good time for dinner."

The joke here is smart enough; but our honest neighbours make many better, when they are quite unconscious of the fun. Let us leave plays, for a moment, for poetry, and take an instance of French criticism, concerning England, from the works of a famous French exquisite and man of letters. The hero of the poem addresses his mistress—

Londres, tu le sais trop, en fait de capitale,
Est-ce que fit le ciel de plus froid et plus pâle,
C'est la ville du gaz, des marins, du brouillard;
On s'y couche à minuit, et l'on s'y lève tard;
Ses raouts tant vantés ne sont qu'une boxade,
Sur ses grands quais jamais échelle ou sérénade,
Mais de volumineux bourgeois pris de porter
Qui passent sans lever le front à Westminster;
Et n'était sa forêt de mâts perçant la brume,
Sa tour dont à minuit le vieil oeil s'allume,
Et tes deux yeux, Zerline, illuminés bien plus,
Je dirais que, ma foi, des romans que j'ai lus,
Il n'en est pas un seul, plus lourd, plus léthargique
Que cette nation qu'on nomme Britannique!

The writer of the above lines (which let any man who can translate) is Monsieur Roger de Beauvoir, a gentleman who actually lived many months in

在魏尔堡［德国地名。——译注］安全登陆，当时正是吃晚餐的时候。”

这个玩笑足够巧妙的了。但我们的邻人并不觉得可笑，因为他们能写很多这样的笑话。让我们暂时离开戏剧转到诗歌上来，以一位法国著名文人的作品为例，看看法国人是怎样评论英国的。诗中的主人公在给他的情妇写信——

> 对伦敦这个首都，你是比较了解的，
> 它的天空寒冷而阴沉，
> 这是一座弥漫着煤味的城市，一个雾都。
> 人们半夜才睡，早晨起得很迟；
> 他们如此吹嘘的盛大交际晚会只不过是个包厢那么大，
> 在他们的大码头上从来也没有梯子或小夜曲，
> 带着行李工去威斯敏斯特［英国议会所在地。——译注］的肥胖的中产阶级低着头从人的旁边经过；
> 船上的桅杆林穿透了轻雾，
> 午夜航行的灯塔点亮了，
> 泽尔琳，你的双眼都比它们明亮，
> 我可以肯定地说，在我读过的小说中，
> 没有一个民族比英国人更迟钝、更无精打采的了！

上面这首诗的作者就是罗杰·德·波伏瓦［Roger de Beauvoir（1806—1866），法国作家。——译注］的作品，他作为波林尼雅克［Polignac，1830年法国首相。——译注］大使馆的馆员在英国生活过一段时间。他把他故事中的女主角安置在一个靠近斯特兰德［伦敦市中心。——译注］的隐蔽处，“房间里有绿色的新百叶窗，一个大大的窗帘，整天都是垂下来的；当你从这个迷人的住所散发着香气的门槛旁经过的时候，你还以为自己进入了亚洲的一个浴室！”他又把她放到——

England, as an attaché to the embassy of M. de Polignac. He places the heroine of his tale in a petit réduit près le Strand, "with a green and fresh jalousie, and a large blind, let down all day; you fancied you were entering a bath of Asia, as soon as you had passed the perfumed threshold of this charming retreat!" He next places her—

Dans un square écarté, morne et couverte de givre,
Ou se cache un hôtel, aux vieux lions de cuivre;

and the hero of the tale, a young French poet, who is in London, is truly unhappy in that village.

Arthur dessèche et meurt. Dans la ville de Sterne,
Rien qu'en voyant le peuple il a le mal de mer
Il n'aime ni le Parc, gai comme une citerne,
Ni le tir au pigeon, ni le soda-water.

Liston ne le fait plus sourciller! Il rumine
Sur les trottoirs du Strand, droit comme un échiquier,
Contre le peuple anglais, les nègres, la vermine,
Et les mille cokneys du peuple boutiquier,

Contre tous les bas-bleus, contre les pâtissières,
Les parieurs d'Epsom, le gin, le parlement,
La quaterly, le roi, la pluie et les libraires,
Dont il ne touche plus, hélas! un sou d'argent!

Et chaque gentleman lui dit: L'heureux poète!

"L'heureux poète" indeed! I question if a poet in this wide world is so happy as M. de Beauvoir, or has made such wonderful discoveries. "The bath of Asia, with green jalousies," in which the lady dwells; "the old hotel, with copper lions, in a lonely square;"—were ever such things heard of, or imagined, but by a Frenchman? The sailors, the negroes, the vermin, whom he

一个偏僻的公园里，天气阴沉、下着霜，

那里有一个隐蔽的旅馆，门口摆着两个破旧的铜色狮子像。

故事的男主人公，一个住在伦敦的法国年轻诗人，在那里并不快乐。

在伦敦这个城市里，

他只能看到茫茫的人海，

他不喜欢公园，

也不喜欢打猎、喝苏打水。

他在斯特兰德像棋盘一样笔直的街道上反复思考，

遇到了海员、黑人、恶棍

和许多零售店的小店主，

还有所有的下等人、糕点商，

爱普生［英国的一个市镇，有赛马场。——译注］的赌客、杜松子酒、议会，

季刊、国王、雨水和他再也领不到一个苏的出版社！

每个先生都对他说：出色的诗人啊！

的确是“出色的诗人”！我怀疑在这个广阔的世界上是否还有人会像波伏瓦先生一样快乐，或像他一样作出了如此令人吃惊的发现。女士住的是“带着绿色百叶窗的亚洲浴室”，“在一个偏僻的地方，一个摆放着铜色狮子像的旧旅馆”——这就是法国人听说过或想象的东西吗？他在街上碰到了海员、黑人、歹徒——所有这些发现是多么伟大和快乐啊！里斯顿不再让快乐的诗人皱眉，“杜松子酒”、“伦敦佬”还有“季刊”对他来说都没什么印象！这位先生在我们英国人当中生活了一段时间，他崇拜威廉·莎士比亚，称他为“严肃的预言家”，但他从来也没怀疑过自己所描述的内容是多么荒谬可笑！

meets in the street,—how great and happy are all these discoveries! Liston no longer makes the happy poet frown; and "gin," "cokneys," and the "quaterly" have not the least effect upon him! And this gentleman has lived many months amongst us; admires Williams Shakspear, the "grave et vieux prophète," as he calls him, and never, for an instant, doubts that his description contains anything absurd!

I don't know whether the great Dumas has passed any time in England; but his plays show a similar intimate knowledge of our habits. Thus in *Kean*, the stage-manager is made to come forward and address the pit, with a speech beginning, "My Lords and Gentlemen;" and a company of English women are introduced (at the memorable "Coal hole"), and they all wear PINAFORES; as if the British female were in the invariable habit of wearing this outer garment, or slobbering her gown without it. There was another celebrated piece, enacted some years since, upon the subject of Queen Caroline, where our late adored sovereign, George, was made to play a most despicable part; and where Signor Bergami fought a duel with Lord Londonderry. In the last act of this play, the House of Lords was represented, and Sir Brougham made an eloquent speech in the Queen's favour. Presently the shouts of the mob were heard without; from shouting they proceeded to pelting; and pasteboard-brickbats and cabbages came flying among the representatives of our hereditary legislature. At this unpleasant juncture, SIR HARDINGE, the Secretary-at-War, rises and calls in the military; the act ends in a general row, and the ignominious fall of Lord Liverpool, laid low by a brickbat from the mob!

The description of these scenes is, of course, quite incapable of conveying any notion of their general effect. You must have the solemnity of the actors, as they Meess and Milor one another, and the perfect gravity and good faith with which the audience listen to them. Our stage Frenchman is the old Marquis, with sword, and pigtail, and spangled court coat. The Englishman of the French theatre has, invariably, a red wig, and almost always leather gaiters, and a long white upper Benjamin: he remains as he was represented in the old caricatures after the peace, when Vernet designed him.

And to conclude this catalogue of blunders: in the famous piece of the

我不知道大仲马是否在英国住过，但他的戏剧同样也显示出他对于英国社会风俗的熟悉和了解。例如在《凯恩》中，舞台监督出现在舞台上，他向正厅后座的观众们讲话，开始是这样说的，“老爷和先生们”，然后就介绍了一群英国妇女（在著名的“煤洞”），她们都穿着围裙，似乎英国的女性都有穿围裙的习惯，仿佛没有了它，她们就会把外衣弄脏似的。还有另一部几年前上演的戏剧，是关于卡罗琳皇后［布伦瑞克的卡罗琳于1795年嫁给了威尔士亲王，即后来的乔治六世，但于1796年分居。1814年，卡罗琳去了国外，并有了男伴。当她的丈夫于1820年登基时，她返回英格兰并要求取得王后地位。鉴于此，当时有人提出一项解除婚姻关系并剥夺卡罗琳王后头衔的议案，后来该议案又撤销。她在当时得到很多人的支持，但被拒于1821年的国王加冕典礼之外，并于不久后死去。——译注］的题材，在那里我们近期崇拜的统治者——乔治六世，变成了一个非常卑鄙的角色；还有西格诺·伯尔加米与伦顿德里勋爵的决斗。在戏剧的最后一幕，出现了英国的上议院，布鲁厄姆先生发表了一段为王后辩护的演说。很快，上议院外面就传来了下层民众的喊叫声，他们叫喊着冲了进来，把纸板、碎砖和白菜帮子扔向议员代表。在这种混乱的场面中，军队部长哈丁先生站了出来召集军队。这一幕就在骚动中结束了，可耻的利物浦勋爵被暴民扔的一块碎砖砸中，跌倒在地上。

这些场景的描述当然不能传达出他们对英国人的总体印象。当舞台上的演员扮演或遇到一位英国绅士的时候，你一定会看到演员是严肃的，听众也非常严肃而认真地听他们说话。我们舞台上的法国人是带着剑的老侯爵，头发梳成辫子，穿着发光的金属片装饰的外套。法国戏剧中的英国人总是戴着红色的假发，穿着皮制的高筒靴，外面穿着一件长长的白色紧身大衣，就像18世纪50年代英法战争结束后［英法两国为争夺北美殖民地而进行的“七年战争”，以英国全胜告终。——译注］约瑟夫·瓦内［约瑟夫·瓦内（1714—1789），法国画家。——译注］在漫画中所画的英国人一样。

"*Naufrage de la Meduse*," the first act is laid on board an English ship-of-war, all the officers of which appeared in light blue or green coats (the lamp-light prevented our distinguishing the colour accurately), and TOP-BOOTS!

Let us not attempt to deaden the force of this tremendous blow by any more remarks. The force of blundering can go no further. Would a Chinese playwright or painter have stranger notions about the barbarians than our neighbours, who are separated from us but by two hours of salt water?

让我们以著名的《美杜莎的遇险》一剧来作个结束吧！这部戏剧的第一幕被设置在英国的一艘战船上，所有的军官都穿着浅蓝或绿色的外套（由于灯光的原因，我们不能正确辨认衣服的颜色）和长统马靴！

我们不要试图去削弱这股被过多的评论所造成的巨大力量。但是这种错误不能再进一步发展下去了。一位中国的戏剧家或画家对于野蛮人的看法也不会比法国人对英国人的看法更让人感到奇怪的了，虽然法国离我们只有两个小时的海路距离。

Meditations at Versailles

THE palace of Versailles has been turned into a bricabrac shop of late years, and its time-honoured walls have been covered with many thousand yards of the worst pictures that eye ever looked on. I don't know how many leagues of battles and sieges the unhappy visitor is now obliged to march through, amidst a crowd of chattering Paris cockneys, who are never tired of looking at the glories of the Grenadier Français; to the chronicling of whose deeds this old palace of the old kings is now altogether devoted. A whizzing, screaming steam-engine rushes hither from Paris, bringing shoals of badauds in its wake. The old coucous are all gone, and their place knows them no longer. Smooth asphaltum terraces, tawdry lamps, and great hideous Egyptian obelisks, have frightened them away from the pleasant station which they used to occupy under the trees of the Champs Elysées; and though the old coucous were just the most uncomfortable vehicles that human ingenuity ever constructed, one can't help looking back to the days of their existence with a tender regret; for there was pleasure then in the little trip of three leagues: and who ever had pleasure in a railway journey? Does any reader of this venture to say that, on such a voyage, he ever dared to be pleasant? Do the most hardened stokers joke with one another? I don't believe it. Look into every single car of the train, and you will see that every single face is solemn. They take their seats gravely, and are silent, for the most part, during the journey; they dare not look out of window, for fear of being blinded by the smoke that comes whizzing by, or of losing their heads in one of the windows of the down train; they ride for miles in utter damp and darkness: through awful pipes of brick, that have been run pitilessly through the bowels of gentle mother earth, the cast-iron Frankenstein of an engine gallops on, puffing and scream-

在凡尔赛宫的沉思

凡尔赛宫这几年已经变成了古玩商店，它古老的墙壁上挂满了几千码[一码等于三英尺。——译注]长的拙劣绘画供人们观看。不知道不幸的游客必须要从多少里格的战役和围攻[战争题材的绘画作品。——译注]旁走过，周围还有一群住在巴黎的喋喋不休的伦敦佬，他们对于法国掷弹兵的英勇事迹从来也看不烦，现在他们完全被那些关于凡尔赛宫的逸事给吸引住了。伴随着一阵飕飕声，尖叫的蒸汽机车辆从巴黎驶向了这里，吸引了一大群马路上爱看热闹的人。以往的布谷鸟全都飞走了，这个地方也忘却了它们。本来它们在爱丽舍宫的树荫下有惬意的住所，但是平整的柏油路、花哨的路灯、庞大而丑陋的埃及方尖碑把它们都吓跑了。虽然布谷鸟不在了，但人们还是禁不住带着某种遗憾来追忆以往它们存在的日子，因为它们给我们这短短的三里格的行程带来了欢乐，谁曾在铁路上得到这样的欢乐呢？有没有读者敢说他在铁路上的旅程是很愉快的呢？冷酷的火车司炉会和别人开玩笑吗？我不信。在火车的每节车厢里，你看到人们的每张面孔都是严肃的。他们严肃地坐在自己的座位上，在旅程中的绝大部分时间内都保持沉默。他们不敢向窗外看，害怕外面的蒸汽烟会把他们的眼睛弄花或是怕自己的头会被后面的列车撞着。他们乘坐在非常潮湿而黑暗的车厢里，石子铺就的轨道无情地压在大地上，铸铁制造的怪物般的火车头喷着烟、尖叫着在轨道上飞奔。有没有人会发自内心地说他喜欢这种旅程呢？——他只不过是在忍受着，不愿意因为表现出任何卑屈的恐惧而被

ing. Does any man pretend to say that he ENJOYS the journey? —he might as well say that he enjoyed having his hair cut; he bears it, but that is all: he will not allow the world to laugh at him, for any exhibition of slavish fear; and pretends, therefore, to be at his ease; but he IS afraid: nay, ought to be, under the circumstances. I am sure Hannibal or Napoleon would, were they locked suddenly into a car; there kept close prisoners for a certain number of hours, and whirled along at this dizzy pace. You can't stop, if you would:—you may die, but you can't stop; the engine may explode upon the road, and up you go along with it; or, may be a bolter and take a fancy to go down a hill, or into a river: all this you must bear, for the privilege of travelling twenty miles an hour.

This little journey, then, from Paris to Versailles, that used to be so merry of old, has lost its pleasures since the disappearance of the cuckoos; and I would as lief have for companions the statues that lately took a coach from the bridge opposite the Chamber of Deputies, and stepped out in the court of Versailles, as the most part of the people who now travel on the railroad. The stone figures are not a whit more cold and silent than these persons, who used to be, in the old coucous, so talkative and merry. The prattling grisette and her swain from the Ecole de Droit; the huge Alsacian carabineer, grimly smiling under his sandy moustaches and glittering brazen helmet; the jolly nurse, in red calico, who had been to Paris to show mamma her darling Lolo, or Auguste;—what merry companions used one to find squeezed into the crazy old vehicles that formerly performed the journey! But the age of horseflesh is gone—that of engineers, economists, and calculators has succeeded; and the pleasure of coucoudom is extinguished for ever. Why not mourn over it, as Mr. Burke did over his cheap defence of nations and unbought grace of life; that age of chivalry, which he lamented, àpropos of a trip to Versailles, some half a century back?

Without stopping to discuss (as might be done, in rather a neat and successful manner) whether the age of chivalry was cheap or dear, and whether, in the time of the unbought grace of life, there was not more bribery, robbery, villainy, tyranny, and corruption, than exists even in our own happy days,—let us make a few moral and historical remarks upon the town of Ver-

别人嘲笑，因此他假装自己是舒适自在的，但实际上他害怕，在这种环境下谁都会害怕。我确信如果汉尼拔［拿破仑手下的一位大将。——译注］或拿破仑突然被关进一节车厢中，他们也会害怕的。人们在车厢里被囚禁几个小时，车轮用这种过快的速度旋转着，你想停也停不下来——遇到危险你可能会死，但你就是不能停下来。发动机或许会在路上爆炸，把你掀起来；或者会脱离轨道，冲进山里或河里。为了享受每小时二十英里的速度给你带来的便捷，所有的这一切你必须承受。

自从布谷鸟消失后，从巴黎到凡尔赛宫的短途旅程中过去感受到的快乐也消失了。我喜欢从国民议会对面的桥上搭乘一辆马车到凡尔赛宫去走走，但现在大部分人都是乘火车旅行。石头塑像也不会比这些乘坐火车的人更冷淡和沉默的了，而在往日的马车厢里，这些人都是非常健谈和快乐的。唠叨的青年劳动妇女和她法学院的情人坐在一起；高大的阿尔萨斯的卡宾枪手在他黄色的胡须和闪闪发光的铜盔下面狞笑着；穿着红色印花棉布衣服的快活的护士去巴黎给她妈妈看看她可爱的孩子——和这些同行的人挤在摇摇晃晃的马车厢中是多么有趣啊！但是马车的时代过去了——火车司机、经济学家和计算家的时代到来了，布谷鸟时代的快乐已经一去不复返了。为什么不为它而哀悼呢？就像埃德蒙·伯克［Burke（1729—1797)，18世纪英国著名的政治家和保守主义政治理论家。他的思想以“对传统的尊崇”和“对自由的保守”而著称于世。——译注］为人类生活的自然状态而哀悼一样，他去凡尔赛宫旅行时不是还在为半个世纪前的骑士时代哀悼吗？

我们在这里就没必要去讨论（就像能做到的那样，以一种相当雅致的风度）骑士制度的时代到底是好是坏，以及在买不到生命之优美的时代是否就没有现在这么多的贿赂行为、抢夺、坏人、专制和腐败，还是让我们对凡尔赛城镇做一些是非功过的评论吧！在铁路和马车的旅行中，我们很快就到了凡尔赛城。

凡尔赛城当然是最具有道德训诫意义的城镇。离开火车站后，你要穿

sailles; where, between railroad and coucou, we are surely arrived by this time.

The town is, certainly, the most moral of towns. You pass from the railroad station through a long, lonely suburb, with dusty rows of stunted trees on either side, and some few miserable beggars, idle boys, and ragged old women under them. Behind the trees are gaunt, mouldy houses; palaces once, where (in the days of the unbought grace of life) the cheap defence of nations gambled, ogled, swindled, intrigued; whence high-born duchesses used to issue, in old times, to act as chambermaids to lovely Du Barri; and mighty princes rolled away, in gilt caroches, hot for the honour of lighting his Majesty to bed, or of presenting his stockings when he rose, or of holding his napkin when he dined. Tailors, chandlers, tinmen, wretched hucksters, and greengrocers, are now established in the mansions of the old peers; small children are yelling at the doors, with mouths besmeared with bread and treacle; damp rags are hanging out of every one of the windows, steaming in the sun; oyster-shells, cabbage-stalks, broken crockery, old papers, lie basking in the same cheerful light. A solitary water-cart goes jingling down the wide pavement, and spirts a feeble refreshment over the dusty, thirsty stones.

After pacing for some time through such dismal streets, we déboucher on the grande place; and before us lies the palace dedicated to all the glories of France. In the midst of the great lonely plain this famous residence of King Louis looks low and mean. —Honoured pile! Time was when tall musketeers and gilded body-guards allowed none to pass the gate. Fifty years ago, ten thousand drunken women from Paris broke through the charm; and now a tattered commissioner will conduct you through it for a penny, and lead you up to the sacred entrance of the palace.

We will not examine all the glories of France, as here they are portrayed in pictures and marble: catalogues are written about these miles of canvas, representing all the revolutionary battles, from Valmy to Waterloo,—all the triumphs of Louis XIV. —all the mistresses of his successor—and all the great men who have flourished since the French empire began. Military heroes are most of these—fierce constables in shining steel, marshals in voluminous wigs, and brave grenadiers in bearskin caps; some dozens of whom gained

过一片长长的、荒凉的郊区，路边有布满灰尘的一排排矮树，树下有几个可怜的乞丐、闲逛的男孩和衣衫褴褛的老女人。树后面就是荒凉过时的房子，它们以前曾是宫殿，在这里（在买不到生命之优美的时代）保卫国家的是投机、抛媚眼、欺诈、密谋。在以前，那里经常有出身高贵的公爵夫人出来去宫殿里扮演杜巴丽［路易十五的情妇。——译注］的侍女、伟大的王子坐着镀金的豪华马车前往宫殿荣幸地去服侍陛下就寝，或在陛下起床的时候给他备好长袜，在他就餐的时候备好餐巾。目前是裁缝师、蜡烛商人、白铁工、可怜的小贩和蔬菜水果商集中在这里营业。嘴上抹着面包和糖浆的小孩子在门口叫喊；每个房间的窗口都挂着潮湿的抹布，在阳光下散发着水气；装在篮子里的牡蛎壳、白菜帮、废纸、打碎的陶器也在快活地晒着太阳。一辆洒水车沿着宽阔的马路叮叮当当地驶来，把水喷洒在干燥的满是灰尘的石子路上。

穿过这些沉闷的街道，我们就进入伟大的凡尔赛镇了。呈现在我们面前的是代表着法兰西荣耀的宫殿。在广阔荒凉的平原上，这座著名的路易国王的府邸看起来矮小而简陋。——在高个儿的滑膛枪手和阔气的警卫不允许任何人进入大门的时代，它是多么尊贵而高大的建筑物啊！五十年以前［1789 年法国大革命。——译注］有上万个情绪激昂的女人从巴黎闯进了这里。现在花一个便士就会有一位衣衫褴褛的专员给你带路，一直把你带到宫殿的神圣入口处。

我们将不再细说法兰西的所有荣耀了，因为这里的绘画和大理石雕像都充分体现了这些荣耀。宫殿里几英里长的油画展现了从法尔梅［1792 年外国对法国的入侵。——译注］到滑铁卢的所有革命战役——路易十四的所有胜利战役——他所有的情妇——从法兰西帝国建立后所有享有盛名的伟人。他们大多数都是军事英雄——戴着闪闪发光的钢盔的残忍治安官，戴着浓密假发的将军，戴着熊皮帽的英勇王侯，还有许多得到过加冕、公国领主职位和公爵爵位的人，几百个掠夺者和军官，在拿破仑的统治下为拿破仑效力而死于非洲沙漠或寒冷的俄国平原的几百万士兵。法兰西的

crowns, principalities, dukedoms; some hundreds, plunder and epaulets; some millions, death in African sands, or in icy Russian plains, under the guidance, and for the good, of that arch-hero, Napoleon. By far the greater part of "all the glories" of France (as of most other countries) is made up of these military men: and a fine satire it is on the cowardice of mankind, that they pay such an extraordinary homage to the virtue called courage; filling their history-books with tales about it, and nothing but it.

Let them disguise the place, however, as they will, and plaster the walls with bad pictures as they please, it will be hard to think of any family but one, as one traverses this vast gloomy edifice. It has not been humbled to the ground, as a certain palace of Babel was of yore; but it is a monument of fallen pride, not less awful, and would afford matter for a whole library of sermons. The cheap defence of nations expended a thousand millions in the erection of this magnificent dwelling-place. Armies were employed, in the intervals of their warlike labours, to level hills, or pile them up; to turn rivers, and to build aqueducts, and transplant woods, and construct smooth terraces, and long canals. A vast garden grew up in a wilderness, and a stupendous palace in the garden, and a stately city round the palace: the city was peopled with parasites, who daily came to do worship before the creator of these wonders—the Great King. "Dieu seul est grand," said courtly Massillon; but next to him, as the prelate thought, was certainly Louis, his vicegerent here upon earth—God's lieutenant-governor of the world,—before whom courtiers used to fall on their knees, and shade their eyes, as if the light of his countenance, like the sun, which shone supreme in heaven, the type of him, was too dazzling to bear.

Did ever the sun shine upon such a king before, in such a palace? —or, rather, did such a king ever shine upon the sun? When Majesty came out of his chamber, in the midst of his superhuman splendours, viz, in his cinnamon-coloured coat, embroidered with diamonds; his pyramid of a wig,[1] his red-heeled shoes, that lifted him four inches from the ground, "that he scarcely seemed to touch;" when he came out, blazing upon the dukes and duchesses that waited his rising,—what could the latter do, but cover their eyes, and wink, and tremble? And did he not himself believe, as he stood

“所有荣耀”（和其他大多数国家一样）绝大部分都是由这些军人建立的。人们以此来嘲讽懦弱并向称为勇气的美德表示深厚的敬意，在他们的历史书中也充满了这类故事，除此之外没有别的。

这里的人随意地在墙上张贴拙劣的绘画作品来加以装饰，当人们穿过这座巨大阴沉的建筑物时，很难想象得到这里住着的是一个家族。它没有像从前的巴别塔一样倒塌，它是一座代表着没落荣耀的纪念碑，在威严地向人们提供历史训诫的素材。路易十四为建立这个富丽堂皇的帝苑花费了十亿法郎。在战争间隙，他召集军队来把山丘夷平或用土堆成山、改变河道、挖掘沟渠、移植树木、修平道路、开凿运河。一个庞大的花园在一片荒地上建立起来了。花园式的宫殿、宫殿外还围绕着一个庄严的城镇，城镇里住满了食客，他们每天都来向这些奇迹的创造者——伟大的国王路易十四表示敬意。马施伦［法国旧教派的代表人物。——译注］奉承地说，“只有上帝是伟大的”，但是紧次于上帝的当然就是上帝在人间的代理统治者路易王了——在路易王面前，朝臣们总是跪着，用手遮住他们的眼睛，仿佛路易王的光辉会像天堂中的阳光一样照得人眼花缭乱。

这样的一个国王真的会像太阳一样发散光辉吗？当国王陛下从他的寝室里走出来，身上散发出神圣的光辉，也就是说，他穿着黄棕色的外套，外套上面装饰着钻石，还有金字塔式的假发[1]、红色的高跟鞋——高跟鞋把他从地面升高了四英寸，“他简直就是触摸不得的”，当他出来的时候，他用身上的荣光照耀着等候他起床的公爵和公爵夫人们——后者能怎么做呢？只有盖住眼睛、不住地眨眼和战栗。当他穿着高跟鞋、戴着芳香的假发站在那里的时候，难道他不认为自己是和普通人一样由命运所支配的吗？

无疑，他是不愿意相信这点的。在一个晴朗的日子里，当他在圣日耳曼宫前的平台上向远处望去的时候，他瞥见了远处圣丹尼斯大教堂［里面是埋葬法国历代国王的陵墓。——译注］的白色塔尖，在那座教堂里埋葬着他的家族成员，他用一种庄严的恩赐态度对他的朝臣说：“先生们，你们必须要记住我也免不了一死。”这些服侍的贵族当然不敢相信国王是认真

there, on his high heels, under his ambrosial periwig, that there was something in him more than man—something above Fate?

This, doubtless, was he fain to believe; and if, on very fine days, from his terrace before his gloomy palace of Saint Germains, he could catch a glimpse, in the distance, of a certain white spire of St. Denis, where his race lay buried, he would say to his courtiers, with a sublime condescension, "Gentlemen, you must remember that I, too, am mortal." Surely the lords in waiting could hardly think him serious, and vowed that his Majesty always loved a joke. However, mortal or not, the sight of that sharp spire wounded his Majesty's eyes; and is said, by the legend, to have caused the building of the palace of Babel-Versailles.

In the year 1681, then, the great king, with bag and baggage,—with guards, cooks, chamberlains, mistresses, Jesuits, gentlemen, lackeys, Fenélons, Molières, Lauzuns, Bossuets, Villars, Villeroys, Louvois, Colberts,—transported himself to his new palace: the old one being left for James of England and Jaquette his wife, when their time should come. And when the time did come, and James sought his brother's kingdom, it is on record that Louis hastened to receive and console him, and promised to restore, incontinently, those islands from which the canaille had turned him. Between brothers such a gift was a trifle; and the courtiers said to one another reverently: [2] "The Lord said unto my Lord, Sit thou on my right hand, until I make thine enemies thy footstool." There was no blasphemy in the speech: on the contrary, it was gravely said, by a faithful believing man, who thought it no shame to the latter, to compare his Majesty with God Almighty. Indeed, the books of the time will give one a strong idea how general was this Louis-worship. I have just been looking at one, which was written by an honest Jesuit and Protégé of Père la Chaise, who dedicates a book of medals to the august Infants of France, which does, indeed, go almost as far in print. He calls our famous monarch "Louis le Grand:—1. l'invincible; 2. le sage; 3. le conquérant; 4. la merveille de son siécle; 5. la terreur de ses ennemis; 6. l'amour de ses peuples; 7. l'arbitre de la paix et de la guerre; 8. l'admiration de l'univers; 9. et digne d'en être le maître; 10. le modèle d'un héros achevé; 11. digne de l'immortalité, et de la vénération de tous les

的，他们发誓说陛下总是爱开玩笑。然而，不论凡人与否，那个塔尖确实“刺伤”了陛下的眼睛，据说就因为这个原因，路易十四才开始建造凡尔赛宫。

在1681年，伟大的路易国王带着包裹和行李——还有护卫、厨子、内侍、情妇、耶稣会信徒、绅士、男仆、费内龙［Fénélons，法国作家。——译注］、莫里哀、洛桑、博须埃、维拉尔斯、威勒罗尔、卢夫瓦［Louvois (1641—1691)，路易十四的军事大臣。——译注］、科贝尔等等——来到了他的新宫殿。旧的留给在英国的詹姆士和其妻子杰奎王琳来法国时住。他们真的来了，詹姆士觊觎他兄弟的王位，据记载是路易十四赶紧收留了他，并发誓会帮助他立即收复那个搅得他不得安宁的兄弟所占有的岛屿。在兄弟之间这样的一份礼物是桩小事，朝臣们互相恭敬地说：“上帝对老爷说，你坐在我的右侧，等我把你的敌人变成你的脚凳。”[2]这句话里没有什么亵渎的成分，相反，它是由一位忠实的信徒以严肃的态度说的，他认为把他的陛下与全能的上帝相比对后者来说并不过分。事实上，如果看看当时的书籍，读者会发现那个时代的人对路易十四的崇拜是多么的普遍。我刚刚读过一本，它是由一位忠实的耶稣会信徒、拉谢兹教堂的神甫写成的，他把这本具有纪念意义的书献给法国尊贵的王子。他把路易十四称做“伟大的路易王——1. 不可战胜的；2. 圣人；3. 征服者；4. 那个世纪的奇才；5. 令敌人恐惧的人；6. 国民崇拜的人；7. 战争与和平的仲裁人；8. 受到天下人赞美的君主；9. 与主人的称号完全相称；10. 完美英雄的榜样；11. 有资格获得不朽，获得整个世纪的敬仰！”

这些实际是一个狡猾的耶稣会信徒对那位国王的言过其实的评价！在三十多年的时间内——1. 战无不胜的他已经被打败过多次。2. 这个圣人是一位精明的老妇人的傀儡，而老妇人又是更精明神甫的傀儡［路易十三在三十七岁时得子路易十四，1642年路易十三去世，路易十四只有五岁，行政大权旁落，由母后及主教马萨林控制，1653年主教马萨林逝世，路易十四重新取得权力，时年二十三岁。——译注］。3. 征服者已完全忘记他

siécles!"

A pretty Jesuit declaration, truly, and a good honest judgement upon the great king! In thirty years more—1. The invincible had been beaten a vast number of times. 2. The sage was the puppet of an artful old woman, who was the puppet of more artful priests. 3. The conqueror had quite forgotten his early knack of conquering. 5. The terror of his enemies (for 4. the marvel of his age, we pretermit, it being a loose term, that may apply to any person or thing) was now terrified by his enemies in turn. 6. The love of his people was as heartily detested by them as scarcely any other monarch, not even his great-grandson, has been, before or since. 7. The arbiter of peace and war was fain to send superb ambassadors to kick their heels in Dutch shopkeepers' ante-chambers. 8. is again a general term. 9. The man fit to be master of the universe, was scarcely master of his own kingdom. 10. The finished hero was all but finished, in a very commonplace and vulgar way. And 11. The man worthy of immortality was just at the point of death, without a friend to soothe or deplore him; only withered old Maintenon to mutter prayers at his bedside, and croaking Jesuits to prepare him,[3] with heaven knows what wretched tricks and mummeries, for his appearance in that Great Republic that lies on the other side of the grave. In the course of his fourscore splendid miserable years, he never had but one friend, and he ruined and left her. Poor La Vallière, what a sad tale is yours! "Look at this Galerie des Glaces," cries Monsieur Vatout, staggering with surprise at the appearance of the room, two hundred and forty-two feet long, and forty high. "Here it was that Louis displayed all the grandeur of royalty; and such was the splendour of his court, and the luxury of the times, that this immense room could hardly contain the crowd of courtiers that pressed around the monarch." Wonderful! wonderful! Eight thousand four hundred and sixty square feet of courtiers! Give a square yard to each, and you have a matter of three thousand of them. Think of three thousand courtiers per day, and all the chopping and changing of them for near forty years: some of them dying, some getting their wishes, and retiring to their provinces to enjoy their plunder; some disgraced, and going home to pine away out of the light of the sun;[4] new ones perpetually arriving,—pushing, squeezing, for their place, in the crowded Galerie des Glaces. A quarter

早先征服领地的诀窍。4. 从宽泛的意义来讲，我们得承认他在那个年纪所做出的奇迹适用于任何人或任何事。5. 令敌人恐惧的人现在反过来恐惧他的敌人。6. 受到人民的爱戴；实际上他是历史上少有的几个受到人民深切憎恶的人，比他伟大的重孙［路易十五，以荒淫挥霍而著称的法国国王。——译注］有过之而无不及。7. 和平与战争的仲裁人却乐意把大使使节推往国外挑起纷争。8. 仍是一句模糊的话。9. 适合做天下的主人，却做不好自己国家的主人。10. 在平凡和粗俗的做派方面是一个完美的英雄。11. 这位应获得不朽的杰出人物在接近死亡的时候，没有一个朋友来安慰或哀悼他，只有年老的孟脱侬［Maintenon（1653—1719），法国女作家兼教育家。——译注］在他的床边为他祈祷，用嘶哑的声音祈祷上帝宽恕他［他们在他临终的时候把他变成了一个耶稣会信徒。——译注］[3] 因为上帝知道他为了能在那个摇摇欲坠的“伟大王朝”出场使用了多么卑鄙的诡计和阴谋。在他八十年荣耀而悲惨的生涯中，他只有一个朋友，他却毁灭和遗弃了她。可怜的拉瓦利埃尔［路易十四的情妇。——译注］，你的经历是一个多么悲惨的故事啊！这时，瓦图先生叫道，“看看这个镜厅”，我们进入的这个房间既让人感到惊奇又有些眩晕，它有两百四十二英尺长，四十英尺高。“这是路易王充分展示皇室豪华、宫廷的壮观和那个时代奢侈风气的场所，以至于这个巨大的房间几乎容纳不了拥挤在君主周围的朝臣们。”妙啊！妙啊！八千四百六十平方英尺的朝臣们！路易王身边有三千个左右的朝臣，每个朝臣要占据一个正方形的院子。想想这三千个朝臣在近四十年的时间内每天又不断地变换着。有些人死了；有些人实现了他们的愿望，隐退到他们的行省内享受他们分到的赃物；有些人失宠了，回到家里，离开了太阳王的照耀[4]；新人又持续不断地来到这里——在拥挤的镜厅里为了找到自己的位置而互相推挤。镜子里面至少映照了二十五万个高贵的面容。微笑着的女士们涂着胭脂，带着钻石、缎带、饰颜片［17—18世纪欧洲贵族妇女脸上的黑色圆形贴片。——译注］；部长、神甫、花花公子和严厉的老指挥官戴着高耸的假发，还有经过修理的光滑的面部、成簇的短髭

of a million of noble countenances, at the very least, must those glasses have reflected. Rouge, diamonds, ribbons, patches, upon the faces of smiling ladies: towering periwigs, sleek shaven crowns, tufted moustaches, scars, and grizzled whiskers, worn by ministers, priests, dandies, and grim old commanders. —So many faces, O ye gods! and every one of them lies! So many tongues, vowing devotion and respectful love to the great king in his six-inch wig; and only poor La Vallière's amongst them all which had a word of truth for the dull ears of Louis of Bourbon.

"Quand j'aurai de la peine aux Carmélites," says unhappy Louise, about to retire from these magnificent courtiers and their grand Galerie des Glaces, "je me souviendrai de ce que ces gens *là* m'ont fait souffrir!"—A troop of Bossuets inveighing against the vanities of courts could not preach such an affecting sermon. What years of anguish and wrong had the poor thing suffered, before these sad words came from her gentle lips! How these courtiers have bowed and flattered, kissed the ground on which she trod, fought to have the honour of riding by her carriage, written sonnets, and called her goddess; who, in the days of her prosperity, was kind and beneficent, gentle and compassionate to all; then (on a certain day, when it is whispered that his Majesty hath cast the eyes of his gracious affection upon another) behold the three thousand courtiers are at the feet of the new divinity. —"O divine Athenais! what blockheads have we been to worship any but you. —THAT a goddess? —a pretty goddess forsooth;—a witch, rather, who, for a while, kept our gracious monarch blind! Look at her: the woman limps as she walks; and, by sacred Venus, her mouth stretches almost to her diamond earrings?"[5] The same tale may be told of many more deserted mistresses; and fair Athenais de Montespan was to hear it of herself one day. Meantime, while La Vallière's heart is breaking, the model of a finished hero is yawning; as, on such paltry occasions, a finished hero should. LET her heart break: a plague upon her tears and repentance; what right has she to repent? Away with her to her convent. She goes, and the finished hero never sheds a tear. What a noble pitch of stoicism to have reached! Our Louis was so great, that the little woes of mean people were beyond him: his friends died, his mistresses left him; his children, one by one, were cut off before his eyes, and great

和灰色的胡须。——哦，上帝，这么多的面孔！每个人都在说着谎话！那么多的舌头发誓说要忠诚并敬爱那个戴着六英寸假发的伟大国王；他们之中只有可怜的拉瓦利埃尔能对波旁家族路易王迟钝的耳朵说句真话。

有一次，当闷闷不乐的路易王退朝的时候，他说：“加尔默罗会修女［信奉宗教改革。——译注］的问题让人棘手，由此我想到了那些为我遭受折磨的人！”——即使是博须埃那样的人也讲不出这样动人的话。当这些悲哀的话从路易十四嘴里说出来的时候，可怜的拉瓦利埃尔遭受了多少年的苦恼和冤屈！这些朝臣对她曾经是怎样的卑躬屈膝，奉承讨好，亲吻她走过的路面，争着在她的马车旁护行，写十四行诗，称她为女神；她在走红的日子里亲切仁慈，对所有的人都很温和，有同情心。后来（有一天，人们私下传说，陛下已经把感情投入到另一个女人身上了）她看到三千朝臣拜倒在陛下新情妇的脚下。——“哦，神圣的女神！我们过去崇拜你是多么傻啊！——女神？——的确是一个‘女神’啊！——还不如说是一个老丑妇，她把我们仁慈的国王蒙蔽了一段时间！看她，这个女人在走路的时候一瘸一拐，以神圣的维纳斯的名义发誓，她的嘴唇都咧到她的钻石耳环那里去了。”[5]这样的故事发生在许多受遗弃的情妇身上。有一天蒙泰斯达拉［法国路易十四的王后。——译注］亲耳听到了这些话并讲了出来，在完美的英雄榜样为此而打哈哈的时候，拉瓦利埃尔的心都碎了，仿佛一个完美的英雄就该这样做，让她伤心，让她用眼泪和忏悔来折磨自己，她有什么权利后悔？她离开路易王去了修道院，这位完美的英雄没有流一滴眼泪。他的禁欲主义已达到一个多么高贵的程度啊！我们的路易王是如此的伟大，他从没有在乎过平凡人物的小烦恼。他的朋友死了，他的情妇离开了他，他的孩子们一个接一个地在他眼前被处死，伟大的路易王也丝毫不受感动！实际上，一个神怎么会被感动呢？

我经常喜欢琢磨琢磨这个奇怪的人物，他确信自己是一贯正确的，教给他的将军们战争的兵法，教给他的部长们关于政府的知识，教给他的才子们怎样培养情趣，教给他的朝臣们怎样穿着；他命令沙漠变成花园，村

Louis is not moved in the slightest degree! As how, indeed, should a god be moved?

I have often liked to think about this strange character in the world, who moved in it, bearing about a full belief in his own infallibility; teaching his generals the art of war, his ministers the science of government, his wits taste, his courtiers dress; ordering deserts to become gardens, turning villages into palaces at a breath; and indeed the august figure of the man, as he towers upon his throne, cannot fail to inspire one with respect and awe:—how grand those flowing locks appear; how awful that sceptre; how magnificent those flowing robes! In Louis, surely, if in any one, the majesty of kinghood is represented.

But a king is not every inch a king, for all the poet may say; and it is curious to see how much precise majesty there is in that majestic figure of Ludovicus Rex. In the Frontispiece, we have endeavoured to make the exact calculation. The idea of kingly dignity is equally strong in the two outer figures; and you see, at once, that majesty is made out of the wig, the high-heeled shoes, and cloak, all fleurs-de-lis bespangled. As for the little lean, shrivelled, paunchy old man, of five feet two, in a jacket and breeches, there is no majesty in HIM at any rate; and yet he has just stepped out of that very suit of clothes. Put the wig and shoes on him, and he is six feet high;—the other fripperies, and he stands before you majestic, imperial, and heroic! Thus do barbers and cobblers make the gods that we worship: for do we not all worship him? Yes; though we all know him to be stupid, heartless, short, of doubtful personal courage, worship and admire him we must; and have set up, in our hearts, a grand image of him, endowed with wit, magnanimity, valour, and enormous heroical stature.

And what magnanimous acts are attributed to him! or, rather, how differently do we view the actions of heroes and common men, and find that the same thing shall be a wonderful virtue in the former, which, in the latter, is only an ordinary act of duty. Look at yonder window of the king's chamber;—one morning a royal cane was seen whirling out of it, and plumped among the courtiers and guard of honour below. King Louis had absolutely, and with his own hand, flung his own cane out of the window, "because," said he, "I

庄瞬间变成宫殿。而当他从宝座上起来的时候，他威严的形象总能激发起人们对他的尊敬和敬畏——那些平滑的头发看起来是多么的高贵；那个君主的节杖是多么的威严；那些华丽的长袍是多么的漂亮！其实，路易王的那套服饰穿在任何一个人身上都会显出王者气派。

所有的文人都会反驳说，仅有王者的外表是不够的，但是王者尊严的意识确实是很强烈地体现在人的外表上。你看，尊贵是由假发、高跟鞋，用晶晶发亮的百合花徽装饰的斗篷所构成的。对于一个身高五尺二、矮小、有皱纹、大肚子，穿着一件夹克和一条裤子的老男人来说，在他身上无论如何也体现不出什么王者威严，然而如果他穿着路易王的那套服饰出来，戴上假发、穿上高跟鞋，他就有六英尺高了。——站在你面前的他就是威严、有帝王气派和英勇的人了！就这样理发师和皮匠制造了让我们崇拜的神，难道我们会不崇拜他吗？是的，尽管我们都知道他愚蠢、冷酷、矮小、缺乏勇气，我们还会崇拜和赞美他，因为在我们的心中已树立了他高大的形象，并赋予他以才智、英勇、非凡的英雄般的地位。

他有什么样的高尚行为呢？我们看待英雄和凡人的行为是有很大差距的，同样的行为在前者身上就是一种美德的体现，而在后者身上只不过是一种尽职的表现。看看那边国王寝室的窗户——一天早晨，人们看到有一根王室的手杖旋转着飞出了窗外，坠落在楼下的朝臣和护卫当中，是路易王亲手把他的手杖投出了窗外，他说："因为我不能降低自己的身份打一位绅士！"哦，宽宏大量的奇迹啊！洛赞没有被手杖打过，因为他恳求陛下遵守诺言，只是在皮格尼路尔监禁了他十年，与被放逐的富凯［路易十四的管理官。——译注］在一起。——关于富凯也有一个非常精彩的故事。

一天，当老孔代［路易十四时期的法国名将。——译注］正费劲地爬宫廷下面的台阶时，国王把威严的头伸出了窗外，他叫道："不要着急，我的堂兄，一个头上顶着这么多荣誉的人是走不快的。"所有的朝臣、仆人、情妇、侍从、耶稣会信徒和厨子都紧握双手，感动得流下了眼泪。直到今天，这个故事仍感动着不少人。一百七十五年来，所有讲述凡尔赛宫或路

won't demean myself by striking a gentleman!" O miracle of magnanimity! Lauzun was not caned, because he besought majesty to keep his promise,—only imprisoned for ten years in Pignerol, along with banished Fouquet;—and a pretty story is Fouquet's too.

Out of the window the king's august head was one day thrust, when old Condé was painfully toiling up the steps of the court below. "Don't hurry yourself, my cousin," cries magnanimity, "one who has to carry so many laurels cannot walk fast." At which all the courtiers, lackeys, mistresses, chamberlains, Jesuits, and scullions, clasp their hands and burst into tears. Men are affected by the tale to this very day. For a century and three-quarters, have not all the books that speak of Versailles, or Louis Quatorze, told the story? —"Don't hurry yourself, my cousin!" O admirable king and Christian! what a pitch of condescension is here, that the greatest king of all the world should go for to say anything so kind, and really tell a tottering old gentleman, worn out with gout, age, and wounds, not to walk too fast!

What a proper fund of slavishness is there in the composition of mankind, that histories like these should be found to interest and awe them. Till the world's end, most likely, this story will have its place in the history-books; and unborn generations will read it, and tenderly be moved by it. I am sure that Magnanimity went to bed that night, pleased and happy, intimately convinced that he had done an action of sublime virtue, and had easy slumbers and sweet dreams,—especially if he had taken a light supper, and not too vehemently attacked his en cas de nuit.

That famous adventure, in which the en cas de nuit was brought into use, for the sake of one Poquelin alias Molière;—how often has it been described and admired? This Poquelin, though king's valet-de-chambre, was by profession a vagrant; and as such, looked coldly on by the great lords of the palace, who refused to eat with him. Majesty hearing of this, ordered his en cas de nuit to be placed on the table, and positively cut off a wing with his own knife and fork for Poquelin's use. O thrice happy Jean Baptiste! The king has actually sat down with him cheek by jowl, had the liver-wing of a fowl, and given Molière the gizzard; put his imperial legs under the same mahogany (sub iisdem trabibus). A man, after such an honour, can look for little else in

易十四的书籍不是都提到过这个故事吗？——“不要着急，我的堂兄！”哦，令人钦佩的基督徒国王啊！他是多么的屈尊啊！这个世界上最伟大的国王应该走上前去说些有良心的话，告诉一个脚步蹒跚的老头儿，由于老人的痛风、衰老和伤口，不要走太快！

在人类的本性中蕴藏着多少奴性啊！像这样的故事应该找出来让人们引以为戒。不知要等到什么时候，这个故事才有可能出现在历史书中，让未出生的后代能读到它，被其感动。我确信那个伟大的国王在那天晚上上床睡觉的时候是愉快的，内心深处确认自己做了一件高尚的事情，会有一个轻松的睡眠和甜美的梦乡——尤其是如果他吃了一顿清淡的晚餐而不影响他的睡眠的话。

还有一个著名的晚餐逸事，是关于波克兰［莫里哀的原名。——译注］的。——它不是也经常被人描述和羡慕的吗？这个波克兰虽然是国王的王室侍从，但他的职业却是演戏，因此宫廷里的达官贵族对他都冷眼相待，拒绝和他一起吃饭。陛下听说了这件事情后，用餐的时候就命令仆人把他的晚餐摆在桌子上，用自己的刀叉割下一只鸡翅膀给莫里哀享用。哦，让巴蒂斯特·波克兰是多么高兴啊！国王确实带着他肉嘟嘟的脸颊坐了下来，在吃鸡的内脏的时候，又分一些给莫里哀吃，把他威严的腿放在同一个餐桌下。一个人能够如此荣幸地和国王吃晚餐，他在世上也就没什么别的乞求了。他已经享受到了可以想象得到的世上最大的快乐，现在只有仰望天空，双臂环抱，死而无憾了。

我们不要因这种荒谬的傲慢自大而辱骂可怜的老路易，应受到指责的主要还是那些相信并崇拜国王的愚人。如果一个人相信自己是一个神，那是因为有数以千计的人告诉他说他是一个神——当然有一半的人是说谎的人，而其余的人在他们奴性深处，几乎就是像他们说的和做的那样崇拜国王。当路易王穿着五亿法郎的外套出现的时候，据说他在泰国大使面前就是这样的，朝臣们都遮住了他们的眼睛并渴望能有一把阳伞，仿佛波旁家族的太阳对他们来说太热了。实际上，路易王相信自己身上有些让人眩惑

this world: he has tasted the utmost conceivable earthly happiness, and has nothing to do now but to fold his arms, look up to heaven, and sing "Nunc dimittis" and die.

Do not let us abuse poor old Louis on account of this monstrous pride; but only lay it to the charge of the fools who believed and worshipped it. If, honest man, he believed himself to be almost a god, it was only because thousands of people had told him so—people only half liars, too; who did, in the depths of their slavish respect, admire the man almost as much as they said they did. If, when he appeared in his five-hundred-million coat, as he is said to have done, before the Siamese ambassadors, the courtiers began to shade their eyes and long for parasols, as if this Bourbonic sun was too hot for them; indeed, it is no wonder that he should believe that there was something dazzling about his person: he had half a million of eager testimonies to this idea. Who was to tell him the truth? —Only in the last years of his life did trembling courtiers dare whisper to him, after much circumlocution, that a certain battle had been fought at a place called Blenheim, and that Eugene and Marlborough had stopped his long career of triumphs.

"On n'est plus heureux *à* notre age," says the old man, to one of his old generals, welcoming Tallard after his defeat; and he rewards him with honours, as if he had come from a victory. There is, if you will, something magnanimous in this welcome to his conquered general, this stout protest against Fate. Disaster succeeds disaster; armies after armies march out to meet fiery Eugene and that dogged, fatal Englishman, and disappear in the smoke of the enemies' cannon. Even at Versailles you may almost hear it roaring at last; but when courtiers, who have forgotten their god, now talk of quitting this grand temple of his, old Louis plucks up heart and will never hear of surrender. All the gold and silver at Versailles he melts, to find bread for his armies: all the jewels on his five-hundred-million coat he pawns resolutely; and, bidding Villars go and make the last struggle but one, promises, if his general is defeated, to place himself at the head of his nobles, and die King of France. Indeed, after a man, for sixty years, has been performing the part of a hero, some of the real heroic stuff must have entered into his composition, whether he would or not. When the great Elliston was enacting the part of King

的东西是不足为奇的，他有五十万个证据来证明这个想法。谁去告诉他真相呢？——只有到他的迟暮之年，颤抖的朝臣绕了好大的圈子，才敢对他低语，在布伦海姆的一场战役中，欧根和马尔堡［他们指挥联合军在一系列的战斗中打败了法国军队。——译注］已结束了他漫长的凯旋经历。

在迎接战败返回的塔拉尔德元帅［路易十四所依靠的法军战场指挥官之一。——译注］时，这个老人对他说，“人到了我们这个年龄就不会幸福了”。他赐予塔拉尔德元帅以荣誉，仿佛他是凯旋归来似的。在欢迎这个战败将军的事件中，国王的表现还是比较宽宏大量的，这个矮胖子不会向命运屈服的。法国的灾祸相继到来，成批的军队被派出去迎战欧根和那个顽固、致命的英国人马尔堡，结果他们都在敌人的炮火中败退。甚至在凡尔赛宫你都会听到轰鸣的炮声，但是朝臣们已经忘记了他们的神，现在谈论的都是怎样离开这个壮观的宫殿。老路易振作精神，绝不允许任何人提到投降。他把凡尔赛宫所有的黄金和白银都用来给军队购买食物，他还果断地当掉了那件五亿法郎外套上的珠宝，命令维拉尔斯［路易十四所依靠的法军战场指挥官之一，六大元帅之一。——译注］去做最后的抵抗，还承诺，如果他的元帅们失败了，他自己会站出来迎战，光荣地死去。实际上，如果一个人在六十年的时间里总是扮演着英雄的角色，他的气质中也一定会渗入某些英雄的品质，不管他是自愿的还是被迫的。当伟大的艾利斯顿［英国著名演员。——译注］在竹瑞街剧院［英国伦敦的一家剧院。——译注］《加冕典礼》这部戏剧中扮演乔治四世国王的角色时，他外柔内刚的气质和威严的举止赢得了观众热烈的喝彩声，艾利斯顿被忠实的观众感动（据说，他还习惯酗酒，可能有些酒精的作用）得掉下了眼泪，伸开他的胳膊大声叫道：“祝福你，祝福你，我的人民!”我们不要嘲笑艾利斯顿的表现和那些鼓掌、赞扬他“好”的观众。这位喝醉的演员在那个时刻真的以为自己就是一个英雄了，观众因为他身上所穿的华丽外套和裤子而兴奋并喜爱他，表达出了真实忠诚的感情，这些都是因为人们心中的敬畏和服装样式的作用。在法国这部漫长的王室戏剧的第五幕，老路易出色地完成了

George the Fourth, in the play of "*The Coronation*," at Drury Lane, the galleries applauded very loudly his suavity and majestic demeanour, at which Elliston, inflamed by the popular loyalty (and by some fermented liquour in which, it is said, he was in the habit of indulging), burst into tears, and spreading out his arms, exclaimed: "Bless ye, bless ye, my people!" Don't let us laugh at his Ellistonian majesty, nor at the people who clapped hands and yelled "bravo!" in praise of him. The tipsy old manager did really feel that he was a hero at that moment; and the people, wild with delight and attachment for a magnificent coat and breeches, surely were uttering the true sentiments of loyalty: which consists in reverencing these and other articles of costume. In this fifth act, then, of his long royal drama, old Louis performed his part excellently; and when the curtain drops upon him, he lies, dressed majestically, in a becoming kingly attitude, as a king should.

The king his successor has not left, at Versailles, half so much occasion for moralizing; perhaps the neighbouring Parc aux Cerfs would afford better illustrations of his reign. The life of his great grandsire, the Grand Lama of France, seems to have frightened Louis the well-beloved; who understood that loneliness is one of the necessary conditions of divinity, and being of a jovial, companionable turn, aspired not beyond manhood. Only in the matter of ladies did he surpass his predecessor, as Solomon did David. War he eschewed, as his grandfather bade him; and his simple taste found little in this world to enjoy beyond the mulling of chocolate and the frying of pancakes. Look, here is the room called Laboratoire du Roi, where, with his own hands, he made his mistress' breakfast:—here is the little door through which, from her apartments in the upper story, the chaste Du Barri came stealing down to the arms of the weary, feeble, gloomy old man. But of women he was tired long since, and even pancake-frying had palled upon him. What had he to do, after forty years of reign;—after having exhausted everything? Every pleasure that Dubois could invent for his hot youth, or cunning Lebel could minister to his old age, was flat and stale; used up to the very dregs: every shilling in the national purse had been squeezed out, by Pompadour and Du Barri and such brilliant ministers of state. He had found out the vanity of pleasure, as his ancestor had discovered the vanity of glory: indeed it

他的角色，当幕布落下来的时候，他以一个国王应有的尊贵的帝王态度穿着威严的服装躺在了床上。

他在凡尔赛宫的继承者路易十五［路易十五（1710—1774），路易十四的重孙。——译注］就没有留下多少具有道德教益的事件。或许附近的鹿苑是他执政期间的最好证明。他伟大的曾祖父路易十四与法兰西的壮观图景似乎是吓住了他。他了解到孤独是一个令人敬慕的人所不可或缺的状态，作为一个神，他所渴望的也只是普通人的生活。只是在女人方面他胜过了他的前辈，如同所罗门胜过大卫一样。他避免战争，如同他曾祖父吩咐他的那样。他除了研磨巧克力和煎薄煎饼之外，就没什么别的爱好了。看，这就是被称做国王实验室的房间，在这里，他亲手给他的情妇做早餐。——这里有个小门，通过这个小门，楼上的杜巴丽就会偷偷地溜下来投入这个疲倦、虚弱和抑郁的老人的怀抱中。但是他很快就对女人厌倦了，甚至煎薄煎饼对他来说也丧失了吸引力。在四十年的执政之后——在对一切事物都已厌倦之后，他还要做什么呢？杜布瓦［路易十五的宠臣。——译注］在他年轻时代为他发明的每个快乐方法，还有在老年时狡猾的勒贝尔［路易十五的宠臣。——译注］对他的服侍方法都是单调和陈旧的。他享尽了人间的快乐，而国库的每个先令也都被蓬巴杜［路易十五的宠妃。——译注］、杜巴丽和那些政府部长给榨干了。他认识到快乐的空虚，就像他的曾祖父认识到荣誉的空虚一样，实际上是到了他该死的时候了。他死了。他的坟墓如同他曾祖父的坟墓一样，被一群饥饿的人围绕着，他们齐声唱着诅咒的歌，不论好歹，这也是他记忆中唯一的墓志铭。

至于朝臣们——骑士和贵族们——在他死后的一分钟之内就把他给忘记了。当国王死了的时候，受命官员打开了国王寝室的窗户，朝下面的院子叫喊，国王死了，说着就折断一根手杖，然后又拿起另一根挥舞着大叫，国王万岁！即刻所有忠诚的贵族都开始大叫国王万岁！这个官员严肃地走了一圈，把大理石院子里大钟的时间固定在了国王死亡的时间上。这是老路易王生前严肃交代过的，但是凡尔赛宫的时钟只固定了两次时间。当后

was high time that he should die. And die he did; and round his tomb, as round that of his grandfather before him, the starving people sang a dreadful chorus of curses, which were the only epitaphs for good or for evil that were raised to his memory.

As for the courtiers—the knights and nobles, the unbought grace of life—they, of course, forgot him in one minute after his death, as the way is. When the king dies, the officer appointed opens his chamber window, and calling out into the court below, Le Roi est mort, breaks his cane, takes another and waves it, exclaiming, vive le Roi! Straightway all the loyal nobles begin yelling vive le Roi! and the officer goes round solemnly and sets yonder great clock in the Cour de Marbre to the hour of the king's death. This old Louis had solemnly ordained; but the Versailles clock was only set twice: there was no shouting of Vive le Roi when the successor of Louis XV mounted to heaven to join his sainted family.

Strange stories of the deaths of kings have always been very recreating and profitable to us: what a fine one is that of the death of Louis XV, as Madame Campan tells it. One night the gracious monarch came back ill from Trianon; the disease turned out to be the small-pox; so violent that ten people of those who had to enter his chamber caught the infection and died. The whole court flies from him; only poor old fat Mesdames the King's daughters persist in remaining at his bedside, and praying for his soul's welfare.

On the 10th May, 1774, the whole court had assembled at the château; the oeil de Boeuf was full. The Dauphin had determined to depart as soon as the king had breathed his last. And it was agreed by the people of the stables, with those who watched in the king's room, that a lighted candle should be placed in a window, and should be extinguished as soon as he had ceased to live. The candle was put out. At that signal, guards, pages, and squires mounted on horseback, and everything was made ready for departure. The Dauphin was with the Dauphiness, waiting together for the news of the king's demise. AN IMMENSE NOISE, AS IF OF THUNDER, WAS HEARD IN THE NEXT ROOM; it was the crowd of courtiers, who were deserting the dead king's apartment, in order to pay their court to the new power of Louis XVI. Madame de Noailles entered, and was the first to salute the queen by

继者路易十五升入天堂加入他神圣的家族时就没有国王万岁的呼声了。

国王之死的奇特故事经常能给我们提供消遣。康邦女士所讲的路易十五之死的故事就挺不错的。一天晚上，高贵的君主从特丽亚农［凡尔赛宫的园林区。——译注］回来的时候就病了，结果被确诊为天花，这种病非常厉害，进入他寝室的十个人都受到传染而死亡。整个宫廷里的人都逃走了，只有国王那些可怜的又老又胖的女儿坚持守候在他床边，为他的灵魂祈祷。

1774 年 5 月 10 日，整个宫廷的院子里都聚满了人，连眼洞窗那么大的地方都是人。法国皇太子决定等国王咽下最后一口气时就赶紧离开。马厩里的人和那些在国王房间里观察的人都相约好了，他们在国王房间的窗户上放了一支蜡烛，等国王一死，就把蜡烛熄灭。蜡烛终于被熄灭了。看到这个信号，护卫、侍从们早已跨上马背，做好离去的准备。皇太子和皇太子妃在一起等候国王驾崩的消息。忽然听到隔壁房间传来一阵很大的噪音，像打雷一样，那是成群的朝臣正离开死去国王的房间，去向新任的国王路易十六献殷勤。娜伊丽斯［法国大将拉斐德的夫人。——译注］女士进入了皇太子和皇太子妃的房间，她是第一个向法国皇后行礼的人，她请国王和王后离开他们的房间去接受王子和宫廷贵族们的致敬。玛丽·安托内特［玛丽·安托内特（1755—1793），法王路易十六的王后，神圣罗马帝国皇帝弗兰西斯一世之女，勾结奥地利干涉法国革命，被抓获交付革命法庭审判，处死于断头台。——译注］靠在她丈夫的手臂上，表情非常动人地用手帕擦拭着眼睛，接受第一批人的拜访。在离开死去国王的房间时，维勒奎尔公爵命令国王的第一任外科医生安德维耶给尸体涂上防腐的药料。安德维耶说："先生，我准备好了，但是在我涂抹的时候，你必须抬着尸体的头部，要完成您的命令必须这样做。"公爵一言不发地离开了，尸体既没有被解开衣服也没有被涂上药料。留在旁边侍奉的几个卑下的用人和贫穷的工人履行了他们最后的职责。外科医生命令他们把酒精撒在棺材上。

他们把国王的尸体卷做一团放进一辆驿站的马车里，在这个马车周围

her title of Queen of France, and begged their Majesties to quit their apartments, to receive the princes and great lords of the court desirous to pay their homage to the new sovereigns. Leaning on her husband's arm, a handkerchief to her eyes, in the most touching attitude, Marie Antoinette received these first visits. On quitting the chamber where the dead king lay, the Duc de Villequier bade M. Andervillé, first surgeon of the king, to open and embalm the body: it would have been certain death to the surgeon. "I am ready, sir," said he; "but whilst I am operating, you must hold the head of the corpse: your charge demands it." The Duke went away without a word, and the body was neither opened nor embalmed. A few humble domestics and poor workmen watched by the remains, and performed the last offices to their master. The surgeons ordered spirits of wine to be poured into the coffin.

They huddled the king's body into a post-chaise; and in this deplorable equipage, with an escort of about forty men, Louis the well-beloved was carried, in the dead of night, from Versailles to St. Denis, and then thrown into the tomb of the kings of France!

If any man is curious, and can get permission, he may mount to the roofs of the palace, and see where Louis XVI used royally to amuse himself, by gazing upon the doings of all the town' s people below with a telescope. Behold that balcony, where, one morning, he, his queen, and the little Dauphin stood, with Cromwell Grandison Lafayette by their side, who kissed her Majesty's hand, and protected her; and then, lovingly surrounded by his people, the king got into a coach and came to Paris: nor did his Majesty ride much in coaches after that.

There is a portrait of the king, in the upper galleries, clothed in red and gold, riding a fat horse, brandishing a sword, on which the word "Justice" is inscribed, and looking remarkably stupid and uncomfortable. You see that the horse will throw him at the very first fling; and as for the sword, it never was made for such hands as his, which were good at holding a corkscrew or a carving-knife, but not clever at the management of weapons of war. Let those pity him who will: call him saint and martyr if you please; but a martyr to what principle was he? Did he frankly support either party in his kingdom, or cheat and tamper with both? He might have escaped; but he must have his supper:

有大约四十人的护送队伍，这天晚上他们要把他从凡尔赛宫送到圣丹尼斯教堂，放入法兰西国王的坟墓中去！

如果有人好奇的话，他可以经允许爬上宫殿的屋顶，看看路易十六平常娱乐自己的地方，他经常用一个望远镜来注视下面城镇居民的行为。看看那个阳台，有一天早晨，他、王后和小皇太子站在那里，拉斐德在他们的旁边，拉斐德亲吻了王后的手，接着，国王被人民簇拥着上了一辆马车驶向巴黎，其实马车并不需要走多远［指 1789 年 7 月 14 日的法国大革命迫使路易十六于 1790 年从凡尔赛宫逃回巴黎，此后凡尔赛宫便冷落起来，并数遭劫难。——译注］。

在上面的回廊里有路易十六的一幅肖像，画像上的他穿着红色和金色相间的衣服，骑在一匹肥壮的马上，手里挥舞着一把剑，剑上刻着“正义”这个词。这幅画像看起来非常的愚蠢，让人不舒服。你看那匹马似乎一下子就能把他给扔下来，至于这把剑，从来也不是为他这样的手而造的，这样的手适合拿一个拔塞钻或一把雕刻刀，而不适合拿战争武器。那些同情他的人称他为圣徒和殉教者，但他是为哪种道义而殉身的呢？他坦白支持或欺骗、干预过他王国中的任何一个党派吗？他都逃避了，但他还记得吃自己的晚餐。当他的家人被杀，王国失去的时候，他却在瓦雷讷镇［1791 年 6 月法国国王路易十六乔装打扮，携全家潜出杜伊勒里宫，逃往荷兰的奥地利军营，但是，在离卢森堡边境不远的瓦雷讷镇，国王一行却被一位小酒馆的老板认出并被当地的国民自卫军扣押。——译注］舒服地喝着勃艮第葡萄酒。还有在 8 月 10 日，他本有机会重建君主政体的，但他是如此的懦弱，以至于差一点出卖了自己的朋友。他背弃了自己的职责和王国，在国民议会上，他竟为了自身安全逃避到一个记者的包厢里。那天有成百勇敢的人死在那里，成了殉道者。可怜的受到忽视的低级朝臣们，他们大多数都已经忘记了国王以前的怠慢和冷遇，离开安全的地方来送死，如果需要，他们会为君主来分担不幸。可他们的君主太懦弱了，以至于无法和他们一起战斗，只留下他们来面对桑泰尔的长枪和分队士兵的威胁。现在，

and so his family was butchered and his kingdom lost, and he had his bottle of Burgundy in comfort at Varennes. A single charge upon the fatal 10th of August, and the monarchy might have been his once more; but he is so tender-hearted, that he lets his friends be murdered before his eyes almost: or, at least, when he has turned his back upon his duty and his kingdom, and has skulked for safety into the reporters' box, at the National Assembly. There were hundreds of brave men who died that day, and were martyrs, if you will; poor neglected tenth-rate courtiers, for the most part, who had forgotten old slights and disappointments, and left their places of safety to come and die, if need were, sharing in the supreme hour of the monarchy. Monarchy was a great deal too humane to fight along with these, and so left them to the pikes of Santerre and the mercy of the men of the Sections. But we are wandering a good ten miles from Versailles, and from the deeds which Louis XVI performed there.

He is said to have been such a smart journeyman blacksmith, that he might, if Fate had not perversely placed a crown on his head, have earned a couple of louis every week by the making of locks and keys. Those who will may see the workshop where he employed many useful hours: Madame Elizabeth was at prayers meanwhile; the queen was making pleasant parties with her ladies. Monsieur the Count d'Artois was learning to dance on the tight-rope; and Monsieur de Provence was cultivating l'eloquence du billet and studying his favourite Horace. It is said that each member of the august family succeeded remarkably well in his or her pursuits; big Monsieur's little notes are still cited. At a minuet or syllabub, poor Antoinette was unrivalled; and Charles, on the tight-rope, was so graceful and so gentil, that Madame Saqui might envy him. The time only was out of joint. O cursed spite, that ever such harmless creatures as these were bidden to right it!

A walk to the little Trianon is both pleasing and moral: no doubt the reader has seen the pretty fantastical gardens which environ it; the groves and temples; the streams and caverns (whither, as the guide tells you, during the heat of summer, it was the custom of Marie Antoinette to retire, with her favourite, Madame de Lamballe): the lake and Swiss village are pretty little toys, moreover; and the cicerone of the place does not fail to point out the dif-

我们已经离开凡尔赛宫十多英里了。

据说路易十六还是一个很聪明的技巧熟练的锁匠，如果命运没有把一顶王冠加在他头上的话，他会靠制造锁和钥匙来谋生，每周挣两个金路易。人们会看到他在自己的工作间里度过有意义的人生。而伊丽莎白女士会在他旁边做祷告，王后则和一些女士欢乐地聚会。阿图瓦伯爵［路易十六国王的幼弟，后来复辟王朝的查理十世。——译注］正学着在绷索［供走索用的。——译注］上跳舞；普罗万斯先生［路易十六的弟弟。——译注］在提高他短文的雄辩水平，研究他喜爱的贺拉斯。据说，这个威严家族的每个成员都会在他们的兴趣和特长中取得成功，大人物的小道消息仍被传播着。在小步舞方面，可怜的安托内特是无与伦比的；阿图瓦在绷索上是如此的优雅，以至于沙纪太太会羡慕他的。唉，只是生不逢时，命运给这些无辜的人安排了险恶的道路！

步行去特丽亚农宫也是非常愉快而有道德教益的。无疑，读者已看过围绕着特丽亚农宫的迷人而美丽的花园，那里有小树林和寺庙、溪流和洞穴（在那里，导游会告诉你，玛丽·安托内特和她要好的朋友朗巴勒夫人常到这里来消夏），湖水和瑞士村庄就像漂亮的小玩具摆设一样。向导还会向你指出那些环绕着湖水的不同小屋，告诉你住在那里的王室成员的名字，他们在这里举行过化装舞会。在那个靠近湖水的狭长的小屋里住着村庄的庄园主，他就是路易十五。皇太子路易十六是司法执行官；靠近他小屋的是阿图瓦伯爵阁下的小屋，他是磨坊主；对面住的是孔代王子，他扮演猎场看守人的角色（或者事实上是其他的角色，因为它并不能表明什么）；他旁边是罗昂王子［王后的崇拜者。——译注］的小屋，他是布道牧师；那边是美丽的小奶牛场，它是归玛丽·安托内特本人管辖的。

我不记得普罗万斯先生是否参加过这个王室的化装舞会。但是看看上面这六个演员的名字，很难想到有什么人会像他们那样将会遇到如此可怕的命运。想想这些成员，在他们幸福的日子里，聚集到特丽亚农宫，坐在湖边高高的白杨树下，亲切地一起谈话。设想这时突然卡里奥斯特［18 世

ferent cottages which surround the piece of water, and tell the names of the royal masqueraders who inhabited each. In the long cottage, close upon the lake, dwelt the Seigneur du Village, no less a personage than Louis XV; Louis XVI, the Dauphin, was the Bailli; near his cottage is that of Monseigneur the Count d'Artois, who was the Miller; opposite lived the Prince de Condé, who enacted the part of Gamekeeper (or, indeed, any other rôle, for it does not signify much); near him was the Prince de Rohan, who was the Aumônier; and yonder is the pretty little dairy, which was under the charge of the fair Marie Antoinette herself.

I forget whether Monsieur the fat Count of Provence took any share of this royal masquerading; but look at the names of the other six actors of the comedy, and it will be hard to find any person for whom Fate had such dreadful visitations in store. Fancy the party, in the days of their prosperity, here gathered at Trianon, and seated under the tall poplars by the lake, discoursing familiarly together: suppose of a sudden some conjuring Cagliostro of the time is introduced among them, and foretells to them the woes that are about to come. "You, Monsieur l'Aumônier, the descendant of a long line of princes, the passionate admirer of that fair queen who sits by your side, shall be the cause of her ruin and your own,[6] and shall die in disgrace and exile. You, son of the Condés, shall live long enough to see your royal race overthrown, and shall die by the hands of a hangman.[7] You, oldest son of Saint Louis, shall perish by the executioner's axe; that beautiful head, O Antoinette, the same ruthless blade shall sever." "They shall kill me first," says Lamballe, at the queen's side. "Yes, truly," replies the soothsayer, "for Fate prescribes ruin for your mistress and all who love her."[8] "And," cries Monsieur d'Artois, "do I not love my sister, too? I pray you not to omit me in your prophecies."

To whom Monsieur Cagliostro says, scornfully, "You may look forward to fifty years of life, after most of these are laid in the grave. You shall be a king, but not die one; and shall leave the crown only; not the worthless head that shall wear it. Thrice shall you go into exile: you shall fly from the people, first, who would have no more of you and your race; and you shall return home over half a million of human corpses, that have been made for the sake

纪西西里的炼丹术士和骗子。——译注］出现在他们面前，对他们预言将要发生的灾难。“你，布道牧师先生，王室的后裔，你热情地爱慕着你旁边那位美丽的王后，但这种感情将会毁灭王后和你本人[6]，你将会在耻辱和放逐中死去。你，孔代的儿子，将会看到你的王室家族被推翻并死于刽子手的刀下[7]。你，圣路易的长子［路易十六。——译注］，将会死于刽子手的斧头下。哦！那个美丽的脑袋，安托内特，同样也会被无情的屠刀割下。”王后旁边的朗巴勒［Lamballe（1749—1792），朗巴勒亲王的妻子，早年守寡，王后玛丽·安托内特的好友。——译注］说：“他们会首先杀掉我吗?”预言者回答道：“是的，命运规定所有爱慕王后的人都会遭到毁灭。”[8]阿图瓦叫道：“难道我不爱我的嫂嫂吗？我请求你不要在预言中忽略了我。”

卡里奥斯特对阿图瓦轻蔑地说：“这里的大多数人都躺进墓穴后，你还可以再活五十年。你将会是一个国王，但不会长久，只能留下王冠。你将会三次被放逐出境。第一次，你会逃离民众，他们不再需要你和你的家族了；但你还会再次回来，五十万人将会因你这个暴君而死亡。你会再次被驱逐出境，而你的死敌又会把你召回来。但法兰西不会被你微不足道的力量控制住，你将会是一个暴君，但成为君王只是你的意愿而已。你将会持有君王的节杖，但很快别人就会从你手中把它夺去。”

“先生，请问抢夺节杖的人会是谁呢?”阿图瓦伯爵问。

我也不知道是谁，因为到这里我的梦就结束了。事实上，我已经在巴黎大街的一个石凳上睡着了，这会儿被一阵马车声和穿着红色制服的国家护卫队、骑兵、骑马的侍从们的咔嗒咔嗒声给惊醒了。路易·菲力浦陛下正要去游览凡尔赛宫，宫里也有一些描述他本人光荣事迹的画像，他把这些都归于法国的荣耀。

of you, and of a tyrant as great as the greatest of your family. Again driven away, your bitterest enemy shall bring you back. But the strong limbs of France are not to be chained by such a paltry yoke as you can put on her: you shall be a tyrant, but in will only; and shall have a sceptre, but to see it robbed from your hand."

"And pray, Sir Conjuror, who shall be the robber?" asked Monsieur the Count d'Artois.

This I cannot say, for here my dream ended. The fact is, I had fallen asleep on one of the stone benches in the Avenue de Paris, and at this instant was awakened by a whirling of carriages and a great clattering of national guards, lancers and outriders, in red. His MAJESTY LOUIS PHILIPPE was going to pay a visit to the palace; which contains several pictures of his own glorious actions, and which has been dedicated, by him, to all the glories of France.

NOTES:

[1] It is fine to think that, in the days of his youth, his Majesty Louis XIV. used to POWDER HIS WIG WITH GOLD-DUST.

[2] I think it is in the amusing "Memoirs of Madame de Créqui" (a forgery, but a work remarkable for its learning and accuracy) that the above anecdote is related.

[3] They made a Jesuit of him on his death-bed.

[4] Saint Simon's account of Lauzun, in disgrace, is admirably facetious and pathetic; Lauzun's regrets are as monstrous as those of Raleigh when deprived of the sight of his adorable Queen and Mistress, Elizabeth.

[5] A pair of diamond ear-rings, given by the King to La Vallière, caused much scandal; and some lampoons are extant, which impugn the taste of Louis XIV for loving a lady with such an enormous mouth.

[6] In the diamond-necklace affair.

[7] He was found hanging in his own bedroom.

[8] Among the many lovers that rumour gave to the queen, poor Fersen is the most remarkable. He seems to have entertained for her a high and perfectly pure devotion. He was the chief agent in the luckless escape to

注释：

[1] 在路易十四的青年时代，他经常把金粉扑在假发上。

[2] 我认为它出自于一本有趣的书，即《凯克（路易十四时期的大元帅——译注）夫人的回忆录》（书名是假冒的，但最可取的就是它的内容和准确性），书中就提到了上述逸事。

[3] 我们忽略了第四个评价，即他是那个时代的奇才，因为这是一个不确切的评语，可以用在任何人或任何事上。

[4] 圣西门记载洛赞侯爵（国王路易十四的宠臣。——译注）的失宠很滑稽和悲哀；洛赞的抱怨和罗利（宠臣。——译注）同样多，罗利被剥夺了拜见他崇拜的皇后和情妇伊丽莎白的权利。

[5] 路易十四送给拉瓦利埃尔一对钻石耳环，这件事情还引起了很多丑闻。一些现存的讽刺文章就因路易十四爱上一个大嘴女人而指责他的审美品位。

[6] 钻石项链事件。（18 世纪晚期的法国，让娜·德拉·莫特瓦卢亚伯爵夫人是个野心勃勃的女人。瓦卢亚家族业已没落，领地和财产均被剥夺。从小受尽贫困和耻辱折磨的让娜长大后，决心不惜任何代价夺回自己失去的一切，并将此作为终生奋斗的目标。当遇到失势贵族卡迪纳·罗昂时，让娜的野心终于找到了突破口。罗昂在王后玛丽·安托内特面前失宠多年，急需重新讨回王后的欢心。然而罗昂本人却并无多大才能，而且对女人和权力充满渴望。这样一个人对于让娜来说，真是再合适不过的工具了。路易十六命人制作了一条价值连城的钻石项链送给王后，让娜得知此事后精心设计了大胆而周密的计划，打算从罗昂手中把项链骗到手。让娜以假造的信件、借据取得罗昂的信任，甚至找来一名与王后长得十分相像的妓女假扮王后与罗昂约会。在让娜的周旋下，她成功地从珠宝商手中骗取了项链。而王后和罗昂都因为那些伪造的凭据陷入了将要身败名裂的境地。——译注）

Varennes; was lurking in Paris during the time of her captivity; and was concerned in the many fruitless plots that were made for her rescue. Fersen lived to be an old man, but died a dreadful and violent death. He was dragged from his carriage by the mob, in Stockholm, and murdered by them.

［7］他被发现吊死在他自己的卧室里。

［8］在谣传的许多爱慕王后的人当中，可怜的费尔斯库是最值得注意的了。他似乎是把所有的热情都投入在了王后身上。主要是他在法国大革命时促成国王和王后逃往瓦雷讷；在王后被捕后，他潜藏在巴黎，想尽一切办法来营救她，但都无济于事。虽然他活到了老年，但他死得很惨，在斯德哥尔摩他被暴民们从马车里拖出来，遭到谋杀。

译后记

我很高兴自己能有这个机会来翻译萨克雷的《巴黎速写》。这是我翻译的第一本书。刚接到译书任务时，还不了解译一本书所要经历的艰难和辛苦，就轻松地答应了下来。在靠着一份恒心坚持到最后时，才不由得佩服自己当初接译稿的胆量。虽然译书的过程很辛苦，但看着厚厚的一沓书稿在一天天、一点点地变薄、变少，我心里也渐渐充满了成功的喜悦。

萨克雷作为一个作家，他的《巴黎速写》无疑会带上一些文学的色彩并牵扯到其相关内容，尤其是19世纪早中期法国的文学状况，这对于关注19—20世纪法国文学的我来说还不至于生涩，加上自己懂点法语，可查阅了解相关的背景资料，所以翻译的过程还不是很艰难。

能在网络时代从事翻译工作对译者来说真是很幸运的。译者在碰到生疏的单词、短语或句子时不用费时费力地跑图书馆、查阅厚厚的工具书，大多数时候只需在网上一搜索，就能得到全面而细致的信息资料。

我在为自己庆幸的同时，不由得对以前的译者更添敬佩之情，他们翻译一本书所要付出的辛劳是我们所无法体会的。

萨克雷在这本书中是以一个英国人的身份和角度来评议巴黎的社会文化风俗的，他对自己的邻居如同对自己的同胞一样，讽刺的笔触毫不留情、犀利直率。希望读者能从这本书中看到一个见解独特、知识丰富、风趣幽默的萨克雷，而不仅仅限于文学名著《名利场》的作者。

在翻译过程中还有一些老师和朋友帮我解决了译文中的疑问和难题，

尤其是曲阜师大英语系的王丽、中文系的颜丽、法国朋友 Thierry Francois 等，在这里一并向她（他）们表示真诚的感谢！

由于译者的水平和能力有待提高，如果译文中有哪些不足和失误，敬请相关专家和读者予以指正，译者必虚心接受。谢谢！

胡明华

2005 年 4 月